KANSAS HOME

*Hearts Adrift Find a Place to Dwell
in Four Romantic Stories*

TRACEY V. BATEMAN

BARBOUR
PUBLISHING

Tracey V. Bateman lives in Missouri with her husband and their four children. She counts on her relationship with God to bring balance to her busy life. Grateful for God's many blessings, Tracey believes she is living proof that "all things are possible to them that believe," and she happily encourages anyone who will listen to dream big and see where God will take them.

ISBN 1-59310-904-0

Published by Barbour Publishing, Inc., P.O. Box 719, Uhrichsville, Ohio 44683, www.barbourbooks.com

Our mission is to publish and distribute inspirational products offering exceptional value and biblical encouragement to the masses.

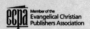 Member of the
Evangelical Christian
Publishers Association

Printed in the United States of America.
5 4 3 2 1

DARLING CASSIDY

Chapter 1

1868, Council Grove, Kansas

T he mid-April wind whipped at Cassidy Sinclair's black muslin skirt as she stood outside the roughly hewn dry goods store, scanning the notices on the wall. Her gaze rested on a poster written in bold, black letters:

WANTED:
WOMAN OF MARRIAGEABLE AGE AND STATUS.
MUST LOVE CHILDREN.

An advertisement for a wife?

Cassidy read it again to be sure.

What sort of man posted an ad for a wife? Her mouth curved into a small, ironic smile at the hope rising in her heart. On the other hand, what sort of woman considered accepting the offer?

The desperate kind of woman with a child to raise, she admitted.

With a heavy sigh, she peered more closely at the notice. Smaller letters declared: IF INTERESTED, INQUIRE WITHIN.

"Aunt Cass?"

"What is it, Em?" she asked absently, keeping her gaze fixed on the post.

Her niece yanked insistently at her skirt. "Aunt Cass!"

Frustrated, Cassidy glanced down, hard pressed to keep the irritation from her voice. "What is it, honey?"

Emily rolled her large green eyes to the side. "Don't look," she whispered, with all the dramatics only a seven-year-old could muster, "but that man over there is watching you."

Cassidy couldn't resist an amused smile at the child's vivid imaginings. "What man?"

Emily's face grew red, and she stomped her foot. A frown creased her brow. "I'm serious this time," she hissed. "There *is* a man watching you. He could be an outlaw."

"Oh, honestly, Em," Cassidy said, shifting her gaze to the possible scoundrel, if for no other reason than to prove to Emily that if there were a man looking in their direction, his interests most certainly weren't focused on them.

Spying the man in question, Cassidy drew a sharp breath. Wavy coal-black hair topped his head, and the shadow of a beard covered his face, giving him a rugged, outdoorsy appearance. He wore a light blue shirt with sleeves rolled midway up muscular, deeply tanned arms. Cassidy's heart did a little flip-flop. He was easily the most handsome man she had ever seen.

Her gaze caught his, and his eyebrows shot up.

Shame filled her at her brazen appraisal of a perfect stranger. And that particular stranger, she admitted, was about as close to perfect as anyone could get.

Stop it! she ordered herself, but she couldn't keep her heart from thundering in her chest.

She held her breath as his glance swept her from head to toe and back again. When he lifted his gaze to meet hers, his cobalt blue eyes held a look of undeniable appreciation.

He flashed her a devastating, but obviously amused, grin, and Cassidy suddenly came to her senses. With a prim lift of her chin, she shot the stranger a reproving look and draped her arm around Emily's shoulders. "Come. Let's go inside."

"Do you think he's really an outlaw?" Emily asked in a loud whisper. Cassidy cast a quick glance back to the stranger, wondering if he had heard. He smiled, showing straight white teeth. With a chuckle, he bowed gracefully, his eyes shifting to Emily, who blushed and giggled at the broad wink he sent her.

"Come, Emily," Cassidy said again more firmly, steering the child toward the door of the general store.

"But he's coming right toward us. It wouldn't be polite to walk away!"

Pretending not to hear her niece's plea for propriety, Cassidy pushed the girl through the doorway and slipped quickly inside, hoping he wouldn't follow.

Unable to resist the urge to venture a little peek outside, Cassidy's breath caught in her throat as the handsome man stepped up to the store window and looked in. Catching her eye, he smiled, tipped his hat, then turned and strode away.

"Somethin' I kin hep you wit', little lady?"

Cassidy whirled around, then stepped back instinctively as a giant with a bushy black beard walked around the counter and towered over her.

She cleared her throat. "Yes. I. . .um. . .I wondered about that notice outside."

"Which un ya mean?" He spit a stream of tobacco juice, missing the spittoon in the corner by a full foot.

With great effort, Cassidy fought to contain the nausea overwhelming her stomach. "The one about a man needing a wife," she said, dropping her voice a notch and glancing cautiously at the other customers.

His booming laughter filled the dusty little store, and Cassidy had a strong urge to reach up and yank his beard to hush him up.

"Well, ma'am, I never thought we'd git a taker so fastlike. Jus' put that up today."

Relief filled Cassidy. No one else had applied, then.

Listen to yourself—applying to be a wife!

Suddenly aware that she was the object of several curious stares, Cassidy felt the humiliation down to her toes. Spinning on her heel, she turned to remove herself from the most embarrassing moment of her life. But she stopped short as her gaze rested on Emily.

Thick, carrot-orange curls twisted into tight braids hung down the little girl's back. Her bonnet, which Cassidy tried to no avail to keep on the girl's head, dangled from the loosely tied laces around her neck. Her tender, fair skin had far too many freckles as it was without exposing it to the sun's burning rays, but Emily hated the confinement of a bonnet and rarely kept it on.

Cassidy's heart sank as Emily's wistful gaze rested on a bowl filled with brown eggs. She knew exactly how her niece felt. It seemed like forever since they'd tasted much more than beans and sourdough biscuits. Emily wouldn't ask for them. She knew the money had disappeared long ago, spent on supplies and unforeseen repairs to the wagon. Eggs were a luxury they simply couldn't afford, no matter how their mouths might water for a change of menu.

Cassidy was so weary of doing without the things they'd taken for granted before William died, leaving a mound of debt and his young daughter for her to raise.

As she observed the longing in Emily's face, Cassidy came to a decision. Her niece would not do without, even if she, Cassidy Sinclair, had to marry a stranger to assure it.

She squared her shoulders and faced the bear of a man. "The notice said to inquire within. Now if you have any information, please pass it along." Crossing her arms firmly across her chest, Cassidy met his gaze, eyes blazing.

Shifting his stance, he folded his massive arms and grinned. "So you wanna be a wife, eh?"

Resentment coursed through Cassidy at the ill-mannered question. "Just tell me how one should go about responding to the notice."

Wondering if she was due another rude remark from the storekeeper, Cassidy held her breath while he assessed her. But when he spoke, all teasing had vanished. "You come in with the wagon train today?"

"Yes, sir."

"How long ya be stayin'?"

"Indefinitely. Emily and I won't be continuing with the others."

The man thought for a moment, stroking his matted beard. "Just gimme yer name, and I'll pass it along to the feller whut put it up."

"All right, then," she replied with a decisive nod. "I'm Cassidy Sinclair, and this is my niece, Emily."

Emily gave him a wide, gap-toothed grin. "Pleased to make your acquaintance," she said with a small curtsy, then stretched out a tiny, freckled hand to the giant.

With a twinkle in his eyes, the man wiped his hand on his dirty buckskin shirt and accepted hers. "Likewise, little missy." He turned back to Cassidy. "One other thing, ma'am."

"Yes?"

"Where kin the feller find ya?"

"Oh." Cassidy hadn't thought of that. "I suppose I'll stay with the wagon train until they pull out day after tomorrow. But if the man who posted the notice doesn't show up by then, we'll find a boardinghouse somewhere."

He nodded. "I'll tell 'im. Now anythin' else I kin do for you and the little missy?"

"No, thank you. We'll be going now. Come along, Em."

With a last longing glance at the bowl of eggs, Emily followed her aunt.

"Ma'am?"

Cassidy stopped just before reaching the door. She turned back to the trader. "Yes?"

He cleared his throat and shifted his huge, moccasin-clad feet. "Um, I'd like to give you a welcoming gift."

She raised an eyebrow. "Whatever for? You don't even know us."

He glanced at Emily, his expression softening considerably. "Fact is, we don' see many redheaded little girls with freckles, an' I'd like to give ya a gift jus' fer the pleasure of havin' her in my store."

Emily blushed and hid behind Cassidy's skirts.

A rare show of timidity, Cassidy thought wryly.

He thrust the basket containing at least a dozen eggs into her hands. "There, that's the gift I'd like to give ya," he said, looking quickly away.

Emily's eyes widened. Cassidy drew in her breath, and her mouth watered as she stared with longing at the treasure. But reason returned, and she shook her head. She didn't know this man. What might he expect as payment?

Regretfully, she pushed the basket back into his large hands.

"Aunt Cass," Emily groaned.

"You're very kind, I'm sure," Cassidy said to the bewildered man. "But we can't accept gifts from strangers. Good day."

She whirled around and slipped swiftly out the door with Emily in tow.

Once outside she looked about the small town, pushing back the anxiety filling her at answering the advertisement. What other choice did she have? Her legs ached from walking all day, looking for a suitable position. From laundress to seamstress, there was simply nothing available, and she couldn't stay in town permanently without a means of support.

Oh, how she longed for the life she'd had before William died. When cholera claimed Cassidy's widowed brother a few months earlier, she'd taken his daughter, Emily, to raise as her own. Cassidy's brother hadn't been the most practical man in the world, and he left the Missouri farm deeply in debt. Within a couple of months of his death, creditors forced her to sell off the farm and equipment to pay the bills, and Cassidy and Emily had no choice but to leave.

Not long before the sale, an excited neighbor spoke of going west, sharing his dreams of a new land where anyone could prosper. His excitement lit a fire in Cassidy, and she decided that she and Emily needed a new start. So with as much courage as she could muster and the small amount of cash left after her brother's bills were paid, she packed up their meager belongings and set off for Independence, Missouri, praying she would find a wagon master willing to accept her into his westbound train. By some miracle, she found a train heading to Santa Fe. The wagon master, Lewis Cross, a red-faced little man with a kind heart lying beneath his gruff exterior, agreed to let her join with one provision. "As long as you don't hold up my train," he'd said.

To Cassidy's dismay, only three weeks passed before the problems started. Her rickety wagon suffered a broken wheel caused by deep ruts in the well-worn trail. A man from the wagon behind Cassidy's offered to fix it for her, but Mr. Cross grumbled about the hours the train was forced to stop.

She had hoped her troubles were over but could have wept when, merely one week later, the axle split in two, once more causing a delay while repairs were made. Mr. Cross took her aside and gently suggested that she quit the trail in Council Grove and find a domestic position.

Assessing her options, Cassidy had to admit that the wagon master was right. A thirty-five-year-old spinster with a niece to raise would never make it to Santa Fe alone. So here she was, five weeks after leaving her Missouri home, trying desperately to find a suitable way to make a living for herself and Emily. With all her options exhausted, there was nothing to do but go back to the wagon and pray someone would come to marry her.

⌒

Cassidy slowly came to consciousness, then sat up with a start. The sun no longer filtered in through the seams of the worn canvas as it had when she'd crawled into the wagon. A pounding headache earlier in the day had sent her to her bed, but she had only meant to lie down for a little while. Poor Emily must be famished.

The fragrance of coffee and bacon from somewhere in the wagon train wafted into the covered wagon, making her empty stomach grumble. For a moment, she wished she had more to give Emily for supper than the ever-present beans and sourdough biscuits.

With a sigh, she pushed back the quilts. Still seated on the bed, she grabbed her boots and slipped them on, then, reaching forward, laced them up.

From outside the wagon, she heard Emily giggle. With a slight frown, Cassidy peeked outside. A gasp escaped her lips. The man she had seen outside the general store earlier now stood over her cast-iron skillet, frying bacon. He looked large and out of place performing the feminine task, and she had the urge to shoo him away and take over. Subconsciously, she smoothed back her hair, then opened the flap wider.

Emily turned to her with a grin and skipped to the wagon. "Evening, Aunt Cass," she said brightly. "You sure slept a long time. Your head feelin' better?"

"Yes, dear," Cassidy replied with a smile, "much better."

The man straightened and strode to the wagon. "Hello. We didn't have a proper introduction earlier." His velvety voice nearly stopped her heart. "I'm Dell."

She accepted his proffered hand and gave it a firm shake.

Looking at their clasped hands, his eyebrows shot up in surprise. She loosened her grip and inwardly cringed. Why couldn't she be dainty like other women?

"Let me help you down," he offered.

Reluctantly, she slid into his arms. The soap-scented smell of him made her pulse quicken, and she pushed quickly away from his arms—too quickly.

He stumbled backward, grabbing at her to keep from falling. Cassidy lost her footing, and they both fell to the hard ground in a tangle of long arms and legs.

"Get off of me," Cassidy spat.

Emily laughed uproariously.

"I'm trying, woman," he grunted. "Be still so I can get up."

She stopped struggling while he disentangled himself from her. Once on his feet, he held out a hand. Warily, Cassidy allowed him to help her up. He brushed at her back, but she stepped away.

"Please," she said, holding up both hands, palms forward. "Stop."

"Only trying to brush off the dust," he replied, a crooked grin teasing the corners of his mouth.

She raised her chin, trying to hang on to her shredded dignity. "I—I can brush off my own dust."

"Now let's start over, shall we?" he said.

"Fine," said Cassidy breathlessly. "I'm Cassidy Sinclair, and this is my niece—"

"Emily," he finished, winking at the little girl. "I know. We've already met."

Emily smiled, her face turning pink.

Cassidy scowled at their camaraderie. Emily was far too easily influenced for her own good. But just as she was about to send the little girl to the wagon while she tried to figure out what this man was doing cooking at her fire, he suddenly frowned and sniffed the air.

Cassidy raised a curious eyebrow just as the acrid smell of smoke reached her nostrils.

"The bacon—" He slapped his thigh and took two strides toward the fire. Grabbing the skillet, he let out a yowl and jerked back his hand.

"Here, let me." With surprising calm, Cassidy lifted the end of her skirt and grasped the hot handle. The pan sizzled as she thrust it into the basin of cool water. "Now," she said, eyeing the stranger, "suppose you tell me what you're doing here, Mr. . . .uh, you never told me your last name."

He returned her frank stare and cleared his throat. "It concerns the advertisement I placed outside the general store."

Clapping a hand to her cheek, Cassidy opened her mouth wide in horror. This was the wife hunter? Why would a man as handsome as he need to advertise for a wife?

His eyes narrowed as he observed her reaction. "Is there a problem, Mrs. Sinclair? You did inquire about the ad, correct?"

"*Miss* Sinclair," she corrected. "You posted it?"

"We didn't exactly get off to a good start, did we?" He gave Emily a sly wink, causing her to giggle again.

What power did this man have over her niece?

"Em, go wait inside the wagon, please," she said, irritation edging her voice.

"Oh, Aunt Cass, I always miss the fun," Emily complained. Nevertheless, she stalked off to do as she'd been told.

Irrational anger boiled within Cassidy. "I should say we did not get off to a good start. Would you please explain to me what you were doing cooking bacon at my fire?"

He opened his mouth, but Cassidy gave him no chance to speak. Humiliation loosened her tongue, and a torrent of words spewed from her lips. "Do you think just because I answered your ad you have a right to come right in and take over? Are you planning to move right into the wagon, too?"

She ignored his blink of surprise and continued, the words spilling from her lips like a rain shower. "If you think I'm the kind of woman who'd—"

He held up his hand. "Miss Sinclair, please let me explain myself."

Cassidy's racing heart settled a little at his soothing voice. "Fine," she said. "Start by explaining where the bacon—which you burnt—came from, and why you were cooking it in the first place."

He lifted a brow and twisted his lips into a smirk. "Well, I hated to invite myself to dinner without bringing the meat. Didn't have time to snag a deer. As to whether or not I move into the wagon," he said with a drawl, observing her with lazy eyes, "now that remains to be seen."

She felt herself blush all the way to her hairline. "Your manners are insufferable, as I observed with the boldness of your stare this morning." She stamped her foot. "And stop looking at me that way!"

"I apologize if my admiration offends you, Miss Sinclair. But if you'll pardon me for saying so—and I wouldn't have brought it up if you hadn't first—I was simply returning a stare from you."

A gasp escaped her mouth. "Sir, you may turn around and go back the way you came. Considering your boorish manners, it's no wonder you have to advertise for a wife."

"Aunt Cass!" cried Emily from the wagon.

An inkling of regret passed over Cassidy's heart, and she wished she could snatch the words back. After all, if he took her at her word and walked away, where would she and Emily go?

Dell's square jaw tightened, and his eyes glittered like sapphires. "You think I'm looking for a wife?"

"Well, aren't you?" Cassidy swallowed hard as embarrassment flooded her. "The advertisement indicated marriage."

He observed her coolly. "I represent Mr. Wendell St. John III. Unfortunately, my employer's business keeps him too busy to attend to such things as meeting suitable women. So he sent me instead. You seem to be the only candidate."

A strange sense of disappointment filled Cassidy. "You don't want to get married, then, Mr. . . . ?"

"Michaels. Dell Michaels. Let's just say I want to find my own wife." With a businesslike air, he cleared his throat and produced a folded slip of paper from his shirt pocket. "This is a contract of sorts, stating that you agree to marry Mr. St. John, or—"

"Now wait just a minute—"

He held up a silencing hand. "Mr. St. John will outfit the rest of your journey," he said with a cursory glance over the worn-out wagon, "beginning with a new wagon. He will also provide material for a suitable trousseau. And I'm sure we can find something for your niece, as well."

Cassidy glanced at her shabby dress and worn-out shoes and felt ashamed. "Mr. Michaels, please. I haven't said I'd go."

"Of course not. No decent woman would agree to such a marriage without further details, which I will provide if you'll stop interrupting."

Cassidy bristled but held her tongue.

"The contract in question is simply this: Once you arrive at the ranch—"

"Mr. St. John is a rancher?" She'd only known farmers.

"Yes." He gave her a stern glance, silencing her. "Once you arrive at the ranch, if you find that Mr. St. John doesn't meet your expectations, you may work as his housekeeper. Or if you prefer, you'll be provided with transportation to wherever you choose to go." He paused. "Well? What do you say?"

"Oh, may I speak now?" she asked, sarcasm dripping from her lips.

With a lighthearted chuckle, he handed her the contract. "You may."

"Where is this ranch, anyway?"

"Southwest of here."

"It's in Kansas, then?"

Dell nodded.

"I'll have to think about this—and pray about it." She scanned the contract. It seemed to be in order. Still, she had to be sure God was behind this. Enough miseries occurred in the world when people jumped into things just because an idea sounded good.

His eyes held a glint of admiration. "The wagon train will probably be pulling out tomorrow or the next day. With all the Indian trouble recently, I'd like to go with them as far as we can. If you can give me your answer early in the morning, we can sign the contract and pick up supplies. I'll have to clear it with the wagon master, but I don't think there'll be a problem."

"Fine. I will give you an answer then, Mr. Michaels."

"Well. . ." He glanced at the charred skillet. "Sorry about the. . .um, bacon. There's more in a crate over there. Enjoy it with my compliments." He lifted a large hand of farewell toward Emily, who peeked out of the opening in the wagon canvas.

Cassidy drew a breath as his gaze shifted to hers. "Until tomorrow, Miss Sinclair." He placed his hat atop his head and mounted his roan mare. With a final glance toward Cassidy, he rode away.

Cassidy thrashed about on the straw mattress, trying to get comfortable enough to fall asleep. Finally, she sat up and shrugged into her dressing gown. Yanking back the canvas flap, she stepped down from the wagon. A cool gust of wind blew across her clammy body, drawing a sigh from her lips. Her mind conjured up the face of Dell Michaels. If only he were the one seeking a wife instead of Mr. St. John. But she wasn't that lucky. Oh, she'd had the dreams of a handsome beau sweeping her off her feet, just like all young girls. But beautiful girls got the handsome beaus, and young women like Cassidy sat like wildflowers among roses, never invited to dances or socials.

Perhaps if she had traveled west sooner, she might have had a better chance at marriage. She had heard women were a rarity in the West—especially single women. Well, she was definitely single. For now anyway.

Lord, is this Your plan for Emily and me? Mr. St. John is a stranger to us, but You've known him since You formed him in his mother's womb. Prepare us for each other, Lord. And maybe. . . No, it was too silly to even ask.

Cassidy lifted her chin and looked into the night sky. The moon shone down on the camp, and a smattering of stars dotted a vast expanse, making Cassidy feel very small in the scheme of things. She remained outside until long after the others had doused their fires and retired to their own wagons. A sense of longing sent an ache across her heart as she heard the hoot of an owl calling to its mate. Everything in nature had a place to belong. Except her.

Still filled with a sense of melancholy, she returned to the wagon and lay down next to Emily. With a yawn, she closed her eyes. *And maybe, Lord, maybe I can even fall in love.* She drifted to sleep with images of a dark-haired man with brilliant blue eyes invading her dreams.

Chapter 2

Dell scanned the wagons camped outside of town until he spied Cassidy standing over her cooking fire. She brushed a strand of hair, the color of ground ginger, from her face, then dabbed at her forehead with the edge of her apron. His heart stirred. *You're a lucky man, Wendell St. John.*

One thing he knew already: Cassidy Sinclair was quite a woman. Strong and solidly built, she stood a head taller than most of the women he knew. A prairie wife had to be tough and work hard. If a man was fortunate, he found a wife who stirred his blood, as well. . .one like Cassidy.

As he approached her wagon, the aroma of smoked bacon wafting his way pulled him from his reverie.

"Good morning, Mr. Michaels." Emily greeted him with a wide grin as he dismounted.

"Good morning." He gently tugged a red braid, then his gaze riveted to Cassidy. "Morning, Miss Sinclair."

"Mr. Michaels." She inclined her head. "Are you hungry? Emily and I were just about to eat breakfast."

The rumble in the pit of his stomach served as a reminder that he had left his hotel room without food. "As a matter of fact, I'm starving." He strode to the fire and peeked into the skillet. Cassidy gave him a good-humored smile but said nothing.

"Ah, so this is how you fry bacon," he said, smacking his forehead with the palm of his hand.

Emily giggled. "What do you have there, Mr. Michaels?" she asked, indicating a small basket he held.

"Emily, don't be rude," Cassidy admonished.

The little girl scowled. "Sorry," she muttered, but she kept her wide, curious eyes on the basket.

Dell struggled to suppress a grin. "Jasper, over at the general store, asked me to give these to you," he said, extending the basket toward Cassidy. "He said you wouldn't take them yesterday."

"Eggs! Aunt Cass, can we please have them now?"

A fleeting look of uncertainty passed over Cassidy's face, then she nodded, reaching for the basket.

"Will you join us, Mr. Michaels?"

"Please, call me Dell."

16

Cassidy tilted her head to one side. Lifting the crispy bacon from the skillet, she slid it onto a platter. "Dell, then. Do you want some breakfast?"

He admired the woman's disposition. As he'd discovered, she wasn't one to hold back. "I don't want to put you two ladies out." He sent Emily a sly wink. "Emily here is eyeing those eggs like a hungry fox."

"I'll share." Emily tried to give him a wink of her own, but her attempt produced a tight blink instead.

He chuckled. "There you have it. If she's sharing, I'm staying."

"Good. You'd better start calling me Cassidy if you're going to eat at our breakfast table." She glanced at the quilt spread over the grass. "Well, our breakfast, anyway." Turning back to the skillet, she cracked open the eggs one by one.

Dell's heart lurched. She was adaptable. That was for sure. He'd only known this woman for a day, but he was finding more and more to admire.

"Cassidy is an unusual name," he said. "I don't believe I've ever heard it before."

"It was my mother's maiden name."

"Lovely," he murmured, keeping his voice low and even. His heart warmed as a modest blush rose to her cheeks.

Emily danced circles around the small campsite, arms stretched wide. "I haven't eaten eggs in years. I can't wait!"

"Think she's exaggerating just a little?" Cassidy glanced in his direction with a wry smile at her niece's antics.

Dell threw back his head and laughed.

Cassidy released a small, wistful sigh as she removed the eggs from the skillet and placed them on a platter. "It's amazing to me, now, what we took for granted living on my brother's farm. We had chickens and cows—all the eggs we could eat and milk we could drink."

"We have plenty of chickens and cows at the ranch," Dell said. "Little Emily here can have as many eggs as she can eat."

Cassidy's eyebrows lifted. "You live on Mr. St. John's ranch, too?"

Dell blinked, then stared. He cleared his throat. "Yeah, I have my own quarters."

"Are there many hands living there?"

"Only the foreman—me—because I don't have a family. All the other hands live on nearby farms."

"Oh."

Emily plopped herself onto the ground and crossed her legs. Her eyes were wide with anticipation as Cassidy handed her a tin plate.

Dell followed her example and sat on the earthen floor beside her. With an indulgent smile playing at the corners of her lips, Cassidy handed him a plate, as well.

"Now, Emily," he said, glancing sideways at the little girl, "I'll show you the best way to eat one of these."

He moved his fork toward the perfectly round yellow center.

"Mr. Michaels, wait!" Emily shouted.

With a start, Dell dropped his fork. "What's wrong?"

"We haven't thanked the Lord yet."

He glanced up at Cassidy. Red-faced, she covered her mouth but couldn't conceal her amusement. Rather than embarrassing him, the action pleased Dell beyond words.

"Well," he said, in what he hoped was a dignified tone, "let's hurry and thank the Almighty, then, 'cause I surely am grateful for this breakfast."

They bowed their heads, and Cassidy said the blessing. Dell studied their reverent faces, and for a fleeting moment, a longing rose within him. Though whether the longing stemmed from a need for faith in his numbed heart or for the closeness of family, he wasn't sure.

"Amen," Cassidy murmured. When she looked up, her gaze found his and locked.

"Amen," Emily echoed and grabbed her fork. "I'm ready now."

Dell tried to respond, but lost in Cassidy's eyes, he found it impossible. His throat constricted, and all he could do was stare.

Emily tugged at his shirtsleeve. "Mr. Michaels," she said, "it's okay for you to show me the best way to eat an egg now. Aunt Cass is done praying."

Cassidy shifted her gaze to Emily. The spell was broken.

"Yes. What is the best way?" she asked.

He cleared his throat and turned his attention to the little girl. "Well, you take your fork in one hand and your biscuit in the other." He grinned at his captive audience. "Stick the fork in the yolk and real quicklike sop it up with the biscuit."

Emily followed his example. "Mmm, it is good this way."

Cassidy handed her a linen napkin. "Wipe your chin, honey."

They laughed and chatted over breakfast. When the meal was over, Dell grabbed his dirty plate and a towel and followed Cassidy to the washtub.

"Why, Mr. Michaels—"

"Dell," he insisted.

"Whatever you say, Dell." She grabbed the towel from his hands. "No man is going to wash dishes in my kitchen."

"May I sit and talk to you while you work, then?"

She hesitated a moment, and he held his breath, afraid she might refuse.

"I suppose that'll be all right."

He sat on a crate and watched her hands move deftly from one dish to another. How long had it been since he'd watched a woman at work? Impatiently, he pushed back the painful memories trying to invade his mind. Now wasn't the time to think about the past.

Cassidy gave him a curious look. "Is something the matter?"

18

"No." His voice was sharper than he intended, and he softened it before his next words. "But I have quite a bit to do today—depending upon your decision, of course. Are you coming with me?" He held his breath, awaiting her answer.

Cassidy's jade green eyes stared frankly behind bristly lashes. "Emily and I are alone now, and if Mr. St. John is offering us a home, I don't see how I can refuse."

Relief washed over him. "Fine. I'll make the necessary arrangements."

"How long will it take to reach the ranch?" Cassidy asked.

She sounded weary, and Dell's gaze traveled over her face. Dark shadows smudged the spaces below her eyes. The trail was hard for anyone, but he couldn't imagine what it had been like for a woman alone with a child to care for. Especially with her pitifully inadequate provisions. All that was over now. He would make sure she never did without again.

"We'll stay with the wagon train for about two weeks. Then we'll turn off and travel another two days until we reach the ranch."

A frown darkened her face.

"What's wrong?"

"Two days with no chaperone? What will the neighbors think of me?"

Dell started to laugh but stopped, realizing by her wide-eyed stare that she was serious.

"Well," he said, swiping a hand over his chin, "Emily can be our chaperone." He laughed aloud.

Her eyes narrowed, and she shook a wet spatula at him, flinging droplets of water onto his shirt. "If you think I'm going to travel two days alone with a man who is not my husband, you have another thing coming, Mr. Michaels."

"Please, please." He held up his hands and took a step back. "I was only kidding. We'll figure something out."

"Oh," she said, appearing slightly mollified. "See that you do 'figure something out,' or the deal is off."

"I promise."

Silence filled the air between them as she resumed her chore.

Finally, Dell shifted and stood. "Can you make a list of the supplies you'll be needing for say, oh, a month to be on the safe side, just in case there are delays?"

"All right," Cassidy said with a nod.

"That includes new shoes." His gaze slid over the black muslin. "And a new dress or two if you deem it necessary. In the meantime I'll go and talk to the wagon master—uh, what's his name?"

A small smile lifted the corners of her lips, captivating him with its soft fullness.

"Lewis Cross. He'll be at the front of the train. His wife and daughter are traveling with us."

He lifted his eyes to meet her gaze. "Can you have a list ready in an hour?"

She nodded. Clearing her throat, she lowered her eyes. "Dell, you are free, of course, to take your meals with us on the trail."

Something inside of Dell softened at the gesture. "I appreciate it," he replied truthfully. "I sure didn't relish the idea of eating my own cooking."

She glanced at him and gave a low, throaty laugh.

Dell swallowed hard. *This is going to be tougher than I thought.*

Placing his hat atop his head, he mounted his horse and rode away.

⁓

Dell found the wagon master enjoying a cup of coffee at his fire. Dismounting, he lifted a large hand in greeting. "Hello, Mr. Cross."

The wagon master's weathered face remained stony. "Should I know you, mister?"

Dell removed his hat and shook his head. "No, sir. There's no reason for you to know me 'til now. Name's Michaels. Dell Michaels."

"What can I do for you, Mr. Michaels?"

Dell cleared his throat and pulled out the signed contract. He handed it over to Mr. Cross and waited while the man read it.

"So Miss Sinclair will be leaving the train with you?"

"Eventually. The turnoff to the ranch is a good two weeks' travel, and I'd sure appreciate it if you'd allow us to continue with the wagon train until then."

Mr. Cross hesitated. "It's been rough going for Cassidy. She must be pretty desperate to consider this without even meeting the man she's agreeing to marry. Fact is, I've been making some inquiries for a position in town. Haven't found her anything yet, though."

"I'll take full responsibility for Miss Sinclair and Emily, of course."

"She might prefer to work as a seamstress."

Dell's throat went dry. He didn't want Cassidy to stay in town. He wanted her company for as long as possible.

"The life she's being offered is a good one. But of course you can give her the choice."

"I just might."

"And if she chooses to go with me?"

The leathery wagon master nodded. "Don't suppose it'd hurt anything to have another pair of hands and an extra gun around here. Those pesky Indians are stirrin' up trouble again. Gonna have to go through Colorado this time around so my people get to Santa Fe with their scalps on their heads."

"Thank you, sir." Dell mounted the roan. "I'll be on my way now so I can stock up on supplies and be ready to move out in the morning."

"Mr. Michaels." The wagon master squinted up at him. "I'm not crazy about this arrangement between you and Miss Sinclair. She's a fine woman and deserves more than marriage to a stranger. I'll be watching you, and if I think there's anything strange about this setup, I'll take her and the little girl all the way to Santa Fe myself."

Dell nodded. "I'd expect no less from you."

"Welcome aboard. We leave at first light."

The two men shook hands, and Dell rode away.

Cassidy grimaced as the reins cut into her raw hands. Worn through from the weeks on the trail, her gloves were little or no protection against blisters, so she didn't bother to wear them anymore.

Why hadn't she thought to put a new pair of gloves on the list? She knew the answer to that. Dell had already paid for so much, including a yoke of oxen to replace the ragged mules, as well as a new wagon. The less she accepted from Mr. St. John, the less she'd have to pay back in housework if she couldn't stand the man.

Or if he doesn't want me.

The thought had occurred to her more than once. After all, no one had taken the slightest romantic interest in her before. This Mr. St. John might want a dainty, doting wife rather than a woman, large and strong. Cassidy knew her face wasn't ugly, but neither was she pretty by any stretch of the imagination. Of course, how handsome could Wendell St. John III be if he had to advertise for a wife?

A flash of lightning caught Cassidy's attention from the corner of her eye. She scanned the horizon, and anxiety gnawed at her as she noted thick black clouds blanketing the sky, threatening to burst at any moment.

"Emily, get back in the wagon," she called. "Looks like we're in for a storm."

"Aw, Aunt Cass." Emily obeyed but let her displeasure be known by a puckered brow.

Cassidy let out a frustrated breath. She'd have to get Emily back under control. Though she knew God expected her to train up the child with discipline, it had been difficult to punish her since her father's death.

Stopping the wagon, she waited for Emily, who flounced over and climbed up.

"I think Mr. Cross will call a halt soon, judging from the weather," Cassidy said, trying to draw Emily from her foul mood.

"Hello, ladies."

Emily brightened considerably. "Hi, Mr. Michaels."

He touched the brim of his hat and grinned broadly at the child.

"Aunt Cass is making me sit in the wagon, and I want to walk."

Cassidy couldn't resist a wry grin at her niece's transparent attempt to gain an ally.

Dell nodded but looked at her sternly. "Couldn't help overhearing. Your aunt Cass is right. The train's already starting to move into a circle. You'd better stay put." He turned his attention to Cassidy. "Lewis thinks we're in for a pretty bad storm, so brace yourself. I came to help you get everything tightened down. Don't want to lose anything."

"Thank you, but it isn't necessary." Cassidy maneuvered her wagon into place in the circle. "There isn't anything here I can't take care of, and there are others who will need your help more than I."

Cassidy wrapped the reins around the brake and jumped down from the wagon. She glanced up at Dell, noting a bewildered look on his face.

"Something wrong?" she questioned, a frown creasing her brow.

"What's that getup you're wearing?"

With a glance at her attire, she smiled. "It's called a bloomer outfit."

"But you're wearing trousers!"

Thunder rumbled, and flashes of lightning were getting closer.

"Technically, they're bloomers," Cassidy replied distractedly, eyeing the sky nervously.

"They look like trousers," he insisted.

"So? I'm wearing a dress over them," she replied with a shrug.

"A short dress." Dell's gaze swooped downward. "It doesn't even cover your ankles." He sounded scandalized.

"The bloomers cover my ankles." She looked down at her loose-fitting dress, which reached midway between her knees and ankles. Why was he acting so silly about it? "Don't you think there are more important things to consider right now? Lightning striking the oxen, for instance."

He ignored the remark. "Doesn't seem like a very good example for a young girl like Emily."

Miffed, Cassidy tossed her head. "You try wearing a dress with all those petticoats and see how comfortable you are out here on the trail." A loud clap of thunder punctuated her heated statement. "Seems to me I'm teaching my niece to have some common sense, even if some menfolk would rather see a woman in a dress on a dusty trail."

"I like Aunt Cass's bloomer outfit. She said she might make one for me, if she has time."

Dell's expression softened at Emily's interruption.

"Is that so, little miss? Are you going to be an independent woman like your aunt?"

Cassidy's cheeks grew warm, but she lifted her chin. She had to be independent, didn't she? She had her niece to care for.

"I don't know," Emily replied.

The tender smile Dell sent Emily melted Cassidy's anger. He certainly would make a fine father. An unreasonable pang of jealousy hit her full in the stomach at the thought of him marrying another woman. She placed a hand over her waist as if to ward off the blow. What right did she have to be jealous? It wasn't as though a man as handsome and wonderful as Dell would ever be interested in the likes of her anyway. And if by some miracle he were interested, it wouldn't matter, because she'd signed a contract with Mr. St. John. At the very least, she owed the rancher a chance to take one look at her and send her packing.

Cassidy shook herself from her thoughts. There was no sense in borrowing trouble. "I'd better unhitch the team before they get spooked and run away," she said, moving to do so.

Dell dismounted and placed a large hand over hers. "I'll do it for you."

Cassidy winced, catching her lip between her teeth.

"What's wrong?" he asked with a frown.

"Nothing." She tried to pull away.

He pursed his lips, turning her hand palm up. "These are badly blistered," he admonished, the concern in his voice warming her down to her toes. Intently, he gazed into her eyes. "Why aren't you wearing gloves?"

Cassidy looked at the ground and swallowed hard. She shrugged. "I don't know."

"Her gloves wore out a long time ago," Emily piped up.

"Emily, get inside the wagon before the rain starts," Cassidy ordered.

The little girl's face clouded over with hurt, but mercifully, she did as she was told.

"Look at me," Dell commanded, placing a finger beneath Cassidy's chin and lifting her head until they were face-to-face. "Why didn't you tell me you needed gloves?"

"I didn't think I would." She jumped as another loud clap of thunder shook the air. "That storm's getting closer, Dell. I really need to get the oxen unhitched."

"Go inside with Emily. I'll unhitch the team." He gave her a gentle nudge toward the wagon.

"B—but what about the others? They need you."

"They can take care of themselves. I'm staying right here."

A large gust of wind whipped at Cassidy's skirt and nearly knocked her off her feet as the sky opened, pouring rain on the band of travelers.

"Get inside." Dell ducked his head against the blast of wind and pushed toward the oxen.

Ignoring his order, she rushed to unhitch the other side. Soon the oxen were free of the wagon.

"Get inside, Cassidy!" Dell yelled again, pulling at the reins. With nothing else to do, she obeyed.

⌒

Heavy rain assaulted the prairie for two days, delaying the train and dumping several inches of water on the ground. Cassidy gave up trying to build a fire after the first day, and she and Emily, with Dell as their guest, subsisted on dried meat and cold beans.

When the skies finally cleared, the people were anxious to head out. But the muddy, rain-soaked ground prevented any movement. Details of women gathered drinking water. The children set about collecting buffalo chips for the fires, and the men took turns guarding the camp and hunting fresh game.

Cassidy's hands were healing, and she dreaded having them blister again once the order was given to move out.

Stepping out of the warmth and dryness of her wagon on the third day after the rain had begun, Cassidy glanced at the puddles of water on the ground and sighed. She'd be soaked before she made it back to the wagon. She dreaded stepping down from her canvas-covered home.

"Might as well get it over with," she grumbled to herself. Gathering her water buckets, she set off for the river a few yards beyond the camp, keeping her eyes fixed firmly on the ground to avoid as many puddles as possible.

"Miss Sinclair?" Mrs. Marcus, wife of Reverend Marcus, stood before her with her own buckets filled.

"Hello," Cassidy said. "How are you faring after all this rain?"

Mrs. Marcus gave her a rosy smile. "The Lord has kept us well and as dry as can be expected, I suppose."

Cassidy inclined her head, feeling suddenly ashamed at her foul mood. "We can be thankful it wasn't any worse."

"Yes," Mrs. Marcus agreed. "As a matter of fact, that's what I wanted to discuss with you. My husband is conducting a service at our campfire tonight, and we would love for you and Emily to attend."

A thrill shot through Cassidy at the thought of having fellowship with other believers again. Thus far on the trail, they'd had few opportunities, and none since leaving Council Grove a week earlier. "We'll be there."

"Wonderful. We'll look forward to seeing you after supper."

Mrs. Marcus continued on her way back to the camp, and Cassidy resumed her trek to the river. Once she reached the grassy bank, she stooped to fill her buckets. At the thought of the meeting that night, anticipation welled in her soul, and she broke into a hymn of praise.

As she straightened, her heart leaped at the sight of Dell leaning casually against a nearby tree, watching her.

"It's a good thing I wasn't an Indian sneaking up on you," he admonished lightly. "If I had been, I'd already have that pretty ginger-colored hair hanging from my belt."

"Then it's lucky for me you aren't an Indian," she retorted, feeling her cheeks grow warm at his compliment.

Dell chuckled and reached for the heavy buckets she carried. "Why are you so happy?"

"Reverend Marcus is holding a Bible meeting tonight." Cassidy couldn't keep the enthusiasm out of her voice. "Will you attend?"

"No."

Cassidy frowned at his clipped answer.

"Aren't you a believer?"

"Let's put it this way. I believe if there is a God, He isn't very interested in humanity."

Cassidy gasped, placing a hand to her chest. "Dell, don't say that."

His mouth curved into an amused smile. "Afraid of thunder and lightning from heaven?" He leaned in closer. "Don't be," he said in a conspiratorial tone. "The skies seem to be clear. As a matter of fact, Lewis gave the okay to move out tomorrow."

She stopped walking and crossed her arms in determination. "Dell Michaels, don't you dare make light of the Lord in my presence again." Cassidy could feel her lips quiver, and tears blurred her vision. "God is the only constant in my life, and I will not stand for blasphemy."

"Cassidy," he said, the regret in his voice unmistakable. "Forgive me, please. I didn't mean to hurt you. Listen, I do believe in God. At one time we were on pretty good terms, but now. . ."

"Now?" Cassidy prodded.

"Let's just say He and I have some things to work out. I'm sorry."

A fleeting look of pain clouded his blue eyes, melting Cassidy's heart. Though there were times she didn't understand why things happened the way they did, she had never considered turning away from God for any reason. But she had known a woman back home in Missouri who had blamed God after losing her little boy to whooping cough. Cassidy's heart twisted as she wondered what had become of her.

"Do you forgive me?" Dell asked, drawing her from her memories.

Cassidy knew it certainly wasn't her place to judge Dell, but if he had gone through a heartbreak similar to that of her friend, he would find no peace until God healed him. She wanted Dell to allow God to do that. Life was difficult enough, even when one drew on a strength from above; without a relationship with God, Cassidy couldn't imagine how anyone survived the hardships.

Slowly, she lifted the buckets from his hands. "You don't need my forgiveness, Dell," she said softly. "But I truly believe whatever issues you have with God will only be settled once you surrender your heart to Him and accept His peace."

Dell remained silent, looking past her, though it appeared he stared at nothing in particular. After a moment, Cassidy realized he wasn't going to respond, so she bid him good day and stepped toward the circle of wagons, sloshing water on the ground as she left him to wrestle with her words.

Chapter 3

Seated on the ground with her back against a wagon wheel for support, Cassidy watched Dell romp with the children. The pleasant aroma of strong coffee wafted from her fire, and the gentle hum of quiet singing could be heard as the women washed their supper pots and went about their nightly rituals, readying their families for bed. This was quickly becoming her favorite time of the day.

Since Dell had only a bedroll and a few personal items, his chores were minimal compared to the duties of the family men in the wagon train. In the evenings, while the other men made repairs to their wagons or cared for their teams, he played tag, blind man's bluff, baseball, or anything else the children could coax him into. Cassidy grinned. It certainly didn't take much to convince him. He was a big kid at heart and loved to play.

She leaned back her head and smiled while Emily tied a handkerchief behind Dell's head and turned him around three times. Dell was such a wonderful man. If only he would come to the Bible meetings, Cassidy knew God would be able to get through to him. He'd said nothing about their encounter during the rain delay, and Cassidy hadn't mentioned it either. But she had prayed for him often. Somehow, she felt she should do everything possible to encourage Dell to reconcile his relationship with the Lord.

The campers had enjoyed the worship service during the three-day rain delay so much that once they returned to the trail, they gathered around the preacher's fire a couple of evenings a week and worshiped together. But Dell never joined them.

"I got someone!" he yelled, yanking the blindfold from his face and tickling the towheaded boy held captive in his arms.

A giggle escaped Cassidy's lips, and Dell raised his head. His eyes still twinkled from the game as his gaze met hers. Her pulse quickened, and she quickly shifted her attention to Emily.

"Time to get ready for bed," she called, waiting for Emily to protest. She wasn't disappointed.

"Aw, Aunt Cass. It's hardly even dark yet."

"Now, sweetheart," Dell admonished the little girl, "you do as your aunt says, or she might not let us play together anymore."

A look of uncertainty clouded Emily's pea-green eyes, and she wrinkled her freckled nose. "Okay." She flounced to the wagon. Bending over, she gave Cassidy a kiss and a hug. "Night."

Dell removed his hat and extended a hand to Cassidy. "Like some help up from there?"

Warily she accepted his assistance but clutched the wheel for support.

Shaking his head, he chuckled, throwing Emily a sideways glance. "A guy drops your aunt one time—just once—and she doubts his manly strength from then on."

"Honestly." Cassidy rolled her eyes but felt her face growing hot.

Her gaze riveted to Dell's head as he ran long fingers through the mass of dark hair molded into the shape of his hat and curling up at the ends. He needed a haircut pretty badly.

"I suppose I ought to find someone who'll cut it for me," he said self-consciously, as though reading her thoughts. "I don't suppose you would. . ."

Horrified, Cassidy opened her mouth to refuse, but Emily interrupted her.

"Aunt Cass always used to cut my pa's hair."

"Emily!"

"Well, you did. Why can't you—"

"Run along now. I'll be in to pray with you shortly."

"Yes, ma'am," she said with a heavy sigh.

"Good night, Emily," Dell called with a wink, flashing the little girl a smile.

She grinned broadly back at him. "Night," she replied, crawling into the wagon.

Slowly Cassidy met his gaze. His eyes pleaded in childlike innocence, amusement written plainly on his handsome face. He was enjoying this a little too much!

A sudden idea formed in her mind, and she couldn't resist a slight smile. Perhaps this opportunity was providential. "Let's make a deal." She stood, her feet shoulder width apart. She folded her arms across her chest and tilted her head to one side.

Dell lifted an eyebrow. "Like a wager?"

"Certainly not a wager. I don't gamble."

"Of course you don't gamble. I didn't mean to imply anything improper." He drew a short breath. "A bargain then."

She nodded. "Yes."

Following her example, he folded his arms over his chest, as well. "Let's hear what you have to say."

"I'll give you a much-needed haircut. . ." Her voice rang with challenge. "If you attend the service with Emily and me tomorrow night."

His eyes narrowed. "Hmm. . . You drive a hard bargain for a woman." A short nod accompanied his next words. "You have a deal, Cassidy Sinclair."

Stunned, she accepted the proffered hand. "I do? Are you sure?"

A wry grin played at Dell's lips. "I guess it's worth it," he drawled. "You're not backing out, are you?"

"Of course not. I'll cut it right after breakfast, then. If you're really sure."

His eyes twinkled at her discomfiture. "I'm sure." His voice was smooth like honey as he gripped her hand, sealing the bargain.

A tremor shot through Cassidy at the warmth of his touch, and she pulled away quickly. "Good night, Dell."

He flashed her a heart-stopping grin and placed his Stetson hat atop his head. "I'll see you in the morning."

Cassidy couldn't drag her eyes from him as he strode into the night, whistling to himself. Once he was out of sight, she clapped a frustrated hand to her forehead. The thought of being close enough to Dell to cut his hair sent shivers down her spine, and warmth crept through her belly. He had made it clear he wasn't interested in the services, so it never occurred to her that he'd really accept. She'd only offered because she wanted another excuse to invite him to the meeting in a way that wouldn't seem preachy.

With an angry toss of her head, she doused the campfire. How dare she have these thoughts and feelings about Dell when she'd signed a contract with Mr. St. John! Of course, she didn't have to marry the rancher. She could simply keep house for him. Then she would be free to marry Dell. Marry Dell! What was she thinking? Dreaming like a schoolgirl—that's what she was doing. It was just that every time he looked at her, he made her feel. . .beautiful.

Well, you aren't beautiful, Cassidy Sinclair, she chided herself. *And you'd better just forget about romantic notions and stick to the bargain.*

Besides, Dell wasn't interested in God right now. She couldn't have these feelings for him. It just wasn't right, was it?

Dell noticed a hesitation in Cassidy's eyes when he approached the wagon. He felt a guilty sense of glee at her discomfiture. When she had given him the challenge, he knew she expected him to refuse. But something inside of him had recognized a good excuse to join the worshipers, and the refusal on his lips had turned to acceptance, surprising him almost as much as it had her.

Emily looked up dully from where she sat on the tongue of the wagon. Instead of greeting him with her usual exuberance, she leaned forward and tucked her chin in her hand. "Morning, Mr. Michaels."

Dell smiled. He'd never seen the little girl so subdued. Hoping to cheer her, he reached out and ruffled her hair. "Hey, kiddo. You in trouble again?"

She shook her head.

Dell frowned.

"What's wrong, honey?" he asked, placing a hand on her forehead. He glanced at Cassidy. "She feels feverish."

Cassidy wiped her hands on a towel and walked the short distance to her niece. Cupping Emily's chin, she looked into the little girl's flushed face. "She certainly does," she said, a worried frown creasing her brow.

"Aunt Cass, I don't feel good."

"Sweetie, do you feel like having breakfast?"

Emily shook her head miserably. "May I lie down?"

"Of course. Come along, and I'll get you all tucked in." Cassidy helped a shaky Emily to her feet and walked around to the back of the wagon. "I'll be with you in a little while," she told Dell over her shoulder.

When she returned twenty minutes later, the worried frown was still in place. "I wish there was a doctor among us."

"Sit," Dell ordered, handing her a tin cup filled with coffee. "What seems to be the ailment?"

"She complains of a headache and sore throat. Plus—"

"The fever," Dell finished.

Cassidy nodded, her shoulders sagging. His heart went out to her. She had already lost her brother. It was inconceivable that she should lose Emily, too.

"Two children have died from sickness since we set out just a few weeks ago. Oh, Dell, I can't bear the thought of losing Emily. She's all the family I have left in the world." Large tears rolled down her cheeks.

Enfolding her in his arms, he stroked her hair. "Emily will be fine, Cass. I'm sure by tomorrow she'll be back to running around making trouble again."

Cassidy pulled away and gazed hopefully into his eyes. "Oh, I hope you're right. Sickness just comes on so sudden out here, and there's nothing anyone can do about it. W—what if it's cholera?"

"Do you want me to get Reverend Marcus to come and pray with you?"

Surprise lit her jade green eyes. "Why, yes. If you wouldn't mind."

"I'll be right back, then," he replied.

A moment later, Dell interrupted the preacher's breakfast with the news of Emily's illness.

Without hesitation, Reverend Marcus grabbed his Bible and kissed his wife good-bye. "I'll be back when I'm no longer needed."

Mrs. Marcus reached up and patted her husband's face. "Take your time, and come back when the Lord releases you. And tell Cassidy if she needs anything to let me know."

Admiration flickered inside Dell, and an odd sense of longing filled his heart.

Reverend Marcus clamped his black hat atop his head. "Let's go."

While the men strode toward Cassidy's wagon, the preacher began to pray. "Father, I ask for Your healing touch for little Emily. And while You work the cure, please give Miss Sinclair peace."

Stirred by the simple prayer, Dell surprised himself by muttering an "amen."

Cassidy was pacing before the wagon as they reached her. Relief lit her face when she spied the reverend. She quickly ushered him into the wagon while Dell watched from outside.

Emily stirred as they prayed, and her glassy eyes fluttered open. "Reverend," she whispered.

"Hello, Emily," the kind man replied, taking a freckled hand in his.

"Preach really good tonight, 'cause Dell's coming to the meeting."

"He is?"

Emily nodded wearily. "Aunt Cass is going to cut his hair. . . ."

The preacher's eyes twinkled as he threw Dell a grin. "Well, that is an answer to prayer."

"Uh-huh," Emily said, eyes fluttering shut.

"I'm going to go now, sweetie. But God is taking care of you. Do you believe that?"

Again Emily nodded, a small, trembly smile touching her lips. She fell asleep before the preacher climbed down from the wagon.

Dell shifted his feet as the minister glanced his way.

"We'll expect to see you this evening," he said.

"I suppose so." Dell swallowed hard.

"I'll reserve a seat for you right close then, so you're sure to hear every word."

"Sure, Reverend. You do that."

"Well, I'd better go prepare something especially good for tonight, per Emily's request."

Just then Cassidy stepped up to them. "Good-bye," she said, shaking the preacher's hand, "and thanks for coming."

"Anytime." He focused his attention back on Dell. "I'll see you later." Stuffing his hands into his pockets, he strolled away, whistling a hymn.

Dell glanced at Cassidy's face, studying the exquisite curve of her chin and the softness of her full lips. Large, luminous eyes gave her an air of vulnerability, and he couldn't help thinking how the delicateness of her face contrasted with her sturdy build. Even though he stood taller than most men, Cassidy almost met him eye-to-eye. She wasn't fat, but neither was she scrawny. Her small waist accented her curved hips. One thing was for certain—he couldn't get her out of his mind. He hadn't thought about a woman this way for a long time.

Her head shifted slightly until her eyes met his gaze.

Clearing her throat, she motioned for him to sit. "I'll get you some breakfast."

"You sit, Cass." He took the spoon from her hand. "Let me serve you today."

He dipped the cinnamon-laced oatmeal into two bowls and handed one to her.

"Thank you."

They ate in relative and unaccustomed silence.

Finally Dell cleared his throat. "Why don't you go sit with Emily? If she gets to feeling better, you can cut my hair later."

"Yes, I think I will," she replied. Throwing him a grateful smile, she set down her half-empty bowl and climbed back into the wagon.

Dell wiped the dishes and left the camp. He smiled as a thought came to him. There was no question about it. He was smitten with Cassidy Sinclair.

＄

Cassidy woke to a light tapping outside of the wagon. She reached over and placed a gentle hand on Emily's forehead. Drenched in sweat, the little girl was cool to the touch.

"Thank You, Lord," Cassidy whispered and crawled to the flap.

Dell stood staring up at her. Those eyes—bluer than the cloudless sky—squinted in the bright sun.

"How is she?"

"Still asleep, but her fever's broken."

Noting the relief on his face, she smiled. "You're fond of Emily, aren't you?"

"Secret's out, eh?" He grinned, reaching to help her down.

Without thought, she slid effortlessly into his arms. Heat rose to her cheeks when he didn't let go. She felt his muscles twitch as her hands pressed flat against his chest. Raising her eyes to meet his, Cassidy caught her breath at the intensity of his gaze.

"You know what?" His voice was low and husky, sending shivers through her.

"Wh—what?"

"I think we're finally getting this right."

"This?"

"No more tumbling to the ground. 'Course, that wasn't so bad, either."

"Dell!"

"I can't help it," he said, his face coming closer to hers. "With you in my arms, all rational thought escapes me."

His breath was warm on her face, and her eyes shifted to his mouth. It curved into a smile, then formed her name. "Cassidy," he whispered.

Swallowing hard, she closed her eyes and waited.

"Hello, Miss Sinclair. Mr. Michaels." A singsong voice broke through the mist, and Cassidy's eyes flew open. She stared, horrified, as the Pike sisters strolled by, curiosity plainly written on their pinched faces.

"Miss Pike." With Cassidy still in his arms, Dell nodded first to one and then the other. "Miss Pike. Beautiful day, isn't it?" He flashed a wide smile, showing perfect white teeth.

The two spinsters blushed to the roots of their hair. "We. . .uh. . .heard little Emily was sick and wondered if there was something we could do."

Cassidy squirmed in Dell's grasp, but his arms tightened about her. "That's very thoughtful of you both," she replied. "But she appears to be over the worst of it."

With a quick glance at Dell's arms wrapped around Cassidy, the two women gave a simultaneous nod and walked quickly past, whispering to each other.

"Thought they'd never leave," he murmured. "Now where were we?" His gaze roved dangerously over her face, resting on her lips.

"Oh no you don't, mister." Cassidy pushed her way out of his arms. "Don't you dare kiss me in public view."

"So you wouldn't mind in private?"

With a gasp at his play on words, Cassidy looked him squarely in the eye. "This isn't a proper topic of conversation," she said firmly. "I have a contract with Mr. St. John, and I intend to hold to my end of the bargain. Shame on you for being so disloyal to the man who sent you to find him a wife!"

"You were about to let me kiss you," he reminded her with a slow drawl.

"I most certainly was not going to let you kiss me."

Dell looked stunned but amused. "Do I still get my haircut?"

With only a moment's hesitation, Cassidy nodded. "Sit. I'll get my shears." She climbed into the wagon and opened her sewing kit, retrieving her scissors. "Oh, Lord. Keep me strong." She cast a glance at the sleeping child and started to climb down.

"Need some help?" Dell called, his voice thick with amusement.

"I think not." Gathering her skirts about her, she carefully climbed backward out of the wagon.

"Are you still mad?" Dell asked when she returned.

"Yes. How could you embarrass me in front of the wagon train's source of information? By nightfall the entire camp will know about this."

"Hmm," Dell said. "You are mad. Am I safe while you stand over me with a sharp object?"

"I assure you, you're safe—from bodily injury anyway." She smiled mischievously. "Of course, there are no guarantees I won't accidentally cut your hair crooked."

Dell gave her a worried frown. "Hey, now. You wouldn't mess up my hair just because I found myself irresistibly drawn to your beauty and tried to steal a kiss, would you?"

How could he tease her about her looks?

"Beauty, huh?" she quipped. "Let's not make this into a fairy tale."

He frowned, but she gave him no chance to speak. "As to whether or not you get a decent haircut. . .that depends on how well you behave yourself."

"I'll be the perfect gentleman." He placed his left hand over his heart and raised his right hand. "So help me God."

"Hmmph. Considering your relationship with God—or rather your lack of one—that doesn't exactly reassure me," she retorted. "Now let's get this over with. You have a promise to keep to my niece."

The worshipers sat on the ground around the glowing campfire, listening to Reverend Marcus's full, rich voice sharing enthusiastically from his worn, black Bible.

Filled with nervous energy, Dell shifted uncomfortably and resisted the urge to bolt from the service. He hadn't attended a church service since Anna died, and even in this open setting, he felt out of place.

He barely heard a word Reverend Marcus spoke as his mind stayed riveted to memories of the day he walked away from God. The God who took Anna and left him with four children to raise alone. It wasn't right. Anna was the gentlest and kindest creature he'd ever known, and the world was a cruel place without her. God should have known how much he needed her. And what of the children? The youngest, four-year-old Jack, had never known his mother. Dell had begged God to spare her life, but He hadn't. She hemorrhaged and was gone without ever laying eyes on their fourth child.

"Dell?" The preacher's gentle voice broke through his hypnotic state, and Dell lifted his head, noting through his daze that everyone was gone but him.

Tears streamed down his face.

"It wasn't God's fault. He kept His end of the bargain. It was mine. I couldn't control myself—couldn't keep my hands off her. She kept having babies until finally. . ." He took in great gulps of air as sobs racked his body. "When our third child was born, she was having such a difficult time of it, and we were afraid we would lose her. I promised if God would just let her live, I'd never touch her again. And then I. . .I killed her." A groan came from somewhere deep inside him. He jammed his fist into his gut to ease the ache. "Why didn't I keep my end of the deal?"

Reverend Marcus placed a hand on Dell's shoulder. "God doesn't bargain with man, son. His ways are too high for that."

"But He pulled her through when I made a deal with Him and took her when I broke my side of the agreement."

The older man lowered himself to the ground next to Dell. "The rain falls on the righteous and the unrighteous, son. There are no guarantees in this life."

Dell frowned. Here he was pouring his heart out to this man, and he was quoting vague scripture verses? Was that supposed to comfort him? Bitterly, he wiped his eyes and stood. He should have known better. There was no peace to be had at a Bible meeting. "Thanks for your time, Reverend."

"Wait. Do you understand what I just quoted to you?"

" 'Fraid not." Dell's lips twisted into a bitter smile.

"It means no one is exempt from life. Your wife could have just as easily died from an Indian attack or a fire."

"But she didn't," Dell insisted. "She died because I didn't stay away from her."

"Did you force yourself on her?"

Dell tensed, resentment creeping through him at the very suggestion. "Of course not. I loved my wife. Things were good between us—that way."

"Then your wife knew the risk of having another child. Correct?"

Dell nodded.

Reverend Marcus placed a firm hand on Dell's shoulder. "She made her choice, and life dealt a harsh blow. Don't blame God. Accept His comfort and move forward."

With a need to be alone, Dell smiled slightly. "I'd best be bedding down for the night, Rev."

"May I give you a bit of advice?"

"Sure."

"I don't know what your relationship is to Miss Sinclair and Emily, but I've seen you together. I strongly urge you to get your heart right with God before settling on a permanent relationship with those two."

"I'll think about it. Thanks." Dell raised a hand in farewell, intending to take a walk down by the river. But as though they had a mind of their own, his feet led him toward Cassidy's campsite.

He spied her leaning against the wagon, the gentle breeze blowing wisps of loose hair around her face and throat as she stared into the night sky. His throat constricted, and he drew a deep, unsteady breath. If everything went well, they'd be leaving the wagon train in a few days. It was time to tell her the truth. He only hoped she didn't run away. Though it might be better for them both if she did.

Chapter 4

Cassidy stood silently, watching Dell approach. Her pulse quickened at the determination on his face. Something was wrong.

"How's Emily?" he asked, concern edging his voice.

"Sleeping. Her fever never returned, thank God. How was the service?"

Dell shrugged. "I've been to worse, I suppose."

Hiding her disappointment, she moved to the fire and poured him a cup of coffee. Settling onto the ground against the wagon wheel, she patted the earth beside her.

"Sit. Tell me what's wrong."

"What do you mean?"

"You're as skittish as a wild stallion. I expect you to bolt any second."

With a heavy sigh, he dropped down beside her and took a sip of the coffee.

"I have something to tell you," he said slowly, avoiding her gaze.

A sense of dread filled Cassidy at his solemn tone of voice.

He cleared his throat nervously, then began to speak. "I should have told you before now, but I was afraid you'd. . ." Raking fingers through his freshly cut hair, he emitted a groan. "Oh, Cassidy, I'm just going to come right out and say it. I'm Wendell St. John. It was my ad posted at the general store."

A knot formed in Cassidy's stomach. "Why?"

"We didn't exactly get off to a good start," he said with a wry, humorless smile. "Remember my 'insufferable manners'?"

She shot to her feet, anger coursing through her veins, and turned to face him. "I'm beginning to," she replied, fearing her trembling legs might not hold her.

"I saw the look on your face when you thought I had posted the ad. You were so mortified, I was afraid you might not agree to come if you knew it was me."

"I see." She folded her arms over her chest. "So you lied."

He nodded. "I'm sorry."

"So why tell me now?" she challenged. "What makes you think I won't change my mind while I can still travel on with the wagon train?"

He reached into his shirt pocket and pulled out a folded document. "Are you forgetting this?"

Cassidy snatched the contract from Dell's hand. She read it carefully by the flickering firelight. Sure enough, there were no clauses for lying, sneaky ranchers. "What are you going to do? Have me hung for breaking this?"

He pulled his legs up, resting his forearms on his knees. With his coffee cup clasped between both hands, he sighed. "Of course not." His gaze caught and held hers. "But I hope you'll consider coming to the ranch with me. My children have been without a mother long enough. They need you."

Cassidy thought back to the notice. It had read, "Must love children." She narrowed her eyes. "How many children do you have?" Her voice was low but firm.

"Four."

It was her turn to sigh. "With Emily that would be. . ."

"Five. I know. I've already counted." His face held a look of hope. "Will you consider marrying me?"

Cassidy ducked her head. Her first marriage proposal. It wasn't exactly as she'd dreamed. No bending on one knee with words of undying love and devotion. Still, who was she to quibble about technique? She wasn't likely to get another offer of marriage anytime soon. After all, it had taken thirty-five years to get this one.

Her heart did a little dance. He wanted to marry her. Dell. Wonderful, funny, handsome Dell. She frowned. No. Not her Dell. Wendell. Lying, cheating, sneaky, say-anything-to-get-my-way Wendell.

"Cassidy?"

She glanced up, fury rising within her all over again. "You took advantage of the precarious position I was in. How do I know I can ever trust you?" She stamped her foot and stepped closer, wagging a finger in his direction. "Maybe you don't even have a ranch or children."

Dell shot to his feet. "I'll be back," he said firmly. "Don't go anywhere."

Cassidy paced along the length of the wagon. *I should just go inside the wagon right now and ignore him when he knocks. Of course, being the kind of man he is, he'd probably just come right in.*

Her cheeks burned at this last thought. "Lord, please tell me what's right," she beseeched.

Before the answer could arrive, Dell was back, shoving a daguerreotype into her hands.

"What's this?"

"The proper question is, who are these lovely children?" he replied with a smile.

"Then what's the proper answer?"

"They're mine."

Cassidy glanced down at the images of four lovely children.

"This is Tarah." He indicated a young lady with soft eyes. Her regal bone structure gave her the appearance of a queen granting favors to her subjects by allowing the image to be taken. "She's sixteen."

"She's beautiful."

36

"Yes," he drawled, a smirk touching his lips. "She knows it, too."

There was pride in his voice, and Cassidy's heart warmed.

"Then there's Sam, next in line. He's fourteen."

"Very handsome."

Dell lifted his eyebrows and flashed her a grin. "Everyone says he looks like me."

Cassidy rolled her eyes. "Who's this?" she asked, pointing to a cherubic, round-faced boy with blond curls covering his head.

"That's Jack. He looks like his mother."

"How old is he?"

"Four. His mother died when he was born."

Dell touched a finger to the last child in the photo, a gangly boy with freckles spread across his nose. A wide mouth curved into what Cassidy could only describe as an ornery grin.

"And this is Luke. He's nine—the prankster in the family." His eyes sparkled with good-natured warning. "You'll have to watch yourself around him."

Glancing at the faces of Dell's children, an ache filled Cassidy's heart. Here was her chance to be a mother to four children who needed her. It could only be that God was filling her too-long-empty arms. First with Emily, and now these four precious souls. Her eyes roved over the face of the youngest boy again. He had never known maternal love. Surely God must want her to agree to the marriage. But how could she marry a man whose heart wasn't completely surrendered to God? Immediately she rejected the troublesome thought. Dell had known God, so he wasn't exactly an unbeliever. He was more of a wounded soul in need of love and comfort to draw him back into the fold. When she raised her head to meet Dell's gaze, only the smallest of doubts remained in her mind. Impatiently she pushed them aside as she became lost in a deep sea of blue eyes.

"All right. I'll marry you."

The expression of shock on Dell's face was soon replaced with relief, then joy. He stepped toward her, opening his arms.

Cassidy stepped back.

His jaw tightened, and the muscle by his left eye twitched as he dropped his arms. "I see. You'll be a mother but not a wife?"

Cassidy opened her mouth to deny his words, but he continued.

"It's probably just as well. Thank you for agreeing to this. . .awkward situation." He held out his hand, and Cassidy placed her hand inside his to seal the agreement. "I promise I'll be a good pa to Emily, too. I guess we'll just have to make the best of things."

Unable to speak through the lump in her throat, Cassidy simply nodded. *Please leave now.* She hadn't meant she wouldn't be a wife to him. She just didn't want to be kissed in public. After all, it would have been her first kiss.

He had said it was just as well she didn't want to be a wife to him. The reason?

He obviously didn't want her for a real wife. He simply needed a mother for his children. Tears pricked her eyes. She fought hard for composure.

As if sensing her desire to be rid of him, Dell withdrew his hand. "First thing in the morning I'll speak to Reverend Marcus about performing the ceremony."

"S—so soon?"

"You're the one who refuses to travel alone with a man who isn't your husband," he drawled.

"Well." Cassidy drew herself up primly. "It isn't proper."

"We'll be splitting off from the wagon party in three days at the most. Would you like for the ceremony to take place the evening before we leave?"

"That'll be fine. Thank you for your consideration."

"Aunt Cass, I'm thirsty," Emily called from the wagon. Cassidy prayed a silent word of thanks for the interruption.

"I'm coming, Em," she called, then turned to Dell. "I'd better. . ."

Reaching forward, Dell placed the palm of his hand against her cheek. With his forefinger, he traced a feather-light line from cheekbone to chin and spoke so softly that Cassidy could barely hear his words. "Good night, darling Cassidy. And thank you." Then he turned and left her.

She shivered and felt her lungs protest until she finally thought to breathe. Had he really called her "darling"?

"Aunt Cass," Emily's insistent voice called.

"Yes, honey. I'm coming."

⌒

Dell stretched out on his bedroll beneath a canopy of twinkling stars. It was a beautiful night, complete with a glorious full moon. From somewhere in the camp, he heard the lazy sound of a harmonica playing "I'll Take You Home Again, Kathleen." The mellow music, combined with a night made for romance, brought tears of longing to his eyes.

Clearly Cassidy wanted a marriage in name only, and he understood her need to provide a home for Emily. He supposed he could live with that arrangement. It would probably be easier. Perhaps neither he nor Cassidy was ready for a romantic relationship.

Though his mind made a convincing argument, his heart couldn't quite believe it. He'd seen longing in Cassidy's eyes when he held her in his arms earlier that day. The same longing, he knew, had been mirrored in his own. If the Pike sisters hadn't interrupted, he would have kissed Cassidy, and she would have allowed it. But that was before she had learned the truth. Oh, how he regretted not being honest with her sooner. Still, Cassidy was a sensible woman. Maybe after she had time to calm down, she'd forgive him, and they could pick up where they left off.

His troubled thoughts began to shift, and Anna's image drifted to his mind. What if Cassidy did change her mind and they became man and wife in truth? Would he lose her, as well? He knew he couldn't live again through the pain he'd felt at the loss of Anna.

With a groan, he flopped over on his stomach and settled his chin into his fist, as his heart flip-flopped between his desire for Cassidy and the fear of causing another woman he loved to die.

What a mess he had made of everything. He had advertised for a wife with the provision that she could be a housekeeper if either decided marriage between them wouldn't work. In truth, that's what he'd intended all along. But he'd never counted on falling in love. And if he gave in to his feelings once they were married, he'd risk losing Cassidy the way he'd lost Anna.

Emitting a weary sigh, he closed his eyes and drifted into a troubled sleep.

⌣

Mrs. Marcus gently placed a bouquet of wildflowers into Cassidy's trembling hands. The vows were supposed to have been said privately before Reverend Marcus, but somehow the Pike sisters had gotten wind of the marriage, and the service had turned into a celebration for the entire wagon train.

At first Lewis Cross had refused to halt the train for the entire day, stating firmly that they must keep going. They had already lost time with the detour to Council Grove and the three-day rain delay.

Although disappointed—particularly the women—they resigned themselves to a smaller, less festive affair.

But by the next day, everyone stood in happy surprise while Lewis announced he had changed his mind. They would remain in camp for the entire day, he'd said, and everyone should go ahead with their preparations. He even called a halt at midday the day before the wedding so the men could hunt for the celebration feast.

No one knew for sure why he'd changed his mind, but it was whispered about that Mrs. Cross had expressed her desire for a break in the rigorous routine. So Lewis gave in but grumbled that he wouldn't be held responsible for any Indian attacks. They were in Indian country, after all, and it was better to keep moving. There was a good possibility, he'd insisted, that all their hair would be dangling from a spear before the night was over. But if they wanted to stop for a wedding—well, that was their choice.

The mention of Indians caused some unrest among the travelers. Still, a wedding didn't happen every day, and everyone looked forward to a break in their rigorous routine. So with excitement, the women of the train had pitched in and helped Cassidy finish the new dress she'd been working on.

She'd bought the white cotton material in Council Grove with part of the money Dell had specified she use for her trousseau.

The collar trailed up the back of her neck but dipped down in front, forming a V a few inches below her throat. The bodice clung to her body, and the skirt widened as far as the petticoats forced it to. Cassidy had opted for short, puffy sleeves before she knew this was to be her wedding dress, but she decided to keep them short anyway. After all, she needed a summer gown to wear to church.

The other women made pies from the wonderful gooseberries found growing wild along the trail. Two deer had been killed, as well as several squirrels. Everyone was looking forward to a tremendous feast following the nuptials.

So there she stood, trembling from head to toe, wondering why she'd ever agreed to this crazy marriage. The laughing, teasing Dell she had grown so fond of had been replaced by a sullen, moody Wendell. Anxiety gnawed at Cassidy's stomach, and she considered backing out of the marriage. But she had given her word and truly believed God had provided this avenue for Emily and herself. He would make a way for their happiness. She was sure of it. Still, although she prayed, the unrest persisted. Finally, she attributed the feeling to premarriage jitters and pushed it aside.

"You're a beautiful bride," she was told over and over. "Simply lovely."

With no mirror to confirm or deny the comments, she listened dubiously to the assurances of the other women.

She had washed her hair in the creek that morning, and when it dried, she left it flowing in waves down her back at Mrs. Marcus's urging. She found out why the woman had been so insistent about the issue when Emily burst into the wagon, holding a wreath of white wildflowers. "Here, Aunt Cass," she said proudly. "I made this for you to wear on your head."

Tears pooled in Cassidy's eyes. "Thank you, sweetheart. It's beautiful," she whispered. "Will you put it on for me?"

Emily nodded. Cassidy bent and allowed the child to place the wreath carefully on her head. "Oh, Aunt Cass," Emily breathed, her eyes glowing. "You're just about the prettiest thing I've ever seen."

Cassidy smiled and decided to let the exaggeration go. Today she had the right to listen to people tell her she was lovely. After all, she was finally a bride.

∽

Dell stood beside Reverend Marcus in the small grove of trees next to the river. The crowd of pioneers gathered in their finest clothes, smiling and lighthearted, ready to wish the happy couple congratulations. . .assuming the bride ever showed up.

Dell cleared his throat and drew an irritated breath. He knew she was only marrying him to mother his children, but couldn't she show a little enthusiasm for the sake of appearances? These folks didn't understand the arrangement.

For the past two days, he'd waffled between excitement over the marriage and dread over the arrangement. Cassidy had been so busy with preparations for the wedding, he'd barely seen or spoken to her. The women tittered around him, inviting him to share meals with their families, obviously an attempt to keep him occupied while Cassidy worked. And worst of all were the sly grins from the married men in the wagon train. Especially since he knew, in all likelihood, he'd be spending his wedding night on the hard wood bed of Cassidy's wagon.

That was if she hadn't changed her mind.

"Don't worry, son." The preacher's gentle gray eyes twinkled in merriment. "She'll be here any second."

"I wouldn't count on—" He stopped midsentence as the crowd parted, and a murmur rose among them. Dell inhaled sharply.

Cassidy appeared like something from a dream. Standing with the sun behind her, she looked surreal. He'd never seen her hair down and flowing free like that, and he felt the urge to sink his fingers into the shimmering tresses. She walked slowly toward him. The wreath atop her head could have been a halo. As though pulled by an unseen force, she lifted her face and cast a luminous gaze upon him, taking his breath away. In spite of himself, he offered up a silent prayer of thanks. He didn't deserve this woman, didn't deserve a second chance, but somehow she was about to become his, for better or worse.

Suddenly Dell's collar was choking him, and his palms became clammy. His knees nearly buckled as he mechanically repeated his vows and listened to Cassidy's quiet, solemn voice respond to the preacher.

"I now pronounce you man and wife. You may kiss your bride."

Dell fought to stay on his feet as his breath came in short bursts, and his head started to spin. Before he could turn to his new wife and seal the vows with a kiss, Dell felt himself sway. Then everything went black.

Chapter 5

A stunned silence filled the air as Dell landed with a *thud* on the hard ground.

"Aunt Cass," Emily shrieked in panic. "Is he dead?"

A low rumble of laughter began in the crowd and grew to a roar as Dell opened his somewhat dazed eyes and sat up, rubbing the back of his head.

"No, sweetie, he isn't dead."

Cassidy extended a steadying hand to her new husband, whose face glowed bright red. "Are you all right?" she asked, speaking softly enough so that only he could hear.

"Everything but my pride," he drawled, accepting her assistance as he stumbled to his feet.

Dell glanced at Reverend Marcus, who wiped tears of mirth from his round face.

"May we continue with the ceremony?" Dell asked.

The preacher gave him a bewildered look. "But the wedding is over. I pronounced you man and wife before your. . .um. . .fall."

The crowd roared again, and Cassidy wished the ground would open up and swallow her. He didn't even remember that they were already married!

"No, sir," Dell argued. "I distinctly recall one more thing you said before I passed out cold." He grinned.

Understanding dawned upon Reverend Marcus's face. "Ah, yes," he said with a merry lilt to his voice. "You may now kiss your bride."

Before she knew what was happening, Dell grabbed Cassidy by her shoulders and turned her to face him. Slipping his hands around her waist, he drew her close. Cassidy's heart thumped wildly as she prepared for her first kiss. His head descended slowly. So achingly slow that she wrapped her arms about his neck and raised on her toes, tipping her face toward his to close the gap between them more quickly. His eyes registered surprise, then he smiled. At the touch of his lips on hers, Cassidy relaxed against him, the spectators fading into the background. There was only the feel of Dell's soft lips and of his arms holding her close.

All too soon, the moment was over, and the look in Dell's eyes left her as breathless as the kiss itself. But there was no time to analyze his gaze or her feelings, for they were surrounded by well-wishers.

As the crowd of men swept Dell away, Mrs. Marcus slipped an arm through

Cassidy's and led her from the rest of the group.

"I've arranged for Emily to sleep in our wagon tonight," she whispered.

Cassidy drew back. "Whatever for?"

A twinkle lit the faded blue eyes of the plump woman standing before her. "Do you want a child in your wagon on your first night as a married woman?"

Mortified, Cassidy lifted her hand and covered her mouth. "Oh my! I never even considered. . ."

"It's all settled, then. Emily will stay with us tonight." Mrs. Marcus gave her a gentle pat on the arm.

She could only nod in response as the preacher's wife moved away to join the women preparing the celebration dinner.

Panic welled up inside Cassidy, and she looked around for a means of escape. Her eyes scanned the camp, stopping short as her gaze locked with Dell's. He shot her a concerned frown. She ducked her head to avoid his eyes and walked hurriedly to the wagon. Climbing in, she sat down, knees to her chest, tears of humiliation streaming down her cheeks.

The flap raised, and Dell stuck his head inside, worry written plainly on his handsome face. His frown deepened at her tears, and without a word, he climbed in and gathered her in his arms while she sobbed. When her tears subsided, he pulled away, holding her at arm's length. "What's wrong?"

"M–Mrs. Marcus is keeping Emily in her wagon tonight so you and I can be alone." A fresh onslaught of tears rolled down her face. "Honestly, Dell, it's all so humiliating."

"Oh." He cleared his throat and appeared to be in thought for a moment. "Cassidy, look at me."

She did so reluctantly. His gaze roamed over her face and came to rest on her mouth. Cassidy held her breath, hoping he'd kiss her once again. Instead, he lifted his hand and cupped her face, wiping away a tear from her cheek with the brush of his thumb.

"If I don't stay here tonight," he said softly, "we'll both be laughingstocks."

"You already are," Cassidy reminded him, then clapped her hand over her mouth. "Oh, Dell, I'm sorry. How rude of me!"

His lips twisted into a wry grin. "It's true. I can't believe I passed out like that. These folks will never forget the wedding where the groom fainted."

A nervous giggle escaped her lips. Soon they were both laughing so hard that tears rolled from their eyes, and Cassidy could feel some of the tension slipping away. Suddenly Dell stopped laughing and drew her close, his face inches from hers. "You've made me very happy," he whispered. "Have you forgiven me for not telling you the truth from the beginning?"

Reaching up, Cassidy pressed a hand to his cheek. She wanted to reassure him, but she became alarmed as she realized how warm his skin felt. Pulling back, she frowned and moved her hand to his forehead, then to his other cheek.

"Dell, you feel feverish. Are you sick?"

His gaze darted away from her. "I think it's just all the excitement. I've never fainted before."

Cassidy was about to pursue the subject further when they heard voices outside the wagon.

"Hey, you two, get out here and join the celebration. You can't leave your wedding guests to fend for themselves."

Cassidy's cheeks burned. How much more humiliation must she endure on a day that should have been the happiest of her whole life?

"Oh, Dell," she groaned.

"They're only teasing. Besides, I have a right to be in here. I'm your husband."

That didn't exactly make her feel any better, especially now that she wasn't sure what to expect from him.

"Let's go join them, shall we, Mrs. St. John?"

The name sounded strange, foreign, but somehow. . .right. "I suppose we should," she agreed with a sigh. "I—if you're sure you feel up to it."

"I wouldn't miss our wedding celebration for anything in the world. Don't worry." Dell hopped down from the wagon and reached up for her.

Cassidy accepted his help, but seeing the gleam in his eyes, she stepped quickly from his arms. "Behave yourself," she admonished.

The newlyweds received a round of applause as, hand in hand, they moved into the center of the circled wagons and sat at their "table" fashioned from boards placed atop packing crates.

The feast was "scrumptious," according to Emily. But to Cassidy, whose nerves were taut, it tasted like cooked burlap. Dell sat by her side. After a while, Cassidy noticed he was less attentive and seemed to pull away from her. His face was noticeably paler, and he barely touched his plate.

"Are you feeling all right?" she whispered.

Dell snapped back to attention, though the spark was noticeably absent from his blue eyes. He reached over and laid his hand on hers. "I'm fine. Don't worry."

Though she tried not to, she couldn't help worrying. She wanted to suggest he retire for the night but knew he wouldn't. So she said nothing.

The sun was descending in the western sky by the time all traces of supper were put away and the music began. Dell leaned in close, his breath warm on her neck. "Dance with me." Standing, he offered her his hand. "Please."

Her heart beat furiously as she allowed herself to be pulled to her feet. It seemed to Cassidy that she floated into his arms. She pressed her head to his shoulder and felt his lips brush her hair. A warm, cozy feeling engulfed her as she closed her eyes and allowed a sigh of contentment to escape her lips.

Suddenly she felt Dell stiffen and tighten his hold. Her eyes flew open, and she looked up to find him glaring over her shoulder. Turning her head, she spied the wagon master striding toward them while, behind him, a group of snickering men stood watching the scene.

"Time to share the bride's dances, Dell," Lewis said, grinning from ear to ear.

"Thought you were worried about an Indian attack," Dell replied in an icy tone. "Shouldn't you be standing guard or something?" He made no move to relinquish Cassidy.

"Come now. Be a sport." The amusement on the wagon master's face made his face even redder as he fought to keep from laughing and clapped Dell on the shoulder. "You'll get her back later."

A thrill passed through Cassidy. He didn't want to let her go. "Dell," she whispered, placing a gentle palm on his chest, "I think I'm supposed to dance with the other men. It's okay."

Dell scowled and released her. "I'll be back," he said, eyeing Lewis.

For the next hour, Cassidy was whirled from one man to the next. Each time Dell started her way, another hurriedly cut in before he could get to her. The men laughed and elbowed each other like it was a merry game. All the men except Dell. Cassidy was beginning to agree with her husband. Enough was enough. Close to tears, she had long since stopped trying to converse with her dance partners when she felt familiar arms encircle her waist. She raised her head to find her husband staring down at her in the flickering light of the campfires.

"Oh, Dell. Thank goodness it's you."

"Had enough dancing?"

She nodded.

Before she could say another word or think another thought, Dell grabbed her by the hand and, without so much as a glance back, led her toward the wagon.

"Dell," she said with a gasp, grabbing his arm for support as he stumbled slightly. "What are people going to say?"

"What does it matter?" He shrugged. "We're leaving the wagon train tomorrow anyway."

That was true enough. Still, the look of bewilderment on the Pike sisters' faces would haunt her for the rest of her life.

When they reached the wagon, Dell stepped aside and held out his hand. Ducking her head, she climbed inside. When he didn't follow, Cassidy frowned. Maybe she'd been wrong after all.

"I'll leave you alone for a while," he said.

She gave a slight nod, wondering at the flush in his cheeks.

"But I'll be back," he said softly and closed the flap.

Dell's saddlebags and rifle rested discreetly in the corner of the wagon, and Cassidy felt her cheeks burn. When had he brought those in here?

Her heart raced like a wild horse running free on the range. She was no fool. She knew what Dell expected of her—or she thought she did. Somehow, through the course of this dreamlike day, the stakes had changed. She knew this would be no marriage of convenience.

Lord, how do I give myself to a man who isn't in love with me? It never occurred to her to ask how she would give herself to a man she didn't love, for in the past few weeks, she had fallen for Dell. His fun and humor, the way he played and teased with Emily, who was slowly healing from the loss of her father. Each kind or protective gesture toward Cassidy or the little girl had endeared him to her more. *Dear Lord, let my love for him be enough.*

She removed her gown. Carefully, lovingly, she folded it and packed it into her trunk. Taking a deep breath, she lifted her new white cotton nightgown. With trembling fingers, she removed the rest of her clothing and slipped the gown on. Then she quickly grabbed her wrapper and drew it around her.

Her mind traveled to the four children waiting for her at home. *My children.* She smiled at the thought. All of them—Dell's four and Emily. She was now mother to five children. How long had she ached and prayed for a family of her own? God had answered her prayers above her wildest hopes. Except for. . .well. . .Dell didn't exactly love her, but he would one day. She felt sure of it. Her God wouldn't leave her in a marriage without love.

⌒

Dell sat beside the creek, watching the moon cast a gentle glow on the rippling water. His head ached, and he knew he was running a fever. With a groan, he placed his hand on his spinning head. He should have been back at the wagon long ago, but he couldn't seem to force his aching body to move.

At first he'd thought it was just nerves—what with the fainting and all. But as the day wore on, he knew he'd caught Emily's sickness. What would he tell Cassidy? Well, she'd probably be relieved anyway. She'd made it pretty clear the marriage was strictly to provide security for her and Emily and to provide a mother for his children. For all intents and purposes, theirs was a marriage of convenience. There were moments, though, when he had begun to wonder if perhaps it could be more. The way she'd responded to his kiss and leaned against him during their dance, for instance. He almost believed. . .

Lights were beginning to go out across the camp by the time he summoned the strength to stand, trembling, to his feet and force his legs to move—one, then the other, until he finally reached Cassidy's wagon.

Leaning against the frame, he tapped, hoping it was loud enough for her to hear, for he knew he didn't have the strength to knock any louder.

The canvas flap opened, and there was Cassidy, clad in white, looking very much like an angel, her hair long and flowing around her shoulders.

"Dell, I was about to come looking for you." The unmistakable concern in her voice filled him with contentment.

"Help me inside," he croaked.

"Are you sick?" Cassidy grabbed his arm and pulled as he climbed. Once inside the wagon, he rolled miserably onto the straw bed.

Curling into a ball, he began to shiver uncontrollably. "I—I think I c–c–caught. . ."

"Oh my, you really are sick, aren't you?"

Dell felt a cool, gentle hand on his forehead, then heard her gasp. "You're burning up. Honestly, Dell, why didn't you say something earlier?"

"I didn't want to ruin the day for you."

"That was sweet of you, but if you were sick all day, you should have said something," she scolded. Sliding on her boots, she grabbed a bucket. "I'll be back. Try to get undressed and under the covers."

Dell tried to sit up but fell with a groan to the bed.

Cassidy returned minutes later. She clucked her tongue, and he felt her tugging at his boots. With a grunt, she removed one, then the other. Next he felt his pants sliding from his body. He tried to protest, but she hushed him. "Don't be silly. You can't rest comfortably in trousers."

He didn't protest further as she removed the rest of his outer clothes, and soon he felt a thick quilt covering him to his shoulders. A cool cloth bathed his face. The last thing he heard as he drifted to sleep was the low, melodious sound of Cassidy's voice beseeching God on his behalf.

The noon sun blazed overhead when Dell emerged, pale and shaky, from the wagon the next day.

"Feeling any better?" Cassidy asked, looking up from stoking the fire.

"Some." He glanced around at the empty campsite. "Where is everyone?"

Cassidy shrugged and waved a hand toward the westward trail. "Oh, they pulled out hours ago."

"Why didn't you wake me?"

The accusing tone caused Cassidy's defenses to rise. "You were in no condition to go anywhere." She placed her hands on her hips. "Now do you feel up to coffee or breakfast?"

Dell shook his head and placed a hand to his stomach. "No thanks. But we need to get going if we're to make any progress before nightfall."

"You can't go anywhere today."

"We can't stay here on the open prairie like sitting ducks, just waiting to get our scalps lifted." He sounded exasperated. "Didn't you hear Lewis talking about the Indians?"

"Well then, I'll get things packed up, and you can tell me which direction to head," she said firmly, giving him no chance to argue. "But you are staying in bed."

"Emily was over her sickness quicker than this," he complained.

"Well, maybe you should have had Reverend Marcus pray over you last night," she retorted. "But since he's gone, you'd better go back to bed and let it run its course."

Within an hour they were on the trail, Cassidy following Dell's instructions that she just "head southwest." She tied his horse behind the wagon, and Emily skipped alongside. Dell slept through the day, and when they stopped at dusk, Cassidy was relieved to note that his color was returning, though he still refused any food.

The next morning they left as soon as the sun peeked over the horizon. Still weak, Dell allowed Cassidy to drive while he divided his time between lying in bed and sitting beside her on the wagon seat.

In the midafternoon heat, Cassidy came to a rippling creek where a trio of oak trees formed a canopy over the grassy bank. It seemed to her that the trees had been placed there on purpose for weary travelers to rest beneath their branches. Unable to resist the compelling shade, Cassidy pulled the team to the water. She waited while the oxen had their fill, then looped the reins over a nearby bush.

"Can I go swimming?" Emily implored. "I'm so hot."

Cassidy nodded. "For a little while, but we can't stay long."

"Yippee!" Emily quickly discarded her shoes and removed her dress. Clad in only her undergarments, the little girl jumped into the river, splashing with delight.

The water seemed to beckon, and Cassidy hesitated only a moment before removing her own shoes and unbuttoning the top few buttons of her dress. Picking up her skirt with one hand, she waded into the shallow water along the bank. Bending, she scooped water over her throat and chest and the back of her neck.

"Now there's a lovely sight."

Cassidy gasped and whirled around. "Dell! You nearly scared the life out of me."

"I've told you before to be more careful. If I was—"

"I know, I know." Cassidy waved a hand in his direction and turned back around. "If you were an Indian, you'd already have my scalp."

"Exactly." The amusement was evident in Dell's voice.

"You seem to be feeling better," Cassidy observed wryly, scanning the water for Emily. She found the redhead not far from them, bobbing in the water.

"Don't go too far, Em."

"I'm not," the little girl threw back.

"As a matter of fact, I am feeling better." Barefoot, with his trousers rolled up midcalf, Dell had waded through the water and now stood beside her. His gaze roved over her neck, a gleam lighting his eyes.

She felt her cheeks grow hot and quickly buttoned her dress. Cassidy swallowed hard. Slowly she waded out of the water, with Dell following close behind.

"Time to go, Emily," she called.

"Aw, Ma."

Cassidy's eyes widened, and she stared in wonder at Dell.

He grinned. "Well, it seems you have a new title. Better get used to it."

Tears swam in Cassidy's eyes. The honor of being someone's mother was something she could definitely get used to.

Dell reached out and squeezed her hand. "This is cause for a celebration. Why don't we stop here for the night?" he suggested. "We only have a couple hours left before dusk anyway."

"I thought you didn't want to stop for very long during the day," Cassidy reminded. "Seems to me I remember something about 'sitting ducks.'"

"Hmm. This is a pretty secluded area. We'll just keep a close eye out."

With a shrug, Cassidy consented. "You're the boss."

"Okay, then. Emily, stay in that water and splash all you want. We're staying here for the night."

"Yippee!"

Cassidy smiled.

Later during supper, Dell ate ravenously of the catfish he'd pulled from the river. Cassidy sighed. It was good to see him well again.

"Play ball with me," Emily pleaded when the last bit of meat was flaked from the fish's bones.

"Oh, Em," Cassidy protested. "Dell probably doesn't feel up to such activity this soon after his illness."

"Sure I do," Dell replied, hopping to his feet for emphasis and sending Cassidy a broad wink. "Come on, Emily, I'll toss the ball to you for a while. Then we'll sit here and I'll tell you a bedtime story. Would you like that?"

Emily clapped her hands together. "Yes, please!"

A smile touched Cassidy's lips as the two played. Even her brother, though always a kind father, hadn't been as involved with Emily as Dell was already. Cassidy sat in awe at the plan God had laid out before her. Her heart did a little dance. They would arrive at the ranch sometime late tomorrow, Dell had said. Cassidy sighed deeply, thinking of her new home. *Thank You, Lord.* She had thanked God so many times in the last few days that she was sure He was tired of hearing it. Well, not really, but her heart was definitely full of gratitude.

The sun had completely vanished by the time the last dish was wiped dry. Dell and Emily had tired of the ball game, and the little girl sat enraptured by the fire, listening to Dell weave a tale about a beautiful mermaid locked away in the lair of an evil sea monster. Cassidy would have preferred hearing about Jonah and the big fish if Dell had to tell a sea story, but she couldn't resist the romantic tale of the mermaid. She sighed audibly when the merprince rescued the young mermaid and whisked her away to his kingdom as his bride, thus ending the story.

Dell glanced her way, lips pursed in an effort not to laugh. Blushing, she snatched up a small twig and tossed it at him. He threw back his head, his laughter ringing in the night air.

With a lift of her chin, she stood. "Come on, Emily. Bedtime."

"Yes, ma'am," the little girl replied with unaccustomed compliance.

Cassidy glanced at Dell and shrugged. She wasn't going to quibble with a blessing, that was for sure.

After the little girl changed into her nightgown, Cassidy reached over and gave her a kiss on the forehead. Emily grabbed her, pulling her close. "I love you, Ma."

"I love you back, sweetie. Very much."

"Do you think my pa would get mad if I called Dell 'Pa'?"

Taken aback, Cassidy sat on the edge of the mattress. "I think your pa is so happy that you have such a wonderful man looking after you, he doesn't care what you call him."

"Think Dell would mind?"

"I think Dell would love it, honey."

Emily seemed to consider the words for a moment, then nodded.

"I guess I probably will, then," she said matter-of-factly. She nodded, and the issue seemed settled in her little-girl heart as she stared up at Cassidy with wide eyes. "Can I say my prayers now?"

Unable to speak past the lump in her throat, Cassidy simply nodded.

Emily bowed her head and was almost asleep before she finished praying.

When she returned to the campfire, Cassidy found Dell lying on his bedroll, hat over his face. He appeared to be sleeping, and relief mixed with disappointment washed over Cassidy.

With a sigh, she strolled the few feet to the river and sat staring out at the reflection of the stars and moon in the perfectly clear night. Gazing at the still, inviting water, she yearned to immerse herself. Impulsively she stood, removed her dress and undergarments, and draped them over a bush. She knew she was alone; still, modesty prevailed, and she folded her arms across her chest while she waded deeper and deeper. Soon only her neck and head were out of the water.

Eyes closed, she tipped back her head until her hair was fully wet, and the tension began to slacken in her shoulders as a gentle breeze blew across her face. With a contented sigh, she opened her eyes. A silhouette at the edge of the water captured her attention, and fear swept through her as her mind replayed Dell's words about the Indians lifting her scalp.

Slowly the figure moved from the shadow of the trees and stepped into the moonlight. Cassidy's heart pounded in her ears as she recognized Dell. His gaze locked on to hers for what seemed like an eternity. Then suddenly, without a word, he turned and walked away.

Cassidy drew a steadying breath and hastened from the river. Trembling, she dressed quickly and walked back to the campsite to find Dell lounging on his bedroll. Propped on an elbow, he stared into the fire. When she approached, his gaze slid up the length of her before locking on to hers. She shivered, hypnotized by the flicker of the campfire reflecting in his blue, blue eyes.

"Sit," he commanded softly.

Her reply was halting, her voice sounding strange to her own ears. "I—have—to get the brush, or my hair will look terrible."

"Get it."

Once inside the safety of the wagon, she closed her eyes and shook her head in an effort to regain some semblance of control over her emotions before facing her new husband again. Grabbing the brush, she returned to Dell.

"Come here," he said. "Sit by me."

Slowly she complied, willing her legs to move—first one, then the other—until she reached him. She sat without speaking a word and brushed her ginger tresses until she felt the warmth of Dell's hand covering hers. She turned to face him. The look in his eyes left her breathless.

"Let me," he said softly, taking the brush from her hand. With long, slow strokes, he smoothed the silky strands. Cassidy's eyes closed involuntarily, and the contentment she'd felt during the dance at their wedding returned.

"Tell me why you've never married," Dell murmured against her ear.

Cassidy felt herself stiffen. "Because no one ever asked me."

"Why is that?" he pressed.

Pulling away from him, she took the brush. "I think all the tangles are out now. Thanks." She moved toward the safety of the wagon. "I suppose I'll go to—"

"Sleep out here with me," he said softly.

Her heart jumped into her throat at the melting glance he sent her.

"We haven't had a chance to discuss our new situation," Dell pressed. "I don't expect anything from you."

Cassidy nodded. "I'll be back." Grabbing a quilt from the wagon, she returned to his side.

Dell took the quilt from her and spread it out over the ground.

She sat. Leaning forward, she began to remove her boots.

Dell raised a questioning brow in her direction.

"I just can't sleep with shoes on my feet," she explained.

With a grin, he took the boots and set them aside before dropping down next to her.

"I didn't mean to upset you earlier."

"Please, Dell," she implored. "I just don't want to talk about why no man ever wanted me before—" She cut off the rest of the sentence. After all, he didn't really want her either—he only wanted a mother for his children.

Dell stretched out on the pallet and looked up at her expectantly.

Gingerly she lay back. His arm crept around her until he pulled her head onto his shoulder. His fingers delved into her hair.

"What's that scent?" he asked, his mouth against her temple, muffling his words. His voice was husky, velvety, and Cassidy's stomach turned over.

"Lilac water."

"Hmm."

"T–tell me about the ranch."

Dell gently removed his arm from beneath Cassidy's head and propped himself up on his elbow. A faraway look came into his eyes, and when he spoke, there was pride in his voice. "We have four hundred acres of grassy fields and three hundred head of cattle grazing on the prairie grass."

Cassidy felt her eyes grow big as he continued.

"I've worked hard to make it what it is. We thrive. My children are well taken care of. . .except for the fact that they haven't had a mother." His gaze roved tenderly over her face. "Until now, that is."

Dell's eyes traveled to Cassidy's lips, which parted slightly as she drew in a breath. His head lowered until he took her mouth with his own. Trembling, her arm clasped around his neck, and she returned his kiss.

After a moment, Dell pulled away suddenly. "Maybe you'd better go on and sleep next to Emily," he whispered.

With a sudden burst of boldness, Cassidy pulled his head back down. He hesitated for a moment as his eyes searched hers. Seeming to find what he was looking for, he closed his eyes and reclaimed her lips.

Chapter 6

Cassidy woke the next morning enveloped in Dell's strong arms. He stirred as she sat up. Staring down at his handsome face, she drew a deep, steadying breath as the memory of the previous night brought a blush to her cheeks.

Dell opened his eyes and smiled. "Good morning." His voice was low and husky from sleep.

Cassidy's eyes darted to the embers still glowing from the campfire. "Good morning," she whispered, then stood. "I suppose I should get breakfast started."

"Cassidy."

Slowly she forced herself to meet his gaze.

"You might want these."

Embarrassed, she reached out and took the boots he held.

"Thanks." She turned and rolled her eyes. *Honestly. Can you make more of a fool of yourself, Cassidy Sinclair? St. John, that is.*

"And, Cassidy?"

Inwardly she groaned, but she still turned back to face him. "Yes?"

He opened his mouth, then closed it again, averting his gaze. "Never mind."

Anxiety gnawed at her stomach. "Something wrong, Dell?"

He pulled his own boots on and stood. Coming close, he wrapped her in his arms. "Nothing's wrong," he said. "Everything's right, and I don't want to tempt the fates by saying too much."

Cassidy pressed her head against his shoulder. "I don't believe in the fates. I believe in God, and He has been so incredibly good to me." She smiled as his arms tightened about her. "All I've ever wanted was a husband and children."

"You certainly won't be disappointed there. With five young'uns running around, you'll have your hands full," Dell said dryly.

"I wouldn't be disappointed to add a couple more," she replied shyly, feeling her face grow hot again.

Dell stiffened and held her at arm's length. He stared pensively at her for a moment, then dropped his hands from her waist. "You'd best wake Em and get breakfast started while I tend the animals. We ought to be going soon if we're to reach the ranch by nightfall."

A chill settled over Cassidy's heart, replacing the warmth of Dell's arms. What had happened? Disheartened, she headed toward the wagon to rouse Emily.

After breakfast, they quickly loaded their things and were soon back on the trail. Dell rode his horse alongside the wagon, while Emily walked on the other side. Merrily she waded through the tall prairie grass, exclaiming over the sunflowers towering above her.

Following a well-worn path, they trudged along, a tense silence filling the air between Cassidy and Dell.

"It's almost noon," Cassidy ventured. "Should we find a place to eat dinner?"

Dell shook his head. "My brother and sister-in-law live just a ways farther. We'll be there within the hour and can have a meal with them."

"All right." Silence once more permeated the air between them.

Emily played alone, occasionally letting out a delighted squeal when encountering a prairie dog or chicken. When she grew tired, she climbed up into the wagon or rode with Dell.

Cassidy's mind wandered back to the morning conversation with Dell. What had she done? Then it hit her. Dell must not want to have any more children! Cassidy almost gasped at the revelation. Her eyes darted to Dell to see if he'd noticed, but he seemed lost in his own thoughts.

Tears welled up in Cassidy's eyes, though she fought desperately to push them back. Not have children! But her greatest desire was to be a mother, to bear her own flesh-and-blood child. *Oh, Lord, what will I do?*

She'd promised to love, honor, and obey her husband. God had already met her expectations and even given her more than she'd asked for. He would make a way for her. She had to trust Him.

Caught up in her own thoughts, she jumped when Dell pointed to a small structure ahead of them.

"There," he said. "That's where George and Olive live."

Cassidy's gaze followed his pointing finger, and a bewildered frown creased her brow. "I've never seen such a home before."

He reined in his horse, and Cassidy followed suit with the team of oxen.

With a low chuckle, Dell dismounted and offered her his arms in assistance. "You'll get used to seeing soddies." He set her carefully on her feet.

"Soddies?"

Dell nodded. "Trees are pretty scarce. Most of the homes you'll see are made of turf."

"Do you mean to tell me that house is made of dirt?"

"That's right." He looked toward the little house. "Anybody home in there?" he called.

A wooden door opened, and a small brunette appeared, wiping her hands on her apron.

"Dell!" He stumbled as she flung herself into his arms. "It's so wonderful to see you." She glanced over his shoulder with a frown, then turned her questioning gaze upon his face.

Dell took Cassidy by the hand. "Olive, I want you to meet my wife, Cassidy.

And this," he said, reaching for Emily, who shyly took his other hand, "is Emily, my new daughter." There was pride in his voice. Emily had been trying out the word "Pa" all day, much to Dell's delight.

Olive seemed flustered but recovered her composure quickly. Smiling, she grabbed Cassidy and gave her a tight hug, then repeated the action with Emily.

"It's so nice to meet you both." Her brown eyes twinkled, and she seemed genuinely pleased. "Well, you must be starving. I was just putting dinner on the table. George is clearing the south pasture, but don't worry, he'll be back anytime." She threw Cassidy a mischievous wink. "I declare, that man can smell my prairie chicken pie five miles away."

Dell chuckled. "Mind if I take care of the animals?"

Olive waved her hand toward the barn, also made of sod. "Of course. Help yourself to feed and water." Turning her attention to Cassidy, she offered a friendly smile. "Come in and rest while I finish putting the food on. You can tell me all about how you two met."

"Excuse me, ma'am," Emily spoke up. "I need to, that is. . ." Her face glowed bright red.

Olive nodded her head in understanding. "It's around back," she said with a small grin playing at the corners of her mouth.

Emily took off running, and the two women turned back to the house.

Cassidy relaxed as she followed Olive into the soddy. The interior of the rustic home was surprisingly cool, a welcome relief from the hot wind outside.

Curiosity getting the better of her, Cassidy glanced around, hoping she didn't appear rude but unable to stop herself. Rag rugs adorned the earthen floor in the attempt, she supposed, to give it a more homey feel. A rough little table sat in one corner, but there were no chairs around it. She wondered briefly where they would all sit for the meal. In one corner of the room stood a wood-framed bed covered with a patchwork quilt.

The sound of Olive's laughter interrupted her scrutiny. "The first time I saw a soddy, I felt exactly the same way," she said.

Cassidy ducked her head. "I'm sorry, I didn't mean to be rude."

Olive waved her hand. "No offense taken, really." She let out a small giggle. "When Mother and I came out here from Georgia four years ago, I was appalled by the 'dirt houses.' Oddly enough, though, I've come to see that they are more practical than the cabins made of logs."

"How so?"

"We're snug and warm in the winter and nice and cool in the summer." She removed a large iron skillet from the oven and placed it on the table. "Log cabins let in all the elements. Plus, the Indians can shoot flaming arrows until they run out of fire, but dirt doesn't burn."

Flaming arrows? Cassidy gulped.

"Tell me about you and Dell." The woman moved on as though she'd never mentioned the Indians.

"Um. . ." How did one tell another woman expecting romantic details that she'd answered an advertisement?

Thankfully she was spared, as just then Dell made his appearance in the cabin, Emily tagging along after him. Behind them, a stocky, barrel-chested man entered. He was slightly shorter in height than Dell. His hair was completely gray, and he looked much older than his tiny wife. He sniffed the air appreciatively, then broke into a huge grin. "Hmm, chicken pie." Grabbing Olive, he picked her up off her feet and hugged her. "My favorite." He gave her a loud, smacking kiss on the cheek, then set her gently on the floor.

Olive slapped him lightly on the arm. "Go on, you crazy man," she said, a flush of pleasure coloring her cheeks.

George turned and stepped toward Cassidy, extending a work-roughened hand.

"I'm George," he said with a good-natured grin. "You must be Cassidy. I'm pleased to meet you."

"Pleased to meet you," Cassidy murmured, accepting the proffered hand.

"Well, let's sit and eat this bounty," George said, rubbing his hands together vigorously.

Sit? Sit where? There were no chairs in sight. Her unasked question was answered as George and Dell grabbed food barrels from the corner and placed them around the rustic table.

Emily grinned broadly and hopped up on one of the barrels. Cassidy couldn't resist an indulgent smile at the child. New adventures kept popping up in the strangest places.

Being on the trail worked up a voracious appetite, and they ate ravenously of the delicious pie. After the meal, Olive surprised them with a fluffy marble cake.

"I made it for the church picnic after service tomorrow," she explained, "but I'd much rather share it now to celebrate Dell's marriage to Cassidy."

Taken aback by the generosity, Cassidy smiled. Her heart lurched as Dell's hand covered her own. She looked hopefully into his eyes and found that his tenderness had returned. Maybe things would be all right now.

Soon after dinner, Dell pushed back from the table. "Well," he said reluctantly, "we'd better get going."

"Oh, so soon?" The disappointment in Olive's voice echoed Cassidy's feelings.

But Dell was firm. "We need to get going. I've been gone two weeks longer than I intended, and there are so many things to do."

There was a hint of weariness in his voice. Was he still ill? No, more likely just tired, as she was.

Olive nodded in acceptance and walked them out.

"Thank you so much for the wonderful dinner," Cassidy said, taking Olive's tiny hands in her own. "It was lovely to meet you."

The other woman pulled her close and gave her a quick squeeze. "Dell deserves happiness. Make him happy, and we'll be friends for life," she whispered in Cassidy's ear.

With a nod, Cassidy hugged her back. "I'll do my best."

George grinned and tugged Emily's orange-red braid. "Well, carrottop, you're my niece now. Be good for your folks."

"Yes, sir," she replied with a wide grin of her own as he lifted her up in his arms and deposited her onto the wagon seat.

Cassidy watched Olive give Dell a hug and wondered if she was whispering in his ear, too.

To Cassidy's surprise, Dell tethered his horse to the back of the wagon. "Why don't you climb in the back, Emily?" he suggested, pulling himself up to sit beside Cassidy as the little girl complied.

Cassidy handed him the reins, grateful that she wouldn't have to fight the lumbering oxen for a while, at least.

Soon they were on their way, while George and Olive stood waving good-bye.

With one last look at the sod house, Cassidy wondered what she would find when they reached Dell's home.

⤳

The sun sank low in the western sky amid a brilliant pink-orange hue as Dell pulled the wagon to a halt. "We're home," he announced proudly.

Cassidy opened her eyes wide at the sight before her. "Oh, it's made of stone." She hadn't meant to speak aloud.

Dell laughed. "Were you afraid you had to live in a little soddy like Olive's?"

"Maybe a little." She smiled up at him.

"The old soddy is over there." Dell pointed to the now-familiar structure a short way from the house. "My foreman lives there now. We lived there for the first couple of years, until I gathered enough sandstone to build the bigger house."

Cassidy turned her attention back to her new home. Wildflowers bloomed in a bed on either side of the stairs leading up to a porch as long as the front of the house. Peeking over the roof from behind stood a windmill. And in the dusk of the evening, a gigantic oak tree cast a silhouette on the barn a few yards away.

The barnyard was surrounded by a wooden fence. A beautiful black mare cantered back and forth, earning the attention a creature so lovely deserved. Her mane, blowing in the breeze, gave her an air of royalty and took Cassidy's breath away.

"That's Abby," Dell said, following her mesmerized gaze.

As if aware of the admiration, the horse stopped at the fence. Then, tossing her head, she neighed what seemed like a welcome and resumed her exercise.

Dell smiled. "It looks as though she approves of you, too. She's yours, if you'd like."

A thrill passed over Cassidy. "Do you mean it?"

"If you want her."

"Oh yes, Dell, thank you. She's lovely."

A look of tenderness crossed Dell's features. "You're lovely," he said, squeezing her hand.

She never quite knew how to respond to remarks like that from him. No one had ever told her she was pretty before. She'd heard things like, "With enough sense, you don't need to worry about your looks." And from old Widower Tridell, who owned the mercantile and was always hinting that she should marry his slovenly son, Merv, "You might not be the best-looking thing in the world, but you sure were built for hard work and having babies." He'd said it like it was something she should take pride in. Cassidy's cheeks burned just thinking about it.

"Why do you always do that?" Dell asked, dragging her back to the present.

"Do what?" She forced herself to meet him eye to eye.

"Look down and blush if I pay you a compliment."

Cassidy shrugged. "It's a little embarrassing, I suppose."

"Why?"

"Look, Ma. Puppies!" Relieved by the interruption, Cassidy tore her eyes away from Dell's smoldering gaze as Emily jumped from the wagon and ran to a pack of wiggling, various-colored pups.

"Those are new to the family. I didn't even have a dog when I left." He sounded just a little annoyed.

"Looks like you have several now," Cassidy observed, finding it difficult to keep the humor from her voice as she watched the giggling Emily romping with the tail-wagging lot of them.

Dell let out a chuckle. "Oh well. I brought a couple of new additions to the family myself." He climbed from the wagon. "Feels good to stretch my legs."

He reached for Cassidy, who went willingly into his arms. "Welcome home, Mrs. St. John." His voice was husky and filled with promise, making her heart lurch.

He released her as the door flew open and a curly-headed tyke ran toward the wagon. "Pa's home!" he yelled. He reached them in no time and jumped into his father's arms. "Pa!"

Dell squeezed the little boy, who in turn held on for all he was worth. He opened his round brown eyes and glanced over Dell's shoulder, spotting Cassidy. Pulling slightly away, he whispered, "Who's that?"

"This is Cassidy."

The front door banged open as more children emerged from the house. The two older boys, grinning and gangly, sauntered shyly to their father. He grabbed them both at the same time and gathered them into a bear hug. With the tension of the initial reunion over, all the boys began to speak at once.

"Did you run into any Indians, Pa?"

"Look at the puppies we rescued," said Jack proudly. "Old Man Taylor was gonna drowned 'em—hey, who's that girl? Those dogs are mine!"

"Did you bring us anything, Pa?" Luke strolled to the wagon and peeked inside.

"As a matter of fact. . ." Moving back to stand beside Cassidy, Dell slipped an arm around her waist and drew her firmly against him.

"Welcome home, Father." All eyes turned toward the house—to the owner of the velvety voice.

This has to be Tarah, Cassidy thought. Her picture, lovely as it was, hadn't done her justice. She stood, one hand holding on to the log rail that framed the porch. Long coal-black tresses flowed down her back. A frown furrowed her otherwise smooth brow as she glanced from Dell to Cassidy and back to Dell again.

Dell's face lit up. He reached the porch in a few strides and gathered his daughter gently into his arms. "You're even more grown up than when I left, honey." He held her at arm's length, shaking his head. "What am I going to do with you?"

Tarah blushed. "Oh, Pa."

Dell took her by the hand and led her down the steps. "Come here. There are a couple of ladies I'd like you all to meet."

The girl threw a wary glance in Cassidy's direction, and even from a few yards away, Cassidy was mesmerized by her brilliant violet eyes.

"Oh, Father, how wonderful," Tarah said in a voice that Cassidy didn't quite believe. "You've hired a housekeeper. Granny will be so relieved. She's been working herself to a frazzle taking care of the cooking and cleaning, and in her weakened condition, she really needs the help."

Granny?

"Get your claws back in, little cat," Dell said with a chuckle.

"Why, what do you mean, Father?"

Cassidy knew exactly what he meant. The little minx was deliberately belittling her presence.

"And stop calling me 'Father.'" He grinned and tweaked her nose. "'Pa' will do, like it has for sixteen years."

Dropping his daughter's hand, he came to stand next to Cassidy. Then, throwing a protective arm around her shoulders, he cleared his throat and made his announcement. "Everyone, I want you to meet my new wife, Cassidy. And this little girl," he said, grinning at Emily, "is your new sister, Emily."

Total silence ensued as four pairs of eyes stared at Cassidy. Three with hostility, one with rapture.

Jack left Emily with the puppies and ran lickety-split to his father's side.

"Do I got a ma now?"

"You sure do, partner." Dell swung his youngest up into his arms and laughed aloud.

"Yahoo!" He wiggled out of Dell's arms, then stopped short, staring at Emily. "She's my sister?"

"Yes," Dell replied with a confused frown.

The little boy walked back to the puppies and picked up a wiggling brown ball of fur. He shoved it at Emily, who still sat on the ground cuddling the pups. "Here. This is Warrior. He's my favorite, but you can have him if you want."

Emily glanced in wonder at the warm little treasure in her arms. She buried her face in Warrior's fur and received a lick on the nose. When she looked back up at Jack, her eyes were filled with tears. "Thank you. I've always wanted a puppy, but my pa. . ." She glanced shyly at Dell. "Well, my other pa always said they made him sneeze."

"Aw, it ain't nothin' to cry about." Jack shook his head and gave his father a look of disgust. "Girls."

A lump lodged in Cassidy's throat, and she could see by Dell's glistening eyes that he, too, was moved.

Shyly, Jack made his way to her. "Do you want a puppy, too?" he asked. "We got five of 'em."

"Why don't we let Cassidy settle in first, and we can talk about that later," Dell said, ruffling the blond curls. "What do you say, partner?"

Jack shrugged. "Okay."

Stiffly, Tarah stepped forward and offered Cassidy her hand. "Congratulations," she said. There was pain in her voice as she glanced at Dell. "If you'll excuse me, I have to finish putting supper on the table. Granny's having another bad spell today."

Cassidy frowned. Exactly who was Granny? Not once had Dell mentioned his mother living with them. Not that it mattered, really. Still, it would have been nice to have had some warning.

Sam and Luke followed their older sister's example, shaking Cassidy's hand. "I'll unhitch the team, Pa," Sam said, his voice quiet and devoid of emotion.

"I'll help him," Luke piped in.

With a frown, Dell watched his three older children make their polite but hasty exits. A thoughtful expression crossed his face for a moment, then he grinned and clapped his hands together. "All right, the rest of you inside now. I can smell that fresh-baked cornbread from here, and it's making me hungrier than a grizzly bear." He glanced at Jack and Emily. "Maybe I'll just eat one of these tasty young'uns and save myself the trouble of table manners." With peals of laughter, the children ran toward the house, five little puppies yipping at their heels, while Dell held up his arms in a menacing, bearlike gesture.

He stopped at the entrance and turned, while Jack and Emily bounded through the door. "You coming in, Cass?"

"What about our things?" she asked, motioning to the wagon.

"The boys'll unload for us later. Now are you coming?"

Flustered, Cassidy forced her legs to move forward. "Of course." She smiled, stepping next to him on the porch. "You're a good father. I'm glad for Emily."

Without a word, Dell swung her up in his arms.

Cassidy gasped, throwing her arms around his neck for support. "Dell, put me down!"

"No, ma'am. I'm not depriving myself of the pleasure of carrying my bride over the threshold."

Dell stepped through the open door. His face was inches from hers, and Cassidy could feel his warm breath growing closer. After placing a soft kiss on her lips, he lowered her gently to her feet and circled her waist, drawing her to him.

"Well, what is this?"

Cassidy jumped back at the harsh words and turned to stare into the hostile eyes of a woman who could only be Granny. The woman stood bent over, supported by a walking stick. Her hair was snowy white and pinned up perfectly. Her glance swept over Cassidy from head to toe, and her nose lifted slightly.

Cassidy felt the urge to step behind Dell, away from the woman's scrutiny.

Dell stepped forward and placed a kiss on the woman's cheek. "Mother," he said, "I'd like you to meet Cassidy."

Cassidy frowned up at him until he added, "My wife."

The older woman's eyes narrowed to dangerous slits. "You dare to bring another woman into my daughter's home?" Her voice trembled with anger, and she stamped her walking stick on the floor for emphasis. "I won't have it. I tell you I will not have it. You may tell Tarah I will take my supper in my room."

With a disdainful glance at Cassidy, she turned and limped away. The *thud* of her walking stick hitting the ground with each step was the only sound in the room.

Dell cleared his throat loudly and looked anywhere but at Cassidy.

"Dell? Is there something you forgot to mention?"

"Cass—"

"I believe there is. Let's see, you mentioned four children. One, two, three, four." She allowed herself the dramatization of counting them off on her fingers for him to see. "Yes, I definitely counted four. But wait. You never mentioned a mother-in-law."

"I'm sorry—"

"So if she's your mother-in-law," Cassidy continued, ignoring his apology, "what does that make her to me? My mother-in-law-in-law? Do I call her 'Mother,' too?"

"Are you finished?" His voice was tight, and the muscles of his jaw jumped.

Cassidy's heart fluttered. Had she gone too far?

"Yes, I'm finished," she answered, still holding on to the anger in her voice. "For now."

"Good. Let's get you settled in and have supper. We can discuss this later."

"Fine."

"Her name is Ellen, and no, I wouldn't suggest that you call her 'Mother,'" he said wryly.

Cassidy threw him a scathing look and went to help Tarah get supper on the table. What in the world had she gotten herself into?

Chapter 7

Dell inhaled deeply, taking in the tantalizing aroma of meat roasting in the oven. His stomach grumbled in anticipation. Glad to be home, he released a contented sigh.

He looked around the room, satisfied at the familiarity of his surroundings, then frowned. It looked like the floor hadn't been swept in days, and a layer of dust coated the hearth. Embarrassed that Cassidy should come home to these conditions, he grabbed the broom from the corner and swept it over the wooden floor, then, reaching up, knocked down the cobwebs in each corner of the room.

Since his mother-in-law's stroke, the place had desperately needed a woman's touch. Dell shook his head. At sixteen, Tarah should have been able to care for things, but she'd never been made to help her granny. Now he could see that they had done her no favors by indulging her laziness. Grabbing the rag rugs from the floor, he stepped out on the porch and vigorously shook each one until no more dust flew into the air.

"Welcome back, boss."

Dell glanced up to find his foreman striding toward the house.

"Johnny," he said, inclining his head. "Glad to see you made it home with the supplies. Have any trouble?"

The young man shook his blond head and lifted his shoulders in a nonchalant shrug. "We saw a few Indians here and there, but they left us alone."

"Good. You're lucky they didn't try to steal anything."

"Yep, that's true enough."

"Well, I'll come by and get the supply list from you in the morning."

"Yes, sir."

A feeling of unease crept into Dell's gut as he watched the young man swagger away. For some reason, Dell didn't quite trust him. He'd only given Johnny the position after Clem, his old foreman, had gotten married a few months before. A young, single man without other responsibilities seemed the logical choice since the other hands had families nearby and lived in homes of their own. It wasn't that he didn't do a good job—he did. But there was an insolence about this newest employee that bothered Dell.

He pushed the troubling thoughts from his mind. Johnny was young. Maybe he just needed a guiding hand. For now, Dell was going to go back inside and enjoy supper with his family.

When he reached the doorway, he stopped. Cassidy stood beside the hearth, her gaze resting on the daguerreotype before her.

"Cass?"

She turned, a frown furrowing her brow. "I don't understand. Why is Olive in this picture with you and the children?"

Dell drew a deep breath. "It isn't Olive."

Her confused frown deepened. "What do you mean?"

"Anna was Olive's twin sister." Why hadn't he told her before?

She set the daguerreotype back on the mantel and drew a deep breath. When she faced him, her eyes blazed with anger and accusation. "Why do you keep letting me find out things the hard way?" she stormed. "Did you think I'd feel threatened by Anna's sister?"

"I don't know." Dell swept a hand through his hair. "Things were so tense between us this morning, I didn't want to add to the problem or make you uncomfortable in their home." He took a tentative step toward her.

Cassidy crossed her arms. "Let's get one thing straight. I am tired of feeling foolish because you conveniently forget to mention certain things to me. From now on, I would appreciate the consideration of your honesty."

She stalked past him, heading for the kitchen, but Dell reached out a hand and caught her by the arm. "Cassidy, wait."

His heart lurched as she faced him, tears pooling in her beautiful green eyes.

"I'm sorry," he said, drawing her into his arms. "I've been selfish and vague. I promise to be straight with you from now on."

Cassidy's arms crept about his neck in a simple gesture of acceptance and forgiveness. Dell tightened his arms, and they stood locked in the comfortable embrace until Tarah's steely voice interrupted them from the doorway. "Supper's ready."

Dell held Cassidy at arm's length, his gaze searching her face. "Is everything all right now?"

She nodded. "Let's go eat."

He blew out a relieved sigh, and they walked arm in arm to the table.

⁓

The children monopolized the dinner conversation, filling their father in on all the details of life on the ranch in his absence. Cassidy sat silently, absorbing the family atmosphere and dreaming of the day when these children would eagerly share their lives with her as they were now doing with their father.

Tarah remained as silent as Cassidy throughout the meal and spoke only when Sam began to tease.

"A new family's living on the Crowley's homestead," Sam said, eyeing his sister.

"Sam." Tarah's voice was thick with warning.

"They got three sons, and all three of them want to court Tarah. But she's smitten with Anthony."

"Samuel St. John, you'd better hush your mouth right now."

"Calm down, Tarah," Dell admonished with a chuckle. "Your brother's only teasing."

"You always take his side." Tarah jumped up from the table and ran out of the room, tears streaming down her face.

A look of bewilderment spread over Dell's features, and he glanced at Cassidy for support.

She shook her head. "Honestly, Dell."

"What?" His brow furrowed into a deep frown. "Females," he muttered. "Boys, if you're finished with your supper, why don't you get your chores out of the way, then unload the wagon."

"Yes, Pa," came the simultaneous reply, and the two bounded out the door.

"And you, partner," he said to Jack. "You run along to bed."

"Aw, Pa, do I have to?"

"No arguments. Come hug me good night."

"Yes, Pa." Jack stood and hugged Dell, then looked shyly at Cassidy.

She smiled at him, and his face lit up with a wide grin showing pretty white baby teeth. He walked two steps until he stood before her.

"Do you want me to hug you, too?"

Taken aback, Cassidy nodded. "Why, yes, I think I'd love for you to do that, Jack." She opened her arms.

The little boy reached up with chubby arms and grabbed her tightly around her neck. She pulled the warm body close, and her heart melted. When he pulled away, his face was glowing. He lifted his chin and planted a wet kiss on her cheek. "G'night, Ma."

Tears sprang to her eyes at his ready acceptance of her place in his life. "Good night, Jack." She reached out and tousled his curly head.

Smiling, he headed to bed.

"Oh, Dell. . ."

"He's a sweet little guy."

Silently Cassidy nodded and began to clear the table. Looking up, she noticed Emily's head practically in her plate as her eyes drooped shut.

Dell followed her gaze to the weary child, and the corners of his mouth turned up in a tender smile. Pushing back his chair, he went to her and gathered her up in his strong arms.

He planted a kiss on her forehead and brought her around to Cassidy.

"Good night, Ma," the little girl said with a yawn.

"Sleep tight, sweetie," she said quietly. "Dell, where will Emily sleep?"

"She'll share Tarah's room. Her bed's big enough for the two of them until I can make Em a bed of her own."

"Wait."

He turned.

"Will this be all right with Tarah?"

"She's had her own room for sixteen years," he said with a shrug. "She'll just have to get used to the idea that she isn't the only girl now."

"I'm sure you know best, but don't be too hard on her if she's upset about it."

Dell gave her a wink. "I promise I'll be kind. I don't want to destroy your faith in my fathering skills." He turned and sauntered down the hallway.

Cassidy smiled after him. She loved her husband and hoped things would go smoothly as the children grew accustomed to her presence in their lives. Her mind riveted to Dell's mother-in-law, and she shuddered involuntarily. The woman had refused to come out for supper, which was fine with Cassidy, but she knew things couldn't continue as they were indefinitely.

Dear Lord, let things work out, and please help me get through the rough times until they do.

She was half-finished washing the dishes when Dell returned.

"Well?" Cassidy asked.

"Well, what?" Dell grabbed a dish towel.

"How did it go with Tarah?"

"Oh, that. She's a little put out, but I think she'll live."

Cassidy sent him a doubtful look, then took the dish towel from his hands.

"I thought I told you I wouldn't have a man working in my kitchen." Cassidy felt her cheeks burn at her bold statement. "I guess this isn't really my—"

Dell took her wet hands in his. "This is your home to care for as you see fit. You're my wife, and everyone will have to get used to it." He bent forward and placed a kiss on her forehead. "But tonight I am going to help you finish these dishes."

"All right," she said with a contented sigh. "But just this once."

They finished cleaning up and had just settled at the table with two steaming cups of coffee when the door opened. Each of the boys came in carrying something from the wagon. For the next few minutes, they carried in crates of books and dishes, pots, and pans—a few mementos from Cassidy's home.

"Where do I put her things, Pa?"

Everyone stopped what they were doing, and Dell cleared his throat. Softly he said, "Put them in your ma's room."

"But, Pa. . ."

The look Dell gave the boy was gentle but firm. "Your ma's room," he repeated.

Luke ducked his head, but not before Cassidy saw tears glisten in his eyes.

"Come on, Luke. Let's do it." Sam spoke with defeat edging his voice.

"The room's been like a shrine," Dell explained once the boys were out of earshot. "No one has slept in there since. . . Anyway, I had it all opened up a few months ago, so it's ready."

Fleetingly Cassidy wondered where Dell had slept since his wife's death but knew this wasn't the proper time to bring it up.

Sam and Luke returned a moment later still carrying Cassidy's things. Their faces were ghostly white.

"What's wrong?" Dell asked with a frown.

"Granny won't let us in there."

"What?" Dell bellowed.

Sam's gaze darted to Cassidy, then back to his father. "Granny said no one is sleeping with you in her daughter's bed." His face grew fiery red as he spoke.

Cassidy's heart wrenched for him. How dare that horrid woman put these children in such an embarrassing situation!

Dell's face grew red with anger. "You boys go on to bed. I'll take care of this."

"Yes, Pa."

" 'Night, ma'am," Sam said, echoed by Luke.

"Good night, boys. Sleep well." She turned back to Dell. "I don't want to cause problems in your home, Dell."

"Nonsense. You're my wife now, and that bedroom is yours. Sit and finish your coffee while I deal with this."

Cassidy returned to the table and sat while Dell stormed down the hallway. She heard him pound on a door until it opened.

"What do you think you're doing?" she heard him demand.

"This room belongs to my daughter," came the icy reply. "I will not have another woman sleeping in her bed."

"Thunder and lightning, woman. This is my room, and I'll give it to whomever I choose."

The woman snorted. "Ha. This was never your bedroom. You slept in the lean-to—most of the time," she added pointedly. "Until you broke your promise and killed my daughter. Now you bring another woman to this horrible country and plan to do it again."

Dell's reply was quiet, filled with controlled anger. "You will remove yourself from this room so that my wife and I can retire for the night."

"No."

"Things will change around here whether you like it or not. Cassidy is my wife, and this is where she'll sleep. With me."

Cassidy heard a strangled sob from the woman. Next came the sound of her walking stick hard on the floor, followed by the slamming of a door.

When Dell reappeared, Cassidy tried to pretend she hadn't heard, but she couldn't stop the tears that flowed.

Silently Dell gathered her into his arms, holding her until the tears subsided, then carried her down the hall. When they reached the bedroom, he hesitated briefly at the door.

"Dell?"

His gaze scanned her face until it rested on her parted lips. He lowered his head and kissed her passionately, almost desperately. Cassidy clung to him, and when he pulled away, she was breathless and wide-eyed.

"Cassidy. . ."

She shivered at the sound of her name upon his lips.

Dell stepped inside and kicked the door closed behind him.

Dell awoke long before the sun rose. He stroked Cassidy's silken hair and drank in the sweet scent of lilacs that always seemed to cling to her.

He glanced at his wife, sleeping so peacefully in his arms. She'd given herself to him the last night on the trail—had been so trusting and willing to be his. She had forgiven him so readily each time he'd asked. Dell pressed a kiss to her head, and contentment settled over his heart as she shifted and snuggled in closer to him.

He had hoped for a better welcome for her. What a homecoming it had been! The children were hurt over his sudden arrival with a wife. Had it been a mistake springing his marriage on the family this way? Maybe he should have just hired Cassidy as a housekeeper until they could get used to her. No! He hadn't wanted her as a hired woman. He'd wanted her exactly where she was. In his arms.

Dell closed his eyes but continued to see the pain reflected in the faces of the three older children. He knew Ellen would continue to spew her venomous words but didn't know how to stop it. It wasn't as though he could throw the children's grandmother out to fend for herself. That she blamed him for Anna's death was obvious. Of course, she couldn't blame him any more than he did himself.

With a silent groan, he threw his free arm over his eyes. He'd made such a mess of everything.

Cassidy stirred in his arms and looked up with sleepy eyes. "Everything all right?" she asked, her eyelids already beginning to close again.

"Shh. Everything's fine, darling," he whispered, placing another kiss on her temple. "Go back to sleep."

Cassidy smiled, and within a few seconds, the steady rise and fall of her chest assured Dell she was sleeping again.

Dell closed his eyes, and suddenly Anna's image invaded his mind. He shifted uneasily at the memory of her sad, pain-contorted face as she told him good-bye. A sudden fear gripped Dell. What if Ellen was right and Cassidy died, too?

Involuntarily his arm tightened about her. Maybe he should settle into the same arrangement he'd had with Anna to avoid that possibility—separate rooms. He cringed at the idea. In the end it hadn't worked anyway. Anna had found her way into his room one night and two months later had announced her pregnancy. When Jack arrived, she'd died—because he hadn't kept his word.

Tears clouded his eyes.

But what if God was giving him a second chance to do the right thing? Maybe he had to prove he could keep his word. If he went back to his own room, peace would settle over the house. The children would still have a mother, and he would have a wife—for the most part. Eventually Ellen and the children would grow to accept Cassidy's presence and maybe even come to love her.

Sitting up in bed, he breathed a resolute sigh. That was the way it was supposed to be. It had to be what God intended all along. He had no right to be in here with Cassidy.

With an ache in the pit of his stomach, he pulled on his clothes and picked up his boots. Throwing one last look at his sleeping wife, he opened the door and tiptoed down the hall toward the lean-to.

⁖

A groan escaped Cassidy's lips as the brilliant sun filtered onto her bed, casting its glow into her eyes. Her grumpy demeanor was soon replaced by a happy smile as she remembered where she was.

Casting a quick glance at the other side of the bed, Cassidy felt her stomach sink. Dell was gone already. Why didn't he wake her before he left?

Rising with a stretch and a yawn, she spread the covers over the bed, then dressed in a faded cotton calico dress. The first thing she was going to do once she settled in was use the rest of the material she'd bought in Council Grove to make herself a couple of new dresses. Emily could use a couple, too. Cassidy wrapped her hair neatly and pinned it back. She knew Dell liked her hair down, but at thirty-five she wasn't about to try to get by with a schoolgirl's hairstyle. As she put the last pin in place, she heard a light tap on her door.

"Yes?"

The door opened with a *creak* to reveal Dell on the other side.

"Why did you knock on your own bedroom door, silly?" Laughing, she reached to place a kiss on his cheek.

With a jerk, he pulled away as though she'd pinched him, then retreated to a corner.

Stung by the rejection, Cassidy stood immobile, staring at him, filled with questions she dared not ask.

Tortured blue eyes met her gaze.

"What's happened, Dell?"

"I have something to discuss with you."

"Go ahead," she urged.

"This isn't easy, Cass, but I want you to know I believe it's for the best." His words tumbled out. "I'm moving my things into the lean-to." He averted his gaze.

She frowned. "Do you mean you and I are moving to the lean-to?"

"No." His reply was short. "Only me."

"H—have I done something wrong?" Tears pooled in her eyes. "I mean, have I displeased you?"

The compassion on his face made Cassidy cringe. She might not have his love, but she refused to stand for his pity.

Dell strode to her and took her hands. "I think the children will adjust better if I'm not sleeping in the same room with you."

"I don't understand." Cassidy caught her bottom lip between her teeth to stop the trembling. "You're my husband."

"You heard Ellen last night. She won't stop throwing a fit as long as we share Anna's room." His voice pleaded with her to understand. "It'll be too upsetting for the children."

"If it's only that," Cassidy said, relieved, "we'll both move into the lean-to."

He dropped her hands and shook his head. "No. It has to be this way."

Humiliated, she did the only thing she knew to do. Moving around the room, she picked up anything that belonged to Dell and tossed it on the bed. "If this is what you think is best, I'll pack up your things."

"Leave them. I'll come back later," he said softly.

With one last effort, Cassidy followed, and when he turned, they were nearly touching. "Are you sure this is what you want?"

He dipped his head and brushed a painfully gentle kiss on her lips. "I'm sorry, but it'll be better for everyone this way."

◝

"Everyone but me," Cassidy muttered three mornings later as she reflected on their conversation. Standing in the barn, she buried her head in her horse's mane and sighed. She hadn't allowed herself the luxury of tears when anyone was around. But when she was alone, they came without warning, and she couldn't have stopped them if she'd tried.

"He doesn't want me after all, Abby," she whispered to the black horse.

She'd been a happy bride for two days. Had felt cherished and hopeful that she could be a good wife and mother. Now it was over. Dell had made it clear that she simply didn't measure up to his expectations and that he regretted the marriage. Oh, he'd said it was for the sake of the children, but Cassidy knew better.

Why did You even make me a bride if I am to live my life in loneliness? she cried out to God.

And that woman! How smug she'd been when Dell had walked past Cassidy's bedroom and retired to the lean-to the night after their arrival.

Cassidy led Abby out of the barn and climbed onto her back. She had to be alone, ached to get away from this place of despair. She wheeled the horse around toward the vastness of the range before her and nudged her to a canter.

"Cassidy, wait." Dell's voice rang in the air, clear and firm.

Fighting the impulse to pretend she hadn't heard, Cassidy tugged on the reins until Abby slowed to a walk, then stopped.

"Where do you think you're going?" Dell's voice was clipped.

"I'm going for a ride, obviously," she said, sarcasm dripping from her lips. "I need to be alone."

Dell grabbed the horse's bridle. "You'll have to find your privacy around here."

"Well, what was the point of giving me a horse I can't ride?" Cassidy glared down at him. "Maybe just a way to make you feel better for reducing me to hired help?"

The pain that crossed Dell's face brought instant remorse to Cassidy. If he had grown defensive or been mean back, she could have stayed angry. But he didn't. She had hurt him.

He recovered quickly and stared up at her with glittering eyes. "You can't go off alone on the prairie. Don't you understand anything you've been hearing about the Indians?"

"I don't know. . . ." Feeling like an idiot, she twisted the reins in her hands and refused to meet Dell's eyes.

"They're stirred up right now. The Sioux and Cheyenne are burning and raiding all over the territory and kidnapping women and children."

The blood drained from Cassidy's face, and Dell softened. "I haven't heard of any raids close by, but please be careful." He placed a gentle hand on her leg. "I don't want to lose you."

Warmth from his fingers spread through Cassidy's leg and down her calf. How could he even say something like that when he'd moved out of her bedroom the morning after carrying her over the threshold? And how could he seem so sincere saying it?

She covered his hand with one of her own. "You won't lose me, Dell." A sadness welled up inside of her, and suddenly she felt very tired. "At least not to Indians."

"Cass. . ."

A sob caught in her throat, nearly choking her as she grabbed the reins with both hands and turned Abby toward the barn.

Once inside, she dismounted and unhooked the saddle. As she started to lift it off the horse's back, she felt strong arms behind her, caging her in. *Dell?*

"Hey, now, you shouldn't be unsaddling your own horse." The voice was smooth as honey and definitely not her husband's.

Cassidy wheeled around, coming face-to-face with Johnny Cooper, the ranch foreman. Ducking under his arms, she glared at him.

"What do you think you're doing?" Anger boiled inside of her. "Don't you ever put your hands on me again."

"Whoa, now," he drawled. A lazy smile played at his sensuously full lips, but his eyes glittered dangerously. "No disrespect intended." Leaving the saddle, he sauntered toward her.

Defenses alerted, Cassidy retreated a step for each step he advanced until her back came up against the barn wall. He was so close, she could see the flecks of gold in his hazel eyes. "Don't come any closer or I'll scream," she whispered hoarsely, fearing she might do just that any second.

He shrugged. "Go ahead; no one will hear you. All the hands are rounding up cattle. Seems a few were rustled during the night." His voice was calm, non-threatening, but fear gripped her.

"What do you want?" she asked, despising herself for being a coward.

He placed a hand on the wall on either side of her head. "Rumor has it the boss is sleeping in the lean-to."

Horror filled Cassidy. The entire ranch knew of her humiliation?

Johnny took a strand of loose hair between a thumb and forefinger. Leaning in close enough so that Cassidy could feel his breath hot on her face, he whispered, "I just thought you might be lonely."

Mustering up her courage, she placed her hands flat against his chest and shoved as hard as she could. Surprise and then anger registered in his eyes as he landed hard on the barn floor.

"Like I said," Cassidy warned through clenched teeth, "don't ever touch me again."

Shaking with anger and fear, she stormed out of the barn and toward the house, only to find Dell walking through the door and strolling her way. So he would have heard her scream after all? Not that he would have cared.

"What's wrong?" he asked.

"Nothing. Just leave me alone."

"Don't be this way. I had hoped we could be—"

"Friends?" Cassidy spat. "Spare me, please. I've heard the 'let's be friends' routine before. Of course, I've never heard it from my own husband."

Leaving him standing with a bewildered expression on his face, she entered the house. She stomped down the hall to her bedroom, only to find Ellen inside with the wardrobe wide open. What next?

"What do you think you are doing in my room?"

The woman turned. "I'm looking for my daughter's shawl. It isn't among the other things I removed from here." She didn't even have the grace to be embarrassed about getting caught or apologetic for the intrusion.

"Well, if I find it, I'll let you know," Cassidy said through gritted teeth. "Now please leave. I'd like some privacy."

"Oh? Trouble already?" A look of triumph leaped into the dull gray eyes. "Dell is a self-centered, difficult man, as my Anna discovered much too late. It looks as though you are discovering it, as well."

A tiny, satisfied smile tugged at the thin mouth, and she limped from the room with the ever-present *thud* of her walking stick ringing in Cassidy's ears.

Cassidy poured a steaming kettle of water into the half-filled tub on her bedroom floor. She had waited all day for night to fall so she could have the privacy of a nice, warm bath and a good cry.

Two weeks had passed since Dell had moved into the lean-to. Rather than help the situation as he thought it would, the three older children were openly hostile. Cassidy felt more alone in this house full of people than she'd ever felt in her life.

She lifted her leg over the side of the tub and stepped down. As her foot touched the bottom, Cassidy frowned. Reaching into the water, she ran her hand over the bottom. Rocks! Those little hooligans had put rocks in her bathwater. It couldn't have been Jack. He loved her. And it was beneath Tarah to pull such a silly prank. It had to have been Sam and Luke.

With a huff, Cassidy snatched up the basin beside her bed and scooped the rocks from the tub. When she settled back into the now lukewarm water, a few pebbles remained and gouged her bare flesh. Miserable, she hugged her knees to her chest and wept bitterly.

In one dreadful day, all of Cassidy's dreams of marriage and family had been dashed. "Why did You betray me, Lord?" she whispered, knowing even as she prayed that God hadn't betrayed her; she had deceived her own heart. Her desperation to marry and provide a stable home for Emily had compelled her to join herself to a man who, admittedly, had hardened his heart against God.

Oh, Lord, forgive me, please, her heart cried. In marrying outside of God's plan for His people, Cassidy knew she'd become one with a man in clear rebellion. How could she have ever believed God would bless the union? Cassidy shook her head, a strangled sob tearing at her throat. She had been so blind.

What do I do now? Should I take Emily and leave? Immediately her ravaged heart spoke the answer. Standing before God, she had promised to love, honor, and obey Dell. Now God expected her to carry out her vows—for better or worse. Dell's rejection knifed through her heart until the pain was almost more than she could bear. But worse still, he had rejected God.

Help me not to be bitter against my husband. I don't want to cause him to pull further away from us both.

Chapter 8

I'm not going." Tarah tossed her head in defiance and folded her arms. "I'm too old to sit in school with a bunch of children."

Cassidy lifted her hands in surrender. "All right, I don't suppose I can force you since your pa's gone. But if you stay home, you'll help me around the house."

"You can't make me do anything I don't want to do," Tarah said with a sniff. "After all—"

"I know." Cassidy rolled her eyes and handed out lunch pails to Luke and Sam, then set about making lunches for the girls. "I'm not your mother. So you've said, more than once."

The last four months had been a tug-of-war between the two of them. If Cassidy wanted Tarah to go one way, she went another. Most upsetting was that the girl didn't even try to hide it, especially during the last couple of weeks since Dell had taken some cattle to sell in Abilene.

"Well," Cassidy replied with a shrug, "I assume if you don't want to go to school anymore, you probably intend to marry and care for a home."

Tarah blushed but eyed her suspiciously.

Ah, so I'm right. She does have a beau.

"How do you plan to do that without learning how? Taking care of a home requires some training. It certainly doesn't come naturally."

Placing her hands on slender hips, Tarah huffed indignantly. "I took care of this family while Pa was away marrying you."

"I don't know," said Cassidy dubiously. "It took me a week to get this place to shine when I first came. My muscles ached for days." *Well, maybe not that long.*

A look of indecision crossed Tarah's features. "Maybe I don't know all there is to keeping house," she said with more humility than Cassidy had ever observed in the girl. "But I'll learn."

Cassidy softened. "I could teach you, if you'd let me."

The moment was broken by a stomp of a small boot on the wood floor. "If Tarah isn't going," announced Emily, "then I'm not either."

Now she was outgunned by both willful girls. Cassidy shook her head and looked pointedly at Tarah. For all of Tarah's hatefulness toward Cassidy, she was Emily's hero. Surprisingly the sixteen-year-old hadn't balked about sharing her room. Cassidy suspected it was because she identified with the little girl's loss of her mother.

Tarah scowled. "Em, you have to go to school. Do you want to grow up to be an idiot?"

"No, but I don't want to go without you," she said, eyes filled with pleading. "I won't know anyone."

"Oh, honestly."

"Maybe you could go just this first week until Emily adjusts to a new school," Cassidy suggested casually. "It would be a big help."

Tarah grabbed their lunches from the table and shoved Emily's into her hands.

"All right. But just this week."

With a sigh of relief, Cassidy watched the four older children set off for town two miles away.

The township of Harper boasted a little sod schoolhouse that would serve as a church as well as a school once they found a preacher willing to stay. So far, services were held only when the circuit rider came through every few months.

The teacher had arrived just the week before and would take turns boarding with the families in the community. Thankfully there were enough families to house her for the three-month term so that she wouldn't need to stay at the ranch. Cassidy couldn't have stood the humiliation of yet another woman knowing about her living arrangements.

As she headed toward the kitchen, a small sigh from Jack brought her up short.

"What's wrong, honey?"

The little boy still sat at the table, his chin jammed onto one chubby palm. "I don't see why I can't go to school, too. Pa says I'm smart."

A smile lifted the corners of Cassidy's mouth. "Your pa's right, of course. But who's going to watch out for Warrior if you go to school all day?"

A frown creased his brow as he considered her words.

"By the time you're old enough for school," Cassidy pressed on, "Warrior won't need quite as much attention as he does right now."

"I guess you're right." He stood and gave her a bright grin. "Think I'll go find him so he doesn't get into trouble."

"I think that's a smart idea."

He beamed up at her and took off out the door, calling for the pup.

Cassidy grinned and shook her head, then turned her mind back to the task at hand. Stepping into the kitchen, she glanced around at the mess. She had postponed the cleaning up until after the children were off to school and was now faced with a pile of dishes to wash. With a heavy sigh, she took the dishpan from its peg on the wall and set it on the counter. Grabbing the fresh bucket of water from the corner, she filled the basin and picked up a dirty plate.

Her stomach turned at the sight and smell of the dried egg yolk crusted on the dish, and she fought to keep from vomiting in the fresh water. She quickly realized it was a losing battle and, dropping the dish, bolted. Rushing through the kitchen door, practically knocking Ellen over as she did, Cassidy ran outside. Bending over the porch rail, she retched violently until she lost every last bit of her breakfast.

She felt a cloth being pressed into her hand and looked up in surprise to find Ellen standing beside her.

"Thank you," she said, wiping her mouth.

"So he's done it to you, too."

Wearily Cassidy sank onto the porch and leaned her head against the rail, fighting a wave of dizziness. "What do you mean?"

"Are you that foolish?" Ellen laughed without humor. "I've watched your bouts of sickness for three months, waiting for you to figure out your condition."

"Do you mean. . . ?" She grabbed the woman's gnarled hand. "Ellen, do you think I'm with child?"

She shrugged, pulling her hand away. "What else?"

"Oh, Lord, thank You," Cassidy prayed, unmindful of the woman standing over her.

"I hope you're still thanking Him when the time comes," Ellen replied with a snort, then turned and limped back into the house.

With a sense of wonder, Cassidy placed a tender hand on her stomach. "Hello, little one," she spoke softly, her heart filling with love for the unborn child. "So you're the reason I've been sick and haven't had my—"

In spite of herself, Cassidy felt her face grow warm. Curiously it had never occurred to her that pregnancy might be the reason she'd failed to have her woman time the past couple of months. She'd been afraid she was passing the time for childbearing. The thought had filled her with dread and despair.

Now she felt indescribable joy and relief. With a gasp, she stopped basking in the joy of her discovery. Anxiety wrapped around Cassidy's heart as she wondered how to tell her husband the news. Given the circumstances, he wouldn't be happy. Well, she just wouldn't tell him for now. She didn't want anything to spoil her happiness.

Cassidy remained on the porch for a while, reveling in the knowledge of the little secret growing inside of her. Finally, with a sigh, she remembered the pile of breakfast dishes awaiting her. Standing on still trembling legs, she made her way through the door and to the kitchen. She stopped short in surprise at the sight that greeted her. Ellen stood over the counter, drying the freshly washed dishes.

Too stunned to speak, Cassidy stood dumbly in the doorway.

Glancing over her shoulder, Ellen grunted when she spied Cassidy. "I won't have you overworking yourself and leaving those children motherless again." Her voice broke slightly. "I'll take over some of the household duties."

"Thank you for your kindness, but I think I'm fine now. You mustn't overdo it," Cassidy said gently, stepping into the kitchen. "I couldn't let you—"

Ellen lifted a hand in silence. "I wasn't here for my daughter, and she died. If I had been, I could have spared her some of this backbreaking work, maybe even saved her life." Her eyes were tortured. "It's no secret that I am not happy to have another woman in the house, but I can't deny you've been good to me. Please, I need to do this," she finished, barely above a whisper, her tone almost pleading.

"Then at least let me make us some coffee and we can sit together and talk. Maybe it's time we got to know each other."

With only a moment's hesitation, Ellen nodded.

Cassidy went about making the coffee while the older woman limped to the table and sat.

As the water boiled, Cassidy sliced some bread and took down a jar of strawberry preserves. Now that her stomach had settled, she found herself ravenous. She placed the bread, preserves, and two steaming cups of coffee on a tray and walked to the dining area to join Ellen.

Lord, please let us become friends. It'll make things so much easier on the children—and myself.

"Here we go." With a smile, she set the tray on the table.

"Thank you," Ellen said stiffly, accepting the cup of coffee.

They sat in uncomfortable silence for a moment until Cassidy found a common topic of conversation. "I met Olive and George on the way here."

From the hungry look on Ellen's face, Cassidy could see she'd chosen the right subject.

"How is my daughter?"

"She seems well. As a matter of fact, I found her delightful. She and George have a cozy little home."

Ellen's face darkened. "She should never have married that man only five years after Peter's death."

"Peter?"

"Her husband. He was killed in the war."

"I—I had no idea."

A faraway look came into Ellen's eyes. "I thought we were doing the right thing by moving here to help Dell care for the children. Peter was gone the first year of the war, and my husband soon after." There was bitterness in her voice as she continued. "The Yankees burned our plantation to the ground when they came through. We lived in the overseer's house until I received word of Anna's death. With my husband gone and the house burned and most of our friends worse off than we were, there was no reason to stay in Georgia. So here we are."

"How awful for you. I'm truly sorry."

Ellen continued as though Cassidy hadn't spoken. "The worst part about it was that Anna didn't have to die. If Dell had just left her alone. . . She was small and delicate, like Olive, and shouldn't have carried one child, let alone four. Dell knew that, but he didn't seem to care."

Resentment welled up within Cassidy at the criticism, but unwilling to lose her newfound ally, she said nothing.

A tear rolled down Ellen's wrinkled cheek. "And now the same thing will happen to Olive."

"I don't know," Cassidy soothed. "Olive seems pretty robust to me."

Ellen's hand came down hard on the wooden tabletop. "It's this country! This wretched land. It's harsh and unyielding for women. We work and work until finally we die, one way or another."

Ellen's thoughtful gaze scanned Cassidy's face, then moved down to her stomach. She drew a breath. "I rattled on too long. You must take care of yourself and stay strong."

Cassidy's mind was reeling from the woman's outburst. Still, her eyes felt heavy as a wave of fatigue swept over her.

"I am tired," she admitted.

"Then you must go and lie down."

With a nod, Cassidy stood and reached to pick up a dish.

Ellen placed a restraining hand on her arm. "I'll just finish my coffee and clean up this mess."

Cassidy hesitated, then nodded. "All right," she said. Making her way to her bedroom, she stopped and turned. "Many women thrive on the prairie and bear children who thrive, as well. I am so very sorry for the loss of your daughter. But you mustn't blame Dell or yourself for her death."

Ellen stared silently at the cup in her hands.

"I'll be going now," Cassidy said softly. "Thank you for your kindness today."

⌒

Dell reined in his roan mare and dismounted. After two weeks away from home, he was ready for a hot meal, a bath, and a comfortable bed.

"Take care of my horse, will you, Johnny?" he asked, slinging his saddlebags over his shoulder.

"Sure, Boss."

They had gotten a good price for the cattle. This had been the most profitable year so far for the ranch, and he'd splurged on little surprises for his family. Anxious to pass out the gifts, he sauntered toward the house, grinning in anticipation. He expected the door to burst open any moment and five happy children to run out to greet him. When the door remained shut, he frowned, wondering where everyone could be.

He opened the door slowly and stepped inside. "Hello!" he called.

"For pity's sake, be quiet. You'll wake Cassidy." Ellen sat in the wooden rocker before the fireplace, knitting in her hands. Something Dell hadn't seen her do in months.

"Mother, it's good to see you feeling well enough to be up in your chair." He glanced around. "Where are the children?"

"Jack is napping. The others are at school."

"Oh, good, the new teacher arrived, then." Dell deposited his dusty saddle-bags on the table. Receiving a scolding frown from Ellen, he snatched them back up and swiped at the dust on the table. He tossed the bags into a corner. "I'll get those out of the way soon as I get something to eat."

"There's some bread, already sliced, wrapped up on the kitchen counter and some preserves in the cupboard. And don't make a mess."

Dell's eyebrows shot up, wondering what had brought about such a change in his mother-in-law. Rather than question her, he decided to count his blessings and let it go.

He grabbed the bread and took it to the table, devouring it ravenously, without the preserves. "Everything okay while I was away?"

"Of course," Ellen replied tersely. "Why wouldn't it be?"

"Did you say Cass is sleeping?" Concern filled him. "She sick?"

Silence filled the air long enough that Dell thought maybe she hadn't heard him. He was about to repeat the question when she spoke up.

"Cassidy needs rest. She does twice as much around here as anyone in the house and just got herself tired out. She'll be fine, but she needs to slow down some."

Concern turned to fear as a gnawing sensation crept through his midsection. "What do you mean?"

"Just what I said." Annoyance sharpened her tone. "You've got to get her to rest more."

If Ellen was concerned about Cassidy, something had to be wrong.

"Mother, just tell me if Cassidy is ill."

"Didn't you hear what I said? She needs more rest, that's all. Make her rest. And she especially needs to stay out of that garden during the heat of the day."

Dell lifted his arms in helpless appeal and let them drop to his knees. "Then what do you suggest I do?" He wished she would stop rocking and knitting and just look at him.

As if she'd read his thoughts, she sat still in the chair and gave him a steady gaze. "It might not hurt to have a little fun around here. Things have been rather dismal since you brought her, through no fault of her own, I might add."

Dell squirmed like a young boy who'd been caught doing something wrong, and he found himself wishing she would go back to her rocking and knitting. Something had most certainly happened while he was away. He never thought he'd see the day Ellen would champion Cassidy.

Ellen shrugged, resuming her knitting. "A late summer picnic down by the creek wouldn't be a bad idea. The children would love it, and the relaxation would do Cassidy some good."

Actually, it was a wonderful idea. Dell stood and closed the distance between them. Bending, he gave her a peck on the cheek. "You're a genius."

She jerked her head away as though the kiss had defiled her. "Do not think I can be charmed the way the younger women can, Dell St. John. I see you for the selfish man you are. You as good as killed my Anna, and now you're doing the same thing to—" She stopped abruptly and returned with a vengeance to her knitting.

With a shake of his head, Dell returned to the saddlebags, reached down, and grabbed them. Strolling down the hall, he reached inside one of the bags and withdrew a small package. He tapped lightly on Cassidy's door, and when he received no answer, he gently pushed it open. His heart lurched at the sight of her sleeping soundly on the bed they had shared one night. With effort, he pushed the image away.

With a frown, he examined her face. Ellen was right. Cassidy was overworking herself. She was pale, and dark smudges colored the skin below her eyes. His heart nearly stopped as she stirred, turning to one side. He laid the package on the bureau, wincing as it made a crinkling noise, and slowly backed out of the room.

~

"Ma!"

Cassidy jolted awake as Emily burst through the bedroom door.

The young girl bounded onto the bed, jostling Cassidy. "I love school! Miss Nelson is just beautiful and so nice." Emily threw her arms around Cassidy and held tightly. "She said I was real smart, Ma."

Returning the embrace, Cassidy breathed a relieved sigh. The little girl had adjusted to her new home better than Cassidy had dared hope. There was an immediate rapport between Jack and Emily, and Tarah had taken her new sister under her wing. Emily adored Sam and laughed uproariously at Luke's antics, thus endearing her to the ornery boy.

"Sweetheart, I'm so glad you had such a nice day."

Emily wiggled free and sat staring with rapture on her face.

"Did you make any new friends?"

Her braids bobbed as she nodded vigorously. "Becky Simpson is my age, too. She just moved here last month and didn't know anyone either, so we decided to be best friends. Her pa's the new doctor. Miss Nelson said she was real smart, just like me."

It appeared the teacher was not only beautiful and nice but pretty smart herself. Cassidy smiled.

Emily hopped off the bed. "I have to go say hi to Pa."

Pa?

"Wait, Em. Dell's home?"

"Uh-huh," the little girl answered as she ran from the room.

Cassidy's heart fluttered. She stood up and smoothed the quilt back over the bed. Walking to the bureau, she grabbed her comb and started to run it through her hair, but she stopped short as her gaze fell on a small brown package.

Realizing it could only be from Dell, she picked it up with trembling hands and carefully opened the gift. Lilac water. Tears welled in her eyes and rolled down her cheeks. He had bought her lilac water. He must have noticed she had run out awhile back.

Is there hope after all, Lord?

She placed a tender hand on her stomach. "You have a wonderful pa, little one," she whispered. "I only hope. . ."

Dell was such a good father, but he had made it clear he didn't want more children.

A smile played at the corners of her lips. It was too late for that now. Their child was growing inside her, and he would just have to get used to it. That is, when she got up the nerve to tell him.

Chapter 9

Squeals of delight greeted Cassidy as she stepped into the sitting room a few moments later.

"Ma, look what Pa brung me," shouted Jack. He was dressed in a war bonnet, long enough to drag on the floor. With a war whoop good enough to put any Indian to shame, he bounded out the front door. Seconds later, the sound of squawking and clucking confirmed he was wreaking havoc on the unsuspecting chickens scratching in the yard.

Dell stood from his place next to the front window and observed Cassidy, his brow creased in an anxious frown. "Here, come and sit," he said, holding on to the back of the wooden chair. "You're still peaked."

Cassidy moved to the seat and lowered herself. "Thank you," she murmured, flustered by his closeness.

"You smell of lilacs again," he said softly.

"Yes, thanks; it was thoughtful of you to realize I was out of my favorite scent."

"It's my favorite scent, too." His low voice brought a shiver up and down her spine. "I've missed it."

Sam cleared his throat loudly. "Thanks for the new rifle, Pa," he said. "Maybe you and me can go huntin' Sunday."

Dell shook his head. "We have plans for Sunday, son."

Everyone stopped and stared at him curiously.

"What plans?" asked Tarah.

"We're going on a picnic down by the creek." He threw a wink at Ellen, who frowned and rocked harder in her chair. "Your granny here thinks we need a little family fun, and I'm inclined to agree." He glanced around the room, eyeing each of the children sternly. "We've been a bunch of old sourpusses too long. We're going to pack us a lunch and take a ball to play with and maybe even take a dip in the creek or go fishing."

"Hey, I can try out the new rod you brought me!" said Luke. Then his face darkened. "Aw, we can't go Sunday."

"Why's that?" Dell asked with a frown.

"The preacher's going to be in town this Sunday," Luke said with unconcealed disappointment. "Mr. Anderson came to the school today and told us to tell our folks."

Cassidy's heart skipped a beat. A real church service. She'd had no fellowship

82

with believers since they left the wagon train. The thought thrilled her to the very core of her being.

"That's right," Tarah confirmed.

Dell's face clouded over. "Well, thunder and lightning," he muttered with a tentative glance at Ellen. "I suppose you'll be wanting to go to the service?"

"Naturally."

"We'll make it another time, then." Disappointment edged his voice. "I'm going to get cleaned up before supper."

Silence descended upon the room as he made his way down the hall to the lean-to.

"Aw, Granny," Sam spoke up, "couldn't we just skip the service?"

"Certainly not, young man. Sunday is the Lord's Day, and if He has seen fit to bless us with a preacher, we will not dishonor Him by going on a picnic instead. Now go do your chores."

"Yes'm," he replied meekly.

Cassidy's heart went out to the group of disappointed children. After all, they hadn't grown up with church services. A picnic sounded like just the thing to cheer them up.

Suddenly an idea came to her. "Maybe we could prepare everything Saturday night and have the picnic after church."

All pairs of eyes turned to Ellen in question.

"Well, I suppose that would be all right," she said grudgingly. "As long as we honor the Lord first."

The children let out a cheer. If Granny said it was okay, then it was settled.

An unbidden quiver of resentment welled up inside Cassidy. She was their mother, after all. Granted, not in the natural sense, but she was in her heart. They shouldn't have to ask their grandmother's permission to do something she suggested. She squelched the irritation with a sigh of resignation. Maybe in time.

The rest of the week passed in a whirl of activity. The children left for school each day filled with excitement. Emily just "loved" her teacher and had found a kindred spirit in her little friend, Becky.

Tarah seemed to enjoy school, as well, and brought homework to complete each night. She didn't mention their agreement about school, and Cassidy hoped the girl would forget all about quitting school and continue her education. Sam, from what Cassidy had gathered from Tarah's teasing, was smitten with the new doctor's older daughter, Camilla Simpson, Becky's sister. And true to his mischievous self, Luke had placed a bent nail on Randall Scott's chair and had been sent to the corner not once but twice during the week. He was severely scolded by his pa, who warned it would be a trip to the woodshed next time.

For Cassidy, the week was filled with the wonder of her pregnancy. More than once, she'd been tempted to reveal her secret to Dell, but he'd been withdrawn and sullen again after the news of the preacher coming through the area. So she enjoyed her secret in silence, hoping Ellen wouldn't tell Dell before she found the right time to do it herself.

Saturday night, Ellen, Tarah, and Cassidy quickly cleared away the supper dishes and went about preparing their picnic lunch for the following afternoon. Dell had slaughtered two chickens earlier in the day, and Ellen cut them into pieces, then fried them to a golden brown. Cassidy carefully shucked and boiled a mound of corn, still on the cob, then mixed together a batch of corn muffins. Tarah completed the feast by baking a fluffy white cake, marbled with brown sugar and cinnamon.

Once the children were settled in bed, Cassidy stepped onto the porch to escape the heat of the kitchen. Catching a cool breeze, she lifted her head slightly and closed her eyes. A feeling of contentment swept over her as she thought of the family God had given her. True, it wasn't what she'd always planned, but she wouldn't trade it for anything in the world. "Lord," she breathed, "thank You so much for the blessings You've brought to my life."

A short laugh startled her, and her eyes flew open. Turning, she spied Dell strolling toward her from a shadowy corner of the porch.

"Honestly, Dell," she said. "You scared me half to death."

"You were completely oblivious. What if I'd been an Indian?"

"Would you stop bringing that up? No Indian is going to sneak up on me while I'm standing on my own front porch."

"You never know." Dell shrugged. He stared intently into her eyes. "You were thanking God for your blessings. Did you mean it?"

Cassidy's mind flew to the child growing inside of her, and joy filled her.

"Oh, Dell, I'm so happy—happier than I ever thought possible."

A sense of glee washed over her at Dell's stung look. Well, admittedly, she could be happier. But it was Dell's decision that they live apart, and she was tired of moping around about it. She wouldn't fight him anymore or be angry with him. For the children's sakes, she would try to give them a natural happy home, even if things weren't natural and happy between their father and herself.

"Will you come to the service with us in the morning?" she asked.

"No." The answer was clipped, meant to end the subject, but Cassidy felt compelled to press.

"It would mean a lot to the children. . .and me."

Dell's expression softened. He reached out his hand and brushed lightly at her cheek.

Cassidy closed her eyes. He hadn't touched her like that in so long, she'd almost forgotten how gentle his hands could be on her. A gentle sigh escaped her lips.

"Cass," he said, his voice husky and low. He stepped forward, claiming her lips with his own.

Cassidy responded with a fervor to match his. *Oh, Lord, please!* She loved her husband and wanted him back where he was supposed to be.

Dell groaned and tore his lips away. "Go inside," he said softly. After a last tortured glance, he walked down the porch steps and headed for the barn.

With a sigh of resignation, Cassidy went back inside. She paused at the boys' bedroom and glanced in. Three angelic sleeping faces greeted her. She paused for a moment, watching them, then closed the door lightly. Next she checked on the girls and found Emily sound asleep, while Tarah sat propped against the headboard, reading a book.

"Good night, Tarah," she said softly.

The girl looked up, resentment in her eyes.

"I wouldn't stay up too late," Cassidy ventured. "We have a busy day tomorrow."

"I'm fine."

Cassidy shrugged. "Good night, then."

She stepped inside her empty bedroom and wearily changed into her nightgown.

Reaching up, she removed the pins from her hair and shook her head, letting the tresses cascade down her back. She gave her hair one hundred strokes, then stood. Making her way to the inviting bed, she pulled back the covers. A gasp escaped her lips as a black snake, free of the confining quilt, slithered from her bed and onto the floor. An ear-piercing scream tore at her throat before blackness claimed her.

⁀

"Cassidy, darling, wake up."

From far away, Cassidy heard Dell's voice breaking through her foggy mind, and slowly she opened her eyes. Dell sat on the floor, cradling her in his arms, while her head rested on his lap. The three older children stood around them, taking in the scene.

"What happened?" Dell asked.

"S—snake." She gulped.

"Snake?"

"There was a snake in my bed."

"How in the world would a snake have gotten into your bed?" Dell wore a perplexed expression on his face.

"I don't know," she said, her head beginning to clear. "Why don't you ask the snake?"

How indeed? Cassidy sat up and glanced around at the faces of Sam, Luke, and Tarah. She was a little surprised to find Tarah's eyes clouded in concern. The boys were red-faced and lowered their heads at her scrutiny.

Sam glanced up and caught Cassidy's knowing gaze. He cleared his throat.

"Uh, Pa," he said slowly.

Cassidy broke in quickly. "Dell, I'm sure it just came in and found its way to my bed accidentally. I've heard of things like that before."

Now why had she defended those little hoodlums? They certainly deserved the whipping Dell surely would have given them.

The looks on the boys' faces as they looked from her to each other registered surprise that matched her own.

"Well, I'll take a look around and see if it's still here," said Dell, helping her to her feet. "Boys, get back to bed. You, too, Tarah. And snuff out that candle. It's bedtime."

"Yes, Pa. 'Night."

Cassidy sat quickly on the bed and pulled her legs off the floor. She was sure she heard laughter coming from the hallway as the boys made their way back to their room. She almost wished she hadn't defended the ungrateful pair.

Dell scanned the room, then looked in every corner and drawer, as well as through the wardrobe.

To Cassidy's relief, the snake appeared to have taken its leave.

"Well," he said, scratching his head, "I still don't know how it could've gotten in here, but I guess it left the way it came."

He glanced at Cassidy, a concerned frown creasing his brow. "You okay?"

She nodded, still trembling from the ordeal.

Dell hesitated. "I could stay for a while."

"That's not necessary. I'll be fine."

He swiped a hand through his hair and headed toward the door. "If you're sure. . ."

"I'm sure."

"Good night, then." With one last worried glance, he exited the room.

Exhausted emotionally and physically, Cassidy sank down in the bed and fell asleep.

Sunday morning dawned bright and sunny, promising a good day for the picnic. To Cassidy's disappointment, Dell was nowhere to be seen when they loaded up in the wagon and headed for town. She had dressed in the white cotton dress she'd worn on her wedding day. Somehow, she'd hoped he would see her and remember the tenderness they'd shared.

The schoolhouse was full when they arrived, so they found seats in the back. The service began with hymns. The sound of voices lifted in praise to God brought a thrill to Cassidy's soul. Although there were no instruments to accompany the voices, she had never heard a symphony that sounded more beautiful.

"Psst. . .psst. . .Cassidy!"

Several people turned around as Tarah gained her attention.

"What is it?" Cassidy whispered.

"I'm not feeling well. May I go to the wagon?"

Concerned, her gaze roved across the girl's face. More than likely she was just sleepy from reading so late, but Cassidy didn't want to take any chances. She nodded. "Do you want me to come with you?"

"Oh no," the girl replied quickly. "I just need to lie down for a while."

They were causing a stir among the congregation, and even the minister was glancing their way.

"Go ahead, then," Cassidy whispered.

Conspicuously Tarah stood and tiptoed to the door, causing every eye to turn. Once she was out the door, the preacher cleared his throat loudly to regain everyone's attention.

Cassidy sat through the rest of the sermon, soaking up the atmosphere. Although she was sorry to admit it, the message was somewhat lacking. The minister bounced from subject to subject—sin to sin. She supposed since he only came through the town once every few months, he wanted to hit on all of the human vices possible to get the little congregation through until his next visit.

Cassidy fought the urge to squirm when he broached the subject of deception. She knew she was deceiving Dell by not telling him about the baby; she would have to tell him soon. *I'm just so afraid of his reaction, Lord,* she prayed, knowing, even as the words lifted from her heart, that the excuse was not a good one. Part of honoring her husband required honesty. Repenting, she determined she would tell him that very day, no matter what the outcome.

Some of the older men were beginning to nod off, and even the most devout among the women were stirring uncomfortably on the hard wooden benches when the preacher finally dismissed the service.

Emily jumped from her seat and grabbed Cassidy's hand. "Ma, come and meet Miss Nelson."

She practically dragged Cassidy to the front of the building. "Miss Nelson, this is my ma," she announced proudly.

The young woman was indeed as lovely as Emily had promised. Her chestnut hair was netted in a stylish chignon, and she looked out at Cassidy from clear blue eyes.

"Why, Mrs. St. John," she said in a low, smooth drawl, "how lovely to meet you."

"Likewise, Miss Nelson," Cassidy replied, feeling herself drawn by the depth of feeling in the woman's voice. "Emily has certainly been singing your praises all week."

The teacher glanced down fondly at the little girl. "Emily and I get along just fine, but. . ." A frown furrowed her lovely brow. "May I speak candidly?"

"Certainly, Miss Nelson."

"Please, call me Aimee," she said with a smile.

Cassidy returned her smile, feeling at ease. "All right. What would you like to talk to me about, Aimee?"

Aimee chewed her bottom lip and glanced cautiously at Emily. Taking the hint, Cassidy turned to the little girl. "Emily, sweetheart, why don't you go to the wagon and tell everyone I'll be right there?"

"Aw, Ma," Emily replied, but she did as she was told.

Cassidy turned expectantly to the teacher, who gestured toward a bench. "Let's sit down," she suggested.

Once they were seated, Aimee drew a deep breath. "It's about Luke."

Tension gnawed at Cassidy's insides as she waited for the teacher to continue.

"He is quite a handful and most disruptive, even destructive, in class."

Tension turned to alarm. "What sorts of things does he do?"

Aimee paused, then the words came spilling out. "He puts nails in the students' chairs, dips ribbons in inkwells, pulls the girls' hair, and just Friday he. . ." She shuddered. "He put a snake in my desk drawer! I almost fainted, Mrs. St. John. Can you imagine the chaos in my school if I had fainted in front of my class?"

Cassidy could well imagine.

"I might have lost my job."

Well, Cassidy doubted that, since there were no other teachers interested in coming to the rustic town for a teaching position that paid only twenty-five dollars for the three-month term. Still, her heart went out to the young woman. Luke was difficult enough to deal with at home under his father's stern hand. In the classroom with only this young woman who was barely older than Tarah, she could imagine how unruly he could be.

She reached forward and placed a hand over Aimee's. "I'll have a talk with him."

Relief passed over the lovely features of the woman sitting beside her. "Thank you." She glanced down at her hands. "This is my first teaching position, and I didn't want the school board to feel I couldn't handle it myself. But standing in the corner is simply another way for Luke to disrupt and gain attention. I—I have never believed in corporal punishment, but a whipping may be what he needs."

Yes, a whipping might be exactly what he needs, unless. . . Cassidy held back the laughter bubbling up inside of her as an idea formed in her mind. She would teach the little monster a lesson. She stood and held out her hand to Aimee.

Aimee stood, as well, and accepted the proffered hand. "I don't want to cause any trouble, Mrs. St. John."

Mrs. St. John. Cassidy loved to be called that. Each time she heard the name, a thrill moved up and down her spine.

"I assure you, you've caused no trouble for anyone who doesn't deserve it. I promise you, Luke will be dealt with, and if he isn't better on Monday, send a note home with one of the other children."

"All right," Aimee agreed, relief evident in her voice.

"I must be going now. We have family plans. But it was very nice to meet you, and don't worry," she reassured the teacher. "You're doing a fine job with the rest of the children. Luke is just a difficult case."

Quick tears sprang to Aimee's eyes. "Thank you."

Cassidy smiled and squeezed her hand before saying her farewell. With a feeling of anticipation, she walked out of the church to the waiting wagon.

She frowned, looking around for Tarah.

"It's about time," Ellen huffed. "We've been sweltering out here."

It didn't seem that hot to Cassidy, but rather than comment, she asked, "Where is Tarah? I thought she came out here to lie down in the wagon."

"We thought she went back inside."

Oh, where was that girl? Cassidy's eyes scanned the little town, looking for the gingham dress Tarah had worn to church that morning.

"Everyone stay here so no one else gets lost," she commanded and left the wagon to begin her search. First she reentered the schoolhouse to be sure Tarah hadn't gone back inside. There was no sign of her. Next she walked outside and checked the privy. Still no Tarah.

Fear and frustration combined inside Cassidy's stomach, forming a large knot. She stopped and asked several of Tarah's friends if they'd seen her, but no one had. Cassidy once again scanned the little town for any sight of the lost girl. Suddenly her eyes focused on a familiar horse tethered outside the general store. It belonged to Johnny, the ranch foreman. Cassidy shuddered, remembering their encounter in the barn.

Now why would Johnny's horse be in town on Sunday? The general store wasn't even open.

Suspicion built inside of her, and she decided to investigate. She walked through the pathway between the store and the building next to it, around to the back. A gasp escaped her lips as she spied the familiar gingham-clad girl in Johnny's arms.

Anger welled up inside Cassidy, and she stormed toward the pair. Grabbing Tarah's arm, she jerked her away. "Johnny Cooper, you get your hands off my daughter, and don't ever let me catch you near her again. Do you hear me?"

"How dare you? You're not my mother!" Tarah's eyes sparked in fury.

"Be quiet and get to the wagon right now, young lady. We'll talk about this later."

Apparently too stunned to argue, Tarah emitted a strangled sob and ran down the alleyway toward the wagon.

Cassidy turned back to Johnny. "I mean it, Johnny. Don't you ever come near that child again."

Johnny stood in stunned silence as Cassidy whirled around and stormed to the wagon. Arms crossed, Tarah sat seething in the back of the wagon, tears of fury still pooling in her eyes. Without a word, Cassidy climbed into the seat and flapped the reins, leading the horses toward the ranch.

First Luke and now Tarah. Give me wisdom, Lord!

Chapter 10

Cassidy's heart did a strange little flip-flop as she pulled hard on the reins, halting the wagon in front of the house. Dell sat on the porch awaiting their return.

Jumping from the wagon, Tarah flounced inside without a word.

Dell raised a questioning eyebrow at Cassidy.

Shaking her head, she shrugged. No sense ruining the day if she could help it. And telling Dell she had caught his daughter with the likes of Johnny Cooper would serve no purpose right now. A twinge of guilt made Cassidy hesitate, but she pushed it back. After all, she reasoned, if Dell found out, he would beat the living daylights out of Johnny and send him packing. And if he did that, Tarah would never get over the despicable man. No. The girl had to see Johnny for what he was and make the decision herself.

"You getting down from there today?"

Cassidy glanced down. Dell stood with a hand extended, ready to help her from the wagon.

"Sorry," she murmured, throwing him a sheepish grin.

"All right, everyone change out of your Sunday clothes and let's get going," Dell called, giving Cassidy support while she climbed down from the wagon.

"Everyone but you, that is. You keep that dress on." His voice was low, husky, and filled with longing. He'd noticed. Cassidy's heart went wild as his gaze caressed her. Was that love reflected in the blue depths of his eyes? Then why did he stay away? She pushed the disturbing thoughts aside for the moment and enjoyed walking to the house, hand in hand, with the man she loved.

Once inside, Dell left her to get the fishing poles while Cassidy busied herself collecting the picnic fare.

"Want me to carry anything for you?"

Cassidy glanced up in surprise to find Sam, hands in his pockets, staring red faced at his boots. *Ah, he's making up!*

"Thanks, Sam. I'd appreciate it," she said, keeping her voice steady as she handed him the platter laden with fried chicken.

"Smells good," he said and walked carefully to the door, then turned to her. "Thanks for not snitching Luke out to Pa last night. He'd got a lickin' for sure."

"He probably deserves one," Cassidy said, giving him a wry smile in spite of herself. "Did he ever find the snake?"

"Nah, it's long gone." Sam shook his head. "We never thought you'd faint, though. Scared us half to death." With that, he left the house. Would wonders never cease?

Emily appeared at the kitchen door dressed in her everyday clothes, bonnet hanging by its strings around her neck. "Can Warrior come with us, Ma?"

Barefoot and wearing his new war bonnet as usual, Jack stood beside Emily. Each child stared at her with imploring eyes.

Tenderness for her youngest children welled up inside Cassidy, and she knew she could deny them nothing at this moment. "I don't see why not," she said with a smile. "He'd probably enjoy a day of splashing about in the creek."

Jack let out a war whoop and threw his arms around Cassidy. "You're the best ma ever!"

Tears stung her eyes as she watched the two children bound out the door, calling for the puppy.

Ellen limped into the kitchen next, and the two women made the final preparations for the picnic. After the wagon was loaded with family and food, Cassidy took a final peek around the kitchen and decided it was time to put her plans for Luke into action. She went to the spice cabinet and took down a small bag she had brought with her from Missouri. Tucking it into her apron pocket, she set out to join her impatient family.

A grinning Dell stood beside the wagon when Cassidy stepped onto the porch.

Cassidy's heart leapt. He'd saddled Abby for her.

"Thought you might like to ride horseback today."

"Oh yes, Dell. I would love it. Thank you." She grabbed the reins and lifted a foot into the stirrup.

"Cassidy," Ellen said cautiously.

"What?"

Ellen gave a pointed gaze at Cassidy's stomach.

Maybe horseback wasn't the best thing for the baby. "O–oh, right." She placed her foot back on the ground and turned to Dell. "Thanks anyway, but I think I'd rather ride in the wagon today."

With a small frown, he helped her up to the seat.

"I'll ride Abby, Pa." Tarah stood in the wagon and jumped down. "Since Cassidy doesn't want to."

"It's your ma's horse. You'll have to ask her."

Cassidy cringed at his reference to her as Tarah's ma. She drew a breath, wondering what Tarah would say.

Eyes blazing, the girl turned to her. "May I?"

Exhaling in relief, Cassidy smiled. "Of course I don't mind. It will do her some good to be ridden."

"Thank you," Tarah replied through gritted teeth. Taking the reins from her father, she mounted and headed off toward the creek.

Dell glanced after her with a puzzled frown, then climbed onto his own horse. "Do you want to explain what just happened between the two of you?" he asked.

"Oh, a little disagreement," was all Cassidy said, and thankfully Dell dropped the matter.

"Let's go, then," he said, following Tarah's lead.

They found a secluded spot surrounded by shady trees and tall prairie grass. Enlisting the help of all the children and Dell, Cassidy had the picnic ready in no time. They sat around a red-and-white-checkered tablecloth spread out on the ground. The tension seemed to fade away. Even Warrior had a feast of the chicken bones, and soon everyone was ready for dessert.

Cassidy cut the cake, serving Dell first, then Ellen, and continuing until everyone but Luke had a piece of the fluffy treat.

"Land sakes. I'm a plate short," Cassidy said, placing a hand to her cheek. "I know I counted right. Wait just a minute." She strolled to the wagon and grabbed the last plate. Glancing cautiously about to make sure no one watched, she gingerly pulled the little packet from her pocket. Sprinkling some of the red powder on the plate, she carefully walked back to the picnic spot. No one paid any attention to her as she cut the last piece of cake and placed it on Luke's plate. They were too engrossed in Dell's story of the Indian chief he'd seen in Abilene.

Luke took the plate from Cassidy's hands. "Hope this is edible." He threw Tarah a sideways glance, obviously trying to get a rise out of her.

Sticking out her tongue in retaliation, Tarah turned back to her pa's story.

Biting the inside of her cheeks to keep from laughing out loud, Cassidy waited while Luke wolfed down two large bites of the cake without stopping to taste it. Suddenly his eyes grew wide, and he grabbed the nearest glass of lemonade.

"Ah—wa—wa—!" he cried, waving his hand over his mouth.

"Cut it out, Luke. We're trying to listen to Pa," Sam said, giving his brother a deep frown.

"Water—gimme water."

"Get your own."

"Luke St. John, you stop your foolishness this minute," Ellen grumped.

"Hot! Hot!" Luke jumped up and ran for the creek.

Ellen shook her head while the rest of the family watched him in irritated silence.

"What that boy won't do for attention," Dell muttered. "I'd better go have a talk with him."

Grabbing a corn muffin, Cassidy stood and glanced around the little group. "I'll see to him. Continue your story, Dell."

When she reached the boy, he was slapping handfuls of water on his tongue. He looked up with eyes smoldering in accusation. "You tried to poison me!"

"Don't be ridiculous," Cassidy replied calmly, dropping to the ground beside him. "Here, eat this. Water will only make it burn worse."

Grudgingly he grabbed the muffin and devoured it, relaxing slowly as it took away the burn in his mouth.

"What'd you put in my cake?"

"That's my secret."

"Why'd you do that to me?" His eyes sparked with anger.

"It's no fun to be on the receiving end of a prank, is it?" she asked quietly.

"I'll say."

"Now I think you and I are even." She eyed him sternly. "But there's the little matter of Miss Nelson."

Caught, the boy swallowed hard and stared into the water.

"She tells me you're still creating problems in class. That true?"

"Well. . .I guess so."

"Hmm. Suppose we make a deal."

Luke eyed her suspiciously. "Like what?"

"I don't want to find any more snakes, frogs, or bugs in my bed. No more rocks in my bathwater. And I don't want to hear of you causing any problems in class. Is that understood?"

Red-faced, he nodded grudgingly.

"And for my part, I'll make sure your food is edible."

"Mas aren't supposed to put hot stuff in their kids' food anyway," he informed her.

"Well, I've never been a ma before, and I'm sorry if I don't do it very well. But the threat of a thrashing didn't seem to keep you out of trouble, so I came up with my own solution. Now do we have a deal?" She held out a hand.

Cautiously he shook her hand and, to Cassidy's surprise, gave her a wide grin. "Aw, I guess you're all right." He stood. "I'd sure like to know what you put on my cake so I can do it to Sam sometime."

"Luke!" Cassidy declared firmly, fighting to keep from grinning back at him. "A deal is a deal. No more pranks!"

He looked at her in disbelief. "Not even on Sam and the rest of the kids?"

"Well, just don't hurt anyone, destroy any property, or do it at school."

"Yes, ma'am," he said and ran back to the little party around the picnic blanket.

A chuckle escaped her lips. Well, a tiger couldn't change his stripes, but he could be tamed, so they said. Fun and games were part of what made Luke who he was, and as long as he didn't get out of hand, she could grant him a little freedom.

What a day this was turning out to be! Cassidy sighed with contentment and stretched out her legs in front of her. She leaned back on her arms, watching the sun shining down on the rippling creek. Suddenly she felt a flutter inside.

She placed a hand on her stomach and felt the flutter again. Her baby was moving! Tears formed in her eyes and streamed down her cheeks.

"Everything all right?" Dell dropped down beside her.

"Yes," Cassidy replied, quickly wiping her tears away with the back of her hand.

"Then why are you crying?" he insisted softly.

"I'm just happy. I have a home and children, and this has been such a wonderful day. I guess I just became overwhelmed with God's goodness." She smiled at him, then threw a glance back to where Ellen was clearing away the food. "I'd better go help."

Dell placed a restraining hand on her arm as she started to get up.

"Mother gave me strict instructions that you are not to move from this spot until she and Tarah finish cleaning up."

Cassidy shrugged. It felt so good to relax that she wasn't going to argue the point.

A loud *splash* caught their attention. Glancing toward the laughing children, Cassidy watched the playful antics of Jack and Emily in the water. Warrior jumped in behind them, barking wildly.

Dell stretched out on the grassy bank, using his arm behind his head for a pillow.

Another flutter from the baby sent a tremor of happiness through Cassidy, and she longed to tell her husband of the child's existence. Swallowing hard, she glanced down at him. "Dell?"

"Hmm?" He opened one eye and stared up at her.

Suddenly Emily screamed. "Jack, come back!"

Cassidy shot to her feet and ran into the water. Jack was caught in a current pushing him downstream.

A scream tore at her throat, and without thought, she dove into the water and swam for all she was worth. "Hang on, Jack. Hang on."

"Ma! Help me!"

The current was rough, and she felt it dragging at her long dress. She kicked hard against the weight. Finally she reached the little boy, but Dell was already there. He grabbed Jack around the waist just as the little boy was pulled under. Jack flailed his arms wildly.

"I have you," Dell reassured. "Be still and don't struggle."

Gulping in a large mouthful of water, Cassidy coughed frantically. Seeing that Jack was safely in his father's arms, she swam as hard as she could toward the nearest bank. Dragging her aching body from the river, she collapsed onto the grass. Dell was right behind her, carrying Jack. Cassidy sat up and held out her arms for the child. Pulling her son onto her lap, she wrapped her arms about him as tightly as she could without hurting him.

"Are you all right, sweet boy?" she asked, tears streaming down her face.

"Yeah, Ma." Jack was already recovered from the ordeal and began to wiggle in her arms.

Cassidy kissed him hard, then let him go. He ran back to meet up with the other children, who hurried along the bank toward him. The way he recounted his ordeal with such enthusiasm, one would have thought it was a grand adventure.

Exhausted, Cassidy lay back on the ground. Closing her eyes, she sent up a prayer of thanks.

Suddenly a shadow fell across her. She opened her eyes to find Dell standing over her, his gaze resting on her stomach. Glancing down, she saw the white cotton dress molded to her body, revealing the small mound where their child grew inside her. The look of horror on his face said it all, and she placed a protective hand across the growing infant.

His gaze traveled from her stomach, up her body, to her eyes. "Are you all right?" he asked.

With a fatigued wave of her hand, Cassidy nodded.

"Are you pregnant?" His tone was guarded and clipped.

"Yes." She met his gaze defiantly. After all, there was no shame in carrying her husband's baby, even if he didn't want her or the child.

"Is this why Mother insisted you get more rest—she knows?"

A short laugh left her lips. "Ellen's the one who told me."

"Why did you keep it from me?"

Cassidy thought she detected hurt in his voice, but when she looked into his eyes, they glittered hard. Disappointment clouded her heart. "Why indeed?" she replied bitterly. "You've been so sweet and tender lately, I don't know why I didn't tell you immediately."

His eyes narrowed at her sarcasm, but Cassidy was undaunted by the warning flash and continued. "Maybe I just wanted to enjoy my happiness for a while before you spoiled it for me!"

She sat up, and a wave of nausea overtook her. Turning her head, she lost her lunch on the bank of the creek. Silently Dell took her into his arms while tears of humiliation fell from her eyes.

"Shh," he crooned. "Don't cry, my darling; the sickness doesn't last very long."

Suddenly Cassidy exploded in frustration. "You ignoramus," she said, jerking back from his arms. "Do you really think I'm crying because I'm sick?"

Dell blinked in surprise and sat dumbfounded as she vented.

"I am thirty-five years old and have never borne a child. I welcome the sickness. I glory in it! I thank God every day knowing there is a life within me."

"Calm down," Dell said softly, gathering her back in his arms.

More frustrated than ever, Cassidy pushed him away from her. "You are a stubborn, stupid man, and I don't know why I fell in love with you." Rising to her feet, she clamped her hands down hard on her hips. "We had two wonderful days and nights together and could have had a lifetime of happiness, but you decided to push me away. Well, be mad all you want about this baby. I'm happy. Ecstatic, in fact, and I will be for the rest of my life. So there!"

Cassidy stomped back to the picnic area before he could say a word. Trembling, she leaned against the wagon and cried. Minutes later, when the tears were spent, she gave a determined lift to her chin, a decision made. She would not cry again. There were too many blessings to count for her to moon about and pine for a man who clearly only wanted her as a mother for his children—his older children, that is. It was time for her to settle in and enjoy motherhood. God was so good. And she would enjoy this pregnancy if it was the last thing she ever did! Dell or no Dell.

Dell lay tormented on his bed that night. He wanted to go to Cassidy, to hold her and reassure her of his love, but something held him back. Once again he bargained with God.

"You took Anna from me when I broke my promise. But I'll keep my end of the bargain this time, God. Let Cassidy live, and I won't touch her again while she's still young enough to have children."

In his mind, the years loomed ahead of him, and unbidden came the words Reverend Marcus had spoken the night Dell had attended the service on the trail. "God doesn't bargain with man. His ways are too high for that."

Dell squirmed on the tick mattress. Well, the preacher was wrong. God did bargain with man. He bargained, and man paid dearly if he didn't keep his end of the deal. Dell had loved Anna, but his own lack of control had killed her. That would not happen with Cassidy. She was like a fresh spring breeze blowing through this dry, dusty land, and he refused to lose her.

When she jumped in the water after Jack, he had thought his heart would pound from his chest as fear rose up inside of him. A knot formed in his stomach at the thought of what might have happened to Jack and Cassidy. And to find out she was going to have a baby nearly did him in!

He'd watched Cassidy carefully the rest of the afternoon and insisted she go to bed as soon as she got home. She'd balked at the pampering but gave in when Ellen agreed with Dell.

"Oh, fine. I'll go lie down, but it really isn't necessary."

When he'd looked in on her fifteen minutes later, she'd been sound asleep, a peaceful smile resting on her lips.

Dell emitted a low chuckle at the memory. How he loved that woman. But God was testing him, and her life was the prize, just like with Anna. The difference was that this time, he wouldn't fail.

Storm clouds invaded the skies the following morning as Cassidy loaded the breakfast table with fluffy hotcakes and sizzling bacon. She looked on with loving amusement while the children and Dell devoured the sumptuous fare as though they hadn't eaten in a month. A rumble of thunder sounded in the distance, and Dell pushed back from his plate.

"Better get a move on before the storm comes," he instructed the children. "I'll take you to school this morning." He reached forward and tousled Jack's unruly curls. "Want to ride along, son?" The little boy's head bobbed as he shoved in one last bite of breakfast. Dell headed outside to hook up the team while the older children grabbed their books.

Cassidy stood at the open door with lunches in hand, ready to pass them out as the children bounded toward the wagon. Jack and Emily each kissed Cassidy before running outside with shouts of "Bye, Ma!" Luke grabbed his lunch and started to head out the door.

"Wait, Luke. Remember our deal."

Throwing her a wide grin, he nodded and ran for the wagon.

Sam grabbed his lunch and paused, then reached over and gave her a peck on the cheek. "Bye, Ma," he said softly. Speechless, she watched him go. With her heart still full of wonder, she faced Tarah's glittering eyes.

"Don't expect me to call you 'Ma.' "

Deflated, Cassidy turned back to the table and sat to finish her coffee. "I don't expect any of you to, but I'm happy the boys are beginning to accept me."

"Tarah, let's go," Dell shouted from the wagon.

"You said I wouldn't have to go after the first week." Tarah's eyes sparked with challenge.

With a sigh, Cassidy went back to the door. "Go on without her. Tarah's staying home today."

"She okay?"

"She's fine. Just go before the rain starts."

With a wave, Dell flicked the reins, and the wagon lurched forward.

Cassidy stepped back to the table and began filling a breakfast plate for Ellen, who was in her bed after the excitement of the day before. "If you're staying home, you can help me."

Tarah opened her mouth to protest, but Cassidy raised a hand. "No arguments. Take this plate to your granny. She's feeling poorly."

"Fine."

"And then come back and help me clean up." Cassidy ignored the anger flashing in the violet eyes and busied herself washing the dishes.

Tarah flounced away. When she returned a few moments later, she grabbed a towel to dry the dishes.

"You had no right to drag me away from Johnny like that," Tarah began. "We were doing nothing wrong."

"You don't consider lying to get out of church, then kissing a man twice your age to be wrong?"

"Well. . .the lying part was wrong, but there was no other way to see him alone."

"You shouldn't be seeing him at all. Let alone kissing him."

Cassidy searched frantically to find the words that would reach the girl.

"Johnny and I love each other," Tarah insisted. "We are going to be married."

A knot formed in Cassidy's stomach. "Tarah, you haven't. . ."

The girl blushed to the roots of her hair, and her eyes grew wide. "Of course not," she gasped. "What kind of a woman do you think I am?"

Relieved, Cassidy gave her a wry smile. "To be honest, I don't think of you as a woman. You're still so young."

Tarah lifted her chin.

"But," Cassidy continued, "I can see that you are close to womanhood, and I wouldn't want you to get hooked up with the wrong man."

"Johnny is not the wrong man!"

"I thought there was another boy you were interested in—Anthony something or other."

Tarah tossed her head. "Anthony Greene. I wouldn't give that child the time of day. Besides, he's smitten with Louisa Thomas."

"I see. . ."

"Are you going to tell Pa about Johnny?"

"I don't know, Tarah. I think he should know."

"But he'll fire Johnny if he finds out."

If Johnny's lucky, he'll get off with just being fired, Cassidy thought. Looking at Tarah, she said, "I can't worry about that. Unless. . ."

Hope rose in Tarah's ashen face but left quickly at Cassidy's words.

"Unless you promise me you won't have anything more to do with the likes of Johnny Cooper."

"You can't ask me to do that. I love him!"

"Then you leave me no choice but to speak to your father."

A sob escaped Tarah's throat, and she threw the towel on the counter. "All right. I won't see him anymore. I can't have him lose his job because of me."

She ran out the door, tears streaming down her lovely face.

Cassidy picked up the towel and finished wiping the dishes, praying for Tarah as she did so. "Mend her heart, Father. Young love is the cruelest love of all."

Chapter 11

Cassidy lay snuggled under her thick quilt, listening to the wind howl outside. She glanced out the window as a bolt of lightning connected heaven to earth in one long, jagged streak. Immediately a crash of thunder followed, shaking the house to its foundation. She shivered at the violence of the storm. "Lord," she prayed, "keep us all safe in Your arms while the tempest rages around us."

As if responding to her voice, the baby gave a hard kick. Cassidy smiled and placed a loving hand over her stomach. "Sorry to wake you, little one, but your ma can't sleep with all the racket outside." The baby rolled inside of her, causing Cassidy to giggle with the wonder of creation.

Suddenly her door flew open, and there stood Dell clad in blue jeans, a flannel shirt open to the waist. "Get up." His gaze rested on her for only a second before he continued down the hall.

Throwing off the covers, she jumped and ran into the hallway as Dell pounded on each door. "Everyone out of bed quickly," he called.

"Dell? What's wrong?"

"The storm is bad. Could be a twister, and I don't want to take any chances. Get your bedding," he ordered. "We're going to the root cellar."

"A twister in the middle of November?"

"When the temperature drops as quickly as it did this afternoon, there are always bad storms. Now hurry!"

Cassidy flew into action as the children gathered around, rubbing sleepy eyes.

"Get a blanket," Dell commanded them, "and come with me."

"What is going on here?" Ellen appeared at her door, clad in her dressing gown.

"We're going to the cellar," Cassidy explained. "Dell's afraid the storm will turn into a twister."

"Hogwash. I'm going back to bed."

As she turned to go, Jack let up a howl. "No, Granny. Come with us. I don't want you to get blown away!"

He threw his arms tightly about her, and she glanced helplessly at the little boy.

"Oh, all right," she said, relenting. "Now stop crying."

Dell grabbed up little Jack and headed for the front door. He began opening it carefully, but the ferocious wind snatched the wooden door away from him, slamming it hard against the outside wall.

"Ma!" Emily screamed in terror, burying her head in Cassidy's bulging middle.

"Shh, it's all right."

She held the little girl tightly as they lowered their heads and struggled against the wind.

"Hang on to the rail," Dell shouted.

The root cellar was between the house and the soddy, and they reached it quickly.

Cassidy waited while Dell helped each child inside, then Ellen.

She took a step toward Dell's outstretched arm but stopped as Warrior barked from across the yard.

"Come on, boy," she called.

Suddenly she heard a yelp as a slat blew off the barn roof and hit the animal, knocking him down.

"Warrior!" screamed Emily.

He lay motionless where he'd fallen.

"Come on!" yelled Dell.

Without stopping to think, Cassidy took off across the yard, fighting the wind. Relieved to find the animal still breathing, she bent and gathered him in her arms. He whimpered as she jostled him. "Come on, boy. I have you." She glanced fearfully at the barn as its door blew open. Abby broke out of her stall and ran out, bucking and neighing wildly around the fenced barnyard.

A flash of lightning brightened the sky, and for a moment Cassidy saw the twister extending from the heavens. Frozen, she could only watch as the funnel swirled toward her, tearing up everything in its path.

Suddenly she felt Dell grab her and half-carry, half-drag her back to the cellar, then pull her inside.

"Are you crazy?" he barked. "Your life and the life of my child are more important than a dog's."

"I—I'm sorry, Dell. I guess I just wasn't thinking straight. I saw him lying there, hurt, and I just reacted. Besides, h—he's not just a dog; he's part of the family."

"Thunder and lightning," he muttered.

He grabbed the door and started to pull it down when Johnny appeared, shaking in fear. "It's a twister!"

"We know. Get in and close the door," Dell said gruffly. Turning, he ordered, "Give me the dog, Cassidy."

Cassidy did as she was told. Dell laid the animal gently on the floor and looked him over. A gash on Warrior's side seeped blood, but the wound wasn't fatal. Dell removed his shirt and wrapped it tightly around the animal to stop the bleeding.

Tarah held Emily protectively against her side but looked out shyly from beneath long lashes at Johnny as he walked to the back wall and sank down.

He threw a cautious glance at Dell, then winked at the girl.

Cassidy bristled and cleared her throat. Receiving the full impact of her stern glare, Tarah shifted her gaze to the dirt floor. Giving Johnny what she hoped was a look of intimidation, Cassidy was rewarded with a very unintimidated, insolent grin.

Tarah had been true to her word the past two months, steering clear of the ranch hand, and had even returned to school. Cassidy's heart sank to realize the girl was still infatuated with Johnny. Perhaps she'd have to speak to Dell after all. She looked toward her husband. His worried gaze was riveted on the closed door above them. In an act of boldness, she went to him and slipped her hand in his. He gripped it hard and turned to her. Tears glistened in his eyes, and Cassidy rested her cheek against his bare arm. "It'll be all right, Dell. God will take care of us."

"Come on," he said quietly. "You need to sit."

He led her back to her space against the wall and sat beside her. Grabbing the quilt, he draped it over her.

Cassidy lifted the edge closest to Dell and pulled it over him. "You'll be sick with no shirt on," she admonished. "Share the covers with me."

His gaze melted into hers, and he lifted his arm, wrapping it around her. The heat from his fingers against her upper arm sent a tremor through her middle.

When the baby kicked again, Cassidy smiled and grabbed Dell's other hand. He glanced down with hesitation in his eyes as she placed his hand on her stomach. The baby greeted his father with a strong kick. Dell pulled his hand away as though he'd touched a hot stove, then placed it gingerly back on the mound. He laid his head against Cassidy's while he became acquainted with his unborn child.

Overwhelming contentment washed over Cassidy, and she snuggled against Dell, enjoying the closeness even while the storm raged over them. *Peace in the midst of the storm, Lord. This is what You've given me.*

They sat huddled together on the dirt floor, wrapped in thick quilts, while the storm spent its rage above them. For a time, they could hear nothing but the roar of the wind and the banging of their belongings flying through the air. Suddenly everything died down, the twister leaving as quickly as it had come, though thunder rumbled and lightning still flashed through the cracks in the wooden door.

"We'll stay here for a while to be certain," Dell informed them. "Storms like this can go on all night."

He was right. Though there were no more twisters, the wind rose and died down several times, and the storm blew until just before dawn.

When morning came, every inch of Cassidy's body ached from her night spent on the hard ground. She dreaded what they would find when they looked outside.

Getting up from beside her, Dell climbed the cellar steps. Drawing a slow breath, he lifted the latch and threw open the door. A blast of cold air blew into the cellar, and white flakes filtered in.

"Is it snowing?" Cassidy asked incredulously.

Dell nodded.

From the back of the room, Johnny groaned. "That's going to make it a bear to get things cleaned up."

Cassidy sent him a scathing glance, then shifted her attention back to Dell.

"How bad is it?" she asked.

"Barn's gone, but the house is fine."

Relief filled her at the news. *Thank You, Lord, for sparing our home.*

One by one, they emerged from the cellar. Dell's shoulders slumped as he stared at the wreckage caused by the storm, and Cassidy's heart ached for him. Chickens lay dead, strewn across the yard. Splintered boards lay on the ground where the tall barn had stood just hours earlier. Tree limbs and slats decorated the area. Cassidy's lips quivered at the extent of the devastation, and she struggled for composure. At least they could thank God that they were all safe and that the house had been spared.

"Darling," Dell said quietly, taking her by the shoulders and steering her toward the house. "I want you to go inside and get into bed."

"But I have to get breakfast," she protested.

Dell's gaze shifted to Tarah.

"I'll help Granny fix breakfast," she offered. "You should lie down like Pa says."

With a sigh, Cassidy nodded. She stepped over fallen limbs and other clutter in the yard and on the porch. Once inside the house, she looked around. A few knickknacks and pictures had fallen, but all in all, everything looked pretty much the way they had left it the night before.

Cassidy made her way back to her bedroom, opened her bureau drawer, and lifted out a fresh nightgown. Changing quickly, she climbed into bed, pulling the covers over her shivering body. It didn't matter that the edges of the quilt were dirty from the cellar floor. She'd wash it later. For now, she was too tired to care.

With a yawn and another prayer of thanks, Cassidy drifted off to sleep, smiling at the memories from the night—of Dell's hand covering her stomach, his arm wrapped tightly about her shoulders. The last thing she remembered before sleep claimed her was that he had called her "darling" in the light of day.

A light dusting of snow fell as Dell surveyed the damage to the barn. Even with five ranch hands working alongside him, it would take awhile to get everything cleared away and begin rebuilding.

Fortunately the horses had emerged from the storm unscathed. For now, they and the milk cow would have to be put back into the old sod barn.

Dell sighed, surveying the work ahead of him. Yesterday he and the hands had rounded up all the cattle they could find. Several had been lost, as well as a few pigs. He'd have to make another trip to Abilene to sell off some more of the stock if they were to make it through the winter. He hated to think of leaving Cassidy alone this far into her pregnancy, but it couldn't be helped.

The snow began to fall faster, and he cast a cursory glance toward the sky. Thick clouds blanketed the heavens, and a knot formed in his stomach. Winter had arrived in earnest after the storm, and those clouds indicated more snow was coming. Spurred into action at the thought, he stepped forward, lifting a splintered board from the pile of rubble. He knew he'd better get to work if the barn was to be rebuilt before the new year.

⌒

Cassidy opened her eyes, then sat up quickly as her ears registered more howling wind.

Not another storm. Oh, God, please, no.

She pushed back the covers and sat up shivering. She swung her feet down to the floor and lifted them up just as quickly. The floor was icy. And yesterday had started out as warm as a day in July! Gingerly she stepped down onto the cold floor, slipped into her house shoes, and walked to the window. A thin layer of frost covered the glass, making it impossible to see outside. With the edge of her nightgown, she made a circle in the glistening white ice. She peeked through the opening but could see nothing in the darkness.

Frustrated, she grabbed her dressing gown and slipped it on. "I'll go look out the front door," she muttered. She lifted her shawl from its peg and threw it around her shoulders.

When she reached the sitting room, she stopped. Dell stood by the front window, staring outside.

She moved forward until she stood beside him. "What is it?" she asked, fearful of the answer.

He laughed shortly. "Welcome to Kansas. First you witnessed a twister; now you get to experience a prairie blizzard."

Relief that it wasn't another twister was mixed with the dread of the snowstorm. She'd never seen a blizzard before, and watching the angry, driving snow sent a shiver through her. Cassidy felt Dell shift, and her heart leaped as his arms captured her from behind.

Resting his hands on her stomach, he pressed her against him. The baby protested the heavy hands spread over Cassidy's stomach.

"This is going to be one strong boy," Dell said with a chuckle.

"Boy? I think not."

"Oh? And what's wrong with having a boy?"

"There are enough men in this family as it is," Cassidy said with a quick lift of her chin. "We need a girl to even things out."

"All right. A girl, then," he said. "One who looks exactly like you."

"Oh no! She mustn't look like me." Years of being overlooked at parties flashed through Cassidy's mind. "I want my daughter to be invited to dances and box socials. I want gentlemen to ask to escort her home when she's a young lady. She has to look like you," she finished firmly.

"Haven't you ever been asked to a dance?"

"Not one single time." In his arms, the sting was gone. Still, she remembered the hurt of her younger years.

"Well, Mrs. St. John. I am formally asking you to allow me the honor of escorting you to the Christmas dance next month."

A giggle escaped her lips. "Mr. St. John, I accept."

With a sigh, she leaned her head back against his broad chest and covered his hands with her own. They stood in silence for a time, Dell's chin resting on her head.

"Cassidy," he said quietly.

"Hmm?"

"I'm glad you decided to come with me."

Her pulse quickened, and she stroked the back of his hand. "Me, too."

He placed a gentle kiss on the top of her head, sending a shiver up her spine. "I love you," he whispered.

"You do?" It was the first time he'd ever said those words.

She felt him nod against her cheek.

"Yes, I reckon I do."

Tears formed in Cassidy's eyes.

"I know it doesn't seem that way, and you don't understand the arrangement we have, but my feelings for you are genuine."

He turned her around to face him in the eerie glow of the fire. "You've been a wonderful mother to my children, and somehow you've even gotten Mother to soften. You amaze me."

"Well, to be honest," Cassidy said, throwing him a saucy grin, "you were the one who got Ellen to soften."

A lifted brow was his response.

"It's true. She started being nice to me after she found out that I—well—about the baby."

At the reminder, Dell shifted. Taking her by the hand, he led her to a chair by the fireplace. "Come and sit," he said.

Grabbing a nearby stool, he brought it closer to the warmth of the fire and sat facing her. "We haven't really had the chance to discuss your condition," he said. "How are you getting along?"

"I'm feeling a little more uncomfortable as time goes by," she admitted. "But not enough to cause concern."

"You sure?" His eyes scrutinized her. "Don't do more than you should. There's no need to hurt yourself when Mother and Tarah can do for you."

Waving away his concern, Cassidy nevertheless felt a thrill that he cared enough to worry. "But there's no need for them do so many of the household duties. Ellen is feeble, and Tarah has her studies to attend to."

The look on Dell's face was firm. "I figure you have about three more months to go. That right?"

Cassidy felt her cheeks grow hot, but she held his gaze. "Two and a half."

"All right, then. For the next two and a half months, and for a few weeks after the baby is born, I expect you to take it easy. No heavy lifting, no more scrubbing over the clothes—"

"Oh, Dell, really," she interjected.

"Tarah is plenty old enough to take care of the washing on Saturdays," he insisted. "It's high time that girl learns to take care of a home anyway."

"That may be, but I can't sit around all day with nothing to do while others tend to the chores I should be doing."

His eyes studied her for a moment, taking in face and body. He drew a breath, then exhaled slowly as he spoke. "You aren't like Anna."

Cassidy's heart sank as his gaze drifted from her up to the daguerreotype on the mantel. She knew he couldn't see the woman's image in the firelit room, but he stared as though he did.

"She was small and dainty. Frail, really. She was in bed almost from the beginning with Tarah. Weak and ill constantly. And it was worse with each child. I should never have. . ." He stood and walked to the window, glancing out into the predawn haze.

A glimmer of understanding dawned on Cassidy. "It wasn't your fault she died. Whatever caused you to think it was?"

A short, mirthless laugh escaped his lips. "When the time came for Luke to be born, she had a rough time of it. I promised myself and God that if she lived, I'd make sure she never got in that condition again—a promise I obviously didn't keep."

"Do you mean to tell me you think God took Anna because she was with child again?" The very thought was ludicrous, insulting to God, really. "He wouldn't do that."

"Well, He did." Dell's reply was clipped and filled with bitterness.

Somehow she had to make him see. "God is merciful. He doesn't let people die out of revenge."

" 'Vengeance is mine; I will repay, saith the Lord.' " He threw her a wry smile. "You see, I know some scripture."

"Don't joke about this, Dell. That verse does not mean God kills for revenge.

That's the way of imperfect man, not a perfect, loving God."

"Then why did she die?" he asked, his eyes beseeching her for an answer.

"You said it yourself. She was frail—weakened a little more with each child."

"And I should have known better. Should have used more control."

Cassidy eased forward in the chair and lumbered to her feet. She went to Dell, wrapping her arms around him from behind. He tensed, but Cassidy pressed in.

"Women know what they want," she said softly, laying her cheek against his back. "If Anna didn't want to have babies, she wouldn't have. Please don't blame yourself anymore."

Dell took a ragged breath and turned in her arms.

The tenderness reflected in his eyes melted Cassidy's heart and caused her to reach out. "I know I'm not Anna," she said, eyes filling with tears, "but I love you, Dell. And you say you love me. Can't we just put the past behind us and be happy?"

He cupped her face between his large hands. "I do love you, more than I ever thought possible."

Joy welled up inside Cassidy. "Oh, Dell."

"I'll be a good husband to you and a good father to our baby, but I won't take a chance on losing you, too."

"You won't lose me!"

"No more babies, Cass. I mean it. And the only way I can assure myself of that is to stay in the lean-to."

"Don't I have anything to say about it?"

"No," he said firmly. "Don't fight me on this. Please."

"All right," she relented. "I won't say any more to you about it." But that didn't mean she didn't intend to discuss the subject with God!

Chapter 12

Dell released a sigh of relief as he left the town of Abilene behind. He hoped the ride home would be quicker than the trip to town had been. Countless troubles had assaulted him and Johnny while they tried to herd ten head of cattle through the deep snow. Now that the stock was sold, the runners on the bottom of the sled should take them home in no time.

He glanced over his shoulder at the supplies loaded in the sled and patted the saddlebags next to him on the seat. Relief filled him that the sale had brought in enough to carry them through the winter and a little beyond. He'd even had enough to buy Christmas gifts for his family and material for Cassidy to make garments for the baby.

His pulse quickened at the thought of the new child. It wouldn't be long now. Just a few more weeks. A sense of dread clenched his gut as he thought ahead. Would he still have Cassidy when it was all over, or like little Jack, would the new baby be left motherless?

Cassidy had waved away all of his concerns, and even Ellen had tried to reassure him that Cassidy was the type of woman who bore children easily. Still, Dell knew from experience that God could be ruthless in His dealings when men broke their word. And he was determined not to break his word this time.

He had found himself praying more lately. For the baby and Cassidy. For the other children, who thankfully were beginning to accept Cassidy into their lives—all but Tarah. Most of all, he prayed for strength to keep his promise to God. In unguarded moments, he wondered if perhaps Reverend Marcus had been right when he said life had just dealt him a harsh blow. That Anna's death had nothing to do with a bargain. And he remembered Cassidy said she didn't believe God was a God of vengeance, either.

Looking out at the glistening snow, Dell knew he was afraid to agree with her. Afraid to give in and be the husband Cassidy deserved, in every sense of the word. In spite of his resolve, somewhere deep inside, hope was beginning to glimmer.

⌒

Cassidy caught her breath as the sleigh glided over the icy ground. The moon, full and bright, cast a silvery glow on the snow-covered plain. Oh, what a perfect evening it would have been if only Dell were there to share it. She sighed aloud, her breath frosty white in the frigid night air.

The first trip Dell made to Abilene only kept him away for two weeks. But this time he and Johnny had already been gone five weeks, and Cassidy was beginning to worry about her husband.

She glanced sideways at Sam, and her heart swelled with pride—mother's pride. He sat with the reins in his capable hands, looking confident, almost manly, as he drove the horses.

Turning, he blushed bright red as he caught her staring at him.

She placed a gentle, gloved hand on his arm. "I was just thinking of what a big help you've been since your pa's been gone." He swallowed hard as she continued. "I truly don't know what I would have done without you."

"I only wish Pa woulda made it back for the dance tonight," he said softly. "I know how you've been looking forward to it."

"I am disappointed," she admitted. "But it couldn't be helped, and there will be other dances your pa can escort me to."

He nodded and turned his attention back to the horses.

Cassidy smiled, remembering the morning Dell had asked her to the Christmas dance. A small ache crossed her heart, making it feel as though it were bruised. She had hoped against hope that he would be back in time to escort her, but here she was again, going alone to a dance. Well, she wasn't really alone, she reminded herself. After all, the children were with her.

A slight twinge pinched her lower back. Mercy, this seat was uncomfortable! Thankfully they were pulling into town. She'd be glad to get out and stretch her legs.

Sam pulled the horses to a stop in front of the little schoolhouse, maneuvering carefully around the other sleighs in the yard.

"Luke, help the girls," he ordered, jumping down. "I'll get Ma."

Sam walked around to her side, almost losing his footing on the icy ground. He lifted the heavy quilt from her lap. "Be careful," he admonished. "It's pretty slippery here."

She took his proffered hand, stepping down carefully. The rest of the children moved ahead of her, unmindful of the ice; but Sam stayed by Cassidy's side. He didn't release her until they were inside the building. Then he helped her out of her coat and led her carefully to a chair.

She patted his arm. "Thank you, Sam. Now go ask someone to dance."

A bright red glow covered his face and spread all the way to his hairline. He glanced around until his eyes rested on Camilla Simpson.

Ah, so he still had a crush on the girl.

Camilla's gaze shifted from the young man who whirled her around the dance floor to Sam, and a pretty blush appeared on her cheeks.

From the looks of it, the feeling was mutual. Well, Cassidy didn't blame Camilla for having a crush on Sam. She only hoped the perky brunette was worthy of her special son.

"Go ahead and ask her to dance," she urged.

"Naw." Sam stuffed his hands into his trouser pockets. "I can't cut in on another fella."

With a sniff, Cassidy waved a hand. "Looks to me like she'd rather dance with you."

Indeed, Camilla seemed hard-pressed to focus on the young man with whom she was dancing, for her eyes kept roving to Sam.

"Think so?"

"Seems pretty obvious," she said with a wry smile. "It's perfectly all right for a man to cut in on a dance. Just go tap her partner politely on the shoulder. If he's a gentleman, he'll move aside."

A look of indecision crossed Sam's features.

"Go ahead." Cassidy gave him a small shove.

With his hands still stuffed in his pockets, he cleared his throat and took a tentative step onto the dance floor.

An encouraging smile touched Cassidy's lips as he glanced back at her. She inclined her head to spur him on. His back straightened, and he tapped Camilla's partner on the shoulder. He received a scowl from the lad, but a shy smile lit Camilla's face.

At the demonstration of new courtship, Cassidy's heart ached with loneliness. Deep in thoughts of Dell, she jumped when a man's voice broke into her thoughts. "It looks like we may end up in-laws."

With an upward glance, Cassidy recognized Camilla's father. She smiled. "Well, I wouldn't count my chickens before they're hatched," she replied. "But you could be right. Sam's pretty smitten."

"He's not the only one." A baritone chuckle escaped the doctor's lips. "Cammie's been miserable for weeks, wondering if your boy would ask her to dance tonight."

"Well, she needn't have worried."

Dr. Simpson took the chair next to her. "Uh, Mrs. St. John, I don't want to appear rude, but I can't help noticing your condition."

Heat warmed Cassidy's face, and a gasp escaped her lips at the man's audacity.

He raised a hand in defense. "Pardon my boldness, but I am a doctor."

"Of course." Cassidy smiled.

"I'd like to offer my assistance when your time comes."

"That's generous of you, but I'm fine, really. I have a woman at home to help me." She shifted in her seat as another twinge pinched her back. Would she ever be comfortable again?

"I realize you've had several children, Mrs. St. John, but you look as though you might deliver at any moment," he persisted. "It wouldn't hurt to have a doctor present at the birth."

"This is my first child, Doctor. And anyway, I have five or six weeks to go."

He frowned, and his gaze shifted to Sam and Camilla.

"My husband had four children before we met," Cassidy explained. "And I took my niece to raise after her parents died."

"And you said you still have a month to go?"

She nodded. "A little over a month."

"Hmm." His gaze roved over her bulging stomach. "You're a large-built woman, so maybe you're just carrying a big baby."

Cassidy winced at the reference to her size. A big baby! She didn't want her girl to be big.

"At any rate," he said, "it might be a good idea to enlist my services when the time comes."

"I'll discuss it with my husband, Dr. Simpson. Thank you for your concern."

The song ended, and the dancers drifted from the floor. Sam and Camilla made their way toward Cassidy.

Sam stretched out a hand to Camilla's father. "How are you tonight, sir?"

The doctor grasped the proffered hand and gave Sam a good-natured grin. "Doing fine, son." He glanced at Camilla. "How'd you like to dance with your pa?"

Camilla dimpled. "I'd love to."

Sam stuffed his hands into his pockets and cleared his throat. "You don't feel like dancing, do you?" he asked, his gaze resting on Cassidy.

Though she felt she probably shouldn't make a spectacle of herself in her condition, she couldn't resist. "I would be delighted."

"Uh, okay."

The hesitancy in his voice caused Cassidy's brows to furrow. "You sure you don't mind, Sam?"

His face colored.

So he was embarrassed to dance with her in her condition. "It's all right," she said, her heart going out to him. "We don't have to."

"No, it's okay. It would be my, uh, honor," he insisted, though Cassidy didn't quite believe him.

The grin that crossed his features was the same heart-stopping smile she'd seen so many times on his father. Another ache crossed Cassidy's heart as he helped her to her feet.

She danced with her son until he stopped abruptly. She glanced up into his face, but his pleased gaze rested beyond her. Cassidy turned. Dell! He stood at the door, watching her, and when he caught her gaze, his face lit up into a smile.

Tears of relief filled her eyes, and she moved toward him as fast as her feet would take her.

Gathering her into his arms, Dell placed a light kiss on her lips.

"Dell," she admonished, "people are watching."

He shrugged and grinned. "If a man didn't kiss his wife after not seeing her for a month, I'd think there was something wrong with him."

Heat rose to her cheeks. "I've been worried sick," she said. "How was the trip?"

"Later," he said, his voice low and husky. "Right now I want to dance with you."

Suddenly feeling light and carefree, she floated into his arms. "I'm so glad you're home." She pressed her head against his chest.

"I couldn't stand you up, now, could I?"

Another twinge pinched at Cassidy's back. She stiffened.

Dell held her slightly away from him, his concerned gaze searching her face. "Everything okay?"

"Oh, I'm fine," she reassured him. "But I would feel better if I sat."

"Let's get you off your feet, then." He led her gently to a chair. "Can I get you anything?"

"A glass of punch would be nice. Thank you."

"Be right back."

As he made his way toward the refreshment table, Cassidy scanned the room, looking for each of her children. Sam again danced with Camilla. Emily and Jack played together with a small gathering of children, and Luke stood in a corner with a group of boys his own age. She continued her survey of the room and frowned. Where was Tarah?

Cassidy's eyes riveted to the door just as the girl slipped outside behind someone. Johnny!

Anger boiled inside of Cassidy. Was she being played for a fool? Tarah must have been seeing him all along!

She glanced back to the refreshment table. Dell was deep in conversation with the doctor. Well, she wasn't going to wait and give Johnny a chance to paw her daughter! Lumbering to her feet, Cassidy grabbed her coat and scarf.

An icy gust caught the door just as she opened it. Stepping outside, she gasped at the intensity of the cold. The ground was slippery as she made her way carefully down the steps, eyes scanning the area for Tarah and Johnny.

Please show me where they are, Lord.

The sound of angry voices caught her ears, and she cautiously moved toward the sound. Tarah and Johnny stood beside Dell's horse.

"You are not going to steal from my pa!" Tarah said hotly.

Johnny's voice came back smooth as freshly churned butter. "I told you, we're not stealing it from him. As soon as we get to Oregon and get settled in, we'll start paying him back."

"Why don't we just wait until we have the money, then? I just don't feel right going about it this way."

"I told you, hon. It's the only way. Your pa'd skin me alive if he knew I was in love with his daughter."

"Oh, Johnny. . ."

The sound of rapture in Tarah's voice made Cassidy bristle. How dare he play on that child's emotions! Without thought, she stepped forward. "Johnny Cooper, I thought I told you to stay away from my daughter!"

"Cassidy!" Tarah groaned.

Cassidy whirled around and pointed a finger at Tarah. "And to think I believed you when you told me you wouldn't see him anymore."

There was no defiance in Tarah's face. "I'm sorry, Cassidy, but I love him. We're getting married."

Rage boiled inside of Cassidy. "Over my dead, cold body are you marrying the likes of that vermin."

"Cassidy," Johnny broke in, amusement edging his voice, "I'm crushed." In his hand he held Dell's brown leather wallet.

"What do you think you are doing with my husband's money?"

"Now don't get riled up. I'm just taking it to the ranch for him."

She squinted, sizing him up. "Uh-huh, we'll see. Come, Tarah," she said firmly. "I think it's time your father knew about this relationship. I never should have kept it from him to begin with."

"Please, don't." Tears glistened in Tarah's violet eyes as she pleaded.

"I'm sorry, but you've left me no choice." Cassidy lifted her skirt and turned.

Tarah gave a sharp intake of breath. "What do you think you are doing?"

Cassidy turned in time to see Johnny's pistol raised above her.

"Johnny, no!" Tarah screamed.

Pain exploded in Cassidy's head, and blackness claimed her.

Dell frowned and glanced around the small room. Cassidy was nowhere to be seen. He motioned Sam from the dance floor.

"What's wrong, Pa?"

"Have you seen your ma?"

Sam shook his head. "Maybe she went to the. . ."

"I don't think so. She's been gone awhile." He grabbed his coat. "Just to be sure, I'll go out and check. You gather up the rest of the kids and ask if any of them have seen her."

Dell returned to the schoolhouse a moment later after confirming Cassidy wasn't in the privy outside. The children were gathered around, concern written plainly on their faces.

"Where's Tarah?" he asked.

Luke shrugged. "I saw her go outside with Johnny awhile ago."

"Johnny Cooper?" Dell asked with a frown. "What would she be doing with him? Besides, I told Johnny to take the supplies home." Anxiety gnawed at his stomach. "Stay here," he ordered.

Dell grabbed his saddlebag from its hook on the wall and opened the flap. Feeling around for his gun, he frowned. His wallet, carrying the money they'd brought back from the sale of the stock, was missing.

"That no-good, thieving. . ." So he had been right not to trust Johnny. He kicked himself mentally. He should have gone with his gut instinct in the first place. Taking his holster from the bag, he slid it around his hips and buckled it into place. There were more important things than money right now. But he'd deal with Johnny once Cassidy and Tarah were safe. Slinging his saddlebag over his shoulder, he hurried into the frigid winter night.

His gaze scanned the schoolyard. Spying something lying a few feet away, he moved toward the object. Cassidy's scarf lay on the ground. As he bent to pick it up, he stared in horror. Drops of blood, crimson against the white of the snow, spotted the area.

Cassidy! Oh, God, no. Please, no.

Panicked, he ran back inside.

"What's wrong, Pa?" Sam asked.

Dell grabbed the boy's arm and led him away from the rest of the children. "I found this outside," he said, holding up the scarf. "And there was blood on the ground beside it."

"We gotta find her, Pa! What do you think happened?"

"I'm not sure, but it looks like Johnny took her and Tarah." Dell swiped a hand across his forehead. "What I can't figure out is why he'd do it. If he just wanted to steal the money from the sale, he could've done that."

"It was Tarah, Pa," Sam said hesitantly. "She told me awhile back they were going to be married as soon as she was of age."

Rage clouded Dell's senses as Sam went on. "Cassidy must have caught them together."

Dell shook his head, still unable to put it all together. All he knew was that he had to find Cassidy and Tarah.

"Sam, I'm going to unhitch one of the horses from the sleigh so I can go after your ma and sister. I want you to be extra careful and take the children home."

"I want to come with you, Pa."

Dell placed a hand on Sam's shoulder. "I know you do, son. But I need you to look after the children for me. Can I count on you?"

"Yes, sir."

"All right, then. I'll be home as soon as I find them."

"Everything okay here?" Dr. Simpson stood before him.

"My wife and daughter are missing." Dell showed him the scarf. "I found this outside on the ground, along with some blood. I'm going after them."

Doc frowned. "You need another man to ride along?"

"I sure could use you," Dell said. "I think my ranch foreman may have kidnapped them."

"Let me get my bag and tell my wife I'm coming with you," he said.

"Thanks. Do you have a saddle horse?"

Doc nodded. "I had a patient to see before I came, so I rode here."

"Good. I'll meet you out front."

By the time Dell loaded the children into the sleigh and sent them off toward home, Dr. Simpson was ready to ride.

"Let's take a moment to pray," the doctor suggested.

"I thought you were a doctor, not a preacher," Dell said gruffly, mounting his horse.

"I am. But I think prayer is in order right about now." He looked sharply at Dell. "I wouldn't want to ride off without His help if it were my wife and daughter out there in danger."

"You're right. Pray as we ride."

They set off in the direction of the tracks made by the sleigh that carried the supplies Dell had brought back from Abilene. The doctor said a quick but fervent prayer.

Dell had to admit he felt better after he echoed Simpson's "amen." "They can't have gotten very far, with that sleigh loaded down with supplies," he said, speaking more for his own comfort than to reassure the doctor.

"We'll be able to cover more ground on horseback than he will with the sleigh and two women," the doctor said.

Dell nodded. *Oh, God, let them be safe.*

⌣

Pain overwhelmed Cassidy as she came to. She tried to sit up but thought better of the idea as a wave of dizziness washed over her. She glanced up at the stars speeding by overhead.

"Cassidy, thank God you're awake." Tarah's tear-filled eyes gazed down at her.

"What happened?"

"Johnny knocked you out so you wouldn't go tell Pa."

"And you still came with him?"

"I wasn't going to, but he pulled his gun on me." Large tears rolled down her face.

Cassidy placed her hand on Tarah's arm. "I'm sorry, sweetheart."

"You were right about him all along."

A gasp escaped Cassidy's mouth as a pain hit her back and crept around to the front.

"What's wrong?"

"I–I'm not sure," Cassidy said through gritted teeth as the pain held on, then gradually subsided. "I think I might be getting ready to have the baby."

The blood drained from Tarah's face. "But it's too early."

"I know." She grimaced.

"Johnny Cooper, you turn around and take us home right this minute," Tarah called from the back of the sleigh where she sat with Cassidy's head on

114

her lap. "My ma is about to have her baby."

"Shut up," he growled. "I don't have time to worry about a baby. We'll drop her off at the next town."

"If you think I'm going anywhere with you now, you have another thing coming!"

"You'll do as you're told unless you want me to drop Cassidy off right now and let her freeze to death."

"I don't know how I could have ever thought I was in love with you."

"Little girl, I don't care if you're in love with me or not, but you're coming with me to make sure I get where I want to go." He turned and eyed her sternly. "Now sit down and be quiet before I gag you."

She turned and looked back down at Cassidy, fear clouding her eyes.

"God will take care of us," Cassidy comforted.

Tarah looked up, and a hand flew to her throat. "I think He just did," she whispered.

"What is it?" Cassidy asked.

Tarah cast a furtive glance at Johnny's back and dipped her head closer. "Pa's coming."

"What do you mean?"

"He's behind us."

Relief flooded Cassidy's heart. God was in control, and Dell was coming to rescue her. She closed her eyes as a defense against the pain that seized her.

Hurry, Dell.

Chapter 13

Dell saw the sleigh speeding along the ice directly ahead of them. He drew his Colt pistol and kicked his horse to spur it on.

"Johnny, stop!" he yelled.

Johnny turned in the seat and whipped the reins hard. The horses sped up. Still, Dell and the doctor closed the distance easily, each going to one side of the sleigh. Dell leveled his pistol at Johnny's head.

"Stop the horses," he ordered.

"You wouldn't shoot me," Johnny hollered back over the pounding of the horses' hooves. "Not with your wife and daughter in back."

"Pull over now," Dell said through gritted teeth, "and I might not kill you."

Fear crossed Johnny's features.

"Look, I'm going to follow you wherever you're headed," Dell said. "And the longer you keep my wife and daughter in this freezing cold weather, the madder I'm going to get. I suggest you pull over right now."

Uncertainty flickered in Johnny's eyes. Seeming to weigh the odds of getting away, he pulled on the reins, gradually slowing the horses to a walk, then a full stop. Dell slipped his Colt back into its holster and jumped from his horse before Johnny could unholster his own gun. He grabbed Johnny's coat and dragged him from the sleigh, then drew back his fist.

"Dell." Cassidy's quiet voice broke through his rage. "Don't hurt him. Let him go."

"Let him go?" He blinked hard.

The doctor glanced up from beside Cassidy. "Better do as she says, Dell. You're about to be a father again."

Dell's grip loosened, and Johnny tumbled to the ground.

The baby was coming now? "It's too early." He groaned. "Just when I was starting to believe God wouldn't do it, it's about to happen again."

"What are you talking about?" the doctor asked, a frown furrowing his brow. "She's a few weeks early, but if we get her to a warm place, everything should be fine."

Dell turned to Johnny. "Get out of here, and don't show your face in these parts ever again. It's a good thing for you that my wife is about to have that baby. Otherwise I'd tear you limb from limb."

"I won't make it to the next town without a horse," Johnny whined.

"I don't care," Dell growled.

Johnny shrank back.

"You can't leave him out here in this weather with no horse, Dell." Again Cassidy's pain-filled voice brought him to his senses.

"Take mine and go."

Not waiting to be told twice, Johnny moved toward the horse, eyeing Dell warily as he walked past him.

"Wait, Johnny!" called Tarah. "Give my pa his money."

Dell had forgotten about the money. Mentally he kicked himself for not thinking to bring the sheriff along. He fingered his Colt and stared hard at Johnny as the scoundrel hesitated.

Finally he shrugged and reached into his coat. He grabbed the leather wallet and tossed it to the ground. Dell loosened his grip on his pistol.

Tarah stomped forward and retrieved it from the snow. Glancing inside, she gave a grudging nod. "The money's there, Pa."

"What'd you expect?" Johnny mounted the horse quickly and grabbed the reins. "I didn't exactly have time to spend any of it." He glanced down at Tarah with an insolent grin. "It's too bad you didn't want to come with me, hon. You and me would've had some good times together."

Dell clenched his fists and started toward him, but Johnny dug his spurs into the horse's flanks and rode away at a gallop.

From the sleigh, Cassidy moaned. Shaking himself from the anger still raging inside him, Dell went quickly to her side. "Is she all right, Doc?"

"She has a nasty cut, but I can tend to that," the man said, pressing a clean handkerchief to Cassidy's head. "What concerns me most is that her pains are coming pretty close together. Let's get her home before we have to deliver this baby in the cold."

Dell tied the doctor's horse to the back of the sleigh and settled into the seat. Tarah climbed up beside him. He flapped the reins, turning toward home.

"I'm sorry, Pa," she said, laying her head against his shoulder.

In spite of himself, Dell tensed at her touch. "I don't understand how you could go behind my back like this."

Her shoulders shook as she wept against him. "I believed him when he said he loved me," she said between large gulps of air. "Cassidy tried to warn me, but I wouldn't listen."

"Cassidy knew and didn't say anything?" He felt betrayed.

"Don't blame her. I promised I wouldn't have anything more to do with him, and she believed me." She lifted her head from his shoulder and sobbed into her hands. "I couldn't bear it if I cause more problems between you and Ma."

At the sound of "Ma" on his daughter's lips, Dell's heart softened. "It's all right, sweetheart. I'm not angry with Cassidy." He pulled a handkerchief from his breast pocket and offered it to the weeping girl. "I'm just relieved you're both all right. Now let's get her home."

Cassidy was barely aware that they'd arrived home, so intense was the pain.

Dell lifted her gently into his arms and carried her inside.

"How is she?" Ellen asked. Four pairs of anxious eyes peered at Cassidy, waiting for the answer.

"I'm fine," Cassidy said, not wanting to alarm any of the children.

"The baby's coming." Dell's answer was clipped. "Fill a basin with water and grab some clean linen."

Once inside the bedroom, he laid her gently on the bed and began to undress her.

"How are you, darling?" he asked.

Cassidy winced. "My head hurts."

Dell glanced down at the pillow, and a groan escaped his lips. "It's bleeding."

"Johnny knocked me out."

Something akin to a roar emitted from deep inside Dell. "If I had known that, I would have killed him."

"I know." Another contraction gripped her, and she squeezed Dell's hand to ward off the pain.

"Doc!" Dell yelled.

"Wait. Get me into my nightgown first." Modesty was too embedded in Cassidy for her to allow even a doctor to see her unclad.

When she was wearing a fresh nightgown, he called the doctor in. Dell cleared his throat and backed toward the door. "Well, I, uh. . ."

"Don't leave me," Cassidy implored, catching his hesitant gaze. She reached for him.

"I—I don't know if I can. . ."

Cassidy knew what he meant. The memories of Anna's death during childbirth were too deep, and he was consumed with fear. She couldn't stop a moan as the next wave of pain seized her.

Dell was back at her side in a flash.

"You're—staying—with—me," she insisted through gritted teeth, digging her nails into his arm.

"That okay, Doc?"

"As long as you keep out of the way."

Dr. Simpson checked her contractions and pressed on her belly. "Everything seems to be right on track," he announced. "Won't be long now."

"Oh, God. Oh, God, please!" Dell said from her bedside.

Irritation rose up inside of Cassidy. "Dell!" she bellowed through the pain. "Be quiet! And don't you dare pass out on me like you did at the wedding!"

The doctor's eyebrows shot up, and a rumble of laughter shook his shoulders.

"Don't cross a woman in labor, Dell," he said, moving to check the cut on Cassidy's head. "It's not bad," he mumbled, as though to himself. "The bleeding's stopped for the most part."

"Is it wrong for a man to worry about his wife?" Dell asked, looking to the doctor for affirmation.

"Yes!" Cassidy exclaimed.

"First you complain that I don't give you enough attention, and now you want me to stop caring?" he growled.

Dr. Simpson looked up from bandaging Cassidy's head. "Uh, this might not be the proper time to—"

"This is the perfect time," Cassidy interjected. "It's the only time I can get him still long enough to talk."

"Why is it wrong for a man to want his wife to live?" Dell directed the question to the doctor, but it was Cassidy who answered.

"I don't know why Anna was taken from you and the children," she said, her voice still sharp from pain and frustration. "But I have no intention of dying. God willing, I'll live to care for my children until I hold my grandchildren, and possibly my great-grandchildren, in my arms."

He winced as she squeezed his hand again. When the contraction was over, she continued as though she had never been interrupted. "You have to stop living your life in fear, dwelling on the past."

"My faith isn't as strong as yours, Cass. I can't bear the thought of losing you."

"Women have babies—they have all through the ages. Sometimes they die, and sometimes they don't. Look at me, Dell."

His tortured gaze met hers, and her heart went out to him.

"There are more ways to lose a person than for that person to die," she said pointedly.

His eyes narrowed. "You saying you're going to leave me?"

"Of course not! I could never hurt God and the children that way. Besides, I love you. But this unreasonable fear you have is causing a wedge between us whether you want it to or not."

Her body went rigid as another pain seized her. She clamped her lips tight, trying not to cry out. Would this pain ever stop?

"It's almost time for you to start pushing, Mrs. St. John. You might want to hold the rest of this fascinating conversation until your babies are delivered."

Did he say "babies"? Must be the pain affecting her hearing.

"Dell, listen to me."

He leaned in closer, tears misting his eyes. "You—have—to—" She let out a deep groan, and tears stung her eyes. "You have to let go of your fear and trust God."

"Cassidy," he moaned. "Please don't try to talk, darling. Save your strength."

Cassidy shook her head. "You have to hear this. I have faith in God that He'll watch me and keep me safe. And when it's time for me to go to be with Him, He'll take me. But I'll tell you this much." She was starting to get riled again. "Whether I live or die has nothing whatsoever to do with you and any silly bargain you made with God! Just how much power do you think you have over a person's life?"

"Okay, I see a head," the doctor announced. "Push with the next contraction."

Another pain squeezed her body, and Cassidy bore down, pushing with all her might.

"Rest a minute," the doctor ordered.

She lay back, exhausted. "If—I—can—trust—God—to—care—for—me—can't—you?" she asked, panting between each word.

He pressed her hand to his lips, wiping her sweat-soaked brow with his handkerchief. "I'll try, my darling."

"Get ready to push again," Dr. Simpson ordered.

Summoning her strength, Cassidy pushed once more, the pain nearly overwhelming her senses. Again and again she obeyed the doctor's orders, until at last, a small but healthy infant made its way into the world.

Dell peeked over Cassidy to the baby. "It's a girl," he cried, tears streaming down his handsome face.

Tears filled Cassidy's eyes. "I told you it would be," she said, managing a smug little smile.

Their infant daughter let out a wail.

"I was right, too. Didn't I tell you she'd take after you?" Dell said with a teasing grin.

Another pain gripped Cassidy's body. "Something's wrong."

"What do you mean?" A look of terror crossed Dell's face.

"I—I feel another pain coming."

"That would be baby number two." Dr. Simpson placed the freshly wrapped infant in Dell's arms.

Cassidy would have laughed if the pain hadn't been so intense. Twins. She'd asked God for a child, and He'd given her twins. The tears spilled over onto her cheeks. How good He was.

"All right, Mrs. St. John, are you ready to do this again?" the doctor asked.

"I'm ready," she said through gritted teeth.

Within moments their second baby arrived—a boy, crying lustily as he entered the world. Soon the doctor had him wrapped and placed in Dell's other arm.

Tears streamed down Dell's face as he looked at Cassidy. "Do you want to see them?"

"Of course. Sit on the bed next to me."

"Only for a moment," the doctor warned. "We need to make sure they stay warm."

Cassidy looked at her red, squalling babies and knew she had never seen or heard anything so beautiful in her life. "Oh, Dell. Isn't God wonderful?"

His tearful gaze captured hers, and he nodded. A thrill passed over Cassidy's heart. She knew her husband was a man who had just had a change of heart.

They heard a quiet tap at the door.

"Open the door," Dell called. "My hands are full."

It was Ellen. "I thought I heard two babies crying."

"You did," Dell replied.

"Oh my. Do you need some help, Doctor?"

"I could use someone to bathe the twins while I finish with their ma. Take them to the front room where the fire is. And make sure they're wrapped tightly after their bath so they don't lose any body heat."

Ellen nodded, then glanced at Dell. "Carry them into the sitting room for me. I'll get Tarah to help."

By the time the doctor was finished tending to Cassidy and Ellen had changed the bedding, a beaming Dell had returned with the babies. He placed one on each side of her. She nuzzled first one, then the other, and sighed with contentment.

"Well, I think my work here is done," Dr. Simpson said. "I must say, this has been the most interesting birth of my career." He looked pointedly at the new parents. "And the most enlightening."

"Sorry, Doc," Dell muttered.

The man placed a firm hand on Dell's shoulder. "Your wife is a smart woman—and most definitely still alive. Do you both a favor and stop being a fool."

Cassidy giggled as Dell blinked in surprise at the candid remark.

"Life and death are in the hand of the Almighty. Even we doctors, much as we'd like to take credit, can't control what God ordains." He zipped his leather bag and lifted it from the bureau. "Now I suggest you stop trying to control how He does His business and relax."

He turned, lifted the latch on the door, and opened it. "Besides," he said with a grin, "your wife is a strong woman, most likely capable of bearing a dozen children."

A gasp escaped Cassidy's lips. A dozen children.

The doctor lifted his hand and exited the room.

"Well, I guess he gave me what for, didn't he?" Dell asked with a wry grin.

"You needed to hear it."

"I suppose. . . ." Dell glanced at the sleeping babies. "What are you going to name them?" he asked.

"I don't know. How about if you name the boy and I name the girl?"

"Sounds reasonable." Dell squinted, deep in thought. "How about Timothy?"

Cassidy wrinkled her nose.

"Matthew?"

"No."

"I thought you said I get to name the boy." Dell's eyes twinkled, and a smile spread over his face.

"Okay, I won't say anything about the next one you pick."

"Hiram," he said with a smirk.

"This beautiful little boy does not look like a—"

Dell threw back his head and laughed heartily. "All right. What do you want to call him?"

Cassidy eyed him. "Can I still name the girl?"

He gave her a wry grin. "I guess."

"All right. Let's call him William, after my brother. It'll mean so much to Emily."

Dell nodded. "Sounds like a pretty good name. Mind if I call him Will?"

"That's fine. But not Willie or Billy. My brother hated those nicknames."

"What about our sweet little girl here?" he asked, cooing at his daughter, whose tiny hand wrapped around his finger.

"I'd like to call her Hope."

Bending over, he brushed Cassidy's forehead with his lips. "Hope and Will. Our babies." He gently unwrapped Hope's fingers from his. "Do you feel up to seeing the rest of the children for a few minutes? They're sort of waiting outside the door."

"Of course."

Dell went to the door and opened it to reveal five excited faces.

Slowly they filed in, one by one, kissing Cassidy on the cheek and running gentle hands over the fuzzy baby heads of their new sister and brother.

Tarah stood before Cassidy with trembling lips. "Forgive me?" was all she could manage before a fresh onslaught of tears.

"Of course I forgive you, sweetheart. I'm just glad everything worked out the way it did." Cassidy grinned at her. "I imagine you'll pay penance enough helping me take care of two babies!"

"Oh, Ma, I truly love you." Tarah maneuvered cautiously around the twins and gave Cassidy a squeeze.

Cassidy's heart leaped from the wonder of it all. God knew what it took to finally make them a family. She stroked Tarah's ebony hair. "I truly love you, too."

"All right," Dell said with authority. "Everyone out. Your ma needs her rest."

The children lifted their voices in protest. But Dell was firm. "You'll have plenty of time to see her and the babies tomorrow, but for now I want you in your beds. No arguments."

They didn't have to be told again, and one by one they slowly left the room.

"Now as for you, my darling," he said, "I want you to get some rest, too."

"I will. I feel like I could sleep for a month."

Dell chuckled. "You'll be lucky to get a couple hours before one or both want to be fed."

"Then you'd better let me sleep."

He pulled the covers up around her, careful not to cover the babies' heads.

"Cassidy, I want you to know I thought about what you said earlier." He reached forward and brushed a damp strand of hair away from her eyes. "About trusting God to care for you."

"Yes?"

"And I think I'm beginning to understand. Anna was tiny and weak from the start. But you. . .you're so strong—strong enough to argue with me the whole time you were having the babies."

"Well, you're so thickheaded," she said in her own defense. "And I was feeling pretty cranky."

"I can imagine," he drawled. "And Doc had a point about me trying to control whether someone lives or dies."

Hope rose in Cassidy's heart. "That's entirely up to God."

"I'm beginning to realize that. Anyway, like the doctor said, you're a very strong woman and could most likely bear a dozen children."

"Dell!" Cassidy gasped.

"Don't worry," he said softly. "I don't intend to have a dozen more. But I wouldn't mind another one or two eventually."

Cassidy stared up at him, eyes wide. "Do you mean you want a real marriage?"

He nodded. "I've allowed fear of losing you to control our relationship. But not anymore."

"Not anymore?" Cassidy repeated, tears welling up in her eyes.

"Nope. Never again."

Cassidy's pulse quickened as his gaze melted into hers. Gently he lowered his head inch by inch until their lips met. His hands went to either side of her neck as he deepened the kiss. When he finally released her, tears glistened in his blue eyes. "I love you more than anything in this world, Cassidy St. John." Lovingly he stroked her cheek. "I'll make it all up to you. I promise."

Cassidy shook her head. "I just want to go forward. There's been too much looking back in this family—too much trying to pay for the past."

"All right," Dell said softly. "There'll be no more talk of the past, then. We start fresh right now."

"What about God?" Cassidy asked. "Our marriage will never be the way it is supposed to be unless we make Him the center of our lives."

"I reckon it's time to start fresh with Him, too."

Cassidy saw the mist in his eyes and smiled. "Behold all things become new," she said wearily, just before a yawn rose from inside of her, catching her unaware.

With his forefinger, Dell gently traced a line from her cheekbone to her chin. "I want you to get some rest while you can," he said softly. "I'll be here on a pallet if you need me for anything."

"Oh, Dell, don't sleep on the floor," Cassidy protested.

He smiled tenderly. "I've spent enough nights alone. From now on, I'm sleeping wherever you are."

After dropping a final kiss on her upturned lips, he blew out the lamp.

Cassidy pressed a kiss to each little head beside her, then snuggled down under the covers. Her mouth curved into a smile as she drifted to sleep.

TARAH'S
LESSONS

Lovingly dedicated to my four children:
Cat, Michael, Stevan, and Will.
You'll learn so many lessons throughout your precious lives,
lessons taught by scores of teachers.
But the most important, by far, are those taught by a loving Father
as He molds you into the vessels He created you to be.
My prayer is that you will learn the lessons well.
Mommy loves you.
Special thanks to Chris Lynxwiler and my mom, Frances Devine,
who have each read this book so many times
for editing purposes, they must know it by heart.

Chapter 1

1871

Tarah St. John stood at the doorway of the little sod schoolhouse and waved good-bye to her departing students. Finally the endless day was over!

Releasing a weary sigh, she pressed her palms to her cheeks and rubbed vigorously, attempting to ease her aching jaw. Whoever had said that "a smile never hurt anyone" had obviously never tried to force one all day.

With purpose, she pulled the wooden door firmly shut and turned to her one remaining student. She narrowed her gaze, set her lips into a firm line, and stomped back to the front of the room, her blue gingham skirt swishing about her legs.

Very near to tears, Tarah rammed her hands on her hips and faced the red-headed boy writing sentences on the slate blackboard. "Luke St. John," she said furiously, "you just wait 'til Pa hears about this."

"Aw," her twelve-year-old brother protested, keeping his eyes on the task at hand, "you ain't gotta tell Ma and Pa."

"I don't *have* to tell them," she corrected. "But it just so happens I want to. Honestly, your orneriness is probably the sole reason Miss Nelson gave up teaching and hightailed it back east." She paced the floor behind him, trying to come up with just the right words to make him thoroughly ashamed of himself.

"Come on, Tarah." He kicked at the ground with a booted toe. "Don't be mad."

Steeling herself against his conciliatory tone, Tarah glared at her brother. She refused to let him off the hook so easily. "You made me look plumb foolish, Luke. Did you have to show off for the new girl on my very first day of teaching?"

Luke stopped his nearly illegible scrawling and turned to her, his green eyes flashing in anger. "I weren't showing off for no girl!"

"*Wasn't* showing off for *any* girl. And you were so. I saw you staring at Josie Raney all during spelling lessons this morning. And from the looks of those sentences," she said with a pointed glance at the board, "you need to concentrate on spelling a sight more than you need to look at a pretty new face. There are two *b*'s in *ribbons*."

"I *wasn't* looking at her pretty face," Luke insisted.

Tarah couldn't resist a teasing grin. "So you *do* think she's pretty."

Caught by his own words, the boy grinned back, showing teeth still rather large for his face. He shrugged. "I reckon."

"Then why in the world did you dip her ribbon in your inkwell? Don't you know they cost money?"

Luke shifted and stared at his feet. "Guess I weren't thinking about that," he mumbled.

"Apparently you *weren't*," Tarah said with a sniff. "Well, you'll just have to buy her a new one."

Panic sparked in the boy's eyes. "But I don't got no money."

She lifted a delicate brow and regarded him frankly. "I suppose I'd be willing to help you out."

"You would?" Hope widened Luke's eyes.

Tarah nodded. "I'll give you a penny a day until you have enough to pay for the ribbons. But you'll have to earn it."

She felt a prick of guilt about bribing him, but after the day he'd put her through, she was just weary enough to offer him anything. If he would just be good until the other children got used to her, his disruptions would be manageable. As it was, he only encouraged unruly behavior among the other students.

Suspicion clouded the hope in his eyes. "What do I gotta do?"

"All you *have* to do is be good in class."

Luke's eyebrows darted upward. "That's it?"

Tarah bit back the smile threatening the corners of her mouth. She knew her brother. He would definitely have to work hard to earn that money. "That's all. Think you can manage it?"

He scrunched his nose, obviously trying to weigh his options. "How much do hair ribbons cost?"

"Five cents ought to get her enough ribbon for a matched pair."

"Two? But I only inked one of her ol' ribbons."

"Yes, but she was wearing a matching set. One of which you ruined. A girl can't go around wearing two different-colored ribbons in her hair."

Luke's shoulders slumped in defeat, and he turned back to writing his sentences. "Aw, who cares if they match anyway?" he muttered.

"She does," Tarah replied firmly. "And so do I. Do we have a deal?"

A heavy sigh escaped his lips. "I guess I don't got no choice."

"Good." Elated by the victory, Tarah didn't even bother to correct his grammar. "I'll buy the ribbon on the way home from school, and all you have to do is behave yourself for a week."

He scowled and nodded.

"Now hurry and finish those sentences so we can get home and help with chores."

Breathing a sigh of relief, Tarah turned and began to tidy up the books scattered across her desk.

The door opened just then, and sunlight streamed into the small schoolhouse. Tarah glanced up as Josie Raney shuffled to the front of the room.

"Why, Josie, did you forget something?"

A deep chuckle emanated from the doorway. "My niece forgot her little brother, I'm afraid."

Tarah squinted against the blinding light, trying to make out the man's features. She caught her breath as he stepped through the doorway into plain view. Anthony Greene. Looking every bit as handsome as ever. He still had the same unruly sandy blond hair and brown eyes, able to melt a girl's insides with one glance in her direction—like now. "Why, Anthony," she said breathlessly. "When did you get back in town?"

"Hello, Tarah." He grinned broadly. "So you *are* the new schoolteacher. I thought Ma was pulling my leg."

Tarah bristled. "Why's that? Don't you think I can be a teacher?" After the day she had just gone through, she wasn't at all sure she could be a teacher, but she certainly didn't need anyone else questioning the fact.

"Sure," he said with a lift of his brow. "I just figured some lucky man would have married you by now."

Heat rose to her cheeks as memories of her schoolgirl crush came rushing back to torture her. She'd had dreams of marrying *him*. But one year her senior, Anthony Greene was the only young man in Harper who had seemed unaware she existed. Much to Tarah's humiliation, he'd preferred the simpering Louisa Thomas.

When he'd left for seminary, no one had expected he'd ever be back. But there he was, as real as Luke's big, ornery, knowing grin.

"Hi, Anthony," Luke said, stepping forward with an outstretched hand. "We've missed you." Tilting his head, he gave Tarah a sly look from the corner of his eye. "Haven't we, sis?"

The lilt in his voice sent a warning through Tarah. Surely he was not going to humiliate her in front of Anthony Greene, of all people!

"Luke. . . ," Tarah warned.

"My hand's awfully tired from writing those sentences, Tarah." Luke's voice rang with challenge.

The boy would pay and pay dearly. "All right," she replied through gritted teeth, taking care to keep what she hoped to be a sweet smile plastered on her face. "I think you've learned your lesson." She'd deal with the little stinker later. Right now she had to thwart any embarrassing comment he might make about her former crush.

"Now," she said, turning her attention back to Anthony and Josie. "What's this about Toby not making it home with you?" she asked the girl.

"I thought he was right behind me," Josie replied, keeping her gaze on the floor.

"I know where he is," Luke spoke up. "I saw him go to the outhouse."

Josie's chin jerked upward, and she stared wide-eyed at Luke.

He cleared his throat. "Yeah, I. . .uh. . .saw him through the window when I was writing sentences."

"And you didn't see him come out?" Anthony asked incredulously.

Luke kept his gaze fixed on Josie's pale face. "Naw," he said with a shrug. "But that old latch is rusty. It gets stuck all the time. Don't it, Tarah?"

"Doesn't it," she corrected. "And Pa just fixed it last week."

"I'd better go check on him," Anthony said. "Come along, Jo."

"I think I'll stay in here and help Luke clean the blackboard," Josie said, giving Anthony a sweet smile. "If that's okay with you, Uncle Anthony."

A flood of color rushed to Luke's cheeks, making his freckles pop out even brighter. "I don't need no—"

"How sweet of you," Tarah broke in, pleasantly surprised by the kind gesture. Maybe Luke's crush on this girl would prove to be a motivating factor for improving his behavior. One could certainly hope, anyway.

Tarah observed Anthony's broad shoulders as he headed toward the door. Her heartbeat quickened, and she hurried to follow him. It was only natural for her to make sure the little boy made it home all right, she inwardly insisted. Her concern had nothing whatsoever to do with a desire to prolong her contact with Anthony. Oh, who was she trying to fool? Anthony had walked out of her life when he'd left town two years ago without so much as a backward glance, and she had no intention of letting it happen again!

"So you're the new teacher. . . ."

"I didn't know you had a niece and nephew. . . ."

They spoke together as they walked around the side of the building.

Tarah laughed. "You first."

He gave a deep chuckle, the pleasant sound causing Tarah's stomach to do somersaults.

"They're my sister Ella's kids," he explained. "She and her husband, Joe, stayed back east when Pa moved the family out here three years ago."

"So your sister and brother-in-law decided to move out here after all?"

He shook his head. "Only Ella and the children came. They'll stay and help Ma for a while. Pa's death was awfully hard on her."

"Oh, Anthony, how thoughtless of me. I'm terribly sorry about your pa's passing."

Anthony swallowed hard and nodded. "It was a shock. If I had known he was ill, I never would have left."

Tarah reached out and gently touched his arm. "You mustn't blame yourself," she said softly. "There was no way you or anyone else could possibly have known."

He stopped walking and turned to her, covering her hand with his own.

"Thank you, Tarah," he said earnestly. "I guess I know that in my heart. But I can't help but feel if I had been here to take on some of the load, his heart wouldn't have given out the way it did."

Tarah opened her mouth to reply but stopped short as a cry broke through the moment.

"L–l–let me out. I w–w–want out."

Together, Tarah and Anthony sprinted the few final yards to the outhouse.

The door was more than jammed. Someone had wrapped a rope around the entire outhouse, obviously locking the little boy in there on purpose.

"Honestly," Tarah said. "Who would have done such a thing?"

Anthony tossed a quick glance toward the schoolhouse. "I think I have a pretty good idea," he drawled.

He quickly untied the simple knot and unwound the rope. The door swung open, and six-year-old Toby stumbled out of the doorway. Fat tears rolled down his chubby cheeks as he grabbed on to Anthony's legs and hung on for all he was worth.

Tarah knelt beside the boy. "Sweetie, who did this?"

"J–j–jo," he said, then dissolved into tears once more.

"You mean your sister, Josie?" she asked incredulously.

"Uh-huh. She said n–n–no one w–w–would miss me and I'd b–b–be here all n–n–night."

Anthony lifted his nephew and held him close. "Well, someone did miss you, scout," he soothed. "As soon as Jo came home alone, your ma sent me looking for you."

"M–m–ma still wants me?" The little boy pulled slightly away and looked at Anthony with wide, hopeful eyes. "Even w–w–with the n–n–new b–baby coming?"

"Of course she does. Who could ever replace our Toby?"

"Jo s–s–said sh–sh–she wants a b–b–boy wh–who d–d–doesn't st–st–stutter."

Indignation filled Tarah. So much for her idea that the girl would be a good influence on Luke. Imagine making the tyke feel as though he were about to be replaced—then locking him in the outhouse to boot.

Anthony disentangled himself from Toby's death grip and set the boy gently on the ground. "You ready to go, scout? Your ma's pretty worried about you. We should go and let her know you're all right."

Toby bobbed his head and swiped at his nose with the back of his hand.

Tarah grimaced as he slipped the same hand inside Anthony's. To her amazement, Anthony smiled affectionately at his nephew and tightened his grip. "Then let's get your sister and go home. You coming, Tarah?"

"In a moment. I think I need to get this rope to a safe place so we don't have a repeat of this incident."

"All right, then. I'm going to round up Jo and head for home. And, Tarah. . ."

"Yes?"

He held her with a long, penetrating gaze, sending her pulse racing. "Thanks for listening to me about. . .you know."

Exhaling slowly, Tarah nodded but couldn't find the appropriate response. He hesitated for a moment, then gave her another heart-stopping smile and turned to go back to the school.

Honestly, Tarah berated herself as the words she should have said spilled into her mind. *Couldn't you have at least said something? Anything would have been better than staring at him like he had dirt on his nose.*

Shaking her head in disgust, she bent forward and picked up the rope from where it still lay in a tangled mess in front of the outhouse. When she stood up, she caught movement from the corner of her eye. Through the window, she saw Luke and Jo—each doubled over in laughter.

Tarah wasn't sure if they were laughing at her or at the cruel joke Josie had played on her brother, but either way she felt the heat rush to her cheeks. She groaned aloud. Not only did she have Luke to contend with—now he had an ally.

Anthony excused himself from the uproar following his homecoming with the two children. That niece of his was a perfect terror, he decided as he walked out the door to the barn. Thankfully chores waited to be done, so he wouldn't be able to hear her howls from the much-deserved whipping she was about to receive.

Poor Tarah! As the schoolteacher, she would have her hands full with Josie, and if her own brother Luke was anything like he used to be, she'd be lucky to stick it out for the whole term.

A grin lifted the corners of his mouth as he stepped inside the barn. That Tarah St. John was still just about the prettiest thing he'd ever laid eyes on. He would have asked for permission to court her years ago, but just when he thought she might agree to such a thing, he'd felt an urge to go to seminary, an urge he knew was from God and too strong to ignore.

He drew in the pungent odor of fresh hay combined with manure. Returning to farm life hadn't exactly been in his plans after he'd accepted the call to preach. He had headed back east to seminary with the intention of returning home only to visit his family. But he knew better than to question God.

"Lord," he prayed while mucking out the first stall, "I know my responsibility is to Ma and the boys." He released a heavy sigh. "I don't begrudge them the help, but sometimes I feel like if I don't get the chance to preach, I'm going to explode."

He cast a sidelong glance at the barn door to make sure he was alone, then turned to the black gelding finishing his supper.

"For God so loved the world," he told Dodger, his faithful four-legged parishioner, "that He gave."

With a complete lack of interest, the horse stamped a hoof on the barn floor and swished his tail at a fly.

"The Lord gave all He had so that you. . .yes," he said, pointing a finger at the long face, "I mean *you*, could have eternal life."

Anthony felt the excitement surge within him, and he dropped the pitchfork. Pacing the barn, he included all the pitifully sinful creatures with a wide sweep of his hand.

"Now if Jesus gave His life—a sacrifice on an altar made by sinful, greedy men—do you dare keep yourself back from His free gift of salvation? Salvation bought with the blood of God's innocent Son?"

Sweat began to bead on his forehead.

"Must the Lord strive forever with man?"

His voice rose to match the excitement of his eloquent message. June, the milk cow, raised her head and stared, clearly captivated by the rousing sermon. Anthony focused on the sorrowful brown eyes gazing back at him. "Oh, wicked and sinful generation, will you harden your hearts forever, or will you return to your God with weeping and a rending of hearts?"

"Uncle Anthony?"

Rats! Just when he was about to give the altar call!

He turned to face Josie. "I thought you were in trouble."

She shrugged. "Ma whipped me."

Must not have made much of an impression, Anthony thought wryly, for the little girl's face held an impish grin.

"What are you doing out here? Come to help muck out the barn?"

A wrinkle creased the perky little nose. "Uh-uh. Ma says I should come talk to you so you can tell me how a Christian girl is supposed to treat others."

"I see." A grin tipped the corners of his mouth. A captive audience.

Josie tilted her blond head to one side and regarded him frankly. "Yeah. But I figure it'll save us both a heap of trouble if we just forget about it and tell her you gave it to me good."

"Josie! That would be a lie."

She released a long-suffering sigh. "Oh, all right. But can we make it short? Reverend Cahill back home used to yak and yak and yak until I almost fell asleep."

Troubled by his niece's lack of reverence, Anthony grabbed a horse blanket from a peg on the wall and spread it out on the barn floor. "Sit yourself down on this blanket, little girl, before I tan your hide."

Anthony "yakked" about kindness and mentioned every fruit of the Spirit from Galatians chapter five while he finished cleaning the barn. Hanging the pitchfork high on the wall, he added a mention of the Golden Rule to his lecture for good measure.

"All right. I think that's enough for tonight." He glanced at Josie. "Let's go inside for supper."

With a sleepy yawn, the little girl stood.

Anthony shook his head. He doubted she'd heard a word of his exhortation any more than the animals had heard his brilliant sermon.

"Uncle Anthony?" Josie asked as they headed back to the house.

"Yeah?"

She looked up at him, her angelic face filled with question. Her eyes serious, she shook her head sadly.

Anthony's heart leapt. Maybe he'd made an impression after all. "What is it, sweetheart?"

"Well, I was just wondering. . ."

"Yes?"

"Do you think there's any hope for that poor cow's soul?" Merriment filled her eyes as she giggled and dashed off across the yard.

"Why, you little. . ." Anthony followed her. "You'd better run, you little stinker. When I catch you, I'm going to tickle you until you recite all the books of the Bible. . .backwards."

Chapter 2

Tarah set a platter laden with golden fried chicken on the lacy tablecloth covering a long, wooden table. She bent and gave her father a kiss on the cheek, then took her seat.

Grateful to be back in familiar surroundings after her harrowing first day of teaching, Tarah smiled at her ten-year-old sister, Emily, sitting to her right. The family members joined hands in preparation for their mealtime prayer.

Pa's gaze roved around the table and settled on Ma's bowed head. "Cassidy?"

Cassidy glanced up, her wide green eyes filled with question.

"Where's Sam?"

"He asked permission to eat supper with Camilla and her family. I didn't think you'd mind."

An amused glance passed between them.

Pa sent Tarah a teasing wink. "Looks like we might be attending Sam's wedding before his big sister's if she doesn't stop sending those young men away."

Tarah gasped.

"Dell!" Ma frowned and shook her head.

"What?"

"It—it's okay, Ma." But Pa's comment stung and only proved a painful reminder to Tarah that she was nineteen years old with no prospects for marriage. She felt her defenses rise. Was it her fault all the boys she'd admired in school had grown up to be dolts? Well, all except Anthony.

Ma stared pointedly at Pa. "Let's just say the prayer, shall we?" she suggested.

Pa shrugged, still wearing a confused frown. Finally he bowed his dark head and prayed. "Father, we thank You for the many blessings You've given this growing family. We ask You to watch over Mother while she's away visiting George and Olive. Thank You for Tarah's new teaching position. May You give her wisdom to teach with grace and patience." He cleared his throat. "And we thank You for the new blessing You are bringing into our lives. A new baby for us to love and. . ."

Emily squealed and leaped from her chair. "Ma!"

"Emily St. John!" Cassidy scolded. "Your pa's praying."

"I'm sorry," she whispered and slowly returned to her seat.

Pa grinned. "In Jesus' name, amen."

Emily's carrot-orange braids flew behind her as she sprinted around the table and grabbed Ma, hugging her tightly.

Luke's face glowed bright red, and he gave Pa a sheepish grin. "Another baby, huh?" He jerked a thumb toward the twins sitting in high chairs on either side of Ma. "Just when those two were starting to grow up and not cry all the time."

Tarah noticed her stepmother's eyes cloud over with hurt until Luke gave her a wide grin. "Hope it's a boy!"

A relieved smile curved Ma's lips. "I'll see what I can do."

Feeling her father's gaze upon her, Tarah rose and embraced her stepmother, then her pa. "Congratulations," she murmured. "This is wonderful news." She sank back in her chair.

"Can we name him Pete?" All eyes turned to Jack. Even at seven years old, his soft brown eyes and mop of unruly curls gave him an angelic appearance.

"That's a dumb name," Emily said haughtily, still standing close to Cassidy. "Besides, it's going to be a girl, and we'll call her Audra."

"Pete!"

"Audra!"

"That's enough, you two," Pa said firmly. "There'll be plenty of time to discuss names later on. Right now you'd better sit down so we can eat this supper your ma cooked before it gets cold."

The revelation that Cassidy was expecting another child came as no surprise to Tarah, who, as the eldest of seven children, had recognized the symptoms in her stepmother over the past couple of months. She wasn't unhappy about the coming baby, but the house was getting cramped as it was. With trees so scarce, Pa and the boys would have to haul sandstone from the river to build on to the house.

Lord, it would be a lot easier all the way around if You would just send me a husband. One or two of the kids could have my room. You know, Anthony Greene came back. . . .

She stopped, uncomfortable with the thought that she might be trying to manipulate the Lord.

Well, she wasn't exactly telling God something He didn't already know. *Besides,* she reasoned, *maybe God sent Anthony back here so we could be married. It never hurts to ask.*

She bit into a slice of buttered bread and tried to focus on what Pa was saying.

"How was your first day, Teacher?" Pa grabbed a piece of fried chicken from the platter and sent Tarah a proud grin.

"Anthony Greene showed up after school," Luke piped in before Tarah could swallow her food and answer.

The bread lodged in her throat, and she coughed profusely while Emily pounded her on the back.

"Tarah," Ma said, "are you all right?"

Nodding, she grabbed her water glass to wash down the mouthful of bread, sending Luke a warning glance over the rim.

He raised his eyebrows and sent her one right back.

Tarah's temper flared. So that was how he wanted to play it. If she mentioned his unruly behavior, he'd tease her about Anthony in front of the whole family. At least Sam was off having supper with Camilla Simpson and her family, or the temptation might have been too great for Luke to resist despite their agreement.

Over a barrel, she drew a deep breath and decided to let it slide. After all, she had his promise of good behavior for a whole week. A promise he'd better keep if he knew what was good for him.

Apparently oblivious to the silent exchange between his children, Pa pointed his empty fork at no one in particular and gave a reflective frown. He glanced at Tarah. "Anthony went to seminary back east, didn't he?"

Tarah nodded, glad the focus was off her disappointing first day of teaching.

"What are you thinking, Dell?" Ma asked.

Tarah looked from one to the other. The love evident in their eyes for each other sent a small ache to her heart. Would she ever find someone to love? With Anthony's return to Harper, her prospects seemed to be looking up. *But only if it's Your will,* she added hastily.

"Well, my darling," Pa said with a grin, "I was thinking we just might have us a preacher."

Ma clapped her hands together, causing the nearly two-year-old twins, Hope and Will, to do the same. "What a wonderful idea!"

"I'll talk it over with the rest of the council at the meeting tonight," Pa said. "And if they agree, I'll probably swing by the Greene farm on the way home. So I might be a little later than usual." He winked at Tarah. "Think you'd mind sharing the schoolhouse with the preacher for Sunday services, little teacher?"

"Tarah wouldn't mind sharing. . . ," Luke began.

Tarah shot him another warning glance.

"Of course she won't mind," Ma said, wiping a glob of potatoes from baby Will's plump chin.

Anthony. . .to be the new preacher. Tarah's heart skipped a beat, and she released a dreamy sigh. What would it be like to be a preacher's wife?

～

Tarah watched proudly as Anthony strode to the rough-hewn wooden pulpit, normally used only twice a year when the circuit rider came through. She'd waited nearly a week to see him again.

Dressed in a black coat, black trousers, and a white shirt, he looked awfully handsome. She smiled at his crooked tie. Once they were married, she'd take care of that little problem for him.

Tarah caught her breath when he looked directly at her as though guessing her thoughts. Almost sure that wasn't possible, she nevertheless felt herself blush to the roots of her hair. Anthony's gaze moved past her, sweeping the congregation. His Adam's apple bobbed up and down as he swallowed hard.

Say something, Anthony.

She watched in concern as his face paled. He grabbed on to the pulpit, his knuckles growing instantly white.

Oh no, he's going to pass out cold!

A gust of cool autumn wind blew into the little schoolhouse-turned-church as the door swung open. Tarah noticed Anthony relax visibly as the latecomer turned the congregation's attention from him to the back of the room.

He looked at her again. Tarah nodded encouragement and returned his smile. "You can do it," she mouthed. She pointed upward, hoping to remind him God would be his helper. His grin widened, and he nodded back to her, then cleared his throat to regain the congregation's attention.

"Excuse me," someone whispered from the aisle next to Tarah.

Irritated to have her attention drawn away from Anthony, Tarah glanced up. Louisa Thomas. What did *she* want?

"May I sit next to you?" the young woman whispered. "There's nowhere else."

Tarah cast a furtive glance around the tiny room, hoping to spy an empty seat and send her on her way. When her search proved futile, she sighed and scooted over.

"I'm so glad I didn't miss Anthony's sermon. Doesn't he look marvelous?" Louisa whispered. "It was worth getting up early to watch him for an hour."

Jealousy stabbed at Tarah's heart. She frowned. "Shh."

Louisa didn't even have the grace to blush for disrupting the service. She looked at Anthony and gave him a broad you-may-begin-now smile.

Temper flaring, Tarah inched a little farther away from the bothersome flirt and bumped into old Mr. Moody, already nodding off on the other side of her. He jerked his head up. "Thanks, little lady," he said aloud, sending her a wink. "Do that again next time you hear me snoring."

The building rumbled with muffled laughter.

Humiliated, Tarah sank down in her seat. *It would be a mercy if the floor would open up and swallow me right now, Lord.*

Anthony cleared his throat again.

Finally!

"Thank you all for coming," Anthony began in a shaky voice. "I'd like to begin with a word of prayer."

Relieved for the chance to close her eyes and shake off the embarrassment, Tarah bowed her head.

"Oh, most precious heavenly Father," he began, dropping his voice at least two notches. "We thank Thee for the opportunity to assemble together in Thy most holy presence."

Tarah frowned. Was it her imagination, or was he trying to be impressive in his prayer? She felt a niggling disappointment creep through her.

People were beginning to shuffle when he finally said "amen" a good five minutes later.

Breathing a sigh of relief, Tarah waited for the sermon to begin. Anthony glanced at his notes for a minute, took a long, slow breath, then stared gravely from the pulpit.

"For God so loved the world," he began, "that He gave. . ."

The tension eased away from Tarah's shoulders, and she felt herself relaxing.

His voice strengthened. "Now if God gave His only Son—a sacrifice on the altar of sinful and greedy men—do you *dare* keep yourself back from His free gift of salvation?"

The flimsy pulpit shook as Anthony's hand slapped down hard on the wooden surface.

Tarah started at the suddenness of the action. Beside her, Old Man Moody jerked his chin from his chest. "What? Amen, Preacher!"

Louisa giggled, starting a chain reaction throughout the room, and soon everyone was laughing.

Anthony's face turned a deep shade of red, and he glanced back down at his notes. When the laughter died, he eyed the congregation and continued as though nothing had occurred. "Salvation bought with the blood of God's innocent Son?"

⌒

"You ever see a person sweat that much before?" ten-year-old Emily asked that afternoon at dinner.

"Emily," Ma admonished, "don't be rude."

But Tarah noticed that Ma placed a napkin to her mouth to hide her smile.

"I saw Mr. Gordon sweat worse than that during harvest last year," Luke offered. " 'Course, that was before Doc Simpson made him lose all that fat. I thought ol' Anthony was going to start dripping on the floor."

"Luke!" Ma said, now nearly choking to keep from laughing aloud.

Pa's blue eyes twinkled. "He did get quite a lather going, didn't he?"

Unable to suppress her mirth any longer, Ma laughed until tears rolled down her cheeks. Pa threw back his head and joined her. And of course, the children couldn't resist.

Sam slapped his hand down on the table, sending half of the utensils flying. " 'You,' " he said, lowering his voice in imitation of Anthony—a very poor imitation, in Tarah's opinion. " 'I mean *you*!' "

Tarah stared at her family with indignation. "I thought Anthony did a fine job," she said with a toss of her head.

The room suddenly grew quiet as her family stared at her, each face registering the same look of disbelief.

Looking around the table, Tarah released a sigh of concession. "Oh, all right.

So he didn't do that great. But honestly, it *was* his first time to preach."

Ma sobered, her gaze searching Tarah's face. Her expression softened, and her lips curved in a smile of understanding.

Unable to abide the scrutiny, Tarah felt her cheeks flush as she averted her gaze and studied the blue-flowered print on her plate.

"Tarah's right," Ma said. "We have to give Anthony a chance to find his own preaching style. I'm sure next week will be better."

"I sure hope so," Luke said, shoving a bite of roasted venison into his mouth. "But I'm bringing a bucket to put under him just in case."

But the next week wasn't an improvement. Neither was the week after, nor the week after that. By the time Anthony had been there a month, the good folks of Harper, Kansas, were beginning to grumble about the hellfire-and-brimstone preacher.

⌒

Anthony awoke with a looming sense of dread. Maybe he could pretend to be sick this morning. His stomach *was* feeling a mite queasy at the thought of facing his unresponsive congregation once again.

He lay in the predawn stillness, his silent pleas stretching from his heart to God's.

Why won't they listen, Lord?

Sometimes he felt like Noah must have, knowing the flood was coming and the people weren't ready. The cows and horses paid more attention to his sermons than his shrinking congregation ever did. And he'd noticed people were beginning to avoid him like a bad smell. Everyone but Louisa Thomas. She seemed to genuinely appreciate his messages. Her smiling face was the highlight of his Sunday mornings.

With a heavy sigh, Anthony drew back the covers and sat at the edge of his bed, trying to muster the enthusiasm to get up and begin the new day.

"This is the day which the Lord has made. I will rejoice and be glad in it," he muttered, feeling anything but joyful. Willing himself to move, he stood and walked barefoot across the small room, poured water into a basin, and grabbed his razor.

A groan escaped his lips as he caught his reflection in the mirror. Even with the overnight scruff of a beard and mustache on his face, he looked like a teenage boy. No wonder no one took him seriously.

Rats! What could he do about his face? He stared into the mirror, wishing for distinguishing gray at his temples or maybe a few lines on his face to indicate wisdom beyond his years. Pushing away the ludicrous train of thought, Anthony sighed and set down his razor. At the very least, he would allow his beard and mustache to grow. That would make him look older.

With that decision made, he dressed quickly and headed to the kitchen, following the heady aroma of bacon frying and biscuits baking in the oven.

"Morning, Ma," he said, bending to plant a kiss on her weathered cheek. He drank in the comfortingly familiar scents of lemon verbena combined with dough.

"Morning, son." She directed him to a chair with a nod of her head. "Blane says not to worry about chores this morning. He was up early and finished."

"That's a blessing." Anthony sank into a chair at the end of the table and stretched out his legs, leaning back in his chair. "Where is he?"

"Cleaning up. He should be in here soon." Ma grabbed a cup from the shelf above the counter. "Coffee?"

Anthony nodded absently. "Thanks," he said and looked up with a smile as she set the steaming cup in front of him.

"Something troubling you, son?"

Breathing a heavy sigh, he waved a hand and shook his head. "Nothing anyone but God can help me with, I'm afraid." Right now, he'd welcome a good talk with his mentor from his church back east. But Reverend Cahill was too far away to be of any help.

"I just don't know what these folks expect."

Ma removed the bacon from the skillet and set it on a platter. "I don't think they expect much, Anthony," she said thoughtfully.

Surprised, Anthony shot a glance at his mother. He hadn't meant to speak aloud.

Setting the platter on the table, Ma stared down at him with a tender smile. "They just want to hear the Word preached with love and authority from someone who knows the heart of God."

Well, that pretty well summed him up, he figured. He loved these people enough to be concerned for their eternal souls and preached with so much authority that it took him all Sunday afternoon to recover from the exertion.

He preached what he had been taught to preach: Show the people their sin, and give them the opportunity to repent. Surely that was the heart of God. Still, if that were the case, why wasn't he seeing positive results?

"I don't know, Ma," he said. "Seems to me the congregation is half the size it started out to be. If I don't do something, I'll lose the rest of them, too." Then he'd be asked to leave at the end of the three-month trial period. The thought of failing clenched his gut.

Ma rested a thoughtful gaze upon him. "Have you prayed about this?"

Raking his fingers through his hair, Anthony released a long, slow breath. "I pray constantly for the people in this town. I've never seen such an unresponsive group." He met her gaze, suddenly feeling the need to unload his frustration. "Do you know the people who have stopped coming to the services are meeting out at the Johnsons' place on Sunday mornings?" It cut him to the core and more than wounded his pride that the folks would opt to share the Word among themselves rather than come to his services.

"I heard something about that." Ma's voice held a twinge of sympathy as she sat and gave his hand a gentle pat. "You just have to concentrate on the members of your flock and not worry about those who feel they need to meet elsewhere."

"I reckon you're right. Still, it's puzzling."

"I don't want to be telling you your business, son, but it might do some good for you to get to know the members of your congregation better."

"What do you mean?"

She shrugged, and her pensive gaze held his. "Seems to me I hear an awful lot of folks inviting you to Sunday dinner, and yet you're always right here at my table."

Anthony shot her a wide grin. "Why should I go eat somewhere else when the best cook in Kansas is right here in my own home?"

"Oh, now. You stop exaggerating." But her eyes crinkled at the corners for an instant before she grew serious once again. "I just think maybe folks would like a chance to visit with you outside of the church. Let them get to know the real Anthony instead of just Reverend Greene."

The thought had never occurred to him before, but as he rolled the idea around, it seemed to make sense. "You think that might make a difference?" Anthony almost cringed at the desperation in his voice.

"Couldn't hurt. People want to know their minister cares about their everyday lives and not just their spiritual condition. Remember, the Bible states that Jesus ate with His disciples. He washed their feet and answered all of their questions. Tending sheep is much more than just feeding and watering."

"Ma, sometimes I think you should have been the preacher and not me." He drained his cup and stood.

"Where do you think you're going? You haven't had your breakfast yet."

He flashed her another grin, feeling more lighthearted than he had in weeks. "Coffee's all I need today. With Blane doing the chores, I didn't have a chance to work up much of an appetite. Besides, I want to get to the church early and look over my notes before the service. If I don't get a move on, I won't have time." He gave her another quick peck on the cheek and headed back toward his room.

"Don't forget to take a razor to those whiskers," Ma called after him.

Anthony stopped and turned to face her. "I thought I might let them grow." He rubbed his hand over his jaw, already irritated with the itchy growth.

"I see."

At the look of understanding on Ma's face, Anthony's ears heated up. He knew better than to think a man's outward appearance mattered. These people were more than willing to give him a chance in the beginning, knowing full well how young he was. A beard and mustache were not going to make a difference if he couldn't somehow find a way to reach their hearts.

Clearing his throat, he turned without another word and strode to his room to dress in his Sunday suit and get rid of those irritating whiskers.

Chapter 3

Tarah closed the door after the last of her students filed into the school-house following their lunch break.

Only two more hours, she consoled herself as she walked to her desk. Then she could go home and nurse her pounding headache—depending on how long it took Luke to write his punishment sentences for the day.

Yesterday she had made him write, "I will not place bent nails in any other student's chair." One hundred times. Today he would have to write, "I will not place frogs in any other student's lunch pail." Why he would want to do such things was beyond Tarah. If he wanted to spend his afternoons writing sentences, that was his choice, even if it meant she had to stay after school, as well.

Rapping on the table with her ruler, she called the school to attention. She released a frustrated breath as the clamor continued. The three McAlester girls screamed and ducked when a slate pencil flew across the room. Tarah rapped again—harder. "Take your seats immediately!"

"Ow! Let go!" Emily's cry of pain echoed off the walls.

"Jeremiah Daniels," Tarah called above the chaos. "Turn loose of Emily's braid and go stand in the corner."

The boy glared back at her, defiance sparking in his eyes.

The room grew quiet as the children watched the exchange. They waited, as did Tarah, to see what Jeremiah would do.

Please, God. Make him obey me.

She met his gaze evenly. "In the corner. . . Now!"

He scowled but slowly slipped from his seat and made his way to the corner.

With a relieved sigh, Tarah turned to the other students. "The rest of you pull out your readers and just. . .be quiet for a few minutes."

Wearily she sank into her chair. *Crunch!*

A sense of dread hovered over Tarah like a thick black cloud about to burst. Pressing her palms to her desk, she pushed herself to a standing position, pinning Luke to his wooden bench with her gaze. She gathered a slow breath and glanced at her chair. Fury rose inside her at the sight of messy egg remains. She twisted and found the rest of the shell and yoke stuck to the backside of her new calico dress.

The children snickered until she glared at the room, hands on her hips. That was it!

"Luke!" she bellowed.

After almost four weeks of absolute chaos, he had finally driven her to her breaking point. Standing in the corner didn't bother Luke, writing sentences certainly didn't deter him, and Tarah had decided telling Pa and Ma was no longer an option. She had to show them she could handle things on her own. And right now, she was going to do just that.

"March yourself up here this instant, young man."

"What'd I do?"

His look of innocence only infuriated her more.

Snatching up her ruler from the desk, she faced him. "You know very well what you did, and it's not going to happen again."

Tarah gathered in another breath for courage. She had never believed in corporal punishment in the schoolroom, but now she understood why other teachers used the ruler on their students. Sometimes other forms of punishment just did not work. "Hold out your hand."

"But, Tarah, I didn't—"

"When we are in school, you will address me as 'Miss St. John' like the other children," she said through gritted teeth. "Now hold out your hand."

"Miss St. John?"

Tarah turned at the sound of Josie's quavering voice. The little girl sat white-faced in her seat, worry clouding her eyes.

Tarah gave her a dismissive wave. Of course Josie didn't want Luke to be whipped. More often than not, they were partners in crime. Well, that was too bad. This time Tarah was getting the upper hand. She'd show them all they couldn't get away with terrorizing her anymore.

"But, Miss St. John—"

"Sit still, Josie. I'll be with you in a moment," she snapped.

Turning her gaze back to her brother, Tarah almost gasped at the tears in his eyes. She pushed away the compassion threatening to melt her resolve and raised her brow. "Well?"

Slowly he gave her his palm.

Tarah flinched as the ruler came down with a resounding *smack*.

"Please, Miss St. John." Josie slipped from her seat and made her way to the front.

"Wh–what is it?" Tarah whispered, unable to pull her gaze from the look of betrayal on Luke's face.

"It wasn't Luke."

"What do you mean?" Panic tore across Tarah's heart.

"I—I put the egg on your seat. Luke didn't know anything about it. Honest." The little girl slowly inched her hand forward, palm up. She squeezed her eyes shut while she awaited her punishment.

All the strength drained from Tarah, and the ruler dropped to the desk with a clatter.

"Luke, I—"

"May I go back to my seat, *Miss St. John*?" Despite his stormy gaze, his bottom lip quivered.

Tarah nodded. With great effort, she faced her class. The wide, questioning eyes and even fearful expressions on some of the younger children's faces were more than she could bear. "School is dismissed for the day," she croaked. "Tell your parents I—I'm not feeling well."

Somehow she managed to stand on wobbly legs until all of her students but Luke silently gathered their belongings and left the school. He walked to the blackboard. Folding his arms, he stared daggers through her.

"What do I write today?"

Filled with remorse, Tarah couldn't blame him for the belligerence in his stance and tone. "N—never mind, Luke. Go on home, and tell Ma I'll be along later."

Silently he walked to his desk and grabbed his things.

"Luke," Tarah said, tears nearly choking her.

"What?"

"I'm sorry I didn't give you a chance to explain."

Luke shrugged. "Didn't bother me none." He slipped outside before she could say more.

Unmindful of the mess, Tarah sank back into her seat. Folding her arms atop the desk, she pressed her forehead onto the backs of her hands. Sobs shook her body.

It's just too hard, Lord. I can't do it.

"I can't give ya any more credit until ya pay what ya owe. And that's all there is to it."

Anthony tried to pretend indifference to the exchange between the ragged stranger and the storekeeper but found himself unable to look away.

"Please, Tucker," the man begged. "You know I got them two youngsters to feed. I'll pay ya soon as I sell off a pig."

Anthony surveyed the man's shabby, thin clothing and greasy hair. He figured it must have taken a lot of courage for a fellow to swallow his pride and ask for help. Compassion rose up within him.

What would it hurt to extend the man credit for a little while? He glanced at the storekeeper, and his heart sank. Tucker was having none of it. "Look, John, ya promised the same thing last month an' the month b'fore. I just can't do it."

Unable to endure the look of misery on the man's face, Anthony stepped up beside him. "Look, Tucker, just put his order on my account."

The creases on Tucker's face deepened. "I don't think that's such a good idea, Preacher," he said, warning thick in his voice.

"You let me worry about that," Anthony replied. He extended his hand to the ragged stranger.

A nearly toothless grin split the man's face as he reached out a filthy hand and gripped Anthony's. "I'm obliged to you, sir. An' dontcha worry none; I'll pay ya every last cent, soon as I sell that pig."

"I'm sure you will. I'm Reverend Greene." Anthony felt his chest swell at the admission. "I haven't seen you before. Just move into the area?"

"Name's Jenkins. Got two fine youngsters at home waitin' fer me."

"We'd love to see you and your family in church on Sunday."

The man shuffled and scratched at his long, matted beard. "Well now, Preacher, we ain't much for religion an' all that. But seein' as how yer bein' so generous an' all. . ."

"Oh no. There are no strings attached to this. But I hope you and your family will come to church anyway. We'd love to have you."

"Here's your order, John." Tucker grudgingly pushed a box filled with supplies across the counter. Anthony glanced inside and frowned at the pouch of tobacco and two bottles of Healy's Magic Elixir lying on top.

Jenkins nearly leaped at the box, grabbed it up, and headed for the door. "Much obliged, Preacher," he mumbled before the clanging bell announced his departure.

Tucker shook his head as Anthony handed him a list of his own. "That was a mistake, Preacher. Jenkins is a no-account if I ever seen one." He moved away from the counter to fill the order. "And I seen plenty of his kind in my day, I can tell ya."

"Took a lot of guts to ask for credit after you turned him down."

"Guts." Tucker snorted and grunted as he lifted a twenty-five-pound bag of flour from the shelf. "He was in here yesterday and the day b'fore and the day b'fore that."

"That so?" Anthony asked, a twinge of unease creeping into his stomach. "I've never seen him around here. Where's he from?"

A shrug lifted Tucker's thin shoulders. "Don't know and don't care. But he owes me seventeen dollars. And he ain't gettin' another thing from this store 'til he pays up."

"Do you happen to know where his homestead is?"

"He ain't got one. Al Garner found the whole slovenly family squattin' in the old soddy he built back in '55 when he first moved into the area. Would have thrown them out, but for the little girl and crippled boy."

"It was the Christian thing for Al to do. I'm sure the Lord is pleased with his generosity."

Tucker set the last of Anthony's supplies in a large crate and snorted again. "It was a fool thing to do if ya ask me. He'll never get rid of that no-account. Already feeds his family most of the time."

Anthony tried to contain his irritation, but Tucker's coldhearted remarks were beginning to go against his grain. "Well, you know the Lord did say if a man asks for your shirt, give him your coat, too."

Leaning an elbow against the counter, Tucker pointed a finger at Anthony, his eyes glittering with determination. "Let me give ya a little advice, Preacher. Get ready for a cold winter, 'cause if ya let Jenkins hornswoggle ya, you'll be goin' without a coat b'fore the week's out. And most likely your boots, too."

"Maybe so," Anthony shot back. "But I can't just turn my back on a family in need."

"Don't that Bible ya like to quote also say something about a man having to work or he don't eat?"

"Well. . ."

Tucker gave a curt nod. "Thought so." As though it settled the matter, he grabbed the account book and began to tally.

"Make sure you add Jenkins's supplies to my account, Tuck."

"That's what I'm doin' right now."

"Good." Anthony clapped his hat on his head and picked up the heavy crate. "And I hope to see you in church this Sunday. We've missed you the last couple of weeks."

"Been busy, Preacher. Now dontcha forget I warned ya about Jenkins."

"I won't. But I think you'll be surprised when he pays you your money and proves you wrong." At least he sure hoped the man made good on his promise. Otherwise Anthony would look like the fool Tucker obviously thought him to be.

Straining under the weight of the crate filled with supplies, Anthony stepped from Tucker's Mercantile into the bright autumn day.

"Why, Anthony, how lovely to see you."

He nearly dropped the wooden box as Louisa Thomas came out of nowhere and clutched his arm.

"Hello, Louisa. Fine afternoon we're having, isn't it?" He smiled politely.

"Just heavenly. I love autumn weather the best." She beamed up at him and tightened her grip. "My, you are strong, aren't you?"

He could hold his own, but those supplies were getting awfully heavy. If she didn't turn him loose pretty soon, he'd be forced to ask her to step aside.

Apparently oblivious to his plight, Louisa continued to smile enchantingly at him. He had to admit the attention was flattering, and he didn't want to be rude, but. . .

"Excuse me, Louisa." His voice sounded strained to his own ears.

"Oh, now don't tell me you haven't the time for a little chat." She pursed her lips into a pretty pout. "I've hardly seen you at all since you got back to town."

"I know, but. . ."

Anthony felt his grip loosen on the crate and feared any second the entire load would fall and land on the lady's toes.

"I am absolutely not going to let you go unless you promise to have a picnic with me after church on Sunday."

He had planned to ask Tarah to accompany him on an outing Sunday, but given the circumstances, perhaps he should accept Louisa's invitation instead.

"Okay. That sounds fine," he said with a grunt.

"Wonderful. It'll give us a chance to catch up on the last two years." Thankfully she turned loose of his arm to clap with delight. "I'll make you a delectable lunch. And a chocolate cake for old time's sake. How does that sound?"

"Sounds pretty good. I'll be seeing you."

Anthony heaved the crate into his wagon and paused to rest for a moment. When he turned, he came face-to-face with Louisa.

Startled, he reached out and grasped her arms to keep from knocking her over.

"Why, Anthony," she said breathlessly, leaning in closer. Her lips pursed as though she expected him to kiss her right there in the street. Abruptly he let her go and retreated a step.

Disappointment clouded her green eyes, but she recovered quickly as the sound of children's laughter diverted her attention to the schoolyard across the road.

Anthony glanced over Louisa's shoulder and watched the children calling good-bye to one another and heading off in different directions.

"That's strange," he mused. "School shouldn't be out for a couple of hours yet. I wonder if something's wrong."

"Oh, who knows?" Louisa said with a wave of her hand. "Tarah probably decided to give them the rest of the day off."

"I wonder why, though. It isn't like Tarah to be irresponsible."

Sidling up next to him, Louisa once again curled her fingers around his arm. "Well, she did run off with that awful Johnny Cooper a couple of years ago."

Now that was an uncalled-for recollection. Anthony felt himself tense. Downright catty, if he had to give it a name.

For some reason, he felt the need to defend Tarah's honor, and he resented being put in the position to do so. Still, he couldn't let the unkind statement go unchallenged.

"If memory serves correctly, Tarah didn't exactly run off with her pa's foreman; he kidnapped her *and* her stepmother." He wanted to be perfectly clear he didn't believe Tarah had been defiled in any way—if that's what Louisa was insinuating. And he had an uncomfortable feeling she might be suggesting that very thing.

A tinge of pink colored Louisa's cheeks, then she lifted her chin. "Well, she was *going* to run off with him until she found out he only wanted to get his hands on her pa's money. At least that's what she told Myra Rhoades."

Louisa snorted in a not-so-flattering manner. "And you know Myra couldn't keep a secret to save her life."

Feeling the need to put an end to the conversation that bordered dangerously on gossip, Anthony gave her a cheery grin. "Well, praise God, Dell and Doc Simpson caught up with them in time to keep them all safe."

A smile curved Louisa's lips. "Oh, I agree completely. I just shudder to think of Cassidy's babies being born out in the snow and cold. God surely was with them that night."

Anthony searched her wide, innocent eyes, looking for evidence of guile. He found nothing. Perhaps he had misjudged her. Most folks had a penchant for gossip more than they should. But that didn't mean Louisa intended anything unkind in her remarks.

"But you must think I'm awful," she said, mist forming in her eyes. "I should never have mentioned poor Tarah's unfortunate incident."

Patting her hand, Anthony gave her a reassuring smile. "Of course I don't think you're awful. But perhaps we should leave those things in the past, as I'm sure Tarah would like to do."

She beamed up at him. "Of course she would like to put it all behind her, poor girl. And I certainly don't blame her. I know I'd just die if anyone knew such horrid things about me."

Unease crept through Anthony's gut. Was she being catty again? At her look of complete innocence, he felt a niggling of guilt. If he was going to be a preacher, he'd have to learn not to judge people so quickly.

Two boys strolled past, heading for the mercantile. Anthony frowned as he overheard their conversation.

"Boy, she gave it to Luke good, didn't she?"

"Well, I don't like her. She's too bossy. Besides, Luke didn't even do anything this time."

"Oh dear," Louisa said, shaking her head, a troubled frown furrowing her brow. "It would appear Tarah's having difficulty with her students."

"I'm going over there to see if there's a problem."

She made no move to let go of his arm.

Frustrated, Anthony searched for a way to get her to let go without being rude. "Louisa, will you tell Mr. Tucker I'm leaving my team in front of the mercantile while I check on Tarah? I'll be back to get it in a few minutes."

Her eyes narrowed but brightened again in an instant. "Of course I will, Anthony. You're so sweet to be concerned. But then, I guess that's why you're the preacher." She squeezed his arm before letting go. "I'll tell Mr. Tucker. Now don't you forget about our picnic on Sunday. I'll have everything ready so we can leave directly after your wonderful preaching."

Releasing a breath, he strode toward the school. Concern crept over him. Josie and Luke sat on the steps. At the sober expressions marring each face, Anthony started to worry.

"But we have to do *something*. It wasn't fair!" he heard Jo declare, indignation thick in her voice. "We're not going to let her get away with—"

"What's going on?" Anthony asked.

Josie's head shot up, worry flickering in her blue eyes. "Miss St. John isn't

149

feeling well, so she dismissed us early," she said. Her gaze darted to her boots.

"Josie, look at me," he said sternly.

Reluctantly she inched her chin upward until he caught her guilty gaze.

"Now what happened? Is Miss St. John really sick?"

Her slim shoulders lifted. "That's what she said."

"Luke?"

"I guess so."

Something wasn't right.

"You stay here and wait for me," he instructed his niece. "I'll drive you home as soon as I'm sure your teacher's all right. I mean it, Jo. Stay put. Do you hear me?"

"Yes, Uncle Anthony."

Anthony opened the door. Alarm clenched his heart at the sight of Tarah, head on her desk, sobbing like a child. He closed the distance between them in a few long strides and crouched beside her.

She didn't look up as he reached forward and drew her close. Slumping against him, she rested her head on his shoulder and cried all the more.

Anthony searched for words of comfort, but finding none, he remained silent. Stroking her hair while she cried, he couldn't help but think how right this felt. As though she belonged in his arms. *Lord, are You trying to tell me something?*

He drew in a breath, the lavender scent of her hair filling his senses.

"D—do you have a handkerchief?" Tarah pulled away and looked at him, her eyes luminous from the tears.

"Huh?"

"Something I can wipe my nose with?"

Rats! He didn't. He gave her an apologetic smile. "I'm sorry."

She scowled.

Should he offer her his sleeve?

Just as he was about to suggest it, he had a better idea. He pulled his arm from around her shoulders and stood. He took out his pocketknife, then untucked a corner of his shirt. While Tarah watched with a furrowed brow, he swiped at the cloth until a piece came off in his hand.

Once again, tears pooled in her eyes as she accepted the makeshift handkerchief and blew her nose. "Thank you. That was sweet."

Anthony's heart soared as he stared into her red, splotchy face. "What's all this about?"

"I'm a bad teacher, Anthony." She hiccupped.

"I'm sure that's not true, Tarah. Toby's learning to read so well. He loves school."

"But the discipline," Tarah countered. Her shoulders shook as she began to sob again.

"Come on, now," Anthony said gently, crouching beside her once more. "It can't be that bad." He reached for her, then pulled back as she shot from her chair.

"It can't, huh?" Her eyes flashed as she glared down at him. "Do you know what I just did?"

Anthony gaped at the quick switch from sorrow to anger.

"I just took my ruler and smacked Luke on the hand for something Josie did." She gave him a satisfied nod. "You see, I can tell by the look on your face how shocked you are."

Rising from his crouched position, Anthony hesitated a moment, not sure he wanted to ask the question begging to be voiced. He drew a breath. "What exactly did Jo do?"

She spun around. "Just look at the back of my dress!"

Anthony groaned. So that's why the girl was so eager to gather the eggs this morning. "But why did you punish Luke if Jo put the egg in your chair?"

All the steam seemed to leave the slender young woman, and she dropped back into her chair. "I—I just assumed it was Luke. He's been so horrid ever since I paid him to be good."

"You paid?"

She nodded, and her eyes filled up again. "He didn't have the money to pay for Josie's ribbons—you remember the ones he inked that first day of school—so I offered to give it to him if he would just stop instigating trouble. I—I thought it sounded like a good solution."

Several questions circled in Anthony's head as he tried to make sense of what he was hearing.

"And he didn't keep his end of the bargain?"

"Oh yes. For as long as it took to pay for the ribbons. Then he was worse than any child I've ever seen, except maybe—" She stopped midsentence.

"Josie," Anthony supplied.

"Yes." Her voice was barely audible as she averted her gaze.

"Do you mind my asking why you didn't just tell your folks? Seems like your pa could deal with Luke with one trip to the woodshed."

"I didn't want them to think I couldn't handle it," she said. "Besides, I don't want Pa and Ma to worry. They have enough to think about with the new baby coming."

"Are there problems with Cassidy's, er, condition?"

"No. But my ma died having Jack, so Pa worries."

Now that was exactly the kind of thing Dell should have come to Anthony about. As preacher, he could have prayed with him and quoted the scriptures about God not wanting His people to be anxious. When would these people take him seriously? He blew out a frustrated breath.

Tarah glanced up, questions written on her face.

Anthony shook his head, inwardly berating himself for thinking about his own problems at a time like this. "I'll take care of Jo," he said firmly, "so you won't have to worry about her causing any more problems."

A shrug lifted Tarah's shoulders. "It doesn't matter, because I'm quitting. Louisa Thomas wanted the position when they gave it to me. Well, she can have it." Tarah stood. "Thank you for being so kind. I'm sorry about your shirt."

"The shirt doesn't matter, Tarah." He placed a hand on her arm. "Things will straighten out. Don't quit just yet."

"I can't face the students after what I did today."

Compassion filled Anthony at her self-loathing. "Listen, how about if I teach your students for a couple of days while you pull yourself together?"

Tarah's full lips parted as she drew in a breath. "I can't ask you to do that! Your ma needs you at home. Besides, won't the town council object?"

"I've been planning to pass on more responsibility to my brothers anyway. Blane's old enough to take care of things now. And I'll be there to help out at night. As for the town council, I'll talk to Mr. Tucker and Mr. Gordon before I leave town. And you can talk to your pa since he's head of the council."

Once again, her eyes filled. "I—I just don't know, Anthony. The look on Luke's face. . ." Tears rolled down her cheeks, and suddenly she was in his arms again.

"Shh. . ." He held her to him, stroked her hair, and felt as though he would never breathe again.

The door swung open, and Anthony caught Josie's stormy gaze. Behind her, Luke still sat on the step. Jo placed her hands on her small hips and stomped her foot. "Are we ever going home?"

Tarah disengaged herself from his arms and gathered her books from her desk. "I—I have to go. Ma will worry when the children get home early."

"Do you want me to come tomorrow?"

After a moment's hesitation, Tarah nodded. "Thank you, Anthony."

Her lovely gaze captured his for a moment. She gave him a tremulous smile and pressed her fingers lightly to his arm. Before he could recover from the shock of her touch, she walked past Josie and left the little school without a backward glance. Luke stood and followed.

As he watched her walk away, Anthony prayed a silent prayer of peace for Tarah.

"Are we leaving now?" Jo's impatient voice drew him back to face a reproving stare.

Anger flashed through Anthony. "Yes. Right now. You and I have some talking to do, young lady."

"I'll say. Me and Luke saw you cozying up to Miss Thomas over by the mercantile." She waved both hands in the air to emphasize her words. "I bet the whole town saw you. And now me and Luke catch you hugging Miss St. John." She gave him a disapproving frown. "Just how many girls are you courting, Uncle Anthony?"

Chapter 4

Tarah waited just inside her bedroom door until she heard Jack, Luke, and Emily head off to school, then she made her way into the front room.

"Tawah!" Hope ran to greet her. Grabbing Tarah around the legs, she hugged tightly.

Tarah snatched the little girl up in her arms and kissed her plump face. Drawing the child close, she pressed her cheek against her little sister's silky head and breathed in her sweet baby smell. A niggling of guilt inched through her stomach. She hadn't spent much time with the twins lately and hadn't even realized until this moment how much she'd missed them.

Not to be outdone, Will clutched at Tarah's skirts. "Me, too."

Laughter bubbled within Tarah. "You two are getting too big for me to hold you both." She knelt on the wooden floor and gathered them into her lap. "What are you playing with?"

Will wiggled free and held up a wooden train engine. "Twain."

"Why, where did you get that?"

"Sam."

"Oh, how nice. What sound does a train make?"

Will's "woo-woos" brought a giggle to Tarah's lips.

Hope scrambled from Tarah's lap and jerked the toy from Will's hand.

"Mine!" the little boy hollered.

"Hope, sweetie," Tarah said, "the train belongs to Will. Give it back."

A scowl darkened the otherwise angelic face. "No!" She snatched the toy back as Will made a grab for it. Clutching the engine tightly to her chest, she ran toward the kitchen, Will close on her heels.

Releasing a sigh, Tarah stood and followed.

The kitchen door opened and Cassidy appeared, holding a mug in her hands. Hope flung herself against Cassidy's skirts. "Ma!"

Relieved to have the situation out of her hands, Tarah plopped into a wooden chair and watched the drama unfold.

"What on earth is going on?" With Hope pressed firmly against her legs, Cassidy inched her way to the table and deposited the steaming cup she held.

"My twain!" Will shouted.

"Was Hope playing with it first?" She looked to Tarah for the answer.

Shaking her head, Tarah gave her a wry grin.

Cassidy bent at the waist until she met Hope eye to eye. "Honey, you can't take away a toy your brother is playing with. That's not nice. Give it back and tell him you're sorry."

With quivering lips, Hope shoved the engine into Will's outstretched hands.

"And tell him you're sorry," Cassidy prodded.

"Sowwy." Eyeing the train as though she would like very much to snatch it back, the toddler didn't look a bit sorry. Tarah ducked her head to hide her grin.

"There's a good girl." Cassidy pressed a kiss to each dark, curly head. "Now go play nicely together for a little while." She dropped into her chair and grinned at Tarah. "Good morning," she said, reaching for her cup.

Tarah knew her stepmother took a few moments for herself each morning. After the uproar and confusion associated with getting everyone out of the house for the day, she needed to relax before cleaning up the breakfast mess.

Cassidy didn't look a bit frazzled by the twins' antics. Her jade-colored eyes twinkled as she glanced at Tarah over the rim of her cup. "I figured you were hiding out until the kids left for school. With those two acting up this morning, you probably wish you'd stayed in bed." She smiled again. "Are you ready for breakfast?"

"I'll get it," Tarah replied, smiling back at her stepmother. "Enjoy your coffee. As a matter of fact, I'll do the cleanup for you, too."

"Why, thank you. I remember a time when I had to practically force you to lift a finger."

Tarah groaned. "I was something else in those days, wasn't I? I don't know why you put up with me."

"When you're part of a family, you don't have a choice. Why don't you go get your breakfast, and we'll have a nice little chat. It seems like ages since we've spent any time together."

"Good idea." Tarah hurried into the kitchen and grabbed her plate from beneath a towel at the back of the stove. She made her way back to the table and settled, once more, into her chair across from Cassidy.

"But you did things so well," she said, picking up the conversation where they'd left off. "Luke and Sam and I, and even Granny, were so horrid to you in the beginning, but you still managed to take care of us and love us in spite of it. I don't know how you did it."

"I certainly made my share of mistakes, though, didn't I?" Cassidy said wryly. "For instance, I should have told your pa about your relationship with Johnny Cooper from the moment I knew about it. It might have saved you a lot of heartache, not to mention the danger my silence put you in."

Tarah shuddered. She didn't want to think about that awful night with Johnny. Still, Cassidy didn't deserve the blame. "That wasn't your fault. I promised you I wouldn't see him anymore. If I had kept my word, he never would have kidnapped us."

"Anyway, those days are behind us, praise the Lord." Cassidy sipped her coffee, then set the cup down. "And look at you now, all grown up and teaching school. I'm so proud of you."

Tarah gave a short laugh and jerked a thumb toward the twins, at last playing peacefully in front of the fireplace. "I can't even get those two to obey me. You should see the mayhem in my classroom." With a gasp, she realized her admission and glanced up from her plate to meet Cassidy's sympathetic gaze.

"Want to talk about it?"

"Oh, I don't know. I'm just not a very good teacher. The children won't obey me. It's a wonder they learn anything at all with all the disruptions from Luke and Jo."

"Luke, eh? Is he still causing trouble in school?" Cassidy shook her head.

"More than ever." Now that she had begun, the words poured from Tarah like a fast-running stream. "I put him in the corner, and all he does is make faces behind my back. The other children think he's just hilarious." Tarah pushed the food around on her plate. With her stomach clenched, she knew she couldn't eat a bite.

"Miss Nelson once told me that standing Luke in the corner was just another way for him to cause trouble," Cassidy said. "Sounds like he hasn't changed much."

Placing a hand to her forehead, Tarah groaned. "I'm so tired of staying thirty minutes after school just so he can write sentences for his punishment. He writes them as slowly as he can just to get under my skin. I've been trying to think of another method of punishment for him, so yesterday—"

Tarah stopped, not sure she wanted to admit to her error.

"What happened that was so bad you had to take a day off?"

Tears stung Tarah's eyes as the memory of the sound of the ruler on Luke's hand came back as vividly as though he were standing before her. She poured out the entire story, omitting nothing, including Anthony's visit afterward. By the time she had blurted the whole wretched tale, tears streamed down Tarah's face.

Cassidy reached out and covered one of Tarah's hands. The comfort of the warm touch made her cry all the more.

"I just can't do it anymore," she sobbed. "I had such high hopes of being a wonderful teacher. I never thought the children would hate me."

"Oh, Tarah, don't be so hard on yourself. Luke is a special case." Cassidy handed her a napkin to dry her tears. "He might act up a little worse for his sister than he would for another teacher, but he definitely caused trouble for Miss Nelson, too. I know it's difficult, but he has to understand that your relationship at school isn't the same as here at home."

Grateful for the support, Tarah voiced the question she had been contemplating since the day before. "Do you think I should talk to Pa about it?"

Cassidy gave a reflective frown. "You could. Your pa would certainly take care of it, I suppose. And I doubt Luke would cause more trouble in school."

"That would be a relief."

"I'm sure." Cassidy nodded. "But he would probably make up for the trouble he can't cause you at school by taking it out on you here at home."

"Oh, Ma," Tarah groaned, hating her whiny tone of voice. "I just don't know what to do."

"Tarah," Cassidy said, "Luke needs to know who's boss. And at school, that just happens to be his sister. I don't argue the fact that you should have gotten the full explanation before you unjustly punished Luke, but don't be so hard on yourself."

"I can't help it. I'm at my wit's end in dealing with him and Josie Raney."

"Luke's ornery; there's no denying that," Cassidy said. "But he has a good heart, and he loves you. Maybe you should try reasoning with him."

"My twain! Ma!" Will's cry cut off Tarah's retort.

Lips twitching in amusement, Cassidy stood. "I'd better find those two something to do before the 'twain' ends up broken." She pushed in her chair, her gaze searching Tarah's face. "It was kind of Anthony to offer to teach today."

Feeling the heat rise to her cheeks, Tarah swallowed hard and nodded.

As if sensing Tarah's reluctance to discuss Anthony, Cassidy gathered a breath and blew it out. "So what do you have planned for your day off?"

Grateful that Cassidy didn't seem inclined to press the matter of Anthony further, Tarah found her voice.

"I thought I'd go for a ride. Down to the river maybe, then into town to see if Mr. Tucker has any mail for us. I was hoping to ride Abby since Lady is about to foal. Is that all right with you?"

"Of course. It'll do her some good. Your pa won't let me near the horse until the baby comes. Make sure you pack a lunch in case you decide to stay out for a while. And, Tarah," she said, a look of hesitancy clouding her eyes.

"Go ahead," Tarah urged.

"If you've prayed about this and it doesn't seem as though God is answering, perhaps you should ask Him if there is a lesson He wants you to learn from your reaction to Luke's behavior."

"My reaction?" Tarah's defenses rose. Her reaction was just as it should be. Luke was the one out of hand, and he was the one who needed to be taught a lesson!

"I don't want to hurt you, and you know I'm not excusing Luke, but often the way we react to pressure teaches us more about our own hearts than we would ever learn if things always worked out smoothly for us." Cassidy regarded Tarah with a sympathetic smile. "Just a thought."

Striding into the living area, she clapped her hands together. "All right, you two, give me that train, and let's go find some wildflowers to decorate the table."

156

Anxious to go for her ride, Tarah grabbed her plate and Cassidy's cup from the table and set about tackling the dishes.

〜

A strong wind blew across the prairie as Tarah gave Abby her head and let the horse run through the tall grass. Breathing deeply of the cool October air, Tarah felt the heavy weight lift from her shoulders.

The confinement of the schoolhouse seemed far away, and she had almost definitely decided to turn in her resignation. Only the thought of Pa's disappointment troubled her about her near decision. And he would surely be disappointed.

Feeling the weight descending upon her once more, Tarah urged Abby on, faster, toward the river. Only when the horse's labored breathing matched Tarah's did she slow down and allow the animal to walk the rest of the way. At the riverbank, she dismounted and led Abby to the water.

Tarah looked out over the river, wishing for the peace usually brought about by the gentle rush of waves lapping against the bank.

So many questions were plaguing her mind. Should she continue teaching? Did she even want to? And if she did, what should she do about Luke and Josie?

Cassidy's words rushed back, bringing a troubling introspection she would rather do without. *Lord, are You trying to teach me something? If so, what? How on earth can I learn anything from Luke and Jo's meanness?*

"Howdy."

Tarah jumped and whirled around, nearly dropping Abby's reins.

A child of no more than seven or eight years stood staring at Tarah, wide brown eyes sizing her up as though she were a cow at an auction. At second glance, Tarah realized the child was a girl, though she wore filthy trousers with holes in both knees and a threadbare button-down shirt that Tarah supposed had once been white. Long, matted hair, which could have been either brown or dark auburn, hung around the girl's shoulders.

"Cain't you talk?"

Tarah found her tongue. "Of course I can talk."

"How come you didn't say nothin', then? When I said 'howdy,' that is." She reached out a grubby hand and patted Abby's rump.

Tarah's cheeks flamed at her own rudeness. "I'm sorry. I was just surprised to see anyone out here today. I thought I'd have the place all to myself."

The little girl glanced up wordlessly and shrugged. Turning, she sauntered away.

"Wait. Where are you going?"

"Thought ya wanted to be alone," she called over her shoulder.

Oh, honestly. Tarah followed, catching up easily. "I didn't say I wanted to be alone. I'm just surprised to find anyone else out here. I'm sorry I made you feel unwelcome."

Stopping, the little girl eyed her. She gave a shrug and nodded. "It's okay. I'm used to no one wantin' me around. Don't bother me. I just don't stay where I ain't wanted. That's all."

Tarah's heart wrenched with the thought that any child could feel unwanted. "Actually, I wouldn't mind some company. Want to come back to the river and talk to me for a while?"

"I reckon," the little girl replied, heading back toward the river without waiting for Tarah. "Ain't got nothin' better to do."

"What's your name?" Tarah asked, falling into step beside her.

"Laney."

"That's pretty. I've never heard it before."

"Short for Elaine." Laney scowled. "But don't call me Elaine. I hate it."

"You have my word." Tarah's lips twitched with amusement.

"So what's yer name?"

"Miss St. John."

"You ain't got a first name?"

"You can call me Tarah, I suppose."

"Nice to meet ya, Tarah." The girl extended her grimy right hand in greeting.

Swallowing hard, Tarah shook Laney's hand, trying with difficulty to hide her distaste.

They settled onto the bank of the river. Downwind from the child, Tarah fought hard not to pinch her nose to keep the stench away. If this girl had ever had a bath, it certainly hadn't been in the recent past.

"Laney, I haven't seen you around before, and Harper's a small township. Are your folks new to the area?"

"I dunno. We been here awhile, I guess." Laney jerked her thumb behind them. "We live over thataway."

"But that's Al Garner's land. He owns all the property between here and town."

"That's right. Pa's a squatter," she said matter-of-factly. "Mr. Garner knows about it, though. Said we could live in the old soddy, long as we don't wreck the place."

"I see." Feeling uncomfortable with her own prying, Tarah tried to think of something else to talk about.

"Usually," Laney continued as though the topic of conversation didn't bother her one bit, "we get thrown off a place 'fore we can settle in real good. We been here longer than anyplace in as long as I can remember."

"Why haven't your ma and pa sent you to school?"

"What fer? I can read good enough, if the words are little. Ain't got no books anyways, 'cept Ma's old Bible, and who wants to read that? And I can do sums up to the hundreds. I figure that's all a body really needs to know. 'Sides, ain't got no ma, just a pa and Ben."

"You don't have a ma?" The words left Tarah before she could rein them in. That certainly explained Laney's appearance. What kind of a pa left a child to fend for herself with no thought to education or cleanliness?

"Nope. She died when I was a young'un. Cholera or somethin', I guess. Pa never talks about it. Ben remembers her, but I don't."

"I'm sorry, honey." Tarah wanted to reach out to the child, to draw her close and give her a woman's touch, but she couldn't quite push through the revulsion. The way Laney scratched her head, she more than likely had lice in her hair. Tarah shuddered at the thought and inched away just a little, praying diligently the child wouldn't notice.

"It don't matter none anyways." A shrug lifted Laney's bony shoulders, and her chin jerked up. "A person cain't miss someone they never knew."

"I miss my mother every day," Tarah said softly.

"Yer ma's dead, too?" Laney regarded her through narrowed eyes.

"Yes. She died when I was a little older than you."

"Too bad." She tossed a twig into the water and watched the river claim it.

"I have a wonderful stepmother, though," Tarah said.

"Yer pa must be a fine man. Ain't a woman alive dumb enough to marry my pa."

"Laney! What a thing to say!"

"It's the truth. And I don't care who hears me say it." With a stubborn set of her jaw, she tossed another stick into the river.

"I'm sure your pa's a fine man." Tarah nearly choked on the words. She had already drawn her own conclusion of the unknown man, and apparently the child held the same opinion.

"No, he ain't, and if you knew 'im, you wouldn't even claim such a fool thing."

Stung, Tarah drew a breath. "Well, no matter what sort of man he is, the Bible instructs children to honor their parents."

"I don't hold to no religion, Tarah. So I don't much care what the Bible has to say about the subject."

Stifling a gasp at the irreverence, Tarah searched for a way to reach Laney, but the girl jumped to her feet. "Look, lady, I don't need no lectures. I'm near twelve years old, and soon as I can, I'm gettin' away from that old drunk."

So the man was not only slovenl; he indulged in liquor. That explained a lot. The girl's age surprised Tarah. She was no taller than seven-year-old Jack and quite a bit skinnier. Surveying Laney critically, Tarah decided the child was half-starved.

"Wait, Laney. Don't go yet. It's a bit early for lunch, but I'm getting a little hungry. Do you want to share with me?"

Laney's eyes grew stormy, her lips twisting into a sneer. "I don't need yer charity."

"Oh, honestly." Tarah stood and made her way to Abby. "I packed more food than I can possibly eat." Knowing she'd be away from the house most of the day, Cassidy had insisted Tarah pack enough food for an army. Tarah had thought it silly at the time, but now she was glad for Cassidy's forethought. "If someone doesn't help me eat it, most of this will go to waste." Tarah pulled a blanket from the saddlebag and spread it on the ground.

"Well. . ." Laney eyed the leftover chicken and thick slices of bread Tarah set on the blanket.

"You might want to go to the river and wash your hands," Tarah suggested.

"What fer?"

"Because they're dirty. You shouldn't eat with dirty hands."

"That so?" She shrugged. "Don't guess it'd hurt nothin' to swish 'em around a little."

"I'm sure it wouldn't," Tarah drawled.

Laney returned a moment later, wiping her wet hands on the filthy trousers. Tarah cringed. It hardly did any good for her to wash. The dirt was apparently ground in so deep, a good scrubbing would be necessary to get her hands clean. Laney didn't seem to notice and ate with abandon, barely swallowing one bite before taking another.

Nibbling on a slice of bread, Tarah watched the girl down three pieces of chicken and two slices of bread. At Tarah's insistence, she accepted the only piece of apple pie left over from supper the night before.

Rubbing her stomach, Laney emitted a loud belch, then groaned. "Don't think I've ever had such good food. You folks eat like that all the time?"

"My ma is a wonderful cook."

"Thought ya said yer ma was dead," Laney challenged.

"She is. I told you my pa remarried."

"Oh." Laney stood. "I best get back to the house 'fore Pa wakes up and starts hollerin'."

Tarah stood and faced the girl. "Laney, I teach in town. Will you consider coming to school?"

"Yer the teacher?" Her brown eyes narrowed suspiciously.

"That's right."

"Then why ain't ya at school?"

Heat rushed to Tarah's face. "I took the day off."

"Never heard of a teacher playing hooky b'fore."

Tarah laughed. "Someone is looking after my class for me. I didn't leave them to their own devices. So how about it? Think you might like to come?"

"And yer the teacher, huh?"

"That's right. I'd love to have you there."

After a moment's hesitation, she shrugged. "Well, seein' as how ya shared yer food with me. . ." She inclined her head. "Guess it wouldn't hurt nothin' to try it out. But if I don't like it, ya cain't make me stay."

Tarah's heart soared. A giddy feeling enveloped her, and she grinned. "Thank you, Laney. I hope you'll like school."

Hungrily Laney eyed the two remaining pieces of chicken and the bread still left on the blanket.

Tarah cleared her throat and stooped to wrap the leftovers in a napkin. "Would you mind taking this home with you? I'm heading into town and would rather not have it in my saddlebag. The smell will attract every dog in Harper."

Light flickered in the girl's eyes. "Guess I could. Ben'll probably like it." Her lips turned down bitterly. "If Pa don't grab it away from him."

"Is Ben your brother?"

"Yep. He don't walk so good."

"Why not?"

"Horse stepped on him a couple years back."

The story grew more heartbreaking with each new chapter, and pity clutched at Tarah's heart for the unknown boy. "Maybe you could slip him the food when your pa's not looking."

Laney grinned. "Think I'll do that, Teacher. You goin' to school tomorra?"

Suddenly Tarah wanted nothing more than to return to her classroom and teach. Luke or no Luke, she was determined to be a success. If she made a difference in only one child's life, it would be worth the effort. "Yes, I am. I really am, Laney."

Giving her a curious glance, the girl clutched the bundle of food to her chest and inclined her head once more. "Reckon I'll prob'ly see ya then."

"I'll look forward to it."

Wordlessly Laney turned and wandered away as suddenly as she had appeared.

With renewed resolve, Tarah turned back to the blanket. She shook it out, then stuffed it back into the saddlebag. Casting one last glance across the wide-open prairie, she watched as Laney's retreating form grew smaller.

If she made a difference in only one child's life. . .

Chapter 5

Releasing a self-satisfied breath, Anthony leaned back in his chair. The day was going pretty well so far. No disruptions. The children attended their studies diligently with only an occasional whisper here and there. Apparently after all the commotion of the day before, they didn't want to push their substitute teacher. Anthony was grateful, but he hoped the compliance would last should Tarah decide to return to her classroom.

Feeling a rumble in the pit of his stomach, he pulled out his pocket watch and noted the time. "All right, children," he said. "Put away your books and stand to your feet. It's time for lunch."

The room rustled with the sounds of books closing, desktops opening then dropping shut, and the children scooting from their seats.

"Who wants to say the blessing before we get our lunches out?"

A shuffling of feet answered, and not one pair of eyes met his gaze. "Oh, come now. No volunteers? I suppose I could pick someone."

He glanced around at the room of suddenly very subdued students. "Jo?"

"Oh, Uncle Anthony. Pick someone else!"

"Come up here," he replied firmly. "You can certainly say a prayer over lunch."

With eyes sparking, she stomped to the front, stopping when she reached the desk.

Soft laughter filled the room.

"That's enough, class," Anthony said. "Go ahead, Jo."

Blue eyes flashed as she jutted out her chin. "Bow your heads, folks," she said. "It's time to pray."

The little scamp could do without the sarcasm and dramatics, Anthony thought. But at least she didn't out and out refuse to obey.

"Our most gracious heavenly Father," she began, her voice deepening. "We thank Thee for Thy most holy presence."

Indignation rose up in Anthony at the obvious imitation of his own prayers on Sunday mornings. The children snickered. He raised his head and opened one eye to look at his niece, then widened his scope to take in the rest of the children. Every eye was open and watching Josie.

She waved her arm with a dramatic flare. "Have mercy on this group of sinners, Lord. They don't know how close they are to the pit of hell."

Now he'd never prayed that in the service. She must have heard his private prayers. *The little eavesdropper!*

"Josie Raney! That's quite enough. Go back to your seat."

With a toss of her thick blond braids, she headed for her desk, a smug grin playing at the corners of her lips.

"Bow your heads," he commanded. After a quick blessing over the food, he dismissed the class for lunch, his own appetite suddenly gone.

While the children ate lunch and had recess, Anthony pulled out a large hollowed-out sandstone he had placed in the desk drawer that morning before the children arrived for school. Inside the stone, he had packed clay made from the soft earth at the bank of the river. He pushed at the mixture to be sure it was still soft, then nodded.

As a preacher, he would be remiss in his duties if he didn't give the children a lesson for their souls as well as for their minds. Knowing how they fidgeted during his Sunday sermons, he had prayed for a creative way to get his message across in a manner children could understand. An idea—too much to be coincidence, he thought—had come to him in the night. Filled with anticipation, he had awakened extra early to go to the river and collect the materials needed to carry out the message.

By the time he rang the bell to end recess, he was ready to begin. When the children were settled and quiet, he decided to let them in on the change in routine.

"We're dispensing with lessons for the rest of the day—"

A cheer rose up from the students.

"But you're not leaving early. We're going to have a little Bible lesson." He picked up his Bible from the desktop.

Walking around to the front of the desk, he eyed the children, noting the look of dread on each face. Heat crept up the back of his neck.

Help me, Lord. Let these children understand the message You've given me to share with them.

He leaned against the desk and opened his well-worn Bible to Jeremiah eighteen and began to read. "Then the word of the Lord came to me, saying, 'O house of Israel, cannot I do with you as this potter?' saith the Lord. 'Behold, as the clay is in the potter's hand, so are ye in mine hand, O house of Israel.' "

Anthony closed the Bible, set it back down on the desk behind him, and looked out over the schoolroom. "Anyone know what that means?"

He received a roomful of blank stares in response.

A sigh escaped his lips as he held up the sandstone for the students' inspection.

"Who would like to try to shape something out of this rock?"

Jeremiah Daniels's hand shot up.

"Jeremiah? You'd like to try?"

"Nah, Preacher. You lived in the city too long. You can't make nothing out of an old rock."

"You don't think so? What would you say if I were to tell you that some folks' hearts are just like this stone?"

Encouraged by the children's now-rapt attention, Anthony forged ahead. "Some hearts are hardened because they don't believe in Jesus. Others believe in Jesus and then allow sin into their hearts until slowly they become hardened again."

A quick scan of the children's faces spurred Anthony to move to the object lesson before he lost them. He pulled out his pocketknife, then sat on the desk. "Anyone who wants to can come up here and gather around the desk. I want to show you something."

The seats emptied as the students made their way to the front, curiosity written upon each face.

"Lord, forgive me of my sins." Slowly Anthony chipped off a piece of the sandstone with his knife. "Lord, I want to live for You." Again he chipped away at the stone. The children watched in silence. *Father, help them to understand.*

"Lord, I want Jesus to be my Savior." Another piece of stone slipped away onto the sod floor.

He stopped when the stone was half the original size. "Any questions so far?"

Jeremiah Daniels raised his hand again.

"Yes?"

"Preacher, you been sinning?"

Anthony felt the wind *whoosh* out of him.

"Oh, Jeremiah. Everyone sins. Even preachers. This stone represents a human heart without God. When we ask for forgiveness, the stone begins to fall away, like so. . ." He chipped away a few more pieces. "You see, it's difficult to do what's right when there is so much sin in our hearts."

He continued to break away the pieces around the clay. "Every sin, every act of disobedience, makes the stone bigger, and it's difficult for God to shape our hearts into what He wants us to be. But when we repent, the stone begins to fall away. Does that make sense?"

"You mean like when I tell a lie to get out of a thrashing, I get rocks in my heart?"

"Figuratively speaking," Anthony drawled.

"Or doing mean things to the teacher?" Emily asked, cutting her gaze first to Luke, then to Josie. Luke's ears turned red. He scowled at his sister.

Anthony nodded. "The Bible says we are to respect those in authority over us. And we shouldn't do mean things to anyone, regardless of who they are. Each sinful act makes it that much easier to do it again unless we repent."

"You know, that's true," Jeremiah spoke up. "First time I stole a sourball from the mercantile, my heart started beatin' real fast. But I didn't get caught, so I figured I'd do it again. And it was a lot easier after that. Think some of that stone built up so my heart wouldn't beat so fast, Preacher?"

Emily spoke before Anthony could answer. "Stealing's just plain wrong, Jeremiah Daniels," she declared, hands on hips. "You probably have more rocks in your heart than all of the rest of us put together, except maybe Luke, since he's so mean to Tarah."

"When was the last time you had a sourball?" Jeremiah asked hotly.

Emily tossed her orange braids. "Just last night. My pa brought us some from Tucker's. But he didn't steal them," she said pointedly. "He bought them fair and square."

"Well, no one's bought me any since *my* pa died last year." He glanced up at Anthony with eyes that begged him to understand. "Sometimes my mouth just itches for the taste of them ol' sourballs. But Ma says there's no money for such things. Guess it's still wrong, huh?"

With great effort, Anthony swallowed past the lump in his throat. He reached out and smoothed the boy's hair, then quickly pulled his hand away so as not to embarrass him. "I'm afraid so, son," he said, finding his voice with difficulty. "Sometimes doing what's right is hard. But it makes a boy into a real man with godly character in the long run."

Anthony decided this was as good a time as any to drive home the point of the lesson. He chipped at the last of the stone to reveal the clay within.

Glancing at Jeremiah's contrite face, he extended his hand toward the boy. "You said I couldn't make anything out of the rock, but what about this? Think you could mold this into something?"

A shrug lifted Jeremiah's thin shoulders. "Sure." He took the ball of clay.

The children remained silent as the mound slowly took shape in Jeremiah's hands.

"It looks just like a turtle!" Emily said, admiration glowing in her green eyes. "Is that what you wanted to make, Jeremiah?"

" 'Course. Or I'd have made somethin' else."

"What if you had wanted to make a turtle out of the clay but couldn't get to it because of the stone around it?"

"I'd do what you did and chip off the stone."

"Well, what if you didn't have anything to chip it off with?"

"Then I don't guess I could've done it."

"Exactly." Anthony's spirit soared. "God wants to form our hearts into what He wants us to be, but if we are hardened against His hands, He can't do it. But the knife here," he said, "is just like telling God you're sorry. It chips off pieces of stone until all that's left is the clay. Then God can begin to mold us just like He wants to." He scanned the small circle of children around him. "Remember the scripture I read when we started?"

Their blank faces confirmed they had already forgotten.

" 'As the clay is in the potter's hand, so are ye in mine hand.' Remember?"

Every head nodded.

"I want you to think about whether your heart is soft and easy to work with or hard like stone."

The door opened, allowing sunlight to filter into the room. Anthony's heart lurched at the sight of Tarah, standing with a confused frown on her face.

"Hello, Miss St. John," he said with a grin. "We were just finishing up a Bible lesson. Think anyone would object if we let them out a bit early today?"

"I suppose that would be all right."

The children cheered and scrambled to their desks to grab their belongings.

Jeremiah hung back. "You know, Preacher," he said, a reflective frown scrunching his brow. "If you preached like this on Sunday, a lot more folks would come and listen to you."

Stung, Anthony didn't know what to say, but he felt like the boy expected a thanks. "Well, thank you, Jeremiah, I'll keep that in mind."

The boy nodded and turned to walk to his desk.

"Jeremiah, do you want to take this?" Anthony held out the turtle.

Flushing with pleasure, Jeremiah walked quickly to the desk and took his creation. "Thanks, Preacher!" Then he was off in a flash.

With a grin, Anthony glanced up at Tarah, who had made her way to the front amid the scramble of children.

She eyed the floor in front of her desk critically. "What in the world did you do, Anthony?"

Tarah scowled, awaiting Anthony's explanation.

"We've been having an object lesson."

"An object lesson?" She glanced into his grinning face.

Anthony nodded. "You don't think I could pass up a chance to preach to a captive audience, do you?"

Tarah tried to hide her horror. *Those poor children!* Then, feeling guilty for her thoughts, she plastered a smile onto her face and swallowed hard. "How did it go?"

Anthony shifted off the desk with a shrug. "Started out a little slow, but I think they got what I was trying to show them." Kneeling down, he began to pick up the pieces of stone from the floor. "We talked about how sin makes our hearts stony, but repentance chips away at the stone until all that's left is a heart easily molded into what God desires us to be. That's what all this mess is about. I wanted to show them instead of just preaching at them."

Tarah's stomach jumped. Was her heart as hard as this stone where Luke was concerned?

Shaking off the thought, Tarah bent down to help Anthony clean up. Her hand brushed against his, sending her heart racing as they reached for the same piece of stone.

Raising his head, Anthony searched her face. Tarah felt heat rush to her cheeks.

"How was your day off?" he asked in a soft, velvety voice.

Tarah stood and brushed at imaginary specks of dirt on her dress, trying to compose herself. "Nice," she said. "I appreciate you filling in for me."

Anthony stood, as well, and moved to the open window. "Should I plan to come in tomorrow?" He tossed out the pieces of stone and pulled the shutters closed. Brushing his hands together, he strode back to the desk.

"No. I met a girl down by the river today who said she might come to school tomorrow. I need to be here just in case she shows up."

"A girl?"

Tarah nodded. "Did you know there is a family of squatters living on Mr. Garner's land?"

Anthony nodded. "I met Mr. Jenkins in the mercantile yesterday, as a matter of fact. But that was the first I'd heard of them. The little girl you met is his daughter?"

"She didn't tell me her last name, but I assume so." Tarah walked around the desk and sank into her chair. "Oh, Anthony, it's enough to break your heart. Laney was filthy and wore torn, thin clothing. Not even girls' clothing, but boys' trousers and a button-down shirt."

With a nod, Anthony hoisted himself back onto the desktop and let his gaze roam across Tarah's face. "Her pa wasn't clean either, and his clothes looked like they might fall apart any moment."

"Children shouldn't have to live that way. Isn't there something we can do for them?"

A shrug lifted Anthony's broad shoulders. "A man has his pride, I guess. I'm not sure how much help Mr. Jenkins would accept. Of course, he did let me. . ."

Tarah waited for him to continue. When he looked away, she frowned. "He let you what?"

"It doesn't matter. Let's just say I believe he would probably be grateful for anything we could do for him."

Though her curiosity was piqued, Tarah realized he wouldn't elaborate, so she decided not to make him uncomfortable by asking questions. Instead, she pursed her lips reflectively. She shifted her gaze to Anthony to find him studying her mouth. Catching her bottom lip between her teeth, she cleared her throat.

Anthony's ears reddened, and he averted his gaze, suddenly intent on studying his hands.

"What do you think we should do?" Tarah asked after taking a moment to compose herself. She couldn't help the excitement flooding her. Was Anthony finally beginning to notice her? Oh, she hoped so!

"I guess basic necessities should come first."

"Huh?" Mentally kicking herself for being swept away on dreams of Anthony courting her, Tarah stared dumbly, waiting for him to repeat himself.

"For the Jenkinses. Basic necessities."

"Oh, of course." *Honestly!* "With winter right around the corner, I suppose they will need clothing first off."

"Yes."

"Do you think we should ask for donations? Maybe Mr. Tucker. . ."

Anthony shook his head. "No. Not Tucker."

"Why not?"

"Jenkins owes him money for supplies over the last couple of months."

"Judging from some things Laney said about him, I guess that doesn't surprise me." Resting her elbow on the desk, Tarah tucked her chin into her palm. "Anthony?"

"Yes?" His soft gaze captured hers, and again Tarah lost the capacity to voice her question. An uncomfortable but short-lived silence hung between them as Tarah recovered her voice. "I was just wondering if you've ever known a man given to drink. Laney told me her pa doesn't work because he's drunk all the time."

Indignation clouded Anthony's eyes. "Is that right? I didn't know that, or I wouldn't have. . ."

Again he didn't elaborate.

"Do you think the folks around here would be willing to help such a man?" Tarah asked.

"I don't know." A frown creased his brow. "Mr. Tucker quoted me the scripture about a man not eating if he won't work. He doesn't seem inclined to do much to help. If he's spoken to any of the other folks about it. . . I just don't know."

"But what about the children? Laney and her brother—Ben, I believe she called him. The boy's crippled."

Compassion moved over Anthony's features, endearing him to Tarah all the more. "Don't fret about it," he said, giving her a gentle smile. "I'll ask around and see what I can do. But even if only you and I help, the family will have more than they would have had otherwise. We can't let the children do without or become sick in the cold weather just because their pa won't lift a finger to help himself."

"Thank you, Anthony. I think this is the right thing to do. I'm so glad you agree and are willing to help me."

Leaning over, he reached out and traced a line from her cheekbone to chin. "I guess I'd do just about anything for you, Tarah."

A gasp escaped Tarah's throat. "Y–you would?"

The door opened suddenly, and he moved away, leaving Tarah to wonder if it had been a dream.

"Why, Anthony, you're still here, aren't you?" Louisa's singsong voice echoed through the schoolroom as she sashayed to the front of the room.

A look of guilt flickered in Anthony's eyes, and he hopped from the desk. Tarah's temper flared. From the tight, possessive grip of Louisa's hand around

Anthony's arm, it was apparent she held some claim on him.

Humiliation started at the top of Tarah's head and drifted to her toes. How dare he trifle with her affections! She would not be fancy's fool again where Anthony Greene was concerned. Shooting to her feet, Tarah gave Louisa her brightest smile. "How lovely to see you. I was just leaving." Turning to Anthony, she was hard-pressed to keep a civil tongue in her head. "Will you close the door on your way out?"

Anthony held a cornered-animal look in his eyes. "Tarah—"

"Oh, Anthony," Louisa said, a tone of reprimand in her voice that Tarah didn't quite believe. "Where are your manners?" She cut her gaze to Tarah, a beautiful smile curving her thin, rosy lips. "Of course we'll close the door when we leave."

"Thank you."

Tarah squared her shoulders and made her way down the aisle to the door.

"Tell me all about your day of teaching school," she heard Louisa ask as she shut the door firmly behind her.

Stomping to Abby, Tarah fought to keep her tears at bay. She unwound the reins from the hitching post in front of the schoolhouse and climbed into the saddle.

Why did Anthony prefer Louisa? He always had. She had been a fool to allow herself dreams of becoming his wife. Jerking her chin, Tarah turned Abby toward home and gave her a nudge.

"Tarah, wait!"

The sound of Anthony's voice brought her about. She pulled Abby to a stop, her traitorous heart racing like a runaway train. Watching as he jogged to catch her, Tarah willed her pulse to return to normal and arranged her face in what she hoped was only a look of mild interest.

"What's wrong?" she asked.

"I'm sorry about. . ."

Tarah followed his gaze to the schoolhouse, where Louisa stood, hands on her hips, lips twisted into a scowl.

"Think nothing of it, Anthony." Tarah attempted a short, teasing laugh. "Far be it from me to interfere with your courting."

"It's not like that—"

"Was that all you needed?"

Anthony swiped his hand through his thick, sandy blond hair, then cupped the back of his neck. "Actually, I thought maybe you would like to ride out to the Jenkins place with me—unless you needed to get home right away. I'd like to meet the children and maybe talk to Jenkins a bit."

"I can ride out there with you."

Flashing her a heart-stopping grin, Anthony nodded. "Good. Let me grab the team from the livery and we can tether your horse to the back."

Tarah watched him walk away, admiring the dignity with which he carried himself. A niggling of regret passed through her. Why did Anthony have to be interested in the likes of Louisa Thomas?

"I hope you had a restful day off." Louisa's irritating voice broke through Tarah's musings. Reluctantly she pulled her gaze from Anthony's retreating form to face the young woman.

"Thank you, Louisa. I did. I look forward to coming back tomorrow."

"I'm sure that's a relief to poor Anthony. It isn't as though he doesn't have enough to do without taking on your duties, as well."

Wishing very much she could think of a crushing retort, Tarah swallowed her anger and met Louisa's deceptively innocent gaze with a smile she was far from feeling.

"I'm sure he will be glad to get back to his own duties tomorrow. But I was certainly grateful he *offered* to help me out today."

"Yes, children can be a challenge at times." Louisa's smile didn't reach her eyes.

"Yes, they surely can. Of course, any job is a challenge, wouldn't you think? Sometimes I wish I had just stayed home to help my ma." Tarah released an exaggerated sigh. "But when the town council asked me to teach, I couldn't very well refuse, could I?"

Tarah felt a guilty sense of glee as Louisa's face colored at the reminder that she had been passed over for the teaching position in favor of Tarah.

"I suppose it must be *nice* to have your pa on the town council," Louisa countered, lifting a delicate brow in challenge.

Temper flaring, Tarah dropped the reins and put her hands on her hips. "Now wait just a minute. That had nothing to do with—"

"All set to go?"

Intent on putting Louisa in her place, Tarah hadn't even noticed Anthony pull up in the wagon. She dismounted and brushed past Louisa. "I'm ready," she muttered.

Anthony hopped down and grabbed Abby's reins from Tarah's shaking hands.

Without waiting for his help, Tarah climbed into the seat while he tied Abby to the back of the wagon.

"Where are you two off to?" Louisa asked in ill-feigned nonchalance.

"We're going to check on a new family in the area. Tarah is concerned for the children, and we're going to see what we can do to help."

"Oh, Anthony," Louisa said breathlessly. "What a wonderful idea. I'd love to help. May I come along?"

If Tarah could have spit to remove the bad taste in her mouth at Louisa's tactics, she would have done so with relish. *Say no, Anthony,* she silently pleaded.

"I don't see why not."

"Wonderful. I just love children. I want a house full of them someday."

Louisa held on to Anthony's hand as she climbed in through the driver's side. "Don't you, Anthony?"

Tarah nearly gasped at the woman's brazenness. Did Louisa have no sense of propriety?

Anthony flushed and settled in beside Louisa. "I suppose I'd like children someday. When the right woman comes along."

Knowing that wasn't exactly the response Louisa was looking for, Tarah turned away to hide her grin.

With a sigh, she looked to the distant horizon and sent another prayer toward heaven. *How many lessons must I be forced to learn at a time?* Dealing with her attitude about Luke was one thing, but Louisa Thomas was another circumstance entirely. Years of animosity couldn't just disappear overnight. And the way Louisa was clinging to Anthony made Tarah want to smack the smug expression from her face. Her nails bit into her palms as she tightened her fists in an attempt to gain control over her raging emotions.

The wagon lurched as a wheel dipped into a rut in the road. Louisa took the opportunity to snuggle in closer to Anthony.

Drawing a long, steadying breath, Tarah wished for all she was worth that she had never agreed to go along. From the raised brows and friendly waves of passersby, she was sure they made quite a spectacle: Anthony, Louisa Thomas, and her.

Chapter 6

"Oh my! This is the most disgraceful thing I've ever laid my eyes on. And the smell! Who on earth would live in such a place?"

The look of revulsion on Louisa's face, as well as the tone of her voice, sent a tremor of irritation through Anthony. This family needed help, not judgment. Admittedly Jenkins was slovenly and a drunk, to boot. But the children weren't at fault for their pa's sins. And after all, Laney and Ben were the reasons he and Tarah felt the need to offer assistance in the first place.

He slid his gaze to Tarah's. Her face held a similar look of revulsion, but when she turned toward him, Anthony observed tears pooling in her eyes. He knew her thoughts were on the children being forced to live in such squalor. Wishing very much that he could pull her close and comfort her, Anthony did all he knew to do and gave her what he hoped to be a reassuring smile.

When he had maneuvered the wagon as close to the soddy as he could amid the clutter strewn about the yard, he tugged on the reins, pulling the horses to a stop. He hopped from the wagon and reached out his hand to assist Louisa.

"I just can't believe people live this way!" she declared, pressing a lacy handkerchief to her nose.

"It is a hard thing to take in," he admitted. "But you might want to keep your voice down a little so we don't hurt anyone's feelings."

Sidestepping a broken wagon wheel, Anthony walked around to help Tarah down. She sat unmoving, staring at the run-down soddy. Anthony followed her gaze. Wagon parts littered the yard, along with a broken washtub and dozens of empty liquor bottles. Anthony couldn't stop the anger from building inside him. How could a man claim to be a pa and allow his children to live in such filth? The way the man had let Garner's place run down was nothing short of shameful.

A wooden door lay on the ground outside the opening to the soddy, and a thin blanket hung in tatters across the doorframe. At the window, a shutter swung loosely by one hinge. At the edge of the house stood a thin, swaybacked mare, pitifully trying to pull up the dead grass from the ground.

"Come on," Anthony said softly. "Let's go see what we can do for those children." Rather than offering a hand as he had to Louisa, Anthony instinctively opened his arms.

Turning sorrowful eyes upon him, Tarah stood and allowed him to lift her from the wagon. Anthony swallowed hard, wishing they were alone so he could ask her permission to court her. In the back of his mind, he knew this wasn't the proper time or place, but at the moment, his rapidly beating heart remained at odds with his head.

His senses cleared as Tarah placed her hands on his arms, still encircling her small waist, and gave them a gentle push. Instantly he released her.

With a furrowed brow, Louisa hurried to stand next to Anthony. "This is all just so. . .horrid." She held tightly to his arm, her long fingernails digging in as though she feared for her very life.

Staring at the devastation, guilt pricked Anthony. This was no place for either young woman. Already his skin crawled at the thought of what they might find inside the soddy.

"Hello?" he called as they reached the doorway. "Anyone home?"

The rusty barrel of a shotgun poked through a hole in the blanket. Anthony stepped back suddenly, pulling Louisa with him. He narrowly missed knocking against Tarah and reached out to steady her.

"Get on outta here, mister," a child's voice commanded. "We got a right to this place. Ain't no one but Mr. Garner gonna throw us out."

"Laney? It's Tarah. Can we come in?"

The blanket was pulled back, and the dirtiest little urchin Anthony had ever seen emerged from the soddy. Her face split into a wide grin at the sight of Tarah. "Whatcha doin' here, Teacher? I told ya I'd be at yer school tomorra."

Tarah stepped forward. "I wanted you to meet a friend of mine."

Anthony disentangled himself from Louisa and stepped forward.

Laney eyed him warily, then gave his proffered hand a firm shake. "You her beau?" she asked, jerking her head toward Tarah.

"He certainly is not, young man." Louisa pushed forward and reclaimed her place at Anthony's side.

"Sor—ry, lady." Laney's eyes flashed as she looked Louisa up and down. "And I ain't no boy. I'm a girl, same as you. Only I'd rather be tarred and feathered than wear a getup like you got on." She squinted and peered closer. "And my pa says only loose women paint their faces. And if there's one thing my pa knows about, it's loose women. Though I wouldn't hold to what he has to say about nothin' else."

A gasp escaped Louisa's lips. Anthony stood in stunned silence, cutting his gaze to Tarah. Her face glowed red, and a hand covered her mouth as she tried hard to hide her amusement.

Louisa held herself up primly. "I do *not* paint my face, young *lady*," she replied hotly. "And I will thank you to keep a civil tongue in your mouth when addressing an adult."

"I'll talk any way I want to, lady. And you are so wearin' paint."

"I am not!"

"Want me to prove it?" Laney shot back, stretching her hand toward Louisa's face.

Louisa recoiled. Anthony caught Tarah's gaze and silently pleaded with her to intervene. Nearly choked with suppressed mirth, Tarah obviously couldn't speak for fear of doubling over and howling with laughter.

Louisa seemed to be managing pretty well anyway, so Anthony left her to her own defense. "Don't you dare put your hands on me! I have never seen such an ill-mannered, filthy child in my life."

"I don't recollect askin' your opinion, lady. And who invited you anyways?"

She had a point there. Anthony strongly regretted allowing Louisa to accompany him. But when that young woman put her mind to something, she had a way of getting what she wanted. Although he couldn't excuse the child's rudeness, neither could he help but feel that Louisa was getting a little of what she deserved from the sharp-tongued girl.

Louisa dropped her death grip on Anthony's arm and placed her hands on her hips. Indignantly she looked from Tarah to Anthony. "Are you two going to just stand there and allow this child to insult me?"

To Anthony's relief, Tarah finally found her voice. "I believe you have equally insulted one another, and you *both*," she said pointedly, lifting a delicate brow as she observed Louisa, "deserve an apology."

Anthony grimaced, anticipating Louisa's reaction.

"I certainly will *not* apologize to that. . .that. . .creature!"

Yep, just as he thought.

"I ain't 'pologizin' to no hoity-toity lady with her nose ten feet in the air, neither. And ain't no one makin' me do nothin' I don't wanna do."

Louisa stamped her foot on the ground. "I will not stand here and be insulted another moment. Let's go."

With that, she swung around and stomped toward the wagon. Stopping halfway to her destination, she looked back. "Well, Anthony? Are you coming?"

"We'll be along in a little while." Completely disgusted with Louisa's behavior, Anthony was in no mood to give in to her whim. "I think you're right, though. It might be best if you wait in the wagon."

Louisa's jaw dropped, and her face grew pinker than usual. Without a word, she spun around and stomped back to the wagon.

"Whew!" Laney said. "That's some girl you got there, mister."

"Just for the record," Anthony said, "she's not my girl."

Laney shrugged. "Two bits says she gets her claws in you and walks you down the aisle, one way or another, if you get my meanin'. Pa says Ma roped him into marryin' up with her 'cause she was gonna have Ben, and he regretted it ever since. So you just watch yerself, mister."

Heat crept up the back of Anthony's neck and seared the tips of his ears.

Tarah cleared her throat, her own face tinged with pink. "Laney, honey, Reverend Greene is the town preacher."

Laney scowled. "We don't hold to no religion, Preacher. I done told Tarah I ain't got much use for the Bible and such."

Still trying to recover from the child's crude statement, Anthony nodded. "Your pa mentioned something about that when I met him at the mercantile yesterday."

With a shake of her head, Laney released a heavy sigh. "I don't know why that Tucker's dumb enough to keep givin' my pa credit. He ain't never gonna get his money."

Taken aback by the disrespectful words, Anthony frowned. "Sure he will, after your pa sells the pig."

Laney chortled. "Preacher, I hate to tell ya this, but if we had a pig, I'da shot it for food a long time ago. Pa sold off every animal we owned when he took to drinkin' a few years back. He'd sell that old nag over there, too, if anyone would buy her."

Remembering the words Mr. Tucker had spoken about being hornswoggled, Anthony felt like a fool. Mr. Jenkins had lied and cheated his way into his good graces.

A twinge of guilt pricked Anthony at the harsh feelings rising up inside, because in truth, he had offered his help to Jenkins. The man hadn't asked him for anything. Not that he hadn't taken advantage of Anthony's good nature—then lied to him about paying him back.

"And if any man will sue thee at the law, and take away thy coat, let him have thy cloak also."

The desire to give the scoundrel a sound thrashing was stronger than ever, and Anthony struggled to contain his anger and focus on the children, who didn't deserve to be punished for their pa's underhanded ways.

"Is your pa around?"

"Passed out cold," Laney said, her lips twisting into a sneer. "Probably won't wake up 'til near dark. Why'd you want to talk to him anyways?"

"I have something to discuss with him."

Laney nodded, curiosity written on her dirty face. "Best time to talk to my pa is between the time he wakes up and when he starts drinkin' again. I figure ya have near two hours a day b'fore he's too drunk. You can come back later iffen ya want."

"Thank you, Laney," Tarah said. "Do you and Ben have anything to eat for supper?"

"Yeah, we got beans left over from last night, and Ben'll have that chicken I took off yer hands earlier."

Anthony pressed a hand to Tarah's shoulder. "We'd better get going."

She nodded her response. "I'll see you at school tomorrow, right?"

"Said I'd be there, didn't I?" Laney replied. "And one thing ya can count on, Tarah. I always keep *my* word." She emphasized "my" as though trying to assure Tarah—and maybe herself—that she was nothing like her pa, who apparently never kept his.

Tarah smiled. "All right, then. I'll see you at eight thirty sharp."

"I'll be there." Laney grinned, showing white teeth, a startling contrast to her smudged face.

"And, Laney," Tarah said hesitantly, "would you mind calling me 'Miss St. John' at school? All the other students call me that, and I wouldn't want them to think I'm allowing you special privileges."

Laney seemed to consider the request for a moment, then her bony shoulders lifted. "Don't see why not. Wouldn't want ya to have no trouble on accounta me."

Anthony smiled at the way Tarah had handled the situation. As they strode back to the wagon, he told her so.

An enticing spot of pink appeared on each cheek at the compliment. "I didn't suppose she would do it if I tried to tell her she had to."

"She's mighty determined not to be told what to do, isn't she?"

"Yes, but she's obviously had to fend for herself and her brother for a long time," Tarah said, rising to the child's defense. "It's no wonder she's so independent."

"True. Still," Anthony mused, "I'm concerned about her bitterness toward her pa. To be so bitter so young is a terrible thing."

"Well, that's no wonder either." Tarah's voice rose. "Honestly, Anthony. The man drinks away any pittance of money he can dig up and lives off the charity of others."

"No one is so far gone that the hand of God can't reach him, though."

Tarah stopped in her tracks and glared up at him. "Anthony Greene, don't you defend that monster to me. I'd like to reach out *my* hand with a nice big skillet and use it over his head! That might be the only way to knock some sense into him." Without waiting for a response, she stomped to the wagon, untied Abby, and mounted. "Good-bye, Anthony, Louisa. I can ride the rest of the way home alone." With that, she turned her horse and rode away in a cloud of dust.

Anthony watched her go. The image of the tiny young woman taking on a man like Jenkins filled his mind, and he chuckled to himself. It would serve the old drunk right if Tarah went after him.

"Anthony, I really must be going home." Louisa's clipped voice broke through his thoughts.

"Coming." Still smiling to himself, Anthony climbed into the wagon and headed the horses toward town. "All set?"

With her back perfectly straight, Louisa jerked her chin and set her lips into a grim line. All signs she was more than a little put out with him.

Rather than feeling distressed by her anger, Anthony felt a sense of relief that she wouldn't be chattering the entire ride into town. Odd how all her ramblings and flighty ways had once appealed to him. Now they were nothing more than irritations. Especially when she grabbed his arm and exclaimed over his strength.

Even as the thought came to him, so, too, did the image of Tarah's wide, luminous eyes and full lips. His mind wrapped around the memory of her slight form in his arms, and the way she had taken a dirty little girl under her wing, determined to do whatever she could to see the child had a chance.

Lord, this is the kind of wife a preacher needs. Someone with a heart of compassion. Of course, it probably wouldn't be a good idea for her to actually follow through with that skillet. Perhaps You could allow her the grace to extend her mercy to include the entire Jenkins family.

∽

"You should just see the place, Pa." Tarah filled Abby's trough with hay and gave her a pat on the neck. "Mr. Jenkins has let it become so run-down I almost didn't recognize it. Remember how Mrs. Garner used to keep it up and plant flowers all around the house? She must be rolling over in her grave about now."

Pa nodded as they walked abreast of each other toward the barn door. He closed and latched the door behind them. Pulling Tarah close, Pa steered her toward the house. "I've heard he'll do about anything for a drink. He must be a lonely, miserable man."

"And deserves no less," Tarah shot back as the run-down soddy and Laney flashed through her mind.

A frown etched his brow. "That's a pretty harsh statement."

"If you could just see poor Laney, Pa. I get so angry just thinking about it."

"Your anger won't do that family a bit of good, Tarah. Only your prayers. Just remember, God's love and grace extend to everyone. Not just the people we think worthy."

"That's what Anthony said."

"He's right." He paused a minute, regarding her thoughtfully. "Is there anything I should know about you and this young preacher?"

Heat rushed to her cheeks, but she shook her head. "He's courting Louisa Thomas." How she wished she could give him another answer.

"You sure about that?"

"Yes. Why?"

He shrugged. "I don't know. I'm sure Louisa's a fine young woman, but she doesn't seem suited to a man like Anthony."

The words sent a strange sense of comfort to Tarah's aching heart. She agreed wholeheartedly with her pa. There was only one woman suited to Anthony, and that woman certainly was not Louisa Thomas.

Moving to the door, Pa gave her a wry grin. "I suppose a man's got to make his own decisions about women. But it'll be a heap easier on him if he makes the right one."

Tarah followed, fighting to hold back the tears clouding her eyes. "If Anthony Greene can't see what's right under his nose, then it serves him right if Louisa sinks her claws into him," she muttered.

Pa stopped before opening the front door. "I thought you might have feelings for him." He studied her face for a split second, then opened his arms wide.

She went to him willingly, taking comfort from the slow *thud* of his heart against her ear. "Oh, Pa. Even back in our school days I favored him. But for some reason, he never saw me that way. It has always been Louisa. When he came back, I hoped he might see me in a different light."

"He did offer to take your class today," Pa reminded her, gently stroking her hair.

"We've become. . .friends, I guess," she admitted.

"Nothing wrong with friendship."

Tarah sniffed. "But I want more than—" She stopped, aware she sounded like a spoiled child crying for a new toy.

Pa held her at arm's length and silently regarded her for a long moment, until at last Tarah felt ashamed and dropped her gaze. He cupped her chin and forced her head gently upward. "And if his friendship is all he has to offer you right now?"

With great effort, Tarah swallowed past the lump in her throat and lifted her shoulders. "Then I guess I'll have to accept it."

He smiled, his approval causing Tarah's heart to soar. "I'm proud of you, sweetheart. But don't give up on him just yet. You never know what God has planned." He reached for the door, then turned back to her with a grin. "Cassidy and I are proof of that."

❦

As promised, Laney stepped inside the schoolhouse at eight thirty sharp the next morning. The room buzzed as the children observed the newest student.

"Never seen so much dirt on one person in my life."

Horrified by Luke's outburst, Tarah pinned him with her gaze until his face reddened and he turned away. Tarah swallowed past her indignation and glanced at Laney, who now stood motionless midway up the aisle. Struggling to keep from pinching her own nose to stifle the odor coming from the girl, Tarah pasted a smile on her face. "I'm so glad you came."

"Said I would, didn't I? And I always keep my word." Laney eyed the other children nervously.

"Yeah, but does she ever take a bath? Pee–ew."

The room filled with twitters of laughter at Josie's loud whisper.

A flicker of hurt flashed in Laney's eyes but left as soon as it had appeared. She squared her bony shoulders and glared at Josie.

Tarah's emotions waffled between compassion for the girl and anger at the children's cruelty. They had no idea the kind of life Laney endured on a daily basis. If Tarah could have her way, she'd march each one of them to the wood-shed and give them the switchings they deserved.

"Josie Raney," Tarah said hotly, feeling Laney's humiliation. "Go stand in that corner. Luke, go stand in the other one. I will not tolerate rude behavior in my classroom."

Laney's brows lifted. "Aw, Tar—Miss St. John. You ain't gotta do that on my account. I'm used to it. Anyways, I don't stay where I ain't wanted." She turned on her heel, headed back down the aisle toward the door, then stopped as Luke brushed past her on his way to the corner. Grabbing his arm, she brought him about to face her. She raised up on her tiptoes and got as close to his face as her tiny body allowed. "Fella," she said. "If I had a face full of freckles like you, I wouldn't be worryin' over a little dirt. Least I can wash mine off iffen I take a notion to."

Squaring her shoulders, she spun around and slipped through the door as quickly as she had come.

Luke's face glowed red as the children laughed at Laney's rude remark. A twinge of sympathy rose within Tarah at his embarrassment. Luke had always been self-conscious about his freckles, and she knew Laney's comment had hurt him.

"I'm sorry, Luke," she whispered as he walked past her.

Surprise lit his eyes. He regarded her briefly, then shrugged. "Didn't bother me none."

She knew he was lying but didn't press the issue. "It bothered me. No one deserves to be treated unkindly." A feeling of unease clenched her stomach as Louisa's annoying face flitted to her mind. Stubbornly she shook the image away. That was an entirely different matter.

Without responding to her comment, Luke turned his back and pressed his nose into the corner.

Tarah turned to the other children. "I'll be right back," she announced. "Take out your readers and keep quiet until I return."

Once outside, she scanned the area for Laney. Her heart raced as she spied the child headed toward the direction of the old soddy. "Laney, wait!" she called.

The little girl stopped and waited until Tarah caught up to her.

With a sinking heart, Tarah observed the stony expression on her face.

"It ain't no use, Tarah. I told ya I weren't stayin' iffen I didn't like it."

"Oh, Laney. You didn't give it a chance."

Laney set her jaw firmly. "I don't stay where I ain't wanted. 'Sides, school's a waste of time anyhow."

"Honey, I'm sorry those children were rude to you." Tarah felt her shoulders slump in defeat. "Believe me, I know how you feel."

Laney's eyes narrowed. "They say you stink, too?" She frowned and, leaning in close to Tarah, drew a deep breath. "I ain't noticed nothin' like that. Fact is, you smell kinda sweet—like I 'magine my ma smelt 'fore she died."

"Thank you, Laney." Tarah's heart ached for the motherless child who had to live in such squalor. "Please come back to school."

"Them kids don't like me."

"They just don't know you yet, honey. After a while, they won't have any choice but to like you—just like I do."

A glimmer lit Laney's eyes. "You like me?"

"Of course I do. From the moment we spoke at the river yesterday, I knew you and I would be friends."

Eyeing her warily, Laney cocked her head to one side. "You ain't just sayin' that so's I'll come back for some learnin'?"

"I promise." Wings of hope fluttered in Tarah's heart, and she prayed as hard as she had in her entire life. *Please, Lord. Change this little girl's heart.*

"Cain't do it," Laney said, shaking her head. "Those kids don't like my clothes nor my smell."

"Well, maybe you could take a bath and put on some different clothes," Tarah suggested hopefully.

Laney scowled. "Pa kicked a hole in the washtub and. . ." She glanced away. "This is all the clothes I got. Sorry, Tarah. Ya been real good to me, and I wish I could go back. But I just cain't. Not with them sayin' such things about me."

Tears stung Tarah's eyes. She couldn't blame the child for not wanting to endure further humiliation. "I understand, Laney. Really, I do. And I'm sorry the other children were so mean." Her voice trembled as she spoke.

Laney's eyes grew wide. "Y—ya really do like me, dontcha?"

Tarah nodded, unable to find her voice.

Laney flew into her arms, nearly knocking her over with the force of her little body. Before Tarah could react, the child squeezed her tightly around the middle, then darted away as fast as her scrawny legs would carry her.

Tears flowed unchecked down Tarah's face as she slowly made her way back to the schoolroom. She drew in a deep, steadying breath, swiped at her cheeks with her palms, and stepped inside. Expecting chaos, she sent up a prayer of thanks when she found her students exactly as she had left them.

Luke turned to face her as she walked toward her desk. For the first time in weeks, no belligerence or teasing marked his expression. Instead, he regarded her with serious eyes, conveying his apology, then he turned and stood motionless with his nose pressed to the wall.

Chapter 7

Tarah shut the schoolhouse door firmly behind her and headed for Tucker's Mercantile. After the fiasco with Laney that morning, the children were mercifully compliant the remainder of the day. But Tarah took only minimal joy in the fact that they learned their lessons well and offered no resistance. Her heart still ached for Laney.

After praying for direction all morning, an idea had come to her around lunchtime. With great effort, she instructed the children in their lessons the rest of the day, impatient for the time when she could dismiss the class.

She walked the short distance to the mercantile, eager to put her plan into action.

"Afternoon, Tarah," Mr. Tucker greeted her as the bell above the door signaled her arrival. "Glad you're here. Got some mail for you."

"For me?"

"Yep." Faded blue eyes twinkled as he handed her an envelope. "Ya got this from some fella over in Starling. Finally courtin'?"

Tarah felt her cheeks warm. "No, sir."

She glanced down to make sure the letter was rightfully addressed to her. Sure enough, her name was written plainly on the envelope: Miss Tarah St. John, Harper, Kansas.

There was no mistake. Her heart did a little jump at the return address: Mr. Clyde Halston, a rancher friend of Pa's from Starling, a small community twenty miles north of Harper. He had come through to buy a horse last summer. The day he arrived, the household was filled with excitement over learning Tarah had been hired to teach in Harper.

At the time, Mr. Halston had mentioned the possibility of Tarah coming to Starling to teach a three-month term in the spring, but she hadn't taken him seriously. Now she wondered if perhaps the town council had taken his suggestion to start a school after all.

"Gonna open it or stand there staring at it all day?" Mr. Tucker asked, leaning his elbows on the counter.

Waffling between the desire to open her letter and wanting to complete her business, Tarah opted to wait. Reading the letter would come later, away from Mr. Tucker's prying eyes. "I think I'll wait. I need to make a few purchases and get home to help with chores," she said, tucking the envelope into her bag.

Clearly disappointed by her decision, Mr. Tucker straightened up and glanced at her over his wire-rimmed spectacles. "Got a letter here for your pa, too." He handed it over. "Looks like it might be from your granny."

Tarah smiled as she read the return address. "Yes, it is."

"When's she comin' back, anyway?" Tucker cleared his throat and gave the letter a once-over. "Some folks been sayin' how they're missin' her."

With great effort, Tarah bit back the smile threatening her lips. She knew Mr. Tucker and Granny had a mutual affection for each other, but so far, neither had lowered their pride enough to admit it.

"I'm not sure, Mr. Tucker," she said. "Perhaps this letter contains that information. We'll all be so happy when she returns to us."

"Make sure ya let me know so I can pass the word along to the folks askin' about her, ya hear?"

"Yes, sir."

"Now what can I get for ya?"

"I need two pairs of boys' trousers. About my brother Jack's size. Do you carry those? And two new shirts, also."

"I got 'em. On that shelf over there."

Tarah thanked the storekeeper and headed in the direction he indicated.

Originally she had toyed with the idea of getting Laney into a dress but dismissed the thought as quickly as it had come. She had the feeling if she tried, the girl would balk and refuse to wear the feminine garment. Next she had thought of asking Ma for some of Luke's castoffs, usually given to Jack, but decided against that, as well. She doubted Laney had ever owned new clothing, and she wanted the child to have something new, something no one else had ever worn.

She rummaged through the shelves until she found two sturdy pairs of blue jeans that looked to be about Laney's size and two shirts—one blue and one brown. On impulse, she grabbed some suspenders, just in case she had misjudged the size. Walking back to the counter, she spied a rack of coats. She glanced at the price and drew in her breath, mentally calculating how much of her meager earnings she would need to part with to buy one.

Reluctantly she turned away, knowing she didn't have enough to pay for the clothes and a new coat for Laney. The shirts were warm enough to shield the child from the cool autumn air for now, but Tarah knew Kansas weather. One day could be hot as July, and all of a sudden, a blizzard could blow up out of nowhere. But there was nothing she could do about it for the time being. With one last glance at the rack of coats, she turned to Mr. Tucker and set the items on the counter. "This is all, I suppose."

"I hate to pass up a sale, but you sure you need those shirts?" Mr. Tucker asked. "Your ma was just in here a few days ago buying material and buttons for new shirts all around. I recollect her mentioning she needed enough to get all her men through the winter."

"Yes. She's busy sewing now," Tarah replied, not wanting to give him more information than necessary.

Mr. Tucker raised his bushy eyebrows and pursed his lips. "Sure ya want all that?"

"Yes, sir." She averted her gaze, feigning interest in a jar of sourballs on the counter.

"Okay, then. Should I put this on your pa's account?"

Tarah turned back to the storekeeper. "Oh no. I'm paying cash."

A curious frown etched his brow as he tallied the items and gave her the total.

Tarah reached into her cloth bag and drew out the money. "Mr. Tucker, how much for that washtub hanging on the wall?"

"Now hold on. Just what are you up to, young lady? I know your pa didn't send you down here for these clothes and a washtub."

A sigh escaped her lips. "All right," she said. "These things are for a needy child. But please don't tell anyone."

"What needy child?"

"Please, Mr. Tucker. Don't ask. I'd rather not say."

"Humph." He eyed her suspiciously. "These for the Jenkins boy? I'm telling you, they'll never fit him. He's about the size of your brother Luke."

Tarah gasped. She'd forgotten all about Ben. She drew in her lip, trying to decide how to proceed. She couldn't really show up with clothing for one and not the other. She had never seen Ben but imagined he had nothing better to wear than Laney.

She glanced down at the items still lying on the counter. One outfit each was better than what they had now. And she could come back next month and get another set.

Snatching up one shirt and one pair of blue jeans, she walked back to the shelf containing the clothing items and selected a larger pair of jeans. Turning to Mr. Tucker, she held them up for his perusal. "Do you think these are about the right size for Ben?"

Squinting, he studied the jeans, then nodded. "Yep. I'd say so."

"All right." Tarah selected a shirt she thought might be the same size Luke wore and strode with purpose back to the counter. "One outfit each will have to do, I suppose."

"You buying trousers for the little girl, too?"

"Yes, sir. I doubt I could get her to wear a dress."

"Suppose you're right about that."

"About the washtub, Mr. Tucker. . ."

He smacked his hand down on the counter and scowled. "Now hold on just a minute."

Tarah drew a breath and steeled herself for the scolding she knew was forthcoming.

"One set of duds ain't enough for a couple of growing young'uns. Get on back over there and pick out another set for each of 'em."

If he'd asked her to marry him, Tarah couldn't have been more shocked, especially after her discussion with Anthony about Mr. Tucker's attitude toward the children's pa.

"But. . ." Her face flushed hotly.

"Go on and do as I say."

"I'm sorry, Mr. Tucker, but I only have enough money to pay for these and maybe the washtub, if it isn't too much. You never gave me the price."

His scowl deepened. He marched over to the wall and grabbed the washtub, then stopped, snatching up two more sets of clothing, and flung the whole lot onto the counter. Next he moved to the rack of coats Tarah had been eyeing, chose two, and set those on the counter, as well. "Now anything else you can think of they might be needin' to get through the winter?"

"I—I really don't know." She also didn't know how she would pay for the items piled up on the countertop. "D–do you think I could open an account?"

"What for? Your pa already has one."

"No. I mean for me. In my name."

"I'd have to talk it over with your pa first," he said. "He might not like the idea of your buying things on credit."

"Then, Mr. Tucker, I'm afraid you'll have to put back the coats and one set of clothing for each child."

With a grunt, he began to fill a wooden crate with the items, completely ignoring her protests.

Desperately Tarah offered him the few bills in her hand—every cent she had to her name. "Please, I'm trying to tell you I don't have enough money for all of those things."

He stopped what he was doing and wagged a bony finger toward her nose. "Now look here, missy. I'm not takin' one red cent from you. And that's my final word on the matter."

"I don't understand."

"It's no secret I don't have much use for a man who won't take care of his own. That Jenkins comes around here wanting credit for tobaccy and elixir when he can't get liquor anywhere else, and he tries to get other useless things that won't help those young'uns of his one bit. Oh, he'll throw in a pound of beans or an egg or two, just to make it look like he's trying to do for his family, but I know better. And I'm not givin' him any more credit in my store. But these shirts and such are for them youngsters, and that's different." Apparently finished having his say, he resumed the task of packing the crate.

Tears pooled in Tarah's eyes. "Thank you, Mr. Tucker. The children will be grateful."

His gaze darted back to hers. "Now don't be tellin' anyone I wouldn't take your money. Folks might come around lookin' for a handout."

A smile tugged the corners of Tarah's mouth. "My lips are sealed. I promise."

"Good. I'll hold ya to that. Now let me carry these out to your wagon for ya."

Clapping a hand to her cheek, Tarah let out a groan. "I walked to school this morning."

"You mean you're aimin' to carry this stuff all the way to the Jenkins place?"

"I—I didn't really think about it."

With a shake of his head, he reached under the counter and produced a key. "Come with me." A deep frown etched his brow, and his voice was close to a growl. "You can use my wagon, but bring it back tomorra." He walked to the door, muttering to himself. "Gonna have to lock up the store and most likely lose customers while I hitch up the team. Women. . ."

⁀

With great interest and more than a little curiosity, Anthony watched Tarah and Mr. Tucker cross the road and head toward the livery. The unlikely pair stood out like a snowy day in July. Mr. Tucker carried a crate in the crook of one thin arm and a bulky washtub in the other. Matching his stride, Tarah spoke with animated gestures, her face bright and smiling. Wishing he could hear their words, Anthony's curiosity suddenly got the better of him.

"Amos," he called to the smithy, "I'll be back in a minute."

The smithy nodded and resumed his pounding on a new pair of shoes for Anthony's saddle horse.

With purpose, Anthony strode the few yards to the livery and stepped inside. He found Tarah speaking pleasantly to Mr. Collins while Tucker hitched up his team.

"Howdy, Preacher." Mr. Collins glanced over Tarah's shoulder and grinned. "How's it goin'?"

"Just fine."

A touch of pink tinged Tarah's cheeks as she smiled a greeting. "What are you doing in town this time of day?"

"My horse threw a shoe." He jerked a thumb toward the smithy. "Amos is getting him all fixed up."

"All set." Mr. Tucker grabbed the bridle of one of the horses and led his team toward the door.

Tarah, Mr. Collins, and Anthony followed until they stood outside the livery.

"Thank you," Tarah said, beaming at the storekeeper. "I promise you'll have your wagon back first thing in the morning. And thank you so much for—"

Raising a weathered hand, Tucker gave her a stern frown. "Now we had a deal. Don't go blabbing."

Lips twitching, Tarah nodded. "I almost spilled the beans, didn't I? I'll have to be more careful."

Anthony's jaw dropped as she raised on tiptoes and brushed her lips to Tucker's wrinkled face. Surprise lit the older man's eyes, then a scowl deepened the lines on his face. "I don't know where you got your manners, going around kissin' people without bein' invited."

A beguiling flush raced to Tarah's cheeks. Anthony's eyes flitted to her full mouth, and he suddenly wished that the kiss had been for him.

Mr. Collins chortled. "Probably the first time you ever been kissed in you. life, Tucker. Probably be the last time, too." He gave Tarah a teasing wink. "If I'd. known the pretty teacher was passing out kisses, I'da offered to let her use my wagon."

With an indignant snort, Mr. Tucker scowled. "There ain't no need to embarrass the girl, Collins. Move on outta my way so's I can help her into the wagon and get back to my store 'fore I lose any more customers."

"Sure you don't want me to help her?" Collins baited the old codger. "She might try to kiss you again."

Anthony's chuckle earned him a reproving frown from Tarah, whose face now glowed red. Averting his gaze, he cleared his throat and tried to stop grin- ning, to no avail. He looked back at Tarah and shrugged an apology. The sight of Mr. Tucker's outraged face was too much. Any moment, Anthony thought the older man might call Collins out.

Tarah finally found her voice. Her eyes sparked fire. "Gentlemen, I assure you I won't be kissing Mr. Tucker again today. Furthermore, I am perfectly capable of getting myself into a wagon." So saying, she hoisted herself up onto the seat and grabbed the reins. "If you'll excuse me, I'll be on my way."

With a stubborn toss of her head, she flapped the reins and maneuvered the horses onto the cut-out road through town.

"Now see what you went and did," Mr. Tucker shot at the liveryman. "She's madder'n a hornet."

Anthony stepped forward before another argument ensued. He clapped a hand on Tucker's shoulder. "I'll walk you across the street. I think I see someone trying to get into the store. You'd hate to lose a paying customer."

"True." He gave Mr. Collins one last look and pointed a bony finger. "Now don't you go blabbin' about that kiss. No need to have folks talkin'." Without waiting for an answer, he spun around and headed back to the mercantile.

Anthony followed. "See you later, Mr. Collins," he called over his shoulder. As soon as they were out of earshot, he turned to Tucker.

"Mr. Tucker, I've been meaning to ask you a favor."

The elderly man glanced up, suspicion clouding his face. "What kind of favor, Preacher?"

Anthony cleared his throat. "I was just thinking you might need some help around the store. With new people coming into town, I've noticed you're getting busier all the time."

Mr. Tucker nodded. "That's a fact. You lookin' for another job? I heard preachin's not goin' too good for you."

Heat crept up Anthony's neck. "The job wouldn't be for me."

"Who, then?"

"There's a young man, a schoolboy actually, who lost his father last year. The family is in dire straits, so I was thinking maybe you could hire him to work here afternoons and Saturdays."

"That's a fine idea, Preacher. Fact is, I been thinkin' of hirin' someone to clean up the place and help stock supplies. What's this young feller's name?"

Anthony averted his gaze. "Jeremiah."

"That Daniels boy?" Mr. Tucker regarded Anthony as though he'd suddenly lost his mind. "You know as well as I do he'd rob me blind. That kid steals from me every time he steps through the door. If his ma wasn't such a good woman, I'd have turned him over to the sheriff a long time ago."

"I know, Mr. Tucker, but maybe the boy just needs a man to look up to. A father figure of sorts."

Mr. Tucker let out a loud snort. "I ain't never been no father, and I don't need to start now."

"I know, but you are a good man. Just the sort of man a boy like Jeremiah can learn from."

The storekeeper seemed to consider it for a moment. "I'll think on it, but I ain't makin' no promises."

"I appreciate it," Anthony said.

Mr. Tucker opened the door. "No tellin' how many customers I lost while I hitched up the team for that girl," he grumbled.

"What's Tarah doing with your wagon, anyway?"

"Guess that's her business." Tucker gave him a sideways glance. " 'Course, it might not be a good idea for her to go out to the Jenkinses' place all by herself. That fella's a no-account if I ever met one."

"Tarah's going out to the Jenkinses' alone?"

"Well, I couldn't close my store and drive her out there, now, could I? I got customers countin' on me."

A lump lodged in Anthony's throat as images of a drunken Jenkins mauling Tarah invaded his mind.

"I'm going after her."

"Might not be a bad idea, at that."

Anthony said a hurried good-bye and broke into a jog as he made his way back to the smithy, praying his horse was ready to go. Thankfully he found Dodger tied up and waiting for him when he got there. Mounting quickly, he glanced down at the smithy. "Put it on my account, Amos. I'm in a hurry."

"Sure thing, Anthony."

Anthony nudged the horse into a trot and headed toward the Jenkinses' place. He nearly groaned when Louisa's high-pitched voice hailed him from the porch of her parents' home at the edge of town. "Yoo-hoo, Anthony."

Knowing he couldn't pretend not to see her, Anthony heaved a sigh. He reined in Dodger, determined not to allow Louisa to keep him talking so long that Tarah would reach the soddy before he could catch up to her.

"Where are you off to in such a hurry?" Louisa called from the porch.

"Got some business out at the Jenkinses' place."

Wrinkling her nose, Louisa shuddered. "That awful place! Anthony, what possible business could you have out there?"

"Personal business." He smiled to take the sting from his words.

Sparks shot from her eyes, and she jerked her chin. "I don't think that place is very sanitary. And that awful child! She deserves a good spanking, if you ask me."

Which he most certainly hadn't. "I think learning about Jesus would do Laney a sight more good than a spanking."

As if sensing his irritation, Louisa smiled invitingly. "We don't have to talk about her, do we? Why don't you come down from there and join me in a nice cup of tea?" she said. "Rosa made some delicious molasses cookies earlier."

"I'm sorry, Louisa," he replied, knowing she could hear the distraction in his voice. He glanced toward the direction Tarah had taken. "I really have to go. Maybe another time."

"Oh, come now, just one little solitary cup of tea? I'll be so hurt if you refuse me."

Hesitating for only a moment at her pleading tone, Anthony shook his head. "I can't today. I'm sorry."

He held his breath as her face clouded over. All he needed was for Louisa to throw a temper tantrum in public. But her angry frown cleared so quickly, Anthony wondered if he'd imagined it.

Fingering the lace on her high-collared neckline, she gave him a pretty smile. "All right. I suppose I can wait until our picnic on Sunday to have you all to myself."

Anthony groaned inwardly. He'd forgotten about the picnic he'd promised her. Knowing he couldn't back out now, he simply nodded and tipped his hat.

"I'll be seeing you, then."

"Bye now."

With a relieved sigh, Anthony left her behind and urged Dodger into a full gallop.

Chapter 8

Tarah, stop!"

The near panic in Anthony's voice sent Tarah's heart racing. She halted the team and spun around in her seat to wait for him to catch up. "What on earth is the matter?"

"Are you crazy?" he thundered, a deep frown creasing his brow.

"I don't know what you mean."

"What were you thinking, driving out to the Jenkinses' by yourself?"

Taken aback by his accusatory tone, Tarah's temper flared. "I have things to deliver for the children. Besides, why shouldn't I go out there alone?"

He slapped his hand against his thigh with a resounding *smack*. "The man's a drunk and a ne'er-do-well, Tarah. You don't know what he might be capable of doing."

"Honestly." Tarah dismissed his words with a wave of her hand, though she had to admit his concern thrilled her to the core. "You heard Laney say her pa sleeps the day away. He probably won't wake up for a couple of hours yet."

"You don't know that for sure."

"I do know if we sit here arguing all day, there's a pretty good chance I'll catch him awake."

"Let's go, then. If he wakes up, I can speak to him about our idea to help with repairs to the homestead."

She cut her gaze upward and flashed a coquettish smile. "Why, Anthony, did you come all the way out here just to accompany me?" she asked in a singsong voice that would have put Louisa Thomas to shame.

His lips twitched, and one eyebrow shot upward. "I wasn't exactly planning to sling you over my shoulder and force you back to town."

Stung by his less-than-flattering response to her attempt at flirting, Tarah tossed her head. "I'd like to see you try," she challenged. "Besides, you needn't have bothered. I'm perfectly capable of taking care of myself."

"I'm sure you're right," he drawled. "But just in case, I think I'll tag along."

"Suit yourself." She flapped the reins to nudge the horses forward.

Astride Dodger, Anthony stayed beside the wagon. Silence hung between them like a heavy fog.

Tarah felt like a fool for believing that just because Anthony worried about her safety, he was growing to care for her as a man cares for a woman. Louisa had set her cap for him, and obviously he had put up no resistance.

Still, in her mind, Tarah replayed the image she often conjured up these days—of Anthony realizing Louisa was not the woman for him. Of his declaring what a fool he'd been and begging Tarah to forgive him and be his wife.

Anthony's voice broke through. "What's in the box?"

Pulled from her dreams of a white gown made of silk and lace, Tarah jumped at the intrusion. "Pardon me?"

"The box? What are you delivering to Laney and Ben?"

"Oh. Some clothes I picked up at Tucker's."

"I thought we were going to ask for donations."

The memory of Laney's humiliation came rushing back, and Tarah spoke with conviction. "We were. But I didn't want Laney to wear the other children's cast-off clothing. I seriously doubt she would anyway."

"Sounds like you are encouraging her to be prideful," Anthony admonished.

Tarah frowned. "I don't mean to, Anthony. But Laney showed up at school today, and the children were horrible to her."

"Not Jo," he said with a groan.

She nodded. "Among others."

"I'm going to have to wear the tar out of that girl. She promised no more shenanigans."

"In this case, it wasn't only Jo. Laney is rather. . .offensive in some ways."

"So I've noticed," he said wryly.

Tarah rose to the girl's defense. "It isn't her fault. She's been raised without a mother to teach her how to bathe and dress. We can't expect her to come by such things naturally with the pa she's got."

"You're right, of course." He grinned. "I hope you got plenty of lye soap to go along with that washtub."

A gasp escaped her lips. "Honestly, Anthony, I forgot all about soap."

Anthony chuckled. "Plain water's not going to do much to cut through all that dirt."

Though tempted to turn the wagon toward home and beg soap from Ma, Tarah put the thought from her mind. Doing so would take another half hour at least, and she didn't want to take a chance on Mr. Jenkins waking before she returned.

"Well, there's nothing to be done about that now. Maybe we can get the first couple of layers off, anyway."

The sound of Anthony's laughter filled the air with a pleasant ring. "Tarah, you're some fine woman. That girl is blessed to have found you."

Her heart soared at the compliment. "I can't help but believe God brought Laney into my life. I was feeling like such a failure as a teacher and just about ready to give up," she confided. "Then, from nowhere, Laney appeared at the river, so obviously in need of love and care. I just knew she was a child I could help."

"God has a way of lifting us from our own problems by showing us how much greater need exists in the world."

The homestead loomed before them, the squalor once again causing Tarah to cringe. Laney stood outside, along with an equally dirty boy who could only be Ben.

"Howdy, Tarah." Laney waved her hand wildly.

Tarah waved back and smiled. "Hello!" She slowed the horses to a stop and wrapped the reins around the brake. Anthony dismounted Dodger and hurried to the wagon.

She accepted his proffered hand, thrilling at the warmth of his touch as their fingers met. Pulled into the depth of his gaze, Tarah climbed down, unable to breathe.

Rather than dropping her hand immediately as propriety demanded, Anthony tightened his grip, causing her pulse to quicken. Oh, how she wished he would draw her into the strength of his arms! As if reading her thoughts, he took a step closer.

Laney's voice brought Tarah to her senses. "You make yer girl stay home this time, Preacher?"

Tarah snatched her hand away and quickly averted her gaze. *Idiot!* she chided herself. *It's Louisa, not you, Anthony wants.*

"I told you, she's not my girl," Anthony insisted.

Laney smirked. "She'll get her claws in you—'lessen you get smart and send her packin'."

Tarah couldn't disagree with Laney's assessment, but from Anthony's pleading gaze, she knew he expected her to bail him out of the embarrassing predicament. "Laney," she said firmly, "that's Reverend Greene's business. Why don't you introduce me to the handsome young man with you?"

An impish grin split Laney's face. "Don't see no han'some young man 'round here." She elbowed the suddenly red-faced boy. "Ain't nobody but my brother, Ben, near as I can tell."

"Aw, hush up, Laney," Ben said, keeping his eyes on his dirty bare feet.

Boots! Tarah groaned inwardly. These children were both barefoot. Why hadn't she thought of buying boots while Mr. Tucker was being so generous?

Stepping forward, she extended her hand. "It's a pleasure to meet you, Ben. I'm Miss St. John. The schoolteacher."

Tarah hadn't planned to bring up the subject of Ben attending school until she had convinced Laney to come back. But the eager light in his eyes spurred her to do just that. "I'd love to see you in school. I have a brother I'll bet is just about your age. Are you twelve?"

"Fourteen."

So he, too, was small for his age.

"Luke will be thirteen soon. That's pretty close to your age. So you see? You already have something in common."

A loud snort from Laney drew Tarah's attention from Ben. "I ain't goin' back to that school, Tarah. And neither is Ben."

"You don't tell me where I am or ain't goin', Laney," Ben said hotly. "Iffen I want to go to school, I'm goin'."

"Then yer about as dumb as Pa says. I tol' ya what them kids said to me. All pluggin' up their noses and sayin' how I was dirty and all."

"They was right. Ya are dirty, and I don't blame 'em for pluggin' up their noses. Ya stink!"

"I ain't takin' none of yer insults." Laney flew at Ben, the force of her weight knocking him off his already unstable feet. She landed atop him. Fists flying, she made little or no contact before his arms came around her, pinning her arms to her sides. "If you don't settle down, I'm gonna have to tie you up."

Tarah looked helplessly at Anthony. He gaped at the pair, disbelief plastered across his face.

"Honestly, Anthony. Do something."

"Sorry," he muttered. "I just can't believe. . ." He shook his head and stepped forward. Grabbing Laney around the waist, he pulled her off Ben.

"Let go of me!" she hollered, twisting and kicking.

Anthony set her on the ground, keeping a firm hold on her arms. "Simmer down."

Raring back, Laney gave him a sound kick in the shin.

"Ow!" Anthony growled. "Why, you little—"

"No one tells me what to do. 'Specially not no preacher."

"Good grief." Tarah shook her head at the spectacle. How in the world had the situation gotten so out of hand? "Laney, would you like to know why I'm here?"

Sudden interest flickered in her eyes, then her face clouded over. "I figure yer here to try and get my pa to make me go to school. But it won't do no good," she said, setting her jaw stubbornly. "I don't go where I ain't wanted. 'Sides, ain't seen Pa 'round here since yesterday. We figure he probably got locked up again."

Tarah caught Anthony's gaze, noting his look of bewilderment, which in all likelihood matched her own.

"You've been all alone since yesterday?" she asked incredulously, thinking of her own small brothers and sisters. "What have you eaten?"

"Aw, Tarah," Laney said, kicking at the ground. "Don't go worryin' about us. Me and Ben can take care of ourselves."

"Now that sounds familiar," Anthony said, the corners of his lips curving into a wry grin.

Tarah felt herself blush. "I'm not exactly a child." She turned her attention back to Laney and Ben. "I'm sure you're very self-reliant—"

"We ain't neither!"

"Hush up, Laney," Ben commanded. "The teacher means we can take care of ourselves."

"Well, ain't that what I just said?"

"Honestly." How would she ever get these children to accept help? Their fierce pride radiated through dirty faces and showed strongly in the stance of their thin bodies.

Helpless fury swept through her, and she had a strong urge to snatch up the pair and take them home with her—kicking and screaming if need be.

Anthony's grip on her elbow brought her to her senses, and she drew a long, slow breath to steady her raging emotions.

"You can't stay alone out here with no food." She waited for the outrage, but mercifully, it didn't come. The children stared at her curiously, as though awaiting the alternative. "So I wondered if you would mind coming home with me—just until your pa comes back."

"Pa'll whale the daylights out of us iffen we ain't here when he gets back," Laney piped up.

"We'll convince your pa that we insisted."

Hope shone in both pairs of eyes. Then Ben's face slowly clouded over with disappointment. "We cain't go, Teacher."

"Why not?"

"Yer folks ain't gonna want us sleepin' on their clean beds and eatin' at their table."

Laney cut her gaze to her brother. "Maybe we could sleep in the barn like we did that time Missus Avery tried to help out."

Crossing her arms across her chest, Tarah looked firmly from one child to the other. "You're not sleeping in the barn, and you're not staying here."

"There is the matter of cleanliness, Tarah." Anthony motioned toward the wagon with his head. "Might be awkward for them bathing at your house with all your brothers and sisters there."

Tarah smiled up at him, warmed by his sensitivity to the children's feelings. Of course the children needed to bathe first. There was no need to give Luke any more ammunition—just in case his good behavior today was a one-time reprieve.

"Hey, who says we're gonna take baths anyways? 'Sides, I done told you, Tarah, Pa kicked a hole in the washtub."

Reaching into the back of the wagon, Anthony produced the new washtub. "Here you go." His eyes twinkled at the expressions of dread on the two faces. "And there are new clothes for each of you where that came from."

Laney's mouth dropped open. "We got new clothes?"

"Yes," Tarah said with a smile. "Now you can come to school without worrying about the other kids making fun of you."

Suddenly Laney's face grew stormy. "Me and Ben don't need yer charity," she spat. "What we got on is just fine. Ya can take them clothes back to the folks they came from and tell 'em we said we don't want 'em."

Oh, Lord, thank You for instructing me to buy new clothing for these children.

"I can't take them back, Laney. They came from Tucker's."

"You got us new clothes?" Ben asked, a hesitant smile peeking around the edges of his mouth. "Really new?"

Tarah nodded. "I guessed at your sizes, so I hope they fit."

"Why'd ya go and do that, Tarah?" Laney asked.

"Because I don't want children to make fun of you. Because I want to see you come to school and learn." Tears sprang to her eyes. "Because I want you to have a chance to grow up and have a better life."

"Pity!" Laney spat.

"Love, Laney, honey," Anthony said softly. "Not pity."

Tarah's breath caught in her throat at the sound of his voice. He, too, seemed choked up, and Tarah thought she might die of love for him right then and there. If the children weren't right under their noses, she would have thrown herself into his arms and begged him to love her back.

She turned back to Laney. All the thunder was gone from the child's face. "Well. . ."

"It's okay, Laney," Ben said, placing a gentle hand upon his little sister's arm. "Let's just take it. This ain't like other folks. I can tell the teacher ain't tryin' to make us feel bad. She just wants to help."

"We don't need her help," Laney mumbled, eyeing the crate Anthony held in his arms.

Ben gazed sadly into her eyes. "Yes, we do. Them britches yer wearin' are gonna come apart 'fore long, and then you'll be nekkid. And this shirt I'm wearin' only gots two buttons."

Folding her scrawny arms across her chest, Laney set her jaw stubbornly. "I don't want 'em if I gotta take a bath."

Tarah's lips twitched. The girl was softening. She looked to Ben, hoping he would keep talking sense into Laney.

A worried frown creased his brow. "Do we *gotta* take a bath to get the new clothes?"

Swallowing hard, Tarah shook her head. "The new things belong to you, Ben. I won't dictate what you have to do in order to have them."

"Good." Laney gave a curt nod. "Reckon that settles things, then."

Tarah's heart sank to her toes.

"Wait, Laney." Ben's hesitant voice made Tarah's dashed hopes rise. "We gotta take a bath."

"What fer? Didn't you hear what Tarah just said? You was right. She ain't like them other folks."

The children continued their discourse as though Anthony and Tarah weren't present. Capturing her bottom lip between her teeth, Tarah caught Anthony's gaze. He winked and gave her a reassuring smile.

"Ain't nobody makin' me take a bath iffen I don't want one," Laney declared hotly, her fiery temper once more blazing.

"It ain't right to smell up them new clothes. 'Sides, we cain't go to Tarah's house like this." Ben glanced at Tarah, then back to Laney. "I know she's nicer than most folks, but that don't mean her ma and pa want us sleepin' in their clean beds."

"Aw, I'd rather sleep in the barn."

Ben grinned and nudged her with his elbow. "Come on. Betcha can't get all that dirt off anyhow."

"Bet I can!"

"It's settled then." Anthony spoke up before another argument ensued. "Ben, come take this crate off my hands. Laney, can you warm water for the baths?"

"Guess I can do that, Preacher."

Ben limped forward and took the crate of clothes, his eyes growing wide at the sight of the wool coats. "Never had a coat that I recollect," he said in awe.

"We got coats in there, too? Lemme see." Suddenly Laney turned to Tarah, her nose scrunching in disgust. "Ya ain't aimin' to try and get me to wear no dress, are ya? 'Cause I ain't wearin' no dress, and ain't no one makin' me do—"

Tarah laughed outright. "Laney Jenkins, do you think I'd try to get you to wear anything you don't want to? There are two fine, sturdy pairs of blue jeans and two warm shirts just your size, I think."

Laney beamed. "Yep, ya sure ain't like them other folks." She followed after Ben, trying to grab at the new things.

"Keep yer dirty hands off my new coat!" Ben hollered.

"Sor–ry. Don't you be puttin' yer hands on my new coat neither, then."

"Anthony," Tarah said, once the children were out of earshot, "can you ride to my house and let Ma and Pa know I'll be along later with guests?"

Anthony scowled. "What if Jenkins comes around while I'm gone?"

"He won't. Besides, I need that soap—and I noticed them both scratching their heads. Better bring some kerosene just in case they have lice."

Anthony grimaced. "You're right."

"Oh, and ask Ma to send along some bread, too. These children probably haven't eaten all day. I want to get something into their stomachs to hold them over until we get them home."

Tenderness flickered in Anthony's eyes. He reached forward and brushed his fingertips along her cheek, sending a shiver up her spine. "I admire what you're doing for these children," he said. "You've become quite a woman, Tarah St. John."

Before she could respond, he mounted Dodger and took off toward the St. John ranch.

The moon hovered full and bright, and a smattering of stars dotted the sky by the time a weary and waterlogged Tarah climbed into the wagon with two very clean, bug-free children.

Laney had sputtered and protested, but Tarah insisted on helping the girl with her bath. They were forced to change the filthy water three times before no more dirt surfaced on her skin.

The child had let out a howl loud enough to put any warring Indian to shame while Tarah poured kerosene through her hair, then soaped the long tresses three times to remove the grime. Once clean, Tarah noticed Laney's hair wasn't brown or dark auburn as she had originally suspected. Laney had beautiful dark blond hair, with just a hint of curl at the ends.

The combing process was long and painful for the girl, who begged Tarah to simply chop it off like Ben's and be done with it. Tarah refused, and once the ordeal ended, she managed to convince Laney that two braids hanging on either side of her head would help keep her hair from matting up again.

Anthony repeated the process with Ben, although he gave the boy more privacy. But he took care of his hair and inspected the dirt removal process just to be certain the lad cleaned himself thoroughly.

The children fidgeted with pent-up anxiety on the ride to the ranch.

"I sure hope yer folks don't mind about you invitin' us to yer house, Tarah," said Laney from the back of the wagon.

"They seem to be looking forward to it," Anthony answered for Tarah.

"Well, they ain't met us yet, Preacher," she shot back.

Tarah turned in the seat and gave the girl a reassuring smile. "I know they'll love you. Don't worry."

"Ain't worried. Just don't stay where I ain't wanted, that's all."

Tarah noticed Anthony's lips twitching and was hard-pressed to bite back her own laugh. Laney was the most stubborn child she had ever met. "I assure you, you are wanted at our home."

Laney let out a snort. "We'll see."

Both children were sound asleep by the time they made it to the ranch. Pa greeted them from his seat on the porch. "I was about to head over to the soddy and make sure everything was all right," he said.

"It took awhile to finish with baths," Tarah replied, glad to be home.

Anthony offered Pa his hand. "You needn't have worried. I wouldn't have let anything happen to her, sir."

Pa grinned. "No, I don't suppose you would. You two had better get those youngsters inside. I'll tie up Anthony's horse and take care of the team."

"Thank you, Pa."

Tarah gently woke Ben while Anthony gathered up Laney and carried her into the house.

Cassidy's face gentled at the sight of the tiny girl snoring lightly in Anthony's arms and Ben limping behind them, a wide, sleepy yawn stretching his thin mouth. She turned to the boy and took his hand. "I'm Tarah's ma, but you can call me Cassidy, unless you're more comfortable with Mrs. St. John. I'm delighted to have you with us."

"Thanks, ma'am. Me an' Laney 'preciate yer kindness."

"Think nothing of it. It's our pleasure. Are you hungry?"

"A mite."

"I have a pot of buffalo stew warming on the stove. You sit at the table there, and I'll be back in a jiffy." She turned to Tarah. "Show Anthony to Emily's bedroom. The covers are already turned down. I put Em in with you in Granny's room for the night."

In the bedroom, Anthony gently deposited Laney onto the bed. Tarah glanced down at the beautiful face bathed in moonlight shining in through the window. "She's lovely, isn't she?"

"Who would have ever thought beneath all that dirt was such a pretty little girl?" Anthony said with a chuckle.

Tarah pulled up the quilt and tucked it securely around Laney's shoulders. The little girl moaned and shifted in her sleep. Anthony and Tarah remained motionless until she lay still and her steady breathing resumed.

Edging toward the door, Tarah motioned for Anthony to follow.

"Got her all settled in?" Cassidy asked when they reached the front room.

Tarah smiled and nodded. "She's sound asleep."

"Good. This fellow will be ready for bed as soon as he's eaten his fill."

Ben beamed at Cassidy. "This is mighty good cookin', ma'am." He reached up as if to swipe his sleeve across his mouth, then stopped, his gaze darting to Tarah. She smiled and inclined her head toward the napkin next to his plate.

"Will you stay and have some supper, Anthony?" Cassidy asked.

"I'd best be getting on home. Ma doesn't know where I am, and I'm sure she'll be worried."

Tarah swallowed her disappointment at his refusal. "I'll walk you out."

"Don't stay out too long, Tarah," Cassidy said. "There's a chill in the air. We don't want you catching cold."

Warmth flooded Tarah's cheeks. Honestly. She didn't need to be treated like a baby right in front of Anthony. But she smiled and nodded, then slipped out the door ahead of him.

"I want to thank you for coming after me today," she said as they stepped into the star-filled night. "I couldn't have managed those children alone."

"My pleasure." Anthony's mouth curved into a smile. "You did a fine job. Although I think I've mentioned that a couple of times today."

"I think so. But I couldn't have done it without you."

Reaching out, he fingered a strand of hair, long since pulled loose from her chignon. "I guess we make a pretty good team."

"Yes," Tarah murmured, lifting her chin a little just in case he wanted to kiss her. "I suppose we do."

Anthony touched her shoulder, then her arm, until finally he took her hand in his. Warmth enveloped her, and a soft, unbidden sigh escaped her lips as Anthony pulled her ever so slightly forward.

A loud cough from the other side of the porch startled them, making Tarah jump. Anthony dropped her hand and took a large step back.

"Guess you two didn't see me sitting here," Pa said with a chuckle.

Tarah's cheeks warmed, and she was glad for the cover of darkness to hide her humiliation.

"No, sir." Anthony's voice cracked like a twelve-year-old boy's.

"Didn't think so. I guess you'll be going now?"

"Yes, sir." Anthony turned to Tarah. "Good night. I'll see you in church on Sunday."

"We're looking forward to it," Pa said, a teasing lilt to his voice.

"Well, good night, then," he said, backing down the steps.

"Night, Anthony," Pa called, a little louder than he needed to, in Tarah's opinion.

A lump of disappointment lodged in her throat as Anthony mounted and rode away. Furious, she turned her gaze to Pa.

"Well, now," he said. "I couldn't have him kissing my little girl right in front of me, could I?"

"Oh, Pa."

"Now there'll be plenty of time for that if he ever says his piece and asks for your hand. And not before. Is that clear?"

"Yes, Pa." Tarah said a curt good night and stomped inside. She'd been sure she was about to get herself kissed. If only Pa hadn't been on the porch, she could have made Anthony forget all about Louisa Thomas!

Chapter 9

Looks like we're not the only ones who thought a fall picnic was a good idea."

Tarah glanced up at the sound of Pa's voice. Dread engulfed her as she recognized the pair seated on a blanket a few yards from the river. She inwardly groaned at the sight.

"Unless my eyes are playing tricks on me," Pa said, thick amusement coloring his words, "I'd say that's Anthony and Louisa up ahead."

"And Josie," Luke piped in, excitement edging his voice. "Hi, Jo!"

From her spot at the riverbank, Josie grinned and waved. Luke hopped from the still-rolling wagon and sprinted to join her, leaving Cassidy to call after him to stay close by.

Tarah felt a low ember of indignation quickly give rise to an inferno of temper as Anthony's beseeching gaze reached out to her. With a jerk of her chin, she averted her gaze, letting him know just what she thought of the situation.

Nearly choked with tears, Tarah felt his betrayal to her toes. After all they had been through just two days ago, she had caught the two-timer having a chummy picnic with Louisa Thomas. And he called himself a preacher!

Seated next to his girl, Camilla, on the wagon flap, Sam gave Tarah an understanding smile. His compassionate gaze searched her face, sending a rush of heat to her cheeks. What did Sam know about unrequited love? He and Camilla had been in love since they were both fifteen years old. And now, seated together with a twin on each lap, they made a picture of domesticity.

Cringing, Tarah realized that Pa's comment a few weeks ago about Sam getting married first might actually come true. She gave Sam what she hoped to be a reassuring smile, then looked away to hide her humiliation.

Anthony rose from the blanket and stepped forward, waving in friendly greeting.

To Tarah's way of thinking, he looked just about as guilty as a dog caught with a Christmas ham.

Obviously thinking the same thing, Pa gave a low chuckle.

"Dell. . . ," Cassidy lightly admonished.

Louisa rose and took her place next to Anthony. Her willowy hand slipped through his arm, and she challenged Tarah with a lift of one delicate eyebrow.

"What's *she* doin' here?" Laney asked, her perky nose wrinkling into a scowl. "That preacher's not too smart. I told him he oughtta send her packing."

Pa laughed outright.

"Dell!" Cassidy turned to the outspoken little girl. "Laney, honey, please don't be rude."

"But that lady ain't nothin' but a—" She broke off the flow of words, apparently thinking better of what she'd been about to say, and ducked her head in submission. "Yes, ma'am."

Resisting the urge to bolt, thus giving Louisa the pleasure of knowing she was upset, Tarah plastered a smile on her face and reined in Abby. She dismounted and tied the horse to the wagon.

"Looks like we're sharing a picnic spot," Pa said, extending a hand to Anthony. "That okay with you?"

"Of course." Anthony accepted the proffered hand and gave a short, dry cough.

"This is just wonderful," Louisa gushed, taking Hope from Sam's arms. Tarah scowled as the little girl went to Louisa without so much as a hint of protest. Her chubby hands grabbed on to a strawberry-blond ringlet. "Pwetty."

The little traitor!

Releasing an annoying giggle, Louisa planted a kiss on the little girl's cheek. "Look," she called to Anthony, who had joined Dell and Sam to help unload the food from the wagon. "She loves me."

"Aw, don't think yer nothin' special," Laney said, reaching up a hand to tickle Hope's belly. "She loves everybody. Don't ya, Hopey Wopey?" Hope laughed outright and threw her body toward Laney. "See?" With a smug grin, Laney took the toddler and headed toward the blanket Cassidy had spread on the ground.

With a great sense of satisfaction, Tarah watched Louisa's cheeks grow red. She silently blessed Laney for putting the bothersome woman in her place. But her guilt got the better of her, and she gave Louisa a genuine hint of a smile. "You three might as well eat with us," she offered, to take away the sting of Laney's rudeness.

"I don't suppose we have a choice," Louisa hissed, "although we'd much rather be alone. It was bad enough we had to bring Anthony's horror of a niece along with us."

A gasp escaped Tarah's lips, and she felt her eyes growing wide. "We certainly didn't interrupt your little outing just to inconvenience you. My family has been coming to this picnic spot twice a year for the last three years. And Anthony doesn't seem at all bothered by our presence."

Louisa's nostrils flared in anger. "Don't think I can't figure out what you're up to."

"I don't know what you mean."

Pursing her lips, Louisa narrowed her eyes. "Come now, don't act innocent with me. We're both women, and we both know what we want. Or rather whom we want. The difference is I already have him. And you never will." She spun on her heel and flounced away to join the others.

Tarah stared after her, fuming and wishing she could refute the other girl's words. Though it grated on her to admit it, Louisa had spoken truthfully. She had staked her claim on Anthony, and it appeared he had no desire to be rescued from her clutches. That was his misfortune, Tarah thought stubbornly. Louisa would make him miserable in the long run, and it served him right for being so ignorant of the ways of women.

"Teacher?"

"What?" she asked in a clipped voice, turning to find Ben standing next to her, looking as if he'd been slapped. "Oh, Ben, I'm sorry. It's not you."

"I heard them things she said to you."

Chafed from the knowledge that this child had witnessed her humiliation, Tarah planted her hands on her hips and frowned. "It's not nice to eavesdrop."

"I wasn't. Just heard it, that's all. Anyways," he murmured, "I wanted to tell ya not to believe what she said. It ain't true."

He started to limp away, but Tarah placed a restraining hand on his arm. "Wait. What do you mean?"

A shrug lifted his bony shoulders. "Preacher ain't gonna ask her to marry him. Near as I can tell, he don't care too much for her."

Tarah's heart soared, then plummeted. What did a fourteen-year-old boy know about love? "Thank you for trying to make me feel better, but you needn't worry. Reverend Greene is perfectly free to court whomever he pleases, and it's immaterial to me."

The look of disbelief covering his face brought a fresh rush of heat to Tarah's cheeks, but she stood her ground. "Anthony and I have known each other for several years," she insisted. "There's nothing but friendship between us."

The boy's gaze darted over her shoulder, and his eyes widened.

"Really, Ben. It's not very polite to look past someone when they're speaking to you."

"Sorry, Teacher."

"Oh, it's all right. I just hope you understand that whatever Louisa said to me doesn't matter, because I'm not interested in Anthony as a beau. You see? He's just a good friend."

Tarah released an impatient sigh as the boy's gaze drifted past her once again. "Honestly, Ben." She twisted to see what he found so interesting.

A knot formed in the pit of her stomach as she realized why Ben had been so antsy. With a sinking feeling, she wondered just how long Anthony had been standing less than five feet behind her.

⌒

Anthony tried to concentrate on his food but found his stomach recoiling at the sight of the meal Louisa had prepared. The talking and laughter from the merry group of picnickers buzzed around him unintelligibly, and he wished for a quick end to the day so he could salvage his wounded pride in private. How could he have been so mistaken about Tarah's feelings for him?

If Dell hadn't interrupted two nights ago, he would have taken Tarah into his arms, and he had the feeling—or had had at the time—that she would have allowed a small kiss before all was said and done. He glanced at her now, observing the fact that she struggled with her appetite just as he did.

As if sensing his eyes studying her, she lifted her head, a question written on her lovely face.

Dear Father in heaven, he prayed, the shock of revelation shooting down his spine, *I'm in love.*

Sorrow, combined with question, filled her eyes. Anthony wanted to look away but found that he couldn't escape the violet depths of her gaze. Surely she knew how he felt. He could shoulder her anger, swallow her disdain, or accept her love, but her pity he could not and would not abide.

Just as he was about to excuse himself from the company, he heard Josie speak up. "Ma says we're going back east as soon as the school term is up. Isn't that right, Uncle Anthony?"

Dragging his gaze from Tarah's, Anthony nodded. "Ma's doing much better. Ella is anxious to get home before the baby arrives, but she wants to let the children finish out the term first."

"Tarah, I imagine you're relieved the school term will be over soon," Louisa piped in. "I hear things haven't gone well."

Tarah flushed and glared at Anthony. Indignation swelled his chest at the accusation in her eyes. Did she really think he had betrayed her confidence about his unruly niece and her brother?

Louisa pressed on before Tarah could answer. "Perhaps the town council will give someone else a chance to teach the children since you apparently aren't enjoying the position." She cast a hopeful sidelong glance at Dell.

"Tarah's the best teacher alive," Laney declared hotly.

"How would you know?" Josie's voice rang with challenge. "You didn't stay at school long enough to sit down, much less see her teach."

Laney's eyes narrowed dangerously, her lips pushing out from her face. "Tarah's a sight better'n *anybody* could be in a million years. And I ain't gotta go to no school to figure that out. And iffen anyone's callin' me a liar, I'll knock 'em flat."

"That won't be necessary, little lightning bolt." Dell cleared his throat and eyed Louisa with a stern glance. "I reckon the job for next term will be Tarah's if she wants to accept it. The council has heard no complaints about her teaching."

Color flooded Louisa's cheeks, and she ducked her head.

"Oh, honestly. I probably won't be here to teach another term anyway." Tarah shot to her feet. "I had planned to discuss this with Ma and Pa privately, but since you all feel so comfortable speaking about my life, I guess I'll just go ahead and tell you."

Dread filled Anthony at her words, and he waited impatiently while she paused to take a breath.

"Tell us what, Tarah?" Cassidy asked, her brow furrowing.

"I received a letter Friday from Mr. Halston—"

"Clyde Halston? From Starling?" Dell asked. "Why would he write to you?"

Anthony wanted to know the same thing. A surge of jealousy shot through him at the thought of another man courting Tarah.

"It seems Starling has come into some funds to build a small school and hire a teacher. And he suggested me."

"But that's nearly twenty miles away!" Cassidy's frown deepened. "I don't think it's such a good idea."

"Darling," Dell said gently, placing a hand on her arm. "Our little girl is old enough to make this decision on her own."

"Now hold on!" Laney hopped to her feet and stood facing Tarah, her features twisted into a scowl. "Ya just cain't get a body to goin' to school and then up and leave 'em. I ain't goin' if *she's* teachin'." She tossed her head toward Louisa without moving her gaze from Tarah.

Tarah's face softened considerably as she stared down at the little ball of fire. "I will finish out my term in Harper." She glanced back up, her eyes shifting between Dell and Cassidy. "They're building the schoolhouse now and would want me to start teaching a winter term. Mr. Halston said the town has the funds to pay a teacher for five months." Tarah glanced around the circle of family and friends, and her voice faltered. "Th–they want me to come right after the new year."

"But, Tarah, you can't go." Emily's lips trembled, her wide green eyes regarding Tarah sorrowfully. "We'd miss you something awful if you left home."

"Oh, honey. I'd miss you, too. But—"

"Well, I think it would be a wonderful opportunity for Tarah," Louisa said brightly.

"Yer just sayin' that 'cuz you wanna steal her job out from under her." The look of disdain on Laney's face could have melted the strongest of men, but Louisa opened her mouth as though ready to take on the tiny creature.

"Laney," Cassidy said before Louisa could voice her retort, "you owe Miss Thomas an apology."

The child stamped her foot and glared at Louisa.

Anthony thought he detected a note of triumph in Louisa's returning gaze. Laney must have detected the same thing, for she jerked her chin and planted her hands firmly on her tiny hips. "Ain't no way I'm gonna 'pologize to her. I stand by what I said, and ain't nobody gonna make me say nothin' else!" With that, she dashed off toward the river, leaving the group around the blanket to stare in disbelief.

"I'll go after her," Tarah offered.

"Well, I certainly hope you give her a good talking to," Louisa said indignantly. "What a spoiled child!"

Anthony shook his head as his anger surged. "Laney is the least spoiled child

I've ever known. It's ridiculous to even say such a thing." Louisa's mouth dropped as Anthony continued. "And I don't believe I'd be remiss in pointing out that she has a wisdom about human nature that many of us lack."

He caught Tarah's wide-eyed gaze. "Would you mind if I go after Laney and have a talk with her?" he asked.

"I—I guess not."

"I'm goin', too." Ben stood beside Anthony. "She can get awfully stubborn."

With a nod, Anthony set off toward the river with Ben close on his heels. He found Laney seated on the bank, tossing stray twigs into the rippling water.

She dashed a tear from her cheek and didn't bother to glance up as Anthony dropped to the ground beside her. Ben took the space on her other side. "I stand by what I said, and I ain't 'pologizin' to that hoity-toit even if she is yer girl. So you can fergit it, Preacher. And you ain't talkin' me into it, Ben. I don't care if Tarah's folks kick us out, neither."

Anthony chuckled. "I didn't come here to try to get you to apologize. You don't need to worry about Tarah's folks kicking you out. And how many times do I have to tell you Louisa's not my girl?"

Laney snorted. "Then yer the only one who don't think so." She tossed a twig into the water. "I even heard that Josie say you'll most likely marry up with her."

"Well, my niece is wrong."

"I wouldn't bet on it if I was you."

Ben kept silent through the exchange. He met Anthony's gaze over Laney's head and held on as though trying to read into the depths of his soul. Anthony looked away from the wizened perusal and released a frustrated sigh. "I didn't come over here to discuss me, anyway."

"Then what'd you want to talk about?"

Suddenly Anthony didn't know. He wanted to reassure her. To gather her in his lap and give her the kind of love a child deserved. Reaching into his heart, he asked the first question that came to mind. "You two haven't been to church much, have you?"

"Ain't never been b'fore today."

"What did you think of the service?"

Laney shrugged. "Don't rightly know. My b'hind got sore sittin' there so long. Ya yelled real good, though. Just like Pa when he's all liquored up."

Anthony felt the heat creep up his neck. He turned toward Ben, suddenly caring what the child thought.

Ben frowned.

With a sinking heart, Anthony gave him a wry smile. "You didn't care for the service either, I take it?"

"Reckon I did," he said quietly.

"You enjoyed the sermon?"

"Cain't rightly say I understood a lot of it. But the part about bein' sinners and how we need God—that part I understood. 'Course, I reckon Laney and me was the only ones in the whole church that didn't already know it."

"What do you mean?"

"You talkin' 'bout that fella that kept talkin' in front of us, Ben?"

Ben nodded.

Anthony waited for someone to elaborate and was just about to suggest it when Laney obliged. "Kept sayin' how there weren't no real sinners in the whole place and how you was spittin' in the wind."

Embarrassment swept over Anthony. Did the whole town believe he was preaching in vain? Didn't Paul say, "All have sinned and come short of the glory of God"? Or was it Peter? Anthony's muddled brain couldn't conjure up a single verse of scripture he could quote with certainty. He raked his fingers through his hair. "I just don't know what to do." Realizing he'd spoken aloud, his gaze darted to the two children. They stared back at him, curiosity on Laney's face, understanding on Ben's. The boy gave a hesitant frown and looked away.

"It's all right, Ben. You can speak your mind."

"Naw."

Curiosity piqued, Anthony felt compelled to hear what the boy had to say. "Go ahead," he urged. "I won't be angry."

Ben took a long breath, then released it with a *whoosh*. "Seems to me," he began earnestly, "that tryin' to tell folks who already go to church that they need God is sorta like tryin' to talk a hound dog into eatin' a rabbit. He already knows a rabbit's good eatin'."

Defenses raised, Anthony stared at Ben. What did this kid know about anything? The strongest lesson Reverend Cahill had taught Anthony was to hammer the salvation message into his congregation. "Many church folks think their lives are just fine," Anthony's mentor had said, "when in reality, they're closer to the gates of hell than they know. As ministers of the gospel, it's our responsibility not to let even the smallest opportunity pass without sharing the truth. And that will more than likely make you unpopular."

Well, it had certainly made Anthony unpopular. His three-month trial period was half over, and he worried he might not have his position extended to a permanent status—despite the fact that he'd visited each of the remaining families this week.

He took comfort from the memory of Reverend Cahill's words. "Always preach the truth, no matter the cost. It's better to lose man's favor than to stand before God and answer why you took the easy road."

With his arms behind him, he leaned on his palms and stared reflectively into the water.

"Sorry, Preacher. I shoulda kept my mouth shut."

"No, Ben," he said. "You pretty much summed up the reason my congregation has been getting smaller and smaller each week. But you have to understand.

Not everyone attends church services for the right reasons. There are many people sitting on benches week after week who don't know the Lord."

"And you figure some of them are sittin' in yer church?"

Anthony shrugged. "I can't see the hearts of men. I only have to preach what I feel God is telling me to preach."

"So yer not mad?"

Anthony smiled. "Not a bit. I think you're a very bright boy with a lot of insight."

Ben flushed with pleasure.

"Anthony?" Louisa's soft voice behind him drew Anthony's attention from his newfound revelation.

"I'm leavin'." Laney shot to her feet and stomped away.

"The boys are planning to play baseball, if you'd like to join them," Louisa offered to Ben as he stood.

"I cain't." He limped away, leaving a red-faced Louisa to stare after him.

"I hoped perhaps we could take a walk while the children are playing," she said, her voice more subdued than Anthony had ever observed.

"Let's sit here for a while instead."

She eyed the ground dubiously, then nodded. "If that's what you prefer." Carefully she lowered herself until she sat beside him. "I know you didn't mean to speak to me the way you did earlier," she said, a hint of her usual cheerfulness returning. "So I've decided to forgive you."

"That's good of you," Anthony drawled. He had intended to apologize for admonishing her in front of the St. Johns, but apparently an apology wasn't necessary.

"Hey, Anthony!"

Anthony turned at the sound of Luke's voice.

"Come play baseball with us. We need a pitcher."

"Oh, Anthony." Louisa's countenance took on a pretty pout. "You're not going to play with the children, are you?"

Relieved at the chance to make a graceful exit, Anthony stood and grinned down at her. "You heard Luke. They need a pitcher."

He heard her huff as he strode toward the players. A niggling of unease swept over him at the thought of the entire town believing they were courting. He wasn't sure how to go about it, but he had to find a way to let Louisa know she had to look elsewhere for a husband. Of course, if she had her heart set on marrying him, as Laney seemed to think she did, he would probably have an easier time trying to convince a rattlesnake not to strike.

Releasing a heavy sigh, Anthony tried to push away his troublesome thoughts. Between Louisa's relentless pursuit, his congregation's lack of response, and Tarah's disinterest, his life wasn't going at all as he had planned.

Chapter 10

After hours spent on his knees bombarding heaven with desperate questions, Anthony still had no answers. Releasing a weary breath, he wiped the tears from his cheeks and stretched out on his bed. He closed his eyes, but sleep eluded him as his mind whirled like a spring twister.

Two weeks had passed since the picnic, and whether Anthony liked it or not, Ben's words weighed heavily on his heart. His nerves were taut with uncertainty.

Conflicting thoughts warred against each other like two great armies on a field of battle. While he didn't want to neglect the salvation message, how could he ignore the spiritual needs of folks who were truly living for God? Should he abandon his firm message of the consequences of sin and begin to teach the fundamentals of godly living as Ben, in his innocence, had suggested?

It would have been so easy to disregard the boy's comments—and he had been prepared to do just that—but last week's message had once again fallen on deaf ears. The apathy on the faces of the few remaining members of his congregation had drained his enthusiasm for his message, and for the first time he doubted his mentor's teachings.

Were these people really hard-hearted and unwilling to hear the Bible preached? If so, why were several families still meeting at the Johnson farm on Sunday mornings to read scripture and sing hymns? Even Tucker, Anthony had heard, was beginning to attend the home group. His congregation was split in half, and Anthony felt the weight of responsibility for the division heavily upon his shoulders.

In preparation for today's sermon, he had prayed and studied the apostles' letters to the churches. Every one of them. But he hadn't received a clear answer. Services would begin in four hours, and he still had nothing to feed his sheep.

Frustrated, he pushed away the heavy quilt covering him and sat up on the edge of his bed. He swiped a hand through his hair and looked up as though the answers might be inscribed on the ceiling.

With his arms bent at the elbows, he held his hands palms up. "What is it, Lord? What am I doing wrong? If I am truly speaking Your message, then why have people stopped attending services?" In the early church, God had added souls daily. Even amid opposition to the apostles' teachings. So why was his church getting smaller and smaller?

With a resigned sigh, he dressed, grabbed his Bible from the table beside his bed, and tiptoed through the house. He snatched an apple from the kitchen table, shoved it into his coat pocket, then quietly exited the house, leaving the morning chores to his brothers.

He entered the schoolhouse in the darkness. After building a fire in the woodstove, he sank onto one of the wooden benches behind a desk. Weary from lack of sleep and spent tears, he leaned his elbows on the desk and stared into the darkness, wondering what he would say to his congregation when they arrived expecting a sermon.

"I guess I could give them an object lesson." He gave a short, bitter laugh. "The children sure loved it." As a matter of fact, his lesson to Tarah's class had garnered the only favorable response he'd received for his preaching since he'd moved back to Harper.

As light from the east filtered in through the window, slowly pushing the inky blackness from the room, so, too, did the fog begin to lift from Anthony's mind.

For the last few weeks, he had been preaching salvation to the saved. Redemption to the already redeemed. The time had come for a new approach.

Concern sifted over Tarah as Anthony walked to the pulpit, the usual spring in his step noticeably absent. Dark smudges appeared under his eyes, and his face was a full shade paler than normal. Clearing his throat, he paused and stared out over the congregation.

When his gaze met hers, he gave her a crooked grin, as though reassuring her. Tarah felt herself flush and quickly averted her gaze.

Though she had been furious with him for taking Louisa Thomas to the picnic, she'd found herself unable to hold a grudge—not after the way he'd defended, then gone after, Laney.

If he preferred Louisa, so be it. Though Tarah's heart couldn't help beating a staccato in his presence, she had resigned herself to his friendship.

"Let's begin with prayer," Anthony said, as he did each Sunday morning.

Tarah held her breath and nearly mouthed the words "Our most gracious heavenly Father" along with him.

"May your words pour like honey on the ears of the listeners today. And may the truth penetrate each heart and mind. In Jesus' name, amen."

Tarah lifted her head and opened her eyes, observing him with the same quiet surprise she was sure was reflected in each face present. Something was different.

Slowly Anthony reached inside his pocket and produced an apple. Then he pulled out a small knife, as well.

Feeling a hand on her arm, Tarah glanced down into Laney's questioning eyes. "How's he gonna preach if he's eatin'?" she whispered. "Yer ma says it ain't polite to talk with yer mouth full."

"It's not polite to talk during service, either," Tarah whispered back, placing a finger to the little girl's lips.

She couldn't imagine what Anthony was thinking, and she wondered if his pale countenance and the dark rings under his eyes were indications of an illness. Twisting around, she caught Dr. Simpson's gaze. He shrugged and sent her a reassuring smile, then glanced back up at Anthony, concern written on his leathery face.

Slowly Anthony sliced through the apple, then held up one half in each hand.

Shuffling noises could be heard throughout the room, and Tarah knew the bewildered congregation wondered if their preacher had suddenly gone daft.

Anthony sent a wry grin around the room. "Bear with me, folks. I'm not crazy yet."

Nervous laughter made its way through the smattering of people present, and Tarah felt some of the tension leave her shoulders.

"Now let me ask an obvious question. What kind of seeds would you say are inside here?"

"What kinda fool question is that?" Mr. Collins asked, earning him a firm elbow in his side from Mrs. Collins.

"It's all right, Mrs. Collins. Don't burn his dinner just to teach him a lesson. I did ask a silly question."

Mrs. Collins blushed as her husband chortled. "Thank you, Preacher," he said. "She just mighta done that."

Again the congregation rumbled with laughter.

A thrill passed over Tarah's heart as she sat watching Anthony speak as though he were passing the day in Tucker's store. For the first time ever, he was reaching his congregation.

"Even the youngest among us," Anthony continued, "understand that inside an apple are apple seeds."

He glanced around the room until his eyes lit on young Sally Hammond. "Sally, when your pa plants his hayseed, what grows?"

The little girl blushed and ducked her head. "Aw, Preacher, you know."

"Answer the man's question," Mr. Hammond said sternly.

"Yes, Pa."

Anthony's features softened. "What grows from hayseeds?"

"Hay," she whispered, her face glowing bright red.

"That's right. Even a child knows that you get what you plant."

He held up the apple once more. "Although you may not know how many apples come from one seed, you can be assured of the kind of fruit it will produce."

Tarah drew a breath and waited for him to come to the point.

"Galatians 6:7 says, 'Be not deceived; God is not mocked: for whatsoever a man soweth, that shall he also reap.'" He swallowed hard and walked around the pulpit to stand directly before the congregation.

"For the past few weeks, I've sown seeds of judgment and criticism to the folks in this town. The fruit I reaped from those seeds were criticism of my preaching and division among the good Christian folks of Harper."

Tarah's eyes moistened as his voice faltered, and she longed to throw her arms around him and reassure him. The silence in the room was deafening as the congregation watched. When he had composed himself, Anthony continued.

"There are only a few weeks left in my trial period. Lord willing, I will preach a series of messages on living a godly life." He swallowed hard. "To those of you who have come each week despite my shortcomings, I thank you for your support and prayers. And I'll do my best to make amends to the folks who felt they had to leave."

The sounds of sniffling filled the room as ladies placed handkerchiefs to their noses and men cleared their throats.

The sight of Anthony standing so vulnerable and open before his congregation tore at Tarah's heart.

"I know it's a mite early, but this is all the Lord placed on my heart to share."

Tarah smiled through tears as he said a short closing prayer and moved down the aisle toward the doorway. She hung back, waiting for her chance to shake his hand.

Her pulse quickened at Anthony's bright smile as she approached.

"You did well," she murmured. He reached out and took her proffered hand, enveloping her with his warmth.

"Thank you, Tarah." His gaze penetrated her, snatching her breath away. "I was wondering—"

Tarah stumbled forward as a flash of blue taffeta and lace brushed past. Louisa claimed her place next to Anthony and clutched his arm possessively. "Oh, Anthony. You were simply wonderful."

Tarah resisted the urge to stomp her foot. Why did Louisa always have to show up and ruin everything?

"Thank you, Louisa," Anthony said, keeping his gaze fixed on Tarah.

Louisa followed his gaze, eyes narrowing dangerously. "Wasn't that just the most clever illustration you've ever seen, Tarah?"

"It was very inspired," she murmured, unable to break Anthony's hold on her.

Louisa's voice continued as though nothing were amiss. She tapped his arm with her closed fan. "I don't know what you meant by apologizing, though. You've always done a wonderful job. I think folks just don't appreciate you."

Anthony cleared his throat and turned his attention to Louisa, a look of faint amusement covering his face.

"If you'll excuse me," Tarah said.

"Wait." Anthony reached forward and placed a restraining hand on her arm.

"Oh, Anthony. Don't be rude," Louisa said, tightening her grip on his arm. "Tarah needs to join her family. See, they're all waiting in the wagon."

Anthony released his hold on Tarah's arm. "I guess it can wait," he mumbled.

Louisa gave a bright laugh that Tarah didn't quite believe. "Besides, I have our picnic all packed and ready to go."

A frown furrowed Anthony's brow as he turned back to Louisa. "Picnic?"

"Why, of course. We were interrupted last time." She glanced pointedly at Tarah. "And last week it was raining."

"Don't let me keep you from your picnic." Tarah sent Anthony and Louisa as bright a smile as she could muster and hoped they didn't notice the tremble of her lips. "Good day."

Without waiting for a response, she hurried to the wagon.

Tarah jammed the needle through the cloth and made yet another crooked stitch in the banner draped in a circle across four laps. Why she had to participate in making the decorations for the end-of-school dance just because she was the teacher, she'd never know. Sewing had always been somewhat of a mystery to her, despite Cassidy's attempts to help her learn.

Listening to Louisa prattle on about how excited she was that Anthony would be escorting her to the silly dance grated on Tarah's nerves like the sound of a squeaky wagon wheel. And the nods of approval from the two matrons present sent Tarah into a tizzy of emotions. She figured she must be the only person in Harper Township except Laney who could see right through Louisa's manipulations. To Tarah's way of thinking, there was nothing worse than knowing what a mistake Anthony was about to make and being unable to stop him without sounding like a jealous schoolgirl.

"Don't you think so, Tarah?"

Tarah started, jamming the needle painfully into her finger. She jerked her hand away, pulling the banner with her. As it billowed to the floor, she felt the disapproval from Louisa's mother. Heat crept to her cheeks, and she quickly snatched up her end of the material. "Sorry," she mumbled. "I—I pricked my finger."

"Well, whatever you do, don't get blood on the material," Louisa squealed. "It'll be ruined."

"Oh, honestly. It isn't bleeding that badly." Tarah hastened to assure the women, whose worried frowns revealed they weren't happy with the threat of being forced to remake the almost-finished banner. She grabbed her handkerchief from the reticule at her feet and wiped away the dot of blood on the tip of her finger, then resumed her sewing.

"Back to what I was saying," Louisa said, as though Tarah's finger weren't throbbing. "Don't you think so, Tarah?"

Oh, don't I think what? Tarah thought tersely.

She would have asked Louisa to repeat the question, but from the way the women stared at her, obviously awaiting her response, she couldn't bring herself to admit her mind had been a million miles away.

She cleared her throat and slid her tongue over her lips. "Yes, I suppose so," she murmured, returning her gaze to her crooked stitches.

"You see, I told you if anyone would know, it would be Tarah. Her pa being on the town council and all." The triumph in Louisa's voice caused Tarah's stomach to do a flip-flop.

What on earth had she just confirmed?

"Do you really think so, Tarah?" asked Louisa's ma. "It would be wonderful if Anthony were kept on as preacher after his trial is over. He's been preaching so beautifully the past few weeks. And now that everyone has started coming to services again, I'd be mighty surprised if the town council didn't approve him as the permanent preacher."

"Oh." How did they expect her to know whether Anthony was to be kept on or not? "It certainly would be wonderful. But I suppose we'll have to wait and see with everyone else."

"But I thought you just said he would be," Louisa challenged, her green eyes narrowing. "Really, Tarah, if you didn't know, you should have just said so."

"I–I'm sorry, I didn't mean to suggest I knew for sure."

"Of course you didn't," Hannah Simpson, the doctor's wife, said soothingly. "Tarah was speculating just like the rest of us."

Tarah could have kissed the woman. She glanced up to give her a grateful smile and caught her breath at the look of sympathy in Hannah's eyes.

"Well," Louisa said haughtily. "One would certainly think the daughter of the most prominent member of the town council would know *something*. I certainly would if my father had ever been elected to the council."

Maybe your father would have been voted to the town council if he hadn't foreclosed on half of the farms in the township in the last four years. Tarah knew it was a sore topic for Louisa that her pa wasn't directly involved in the town business. But the banker was ruthless, she had heard her pa comment. Never once had he extended mercy. If a person was late on a payment, the bank took the land—lock, stock, and barrel.

Thankfully Pa had made a success of the St. John ranch before the area was heavily settled. He didn't have to rely on good crops to make ends meet, and as long as the cattle and horses did well at auction, the ranch thrived.

"My pa doesn't share town business with me, Louisa. And I wouldn't ask him to."

Louisa sniffed and resumed her delicate stitching. "Still, I'd find a way to make sure Anthony was kept on. But I guess that's because he and I. . ." A delicate blush appeared on her cheeks as she slid her gaze to Tarah's. "Well, I suppose I shouldn't say anything yet. Anthony wants to wait until he knows for sure he has a way to support us."

"Why, Louisa." Mrs. Thomas stopped sewing and stared with delight at her daughter. "Why haven't you told me?"

"W–well," Louisa's voice faltered, and she glanced from Tarah to her mother. "We haven't made any firm plans yet."

Tarah felt the high collar of her gown choking her. Her throat went suddenly dry, her palms grew damp, and she was almost sure she felt a faint coming on. She stared dumbly at Louisa as her mother wrapped her arms around her and squealed gleefully.

"My baby, finally getting married. We'll have to order a copy of the latest *Godey's Lady's Book* to see what is in fashion for wedding gowns. And of course we must order the finest silk and lace from Paris." Her eyes widened with inspiration. "Your brother Caleb will be coming home from the university in a couple of weeks. Wouldn't it be wonderful if he stood up next to Anthony at the wedding?"

"Well, I don't know, Mother," Louisa mumbled. "Anthony has brothers he might prefer."

Mrs. Thomas waved away Louisa's comment. "And, oh, Tarah," she babbled on, as though Tarah's heart weren't nearly breaking in two, "do you think Cassidy would be available to make the gown? She did such a fine job on Louisa's ball gown last year."

Choking back the tears, Tarah spoke around a lump in her throat. "Why, I don't know. Pa doesn't want her taking on too much with the new baby coming."

"Oh, well, we don't need to speak about such an indelicate topic, dear," Mrs. Thomas reproved. "I'm sure Cassidy would be appalled by your manners."

Mrs. Simpson chuckled. "Around a doctor's home, childbirth is hardly an indelicate subject."

Thankfully Mrs. Simpson had volunteered to head up the decorating committee.

Mrs. Thomas's lips thinned into a tight smile. "I never have quite gotten used to the crudities of life out here. In Charleston, we would never consider speaking of such things in the parlor."

"I do apologize, Mrs. Thomas," Tarah said. "I don't know what I was thinking to bring up such a subject."

Mollified, the older woman nodded and gave a delicate wave of her hand. "Oh well. I suppose I should expect such manners from a young lady raised in these parts," she said charitably. "We can hardly fault you for your manners."

Tarah's temper flared. She opened her mouth to speak, but Mrs. Simpson spoke up first. "How about some coffee and apple pie, ladies? I think we're about finished for today. One more session, and the banner will be completed." She laid the banner aside with care and turned to Tarah. "Will you help me bring in the refreshments, Tarah, dear?"

Grateful for the opportunity to escape, Tarah lifted the banner from her lap and fairly bolted from the room.

Once inside the kitchen, Mrs. Simpson took hold of Tarah's arms and fixed her with a firm gaze.

"Now you listen to me, Tarah St. John. Don't let them make you feel like you're less than they are. You hear?"

Hot tears sprang to Tarah's eyes. Unable to utter a word, she nodded.

"You come from the finest family I know, or I wouldn't be allowing my Camilla to marry your brother, now, would I?"

"M—marry?" Tarah croaked.

Mrs. Simpson's eyes grew wide, and she released Tarah's arms. "You mean you don't know?"

"Know what?" *Could this day bring any more bad news?* Surely Mrs. Simpson was speaking of the future when Sam and Camilla would inevitably become betrothed.

"Oh, honey. I can't believe they haven't told you yet. Your ma and pa gave their blessing a week ago."

"B—blessing?" she croaked. Panic welled up in Tarah, and dread knotted her stomach, making her suddenly ill. "Do you mean Sam and Camilla are. . . ?"

A worried frown creased Mrs. Simpson's brow. "It never occurred to me you didn't know. I can't imagine why. . ." She studied Tarah's face for a moment, then nodded. "You're in love with Anthony, aren't you?" Compassion filled her eyes. "I thought I saw it while we were sitting in there, but I wasn't sure."

Unable to deny the statement, Tarah sank into a kitchen chair and rested her chin glumly in her palm. "I guess my family didn't want to hurt me with the news my younger brother is getting married. Especially when the man I love is marrying someone else."

Mrs. Simpson snorted. "I wouldn't be too sure of that."

Tarah's gaze darted to the older woman. "What do you mean?"

"Well." She glanced toward the kitchen door and dropped her voice a notch. "I'm not one to gossip, but did you notice how quiet Louisa got when her ma started talking about ordering silk from Paris?"

Now that she mentioned it, Louisa had seemed a mite nervous.

"You see? You noticed it, too." Mrs. Simpson gave a quick nod and collected four plates, four cups, and a tray from the cabinet. She allowed Tarah to digest the hopeful news while she cut four generous slices of apple pie. "I'd bet my right arm Louisa was just trying to get under your skin and got herself dug into a hole instead." She gave a quick laugh. "I'd love to see her try to scratch her way out."

Tarah shrugged. "It doesn't matter. Eventually he'll ask her. And if I know Louisa, she'll make it happen pretty quickly now that her ma thinks she's already snagged him."

"If that day ever comes, I'll be the most surprised woman in Harper," Mrs. Simpson retorted. "I've watched him, and I'll tell you, our young preacher's in love. But not with Louisa."

Tarah groaned inwardly. Bad enough to lose him to Louisa, but at least she could console herself that he was being fooled. What other woman could possibly have won his affections without Tarah's notice?

"You really don't see it, do you, honey?"

"See what, Mrs. Simpson?"

"Unless I miss my guess—and I rarely do—our preacher is head over heels in love with a certain Miss St. John."

"Oh, Mrs. Simpson, you don't have to say that. Anthony and I have become friends. But he's smitten with Louisa."

Lifting the tray, Mrs. Simpson sent Tarah a confident smile. "Mark my words. Anthony may not know it yet, but you're the woman for him. You just have to make him see it."

Tarah lifted her chin, remembering the humiliating experience of Anthony's amusement the one time she had attempted to flirt. "I won't resort to manipulating him like. . .well, like some people would. If Anthony can't see the truth, then that's his own misfortune."

Mrs. Simpson chuckled and walked to the door, then turned back to Tarah. "Anthony knows you're not like Louisa. But do you have to be as bristly as a cat getting ready to pounce all the time?" she whispered. "He's probably scared to death you'll scratch his eyes out if he ever speaks his mind." She opened the door before Tarah could reply.

"Now who's ready for some of my famous apple pie?"

Chapter 11

Anthony drove the last nail into place, then tested the shutter to see if it would swing properly.

"Ya did it, Preacher," Laney said, nodding in grudging approval. "Reckon Mr. Garner's gonna be mighty glad we come out here to fix up the mess my pa made of the place."

"Reckon so," Anthony replied. He knew Laney still thought he was courting Louisa, and it gave him no pleasure that he was unable to convince her otherwise. Even more embarrassing was the fact that this little urchin had doubts about his intelligence because of that belief.

"Me an' Ben finished puttin' all the junk in a pile. Can I light it on fire?"

"I think I'd better do that," Anthony said. "But you can pour the kerosene over the pile."

She brightened at the idea. "Can I do it now?"

"Yes, but don't try to light it."

Flashing a quick grin, Laney took off across the yard.

Anthony glanced through the open shutter at Tarah, who labored to clean up the filthy soddy. "How's it going in there?"

She looked up, a weary smile on her lips. "I should be finished sometime around Christmas, I figure."

"We're just about finished with the outside," he replied, chuckling at her remark. "Then we'll all come inside and pitch in."

"I'd welcome your help." Tarah planted her hands on her hips and scowled. "Honestly, Anthony. How can a man allow his home to become so filthy? I wouldn't let my favorite pig live in this place."

"Jenkins must have been mighty miserable. I pray he finds the Lord, wherever he ends up."

The scowl left Tarah's face, and she drew in a deep breath. "I suppose you're right. I've been awfully hard on him. I just can't seem to help myself. When I think of the treasure he possessed in those precious children, only to throw them away as if they meant nothing, it just makes me want to scream." She waved to emphasize her words, and her hand knocked against the kettle warming on the stove. A look of pain flickered across her face. Instantly Anthony sprang from his place at the window and ran into the soddy.

"Are you okay?" he asked.

She held on to her wrist and blew on an angry red mark already beginning to blister on the back of her hand. "I'm all right. This is my own fault for being so angry I wasn't paying attention to what I was doing."

"Here," Anthony said, "let me see it."

Offering her hand with the trust of a child, Tarah drew in her bottom lip.

"This is a pretty bad burn," Anthony observed, inwardly berating himself for distracting her in the first place. "We'd better get you home so you can tend to it."

"Honestly, it's just a silly little burn. I want to finish up here."

"No," he said firmly. "I'm taking you home right now. The cleaning will keep until another day."

Tarah's eyes grew stormy, and she narrowed her gaze. "What do you mean, no? If I want to stay and finish cleaning, I will."

In spite of himself, Anthony laughed outright. "Now you sound just like our little Laney. Who's teaching whom?"

A pretty blush rose to her cheeks, sending a rush of warmth to Anthony's heart. He loved this woman so much it hurt. But the knowledge that he rated only friendship in her heart made his stomach clench so tightly at times, he could barely stand the ache.

"Really, Anthony, it's nothing to be concerned about."

"It is something to be concerned about. You can't work in this filth with a blister on your hand. It could become infected."

Glaring at him, Tarah finally sighed in concession. "Oh, all right, but I think you're making a lot of noise over nothing."

"It isn't nothing to me, Tarah," he said. "I just don't want to see you sick."

All the thunder left her face as she met his gaze.

Still holding her hand, Anthony stepped closer. He brushed at a smudge on her cheek, marveling at the softness of her skin. "Tarah," he whispered, darting a glance to her slightly parted lips. Anthony's insides quivered as he drew her close. He longed to kiss away any thoughts of mere friendship from her mind and show her it was she, not Louisa Thomas, who held his heart. And heaven help him, he was getting ready to do just that.

"Just kiss her, would ya? Ya know ya want to."

Tarah gasped at the sound of Laney's voice and quickly moved away. "No one was going to kiss anyone. I—I just hurt my hand, and Anthony was looking at it for me, Laney."

"That ain't the way it looked from where I'm standin'," Laney said with a snort. "So are we gonna light up that pile of junk out there, or ain't we, Preacher?"

"Like Tarah said, she hurt herself. We're going to take her home first. Then we'll come back and light the fire."

"Ya really hurt yerself?" Laney frowned and strode to Tarah's side. "Think we oughtta take her to the doc, Preacher?"

A tender smile curved Tarah's lips as she looked at Laney. "I'll be all right, honey. I just need to put some butter on it for the pain. Reverend Greene is afraid I might get it dirty, and that could make me sick."

Laney turned on Anthony. "What're ya doin' just standin' there? We gotta get Tarah home 'fore she gets sick." She hurried out the door. "Ben," she bellowed. "We're leavin'. Hurry up."

Shaking her head, Tarah gathered up her reticule. "I suppose I should be glad I have so many people to worry about me."

"People who love you," Anthony corrected.

Eyes wide, Tarah stared silently at him until he felt himself blush beneath her questioning gaze.

He cleared his throat, ready to declare his love and take his chances.

"What are ya waitin' fer?" Laney stuck her head through the doorway, a scowl marring her features. "Do ya want Tarah to get sick?"

Sighing in frustration, Anthony took Tarah by the elbow and steered her toward the door. "If we don't get out to the wagon, that child is likely to try to carry you out there herself."

During the drive to the St. John ranch, Anthony watched for signs that Tarah had been moved as much as he during their closeness at the soddy. Disappointment crept through his gut as she talked and laughed with the children, looking as though the almost-kiss had never happened.

In view of her apparent lack of emotion, Anthony felt relief that he hadn't put his heart into her hands by telling her he loved her.

Help me to accept this, Lord.

If friendship was all this amazing woman had to offer, he would accept it, no matter how much it hurt. Her friendship was better than nothing at all.

⌐

As the days grew shorter and the time grew closer for the school term to end, Tarah was filled with uncertainty. She had to give Mr. Halston an answer before Christmas so Starling's town council would have time to secure another teacher should Tarah decide not to accept the position. The school term was to begin in February, he informed her, and the schoolhouse now sat completed at the edge of the small town.

As the chilly autumn air gave way to a mid-November freeze, Tarah still hadn't made a decision.

Glancing out at her empty schoolroom, Tarah allowed her mind to imagine what it would be like to move away from home for a few months and teach a new group of students. Excitement warred with uncertainty, feelings all too common in the past few weeks.

Try as she might, she couldn't bring herself to heed Mrs. Simpson's advice and allow Anthony to see how deeply she cared for him. Fear wrapped around her heart each time she considered the possibility. It was just no use. Besides, the only time she saw him anymore was after service on Sunday, and Louisa always claimed her place by his side, clinging to his arm with either a picnic lunch packed for the two of them or an invitation to her parents' house for dinner. Tarah held her breath each Sunday morning, praying Anthony wouldn't announce their betrothal from the pulpit. So far, he hadn't. But Tarah feared the day was fast approaching.

With a sigh, Tarah stood and began to tidy her small desk. Only two weeks remained in the school term. She had hoped by now that Anthony would have come to his senses like Mrs. Simpson believed he would. In her favorite daydream, she always penned a letter to Mr. Halston, thanking him for his patience but informing him she was to be married soon, so teaching in Starling was out of the question. So far, her dreams were only that: dreams. The wretched reality was that Anthony still seemed mesmerized by Louisa Thomas.

Gloomily Tarah gathered her belongings and headed down the aisle, just as Ben and Laney burst through the door. Pale and visibly shaken, their breath came in short, quick bursts.

A knot formed in Tarah's stomach at the fear widening each pair of eyes. "What is it?"

"W—we just seen Pa comin' out of Tucker's," Ben said.

Tarah gripped his shoulders and hurriedly scanned his face. "Ben, are you sure?"

"It were him, all right," Laney said, her lower lip trembling. "I ain't goin' back, and ain't nobody makin' me do it."

Ben limped to the window and peeked out. "Tarah, he's headin' over here. He musta seen us." Ben's voice shook with fear as he turned from the window. "We gonna have to go back?"

"I don't know, Ben." Helpless fury engulfed her at the thought of that man waltzing into town after weeks of abandonment and expecting to take the children back.

Over the past few weeks, Laney and Ben had lost the haunted expressions in their eyes. Now the hopelessness had returned.

"Well, you ain't just gonna let 'im take us back, are you, Tarah?" Laney's voice reflected her challenge, but her eyes held pleading.

Tarah lifted her chin, determination rising inside of her. "I'm going to do everything I can to keep him from it. You two go to the front of the room and stay by my desk while I speak with your pa."

Squaring her shoulders, Tarah moved toward the door, preparing for confrontation, praying for wisdom.

"Be careful, Tarah," Ben warned. "He can get downright mean if he's been drinkin'."

"Don't worry about me. I'll be fine." Tarah spoke with more confidence than she felt. Her insides quivered at the thought of confronting the man who had forced his children to live in squalor, practically starved them because of his laziness, and then abandoned them to the care of others. He was not worthy of his children, and she wouldn't let them go without a fight.

Oh, how she prayed God would make him see reason.

She drew a steadying breath, gathering her courage as the door swung open and Mr. Jenkins appeared at the threshold. He stared at her through narrow black eyes. "I heared you got my young'uns."

"Th—they've been staying at the ranch during your absence, yes."

"Well, I come fer 'em."

"I—I wanted to discuss that with you, Mr. Jenkins." Tarah motioned to a nearby desk. "Would you care to sit?"

"No, girlie, I don't wanna sit. I want my young'uns."

"But they've been so happy with us. They've even come to school and made friends." She looked into his unrelenting eyes and nearly sobbed. "Please let them stay."

He leaned toward her, his lips twisting into a sneer. Instinctively Tarah stepped back, despising her cowardice.

"So ya don' think I'm a fittin' pa, eh?"

"I didn't say that, Mr. Jenkins. But I—I know how much trouble you've had caring for them."

At the angry flush appearing in his cheeks, Tarah wished she could snatch the words back. The first unwritten rule in trying to get a man to see reason was to never wound his pride. And she had done just that.

"I'm sorry," she murmured. "I didn't mean to imply—"

"Where are they?" he demanded.

Couldn't the man see past the end of his nose? With a frown, Tarah turned toward the desk. A wave of relief swept over her. Laney and Ben were nowhere to be seen. "Wh—why, I don't know where they are," Tarah replied truthfully, though she had a feeling the pair was hiding under her desk.

"Well, I ain't a-gonna try and find 'em." He squinted his beady eyes and wagged a filthy finger inches from Tarah's nose. "Ya make sure them kids git their no-good hides to the soddy b'fore dark, or I'll be a-goin' to the sheriff."

He shuffled toward the door and slammed it shut behind him.

Weak with relief that the man was too lazy to look in the most logical hiding place available to the children, Tarah sank down in the nearest desk and glanced toward the front of the room. "You can come out now. He's gone."

The cloth covering her desk moved, and Laney and Ben crawled out.

Laney hopped to her feet and ran down the aisle. She hurled herself into Tarah's arms. "Don't let 'im take us back, Tarah. I promise I'll do chores w'thout complainin', and I won't trip Luke no more just 'cause he's walkin' by; and next time I pitch the baseball at recess, I won't throw it at that Josie Raney on purpose and try and hit her. A—and I can even say them words to Jesus, like Preacher wants me to." She gathered in a deep, shuddering breath. "I'd do anythin' to stay with ya."

Hot tears burned Tarah's eyes. She blinked them back and swallowed hard, holding Laney at arm's length. The tear-streaked face stared back at her with more vulnerability than Tarah had ever seen in the child.

"Let's go home and talk to my pa," she said when she recovered her voice. "If anyone can change your pa's mind, it'll be my pa."

"Do you really think he might wanna keep us, Tarah?" Ben's face lit with hope. "It's awfully crowded at yer place."

Tarah's lips curved into a soft smile. "Of course he'll want to keep you. You're part of the family now. Aren't you?"

"We are?" The expression on Laney's face mirrored her brother's. A mixture of disbelief and hope.

Gathering the child back into an embrace, Tarah brushed a gentle kiss on her head. "Of course you are."

"I—I love ya, Tarah."

"I love you, too, Laney." She glanced up at Ben over the little girl's head. "And you, too, Ben."

The boy's face glowed, and he looked away quickly, dashing a tear from his cheek.

Laney stepped out of Tarah's arms, a frown creasing her brow. "Aw, he ain't gonna give us up. Folks only give 'im charity 'cause of Ben and me."

Ben's face clouded over at his sister's words. "Laney's right. He ain't never gonna give us up. We'd better just git on home."

"But let's at least give it a try. Maybe my pa can convince him."

Shaking his head, Ben steered Laney toward the door. "It ain't no use." He stopped before stepping outside and turned back to Tarah. "Ya been awful good to Laney and me," he said. "Nicer than anyone I can ever r'member, 'ceptin' our ma—but Laney don't r'member her."

Tears flowed down Tarah's cheeks at the hopelessness reflected in each face. "Can't you just wait? I'm sure my pa—"

"I figure it ain't right to ask yer pa to do that. 'Sides, don't that Bible say, 'Children, obey your parents, fer *this* is right'?"

"Well, yes, but, Ben—"

"Then this is the right thing fer us to do. It's better iffen we just head on home. And, Tarah, I'm askin' ya to promise me ya won't ask yer pa to come to the soddy."

"But—" Tarah stopped at Ben's pleading glance. She nodded. "I promise."

With his arm still firmly about Laney's shoulders, Ben steered her out the door and limped away. Tarah watched as the two bravely headed through the freshly fallen snow in the direction of the soddy. When they were out of sight, she pressed her hands to her face and wept.

～

The sound of thundering hooves accompanied the *thud* of Anthony's ax as he brought it down hard, splitting a log in two.

He straightened up and swiped an arm across his sweaty brow, glancing toward the cloud of dust headed in his direction. Recognizing Tarah, he dropped the ax and ran toward her, his heart hammering against his chest.

Abby skidded to a halt a mere foot from him. One glance at Tarah's tear-streaked face confirmed something was horribly wrong.

She slid into his outstretched arms and clung to him, babbling nonsensical words that were muffled by his shoulder. Heart in his throat, Anthony held her, stroking her hair while she sobbed. When the tears were spent, she pulled away until he held her at arm's length.

"What is it?" he asked and fished a handkerchief—which he'd started carrying after the first time she'd wept in his arms—from his shirt pocket. He pressed the cloth into her hands.

"Thank you," she said, lips trembling.

Anthony gathered her close to his side with one arm about her shoulders and steered her toward the house. When they reached the porch, he motioned for her to sit. She sank onto the step and twisted the handkerchief in her hands until her knuckles grew white.

Dropping next to her, Anthony waited while she drew a ragged breath, then spoke, her voice thick with tears. "Mr. Jenkins came back and took Ben and Laney away."

Dread engulfed Anthony. "When?"

"Just after school today."

"I thought we'd seen the last of Jenkins."

"So did I," Tarah replied glumly. She turned to him, her violet-colored eyes wide with fright. "What if he takes them away where we can't look out for them?"

"If the man has any sense at all, he won't go anywhere with winter setting in." Anthony wasn't at all sure Jenkins had a lick of sense, but it was the least he could say to try to relieve Tarah's fears. By the dubious expression on her face, Anthony knew she was thinking the same thing.

"That's not too reassuring, Anthony," she said.

"I know."

With a groan, she pressed her cheek against his shoulder. "What are we going to do?"

Anthony felt his senses reeling at the lavender scent of her hair and the sweet warmth of her cheek through his shirt. He drew a breath and exhaled slowly, willing the moment to last forever. "Have you spoken with your pa yet?" he asked, his voice a hoarse whisper.

He felt her shake her head. "Ben made me promise not to. I came straight here from school."

"Why would Ben make you promise such a thing?" Anthony asked, his heart soaring at the knowledge she had come to him for help.

A shrug lifted her slim shoulders. "He doesn't feel right putting Pa in that position. A–and he quoted the verse about children obeying their parents." She raised her head and captured his gaze. "Honestly, Anthony. Sometimes I think Ben is the oldest person I know."

"I know exactly what you mean. That boy is special. I wouldn't doubt it if he becomes a preacher someday." He slapped his thigh in a moment of decision. "I'm going to go talk to Jenkins."

"Oh, Anthony." Tarah smiled through her tears. "I hoped you would."

He regarded her warmly. "All you had to do was ask. I told you once before I'd do anything for you."

Twin pink spots appeared on her cheeks, and she pulled away, ducking her head. "You're a true friend. But this isn't for me." She stood and met his gaze, determination sparking in her eyes. "We have to do this for Ben and Laney."

Anthony shot to his feet. "What do you mean 'we'?"

"I'm going with you, obviously."

"I don't think so, Tarah. No telling how Jenkins might react."

Planting her hands firmly on her hips, Tarah sized him up, ready for a fight. "If you're going, so am I, Anthony Greene. Those children are as dear to me as my own flesh and blood. If I had a husband, I'd adopt them as my own, so don't you dare try to stop me."

"I'll marry you," he drawled. He searched her face, trying to gauge her reaction. "Then we can adopt them together."

Tarah scowled. "Very amusing, but I'm sure Louisa Thomas would have plenty to say about that."

Anthony was about to set her straight about his lack of romantic feelings toward Louisa, but she gave him no chance to speak.

"And don't think you'll marry her and adopt them if their pa agrees to let them go. Laney doesn't care too much for Louisa. I doubt she would want to live with her."

"And no one's making her do anything she doesn't want to do." Anthony chuckled to hide the sting as the truth of Tarah's feelings rammed into his gut once again.

A smile lifted the edges of Tarah's lips. "She's so special. Ben, too." A look of urgency filled her eyes. "Let's get going, Anthony. I don't want them to have to spend one night under the same roof as that wretched man."

Anthony followed as she headed toward the barn, obviously intent on getting Dodger saddled.

"I'm still not crazy about their lack of respect for their pa," he said. "Even if he is a no-account."

Tarah sniffed and glanced back over her shoulder. "I think they showed a great amount of respect by going back to him. I wanted them to hide out at the ranch while Pa tried to talk Jenkins into letting them go."

Anthony grinned and shook his head. "The man who marries you will have his hands full. I'll pray for him."

Tarah threw him a cheeky grin. "And you proposed just five minutes ago. Bet you're glad I didn't take you seriously."

But I was serious. I'd marry you tomorrow if you'd have me. The words were on the tip of his tongue, but he bit them back just in time. Why humiliate himself any more than necessary? Besides, they had other things to attend to at the moment. *If it's Your will those children leave their pa, please give me the wisdom to know what to say.*

Chapter 12

Tarah's thoughts whirled with what-ifs as she and Anthony rode to the Jenkinses' in relative silence. What if Anthony had been serious and really wanted to marry her? What if Laney and Ben could be their very own children? Then a bleak thought entered her mind. What if Mr. Jenkins refused to let the children go?

Tarah stiffened as they approached the soddy. The door was already off its hinges, another tattered blanket hanging from the doorframe. Several bottles littered the yard. Tarah stared in disbelief and disgust. And the man had only been back for one day!

They reined in their horses and dismounted as Mr. Jenkins stepped through the doorway, his fingers wrapped firmly around a half-empty bottle.

Laney darted around her pa. A cautious smile lit her face. "Howdy, Tarah, Preacher."

Roughly grabbing her skinny arm, Jenkins pulled her back toward the door. "Git inside, gal," he said. Lifting a booted foot, he kicked her backside, then stumbled against the outside wall.

"That does it, Anthony," Tarah hissed. "If he refuses to let me have Laney and Ben, we'll wait until he passes out drunk, then steal them away."

Anthony reached out and lightly pressed Tarah's shoulder. "Let me do the talking, all right?"

"All right, but if he doesn't listen, we're doing it my way. I couldn't live with myself if I left those children in that horrid man's clutches."

Anthony gathered in a deep breath and plastered a smile on his handsome face. "Afternoon, Jenkins. When did you get back in town? We've been wondering about you."

Tarah gaped. Why was Anthony bothering with small talk? *Get to the point*, she inwardly urged.

Mr. Jenkins snorted. "Been expectin' company. 'Course, I figgered it'd be her pa," he said, waving the bottle in Tarah's direction. "Yer wastin' yer time, Preacher. Them's my young'uns, and I don' aim to be givin' 'em away."

Tarah couldn't hold back. She shook off Anthony's restraining embrace and stepped forward. "Please, Mr. Jenkins. This is no life for Laney and Ben."

Tipping the bottle, Jenkins took a swig, then wiped his mouth with his sleeve. His lips twisted into a cruel sneer. "Yer kind," he spat. "All the time thinkin' yer so much better'n me. Always thinkin' I don' do right by my young'uns." His bold, dark gaze raked over her, and Tarah felt the urge to duck behind Anthony.

As if feeling her discomfort, Anthony drew her close to his side.

"You and folks jus' like ya, all the time comin' around in yer fancy clothes an' holier-'n-thou attitudes. Well, Teacher Lady, I don' need the likes a you a-tellin' me how to live."

Tarah's temper flared, and she stepped away from Anthony once again. She planted her feet to give herself courage and drew herself up as tall as she could. "Frankly, Mr. Jenkins," she said, meeting his steely gaze head-on, "it's immaterial to me how you live your life. You can drink yourself into a roaring drunk and stay there if you wish. But I love Laney and Ben a great deal. And if you care anything at all for them, you'll let me have them."

"I don' give nothin' away for free, girlie." He cocked his eyebrow. "Iffen you catch my meanin'."

Tarah gasped, and her mouth dropped. The scoundrel was offering to sell his own children! Disbelief quickly became revulsion at the very thought. Then elation set in. She mentally calculated the money she had saved from her two months of teaching. She still had most of it. Almost fifty dollars.

"And just how much do children go for these days, Mr. Jenkins?"

"Tarah!" Anthony grabbed her arm and pulled her back. He eyed Jenkins. "Are you seriously suggesting we buy your children from you?"

"Iffen ya want 'em, I expect to be paid fair and square."

Anthony's voice rose considerably. "Laney and Ben are not animals to be sold off. They're living human beings. How can you even suggest such a thing?"

"Take it or leave it, Preacher." He slurred his words, and Tarah knew they didn't have much time before he was too far gone to be reasonable.

Fists clenched, Anthony stepped forward. Tarah's eyes widened. She couldn't let the preacher get into a brawl with a drunken man. Even if Anthony could take him. She grabbed his arm to halt him.

"Will you excuse us for just a moment, Mr. Jenkins?"

"Take yer time," he said and tipped the bottle again.

Tarah pulled Anthony back to the horses where they could speak in private.

His brown eyes blazed. "Forget it," he said. "We are *not* buying those beautiful children from that skunk. I've half a mind to go to the sheriff and have him arrested."

"He'd just deny it." Tarah grabbed on to Anthony's muscled arms. "Now you listen to me, Anthony Greene. As if he wasn't despicable enough, now we see how horrid he really is."

Anthony groaned. "Tarah. . ."

"He probably never thought of selling those children before. But we put the thought into his head by wanting to take them from him. What if he tries to sell them to someone else?" Tarah shuddered at the thought. "Someone who won't love them?"

A flicker of doubt appeared in Anthony's eyes, spurring Tarah to fight on. "Don't you see? We have no choice. I won't take a chance on losing them forever to who knows what kind of life."

Nodding, Anthony grabbed one of her hands and pulled her back to the soddy. Mr. Jenkins tossed the now-empty bottle aside and folded his arms across his sunken chest. "Well?"

"What are your terms?" Anthony asked.

Jenkins scratched at the gray stubble on his chin. "Let's see here. A hunnerd a head oughtta do it."

Tarah gasped, and her heart sank to her toes. "I only have fifty."

"Well then, girlie, ya got yerself a problem, dontcha? Guess iffen ya really wanted 'em, ya could come up with the price."

"The children are priceless, Mr. Jenkins, and I'd give my last cent to take them home with me. But I don't have two hundred dollars." Tarah caught Anthony's gaze. The sickened expression clouding his face dashed her hopes.

"I'm afraid two hundred dollars is out of the question," Anthony said. "I don't have much cash money. No more than twenty dollars. Will you take seventy?"

"Well now, don' see as how I could." Mr. Jenkins scanned the horizon over Anthony and Tarah's head. "Say, Preacher. That's a mighty fine animal ya got there. Might be we could work somethin' out."

"You want my horse?"

"I gotta have somethin' to git me where I'm goin'. That ol' nag up and died on me a couple weeks ago. 'Course, I'd a-be needin' the saddle, too."

Anthony swallowed hard and glanced at Dodger. He clenched his jaw and turned back to Jenkins. "That horse is easily worth two hundred dollars. We'll make it an even swap. Tarah gets the children, and I throw in the saddle."

Tears filled Tarah's eyes at the thought of the treasure Anthony was willing to give up for the children's sake. She wanted to protest, to tell him he couldn't give the scoundrel his beloved Dodger, but her mouth refused to open. And one look into Anthony's eyes confirmed her feelings. No price was too great.

"Do we have a deal, Jenkins?" Anthony asked, his voice curt, almost gruff.

"Well, I'm needin' some cash money."

Tarah dug quickly into her bag and pulled out ten dollars. "This is all I have with me. Ten dollars and the horse."

His eyes lit with greed, and he reached out eagerly.

Tarah snatched her hand back. "Not until I see those children safely on my horse."

A scowl darkened his features. "Ben! Laney! Git out here."

Laney appeared. Then Ben. Tarah gasped at the sight of the boy. A bruise marred his eye, and he limped with greater care than normal, holding his side.

"You want us, Pa?"

"Nah, I don' wantcha. The teacher here does." His lips twisted into a cruel smile. "I don' know why she'd want a couple a worthless young'uns like you two. But yer hers now."

"You mean yer givin' us away? Just like that?" Laney's brow furrowed, her eyes filled with confusion.

"Go on. Git outta here," Jenkins bellowed. "An' don' bother to come back, 'cause I won' be here."

Hurt and anger flashed in Laney's eyes. She placed an arm around Ben's shoulder. "Come on, Ben. We don't stay where we ain't wanted."

Ben shrugged off her arm. "I don't need yer help."

"Fine," she shot back. "Fall on yer face, and see if I care!" But Tarah observed that she didn't leave his side.

Anthony strode to his horse. His hand curled around the leather reins, and he patted the black neck, whispering into Dodger's ear. Tarah watched as he gathered in a slow breath and handed over the reins.

"Laney, go climb up onto Abby." She slid her gaze to Ben. "Can you make it up, or should Anthony help you?"

Ben's soulful eyes stared back at her. "What about you? It's a good five miles to the ranch."

Tarah gave him what she hoped was a reassuring smile. "The walk will do me good. I've grown soft sitting in that schoolroom all day for the last two months. Come on now. Let's hurry." *Before he changes his mind.* "Can you make it up on your own?"

Ben nodded, seeming to understand.

When the children's backs were turned, Tarah hurriedly slipped Jenkins the ten dollars and spun around to join Laney and Ben.

Jenkins chuckled to himself, but no further words were spoken.

Squaring his shoulders, Anthony fell into step beside Tarah, and with the children on Abby, they headed for the St. John ranch.

In a bold move, Tarah grabbed Anthony's hand to comfort him. He laced his fingers with hers and held tightly, as though drawing on her for strength.

"I cain't believe Pa just up and gave us away," Laney said hotly.

The relief Tarah had expected from the children was replaced by the reality of indignation and hurt, emotions she had never expected from them.

"He ain't givin' us away, Laney," Ben said with a scowl.

"Do ya think I'm dumb? I got ears. Pa said we was Tarah's now. If that ain't givin' a person away, I don't rightly know what is."

"Pa sold us," he said curtly.

"Yer crazy," Laney retorted.

"Why do ya think Anthony and Tarah's walkin'? Pa got ol' Dodger, and I seen Tarah give 'im some cash money, too."

Laney's mouth dropped open, and she regarded Tarah and Anthony with disbelief. "You mean, you bought me and Ben like we was slaves?"

"No, sweetie," Tarah said. "We did what we had to do so you don't have to go back to your pa."

"Ya said we was like family," Laney said bitterly. "But we ain't. We're just slaves, bought and paid fer."

Tarah grabbed the reins and halted Abby. She laid her palm on Laney's jean-clad knee and met her accusing glare.

"You know Cassidy isn't my blood ma, right? And Emily isn't my blood sister?"

Laney nodded.

"But I love them as dearly as if they were blood kin. And Hope and Will are no less my brother and sister than Luke and Sam and Jack and Emily," she said, giving Laney a gentle smile. "It doesn't matter how you become a family. All that matters is that you love one another."

To Tarah's relief, Laney's face softened reflectively.

"And you really can keep us always?"

"Always."

Laney inclined her head. "Then I reckon we oughtta be gettin' home b'fore yer ma starts worryin'."

Anthony's wide smile greeted Tarah as she dismounted Abby two days later. He strode toward her from the front porch of his house, curiosity filling his brown eyes.

He gestured toward the other horse she led. "What's this?"

Tarah sent him a cheeky grin. "This, Anthony, is what is commonly referred to as a horse."

"You don't say," he drawled, patting the mare's chestnut neck. "She's a beauty."

"I'm glad you think so." Tarah could barely contain her excitement as she presented the gift to Anthony. "She's yours."

Accepting the reins with reluctance, Anthony's brow furrowed. "Mine?"

"My pa sent her over—our way of saying thanks for what you did for Ben and Laney."

"This isn't necessary, Tarah. I figure after next harvest I can get another riding horse. In the meantime, there's always the wagon horses."

"You don't like her?" Tarah asked, disappointment reaching to her toes. "Pa said you can pick out another one if you prefer, but I thought you'd like this one the best. I know she can't replace Dodger. . . ."

The gentle caress of Anthony's finger upon her lips silenced her. "I didn't say I don't like her."

Trying to calm her racing pulse at Anthony's touch, Tarah stepped back, causing his hand to drop. "Then why not take her?"

"Would it mean so much to you?" he asked, his gaze searching her face.

She nodded, unable to find her voice.

A gentle smile lifted the corners of his mouth. "Then tell your pa I accept."

"Wonderful. He'll be pleased."

"How are Ben and Laney getting along?" Anthony asked, tethering the new mare to the rail spanning the length of the porch.

Tarah wrapped Abby's reins around the porch railing as well, then turned to Anthony. "They're doing wonderfully. Though Luke and Laney fight like a couple of wild dogs over a piece of meat." Tarah shook her head. "Honestly, Anthony. If it isn't one thing, it's another. And Luke is acting up in school again, too. I was afraid the reprieve was too good to last."

"And Jo?" He leaned against the rail and folded his arms across his broad chest.

Tarah hated to be a tattletale, but neither could she look Anthony in the face and lie. "Well, they aren't as bad as they used to be," she said, trying to sound nonchalant. "I suppose I can put up with them for a couple more weeks."

"I can speak to her ma about her."

Tarah shook her head. "Don't, Anthony. Your sister doesn't need to be upset in her delicate. . .well, you know."

A flush reddened Anthony's neck and cheeks, and he reached out, absently patting his new horse. Silence loomed between them momentarily until Anthony spoke. "Have you decided whether or not to accept the teaching position in Starling?"

Studying his face for any signs that he might want her to stay, Tarah felt her stomach drop as his eyes reflected only interest. No worry, no dread. Just interest.

She shrugged. "I haven't replied just yet. I have a few more weeks, but I suppose I'll go. The town council in Harper offered me another certificate for next term. So teaching in Starling will pass the time."

A heavy sigh escaped Anthony's lips. "So you won't be gone for good."

Tarah frowned, not sure if Anthony's sigh meant he was glad or disappointed that she'd be back. "No. Pa said the council is close to approving a full school term like in the cities, so once I'm back, I suppose I'll teach for as long as they'll have me."

"How do you think Laney's going to take the news you're going to Starling for five months?" Anthony sent her a crooked grin.

"I'll take Laney and Ben with me, of course," Tarah replied without hesitation.

Anthony's eyes widened. "You will?"

"I've already spoken to Pa and Ma about it. Laney and Ben are my responsibility, and I love them dearly. I want to take care of them." Tarah shifted her weight and regarded Anthony frankly. "I've spoken to Pa and asked him to consider building a small teacherage in town where the three of us could live once we return to Harper."

"And he agreed to that?" Anthony asked incredulously.

"He's agreed to speak with the council about it." Tarah's eyes narrowed. "Why shouldn't he?"

A shrug lifted Anthony's shoulders. "You're mighty young and, well, small to be taking on a ready-made family, don't you think?"

Tarah bristled and folded her arms across her chest. "If I thought so, I wouldn't be doing it. And what does being small have to do with raising a couple of kids?"

"I don't know." Anthony raked his fingers through his thick hair and scowled. "Why do you have to get so riled up about things?"

"I don't know!" Tarah stomped to the railing and untied Abby just as the door swung open.

Anthony's gray-haired mother appeared at the threshold. "Where are you going, Tarah?"

"I was about to go home."

"Her pa sent me a horse," Anthony said sheepishly.

"How kind of him." A broad smile split her plump face, and she gave a cursory nod toward the new animal. "It's lovely. Anthony, have you forgotten we have a guest for dinner?"

Anthony's ears turned red. "I suppose I did."

"Well, you've left her to us long enough. You'd better get back inside." She turned to Tarah. "Honey, tie that horse back up and come on in. Your ma will know you're taking supper with us."

"Oh no. I couldn't intrude. Really. Especially if you have a guest." And especially if that guest was who Tarah had a feeling it might be. The thought of watching Louisa Thomas fawn all over Anthony through dinner not only robbed Tarah of her appetite—the unwelcome image made her positively ill.

Mrs. Greene waved away her protest. "Nonsense. There's always plenty in this house," she insisted. "And you haven't been out here since Anthony and Ella came back from the East. Anthony, tie up Tarah's horse, and both of you come in to supper." With that, she returned inside and let the door swing shut behind her, leaving no room for more argument.

Tarah glanced helplessly at Anthony.

"Ma doesn't take no for an answer," he said with an uneasy grin. "You'd better do as she says."

"Oh, all right."

Anthony cleared his throat as they walked together up the steps. "Tarah, there's something you should know about our dinner guest."

"Louisa?"

His Adam's apple bobbed as it always did when he was nervous, a habit Tarah found endearing, even now. He nodded. "I'm sorry. She just dropped by to bring Ma some quilting patches. And you know Ma. . . ."

"She can't help but take in wandering females?" Tarah gave him her best forced smile. "Don't worry, Anthony. I can be civil to your young lady for a couple of hours if I have to." She brushed past him and, without waiting for him to open the door, slipped inside, trying to choke back her humiliation.

Louisa's icy smile greeted them. "Why, Tarah, how lovely you dropped by—just at suppertime."

Heat rose to Tarah's cheeks at the implication.

"Tarah knows she's always a more-than-welcome guest in this house," Mrs. Greene said, giving Tarah a pat on the arm.

Louisa's nervous laughter filled the air, ringing Tarah's ears. "Well, of course she is. In every town the schoolteacher and the preacher are fixtures at one table or another, aren't they?"

"And even more so when they happen to be cherished friends," Mrs. Greene shot back.

Tarah looked between the two women, wondering if either realized what the exchange sounded like. From the embarrassed look on Ella's and Anthony's faces, she had a feeling she wasn't the only person in the room who recognized Anthony's mother as her champion. Unbidden sympathy welled within her at Louisa's red face.

Anthony held out Tarah's chair for her, and she sat gratefully, knowing her trembling legs would give out at any moment if forced to continue standing.

Rounding the table, Anthony took a seat next to Louisa. The smug smile curving Louisa's mouth said clearly, *I belong here, and you don't.*

Tarah kept silent during the meal, speaking only when spoken to. She fought to maintain her composure amid the humiliating experience and longed for the last bite of dessert when she could be on her way.

Louisa's incessant chatter grated on Tarah's already taut nerves until she wanted to cover her ears and scream.

"Tarah brought Anthony a beautiful mare from her pa," Mrs. Greene said during a pause in Louisa's prattle.

"Oh, you're buying a horse from the St. Johns, Anthony?" Louisa asked, a frown creasing her otherwise flawless skin. "I'm sure you could have gotten a better price in Abilene."

What does Louisa Thomas know about the price of horses? Tarah thought, defenses rising at the possible slight to her father's pricing of their animals.

"The St. John ranch has the finest reputation for quality stock around," Anthony said, his voice tense. "At an auction I wouldn't know what I was getting. Besides, I couldn't have asked for a better price. The horse was a gift."

"A gift?" Louisa's gaze riveted on Tarah, her eyes narrowing to two green slits, reminding Tarah of blades of grass peeking through the slats in the outhouse wall.

"My pa gave him the horse because of—"

"Because I lost Dodger," Anthony broke in.

Eyes widening, Tarah stared at Anthony. He hadn't told Louisa about Mr. Jenkins?

Seemingly oblivious to the exchange, Louisa pressed on. "Oh well, Anthony. I'm sure my father would be more than happy to buy you the finest horse in the state. Do be sensible and tell Mr. St. John you can't accept his gift."

Anthony's lips twitched. "Thanks all the same, but I believe I already have the finest horse in the state. And I'm not about to part with her."

He smiled at Tarah, sending her heart into a flutter.

"All right, Anthony, you keep whatever horse you want," Louisa said, placing a slender hand upon his arm. She glanced around the table. "I'd much rather talk about the dance anyway. Of course, your country dances are nothing like the balls I attended when we lived in Charleston, but these little diversions every now and then do tend to break up the dreariness of life out here." She turned to Ella. "I'm sure Tarah doesn't know what I mean, having lived here her whole life, but you certainly do, don't you?"

Ella sent her a kind smile. "We rarely attend fine balls, Louisa. I suppose we're just country folk at heart. I am greatly looking forward to the dance. I only wish my Joe were here."

"Uncle Anthony will dance with you, Ma," Josie piped in.

"You can d–d–dance w–w–with m–m–me, Ma," Toby said, regarding his mother with wide, adoring eyes.

Ella's face softened considerably. "Thank you, darlings," she said. "And just two days after the dance, we'll all go home to your father."

Mrs. Greene cleared her throat and stood. "Well then," she said, her voice faltering slightly. "Who's ready for dessert?"

Tarah's heart went out to Mrs. Greene, knowing how much she would miss her daughter and grandchildren when they returned to the East. "May I help you bring in the dessert, Mrs. Greene?"

Louisa shot to her feet. "Of course, where are my manners? Do let me help you."

The older woman gave a smile to include them both. "You two girls sit here and enjoy the conversation. You're guests, after all."

Louisa sat gracefully back into her chair.

Tarah stood. "I insist," she said, noting the mist forming in the older woman's eyes.

Once they reached the kitchen, Tarah lovingly reached out to comfort the older woman. "I know you'll miss Ella and the children dreadfully, Mrs. Greene. I remember how it nearly broke my granny's heart every day thinking of my aunt Olive not being nearby. Now that she's been visiting Aunt Olive for a few months, she misses us dreadfully and can't wait to return."

"I suppose when your children are grown, it's too much to hope they'll all stay close to home." Mrs. Greene wiped her eyes with the edge of her apron and smiled at Tarah. "I promised myself I wouldn't cry until Ella and the children were gone. But I suppose when the tears need to come, they just do, and there's nothing a body can do about it."

"No one expects you to be strong. And as happy as Ella is to be going home to her husband, I'm sure she'll shed a few tears of her own when the time comes to leave her ma."

Reaching up, Mrs. Greene pressed a hand to Tarah's cheek. "Such a good girl. Any mother would be proud to have you for a. . .daughter."

The kitchen door swung open, and Louisa burst in. "I thought I'd come and help, too."

"Thank you, dear." Mrs. Greene stepped back and moved to the counter.

Once Mrs. Greene's back was turned, Louisa threw Tarah a scathing look. Leaning in close, she whispered, "I know you're trying to make me look foolish, but it's not going to work. If all goes as planned, Anthony and I will have an announcement to make at the dance."

Before Tarah could respond, Louisa stepped forward. "Let me take that tray for you, Mrs. Greene."

"Thank you, Louisa. That's very sweet."

Louisa beamed. "Oh, I just love doing domestic things. I rarely have the chance at home, what with having Rosa to take care of menial tasks. You know, Rosa has been with our family ever since I can remember. Of course, we pay her now since we lost the war, but she doesn't try to throw that in our faces one bit."

Tarah released an exasperated sigh, then glanced quickly to see if the other two women had noticed. She found Mrs. Greene's gaze studying Louisa, a worried frown etching her brow.

"Well now. Let's not keep my family waiting on their dessert," she said, opening the kitchen door ahead of Louisa. Tarah trailed behind, wondering again what in the world Anthony saw in Louisa Thomas.

Chapter 13

In the light of the full moon, Anthony watched wistfully as Tarah headed off toward the St. John ranch with his brother Blane as her escort. He climbed into his saddle and smiled as best he could at Louisa, who sat astride her own mount. "All set?"

Louisa eyed his horse dubiously and nodded, nudging her mount forward. "I know you were trying to be polite, Anthony. But I really think you could find a higher-quality animal."

Irritation rose in Anthony. "I'm happy with this one, Louisa, but thank you for the offer."

"Oh well, let's not talk about that now anyway," she said brightly. "I'd much rather discuss the dance. I'll be the envy of all the girls, walking in on the arm of the most handsome man in town."

Anthony felt the heat rush up his neck and burn his ears. He still wasn't quite sure how Louisa had finagled the invitation from him, but he'd regretted it ever since. Still, she deserved to have a nice evening. And maybe—if God allowed him—he could snatch one dance with Tarah. Preferably a waltz.

As if reading his thoughts, Louisa released a regretful sigh. "It really is a shame Tarah doesn't have an escort. I suppose I could ask my brother, Caleb, to invite her. Although she isn't really the elegant sort of young lady he normally courts. And there is also Tom."

"Tom?"

"A friend of Cal's. He accompanied my brother home from the university. He's even considering setting up a law practice in Harper, what with all the new people settling in the area. Of course, I don't see how he'll make the sort of living he could make in a city, but that doesn't seem to concern him a bit." Louisa paused to take a breath, then continued on as though speaking to herself. "Yes, I believe I'll suggest Tom invite Tarah to the dance. He's rather handsome. I suppose Tarah will be quite taken with him. I'll have to warn him not to give her any false hope. B—because, Anthony, there is nothing worse to a girl than receiving false hope from a man she fancies."

The way her voice faltered brought Anthony up short. He had supposed she had no idea how he felt. He'd taken great pains not to hurt her feelings over the past couple of months, but now he realized he had done her no favors by not being firm and refusing invitations. And furthermore, she was aware that he had been doing just that.

Taking a deep breath, Anthony sent up a silent prayer. "Louisa. . ."

The ring of false laughter filled the air as Louisa nudged her horse closer and reached out to place a hand on Anthony's arm. "Father just said this morning that he would be asking your intentions soon if you don't speak up. But I—I assured him you are too fine a man to trifle with a girl's affections. Aren't you, Anthony?"

The cautious hesitancy in her voice fanned Anthony's feelings of guilt, and he swallowed hard past the lump forming in his throat. Louisa might be flighty and annoying at times, but this new show of vulnerability sent a wave of compassion through Anthony. The time had come to stop the charade before she was hurt any more than she inevitably would be now.

"Stop for a minute, Louisa," he said, reining in his horse.

She did as he asked, and in the brightly lit night, Anthony saw the tears shimmering in her eyes. Her lips trembled as she stared back at him, a look of dread covering her delicate features. "Oh, Anthony," she whispered. "Please don't say it."

"I'm sorry," he mumbled. "I never should have led you on the way I did when I'm in love with—"

"Tarah," she said bitterly.

"Yes."

"Then why, Anthony?" she said, her voice thick with tears. "Why did you take me on picnics and ask me to the dance?"

What could he say without humiliating her? He had never asked her to go one place with him. He had even tried to refuse invitations from her, but she wouldn't take no for an answer. "I suppose I've been a cad, Louisa. I hope you'll forgive me."

"I don't know, Anthony," she said stiffly, jerking her reins and nudging her horse forward once again. "After all, you did lead me on. You aren't going to back out on escorting me to the dance, are you? Why, I'd be the laughingstock of the entire town."

Relieved that indignation had replaced the tears, Anthony smiled into the darkness and followed her. "I'm not backing out on the dance."

"That's little comfort for the humiliation I'll endure when the whole town finds out you preferred that mousy little country schoolmarm to me," Louisa huffed. "But it's better than the alternative."

The thought of his beautiful Tarah as a mousy little country schoolmarm brought a sudden smile to Anthony's face. Spunky, tenderhearted, and generous were traits that came to mind. He prayed she would hold off on answering Mr. Halston until after the dance so he could speak his heart freely. If only she shared a portion of his feelings, there was hope.

⁓

Dear Mr. Halston,

I am pleased to inform you of my recent decision to accept the teaching position you have so graciously offered to me. I will make arrangements to travel to Starling shortly after the New Year. Further correspondence will follow to inform you of the specific date of my arrival.

Sincerely,
Miss Tarah St. John

Tears blurred the words on the page as Tarah attempted to reread the letter. Once this was posted, there would be no turning back. She hadn't informed the family of her decision because she had just decided this very night to accept the teaching position. Louisa's presence at Anthony's house had proven she was holding on to a foolish dream.

Her heartbreak knew no bounds, but she couldn't be angry with Anthony. She loved him too much, and his happiness meant the world to her. But neither could she stay and watch as he became another woman's husband.

A soft rap sounded on her door. "Come in," Tarah said, tears thick in her voice. She tried to compose herself as Cassidy stepped into the room.

"I wanted to say good night."

Tarah nodded, afraid to trust her voice.

"Tarah?" Cassidy stepped closer. Cupping Tarah's chin, she inched her head up until they met eye to eye. "What's wrong?"

Hot tears sprang to Tarah's eyes, and she handed Cassidy her letter to Mr. Halston.

A troubled frown creased Cassidy's brow as she read. Gathering a deep breath, she gave the letter back to Tarah and sank down on the bed next to her. "I see you've made your decision."

"Yes."

"You'll need to tell your pa soon."

"I will." Tarah sniffed and brushed away a trail of tears with her fingertips.

"You don't seem very happy with your decision," Cassidy said, her eyes searching Tarah's face. "Are you sure you want to do this?"

A shrug lifted Tarah's shoulders. "I don't have a choice. Anthony is going to marry Louisa." With that she threw herself into Cassidy's arms and sobbed.

"Oh, Tarah, I'm so sorry. When did they make their announcement?"

"Huh?" Tarah pulled back and stared at her stepmother.

"Their betrothal announcement. When did they make it? I hadn't heard."

"Oh," Tarah said, waving a hand in dismissal. "They haven't yet. But it's only a matter of time."

"I see."

But Tarah could tell from the confusion on Cassidy's face that she didn't see at all. "I just can't stay here and watch Anthony marry her!"

"Are you sure this is what God wants you to do, Tarah?"

"I—I don't guess I've really prayed about it, Ma. I've been waiting to see. . ."

Cassidy drew an exasperated breath and planted her hands firmly on her hips. "Do you mean to tell me you are running off twenty miles from home just because the man you love doesn't love you in return?"

When she puts it that way. . .

Still, Tarah felt her defenses rise. Her life had been perfectly wretched the last few months. Between Luke and Jo making trouble in class, Anthony's love for Louisa, and Louisa always rubbing her nose in it, she needed to make a fresh start to regain her shattered dignity. And Starling was as good a place as any to do it.

Cassidy stood. "Honey, there's not a lot I can say. You have to make this decision for yourself, but running away is never the answer. If Anthony isn't the man God has for you, then He's preparing someone else. One decision has nothing to do with the other."

She strode toward the door, then hesitated. "Just make sure it's His will before you run off half-cocked because of your wounded pride. I'd hate to see you do something you'll regret later on."

Tarah said nothing as Cassidy slipped from the room, leaving her to wrestle with her words. Wounded pride, was it? She jerked her chin, then her shoulders slumped as truth rushed in like a raging tide. Was it wounded pride? She groaned aloud. Of course that's what it was. She loved Anthony, but he loved Louisa, a woman who clearly didn't understand or deserve him. Yet she, Tarah St. John, would have been the perfect wife for a man in his position. Thinking back, she remembered how her determination to love Johnny Cooper had almost killed her, Cassidy, and the twins.

Oh, God, I thought I had learned my lesson back then. Will I ever learn to trust Your will even when the answer is no?

Stretching out fully on her bed, she rolled to her stomach and allowed the tears to flow unchecked as she let go of Anthony, the most precious dream she had ever held in her heart.

In a flash, Cassidy's words from weeks before came back: *"Often the way we react to pressure shows us more about our own hearts than we would ever learn if things always worked out smoothly for us."* Her mind replayed every encounter she'd had with Louisa Thomas over the past few months since Anthony's arrival in Harper, and she saw how bitter and jealous she had become, growing more so with each meeting.

God, she prayed, *I was so sure You'd sent Anthony back here for me. But all the time he was only a test to see how I would react to his taking up with Louisa again.* And she had failed the test miserably. Her resentment toward Louisa had only hardened her heart. Sobs of repentance shook her body. *Mold me, like a potter molds clay, Lord. And please teach me to accept Your will for my life instead of always trying to manipulate my own course.*

Suddenly Tarah thought of the letter on her night table, and she sat up. All the weeks of indecision seemed to fade away, and she realized Cassidy was right. Her decision to leave was based on a desire to run away.

Even if she went to Starling, she would have to face Anthony and Louisa when she returned. And the thought of uprooting Laney and Ben didn't sit too well with her. They loved the family life she had always taken for granted. The more she thought about it, the more Tarah recognized that she wasn't ready to make such a drastic move either. Even if the town council approved the building of the teacherage, she would have months to prepare to set up housekeeping on her own. If she tried to do that now, she would be completely unprepared.

She stared at the letter for a moment longer, then knew what she had to do. She snatched it up and ripped it into pieces, feeling the pressure loosen in her chest with each tear.

Drawing a long, cleansing breath, Tarah stretched back out on her bed. She would stay in Harper and learn to get along with Louisa. Even now her bitterness toward the woman was abating, and she knew God would somehow take care of the rest. Her strong love for Anthony concerned her, but she felt confident God would take care of that as well. And if God willed her to fall in love again, He would send her a man who would return her love. But until then, she would keep her hands off God's business and trust Him to know what was best for her.

Chapter 14

Tarah hesitated at the double-doored entrance to the crowded livery stable, which had been transformed for the dance.

"Coming, Tarah?" Pa asked, holding out his arm. Cassidy looked radiant at his other side, dressed in a slightly snug gown of cream-colored satin.

"How could I resist being escorted by the most handsome man at the dance?" Tarah said, slipping her gloved hand inside the crook of his arm.

"Then let's make our grand entrance." Pa grinned to include Laney and Emily, who each held on to one of the twins. "I'm the luckiest man at the dance with all these beautiful women in my company."

Tarah had to admit they were a handsome group. Even Laney had acquiesced to wearing a dress, but she had made it clearly understood this was not to be an everyday occurrence.

Tarah grinned. Wearing a gown of blue velvet fashioned from material Cassidy had insisted was made just for Tarah, she felt confident in her appearance. But only for a moment. As she stepped inside, she spotted Louisa whirling past in Anthony's arms. Her gown of emerald-colored silk clung to her body and perfectly offset her green eyes, pale skin, and strawberry blond hair. Tarah had to admit, Louisa was breathtakingly beautiful, and suddenly she felt dowdy by comparison.

Anthony looked handsome in his Sunday suit and his tie, crooked as ever. Tarah couldn't keep an indulgent smile from curving her lips, though her heart ached at the sight of him dancing with Louisa.

She had barely removed her wraps when she was asked to dance. The evening whirled by with partner after partner vying for her attention until her self-confidence returned and she felt like the belle of the ball. She would have been on a cloud if only Anthony had once asked her to dance. But she knew it was just as well.

Standing next to the refreshment table, Tarah graciously refused a would-be dance partner and sipped a glass of lemonade, wishing she had brought a fan to cool herself off.

"Good evening, Tarah. Lovely dance, isn't it?" Louisa's singsong voice tore Tarah's attention away from watching Anthony waltzing with pretty Camilla Simpson.

In no mood for a confrontation, Tarah eyed Louisa cautiously, her stomach tense, awaiting the insults. But for once, the young woman smiled pleasantly. "I've made a decision, Tarah," she said, graciously accepting a glass of lemonade.

"Oh?" *Do you want me to be a bridesmaid?* Feeling a twinge of conscience, Tarah sent up a hasty prayer of repentance.

"Yes, I've decided Anthony is not the man for me after all. So you can have him."

Tarah felt her mouth drop at the sudden revelation. "What do you mean?"

With her gaze fixed on the dancers, Louisa inclined her head toward a young man Tarah had danced with earlier in the evening. "That's Tom Kirkpatrick, a friend of my brother's from the university." She cut her gaze to Tarah, apparently expecting a response.

"Handsome," Tarah obliged.

"Yes, isn't he?" Twin spots of pink dotted Louisa's cheeks. "We have discovered we have ever so much in common, and Mother and Father agree Tom is more suited to me than Anthony could possibly ever be."

Poor Anthony! "But what about your betrothal?" Tarah asked indignantly. "You can't just throw Anthony over for another man. It isn't right."

Louisa shrugged as she caught Tom's eye. The two shared a smile. "Better I find out now than after we're married. Don't you think?"

Tarah's temper flared. "I don't see how you can do this to Anthony after all this time of making him believe you would welcome a proposal."

Giving Tarah her full attention, Louisa lifted a delicate brow and regarded her reflectively. "I rather thought the news would please you. It's no secret how you feel about Anthony."

Heat rushed to Tarah's cheeks, but she met Louisa's gaze head-on. "How I feel isn't the point," she said, not caring that she had just made an admission. "Anthony's feelings are all that matter right now. And he'll be so hurt."

An amused smile played at the corners of Louisa's lips. "A bright girl like you should be able to find a way to help him feel better." She let out a short, mirthless laugh. "In fact, I wouldn't be surprised if he turns to you before the evening is over."

A retort fell short of Tarah's lips as her pa stood on the rough-hewn platform at the front of the room and held up his arms. "Ladies and gentlemen, may I have your attention, please?"

The room stirred for a moment, then quiet ensued as all eyes turned with interest toward Pa.

"You all know how long we've been praying and searching for a preacher. It seemed like God raised one up right in our midst when Reverend Greene came back to Harper."

Tarah's gaze darted to Anthony. His face glowed red, and a look of dread covered his features.

"Now the reverend's the first to admit things started off a mite rough, but I think we all agree God has made quite a turnaround in our church in the past few weeks."

Heads nodded in approval. Mr. Tucker slapped Anthony on the back. "Doin' a fine job, Preacher."

Tarah's heart soared as she realized her pa was about to confirm Anthony's position as pastor. She glanced at Louisa, whose gaze was fixed on her new beau, her face glowing with the joy of newfound love.

Tarah bristled. Anthony should be sharing this moment with the person he loved. Instead he was about to be given the boot right out of Louisa's life. *Lord, it just isn't right. I know Anthony doesn't love me, but please don't let him be too hurt over Louisa.*

Without thought, she nudged Louisa. "Can't you wait until tomorrow, at least? Give Anthony this night to enjoy getting the permanent position."

"Too late," Louisa replied without averting her gaze from Tom Kirkpatrick. "I told Anthony during our last dance together."

Pa again lifted his arms to quiet the commotion brought on by his last statement. "I guess you've pretty much figured out what I'm going to say next. Come on up here, Reverend Greene, and let everyone have a good look at Harper's new pastor."

A wide grin split Anthony's achingly handsome face as he strode forward and stood before his friends, family, and congregation. Pa shook his hand vigorously. "Congratulations, Reverend. I pray you'll shepherd this flock with the compassion of David, the wisdom of Solomon, and the love and sacrifice of the Great Shepherd, Jesus Christ."

Tears sprang to Tarah's eyes even as Anthony smiled, his own eyes glistening in the lamplit room. "I thank you all for the trust you've placed in me. I ask that you pray for me as often as you will."

Pa stepped forward again and clapped Anthony on the shoulder. "I have one more announcement to make, then the band will play the last waltz of the night." He grinned at Anthony. "God has blessed our town with new folks moving in all the time, and we don't want it said we don't take good care of our preacher. So the town council has approved the building of a new church. And not a sod building, either."

A cheer rose up from the crowd. Pa waited for quiet to resume before continuing. "Mr. Thomas, our distinguished banker, has approved a loan and donated the first fifty dollars for shipping in enough wood for the church and a small parsonage."

Anthony's mouth dropped at the news, and everyone turned to the banker in a mix of disbelief and astonishment. Mrs. Thomas stood beside her husband, her chin lifted with pride, shoulders straight with the dignity this effort afforded them.

"You see what a generous man my father is?" Louisa asked smugly. "Now maybe the town will vote him onto the council."

"I hope so, Louisa." And Tarah was surprised to discover that she really did.

Mr. Thomas was in a position to help the townsfolk, and a little mutual respect might be called for now that Harper was becoming a real town.

Anthony cleared his throat and inclined his head. "Again, I thank you folks and you, Mr. Thomas, for your generosity. I will try to earn your faith in me." With that, he shook Pa's hand again and stepped off the little platform as the band began to play a reel to start off the last waltz of the night.

Tarah found her gaze fixed on Anthony, her heart beating time to the reel. Unable to look away, she watched as he stopped to speak to well-wishers. Then in an instant, he found her. Tarah's breath caught in her throat at the intensity of his gaze, and she couldn't have looked away if she had wanted to. He strode toward her and smiled. "Will you give me the honor of the last dance, Miss St. John?"

Heart pounding, Tarah nodded and placed her hand in his. He pulled her as close as propriety allowed, but Tarah was sure he could feel her heartbeat as he swept her around the dance floor.

"Congratulations, Anthony," she said when she found her voice. "I'm so happy for you."

He grinned. "I was a little worried when your pa started off talking about how rough the first few weeks were. You don't know how relieved I was when he went on."

Tarah let out a giggle. "You should have seen your face."

"You were watching me?" His gaze searched her face.

She tried to think of a flippant answer, but nothing came, so she simply nodded. He drew a quick breath, his eyes serious. "Tarah," he said hesitantly, "now that my future is secure in Harper and we're building a parsonage, I'll be in a position to marry and settle down."

Tarah's heart plummeted. Maybe he didn't understand Louisa's change in affections after all. "Oh, Anthony—"

"Now wait. Before you say anything, I know you're planning to go to Starling in another month or so, and I wouldn't try to stop you if that's really what you want to do."

A frown furrowed Tarah's brow as Louisa's words came back to taunt her. *I wouldn't be surprised if he turns to you before the evening is over.*

"Why are you looking at me like that?" Anthony asked. "All I'm asking for is a chance to court you like a gentleman." He sent her a heart-stopping grin, which only fueled Tarah's anger.

She stopped midstep, then winced as Anthony stumbled and ground his boot into her slipper-clad foot.

Suddenly the air in the room was stifling, and Tarah's chest heaved, her palms growing moist. Without a word, she glared at Anthony and stomped as best she could with a limp toward the door. She snatched her coat from a peg on the wall, and brushing past Pa and Cassidy, she hurried out the door, desperate for a private spot where she could spill the threatening tears.

"Tarah, wait." At Anthony's voice, she spun around to find not only Anthony staring at her, but Pa and Cassidy and Mrs. Greene.

"What happened, Tarah?" Cassidy asked. "Is something wrong with your foot?"

"What? Oh, Anthony stepped on it. But I'm fine."

"Then why are you so upset, honey?" Pa asked.

Heaving a frustrated sigh, Tarah glanced at Anthony to see if he would speak up and admit what he had done. The look of bewilderment on his face boiled her blood.

She knit her brows together and took a step closer to him. "Ask him!" she said, never taking her gaze from Anthony's face.

"Anthony, what have you done?" Mrs. Greene's voice trembled.

"Is there something we should discuss in private, son?" Pa asked, a hard edge to his voice that Tarah had rarely heard.

"I—I'm not sure, sir. All I said was—"

Tarah had had all she could take. After months of dreaming about him, she'd had to watch Louisa hook him, then throw him back. After the heartbreak of releasing him to God, now he asked her for permission to come calling!

She took another step closer to Anthony until they were close enough to touch. "All he said was that he wanted to court me! Can you believe that, Ma? After all this time? Now he wants to court me!"

A look of faint amusement covered Cassidy's features. She opened her mouth, then closed it again and shook her head as Tarah continued to rant.

"After mooning over Louisa Thomas for as long as I've known him, he suddenly wants to court me. And do you know why, Mrs. Greene?"

"You're a very pretty girl, Tarah," she replied, the same look of amusement on her face. "Anthony has always thought very highly of you."

"Ha!" Tarah let out an unladylike snort and turned to Pa, knowing she could count on him to understand. "The reason he suddenly wants to court me is because Louisa threw him over for that university fellow tonight."

"That's not exactly—"

"Oh, Anthony," Tarah said, her energy suddenly drained, "you're not going to deny it?"

"Tarah, please." Louisa's voice broke through the silence that had suddenly permeated the tension-filled air. "Keep your voice down before the whole town hears you make fools of all of us."

Tarah spun around and glared at Louisa. "What are you doing out here?"

"Tom and I came out to get a breath of air."

"And you decided to eavesdrop?" Sarcasm dripped from Tarah's lips.

Louisa scowled. "It isn't as though I had to struggle to hear you hollering at poor Anthony."

"Poor Anthony? As if you care about his feelings," Tarah snapped, her gaze darting to the young man holding protectively to Louisa's elbow.

"Dell, perhaps we should leave these young people to work all this out between them," Cassidy suggested quietly.

"No!" Tarah said, keeping her gaze fixed on Louisa. "I want you to stay."

Louisa glanced nervously about the little gathering. "I'm afraid this misunderstanding is all my fault."

Tarah's mouth dropped open as she stared at the contrite face that only a moment before she would have loved to slap. Louisa gave a resigned sigh and continued. "It's true I cared for Anthony a great deal—or thought I did," she added, smiling at Tom. "But as kind as he has always been, he never felt the same way about me."

"But I thought—"

"You thought what I led you to believe," Louisa said, a wry grin twisting her lips. "But Anthony had nothing to do with it. I'm sure you remember the night we both had dinner at the Greenes'?"

Tarah nodded, reliving the humiliation.

"Anthony told me that night that he is not in love with me and never could be because he's in love with someone else—you. He only brought me to the dance instead of you because I begged him not to humiliate me in front of the whole town."

Eyes widening, Tarah's gaze darted to Anthony, who stared at Louisa in astonishment.

"And, Anthony," Louisa said, "I think you'll find the feeling is returned."

Pa snickered behind them, adding to Tarah's humiliation. So much for understanding.

"Dell," Cassidy admonished.

Tarah planted her hands on her hips and struggled to maintain her composure. "Now hold on, Louisa Thomas. Who do you think you are to speak for me?"

Completely unintimidated, Louisa lifted a brow and smirked. "Come now, Tarah. We're all being honest here. If I can humiliate myself with the truth, why can't you? And if the truth be told, all this is your fault to begin with."

Tarah gasped. "Mine? You just admitted it was yours."

Her slim shoulders lifted. "I've changed my mind. If you had let Anthony know how you feel about him in the first place, you would have been the one to go with him on all the picnics and horseback rides. And you would have come with him to the dance instead of me. Then all of this could have been avoided. But you have your pride, don't you?" She smiled up at her escort. "Shall we go, Tom? I think I've done all I can do here."

Tarah watched them leave arm in arm. Her mind whirled, trying to absorb the shocking revelations of the past few minutes. Anthony loved her? But what about the lessons she had learned about letting God direct her life? Was it even possible that Anthony was hers all along? Then it struck her. She had let him go, and God had given him back. It had been a hard lesson to learn, but she knew she was stronger spiritually as a result than she ever could have been without learning to surrender her will to God's.

Her anger drained away as she turned slowly and caught her breath at the intensity of Anthony's gaze. He stepped forward and took her hands, and everything and everyone present faded away.

Pa cleared his throat, making them both jump. "I still expect you to court my daughter properly, young man."

"Yes, sir," Anthony said without removing his gaze from Tarah's.

"Then I suppose we can go now. Unless you want us to stay, Tarah?"

"No, Pa. You can go."

"Ladies?" he said, turning to Cassidy and Mrs. Greene. "Shall we return to the dance?"

Tarah could hear them laughing as they strolled away, but she didn't care. All that mattered was knowing Anthony shared her feelings and that her love for him was part of God's plan all along.

She stared at him, not daring to speak for fear it had all been a dream that would float away if she broke the silence.

Anthony searched her face, his warm hands still enclosing hers. He drew a ragged breath and tightened his grip. "Do you love me?"

"Do *you* love me?" Tarah whispered.

Anthony's lips curved into a wry grin. "I've been trying to tell you for weeks how much I care about you."

"You have?"

He nodded. "Remember me telling you I'd do anything for you? I even offered to marry you, but you didn't think I was serious. I love you." He paused. "Now you. Was Louisa speaking the truth?"

Heat rushed to Tarah's cheeks. She dropped her chin and nodded. "Yes, it's true."

Releasing a sigh, Anthony pulled her closer.

Tarah met his gaze head-on and held her breath.

"I want to ask you to marry me. Do you think your pa would give his blessing without a courtship? Because I'm willing to wait however long it takes, but I'd prefer to be married as soon as the parsonage is built."

Amusement washed over Tarah, and she tilted her head to one side, a grin tugging at the corners of her lips. "Have I ever told you how Pa and Cassidy met?"

A frown furrowed Anthony's brow. "No. Do you want to tell me right now?"

Tarah giggled and nodded. "My pa placed an advertisement for a wife. Cassidy answered, and they married less than three weeks later with no courting whatsoever. And I've never seen two people more in love. Have you?"

His lips twitched. "Now that you mention it, I haven't."

"So you see, I don't think my pa or Cassidy will raise any objections to our marriage."

"Are you saying yes?"

"Yes, Anthony." Tarah closed her eyes as his head descended, and she knew this time she was going to be kissed. At the first touch of his lips on hers, Tarah wrapped her arms about his neck. The gentle caress sent shivers down her spine as she gave herself over to the heady sensations filling her for the first time.

Just as Anthony drew her closer and deepened the kiss, a sudden thought popped into her mind. She gasped, tearing her mouth away. He drew back immediately as her eyes flew open.

"What is it?" He shook his head. "I'm sorry. I should never have been so forward."

"No, Anthony. Of course I welcomed your kiss. It isn't that."

"Then what is it, sweetheart?"

Tarah drew a steadying breath and regarded him frankly, feeling her heart racing within her chest. "When I marry, Laney and Ben come with me. And I don't want a man who puts up with them but secretly resents them. They need a good man in their life—someone who will love them. Otherwise, they'd be better off with no man at all."

Relief washed over Anthony's face, and he smiled, pulling her close once again. "I know those children are part of the deal. And I wouldn't have it any other way. But do you think they'll want me in their lives?"

"I think so. Ben idolizes you already, and Laney's coming around."

"That's a good thing," Anthony said with a teasing smile. " 'Cause I don't stay where I ain't wanted."

Anthony's head descended once again, and his lips captured Tarah's, muffling the sound of their laughter.

LANEY'S
KISS

For my sister, Sandy.
Your strength of character amazes me.
Your ability to consistently achieve your goals inspires me.
Your humanness humbles me.
In all of your strengths and weaknesses—
to God be the glory for making you who you are.
All my love,
T

Prologue

From *Tarah's Lessons*

I cain't believe Pa just up and gave us away," Laney said hotly.

The relief Tarah had expected from the children was replaced by the reality of indignation and hurt, emotions she had never expected from them.

"He ain't givin' us away, Laney," Ben said with a scowl.

"Do ya think I'm dumb? I got ears. Pa said we was Tarah's now. If that ain't givin' a person away, I don't rightly know what is."

"Pa sold us," he said curtly.

"Yer crazy," Laney retorted.

"Why do ya think Anthony and Tarah's walkin'? Pa got ol' Dodger, and I seen Tarah give 'im some cash money, too."

Laney's mouth dropped open, and she regarded Tarah and Anthony with disbelief. "You mean, you bought me and Ben like we was slaves?"

"No, sweetie," Tarah said. "We did what we had to do so you don't have to go back to your pa."

"Ya said we was like family," Laney said bitterly. "But we ain't. We're just slaves, bought and paid fer."

Tarah grabbed the reins and halted Abby. She laid her palm on Laney's jean-clad knee and met her accusing glare.

"You know Cassidy isn't my blood ma, right? And Emily isn't my blood sister?"

Laney nodded.

"But I love them as dearly as if they were blood kin. And Hope and Will are no less my brother and sister than Luke and Sam and Jack and Emily," she said, giving Laney a gentle smile. "It doesn't matter how you become a family. All that matters is that you love one another."

To Tarah's relief, Laney's face softened reflectively.

"And you really can keep us always?"

"Always."

Laney inclined her head. "Then I reckon we oughtta be gettin' home b'fore yer ma starts worryin'."

Chapter 1

A man's heart deviseth his way:
but the LORD directeth his steps.
PROVERBS 16:9

1879, Kansas

Laney Jenkins glared at the man sitting tall astride a gelding as red as its master's hair. "One more word, and I'm going to flatten you, Luke St. John."
She could admit she was a little dusty from the trail, and who wouldn't need a bath to wash away the smell and grime after two weeks of herding cattle? But that didn't give Luke any right to insult her.

A shrug lifted his well-muscled shoulders. "I stand by what I said. You're as dirty as you were the first time I laid eyes on you." Luke's lazy grin infuriated Laney all the more. "I remember you walked into the school looking and smelling like you'd just had a tumble with a herd of pigs."

Laney's ire rose, and she clutched the leather reins, fighting for control over her raging emotions. She felt grimy from driving the cattle to Abilene, tired from her turn at keeping watch last night, and her behind ached from day after day of sitting on the hard seat of the supply wagon.

She hated the trip more each time she made it. Going along with Papa Dell and the ranch hands had started out as an adventure, but she would have stopped after the first drive if not for Luke suggesting she was too much of a tenderfoot to endure the hardship. Now, enduring the hardship was a matter of principle.

But she'd made her point once again, and home was only a few miles away. She longed for a leisurely hot bath, a home-cooked meal, and a good night's sleep in her own bed. She certainly didn't need Luke's insults. Nor would she stand for them.

"Luke," she said slowly, warning thick in her voice. "I mean it. You hush up, or I'm going to knock you off that horse and give you a sound thrashing."

"I doubt you could," he challenged, his grin firmly planted on his freckled face. "Besides, when are you going to start acting like a girl? Or do you even know how?"

"I—you—" she sputtered. Oh, why could she never come up with a good retort to put him in his place?

"Close your mouth before you swallow a bug," Luke baited.

"That's it!" Laney shot from the wagon seat, propelled her body toward

253

Luke, and knocked him from his horse. His startled cry gave Laney more than a little satisfaction as they landed together on the rain-deprived earth. Ignoring the pain in her left leg, she held on to his shoulders and rolled, waiting for an opportunity to whale the daylights out of him. In a flash, he overpowered her. He straddled her, pinning her hands to the ground with his palms.

"Stop it," he growled, his green eyes flashing mere inches above hers. "You know I can't hit you back."

"You couldn't get close enough to hit me, Luke St. John!" She glared up at him.

The corners of his lips twitched at her ridiculous statement. Something akin to a growl gargled in her throat, and she kicked fruitlessly against the ground beneath her heels. She gave a violent twist, trying to free herself.

"Cut it out." Luke pressed harder on her hands, his face screwed up in disgust. "I don't know what's got into you lately. You can't even take a little teasing anymore."

"Maybe I'm just sick of you," she spat. "Ever think of that?" Being this near to Luke, feeling his warm breath on her face, was too achingly close for comfort. If he didn't let her up soon, she'd most likely do something stupid like throw her arms around him and declare her love right then and there.

"I'll let you up if you promise to stop acting so ignorant and get back in the wagon."

"Sounds like a good idea." A shadow fell across them, accompanying the stern voice. Laney glanced up to find Luke's tall, lean pa astride his mount. Brows furrowed, he glared down at his son. "Get off of her. I didn't raise you to manhandle women."

Luke's face reddened, making his freckles pop out even farther. He stood and reached down for Laney.

Laney grasped his hand and felt herself being hauled upright. The thick tension passing between father and son felt almost tangible, and guilt pricked her.

"It was my fault, Papa Dell. I—I took offense to something Luke said."

Dell glanced sternly at Luke. "What have I told you about the way you speak to Laney? I've half a mind to let her give you a sound whipping."

Luke slapped his Stetson hard against his thigh. Laney cringed, knowing his action was more from frustration than the need to dust off his hat. Now he'd be madder than ever. Mad at her.

With his eyes as cold as emeralds, Luke pressed his hat against his chest and gave her an exaggerated bow. "I apologize from the bottom of my heart, fair Laney. I should never have suggested you aren't the epitome of ladyhood."

Laney wasn't sure *ladyhood* was even a word, but the implication hit her full in the stomach. Heat rushed to her cheeks. She clenched her fists and swept a sideways glance at Papa Dell. No. She'd better not tear into Luke right now, or she'd get the same scolding he was getting.

"We can do without the sarcasm," Papa Dell drawled. "Now mount up, and let's get home."

"Yes, Pa," Luke mumbled.

With a satisfied nod, Papa Dell turned his horse and rode after the three ranch hands who appeared as mere dots on the horizon. Luke's gaze followed his pa's retreating form. Laney could see the struggle in his expression, and her heart went out to him, sifting the anger from her like a sieve. The two men often disagreed about the ranch. Luke complained that his pa was too set in his ways, and the older man always said there was no reason to change what had worked well for over twenty years. No one could deny that the St. John ranch prospered more than any ranch in the area, but Laney had to wonder why his pa couldn't at least consider some of Luke's ideas.

Clearing her throat, she reached out tentatively, then stopped short of touching Luke's arm as he turned to her, eyes blazing.

"Get in the wagon, and let's get out of here."

That was the last time she'd try apologizing to him! "Well, you don't have to be such an ol' bear about it. It's not my fault your pa rode back to check on us and caught you pinning me to the ground."

"Which," Luke said through gritted teeth, "I wouldn't have been doing if you hadn't knocked me off my horse in the first place."

Hands on her hips, Laney stamped her foot and glared back at him. "You shouldn't have suggested I don't act like a girl."

"Suggested? I'm saying plain as day you don't act like a woman. Just look at you." Reaching forward, he flicked her Stetson from her head.

"Hey!" Snatching at the air, Laney made a futile attempt to catch the hat before it landed on the ground. Leaving it, she glowered. "Wearing britches and a hat don't make me no less a woman than a person in ruffles and petticoats."

"I didn't say you're less of a woman. I said you don't act like the rest of them." He gave her a pointed look. "And you don't."

Narrowing her gaze, Laney sized him up. She cocked her head to the side. "What do you know about women anyway?"

Deep creases etched his brow. "Just forget about it, okay?"

"No," she challenged. "I want to know. Just how do you think a woman is supposed to act?" The air between them grew still as she waited. What sort of woman was Luke looking for? Could she ever measure up?

He hesitated a moment, regarding her frankly. "You know, all soft and. . . womanly. I don't know, Laney. Just let it be."

"Womanly?" Dejectedly Laney glanced down at her faded britches and ripped shirt. Soft and womanly pretty much excluded her from the list of possible candidates for Luke's affection.

He looked pensively toward the orange horizon, where the sun was making a final bow before disappearing into the night sky. A sense of foreboding coursed through Laney at the faraway look in his eyes.

"What do you mean by 'womanly'?"

He shifted his gaze back to her, searching. Laney's heart pounded in her ears at his uncharacteristically intense manner. He spoke slowly, thoughtfully. "A man wants a woman he can take into his arms and feel like she needs him to protect her." Laney stiffened as a hint of the old teasing creased the corners of his eyes. "In all the years I've known you, you've never once even let me lead a dance."

Laney smarted under his criticism and was about to retort when he strode forward and retrieved her hat from the ground. He towered over her tiny frame. The angry words fled her mind as he placed the Stetson gently atop her head and looked down into her eyes. "You're a pretty girl, Laney."

Laney's hopes soared at his words and then sank as he continued. "But pretty isn't all a man wants." He smiled an almost bitter smile. "You don't need anyone to take care of you. You can outride, outshoot, and outtrack most of the men living in and around Harper, and everyone knows it. A fellow doesn't want a wife who's more of a man than he is." He laughed. "You'd probably expect your husband to scrub the floors and cook the food you shoot."

His laughter was all the humiliation Laney could take. There was only one way to prove to him she was as much of a woman as any of the frilly, eye-batting, teeth-flashing ninnies of Harper out to trap him into matrimony.

With a determined lift of her chin, she took a step closer until she stood mere inches from him.

"What are you doing?" Suspicion thickened his tone, and he moved back.

Silently she took another step forward without breaking his startled gaze. Then before she could change her mind or he could get away, she inched her arms upward until they clasped behind his neck.

"What do you think you're—"

Without a word, Laney rose up on her toes and kissed him full on the lips. He stood motionless for only an instant, then his arms encircled her waist, pressing her closer. Laney's senses reeled as her plan backfired and Luke took control. His mouth moved over hers until she clung to him. When he gently released her, they stood for a moment, gazes locked, chests heaving.

"Do you want to tell me what that was all about?" Luke asked, visibly shaken, but scowling as if he hadn't responded to the kiss.

Laney stepped back.

"Well?" he asked.

"D—don't ever say I'm not a woman again!"

Giving him no chance to respond, she spun around on the heel of her boot and stomped to Luke's horse, Rusty. She mounted the gelding.

"What do you think you're doing?"

"I'm sick of that wagon." She glared down at him, daring him to try to stop her. "You take it to the ranch. I'm going straight home."

"Okay, fine. I'll be over tomorrow to pick up my horse."

"Fine." Needing to distance herself from him as quickly as possible, Laney nudged the horse into a gallop and left Luke standing beside the wagon.

The memory of Luke's lips on hers taunted Laney as she headed for Harper. She squirmed under the humiliation. How could she have been so stupid? Now Luke would know she cared for him. Things would never be the same again.

A cloud of dust rose up around Laney as she sped away. Luke stared after her, shaking his head. *She ought to have more sense than to ride Rusty so hard after weeks on the trail.*

He climbed onto the wagon seat and flapped the reins. What had crazy little Laney been thinking, kissing him like that? She couldn't even let a man make the first move. Not that he ever would have. He'd never thought of Laney romantically. But he had to admit, their kiss was something. Even now, the memory of her soft, full lips beneath his stirred him.

With a frustrated grunt, Luke tried to remove the image of her wide, doelike eyes staring up at him in wonder after he released her. It wasn't like he'd never kissed a girl before. He'd stolen plenty of kisses behind the schoolhouse and on buggy rides, but none had affected him like this one.

Whatever possessed him to draw her into his arms and respond to her kiss the way he had? Laney, of all people! She'd grown up in his older sister, Tarah's, home. Luke and Laney had played together, fished together, hunted together, and for the past two years worked the ranch together. But mostly they fought. Luke grinned in spite of his confusion. Laney could get riled up quicker than an ol' tomcat stuck in a tree, and he knew just how to get her spittin' mad. To her credit, she never held a grudge. Once she said her piece, that was that and she was ready to be friends again.

His friend, his buddy, his pal. . .or was their kiss an indication there was more than friendship between them?

Luke chided himself for the idiotic thought worming its way into his mind. He shook his head. How could there be anything romantic between them? That was about the dumbest thing he'd ever thought of. And it was her fault. If she hadn't been so fired up to prove she was a woman—and she'd pretty well made her point—he wouldn't be so addlepated about everything.

He stared into the dusky sky. Things would never be the same between them again. She'd expect him to court her now. And she'd be within her rights to expect it after the way he'd kissed her.

Luke slapped at his thigh. He'd made a big mess of things by not throwing her away from him and giving her a good chewing out for even trying to kiss him. If only it hadn't seemed so right. . . .

"What do you mean, you aren't going to the dance tonight?"

Seated on the edge of her bed, Laney forced herself to meet Tarah Greene's gaze head-on. "Exactly what I said. I'm staying home."

"Now you listen to me, Laney Jenkins. You've been moping around this house for two weeks—always making excuses not to go to the ranch or even to church. Are you going to tell me what happened on that trail, or am I going to have to go ask Pa?"

Laney knew better than to try to skirt around the issue any longer. When Tarah tossed her head of coal-black hair, she meant business.

Laney threw herself across her bed, landing on her stomach, chin planted firmly in her palm. "I kissed Luke," she admitted flatly, wishing for all she was worth the episode had been only another of her delicious dreams instead of a wretched bit of reality.

After a moment of silence, Laney turned her head to see if Tarah was still in the room. Tarah grinned as Laney's gaze found hers. "Are you telling me you and Luke are courting now?"

"No. He was teasing me, as usual, about not acting like a girl, and I just. . . up and kissed him." Laney emitted a low groan. "He makes me so mad, Tarah. Always insinuating I'm somewhere between a male and female just because I like to wear britches and boots." Laney gave a frustrated wave of her hand. "So what did I do? I had to go and show him I'm all woman."

Tarah lowered herself carefully to the bed beside Laney. "Believe me," she said, her lips twitching, "as Luke's sister and former schoolteacher, I know how infuriating he can be. The thing that surprises me is your reaction to it after all these years. I would have expected you to ignore him or punch him. . .but a kiss? Where did that come from?"

"From me, unfortunately." Laney heaved a sigh as she stared morosely at the ceiling. "Now he'll probably think I want him to court me like some weak-kneed sissy-girl with a lacy parasol."

"You know, Laney, there's no shame in being a woman. And looking like one," Tarah said with a pointed glance at Laney's faded britches. "And there's nothing wrong with wanting a man to court you."

She shrugged. "It's okay for other women—just not for me, that's all. It's not like I don't wear skirts when I go to town or for church on Sunday. But I have to wear britches on the ranch. How can I herd cattle in a dress? And if Luke wants the kind of woman who faints and flutters, then I wasted a perfectly good kiss on a big, dumb. . .dumb. . . !" She hated it when she couldn't think of just the right insult, even if he wasn't in the room to hear it.

"Honestly, Laney. Don't fret about it." Tarah stood as gracefully as her protruding stomach would allow and planted her hands on her hips, rounded from bearing three babies in the past eight years. "Don't wear a dress on the ranch and at home if you'd rather not—you know, no one in the family cares about that. And don't waste any more kisses on Luke—although it served him right that

258

you gave him one in the first place. But you *have* to come to the dance. Half the women there will be wearing gowns you made. You never know how many orders you might get for more, once word gets out that you made the prettiest dresses at the dance."

The thought was tempting. Laney's mind floated to her growing nest egg. If she could sell a few more dresses, she'd have enough to put a down payment on the old soddy Mr. Garner was willing to sell to her along with five acres now with an option to buy more.

As if reading her mind, Tarah sighed heavily. "I hate the thought of you moving out. You should stay with us until you marry. Then you and your husband would have a fine start with the money you've socked away."

Laney's eyes widened. "Give my money to a man? Are you crazy, Tarah? Pa took everything we had and drank it away. I'm going to make sure I have everything I need, and I'll never let a man boss me. No siree. That might be okay for some women, but not me—ever! When I marry, I'll make sure my property is protected so he can't take it and squander it all away. My young'uns will be taken care of."

Tarah gave her a pitying smile—one that carried a secret Laney felt she would never be privy to. "Laney, honey," Tarah said, "when you find a man who really loves you, he won't want to boss you around. You'll be partners."

Laney snorted.

"It's true." Tarah's smile widened, and she sent Laney a wink. "And you know what else?"

"What?" Laney asked, narrowing her gaze in suspicion.

"You'll gladly give him all the money you have, because you'll be able to trust him to use it wisely, and if he is a smart man—which I have no doubt he will be—he'll want all the input from you he can get about how to spend it."

Laney stood, inclining her head in a jerky nod. "I won't marry a dumb man. That's for sure. Still, I reckon I'll do it my way just in case he takes to drinking. That makes a man stupid real fast."

Tarah chuckled and hugged Laney tightly. "Oh, Laney. God has such a wonderful plan for your life. I only hope you're not too stubborn to let Him unfold it for you."

"God gave me a good head on my shoulders and two sturdy hands. I reckon He expects me to do the rest. And, Tarah, I fully intend to make sure I can take care of myself."

Laney squirmed under that pity-smile again.

"Then come out to the Moodys' farm for the dance. I could use your help with the kids."

Laney gave a short laugh. The whole town loved Reverend Greene, Tarah, and their three children. Once she walked through the barn doors, Tarah wouldn't see those children again until they were ready to leave.

Caught in her manipulation, Tarah gave her a sheepish grin and shrugged. "Okay, maybe I won't need help with the children, but you still have to go. We won't have nearly as much fun without you. Now come on. I took your blue skirt off the line today. I noticed it's getting a bit thin. You may want to take time out to sew another one before it's too threadbare to do any good. Anyway, the tub's filled and waiting for you in the kitchen."

Unable to withstand Tarah's pleading eyes, Laney relented. "All right. But only because I might get some business out of it."

"Wonderful!" Tarah said, her violet eyes sparkling. "I'll leave you to get ready for your bath, then."

Laney watched the door close behind Tarah. Her stomach jumped at the thought of seeing Luke for the first time since their kiss. Would he act any differently? Would he ask her to dance like old times? She'd be careful to let him lead this time. Following wasn't easy for her, but she could do anything she set her mind to. Especially if it meant proving to Luke she was a woman.

Fleetingly her mind drifted to the blue silk gown in her wardrobe. The fashionable bustle was sure to make Luke take notice. As far as Laney knew, no one else would be wearing a bustle this evening. The woman who had commissioned the gown had gained at least fifteen pounds between the time she had ordered the dress and waited her turn for Laney to sew it. There wasn't enough material to make it fit, so Laney had to take a loss on the sale.

She walked to the wardrobe, opened it, and fingered the delicate material. The loss of money might be worth the look in Luke's eyes when he saw her wearing this.

"Laney?" Tarah's voice drifted through the door.

Laney jumped and snatched her hand away as though she were a thief caught stealing priceless jewels. "What?" she snapped.

"If you don't take your bath right now, we'll be late for the dance."

"You all go on ahead of me. I'll get ready and follow on Colby."

"Are you sure, Laney? We can wait if you'll hurry."

"I'd rather ride."

Laney felt Tarah's hesitation.

"Honest, Tarah. You go on. The preacher's family can't be late. I'll be along soon. I promise."

"All right. We'll see you there."

Laney smiled at the relief in Tarah's tone. Laney always kept her promises. Tarah knew that and trusted her. The knowledge warmed Laney.

Laney Jenkins didn't lie, she didn't cheat, and she never, ever went back on her word no matter how much it cost her. She grabbed her simple muslin skirt and fresh blue gingham shirt from the wardrobe, then slammed the wardrobe shut. Most of all she never, ever resorted to frills to win a man's attention. Luke would have to take her as she was, or he could forget it!

Dejectedly Laney studied her reflection in the vanity mirror. Luke had already told her what kind of woman he wanted, and she didn't come close to fitting his ideal. She jerked her chin. Oh well. Let him marry some snippy, drippy, fainting ninny. Laney Jenkins would be just fine on her own. Everything was going according to plan. If her dresses kept selling, she would soon have the down payment on her own land. She'd be self-reliant, and the Jenkins name would be brought to honor instead of the shame her pa had made of it.

Who needed Luke St. John, anyway?

Chapter 2

Laney's head pounded to the beat of "Camptown Races," and her toes suffered under the punishment of Clyde Hampton's shiny new boots.

She cast another hopeful glance toward the double doors of Mr. Moody's barn—which had been transformed for the harvest dance, as it was every year. The dance had been well under way for the past forty-five minutes, and still no Luke. Not that Laney cared if he missed the harvest dance. Why should she?

"Ow." Laney turned her gaze from the door and glared up at her dancing partner as pain shot through her big toe and up to her ankle. "Clyde, where'd you learn to dance, anyway?"

"I'm sorry, Miss Laney." The middle-aged sheep rancher's face turned as red as the handkerchief tied around his long, skinny neck. "Don't know what's got into me tonight. Seems I got two left feet."

"Oh, Clyde." Laney gave him an apologetic smile, suddenly feeling guilty for her churlish manner. "You're not that bad."

His face brightened. "Mighty kind of ya to say so, Miss Laney."

"May I cut in, Clyde?"

Laney's palms dampened at the sound of Luke's voice.

"Be my guest."

All the feelings of compassion she had previously felt for the bad dancer fled at the relief in Clyde's tone and the way he practically pushed her into Luke's arms.

"Clumsy oaf," she muttered as the rancher hurried from the dance floor. "I won't be able to wear my boots for a week."

Luke laughed and pulled her into the circle of his arms. "It's your own fault if your toes are bruised. You should have let him lead."

Laney huffed and stepped to her left, then stopped short as Luke stepped to her right. He laughed again. "See what I mean? Now concentrate real hard and try to follow."

"I wouldn't follow you if you were the last man on earth with two good legs, Luke St. John!" Laney squirmed, trying to free herself from his embrace.

"I'm probably the last man on earth even willing to dance with the likes of you, Laney Jenkins," he retorted, releasing her.

Fury washed over her. "I can get any man here to dance with me, and they'd be proud to do it!"

"Simmer down. People are staring."

Laney glanced quickly around the room, observing the raised brows from a group of gray-haired matrons chatting in the corner and Papa Dell's disapproving frown from the other side of the room, where he stood talking with Anthony. She drew in a long, calming breath. Luke had the uncanny ability to get her riled enough to make a complete fool of herself, but this time she would not allow him to bait her.

With a step forward, she placed her hand on his shoulder and waited for him to take the other. "Lead," she commanded through gritted teeth.

Luke pulled her to him once more just as the music ended and the band struck up a new tune. "You up for a waltz?" he asked, brow raised in skepticism as though he didn't quite believe it was a good idea.

"I'm up for anything you are. Just make sure you get the steps right."

He narrowed his gaze. "Just make sure you follow, or we'll both end up on the floor."

"Fine."

In spite of her determination to remain rigid, Laney's anger sifted from her almost immediately, and she felt the tension leave her shoulders. Enjoying the feel of Luke's strong hand cupping her waist, she closed her eyes, allowing herself to be swept away by the music. Luke spun her around the room without missing a beat.

A soft, contented sigh escaped her lips.

At Luke's sharp intake of breath, Laney opened her eyes. He stared down at her, his green eyes serious and searching. Laney's pulse quickened as his gaze moved across her face, then settled on her lips.

He leaned forward. "Let's get out of here," he said, his voice low against her ear.

Laney shivered from the tickle of his breath, and wordlessly she nodded. She barely noticed the other dancers or the people huddled around the refreshment table as Luke ushered her outside and behind a nearby tree. He leaned back against the oak and took her hands in his as they faced each other.

"What's happening between us, Laney?"

At a loss for words, Laney stared into his dear face, joy invading the very depths of her soul.

He pulled her closer. "I can't sleep for thinking about you and that kiss. What did you do to me?"

A lump lodged deep in Laney's throat, cutting off any reply.

"If you don't stop looking at me like that and say something. . ." Luke growled. He released her hands and pulled her into the circle of his arms. Even before his head descended, Laney knew she was about to be kissed.

His lips brushed against hers once. . .twice—soft and achingly sweet. Laney moved closer as his arms tightened. He pressed his forehead against hers. "My Laney, why didn't I know I've been in love with you all these years?"

Giving her no chance to answer, Luke captured her lips once more.

"Yuck!"

Laney tore herself away from Luke and turned to Tarah's oldest boy, Little D, named for Papa Dell. He sneered in disgust as he observed them.

"I found 'em, Pa!" He turned toward the barn.

"Little D, wait!"

Laney cringed as he hollered, "Uncle Luke's kissing Laney!"

"Get back over here, then, and give them some privacy." Anthony's amused voice brought heat to Laney's cheeks.

"Yuck!" Little D repeated, then took off lickety-split.

Still imprisoned in Luke's iron grip, Laney turned her gaze back to his teasing eyes. He grinned down at her. "Guess I'll have to marry you now that the whole town knows I've been stealing kisses behind the kissing tree."

As usual, the appropriate quip eluded her. "You will?" she whispered.

All traces of teasing fled his expression. "I was just getting around to asking."

"You were?"

"What do you say?"

Yes, yes, yes. The words remained stuck in her throat.

"What? Don't you want to marry me?"

At the hurt expression in his eyes, Laney found her tongue. "I can't imagine marrying anyone else. I just can't believe you're really asking."

A grin spread across Luke's face. With a loud whoop, he snatched her up, spinning her around until she laughed and beat lightly on his broad shoulders.

He set her on her feet. "Do you mean it?"

"Do you?"

"You bet I do."

"Then so do I."

He dipped his head and kissed her again, leaving her senses reeling by the time he pulled away.

"What do you say to a late winter wedding?" Luke asked. "We'll head west as soon as we can hook up with a wagon train in the spring. We'll be in Oregon by the fall of the year and stake our claim. By the following spring, we'll be ready to start a herd of our own."

Laney's stomach sank to her toes as she watched Luke grow more excited with each word he spoke. "What do you mean, you want to go west, Luke? I haven't heard you mention it since we were still in school. I—I thought you gave up such notions after you started working with your pa."

Luke kissed her hard, then pulled back with a grin. "I've never stopped wanting to go. With you at my side, we'll raise a herd even larger than my pa's."

Laney jerked away from his arms. "So this moving west is all about proving you can outdo your pa? That's just dumb, Luke. And you're dumb for thinking of it."

The line of Luke's jaw tightened. "That's not it. I don't want to build on another man's foundation. I want to make my own way and leave a real legacy to my own son or daughter." Gently he took her hand. "*Our* sons or daughters."

Forcing her gaze from his, Laney turned her back, knowing she'd never be able to say what must be said if she faced him. "I'll bet that's what Papa Dell thought, too. He'd build a herd and leave a real legacy for his sons. Only Sam decided to be a doctor, you're leaving, and Jack and Will are too young to be any real help. If you go, what's your pa going to do? You should wait until Jack is old enough to take over, at least. That'll only be two more years."

Luke shook his head. "Jack's been reading law in Tom Kirkpatrick's office. He's convinced he wants to become an attorney. Pa's offered to send him to Harvard when he passes the last of his courses at the town school."

Laney spun back around. "Then you'll just have to wait until Will grows up. That's only seven or eight more years. You wouldn't even be thirty years old yet."

"By then all the land will be gone! Besides, my pa has plenty of hired hands, just like he did before Sam and I were old enough to help out around the ranch. Just like we will in Oregon."

"It's not the same. It's going to break his heart to see you go."

Luke took her hands in his once more. "Laney, honey, families move off from each other all the time. It's the way of the world. They'll miss us, of course, just like we'll miss them; but we can come back for a visit every two or three years, and Pa and Ma can visit us."

With grim determination, Laney pulled her hands away and planted them firmly on her hips. She shook her head decisively. "Not 'us,' Luke. I'm sorry to go back on my word about marrying you, but I'd rather swallow a live tadpole than move off to *Oregon*. I like it right here in Harper. Besides, now that my brother is marrying Josie Raney, he'll be moving to Virginia as pastor of his own church."

A sickened expression covered Luke's face. "What does Ben have to do with whether or not you marry me?"

So disappointed was she at the unexpected turn of events, Laney didn't even attempt to be patient. "Don't you know anything? Every preacher alive has a passel of young'uns, and they never have enough money to feed themselves, let alone enough to pack them all onto a train to go off visiting a long-lost sister. I'd never see him again."

"We'll work it out. Won't you at least consider it?"

Squaring her shoulders, Laney forced back the tears tickling her throat. "No, I won't. Ben's all I have in the world, and I won't take a chance on never seeing him again. Besides, ten ladies ordered gowns tonight that have to be ready in time for the Christmas ball. After they pay me, I'll have enough for a down payment on the old soddy."

Luke's mouth dropped open. "You mean you aim to buy the soddy you lived in when you and your pa and Ben first came to Harper?"

"That's right. I've been saving every penny from sewing and working your pa's ranch for the last two years." Laney lifted her chin stubbornly. "Mr. Garner is selling for a right fair price, and he's willing to carry the note himself if I come up with a big enough down payment to prove I'm serious about it. He's selling me five acres to boot, and I can buy more as my own herd grows." She gasped as a wonderful idea flooded her mind. "Luke!"

Luke shook his head. "Don't even suggest it, Laney."

"But why? We'd still be starting our own herd. Only it would be here and not off somewhere away from the family. This is perfect." Laney beamed up at him, then, as emotions got the better of her, there didn't seem anything to do but throw her arms around his neck. So that's what she did. "Tarah was right, as usual," she said over his shoulder. "I don't mind sharing my money with the right man. But don't take to getting liquored up, Luke, or I'll have to hide every cent from you, and I'd never give it up even if you beat me to a bloody pulp."

He gave an exasperated sigh. "You know I'd never take a drink or hit you."

Laney clasped him more tightly around the neck. "Then it's all settled."

Luke's large, steady hands encircled her wrists and pulled her away from him. "I don't want to stay in Harper. I'd always be the 'St. John boy following in his father's footsteps.' Out West I can be my own man. Can't you understand how important that is to me?"

"So you just ask a girl to marry you and then take it back?" Anger burned inside Laney as realization struck her.

"I'm not taking anything back. I'm just saying if you want to marry me, you'll have to go west, because that's where I'm headed next spring."

"Who says I want to marry you, anyway? I wouldn't marry you even if you was stayin' in Harper." Disappointment loosened her tongue and caused her to revert to her childhood speech. "I'd rather marry red-faced ol' Clyde and raise all five of his poor, motherless children—even if he ain't much of a dancer—than have to marry you."

"That suits me just fine."

"Fine!"

"We might as well head back inside, then," Luke said, taking her by the elbow.

Laney jerked away. "Turn your back so I can get out of this skirt."

"What?"

"The skirt. I can't ride home with it on, now, can I?"

Luke shook his head and turned his back. "I don't know why you bother putting it on over britches, anyway. Everyone knows what you're wearing underneath."

Staring at Luke's back, Laney slipped off the skirt and wadded it into a ball. She tucked it under her arm. "All right. You can look now. Tarah and Anthony take too much criticism over me wearing britches, though it seems more indecent to me for everyone to be thinking about what I'm wearing under my skirt than for me to just wear the britches out in the first place."

"When you put it that way. . ."

She shrugged. "Doesn't make much sense, but I guess to some people, as long as they don't have to *see* what's underneath, it doesn't make them uncomfortable knowing what's there."

"I guess."

Still smarting from the disappointing evening, Laney stepped toward the hitching post to get Colby. "Anyway, tell Tarah I rode on home," she said over her shoulder.

Luke grabbed her arm and spun her around to face him. "You're not going by yourself."

"You don't tell me what to do! If I want to ride home by myself, I will!"

"Fine, you stubborn-headed mule. See if I care." Too angry to speak, Laney spun around and headed for her horse. Tears of disappointment forced their way down her cheeks despite her best efforts to keep them at bay.

Who wanted to marry that big, dumb. . .dumb. . . Well, who wanted to, anyway?

Luke quickly stepped inside the barn, knowing it would take Laney no time at all to get saddled and hightail it to the edge of town. Normally the short ride wouldn't cause concern, but after seeing the WANTED poster the sheriff hung up in Tucker's Mercantile just that afternoon, Luke worried for Laney's safety. Her no-account pa had not been seen anywhere near Harper for years, but according to the poster, he and a couple of men he rode with had robbed the home of a wealthy businessman in Topeka not two weeks ago. Topeka was too close to Harper for Luke's comfort. He'd feel better if the man were clear across the country. If Mr. Jenkins decided to head this direction and look up his children, he'd be able to spot Laney like a red barn in a green field. She hadn't changed all that much in eight years. She still wore britches except for in public places, and her hair hung in a thick, dark blond braid down the center of her back. No bigger than a twelve-year-old boy, she would be an easy target if someone wanted to grab her. She'd put up a good fight, but her size would be a disadvantage.

"Where's Laney?" Tarah's eyes twinkled with teasing. "Little D is completely disgusted that you've joined the ranks of the kissing men, Uncle Luke. I don't believe he will ever trust you again."

Luke felt his ears heat up. "He can lay his fears to rest. I just came back over to the other side."

She chuckled and rubbed her protruding stomach. "That didn't take long."

"That's what I came to tell you. Laney and I had words, and she took off for home. I'm going to make sure she makes it all right."

"You two are hopeless." In spite of her words, Tarah's lips twitched. "It's not that far, Luke. I'm sure she'll be fine. Why don't you stay and enjoy the dance?"

"I'll explain it to you some other time. I have to go."

Without waiting for a reply, Luke left. He quickly mounted his horse and headed toward the parsonage. To his relief, a soft glow came from inside the stable. He dismounted and tethered Rusty to the hitching post outside the church. Striding purposefully toward the stable, Luke determined not to be dissuaded from his mission to see her safely inside the house. As he approached, the sound of wrenching sobs stopped him in his tracks.

Laney! He had never heard her cry before—hadn't really thought her capable of shedding tears. Compassion mingled with his own disappointment. He longed to hold her. . .to comfort them both. Without thinking, Luke stepped inside the musty stable. Pungent odors of manure and fresh hay assailed his senses. "Laney?"

She glanced up sharply, swiping her gingham sleeve across her face. "What are you doing here? I thought I told you I didn't need you following me home."

"I just wanted to be sure you were safe."

"I'm just fine. And don't think I'm crying because of you, because I'm not. I—I just. . . Well, I'm just. . ." She kicked at the wood stall where her horse munched on hay. "It's none of your business why I'm crying, so just go home and don't you dare tell anyone, or I'll flat out deny it."

"I wouldn't dream of telling."

"Make sure you don't," she warned, obviously unappeased by his smile.

"I need to tell you something."

Laney sniffed. "Please, Luke," she said wearily. "I don't think I can take any more of your news tonight."

"It's important."

Her chest heaved with a long-suffering sigh. "All right, but make it fast so I can be in bed before the family gets back from the dance. I don't feel like dealing with Little D."

Luke told her about the poster. Her expression changed from sadness to horror as she listened, her eyes widening in fright.

"Do you think he'll try to come back here and get me to help him hide from the law?"

"I don't know, honey. But you need to be on the lookout for him, just in case. I'll be watching, too. Try not to go off riding by yourself."

"I can't stay locked up like a prisoner." Determinedly Laney grabbed the lantern from its nail. She walked with purpose to the doors and glanced expectantly at Luke. He followed, wishing the events of the night had not unfolded as they had. They should be celebrating their betrothal with family and friends right now—not standing outside in the cold autumn night, about to get into another argument because of Laney's stubbornness.

"You have to be more careful. No other woman in this town would gallivant the way you do without a chaperone."

A snicker escaped her. "Tarah rides out to the ranch all the time by herself, and Anthony doesn't mind."

"All right. I should clarify that only the women in my family would ride around alone."

"If Pa wants to find me, he will—whether I'm hiding out or riding alone on the prairie. I'm not going to hole up like some coward. I just can't." They reached the parsonage steps, and Laney turned. "Thank you for the concern, Luke. I appreciate it. But I've always looked after myself. I'll be all right. Good night."

Luke watched her step inside and close the door, knowing there was nothing he could say. He wished he could go back and relive the past couple of hours. He had added to Laney's hurt tonight by asking her to marry him before he shared his plans to move west. He had been too caught up in her large doelike eyes and her soft, rosy lips and wasn't thinking clearly.

Still, if a woman loved a man enough, wouldn't she be willing to go with him? Luke pondered the question as he rode the few miles out to the St. John ranch. The thought tightened his stomach. He wished for all he was worth he had never teased her on the way home from Abilene. Then she wouldn't have kissed him, and their friendship would never have been distorted. But it was too late for regrets. No matter how many miles separated them, Luke would never forget the joy of holding her in his arms or the sweetness of her kiss.

Chapter 3

Laney stared at the wanted poster on the wall in Tucker's Mercantile. The man in the sketch looked older and thinner than she remembered, but there was no denying the cold eyes staring back at her. Memories she'd thought were long buried assaulted her. Laney shivered. Pa was back.

"Afternoon, Laney."

She jumped as Mr. Tucker entered from the back room. Dragging her gaze from the poster, Laney stepped up to the counter, trying to pretend nonchalance.

Tucker nodded toward the wall. "Thought he looked an awful lot like yer pa, even if he is goin' by the name Hiram Jones."

"Yeah, it's him." Laney lifted her shoulders in an it-don't-bother-me-none shrug.

Tucker raised his gray, bushy brows. "You just mind yerself and be careful. Ya hear?"

"I can take care of myself." Laney lifted her chin. Why did everyone think she needed to be protected?

Tucker let out an unpleasant snort. "Yer barely big enough to look over this counter without standing on your tippy toes, gal. What makes you think you can hold yer own against someone as big and mean as yer pa?"

Laney pulled back her sheepskin coat and revealed the gun belt hanging from her boyishly small hips, over her new wool skirt. "I'd say this just about evens the odds, wouldn't you?"

The old man's eyes narrowed. "Now see here. Does yer family know yer totin' a Colt?"

Letting the coat drop back into place, Laney met Tucker's gaze head-on. "No. And don't you go blabbing, either. You'll just make Tarah worry, and she doesn't need to be doing that in her condition."

"I ain't makin' no promises, missy, so don't try to bully me. If I feel the need to spill yer little secret, I will."

Laney glared at the old codger. Tucker wasn't one to back down from a fight. Even though he'd become a Christian years ago, he was still as formidable as ever.

"Have it your way, then." She rose up on her toes and leaned her elbows on the tall counter. "Anthony said you wanted to see me."

Tucker nodded. "That's right. I got a proposition fer you."

Laney's eyes widened, and she inwardly retreated. Was Mr. Tucker losing his mind? "Mr. Tucker, maybe you should think about this some more before you—"

The storekeeper shook his head. "Nope. Got my mind made up. Yer just what I been lookin' fer."

Stepping away from the counter, Laney glowered. "I like you fine, Tucker. You're a real hard worker and nice enough when you take a notion to be, but I ain't marrying up with a man old enough to be my pa's uncle!"

Brows knit together, Mr. Tucker turned red beneath his scraggly whiskers. "Are you goin' soft in the head? I ain't askin' you to marry up with me, gal!"

Mortified, Laney lowered her gaze as heat suffused her cheeks. "What other proposition did you have in mind?"

"What are you two yelling at each other about?"

Neither Mr. Tucker nor Laney had heard the bell above the door signaling Luke's entrance into the mercantile.

Laney stared at the floor. "Nothing," she muttered.

"Just a misunderstanding," Mr. Tucker confirmed.

Laney could have kissed the old coot for sparing her more humiliation in front of Luke.

"I was just telling Laney here that I got a proposition fer her."

"What proposition?" Luke asked. His eyes narrowed, and Laney knew instinctively he had made the same assumption she had. The thought warmed her.

"A *business* proposition."

Laney's ears perked up. "What'd you have in mind?"

"How'd you like to work for me, sewing dresses for the store?"

"And split my profit?"

" 'Course."

Laney's brow furrowed. "Why would I want to do that? I get to keep all my money when I drum up my own business."

"Yeah, but how much business do you drum up?"

Laney drew herself up to her full height. "I got myself ten orders at the dance last week."

"Party dresses?"

"That's right."

"Well, that ain't what I'm talkin' about, missy. So how's about you closin' yer trap and hearin' me out?"

Smarting under the reprimand, Laney sized him up for a minute. Mr. Tucker wouldn't suggest something that wouldn't benefit her. He was like a grand old uncle. "I'm listening."

Luke shifted his weight and leaned against the counter. Laney felt his nearness as keenly as if he had embraced her. She cleared her throat and tried to concentrate on Mr. Tucker's voice.

"Now them hoity-toity ladies movin' to Harper from the cities come in here all the time lookin' fer ready-made dresses. I'm losin' business if they order from them books." He leaned forward and pointed a gnarled finger toward her face. "If you and me was to partner up, we'd both stand to make a profit."

"I understand that, Mr. Tucker, but why shouldn't I just get my business straight from them?"

He sent her a scowl fierce enough to intimidate a grizzly. Laney's eyes grew wide, and she stepped back. "It ain't right for you to take my idea and go lookin' fer business after I'm the one that brought it up in the first place. Ain't living with that preacher all these years taught you nothin', gal?"

Luke chuckled. "He has a point."

Laney turned the full force of her glare upon him, then focused her attention once more on Mr. Tucker.

Luke was right; Tucker did have a point. Still, she could have kicked herself for not thinking of advertising for her own business in the first place. "All right. Let's hear your terms."

She listened carefully and had to admit she would save the funds to buy her soddy and start a herd much quicker if she accepted the proposal.

"Throw in the dress goods and I might consider it."

Tucker stared at her as though she had lost her mind. "You expect me to provide the dress goods *and* split the profits fifty-fifty?"

Laney shrugged. "I have to do all the work. Seems fair to me."

Tucker squinted at her as if considering. "All right," he grumbled. "But it sounds like highway robbery to me."

Elated, Laney nodded, trying not to glow with victory. She'd never expected Tucker to give in so easily. "And I broke the handle on my shears last week, so I'll need a new pair."

Tucker gave her a wry grin. "You can pay for those, can't you?"

Luke chuckled. "Seems to me that's the least you can do, Laney."

Grudgingly Laney handed over the money. "All right. You willin' to put all this in writing?"

Laney winced as Mr. Tucker's mouth turned down in indignation. "What do you take me fer? Some thief? We got a witness right here." He jerked his thumb toward Luke.

"That's not what I mean. I want to show Mr. Garner proof of a steady income so I can get my soddy. I won't have room to work at Anthony and Tarah's with all those kids running around."

Appeased, Mr. Tucker nodded. "Reckon I can do that."

Twenty minutes later, with signed proof of a steady income, Laney strode from the mercantile and headed for her horse.

Luke followed. "Congratulations. Looks like you're getting what you wanted."

"Looks that way." Then why did she feel so empty when she gazed at the familiar freckled face staring back at her? "How about you? You told your ma and pa about your plans?"

Luke's jaw tightened. "Not yet."

"It'll be all right, Luke. You have a right to be your own man. Your pa will understand that."

A short laugh lifted his shoulders. "But you can't understand it?"

"I just don't see why you'd want to leave your family. If you'd stay here and help me start my herd. . ."

"Your herd?"

"Well, it would be ours. Yours and mine. If you'd stop being so stubborn about letting me share it with you."

Luke smiled at her. "I have money saved. I could help you buy the soddy and start the herd."

Hope lifted Laney's drooping spirits.

"But that's not the point. I want to go west and be my own man."

"But, Luke, if you stay here and we got mar—" Laney stopped. She would not beg.

Luke's brow arched. "If we got married?" He reached for her hand, sending warmth through her belly. Luke's gaze searched hers, drawing Laney in until she was certain. "Don't go put that money down on the soddy, Laney. Marry me. Come west and let's build a life together. Don't you see how good it would be between us?"

Looking into Luke's emerald green eyes and remembering the warmth of his kisses, Laney almost relented. But reason prevailed. She snatched her hand away. "I can't do it, Luke. I just can't." Quickly she mounted her horse. She stared down at him. "You got your plans, and I got mine. They just don't match up, that's all." Without giving him a chance to respond, she whipped her horse around and headed off toward Mr. Garner's property. She knew if she stayed any longer, she would fall into Luke's arms and never leave them. But Harper was home. Tarah and Anthony and their brood were home. How could she give them up? No. This way was for the best. Luke would go to Oregon and fulfill his dreams, and she would stay here and fulfill hers.

It was for the best. . . .

Luke drove in the last stake for the new fence and stepped back to wipe the sweat from his brow. "There," he said, taking the proffered canteen from his pa. "If that doesn't keep Ol' Angus in his own pasture, nothing will."

He took a swig of the tepid water, wiped his mouth with the back of his arm, and screwed the lid back on the canteen.

Pa leaned his weight against the newly repaired fence. "I thought I'd go ahead and buy a new bull next year in Abilene." He stared at the bull with a troubled expression. "Ol' Angus has just about worn out his usefulness, and he's getting meaner than a grizzly from what I can tell. I'm worried he'll get loose and gore a young'un walking home from school."

Luke nodded, clenching his teeth to refrain from mentioning that he'd been suggesting that very thing for the past year. The aging bull had knocked this same fence down twice in the past six months trying to get at a passing rider or someone walking through the north field. If Pa had listened in the first place, they wouldn't have had to waste time making the repairs.

"Reckon you already knew that about Ol' Angus, huh?"

Luke stared off into the blue horizon. "I reckon." What else could he say?

"I should have listened to you." Pa kept his own gaze fixed beyond the brown field.

Luke knew what the admission had cost his pa. He remained silent, sensing there was more to this conversation than Ol' Angus's foul temper.

Pa cleared his throat. "I know I've been pretty hard on you, son. There were times when I could have taken your advice and should have but didn't. I guess my pride got the best of me. It's not easy to admit my son might know more than I do about ranching." A chuckle rumbled his chest, and he coughed, then pulled out his handkerchief and blew his nose.

"You taking a cold, Pa?"

"Must be. But don't go telling your ma, or she'll have me sitting in front of the fire sipping hot tea and all wrapped up in a quilt."

Luke grinned. His pa carried on, but everyone knew he loved Ma's attention. Marrying late in life, Luke's stepmother, Cassidy, had years of nurturing to catch up on, and she babied anyone who would allow it. Luke could scarcely remember a time when she hadn't been a part of their lives. His memories of his own ma were misty, and except for the daguerreotype sitting on Tarah's mantel, he wouldn't remember her at all. Cassidy had filled that empty space long ago, and he couldn't love her more if she truly were his mother.

Pa sneezed, drawing Luke's focus back to the present. "I reckon we oughtta head back to the house. Ma'll tan my hide if I let you catch pneumonia."

"In a minute." Pa turned to face him. "I want to talk to you about something."

At Pa's serious tone, a gnawing sensation nearly overwhelmed Luke's stomach. Had he somehow caught wind of Luke's plans to move west? Luke knew it was time to come clean, but he dreaded the conversation. "What is it, Pa?"

"I've decided it's time you start taking on more responsibility around the ranch. I've never had a manager before, but I'm offering you the position, son."

"Manager? You have a foreman."

Pa shook his head. "I need someone to oversee the ins and outs of the ranching—not just to watch over the hands—do the hiring and firing, accounts, keep track of the buying and selling. That sort of thing."

"But you do that."

"I have. And now I'm ready to hand it over. Sam never was interested in ranching, and of course Jack is headed for college in a couple of years. Will might enjoy ranching, but you'll get the lion's share when I'm gone. Thought you might like a chance to put some of your ideas into practice without me standing over you telling you no all the time. You can run the ranch any way you see fit."

Luke tried to make sense of Pa's words, but he couldn't quite wrap his mind around the truth of the matter. "But if I take over for you, what are you going to do?"

Pa chortled, then coughed again. "Don't worry, I'll be around, getting in the way. I'm just ready to hand over the responsibility." He peered closer at Luke, his brow creased. "I thought this would be good news. Am I wrong?"

Just say it. You can't take on a position like this and then up and quit come spring. Pa deserves to know the truth so he can make other plans.

"The fact is, Pa. . ." Luke cleared his throat, then braced himself for whatever reaction Pa would give. "The fact is that I got other plans."

"What kind of plans?" He sounded hurt, confused, and worried all at the same time.

Luke nearly relented, but he knew he couldn't. The thought of running the St. John ranch for the rest of his life left a bitter taste in his mouth. He had to make it on his own.

"I don't mean to sound ungrateful. I love the ranch; you know that. I'll do whatever I can to help—until I move west in the spring."

Pa drew in a long, slow breath, the kind he always drew when trying to maintain control. "When did you decide this?"

"I've always planned to, but lately it's all I can think about." Despite the intensity of the moment, Luke's excitement rose. "I've been saving every penny to start my own herd." Luke's plans spilled from his lips like water over a fall. When he stopped and glanced at his pa, the man's eyes were moist, but a smile lifted his lips.

"I see you've thought this through." Pa clapped him on the shoulder and strode toward his gray mare. "Let's get back. I promised your ma we'd be back in plenty of time to clean up and get to church." With a sad smile, he mounted the horse.

Luke's stomach clenched. He climbed into Rusty's saddle and urged the roan forward. "Pa, I could stay on until Will's old enough to take over." He heard his voice but couldn't quite believe he'd made the offer.

"I appreciate that, son. But it'll be a few years yet before your little brother is old enough to break a horse, much less run a ranch. But that's my concern, not yours. I won't have it said I held back any of my children from their dreams. Sam's a doctor, Jack's going to practice law, your sister is married with a brood of her own, and they're a happy bunch." He gave a short laugh. "Even little Laney is doing just what she's been bragging she'd do for the past five years. She's got herself that little soddy and plans to start a herd of her own in a couple of years."

Pain stabbed at Luke's heart. Laney had made herself pretty scarce the past three weeks. He'd heard from Tarah and other female members of his family that she was sewing her fingers to the bone and happy as a pig in slop to be doing it in her own home. It stung his pride to know she was so happy without him. "So I heard," he said, trying to keep his voice even.

"Don't you think your happiness is just as important to me? If you want to go off and make it on your own like I did when I came here to Kansas, I won't be the one to try and stop you."

Relief flowed over Luke like a cool summer shower. "You're not mad?"

"Nope. I just assumed because you have ranching in your blood like me that you'd be content to stay on and take over for me. I should have asked you what you wanted instead of taking it for granted. I'm sorry you found it so hard to share your dreams with me, son. Cassidy is right. I can be mighty thickheaded at times."

"You're not the only one."

Riding back to the house next to his pa, Luke felt a kinship like he'd never felt before, even though they'd worked side by side for as long as Luke could remember. His insides quivered with excitement now that the last barrier to his dream had been knocked over. Only one thing would have made everything perfect: if Laney would share the dream with him; but she had made her choice and had found happiness in fulfilling her own plans. He had to accept that and move on without her. But how did one function when he felt incomplete—as though he were only half a man?

Chapter 4

Laney suppressed a yawn while she waited just inside the church doors for the crowd surrounding Anthony to diminish. She eyed the side door, wishing she could slip out unnoticed and head for her little soddy.

With a gnawing sense of dread, she envisioned the enormity of the task awaiting her when she arrived home. She still had one Christmas gown to finish for Mrs. Thomas and one for Mr. Tucker's mercantile before next Saturday. How she was going to get everything done, she'd never know.

"Laney, honey, you okay?"

Laney turned at the sound of Mama Cassidy's voice. The older woman's worried tone warmed Laney. Tired as she was, she would like nothing better than to lay her head on Mama Cassidy's shoulder and close her eyes for ten minutes.

"I'm all right. Just a little tired." She gave what she hoped to be a reassuring smile; but from the deepening skepticism on Mama Cassidy's face, she knew she hadn't been very convincing.

"You have circles under your eyes." She cupped Laney's chin. Mama Cassidy's green-eyed gaze studied every line of her face, then swept over the rest of her. "And you've obviously lost weight. My guess is that you haven't been sleeping or eating since you moved out on your own."

Unable to deny it, Laney shifted her weight from one booted foot to the other and dropped her gaze to the wooden floor.

Mama Cassidy gave her a one-armed hug and a gentle smile. "That's all right. You'll eat at the picnic and take a nap afterwards. You'll be sick if you don't take care of yourself."

Clearing her throat, Laney gathered her courage to broach the topic of the picnic. She would need to tread lightly if she was to get out of it without too much outcry from her large adoptive family. "To be honest, I—"

"Mama, you look lovely this morning."

Laney stopped as Tarah joined them, carrying little Olive in her arms. She brushed a kiss on her stepmother's cheek. When she turned to greet Laney, the smile faded from her lips, to be quickly replaced with an indignant frown.

"Laney Jenkins, you promised you'd get more rest."

"I did," Laney mumbled.

Tarah's gaze traveled over her. "Not much, from the looks of you. Have you been eating the food I've been sending over, or is it going to waste?"

"I eat some of it." A few bites here and there, when her fingers weren't too busy to pick up a fork.

"Not much, I'd say." The thump of a cane hitting the wooden floor accompanied a sharp voice.

Laney inwardly groaned. If Granny Ellen joined the hovering women, she might as well forget about skipping the picnic. With as sweet a smile as she could muster, she faced the women, feeling as though she were standing before a jury—only these jurors had already made up their minds. She was guilty of not taking care of herself. If she didn't control the situation, not only would they force her to attend the picnic; they'd take turns standing over her to make sure she was eating to their satisfaction.

"You all are dear to worry so much about me. I promise to take better care of myself. I declare, sewing for Mr. Tucker has me busier than a fox in a henhouse." Laney cleared her throat. "As a matter of fact—"

"Harrumph." Granny Ellen narrowed her gaze. "Don't try to sweet-talk your way out of the picnic today. I can see plain as day you want to go home and sew." She thumped her cane on the floor for emphasis. "I'll not have a member of my family working on the Lord's Day, so you get that notion right out of your head. And don't go blaming it all on Mr. Tucker, either. He would never approve of your working on the Lord's Day! So there, girlie."

"Laney!" Tarah's eyes widened. "You know very well it wouldn't be the same without you. No one would have a bit of fun."

Fully prepared to put up a fight, Laney glanced at the determined faces and changed her mind. If she knew Tarah and the rest of the St. Johns, they'd hog-tie her and throw her into the back of a wagon before allowing her to skip the picnic. And as much as she'd like to be irritated at the whole situation, something about the reminder that so many people loved her warmed Laney to her toes.

With an exaggerated sigh of defeat, she nodded. "All right. I'll go to the picnic. But only for a little while. At sundown I have to get back to sewing, or I'll never finish."

⌒

Relief coursed through Luke at the sight of Laney riding alongside Tarah and Anthony's wagon. He hadn't been at all sure she'd even show up to the picnic. As she drew nearer, alarm shot through him. She looked downright worn to a frazzle. When she dismounted, he noticed the usual spring in her step had been replaced by a weary stride.

He moved quickly to her side. "You look like you haven't slept in a week."

"So I've been told," she said dryly. She grabbed a basket of food from the back of Tarah's wagon and headed for the picnic site.

Luke fell into step beside her. "You're working too hard."

She glanced up, and alarm seized Luke at the dark smudges beneath her eyes.

"It's not possible to work too hard." She stifled a yawn. "Hard work gets you where you want to go in life."

"Working too hard gets you dead, or sick at least. Give me that basket."

Alarm clenched his throat like a hangman's noose when she let out a weary sigh of relief upon relinquishing the load. He stopped in his tracks.

She halted beside him. "What's wrong?"

"You. You're worn to a frazzle. I'm talking to Tucker about getting you some help, and you're going to have to stop accepting so many orders."

"Oh, Luke, mind your own business." Turning, Laney ambled away without putting up a fight, which only fueled Luke's concern. He went after her, took her by the arm, and turned her to face him. "I think you should have Sam check you over."

A slow smile tilted her lips, making Luke wish he were free to swoop her up in his arms and force her to rest.

"I'm not sick, Lukey."

The childhood pet name used to make him mad back when he was a boy, but now he delighted in the familiarity, accepting the name as an endearment from Laney's lips.

She passed her slender hand across her forehead. "I'm just tired. Once I finish this order for Mr. Tucker, I'm going to take some time to rest. I promise. Now come on, they're waiting for that food."

"Laney, come play ball with us!"

Little D's shrill voice cut through the air just as Luke was about to insist Laney go lay down in the back of the wagon until Cassidy called them to eat. He addressed his nephew instead. "Laney's too tired to play today."

"Aw! Who's going to pitch?" Little D ran to them.

"Find someone else," Luke replied firmly.

Little D kicked the ground. "But no one else can get it over the plate!"

"Too bad. Laney needs to rest."

Laney planted her hands on her hips. "Wait a minute. Who said I was too tired to play ball?"

"It's obvious," Luke replied.

"You don't speak for me, Luke St. John. If I want to pitch for the kids, I will!"

She draped her arm over Little D's shoulders. "Come on, let's go."

Helplessly Luke watched them go. He shook his head. Laney would be stubborn enough to play with the kids just to show him he couldn't boss her around.

Turning, he headed to the picnic spot and handed the basket to Tarah.

"What are we going to do about that girl, Luke?" she asked, concern edging her voice.

"There's not much we can do. She's as stubborn as a mule in a briar patch and kicks twice as hard when anyone tries to help her. I say let her work herself into an early grave. It'll serve her right."

"Honestly," Tarah huffed. "You know full well you don't mean that. When you want to be reasonable, we'll talk."

Luke opened his mouth to let her know just how much he meant what he'd said, but a cry from the ballplayers drew his attention.

"Look at her fly!"

"Run, Laney!"

Luke walked toward the game, shaking his head. That Laney just had to go and hit a home run to prove him wrong. He grinned in spite of himself. Maybe she wasn't as frail as she appeared after all.

She rounded second base, flashing him a triumphant smile. Just as quickly, the smile faded and she slowed to a walk, her hand pressed against her forehead.

"Laney?"

A look of bewilderment clouded her face, and in a flash, she crumpled to the ground. Luke's mouth went dry. He broke into a trot and quickly closed the distance between them.

"Little D, go get Sam!" He knelt beside her and took her limp hand in his, breathing a sigh of relief at the steady beat of her pulse. Laney had always been tiny, even for a woman; but lying on the ground, her skin pale, her lashes brushing her cheeks, she looked like a doll. Running a thumb gently across the back of her hand, Luke prayed a silent prayer. *Let her be all right, Lord. As much as I'd like to strangle her at times, I couldn't stand it if something were seriously wrong.*

A shadow fell across Laney's still form. Luke glanced up to find his brother standing over them. "Move out of the way, Luke," Sam commanded. "Let me take a look."

Reluctantly Luke released her hand and stepped back.

"She's exhausted," Sam announced after a short examination. "But I think that's all that's wrong."

By now the family had encircled the unconscious girl. "That settles it," Mama Cassidy announced with an air of finality. "Laney is coming home with us. Luke, carry her to the wagon, and we'll take her home right now."

"No, Mama," Tarah said. "She should come home with Anthony and me. Put her in our wagon, Luke."

Mama Cassidy set her lips into a grim line. "Honey, I know you love Laney, but she wouldn't get any rest at all with the children running around."

Luke scooped Laney into his arms, wondering which of the strong-willed women would relent.

A sigh escaped Tarah's lips. "You're right, of course." She nodded to Luke. "Take her to Ma and Pa's wagon. We'll be over later to check on her."

Luke glanced down into Laney's pale face, and his heart lurched. Who would be there to take care of her after he was gone?

⟿

Laney snuggled deeper into the fluffy goose feather mattress and sighed. She felt more rested than she had in ages. Her mouth stretched into a wide yawn, then curved into a contented smile. With a start, her eyes flew open. Rest could only mean one thing: She'd slept too long, and Tucker's dresses wouldn't be done in time.

Glancing around the familiar room, confusion settled over Laney. What was she doing in Granny Ellen's room at the ranch, anyhow? Then the memories rushed back to haunt her. She remembered running the bases and feeling fuzzy in the head. A gasp escaped her throat. Horror of horrors! She'd fainted! Like a girl—a weak-kneed, eyelash-batting, dress-wearing girl! She'd never live this down in a million and a half years.

She groaned, picturing the stupid, teasing grin sure to be on Luke's face the next time she saw him—which wouldn't be long, since she was at the ranch.

Throwing back the rose-colored coverlet, she stiffened in resolution. There was no way she'd stand for Luke's insults. Besides, she had a ton of work to do, and she couldn't very well finish those dresses while lying abed.

The sun shone bright outside, so Laney figured she hadn't slept too long. If the family was still at the picnic, she could sneak out and get back to the soddy before anyone could stop her and insist she eat supper or spend the night.

She swung her legs over the side of the bed, and her brows lifted in surprise. When had she changed into a nightdress? Mama Cassidy probably changed her. They must have assumed she would sleep all night. Laney hated to hurt anyone's feelings, but she couldn't take the time to stay here and be pampered, although she had to admit it would have been nice.

Now where were her britches? Hands on her hips, she glanced around the room.

It was a conspiracy! They had brought her here against her wishes and hid all of her clothes so she couldn't go anywhere.

She stomped across to the door and jerked it open. Her scream mingled with Mama Cassidy's as they came face-to-face at the threshold.

"Honestly, Laney, you nearly scared the life right out of me! What are you doing out of bed, anyway?"

"I'm sorry, Mama Cassidy. I didn't know anyone was home from the picnic." Laney waved toward the bedroom. "I need to get home, but I can't find my clothes."

"The picnic?" Cassidy's face lit with amusement. "Laney, honey, you've been sleeping for two days. It's Tuesday afternoon."

"Tuesday?" That just couldn't be! She'd lost two whole days of work!

"I was just getting ready to wake you so you could eat something."

"Oh, Mama Cassidy! I have to get home. I have so much work to do. Please tell me where my clothes are."

"Nonsense." Taking her by her upper arm, Cassidy steered Laney back toward the bed. "You get back under those covers, and I'm going to go warm up some venison stew and biscuits for you."

An upraised hand silenced Laney's protests. "Don't worry about the gowns. Granny and Tarah are working on the two you need to finish this week, and the others can wait until you get home next week."

"Next week! Tarah has plenty to do without taking on my work, too. What is she thinking?"

"She's thinking that the girl she's loved and cared for all these years is so stubborn that instead of asking her family for help, she worked herself sick."

Ashamed, Laney fixed her gaze on her broken fingernails. "I'm sorry," she mumbled. "I didn't mean to worry anyone." Without more protest, Laney allowed herself to be tucked into bed. Mama Cassidy sat beside her and adjusted the coverlet around her shoulders.

"I know you didn't, honey. But after all these years as part of this family, you should know we'd do anything to help one of our own. Your dreams are our dreams, too. We're all so proud of you."

Tears pricked Laney's eyes. How she loved this family! Luke was an idiot to even consider leaving.

Cassidy patted Laney's hand. "You just stay right here and rest while I go get you something to eat."

Unable to argue, Laney nodded. She watched Mama Cassidy leave the room and closed her eyes, drinking in the scents of lemon verbena combined with liniment, which always seemed to cling to Granny Ellen.

She snuggled back down into the comfort of the fluffy mattress and coverlet and closed her eyes. Immediately the image of Luke standing over her, asking her to marry him, came back to her mind as vividly as if the dance was just yesterday. Before she could push the memory aside, the feel of his arms and the touch of his lips flooded back to torment her.

"Lukey," she whispered. "Why did I have to go and fall in love with a man itching to move out west? We could have been so happy together raising a passel of young'uns right in the middle of this big family. Why can't you just be content with what you've been given?"

Hot tears escaped her closed eyes and slipped down her cheeks. With an angry swipe, she brushed them away. First she'd fainted; now she was crying for no good reason! Loving Luke had turned her into just the sort of woman she'd always held in contempt.

She released a resolute sigh. The fact was, tears or no, she couldn't help loving Luke. And whether she wanted to or not, she would go on loving him forever.

Chapter 5

Laney entered her soddy, a smile spread across her face. A contented sigh escaped her lips. *Home.*

Upon further inspection of the room, warmth flooded her cheeks. The house was twice as clean as it had been when she'd left for church the previous Sunday. It didn't take much for Laney to picture Granny clucking and shaking her head while she picked up the clutter.

Shaking off the embarrassment, Laney moved across the room, determined to get in as much work as possible before nightfall—the time she'd promised Mama Cassidy and Tarah that she would stop working, eat a bite of food, and head to bed for a full night's sleep. When her gaze reached the corner of the room where she had set up her work area, her mouth dropped open. Shelves stood before her, reaching from the ceiling to the earthen floor. She tested the smooth wood with her fingertips, marveling at its softness. Her dress goods were folded and arranged on shelves according to fabric. Smaller shelves contained other necessary items such as thread and shears.

"Do you like it?"

Laney spun around, her hand pressed against her heart. "Luke, do you have to sneak up on a person?"

A grin split his face. "Sorry." He inclined his head toward the shelves. "What do you think?"

"What do I think?" She clasped her hands together to keep from making a fool of herself by clapping with delight. "It's the most beautiful thing I've ever seen. Who made it?"

Luke's face reddened, and his Adam's apple bobbed in his neck.

Laney's eyes widened. "You did this?"

"Yeah," he mumbled, then cleared his throat. "Where do you want Granny's trunk?"

"Luke, I don't know what to say. I'm so grateful, I—" She stopped short as her mind registered his last question at the same time she noticed the oak trunk at his feet. "What do you mean, where do I want Granny's trunk?"

"You didn't expect her to come with just the clothes on her back, did you?" Luke's lips twitched with amusement.

"Luke, what are you talking about? Why is Granny coming?"

He studied her face a moment, bewilderment registering in his own expression. Then he threw back his head and howled with laughter. "They didn't tell you!"

A sense of dread tightened Laney's stomach. "Tell me what? Stop that cackling this minute, or so help me, I'll flatten you."

"Granny is coming tomorrow to stay with you."

Weakness settled in Laney's knees. She grabbed a nearby chair and sat before she lost the ability to stand. "Tell me you're joking," she whispered.

" 'Fraid not," he drawled. "And it's your own fault for making yourself sick."

"How long is she staying? A week?" That sounded fair. After all, Laney had shared her room for a week.

Again, Luke's lips twitched. "Guess again."

"Two?" Laney gulped.

"Laney, Granny's moving in—lock, stock, and barrel."

A groan escaped Laney's throat. "Think it would make a difference if I promise to eat and sleep more?"

"Not a chance. You know Granny; she's convinced that you need her, and she's going to stay here no matter what." He hoisted the trunk across his back. "Where to?" he asked, groaning under the weight.

"Oh, who cares?" she replied, giving him a distracted wave. "Anywhere you can find a spot for it is fine." What difference did it make? This was no longer her home. Granny would move in and take over completely. Laney might as well move back in with Tarah and Anthony for all the freedom she'd have now.

Luke deposited the trunk in a spare corner, then turned. "It might not be so bad. Personally I feel a lot better knowing Granny's going to be here to look after you."

Laney's ire rose. She stood, stretching to her full height. "I don't need anyone looking after me. I can take care of myself."

With a smirk, Luke headed toward the door, then turned and faced her. "I guess I could remind you where you just spent the last week—and why; but knowing you, you'd deny the whole thing just to try to prove a point. Regardless, you'd best get used to the idea. Granny's moving in, and there's nothing you can do about it."

He turned his back and ducked through the doorway. Laney stomped across the room, intending to slam the door behind him; but when she peeked out, she realized he wasn't finished unloading the wagon.

Granny had brought all of her bedding, as well.

"Move back so I can get it through the door. Oh." Luke pulled a bottle out of his pocket. "Granny's liniment."

Tears of condemnation sprang to Laney's eyes. "I'm rotten to the core, Luke. Here I have been thinking about Granny invading my house and taking away my privacy, and really she's the one sacrificing her comfort for me. She'll ache all the time, what with the arthritis in her hip. And you know I'll have to fight her to take my bed and let me take the floor."

Luke reached forward and captured Laney's hand. "The last thing you are is rotten to the core, honey. And I know exactly how you feel. As much as I love our family and thank God for them, sometimes it can feel like you're being smothered."

Laney nodded, still inwardly berating herself for her pathetic lack of loyalty to the family who took her in and loved her as though she were one of their own. She barely noticed when Luke stepped closer, until he was so close she had to look up to meet his gaze.

"Now that you understand how I feel, won't you change your mind and come west with me? We'll have the wide-open range and all the freedom we could possibly want."

Laney glowered, shocked beyond words at the very suggestion. When she recovered her voice, she gave it to him with both barrels blazing. "Luke St. John, how can you even suggest I leave these wonderful people after all they've done for me?"

Luke's jaw dropped open. "Six seconds ago, you were ready to throw poor Granny out on her ear to have your privacy, and now they're too wonderful to leave behind?" He grabbed his Stetson from the table and headed toward the door. "You're crazy!"

Laney stormed after him, but he was already in the wagon before she reached the threshold. "Oh yeah?" she called after him. "Well, you're. . .you're— *Rats!* He was already driving away. She reared back and slammed the door as hard as she could. Gaining little satisfaction, she kicked at the closest chair.

As pain laced her toes, bringing her back to her senses, Laney felt the heat creep to her cheeks. She had to stop letting Luke rile her so much. Especially after Anthony had just preached a sermon yesterday about a person not sinning even when they are mad as all get-out. And she hardly ever got mad at anyone besides Luke. So he pretty much was the only reason she'd sinned in the first place. She knew she had to stop allowing Luke to goad her into getting so angry. Of course, he would be gone in a few months, and that would be the end of that.

Sobered by the last thought, Laney felt her shoulders slump. During the past week, each conversation she had shared with Luke inevitably steered toward the topic of his heading to Oregon. Laney couldn't stop the despair from flooding her at the memory of his green eyes shining with excitement as he spoke of raising his herd and leaving a legacy for his children. His children. Pain knifed through Laney. Children he would share with another woman. White-hot hatred flared inside her toward that other woman—the nameless, faceless woman who would share Luke's dream and win his love away from Laney.

Suddenly she hurried to her bed and knelt. She planted her elbows on the mattress and closed her eyes. Unable to bring herself to talk aloud in the empty room, she silently petitioned God.

I know You're up there looking out for me, God, just like You have ever since I was just a tyke. I want to thank You again for not letting me grow up with that drunken, no-good pa of mine.

I haven't asked for much all these years since I received Your Son, Jesus, as my Lord and Savior. I know I don't have the right to ask for more than You've already given me. But I thought seeing as how it's been so many years, and I haven't asked for anything up to now, maybe You wouldn't mind doing me a little favor. I was wondering if You could sorta fix it so Luke decides to stick around these parts. And just so You know, if it don't happen, I won't hold it against You.

Well, she'd done all she could. Now it was up to Luke and God. She had work to do.

Luke paced the hallway outside of Pa's bedroom door. Panic gripped him at the groans of pain coming from beyond the walls.

"I brought you some coffee."

He turned. His adopted sister, Emily, approached and handed him a steaming mug.

He took the cup gratefully and leaned against the wall. Another moan escaped through the walls. Luke's stomach knotted even tighter, and he shook his head.

"You can't blame yourself, Luke." Emily's own expression was filled with pain at the sounds of agony coming from their pa's room.

"I should have insisted on getting rid of that old bull last year. It's almost like Ol' Angus knew he was about to be sold and wanted to punish Pa for it."

"Oh, Luke. Don't be silly. Ol' Angus just got through that fence at the wrong time, and Pa took the punishment for it. It was an accident. Just be glad you were there to take him down before he could kill Pa. God sent you along at the right time."

Luke sipped his coffee and studied Emily over the rim of the mug. Two years his junior, she could have passed for his twin with her carrot-orange hair, green eyes, and freckles. He couldn't count the times they'd been mistaken for blood relatives even though, in truth, Emily was Cassidy's niece. When her real pa had died of cholera, Cassidy had taken over Emily's care and had brought her along when she married Pa.

As though unaware of his scrutiny, Emily gave him a tender smile. "Really, you're a hero. Pa wouldn't be here at all now if not for you."

"I'm glad I was there, but it doesn't change the fact that I knew we needed to put in a new fence where Pa's crazy bull keeps getting out. Instead, I just patched it up again. If I had just gone with my gut, Pa wouldn't be laid out flat in there. What if Sam can't save his leg?"

Luke shuddered at the thought. What would Pa do if he lost his leg?

"We just have to pray hard," Emily replied firmly, reaching for him. Luke accepted the proffered hand and closed his eyes.

"Dear Lord," Emily prayed. "You see our pa in there, and You know how serious his condition is. We ask You to spare his life. That's the most important thing. Please give Sam wisdom and guide his hands. If possible, please help him to save Pa's leg. But if it's already too far gone, please give Pa the grace to accept it and to live with it. In Jesus' name, amen."

Luke pushed away the thought. He didn't want to consider the possibility that God wouldn't save Pa's leg. God could do a miracle. He'd done plenty, and Luke had even witnessed a few. Surely saving Pa's leg wasn't too much trouble.

"Why don't we go sit with Ma awhile?" Emily suggested. "She's pretty shaken up. Sam won't let her anywhere near the bedroom."

"It's just as well she can't hear Pa groan." Luke cast a glance at the closed door and headed into the sitting room.

Hours later, Sam emerged, pale and shaken.

"How is he?" Cassidy asked, her eyes wide with fright.

Sam sank to the nearest chair and jammed his fingers into his thick hair, raking back the black locks with one quick swipe. He leaned his elbows on his knees and regarded his family wearily. "I've never seen so many lacerations on one leg. I lost count of the stitches."

"You saved the leg, then?" Luke asked.

Sam's blue eyes filled, and his voice faltered. "I don't know. We have to keep the wounds clean and pray infection doesn't set in. To tell you the truth, even if Pa gets to keep his leg, there is no telling how much damage that bull did to the muscles. Pa may never have use of it again."

As though the burden of the past hours overwhelmed him, Sam buried his face in his palms and wept like a baby.

Cassidy stood immediately and went to him. She knelt on the wooden floor and took him into her arms. "Shh. You did all you could."

"What if it wasn't enough? Why did Doc Simpson have to be out of town now, of all times?"

"You are a capable doctor. Would your father-in-law have done anything different than you did?"

"I don't think so. There wasn't much to do but stitch him up and pray for the best."

"All right, then," Cassidy said with a nod. "I remember Doc Simpson saying once that even doctors can't control what God ordains. You just have to do the best you can and leave the rest up to the Lord. Your pa knows that. No matter what happens, you have to believe God is in control. That way, you can't take the credit for the successes or the blame when things don't work out." She smiled and stood. "May I go to him?"

"I have him heavily medicated with chloroform," Sam replied, once again the professional doctor rather than the broken son. "Hopefully he'll sleep through the night. When he wakes up, the pain will be nearly unbearable."

"I'd still like to sit with him," Ma insisted.

Sam nodded. "Go ahead. But there'll be a lot of moaning in his sleep. Make sure you come out if it begins to bother you. Pa won't even know you're there, much less when you leave."

"Thank you, Sam. Emily made up your old bed for you. Go get some rest. I'll wake you when your pa rouses."

"Want me to ride over and tell Camilla you'll be staying over tonight?" Luke asked, feeling suddenly as though he needed to do something. . .anything to feel useful.

"No need. She'll expect it." Sam stood. "I'm going to try to catch a few hours of sleep. Wake me if you need me."

"Thank you for everything, Sam. Try to cast the worry of this over on the Lord and get some rest," Ma said. "Good night."

"May I come with you and sit with Pa for a few minutes, Ma?" Emily asked softly, her voice trembling.

"Of course." Cassidy slipped her arm about Emily's shoulders, and they headed down the hall to the bedroom.

Luke watched as Sam followed, then turned at the bedroom they had once shared.

He released a heavy sigh and stoked the fire, watching the sparks fly upward. What if Pa never regained use of his leg again or lost it altogether? Then Luke would have no choice but to stay on indefinitely and run the ranch for the family. He would never get to Oregon. His mind rejected the thought instantly as guilt crept over him. How could he even think about himself at a time like this?

With a sigh, he added a log to the fire. After he was satisfied it would keep the house sufficiently warm until he returned, Luke slipped into his coat and wrapped a scarf around his neck. Feeling the heavy weight of responsibility on his shoulders, he stepped into the blustery November night to attend to chores and make sure all was well on the ranch.

Chapter 6

Laney waved hello to Emily and pulled Colby to a stop in front of the St. John ranch house. She leaned forward and rested her elbow on the saddle horn. Emily smiled a greeting and stooped over the scrub board, attempting to clean a pair of trousers.

"Morning," Laney said, noting that Emily's hands were red from the December cold. "Why are you washing out here on such a cold day?"

Emily shrugged and smiled. "Ma's getting caught up on the cleaning. I didn't want to be in the way."

"Where's Luke?"

Emily straightened and gave her a weary smile. She pressed her hands against her back and stretched.

"Down by the creek." She squinted and cupped her hand over her eyes to shield them against the sun's bright rays. "Haven't seen you around in a few days. You heard about Pa?"

Laney gave her a sober nod. "That's why I'm here. How's the leg looking today?"

It had been three days since Anthony had ridden out to the soddy to let them know about the accident, but Laney hadn't been able to bring herself to face the family. Guilt bit her deep. She had prayed for God to keep Luke in Kansas, so she figured her prayer was to blame for Papa Dell's condition.

Emily's shoulders rose and fell. "Not good. Sam's trying to put on a brave face, but you know how hard it is for him not to show his emotions. I'd say it's only a matter of time before he takes the leg." Her voice faltered. "Poor Sam. I can't imagine what he's going through."

And poor Luke. Laney knew Luke must be feeling torn between his responsibility to his family and grief over the loss of his dream.

"Do you want to come in and say hi to Pa? He'd probably welcome the distraction."

Laney just couldn't look Papa Dell in the eye, knowing she was responsible for the accident. "Maybe another time. I think I'll go find Luke."

"I think he just needed to get away from the ranch and try to think straight. You know he'll have to postpone his plans to head west?"

"Yeah, I reckon he will." That was her fault, too. "I'll see you around, Em."

"All right. If you find him, tell him not to worry about evening chores. Will and Hope are pitching in to get them done."

"Hope?"

Emily grinned. "I promised her I'd bake an apple pie."

Laney shook her head and returned Emily's smile. "If that little sister of yours doesn't stop being ruled by her belly, she'll be as fat as Mr. Moody's prize sow."

"It's just baby fat," Emily replied, defending the chunky young girl. "She'll grow out of it."

"Probably." Laney glanced uncomfortably toward the direction of the river. She wanted to leave before Mama Cassidy discovered she was out here and insisted she go inside. "Well—"

"Sure you can't come in and say hi to Ma and Pa?"

"I'd better go find Luke. Tell Papa Dell I'm praying for him and that I'll be over soon to see him."

"Okay."

Laney could tell Emily was confused. But for the moment, Laney's need to find Luke ruled her reluctance to hurt the young woman, dear as she was.

Laney turned her mount toward the river and rode off at a gallop. Her heart picked up a beat when she reached the river and spied Luke seated on the bank. He glanced up and waved as she dismounted and slipped Colby's reins around the branches of a nearby bush.

"What are you doing here?" he asked, his voice laced with sarcasm. "Rumor has it you're busy as ever, even with Granny's help—too busy to come to the ranch and see how Pa is."

It was true. She was busier than ever. The addition of ready-made dresses to Tucker's Mercantile had been such a success with the ladies of Harper, Tucker had offered her a 10 percent increase in her profits to take on more orders. Even with paying Granny a salary, she was coming out with more than before Granny moved in. If things continued as they were, the soddy would easily be paid off next spring—on time and in full. She couldn't help the thrill she felt as she watched her dream draw closer and closer to becoming a reality.

She chose to ignore Luke's comment about her not coming to the ranch to see Papa Dell and focused instead on the business. "Will came by and drove Granny into town to drop off the gowns we finished this week and to pick up some more orders from Tucker." Laney dropped to the cool ground next to him and sent him a sideways grin. "Between you and me, I think Tucker and Granny are sweet on each other. I won't be surprised if there's another wedding in the family before long."

Luke grinned. "Wouldn't surprise me, either." The grin faded almost as quickly as it had appeared, and he leaned in closer. Laney shrank back at the intensity of his gaze. " 'Course, that's not the family wedding I had hoped to attend next."

"Oh, Luke. Please don't start a fight." Laney turned and stared out across the rippling water. "I came out to tell you how sorry I am about your pa."

"Are you?" He gave a short laugh and tossed a stick into the water. "Looks like things worked out just the way you wanted them to."

Laney's blood heated at the insinuation, but she knew Luke was spoiling for a fight as a way to relieve his frustration. She prayed for patience.

"You think I'd want you to stay here for my sake, at your pa's expense? You must not think very highly of me."

His brow furrowed in suspicion. "It never occurred to you that now I'd have to stay and run the ranch?"

"Of course it occurred to me. But not for the reason you suppose. I wouldn't marry you and be second choice to your dreams, anyway. Besides, maybe Sam will be able to save the leg, and you won't have to postpone your move after all. If that's all you care about." He was getting her riled again.

Luke's face darkened. "Even if Pa doesn't lose his leg, he'll probably never gain use of it again. If I don't run the ranch, who will?"

"I could." She'd thought of it before. It would mean sacrificing her herd for a while, but it seemed to be the least she could do after praying for something to happen to change Luke's mind about leaving. She'd rather run the ranch herself than to live with the guilt.

He studied her so intently, Laney felt warmth creep to her cheeks. "What about your soddy and the herd?"

She shrugged. "I almost have enough saved to pay off the soddy. I can wait until Will's old enough to take over the ranch before I build my own herd."

"You really think you could handle running the ranch?"

Was he thinking of letting her try?

"Why not? I've worked with you and Papa Dell long enough to know the ins and outs of St. John Ranch. I could probably run it in my sleep."

A sigh escaped from deep within Luke. "No, you couldn't. I have to be the one to stay—as usual."

Laney shot to her feet. She glared down at Luke, hands on her hips. "Luke St. John, you are acting like a—" Oh, what was he acting like? She stomped her foot on the ground. "You know how you're acting! And Papa Dell would probably rather sell off this place to the highest bidder than to let you run it with that attitude. He's up there in the house, about to have his leg chopped off, and listen to you—throwing sticks in the river and crying like a baby because you don't get to go west and build a bigger herd than your pa's."

"I am not crying!"

"You might as well be." She stomped to Colby and grabbed his reins from the bush. "I'm ashamed of you."

⮑

Luke felt his ears burn as he watched Laney ride away at breakneck speed.

Serves you right, he chided himself. Everything Laney said was true. Shame seared him. Not only had he insulted her by insinuating she was glad he had to stay in Kansas, he had made a fool of himself, complaining about running the ranch for his injured pa. What kind of man was he, anyway? This proved he didn't have half the backbone he'd always thought he had.

He knew Laney had been serious about putting her plans for her own land on hold so he didn't have to postpone heading west. She had more character than he did. Suddenly he knew he had to do what was right and stop complaining about it. God knew what was best.

Forgive me, Lord.

A heartfelt prayer. So powerful in its simplicity. Luke felt the change immediately and smiled. God had a way of changing a man with the smallest of adjustments.

And with that adjustment, Luke determined not to make any more plans to head west. Instead, his imagination headed in another direction: Laney. What if he married her and helped her start a herd for them next to his pa's ranch? Of course, they'd have to wait awhile to see what happened with Pa.

The sound of hooves pounding hard on the earth drew his attention back to the present. He glanced up to find Laney heading back. Luke grinned. She would love to hear that she'd actually won an argument, even if she hadn't stuck around to see him admit to being wrong.

His grin faded abruptly when he saw her pale face. She brought Colby to a skidding halt a few feet from where Luke stood.

He hurried to her and grabbed the horse's bridle. "What's wrong?"

"Get home, Luke. Your pa's leg's turned gangrenous. He's delirious from a high fever, and Sam is going to amputate. He needs your help."

∽

"Oh, Luke, thank heaven you're here." Ma's tear-streaked face greeted him when he walked in the house moments later. "Sam needs you."

"What can I do?"

"Honey, you'll have to hold your pa's leg still while Sam amputates." Her voice broke. "I'm sorry, but Sam says it needs to come off immediately."

The blood drained from Luke's face. He felt the pressure of Laney's hand on his arm, but he couldn't respond.

Sam emerged from the bedroom. He gave Luke a cursory glance. "Good. You're here. Let's get it done before that poison spreads. Pa's fever shot up in a matter of minutes."

Luke swallowed hard and hung back. The pressure of Laney's hand on his arm increased. "Luke, you can do all things through Christ who strengthens you. Trust God to get you through this. But you have to go help. Sam needs you. Your pa needs you."

Her words shook him from his numbing state of dread. He covered her hand with his and squeezed. "Thank you, Laney. Pray for us."

Tears pooled in her eyes. "I am."

He gathered a shaky breath and followed Sam to their pa's room.

Laney prayed throughout the night. She prayed for Luke, for Sam, and most of all for Papa Dell. *Oh, God, he doesn't deserve this. I'm so sorry. I'll do anything if You'll just keep him alive.*

Finally Luke emerged, tears streaming down his face. Heedless of Mama Cassidy, Emily, and Tarah's presence, Laney jumped from her seat and went to him. He dropped to his knees and grabbed on to her, holding so tightly, it seemed he would crush her with his iron grip. She wrapped her arms about him and stroked his hair. Sobs shook his body, and Laney held him more tightly, her own tears flowing unchecked down her face.

They stayed wrapped in each other's arms until Sam appeared several minutes later. Laney withdrew first. Luke stood and grabbed his handkerchief from his pocket, then crossed the room. "I'll be back," he said to no one in particular. Laney let him go, sensing his need to be alone.

"How is your pa, Sam?" Cassidy's face showed the signs of her worry. She seemed older than Laney had ever noticed.

Sam pinched the bridge of his nose. His shoulders slumped. "The next few days will tell. We need to keep the wound clean, which means changing the bandages more often than I can be here to attend to it."

"Show me what to do next time they have to be changed, and I'll tend my husband."

Sam nodded and squeezed her hand. "His fever is extremely high. I'm going to pack ice around him to get it down. We still have a rough few hours ahead of us. Luke is hitching the wagon now to go into town and get some ice from the icehouse."

"Is Luke going to be all right?" Mama Cassidy asked. "He fell apart as soon as he came out of the room, but Laney was here to comfort him."

Embarrassed at the memory of Luke in her arms right in front of the family, Laney shifted her gaze downward and studied the floor's wooden slats.

"He was a rock in there. I couldn't have done it without him. To tell you the truth, I was wishing for my wife's arms when I left that room. Sometimes no one can comfort us like the women we love. Luke will be all right. Don't worry."

The woman he loves. Does Luke still love me?

Chapter 7

Luke pushed his Stetson off his forehead, taking in the scene before him. He reveled in the beauty of the wide-open prairie blanketed in the first snowfall of the year.

Did Oregon smell this fresh and crisp in early winter?

Impatiently he pushed the thought aside, determined nothing would spoil the moment for him. He always looked forward to coming out to the south pasture and looking over St. John land at the first snowfall. The difference this year was that Pa wasn't with him as he always had been for the snow ride. Luke released a heavy sigh and turned Rusty back toward the house.

Three weeks had passed since Pa's operation. Two days after the surgery, his temperature returned to normal and he regained consciousness. His stump showed no signs of infection, and Sam was growing optimistic about his chances of recovery.

Sam said they could eventually order an artificial leg, and Pa should be able to lead a fairly normal life. Until then, the most important thing was that he gain strength. For now, even the briefest excursions from bed exhausted him.

Pa never complained. . .had even made a joke about having a funeral for the missing leg. But Luke knew the weakness had to be difficult for him.

Despite the tragedy of Pa's getting his leg amputated, Thanksgiving had held special meaning for the entire St. John family this year. "Thank You, Lord" seemed to be more heartfelt than ever before.

As Luke approached the ranch, he noticed a commotion and nudged Rusty to a trot. Disheveled and unshaven, Anthony sat in his wagon seat, his face drained of color.

"What's wrong?" Luke asked.

"Tarah's time has come. I brought the kids over for Emily to keep an eye on, and your ma is coming with me to the house."

"Sam know?"

"He knows, but as usual, Tarah refuses to allow him to deliver the baby. He's there just in case there's trouble, but she wants Granny and your ma. I'm headed over to Laney's next to get Granny."

"Want me to ride ahead and let her know you're coming?"

"Would you? That'll save us some time."

Luke grinned as he rode off toward Laney's soddy. After a man had been with his wife through the births of three children, number four should be a matter of course. But Anthony fell apart with each birth.

As Rusty made steady progress in the newly fallen snow, Luke allowed his mind to wander toward the future day when he would have his own children. He continued to daydream until Laney's soddy came into view, then he rode with purpose.

Recognizing Luke's horse through the window, Laney inwardly groaned. What was he doing here at this time of day? And why did Granny have to choose now to fix the hem on little Sarah Jean Taylor's dress? It was humiliating enough for Laney that a ten-year-old's dress fit her, but Luke would tease her unmercifully.

"Hold still," Granny scolded. "How will I ever get this hem straight with your fidgeting?"

"Sorry, Granny. Luke's here."

"Well, whatever he wants will just have to wait until I finish pinning this hem."

As if on cue, Luke tapped on the door.

"Come in, Luke," Granny called.

The door swung open. His gaze swept her, his eyes growing wide in surprise. He cleared his throat and averted his gaze. Heat burned Laney's cheeks. She knew what a spectacle she made, and she knew he was fighting to keep from laughing out loud at the sight of her.

He cleared his throat. "I'm sorry to interrupt, Granny."

"You should be. It's not as if we aren't working our fingers to the bone to get these gowns to Mr. Tucker. There's no time for constant interruptions."

"I know, Granny. And again, I'm sorry, but Anthony's on his way over with Ma. Tarah's time has come, and you know she won't have the baby without you."

"Now why didn't you say so? Help me up from here."

Luke strode across the room and took Granny's arm as she struggled to her feet. "The hem is pinned, Laney. You can sew it and deliver the dress to Tucker by tomorrow with the rest of the gowns, right? Mrs. Taylor has been hounding the poor man for a week about this dress."

Laney snorted and hopped off the chair. "Yes, we don't want Mrs. Taylor to pop her corset strings, worrying about her little girl's dress being ready in time for the Christmas dance."

"Don't be impertinent. I know you never liked the woman, but she's still your elder. And you shouldn't be discussing ladies' undergarments in front of Luke."

Amusement tipped the corners of Luke's lips. "I think you should make yourself a dress just like that one, Laney. It's nice to see you in girl clothes for a change—even little girl clothes."

The ruffly dress only reached Laney's midcalf. She straightened her shoulders, pretending she didn't care what he thought. "You know Sarah Jean is big for her age. Can I help it if she's as tall as I am?"

"No need to get riled. I think you look very sweet," he baited.

"Luke. . . ," Laney warned. "Will you get out of here so I can take off this ridiculous getup?"

"Too late." Luke chuckled and opened the door.

Laney heard the wagon rattle to a halt just as Luke spoke. She groaned aloud. Must everyone in the family see her dressed like a little girl?

Luckily Granny had a bundle ready and quickly headed toward the door. "Now don't you work yourself to death while I'm gone, you hear? I'll be staying with Tarah for a few days to help out."

Laney kissed the leathery cheek. "Don't worry, Granny. I'll be fine. Give Tarah my love, and tell her as soon as she's up to it, I'll be over to see her and the baby."

After the wagon rolled away, Laney braced herself for more teasing. Instead, Luke turned to her. "I'll go outside while you change, but I'd like to talk to you for a few minutes before you get back to work."

"Sure." Laney's stomach jumped at the seriousness of his tone. When the door was safely closed behind Luke, she hurriedly removed the dress and laid it across the table to be sewn. Then she slipped on her shirt and jeans and pulled on her boots. She only prayed Papa Dell hadn't taken a turn for the worse.

"Come on in, Luke," she called. "I'm decent."

He came back in and smiled, his gaze sweeping her. "Now that's my Laney."

Her stomach hopped at his tone. Was she his Laney?

"What did you want to tell me?"

Luke hesitated. "I don't know how you feel about this," he began, his voice shaky, words stilted.

"About what?"

"Well, just hang on. I'm trying to tell you."

Laney's defenses rose at his impatient tone. "Sor—ry! I don't got all day to wait on you, Luke St. John. You know I have a pile of work to do since Granny's going to be at Tarah's."

Slapping his Stetson against his thigh, Luke let out a growl. "Just forget it, Laney. I declare, a fella can't even propose to you without a big argument!"

He stomped off and mounted Rusty. He galloped away, leaving Laney to stare after him.

Propose? Excitement wiggled around in her stomach. If Luke was ready to propose again, he must have made the decision to stay and run the ranch for Papa Dell. She inwardly berated herself. If she didn't stop running him off, he might never marry her!

She tried to get back to work, but she couldn't help casting frequent glances toward the window, hoping Luke would come back. If he did, she would greet him at the door with a smile and be ready to throw herself into his arms if he decided to ask her to marry him again. She waited the rest of the morning, but hope gave way to despair when lunchtime arrived and he still hadn't returned.

After shrugging into her sheepskin coat, Laney grabbed the water pail and made the short walk to the creek. She planned to dig a well come spring, but for now, the daily trip wasn't too awfully bad. It gave her a good excuse to escape the confines of the soddy and stretch her legs for a few minutes.

She squatted down beside the creek where the clear water rippled over a bed of rocks. Suddenly an eerie feeling slithered over her. The hairs on the back of her neck stood up. Laney hurriedly finished filling her pail and rose. Why hadn't she thought to buckle on her Colt? That would have made her feel a sight more comfortable right now.

Casting a wary glance over her shoulder, Laney picked up her pace, sloshing water from the pail. "Luke? Is that you? You're not scaring me, so you might as well show your face."

A twig snapped behind her, and Laney grinned and swung around. Expecting to startle Luke and get the upper hand, she stopped short and gasped as she came face-to-face with a tall man dressed in black. His brilliant blue eyes swept over her, and a smirk tipped the corners of sensual lips.

She willed her hands to stop trembling and made a mental note to get herself a big dog. "Who are you?" she demanded, her heart pounding like Indian drums during a rain dance. "And what are you doing on my land?"

He cocked an eyebrow. "Your land? Since when do they hand out property to children?"

Laney sneered. "I'm no child, mister. I'm a grown woman, and I own this patch of land your no-good carcass is standing on."

A slow smile slid across his face. "A woman, eh? Well, in that case. . ." He reached for her. Laney recoiled and drew back her arm, ready to strike if he dared to lay a hand on her.

"That's enough, Matt. No one said you could manhandle my daughter. Look at her. She ain't worth the bother, nohow."

Laney froze, fear causing the bile to rise in her throat. She'd know that voice anywhere. Slowly she turned. "Pa," she whispered. The sight of him shocked her. This man was a mere shadow of the pa she remembered.

"That's right. It's me. Looks like you done real good fer yerself, girlie."

"Wh—what do you want? You know there's a wanted poster up at Tucker's with your face plastered on it?"

"Then it's lucky fer me an' Matt here that I got me a girl with her own place."

Laney gave him a short laugh. "You don't think you're staying with me?"

His face darkened. "You ain't changed a bit. Still as mouthy as ever." He brought his hand hard across her cheek. The ground came up to meet her, and she sprawled in the snow, tasting blood. He stood over her, intimidating even with sunken cheeks and bony arms.

She swiped at her mouth with the backs of her fingers and glared up at her pa. Her lips curled into a sneer. "You haven't changed either. Still enjoy bullying anyone smaller than you."

He moved closer, but Matt stepped between them. "Leave the girl alone. How's she going to go into town for supplies if she's all bruised up?"

Matt reached down. Ignoring his outstretched hand, Laney hopped to her feet. "What makes you think I won't go straight to the sheriff if you let me go into town?"

"I'll show you," Pa said, a coarse grin twisting his thin lips. He turned toward a nearby tree. "Get out here."

Laney watched in bewildered silence as a young girl of no more than five or six years stepped slowly into view. Even with her hair matted and her face covered in dirt, Laney could see the unmistakable resemblance to her own hair and features. This child was family.

Laney glowered at her pa. "Don't tell me you found another woman dumb enough to marry you."

Matt chuckled.

Her pa's eyes glittered dangerously. "I didn't marry her. But that didn't stop her from getting in a fix with this one." He jerked his thumb toward the little girl.

Laney ignored his crude comment and focused on the child. She smiled, trying to wrap her mind around the fact that now she had a little sister to look out for. Wait 'til Ben found out about this! For the first time, Laney was glad her brother had gone east to seminary. At least he would escape Pa's meanness this time around. "What's your name, honey?" she asked.

The little girl ducked her head.

Pa nudged her forward. "Yer big sister's talkin' to you, girl."

"Leave her be, Pa. She's just a little girl—not that showing kindness to children was ever your strong suit."

The little girl glanced shyly at Laney. Laney smiled at her and winked. Beautiful blue eyes grew wide, and she smiled back, revealing a missing front tooth.

"What's your name?" Laney asked again.

"Jane," she said in a barely audible voice.

"The perfect name for a sister."

Jane's face lit up. Laney could well imagine how she felt. She knew from experience that one kind word from a stranger could make all the difference in a lonely child's life. Stepping toward her sister, Laney reached for her hand. "Are you hungry?"

Jane nodded.

"Well, let's go find you something to eat."

The little girl slipped a dirty hand inside Laney's, then to Laney's surprise, she turned and reached for Pa. He cleared his throat. "I'm coming."

Laney ignored the two men, though she knew they were following. Her mind raced. What was she going to do? Her Colt was hanging on a hook just inside the door. What if she could get inside first and grab it before Pa and his thug friend could stop her? She picked up her pace a bit, pulling Jane along with her. When she reached the soddy, she quickly pushed open the door. She stopped short and gasped. A man sat at her table, a cigar between his teeth.

Her gaze flew to the peg where the gun belt usually hung.

"Looking for this?" The man at the table held her Colt in his palm.

Laney shuddered in anger. Her pa was a good-for-nothing varmint to bring these rascals to her house.

She heard a chuckle next to her ear and spun around, once again coming face-to-face with Matt. Laney shuddered at the clear message written in his dark eyes. She couldn't escape, so she might as well forget the idea. But he didn't know Laney Jenkins. She'd get out of this mess one way or another. They'd be sorry they ever tangled with her in the first place!

Chapter 8

He's another good-looking baby, Tarah," Luke fibbed. Just a little fib—no use hurting his sister's feelings, even if the wrinkly, squalling infant was slobbering all over the front of his shirt.

Tarah took the baby and cuddled him close, instantly halting Johnny's wails. A laugh erupted from the four-time mother. "Don't worry, Uncle Luke. He'll get better looking every day." She kissed the top of her baby's head and lowered herself into a rocking chair next to the cozy fireplace.

Luke averted his gaze while his sister prepared to nurse Johnny. When she was settled and covered with a shawl, she said, "Your first few days on this earth, I was so embarrassed, I begged Ma and Pa not to take you anywhere."

Luke sent her a sheepish grin. "I couldn't fool you, eh?"

"Don't worry about it. I think he's just beautiful. So how are things at the ranch?"

"Running smoothly."

"And Pa? How is he?"

"Stronger every day. Still a long ways from running a ranch, though."

"I'm sorry, Luke. I know it doesn't seem fair that you have to put your plans on hold."

A shrug lifted his shoulders. "You know, at first I was bitter about it. But after a good tongue lashing from someone near and dear to us both, I saw that I was just being selfish."

Tarah laughed. "Our Laney has a way of getting straight to the heart of the matter, doesn't she?"

He grinned. "I guess so."

"Speaking of Laney, I thought she'd have come to see Johnny by now."

"She hasn't been by?"

Tarah shook her head. "I suppose she's extra busy since Granny's staying with me, but I thought she'd have taken a few minutes to come meet the baby. You know how she loves to cuddle newborns."

Laney's adoration of infants was legendary in the family. Anthony good-naturedly said it was like trying to wrestle a piece of meat away from a grizzly to get to hold his own children when they were babies.

"Doesn't sound like Laney, does it?"

"Has anyone checked on her in the last few days?"

Luke shifted uncomfortably in his chair. "I don't guess so."

"She's probably working herself to death, with no one to make sure she's eating and sleeping properly. Could you run by there after you get Ma's supplies from Tucker's?" She stopped short and stared at him. A frown furrowed her brow. "What?"

"What, what?"

"You're staring at your boots. What's wrong?"

"Laney and I got into it last time I saw her. I doubt she'd want to see me."

Shaking her head, Tarah huffed. "Honestly. You two beat all I ever saw and then some. You're either kissing or arguing."

"Who's kissing?" Little D entered the room, trailing mud. "Uncle Luke and Laney? Yuck. Not again."

"Little D! Look at the floor. Granny just scrubbed it yesterday. She'll tan your hide for this." Tarah gave him a stern look. "Take off those boots, and go get a bucket of water. You can just clean it up before she sees it."

Little D looked scandalized. "You want me to do women's work?"

Luke bit back a grin and stood as Tarah's eyes narrowed. The boy was about to get a stern lecture, and Luke didn't want to be around to witness it.

Obviously Little D caught the look, too, for he scooted off to fetch the water.

Tarah's glance swept upward until her gaze caught Luke's. "Will you go by Laney's? She's probably forgotten all about your argument. Besides, I'm a little worried about her."

Luke grabbed his hat from the table and headed for the door. "All right. I'll swing by there after I pick up Ma's supplies from Tucker's."

A relieved smile crossed Tarah's lips. "Thank you."

Luke bid her good day and stepped outside. The sun, beating brilliantly against the snow, nearly blinded him, and he squinted against the brightness. He climbed into the wagon and made his way to Tucker's.

Tucker glanced up and grinned as the bell above the door announced Luke's entrance into the dusty mercantile.

"Howdy, there, Luke. How's that pa of yers doin'?"

Luke's spine stiffened. It was one thing to give family news to other family members like Tarah, another entirely to give the townsfolk more to gossip about. Nevertheless, he attempted a cheery response. "He's gaining strength every day."

"Glad to hear it," Tucker said, nodding. "I hated to hear about such a fine man losing a leg, but I guess the good Lord knows whut He's a-doin'."

"He always does," Luke replied, handing Tucker his list. "Ma sent me in for these."

"I'll git right on it." He scanned the list, then turned and pulled a large sack of flour from the shelf behind him. "I hear the reverend and Tarah got another blessin' t'other night."

"Yep. Another boy to keep Tarah on her toes."

"Not much of a looker, from what yer granny says. 'Course, I ain't likely one to judge, bein' as I ain't never had one of my own."

Luke grinned. "Tarah says they all look like that in the beginning, but she's convinced he'll handsome right up with time."

"I'm sure that'll be a relief."

Tucker continued to fill the order for Cassidy, then he paused and squinted at Luke. "You seen Laney, by any chance?"

Why did everyone seem to think he should be keeping up with Laney? Irritation taunted Luke, daring him to spout off to the old man, but he bit back a retort, determined not to offend. "I haven't seen her in a few days."

Tucker shook his head, his brow furrowed. "That's right peculiar."

"What is?"

A shrug lifted his shoulders. "She came in for supplies yesterday, but she didn't bring the gowns she owes me. Nearly bit off my head fer asking about 'em. Then I seen her duck into the saloon."

"The saloon? Laney hates the sight of that place."

"That's whut I thought, too. That's why it struck me as peculiar to see her go in there." The storekeeper leaned across the counter and lowered his voice. "You don't think she's been working so hard it finally got to her, do you?"

A frown creased Luke's brow. "What are you saying?"

"Think Laney coulda took to the drink like her pa?"

"Laney?" Luke laughed at the thought.

"Been known to happen." He shoved his finger toward Luke. "It's a sorry enough sight to see a man all liquored up, but a drunken woman is downright shameful."

Still grinning, Luke paid Tucker and grabbed the crate. "You don't have to worry about Laney turning to the drink. For one thing, she hates it because of her pa; for another, she's a Christian. She wouldn't do it because she believes it's wrong."

"Then what was she doin' sneakin' into the saloon?"

That was a puzzle. "I'm not sure, but let's give her the benefit of the doubt, okay? And I'd sure appreciate if you didn't mention it to anyone else."

Tucker's face darkened. "What do you take me fer, some gossipin' woman?"

Luke hid his amusement and turned. His eye caught the WANTED poster on the wall, and his mouth went dry. What if. . . ?

"I have to be going now, Mr. Tucker. Remember, don't mention Laney to anyone else."

Mr. Tucker's indignant response was lost on Luke's ears as he hurried from the mercantile, set the crate in the back of the wagon, and quickly climbed into the seat.

One thing was for certain. If her pa was back, Laney was in trouble. Luke's jaw clenched. But not as much trouble as the old man would be in if he laid one hand on her. Remembering that there were two men on the WANTED poster with Jenkins, Luke decided to stop off at the sheriff's office.

Sheriff Boggs, a middle-aged bachelor with graying temples, greeted Luke cordially. "What can I do for you, Luke?"

"I think Jenkins and his gang might be holding Laney out at her place." No point wasting time with small talk when Laney might be in trouble.

The sheriff's gaze narrowed, and he leaned forward with interest. "You saw them?"

"No, but Tucker noticed Laney headed into the saloon yesterday."

"Well, if she was in town, they aren't likely holding her." Sheriff Boggs scowled and tipped his chair back to rest on two legs.

"Unless they sent her to town for supplies—including liquor."

"That's an awful lot of supposin'. If I jumped to conclusions every time someone went into the saloon. . ."

"This is *Laney*. She'd never take a drink."

"I can't go rushing off to her place just because you don't like that she went into the saloon."

Luke wanted to grab the apathetic sheriff by the collar and send him across the room; instead, he reined in his anger and tried to reason with the poor excuse for a lawman. "Tucker said she snapped at him yesterday, and Tarah says she hasn't even been by to see the new baby yet."

Emitting a short laugh, the sheriff stood. "Listen, Luke. Laney Jenkins is as snarly as a bear most of the time, and if she hasn't been by to see your sister's new young'un, it's probably because she's busy sewing for Tucker."

Luke searched for something else to convince the sheriff. The man had a point on all accounts. Those things didn't necessarily mean Laney was in trouble, but Luke knew she was. He could feel it. And he hated to walk into a situation outgunned.

"Look, Sheriff, I'd be obliged if you'd just trust me and ride out there with me. Maybe I'm wrong, and if I am, Laney'll give me an earful; but if I'm right, we'll have saved her, and you'll have captured three outlaws."

The sheriff seemed to consider the idea for a moment and appeared as though he might give in when the door flew open.

"Sheriff, come quick. There's trouble down at the saloon. Some fella's been caught cheatin' at cards, and it looks like they're about to shoot him."

Sheriff Boggs grabbed his rifle from the wall and shrugged at Luke as he walked past him to join the messenger. "Sorry. I'll ride out there with you later, but I have to go put a stop to this before someone ends up dead."

Expelling a frustrated breath, Luke watched him go. Laney could just as easily be in trouble. He drove past Sam's office and stopped just as a man hurried inside carrying a small boy. The child appeared to have broken his arm. Sam would be busy for quite some time.

Determined not to waste another second, Luke said a hasty prayer and turned the horses toward Laney's soddy.

Laney jumped and glanced up from her sewing as a plate sailed across the room and hit the wall, flinging its contents all over the floor.

"This ain't fit to eat. How come you ain't never learnt to cook?"

Laney glowered at the unkempt cowboy called Abe. "Who taught you manners? At least I tried to cook a decent meal!"

"There ain't nothin' decent about that mess you tried to pass off as venison stew. That was just a waste of meat and vegetables."

"No one said you had to eat it!" Laney retorted.

"You best watch your sass, little girl, or I'll make you wish you'd been nicer. Now get yourself up and cook something we can eat."

"Cook it yourself," she shot back, returning her attention to her sewing.

Abe sprang from his chair and towered over her, his breath fouling the few inches of space between them. He grabbed her arm in a flash of movement, his fingers biting cruelly into her soft flesh.

Determined not to show the fear creeping into her belly, Laney met his gaze evenly. Sneaking vinegar into the stew had made her feel better, but maybe it hadn't been such a good idea after all. Of course, she'd dipped a little out for Jane and herself first, but Abe didn't have to know that.

"Leave her alone," Pa growled from a pallet next to the fire. "Can't you see she's busy?"

Obviously as surprised as Laney, Abe released her arm and turned to Jenkins. "Have you tried to eat the mess she's passin' off as grub? My dog wouldn't eat that slop."

"Then fix yer own grub and leave the girl be."

Her pa erupted in a deep cough, and for several minutes no one spoke while he hacked. Laney frowned. He had been coughing like this since he arrived. She tried not to care, but she couldn't help herself. He spent the majority of his time stretched out on a thin pallet in front of the stove. When he rose, he trembled with weakness.

"I'm goin' out to try to find a rabbit to roast." Abe glared at Laney and yanked open the door, letting in a blast of cold air. "And don't think yer gettin' a bite of it!"

"I wouldn't take food from you anyway."

"What's wrong with you, Pa?" Laney asked after Abe slammed the door.

"Worried about your old pa, are ya, girlie? Must be gettin' soft. The girl I left would've been countin' the days 'til I keeled over."

"Forget I asked." Laney gave a short, bitter laugh. "And you didn't leave a girl behind. You sold me to the highest bidder like I was a slave. And Ben, too. You do remember Ben, don't you? Or have you forgotten about your son?"

"I ain't forgettin' him. I just figured he must be dead since you didn't mention him."

Laney fought to keep her temper in check. "I didn't mention him because you didn't ask. But I guess that's to be expected of someone like you."

His eyes narrowed, and his expression darkened. "Well, where is he, then? He couldn't be farmin' or ranchin' around here with that bum leg of his."

"Not that it's any of your business, but he happens to be back east, married to a pretty wife. He just finished seminary and was offered a church somewhere in Virginia."

"You mean to tell me my son's a preacher? A no-good, thievin' preacher?"

A coughing fit seized him as it did when he got too excited.

When he calmed, Laney met his gaze. "Ben's a preacher, but he's not a thief. Besides, you calling anyone a thief is sorta like the pot calling the kettle black, wouldn't you say?"

Jenkins shook his head in disgust. "I shoulda known better than to give you to that teacher and her preacher beau." He raised his brow in question. "I reckon they got hitched?"

"That's right. Tarah and Anthony took us in and raised us." She gave him a pointed look. "And you didn't *give* us away. You sold us."

"You don't have to keep reminding me of that, Laney-girl. I remember it like it were yesterday. So just shut up about it before I whale the daylights out of you."

Laney blinked in surprise. Not only was this the first time he'd used her name since he'd returned to her life, he seemed bothered by the memory of what he'd done. The thought raised her ire. She didn't want him to suddenly grow a conscience about it. If he cared, she might not be able to hate him, and he deserved her hatred—every bitter ounce that she'd harbored for as long as she could remember, and even more so since the day he'd taken ten dollars and a horse, then walked out of her life.

She wanted him gone. Out of her life again. "What do you plan to do, Pa? You know you can't hide out here forever."

He nodded. "Matt has plans for the bank in town. After that, we'll leave."

"You're going to rob the bank? Are you crazy? You can't do that." A gasp escaped Laney's lips. "My money is in that bank!" Her dreams for the future. "I'll lose my soddy and my land without that money."

His gaze searched hers. "I know you worked hard trying to buy this property. Don't know why you'd want it, but I know what it's like to lose. Wish it could be different, but Matt has his mind set on the bank. We need more money, iffen we're to get fer enough away that the law can't find us. After we do a number on the bank, we can split up."

"What makes you think I won't warn the sheriff next time you send me in for supplies and whiskey?"

He gave a short laugh. "You think I'd have told you if we was goin' to be around long enough? Matt's in town checkin' the layout of the place, and we're leavin' out tonight. 'Course, we'll have to tie you up when we go so's you don't go running to the law or those St. Johns. But I figure you'll get yourself loose pretty fast. From what I can tell, yer one smart girl."

"What about Jane?" Laney asked, ignoring the compliment.

"She ain't yer affair."

"She is, too. She's my sister!"

"You want her?"

"What's your price?" Laney curled her lip.

His face grew red, though from embarrassment or anger Laney wasn't sure. Nor did she have a chance to find out, as a coughing fit seized him.

"You shouldn't go out in this weather. What if you have pneumonia?"

"Don't tell me what to do, girl. Ain't no woman yet got by with orderin' me around, and I ain't starting with the likes of you."

"Fine. Catch your death, then. See if I care. What about Jane?"

"You can have her."

Laney hesitated, waiting for him to go back on his word. When he didn't speak, she finally broke the silence herself. "You mean it?"

He shrugged. "Like ya said, I'll probably be dead sooner than later, and ain't no sense takin' the girl when she'll most likely have to fend for herself 'fore long."

Laney caught his gaze, searching for a trace of deception in his dark eyes. He stared back frankly, and when he looked away, Laney had the uncomfortable feeling it was from shame. Again, anger seized her at the compassion seeping in despite her determination to hold a grudge.

I don't want to feel sorry for him, Lord. He doesn't deserve it. Don't make me feel sorry for this worthless excuse for a man.

She glanced to the bed where Jane napped, one strawberry blond braid slung across her face. Laney's heart swelled with love. This little girl was her own flesh and blood. Laney smiled. Her sister would have roots here in Harper. She'd never feel like she didn't belong. She would grow up with Little D and the rest of Tarah and Anthony's children. Most of all, she would know her sister loved and wanted her.

Glancing at her pa, she couldn't help but notice he shivered, despite his close proximity to the fire. His back was turned, and even through the thin blanket, Laney could see his bones poking through. He wasn't long for this earth. A thought seized her. If her pa died, he wouldn't go to heaven. Her stomach quivered.

"Pa?"

"What?" he growled.

"Don't die without knowing Jesus."

"Shut up, girl, before I shut you up. You know I don't have no use for religion and such." He coughed. "Leave me alone and let me rest."

"Fine. I tried."

Laney turned back to her sewing.

Please send help, Lord. It's been four days, and no one has even come to check on me. Don't they notice I haven't been around? If I lose my money, I won't have a home for Jane. I can't bear the thought of her growing up without a sense of belonging like I did. Please, Lord. After what You did to Papa Dell, I've learned my lesson. I'm not asking for myself; I'm asking for Jane.

Chapter 9

Luke crept stealthily alongside the soddy until he drew near the window. Pressing his back against the outside wall, he craned his neck and peeked sideways through the window. Relief flooded him at the sight of Laney working diligently as though there wasn't an unkempt outlaw glaring at her from across the table. She glanced up and sneered at the dirty buckskin-clad man who tore off a bite of roasted meat, then licked his fingers.

Across the room, a man lay on a pallet close to the woodstove, and a small girl sat quietly on the bed, her gaze fixed on Laney. Luke studied the rest of the room. There were only two men. He couldn't move in until the third man showed up. Otherwise, the missing outlaw might come in at the wrong time and overpower Luke. Then he'd be no help for Laney.

Luke retreated slowly until he found a safe place away from the soddy where he could watch without being discovered. He lay flat on his stomach. Snow soaked into his shirt and the front of his trousers, adding irritation to his anxiety.

Although he hated the thought of Laney staying in the soddy much longer, he couldn't help but feel a bit of relief that she appeared unmolested. Still, he'd feel a lot better when the other outlaw showed up. Once he did, Luke knew he could move in and get her out of there. A thought occurred to him. *What if the three men split up and the third outlaw isn't with them anymore?* Luke groaned inwardly. Laney might be in there with those men for nothing. *Show me what to do, Lord. I don't want to put Laney in danger.*

It seemed like an eternity of waiting without an answer from heaven. After two hours, Luke made up his mind. He was moving in. He started toward the soddy. A twig snapped behind him. Luke spun around, expecting to find the third outlaw poised to jump him. Instead, the sheriff stood before him, his six-shooter cocked and pointed.

"What are you doing here, Sheriff?" Luke whispered.

"You were right. The outlaws are holed up at Laney's."

"What changed your mind?"

"I arrested one of them in the saloon today." The sheriff chuckled. "Not very smart for a wanted man to cheat at cards, if you ask me. Have you checked out the soddy?"

Luke nodded. "There are two men—although one of them appears to be sick. That one must be Jenkins. I recognized the other man from the poster. He's the only one with a gun. Besides those two, there's a little girl and Laney."

"All right, then," the sheriff said. "You go to the window and be ready to fire if necessary. I'll bust the door open and try to gain the upper hand without getting those two females hurt."

Soon they were in place. The second outlaw sat with his legs stretched out, his hat down over his face. His chest rose and fell evenly as though he slept. Suddenly the door burst open and the sheriff appeared, his rifle in one hand and a pistol in the other. The younger man started awake and nearly fell out of his chair as he recognized that he'd been caught. He stood and reached into the air. Laney grabbed his guns.

Luke moved around the soddy and entered.

Laney glanced up and gave him a cursory smile, then she turned back to the sheriff. "That's my pa over there, Sheriff," she said. "He's pretty sick."

"We'll get Sam over to take a look at him once I get him all locked up in the jail."

"Just get him out of my house, please." Her voice trembled slightly, and she passed her hand wearily across her forehead.

Luke strode across the room until he stood next to Laney. "Are you all right?"

She gave a nonchalant wave. "Oh, I'm fine. But they put me even further behind with Tucker. Think Granny's about ready to come back?"

Luke knew she was shaken and trying not to show it. Tenderness rushed through him. He brushed his thumb down her cheek, testing its softness. "I'm sure she'll be ready soon." He wanted to take her into his arms to reassure himself that she was truly all right, but he knew she'd balk at the gesture in front of anyone.

"Well, I suppose I'll get these two where they belong." The sheriff eyed Jenkins critically. "You don't look much like the man you used to be, Jenkins. I guess this is what hard living does to a man."

"Save your sermon, Sheriff," the bone-thin man replied with a sneer. "Just do what you gotta do."

"Can you sit a horse?"

"I'll hitch Laney's wagon and drive him into town," Luke volunteered. He'd left his own wagon a mile from the soddy to enable him to approach silently.

"No need for that," Jenkins growled. "I can sit a horse just fine." His last words were followed by an onslaught of coughing from deep within his chest.

Laney snorted. "Hitch the wagon, Luke. He couldn't ride ten feet without falling off."

Sheriff Boggs shoved the other outlaw out the door. "I'm taking this varmint on ahead. You follow as soon as you get the wagon hitched, will you, Luke?"

"Sure, Sheriff. We won't be long."

"What makes you think I won't make a run fer it?" Jenkins said, his voice trembling from his last coughing fit.

"You couldn't make it to the outhouse, let alone run away, Pa."

"You better just watch yourself. I can still tan your hide."

Laney snorted again, but the sheriff interrupted before she could reply. "We'll be going now."

"Might as well sit and wait," Jenkins grumbled, obviously too sick to keep up his grisly facade.

Once the door was closed behind the sheriff, Luke turned to Laney. "Why don't you pack a few things and ride along?" he suggested. "I'll drop you off at Anthony and Tarah's for the night so you don't have to stay alone."

"I told you, I have work to do. Besides, I won't be alone. Will I, Jane?"

Luke shifted his attention to the little girl on the bed. He'd forgotten she was even there. "Who's this?" he asked, smiling at the child. She ducked her head and trembled.

"I'm sorry," he said. "I didn't mean to scare her."

"It's all right," Laney said softly. She walked to the bed and pulled the girl in her arms. "This is my sister. I guess she'll be staying with me from here on out."

Luke raised his brow, trying not to show his shock at the news. He eyed the little girl and smiled. "It's nice to meet you," Luke offered. "I'm Luke, a good friend of your sister's. I hope we'll be friends, too."

Jane glanced at him, eyes wide, but she didn't speak, nor did she smile.

Luke cleared his throat. "I suppose I should get that wagon hitched."

Laney watched Luke go, not sure what to say to her pa now that he was headed to jail. She turned and observed him wrapped in his blanket at the table.

White-hot anger burned inside of her. She wanted to be glad he was going to get what he deserved, but her anger warred with the compassion rising inside of her. He could be sentenced to hang, and if he did, he would die a sinner. He wouldn't last a week in prison.

God, what can I do about it? I already tried to share with him about Jesus, and he won't listen.

"Stop starin' at me like that, girl. I ain't no charity case."

Laney laughed at the ludicrous statement. "As long as I can remember, we lived on folks' charity, Pa. When did you suddenly grow a sense of pride?"

Jenkins glowered at her. "Maybe I wanted to make life easier for her," he said, jerking his thumb toward Jane.

"So making her travel with an outlaw gang and threatening to hurt her if I didn't cooperate was your way of making things easier? That doesn't seem too likely, Pa."

"I was just blowin' smoke. I ain't never hit her even once, and I never would."

A bitter laugh erupted from Laney's lips. "First thing you did was knock me to the ground. Just like old times." Impatiently she pushed aside the hurt trying to shove its way in through the memories she'd tried to forget. What did she care if her pa loved her little sister but had never loved her?

He grimaced. "I know how stubborn you are. How was I supposed to keep ya in line without some sorta hold over ya? If I didn't remind ya who was boss and threaten to beat your sister, ya never would have obeyed. Then I couldn't have protected you from Matt and Abe, no matter how much rough talkin' I did."

Choosing to ignore the implication that he cared anything at all about her, Laney stepped closer and lowered her voice so Jane couldn't hear. "If you care so much about Jane, why didn't you take good care of her, Pa?"

His features darkened. "There was supposed to be enough money in that old fool's safe to make all three of us rich," he growled. "I was gonna buy us a little house somewhere where Janey could go to school like other little girls. I wanted her to be proud."

He began to cough again before Laney could reply. She regarded him silently. Could he possibly be telling the truth? She recalled the last few days. He had protected both her virtue and well-being against Matt and Abe numerous times. She had to admit Jane wasn't afraid of him in the same manner she and Ben had been as children. And he seemed almost gentle when dealing with the little girl.

While Laney pondered these last thoughts, Luke returned. The door opened, letting in a blast of cold air and a swirl of snow.

"It's snowing again? Honestly, Luke. My pa will catch his death if he goes out in this."

Luke shrugged. "I don't see as how we have a choice in the matter."

"Go tell the sheriff we'll bring him in tomorrow if the snow has quit falling. No sense in having him keel over before the circuit judge comes through."

Laney noted the hesitation in Luke's eyes. His concern warmed her, and her lips tilted upward in a small smile. "Don't worry, Lukey. I'll be fine. Pa couldn't hurt a puppy in his condition."

"I suppose you're right. I'll run to town and talk it over with the sheriff, but if he objects, I may have to come back and get your pa."

Relief washed over her. "Thank you. I appreciate it."

"Can you walk me out?" he asked, lifting her coat from its peg next to the door. The intensity of his gaze sent a rush of warmth through Laney. He held her coat while she slipped her arms in it. Laney could feel the insistent pressure of his hands on her shoulders, and another wave of warmth covered her.

Laney turned to Jane. "Help Pa to his pallet, honey. I'll be right back."

Jane scooted off the bed and shuffled to Jenkins's side. "Come on, Pa," she said quietly. "Laney says you ain't gotta go nowheres tonight."

Laney's heart ached as she watched her pa smile at the child. In the first twelve years of her life, he had never once looked at her that way. She welcomed the frigid air as she stepped into the night. Luke snatched up her hand and tucked it through his arm.

"I'm going to ask Sam to come and take a look at Jenkins," Luke said. "So don't bring him in too early tomorrow. Wait for Sam."

"The sheriff said he'd have Sam take a look at him at the jail." Standing so close to Luke, Laney had difficulty concentrating.

"Your pa seems pretty bad off. If Sam suggests it, the sheriff might let him stay with you until the judge comes. You know as well as I do that could be anywhere from a week to two months, depending on where he is and how much crime there's been in the county."

Laney cringed inwardly at the very thought. Judges sometimes took months to respond to a summons. She didn't want Pa staying with her for days or weeks or months. Why shouldn't he be locked up like Matt and Abe? It was one thing to keep him overnight while it snowed, but two months? How would she ever put up with him that long? Why should she have to? He had sold away his rights to her eight years ago.

"Well?" Luke's voice broke through her bitter thoughts.

Laney shrugged. "I guess we'll wait and see what Sam thinks."

"What do you think?" he insisted. "If you don't want him here, I'll take him right now. It's your decision."

Laney tilted her head and regarded him frankly. "He'll stay the night, and after that, I just don't know."

They reached the wagon. Luke released her to pull the team back into the sod barn. Laney followed and helped him unhitch the horses.

When they finished, Luke leaned against the wagon and faced her. He captured both of her hands in his. "Are you all right?" he asked, his voice shaky with emotion. "They didn't hurt you?"

Laney smiled and shook her head. "They didn't lay a finger on me. Pa wouldn't let them, actually."

Relief washed over his features. He drew her close. Laney went willingly into his arms and nestled against his broad chest. She felt his hand stroke her hair. A sigh escaped her lips, and for the first time in days, the tension left her shoulders. "Thank you for coming for me, Luke."

Luke pulled slightly away and tipped Laney's chin upward until she met his gaze. "I'm sorry I let my pride keep me away as long as I did. I could have spared you sooner if I had come by to check on you."

Reaching up, Laney pressed her palm against his rough cheek. "None of this is your fault," she said softly, swallowing hard as she recalled the last thing Luke had said to her that day. He had wanted to propose. "I wasn't exactly nice to you last time we spoke."

"We do seem to bring out the temper in each other." Luke grinned and covered her hand with his. "But I'd rather be mad every day of my life and have you with me than live in peace with anyone else."

What exactly was he trying to say?

"Marry me, Laney."

She glanced at him cautiously. "Where have I heard that before?"

He sent her a heart-stopping grin. "I'll keep asking until I get you in front of a preacher, Laney Jenkins." He slipped his hands around her waist and pulled her close. "You're the only woman for me."

Laney's knees felt watery, and her senses reeled at the proximity of the man she loved. She swayed forward as his head slowly began to descend. Then, although it required every ounce of her will, she pressed her palm against his chest to deter him. "Wh–what about Oregon? I still can't move off away from here—especially now that I have my little sister to raise."

"I've decided not to go." Luke's eyes momentarily seemed to cloud in the soft glow of the lantern light.

"Why would you decide something like that?"

"Pa won't be up to sitting a horse again for quite a while, if ever. He needs me to run things for him. We might have to put off building our herd for a few years while I keep his operating until Will can take over. That okay with you?"

"Of course it is, Luke. I'll continue sewing for Tucker, and we can keep saving money." Laney's excitement grew with each word. "By the time we're ready, we'll have enough to buy a right fine herd to start us off."

A grin split Luke's face. "Are you saying yes, then?"

Laney's cheeks heated. "Of course my answer is yes!" She flung her arms around his neck and giggled when he lifted her off the ground.

He set her down and kept a steadying hand on her arm, allowing them both to regain their composure a moment before he pulled her close. "Thank you, Laney. I promise you'll never regret becoming my wife."

"I know I won't," she murmured just as his lips moved slowly over hers, drowning her words and pushing aside the doubts creeping into her mind.

Later, while she lay in the darkness next to Jane, listening to her pa's loud snoring, Laney recalled the faraway look in Luke's eyes when he told her he'd decided to stay in Harper and run St. John Ranch.

Unease gnawed at her. She had said she would never be second choice to Luke's dream. Would she ever believe he was staying because he wanted to run the ranch and marry her, or would this anxiety always creep in during times of uncertainty? She tried to push the worry away. After all, she was getting every-thing she wanted—her own place, a means of making and saving money, her own herd eventually, and now the most important dream of all. . .she would soon marry Luke. So why was her stomach twisted in knots?

Closing her eyes, she tried to pray, but the words wouldn't come. Finally, after hours of trying not to toss and turn, she got up and stoked the fire to make sure Pa stayed warm, then she pulled out her sewing and went to work. Things were changing so fast, she was having trouble wrapping her mind around the reality of it all.

As she tried to sort it all out, her thoughts wandered away from the task at hand. She pricked her finger with a pin, and sudden tears sprang to her eyes. Then, as though she had opened a floodgate, the tears continued in a steady stream down her cheeks until the sobs wrenched her body.

Lord, I have everything I have ever dreamed of, and still I feel like there's a hole dug in my heart. What's wrong with me?

She felt a soft hand slip inside hers and looked up. Jane's brilliant blue eyes were flooded with tears, and she leaned her head against Laney's shoulder. "I been crying, too," she whispered. "I think Pa's real sick. Is that why you're crying, Laney?"

Laney held Jane more tightly, taking comfort from her warm little body as she pulled her onto her lap. "Partly, honey."

She stared at the child and wondered at her ability to love their pa. Maybe if he had treated Laney and Ben with an ounce of the affection he seemed to feel for Jane, she would be able to feel something for him, too. As it was, she was willing to let him stay until the judge came through—for Jane's sake, if nothing else. But once he was sentenced to his fate, she was through with him. For good.

Chapter 10

A persistent knocking at the door awakened Laney after barely two hours of slumber. Pa's coughing was getting worse, and sleep was sporadic, at best. The knock came again as she pushed back the quilts and swung her legs over the side of the bed. Turning, she replaced the covers over Jane.

"I'm coming," she called, her voice husky from sleep and irritation.

She grabbed her dressing gown and padded across the sod floor strewn with rag rugs. She lifted the latch and swung open the door.

"I declare. Who stays in bed two hours after sunup? Where is your sense of propriety, gal?"

"Granny! What are you doing here?" Glancing past her, Laney spied Anthony grinning broadly as he lifted his hand in farewell and flipped the reins at the horses.

"Humph." Granny walked right in, thumping her cane against the floor. "I live here, remember—or have you thrown me out since I've been helping Tarah with her new baby?"

Laney felt her cheeks grow warm. "Of course I didn't throw you out. It's just that. . ."

Granny waved toward Jenkins's pallet. "Oh, him. Well, I know all about that rascal."

"My pa ain't no rascal!"

Laney started at Jane's outburst.

Granny cackled. "Heard about her, too. 'Course, I heard she was quiet as a mouse and not a thing like you. Maybe she's more like you than Luke gave her credit for."

"Maybe." The thought didn't entirely displease Laney. A woman needed a voice in this world.

Making her way to the bed, Granny eyed Jane sternly. "Now look here, I am your granny now, so you must watch how you speak to me. Is that understood?"

Jane trembled beneath the covers. Laney only prayed she didn't wet the bed from fear.

"Speak up. You weren't afraid to voice your opinion a minute ago."

"Yes, ma'am," Jane squeaked out.

"That's fine." Granny's stern face lit, and she smiled. "Now I showed some mighty poor manners by calling your pa a rascal right in front of you. But I'll forgive you for sassing if you'll forgive me for my bad manners. How's that?"

Jane gave her a shy smile. "That's just fine, ma'am."

"I thought you looked like a girl with some good sense. Now you must call me Granny."

"Yes, Granny."

Laney stared in wonder at the exchange. Granny was a crotchety old woman, but she never ceased to amaze her.

"Get yourself dressed, Laney-girl. I'll put some coffee on to boil and start breakfast."

"But, Granny, you can't. . .well, I don't see how you can stay here. My pa has some sort of lung sickness. When Sam came by yesterday and examined him, he said we'd best keep him away from folks just in case it's contagious."

"Hogwash. I've nursed my share of disease-riddled men. I haven't taken even one man's sickness, and I don't figure to start at this late date."

Laney cleared her throat. "That's not the only reason. You might have noticed. . ."

"Oh, stop trying to be polite. Of course you don't have room for me to sleep here. Anthony will be back to pick me up this evening after supper. In the meantime, I hear you're behind on your sewing for Mr. Tucker. I'm here to help."

"I don't know what to say."

"Don't say anything. Just go get dressed, and make the bed so we can get our day started. Now, Jane, I have a couple of sourballs and a book in my bag. After breakfast, if you'll sit quietly and look at your book, I'll let you have one sourball. How's that sound?"

"Just fine, Granny. Just fine!"

For the next two weeks, Granny came every day but Sunday. Laney's nest egg continued to grow, and she looked excitedly to the day she could slap down a large last payment and get the deed to her property.

So far no one had said a thing about the engagement—neither Granny, nor Mama Cassidy at church, nor Tarah. Obviously Luke hadn't mentioned his proposal to anyone. Laney felt a little disappointed. Her growing pessimism over Luke's sincerity wasn't helped by the fact that she had only seen him at church on Sunday during the past two weeks. During those times, their conversations had been brief, almost too polite. Miserably Laney feared that Luke had changed his mind and just didn't know how to tell her. She took comfort from the fact that she would soon be at the ranch for Christmas Day and would get to the bottom of things.

After conferring with his father-in-law, Doc Simpson, Sam had concluded that whatever Pa's illness, it likely wasn't the contagious sort, so he okayed an outing for Christmas dinner.

Thankfully, though the air was icy, no snow fell on Christmas Day. Jane was beside herself with excitement over the new dress Laney and Granny had made her. Predictably Pa balked about going to the St. Johns', but Laney dug in her heels and refused to budge.

"You're going if I have to get Luke over here to carry you to the wagon. Besides, don't you want one last Christmas with Janey? Think of what it will mean to her."

Finally he relented and even agreed to a bath and a shave. Laney had bought him a new pair of britches and a nice warm flannel shirt at Tucker's. He seemed to perk up and didn't complain even once during the ride over.

Laney's palms grew damp as the ranch came into view. She hadn't seen Papa Dell since Thanksgiving; and at that time, he hadn't been out of bed yet, so she'd barely spoken to him. She knew he was sitting up for longer and longer periods of time now, and she hated the thought of having to face him. The guilt of her prayer that Luke would have to stay in Harper tore at her most of the time. She wanted desperately to confess, throw her arms around him, and beg his forgiveness, but deeper than her need to confess was her aversion to the thought of Papa Dell being disappointed in her.

Luke was on hand to greet her when the wagon rolled next to the house. "Merry Christmas," he said, his voice husky and filled with longing.

All at once, relief flooded Laney. The way Luke gazed at her was definitely the look of a man in love. At least that was one worry she could lay to rest today. Now if only she could put aside her guilt over Papa Dell as easily. She squared her shoulders and ascended the porch steps.

She grinned as Jane immediately went off to play with Cat, the youngest member of the St. John clan.

As gracious as ever, Mama Cassidy gave Jenkins the best chair in the house and insisted on giving him a quilt to lay across his lap. To Laney's amazement, her pa seemed honestly grateful as he snuggled under the covers and watched the comings and goings of the St. Johns.

Papa Dell sat in the chair opposite him and immediately struck up a conversation. Laney noticed her pa relax visibly, and she felt the tension leave her own shoulders, as well. Everything would be fine.

Thirty minutes later, Laney groaned to herself as Papa Dell called to her. How could she have thought everything would be fine? Luke had taken off without telling her where he was going or inviting her along, and once again, all of her earlier doubts began to surface.

Laney sat on the hearth, feeling the warmth from the fire heating up her backside.

"How are you doing?" Papa Dell asked, his eyes filled with genuine concern and love.

Unable to hold his gaze, Laney studied the scuff marks on the tips of her boots. "I'm fine," she mumbled.

"Glad to hear it. I know you've been mighty busy, but it's good to see you."

"Yeah, between Tucker's orders and now Pa and Jane. . ."

"I understand, believe me. Sometimes life makes it impossible to find time for anything other than work and church meetings. I'm just glad you're with us today."

Laney could bear no more. Tears stung her eyes, and she laid her head on Papa Dell's lap. He hesitated briefly, then he stroked her hair.

"What is it, honey?" His voice sounded worried, his concern only fueling Laney's guilt.

"Oh, Papa Dell, I'm so sorry."

"What are you sorry about?"

"I did something terrible."

"I know you couldn't do anything truly bad, Laney."

"I did."

"Well, look at me and tell me what has you so upset."

She lifted her head from his lap but still couldn't bring herself to look at him. "I—I—Papa Dell. . . It's all my fault you got hurt."

"What do you mean? How could it possibly have been your fault?" Papa Dell cupped her chin and pressed gently until she had no choice but to look him in the eye.

Laney's stomach dropped. Now was the time for honesty. She couldn't put it off any longer. "I—I didn't want Luke to go out west, so I prayed for God to make a way for him to have to stay in Harper."

"And you think God answered your prayer by letting Ol' Angus tear into my leg?" He asked the question thoughtfully, and to Laney's relief, there was no anger in his tone.

"I reckon that's about the end of the matter, though I can't say how sorry I am about it. And if I could do it over, I'd just let Luke go and marry someone else. Honest, I would."

Papa Dell's lips twitched. "Those are some mighty powerful prayers you have there."

Laney nodded miserably. "I reckon I just have the praying touch. That was the first time I ever prayed for something for myself, Papa Dell, and look what happened. But don't worry, I'll never do it again."

"Well, don't give up on prayer altogether, honey. Do you think God would harm one of His children just to answer the prayers of another?"

"It appears that way."

Papa Dell gave her an indulgent smile. "Can you see me cutting off Luke's leg just to give Sam experience doctoring?"

" 'Course not!"

Papa Dell nodded. "God loves us the same. And what happens to one of His children has nothing whatsoever to do with His answers to another."

"But. . .your leg. . ."

"My own stubbornness caused that accident. Luke told me a year ago we needed to sell Ol' Angus before he hurt someone. Since I let my pride stand in the way of a sound decision, I lost money putting Ol' Angus down, not to mention that now I have to wait until spring to buy another bull, and I'll lose out on one breeding cycle. My pride was pretty costly. But I promise, honey, this missing leg of mine isn't your fault."

Laney smiled. For the first time since the accident, the guilt lifted, and she felt almost giddy with relief. She threw her arms around Papa Dell. "Thank you."

"Now I expect to be seeing you a lot more around here. I need my dose of Laney every now and then to keep me laughing." He pulled his handkerchief from his pocket.

"I promise," she replied, accepting the proffered hanky.

The rattle of a wagon outside captured her attention. She turned to Papa Dell. "I didn't realize anyone else was coming."

"Yep," he said noncommittally.

A moment later, Luke burst in, his cheeks red from the cold. He grinned at Laney. "Are you ready for your Christmas present?"

Laney's cheeks warmed. "I can't open my present before the kids!" What was Luke thinking?

He shrugged. "Have it your own way, but they'll get mighty cold standing on the porch until Christmas dinner is over and we gather round the tree."

"Honestly, Luke. What are you talking about?"

He stepped aside and swung open the door.

Laney gasped, shrieked, then flew into her brother's arms. "Ben! How'd you ever make it home on your preacher's salary?"

Then she gasped again at the rudeness of her question.

Ben laughed and lifted her into a crushing bear hug. "Papa Dell wrote us a letter, inviting us, and sent the tickets. We've been holed up at Tarah's since the train rolled in yesterday morning."

"I just can't believe you're here."

"What about me?" At one time Josie Raney's honeyed tone would have sent shivers of annoyance down Laney's spine, but now that she had made Ben so happy, Laney was willing to put aside past bad feelings and welcome her as a sister. Moving from Ben's arms to Josie's, Laney said, "Of course I'm thrilled to see you, too! You look downright beautiful."

Josie gave a pleasant laugh. "And you haven't changed one bit, Laney Jenkins. You're just as boyish as ever."

Laney stiffened. Maybe marrying Ben wasn't enough to redeem Josie after all. Laney felt a warm hand on her back and turned to find Luke grinning down at her.

"I hardly think anyone could call Laney boyish anymore." He chucked her chin. "She's too pretty for that."

Laney felt the warmth from her head to her toes. She could have hugged him right then and there and probably would have, if not for the sound of a raspy cough filling the air and silencing all banter and laughter—a reminder that Ben had a hurdle to get over before they could get on with their reunion.

"Ben, there's something you should—"

"It's all right, Laney. I knew he was here."

Ben moved slowly across the room, his limp more pronounced than Laney remembered. She started to follow, but the pressure of Luke's hand on her arm stopped her. Turning, she glowered at him, trying to jerk away, but he held firm.

"Let Ben handle this alone."

She nodded, and he loosened his grip, sliding his hand downward to grasp her hand. A delicious thrill shot through her, and she moved a step closer to him, enjoying the warmth of his arm pressed against hers.

"Hello, Pa," Ben said, his voice trembling slightly. Laney wondered if he was fighting for control or if he was truly glad to see their pa. Ben always was the more forgiving of them. Even when they had a chance to run away and live with Tarah, Ben had insisted they had to go home and honor Pa like the Bible said. Only days later, Pa had sold them to Anthony and Tarah—but by then, Ben had a black eye and bruised ribs from another undeserved beating.

Laney fought to control her anger at the memory. She wanted to rush forward and grab Ben away. He shouldn't be nice to Pa. The old rascal didn't deserve it.

Give him a good piece of your mind, Ben! She knew full well it wasn't in Ben's nature to hold a grudge—his marriage to Josie Raney was proof of that.

Pa's reply was short. "I see yer all growed up and probably think yer too good for yer ol' pa—just like her." Laney glared as he jerked a thumb at her.

Ben gave a good-natured chuckle. "True, I am all grown up, but no, I don't think I'm too good for my pa. As a matter of fact, I'd like you to meet someone." Ben turned and reached for his wife. Josie walked to him hesitantly, a tentative smile plastered on her face. Laney could tell she was fighting for her own control. The realization went a long way toward Laney's overlooking the earlier "boyish" comment.

"Least you got yerself a looker," Pa said with a knowing grin that made Josie blush to the roots of her blond hair.

Ben gathered her protectively around the shoulders and pulled her close. "She's beautiful on the outside, that's true, but her inward beauty is what made me fall head over heels in love with my wife."

Laney held back a snort. Boy, did Josie have her brother fooled.

Ben cleared his throat loudly and glanced about the room. "We actually have an announcement to make."

Laney waited impatiently. *Oh, please let him say he's moving back.*

"We just found out that God is blessing us with a new addition to the family.

Looks like you're going to be a grandpa, Pa."

Pa squinted and eyed him for a moment. Laney hurried forward before Pa could ruin things with another crude comment and hugged Ben tightly. "Congratulations. Never thought I'd see the day you'd be a pa, but I know you'll be a good one." *A sight better than our own pa ever was.*

The family surrounded the happy couple, and for the next few minutes, the sitting room buzzed with congratulations, good-natured ribbing, and advice until Luke grabbed Laney's hand once again and cleared his throat. "I can't let Ben outdo me on Christmas," he said, grinning. "Laney and I have an announcement to make, too."

He paused long enough to search her face for approval. She smiled and nodded.

"Don't tell me ya got my daughter in a fix!"

Pa's outburst brought a collective gasp from the women. Laney would have gladly clobbered the old coot, but Luke squeezed her hand to silence her.

"Actually, our good news is that we're getting married."

"Finally!" Tarah stepped forward and grabbed them both, hugging them tightly. "I thought the two of you would never stop fighting long enough to actually realize you love each other."

The room exploded into laughter. The door opened, bringing a blast of cold inside as the children tromped in from their playing.

"We're starving," Little D complained. "Is the turkey done?"

"Little D," Anthony said, his tone taking on a rare sternness. "You're being impolite. I think you owe Grams an apology."

"Sorry, Grams," Little D muttered.

Cassidy sent the little guy a wink. "Accepted. And yes, the turkey will be coming out of the oven in just a few minutes, so you children get out of those wraps and come help us set the table."

Laney stepped forward to help Jane out of her coat and scarf. "There's someone I want you to meet," she whispered to the little girl.

She nestled her little sister in the crook of her arm and pulled her close, moving toward Ben. He apparently had been made aware of their new little sister, for his expression gentled.

"Ben, meet our little sister, Jane. Jane, this is our big brother, Ben. He came all the way from Virginia to meet you and to have Christmas dinner with us."

Josie gasped. "Why, she looks exactly like Laney!"

Jane and Laney glanced at each other and grinned. "Thank you," they replied in unison, then joined the laughter once again filling the room.

Ben knelt down in front of the little girl. "It's nice to meet you, sweetheart. This is your new big sister, Josie. She's my wife."

"Hi," Jane said shyly, her eyes wide in admiration for Josie. A surge of jealousy shot through Laney, although she understood. As a young girl, she had looked upon Tarah with the same adoration. Jane loved frilly, dressy things, so it was only natural she'd admire Josie's beauty and ladylike manner.

"May I go help with the table settin'?" she asked Laney.

"Sure you can, honey."

Jane hurried to join the other children.

Laney sighed as she watched her go. "She's a wonderful little girl, Ben. Anyone would be proud to have her as a sister."

She felt the warmth of his arm as he pulled her to him. "You're quite a wonderful sister, too, Laney. I'm right proud of you. Let's go outside and talk for a few minutes."

Laney nodded. They grabbed their wraps and headed outside. No one asked where they were going or whether or not they wanted company. Everyone seemed to sense that the two needed a few minutes of privacy.

"It took a lot of gumption taking Pa in the way you did, especially under the circumstances."

Laney leaned over the porch rail, resting her elbows on the rough wood. "You heard about him holing up at the soddy with those two varmints?"

Ben gave her a solemn nod. "I did. He looks pretty bad, doesn't he?"

"Sam says he's dying."

After a long silence, Laney turned to glance at Ben and straightened in shock to see tears streaming down his cheeks.

"What are you crying for?" But she knew. She had felt it, too. No matter how mean he'd been, he was their pa, and his soul was in danger of eternal darkness without Jesus.

"Oh, Laney. We can't let him die a sinner."

"I tried talking to him about Jesus one night," Laney said, defenses raised. "He told me to shut up."

"Don't give up on him. Jesus never gave up on us."

Sudden shame gripped Laney. All she'd been focused on was Pa's trial date so that he would leave her house. *Give me another chance, Lord, and I'll share with Pa about You.*

Chapter 11

Amid kisses and hugs, tears, and promises to keep in touch, Ben and Josie boarded the train for Virginia two weeks after Christmas. A month later, the sheriff finally brought the news that the circuit judge would make an appearance in Harper within three weeks' time.

Laney approached the day of reckoning with a combination of relief and dread. Pa was a difficult patient, at best. At worst, a trial by fire. His orneriness and deliberate jibes were almost more than she was willing to take. His only redeeming quality, as far as she could see, was that he loved little Jane. And the child loved him—the one fact that saved his scrawny carcass from being hauled into town and turned over to the sheriff for the duration.

Despite her guilty conscience, Laney tried to ignore him as much as possible. The task wasn't as simple as it seemed, for he wheezed and coughed all night until Laney was sure he did it on purpose just to spite her and keep her awake. When she was rested, she recognized the thought as ridiculous; but at three in the morning, after thrashing about all night, it was almost impossible to convince her sleep-deprived brain of anything that made sense.

"There now, that just about does it for this one." Granny smoothed the red satin gown and prepared to pack it for transport into town.

"Doesn't Miss DuPres wear the prettiest dresses?" Emily asked.

Laney glanced at the newly made gown, ordered from Tucker by the newest addition to the town—a singer named Vivienne, with raven hair and flawless skin that looked as though it had never seen a ray of sunshine. Laney thought she looked downright ghoulish; but the men in town, including Luke—much to Laney's annoyance—seemed to think her quite becoming. Laney regretted allowing Emily and Luke to talk her into going to the schoolhouse the previous night to listen to the indecent woman. It was a waste of good money when she could listen to Anthony sing hymns on Sunday morning for free.

Emily had stopped by early this morning to discuss the concert. To Laney's irritation, her adopted sister was mesmerized by the singer's "charm and beauty" and raved until Laney wanted to throw her out of the house—but to do so would be an admission of jealousy, and Laney Jenkins wasn't jealous of anyone.

So she sat pushing her needle through the fabric while Granny finished up the red silk and Emily sipped tea—for coffee was now simply too crude a drink for a lady—and talked nonstop about the lovely and wonderful Miss Vivienne DuPres.

"If only I didn't have this horrible red hair and freckles," Emily lamented for

323

what seemed like the twentieth time in as many minutes. "Miss DuPres says all the really famous singers have perfectly white skin and hair as soft as silk."

Laney gave a loud snort but continued to work, hemming Louisa Kirkpatrick's latest gown, a replica of a gown she saw in *Godey's Lady's Book* and designed specifically to keep Louisa firmly in the seat of fashion superiority, regardless of the newest woman in town.

"Did you say something, Laney?" Emily asked.

"Nah."

Granny cackled. "What have you got against Miss DuPres?"

Laney turned and stared hard at Granny. How did the old woman always seem to know what she was thinking? "I don't have anything against *Vivienne*. I don't even know her. I just think Emily should be happy with the looks God gave her and stop trying to look like some floozy saloon girl."

Emily gasped. Laney cut her a glance and noted with concern that, between the freckles, her face was every bit as pale as Vivienne's.

"Laney Jenkins, you take that back," Emily declared hotly, the color returning to her face and going beyond natural to an angry pink. "Miss DuPres is as decent a woman as you or I. And she is *not* a s—saloon girl. You know very well she is a wonderful singer using her talent to support herself. Furthermore, if Pa and the rest of the town council, *including* our preacher, think there's nothing improper with her singing in town, then I don't see how you have the right to call her names. So there!"

Laney blinked in surprise at the outburst. She shrugged and tried to pretend she didn't care that Emily was defending an interloper. "Honestly. Don't get in a snit about it. I'm sorry I said anything." She glanced back at her sewing. "But I got a right to my opinion," she mumbled.

A coughing laugh sounded from the bed. "Yer just jealous, girlie. What's a matter? That man of yourn cast sheep eyes at a woman pertier and softer than you?"

Laney eyed the shears and debated the consequences, then decided to stab him with the truth instead. "Luke doesn't cast 'sheep eyes,'" she declared through gritted teeth. "And especially not at some floo—" She cast a cautious glance at Emily. "Especially not at another woman. Not all men are like *some* men." She gave him a pointed look.

Rising on his elbow, he pointed a shaky finger and gave her a squinty-eyed glare. "One man's just like another, and you best find that out sooner than later, girl. Yer precious 'Lukey' would leave for greener pastures if he could, and you know it. Yer gonna be mighty lucky if he sticks around after yer all fat and have two or three young'uns hanging off yer dress."

"Oh, hush up and lay back down, you old fool," Granny commanded. "Don't compare my grandson with the likes of you."

"You tryin' to tell me he didn't give up his plans to go west because his pa had an amputation? You don't think he'll hightail it to Oregon just as soon as that ranch is off his neck?"

Now how did he know all about Luke's plans? The old eavesdropper! Still, his words rang with a smidgen of truth, bringing Laney's fears back to the surface.

As Granny launched into a list of Luke's attributes, thereby proving his superior character, Laney pondered her pa's words.

What if Luke did decide he couldn't go through with the marriage?

The sun filtered in through the window, causing the ring on Laney's left hand to glimmer. She didn't need the garnet ring, which Luke had presented to her on her birthday the day after Christmas. A wedding band on the day they said their vows would have been enough, but Luke had insisted. He loved her that much, she thought with a sense of satisfaction. "No, Luke wouldn't leave. He gave me his word." She jerked her head in surprise. She hadn't meant to speak. Heat flooded her face as Pa gave her a knowing grin, which clearly asked the same question she'd been pondering for the past few weeks: Did she want to keep Luke here because of a promise? If she held him to it, would he resent her forever and wish they'd never married? Laney knew she couldn't live with that, but could she live without Luke if she released him from his promise?

Returning her attention to her sewing, she tried to push the thoughts aside but found she kept returning to the troublesome issue. Luke was doing a fine job of running the ranch, and they all looked forward to the four expected foals and many calves due this spring.

Papa Dell still struggled to walk with the use of crutches he had carved for himself while sitting before the fire day after day. Though all were thrilled with his progress and he seemed in better spirits since he could get around on his own, everyone knew that hobbling with crutches was a far cry from sitting a horse and running a ranch.

So, for now, Luke seemed to have resigned himself to the task at hand, which allowed Laney to push aside her fears. But she knew sooner or later, Papa Dell would be fully healed, learn to ride again with a missing leg, and take over. The question was, would Luke be content to stay in Harper, or would he keep his promise, marry her, and regret it for the rest of his life?

⁓

Laney pulled on the reins to make Colby walk calmly next to the wagon. On the wagon seat, Luke held the reins while Granny sat primly next to him, her back straight, gaze forward, hands folded in her lap. Anticipation shone in her faded gray eyes. Laney grinned. Mr. Tucker would be happy to see her, as well.

She cast her glance to the back of the wagon. Pa sat up, determined he would not ride to his court hearing lying in the back of a wagon like some invalid. Jane sat next to him.

Luke reined in the team in front of Tucker's and hopped down to help Granny from the wagon. Laney dismounted Colby and tethered him to the hitching post.

She glanced in the back of the wagon. "Jane, honey, can you please stay here and keep Pa company while we go inside and attend to business?"

The child smiled her missing-tooth smile and nodded. "We'll play a game. Won't we, Pa?"

"A game?" He scowled, but after seeing the child's sudden pout, the harsh lines in his face softened. "What sorta game?"

Laney and Luke exchanged a smile at Pa's expense while Luke grabbed the crate containing the finished gowns. Granny preceded them up the steps to the mercantile. Laney nudged Luke when the older woman stopped at the door and patted her bonnet in the window reflection, as though patting her bonnet would straighten any mussed hair beneath its cloth folds. She touched the cameo clasped at her collar before opening the door and stepping inside.

"Think those two will ever tie the knot?" Luke asked.

Laney gave a short laugh. "I wouldn't be surprised if they make it to the altar before we do."

"Don't count on it," he said, capturing her gaze. Laney gulped at the hunger burning in his eyes. She thought he might kiss her right in front of the whole town of Harper, but a honey-toned call from the road caught their attention.

"Oh my goodness. Hold the door, please."

Laney turned to see who had ruined her moment and fought back a biting comment as Miss DuPres joined them—out of breath from running ten feet in a dress pulled so tight in the middle that Laney was surprised she was conscious, let alone walking and talking.

Luke stood before the door, holding the crate and, to Laney's chagrin, gaping at Vivienne like an imbecile.

"Move out of the way so I can open the door, Luke," she grumped, pushing him aside as roughly as she could and wishing she could just flatten him right then and there.

"I declare, it's an absolute gale out here. My hair will be down any moment."

"Seems pretty calm to me," Laney observed just as a gust of wind nearly knocked her off her feet. "Maybe you oughtta use more pins in your hair if you need to have it in all sorts of twists and curls." Laney thought it was just about the dumbest hairstyle she'd ever seen—much too loose for a March day in Kansas. A long braid down the back was the only way to keep hair from flying and falling during spring weather. Some women just plain weren't as smart as they were pretty—not that she thought Vivienne pretty.

"Why, thank you. What a wonderful suggestion," Miss DuPres replied, beaming at Laney as though she had just elected her president. "I'll just pick up some more pins while I'm here."

Stunned into silence, Laney stepped aside while Miss DuPres glided between Luke—who still couldn't seem to find his tongue—and Laney, who was just about to suggest he go wait in the wagon. Miss DuPres's lavender scent drifted between them. Laney noticed Luke swallow and raise his brow to Laney. "She's something, isn't she?"

"Yeah, she is." *A fancy-pants, powder-wearing, toilet water-drenched, man-stealing floozy.* And Laney wasn't going to put up with it. She'd rather lose Luke to the westward fever than have him trapped by dangly eardrops and low-cut gowns.

With purpose, she punched Luke's arm—a little harder than necessary—to gain his attention.

"What was that for?"

"Stop gawking at the singer. You're holding up the door. We're going to be late for Pa's hearing."

"Who's gawking?" Luke turned red and maneuvered the large crate through the doorway.

"You are," she replied with a huff.

"Well, it ain't like *that.* So stop being all green-eyed. I just haven't ever seen anyone so. . .I don't know. . .like her."

Laney knew what he meant, even if he didn't. Miss DuPres was exactly the "ideal woman" Luke had described right before that fateful kiss. But there was no way she was going to bring that up and remind him that she would never be the type of woman he truly wanted.

When they reached the counter, Vivienne took her red gown and held it up against herself. She glowed with excitement. "It's just the most beautiful thing I've ever laid eyes on." Her eyes shone with admiration as she regarded Laney. "And you make gowns like this all the time? Why, you'd make a fortune in the city."

Maybe the lady isn't quite so bad, Laney conceded.

"Whoa now, little lady," Tucker growled. "We got us a deal. Don't be puttin' ideas in that girl's head. If she thought she could make a dime, she'd ride four days on a half-dead pony and scoop up cow patties."

Miss DuPres giggled. "Well, I suppose I would, too, Mr. Tucker. A lady has to make a living somehow. We can teach, sing, or find work as a seamstress if we have the gift for it. And my, oh my, miss, you have the touch."

Laney cleared her throat. "Thanks," she mumbled. "It's nothing."

"Nothing? Oh, Miss. . .what is your name?"

"Laney."

"Well, Miss Laney. This is absolutely the best seamstress work I've ever seen in my life. Oh, if only I. . ."

Her face suddenly turned just about as red as the gown, and she turned to Mr. Tucker. "I—I don't know how to tell you this, sir, but. . . Well, it's just that my manager, you know the man I traveled with? He. . ." Her face crumbled, and she burst into tears—not the delicate tears one would expect from a dainty woman of refinement.

Tucker's gaze swept Granny, Laney, and Luke, horror smoothing the age lines extending from the corners of his eyes to his cheeks. "There, there, miss," he said awkwardly, his expression going from horror to horrified pleading.

Granny came to his rescue and stepped forward. Tucker gladly moved aside, faster than Laney ever would have thought him capable of moving.

"Now, honey, tell us what's wrong."

Vivienne swiped the back of her hand across her nose.

"Luke," Granny said, "give the poor girl your hanky."

Luke cleared his throat and fished his hanky out of his pocket. "Here, Miss DuPres," he said, extending the handkerchief.

"Thank you," she gulped out. Rather than patting the cloth daintily against her nose, Miss DuPres gave several hearty blows while the onlookers waited for her explanation.

Finally she gave a nervous little laugh and glanced around. "Goodness, I've certainly made a spectacle of myself, haven't I?"

Laney had to agree, but she also had to admit it made her like the singer a little more. A little, but not much.

"Why don't you tell us what's wrong?" she said impatiently.

Miss DuPres chewed her lip. "I really. . .well, you're strangers; I don't know if I should. . ."

"Well, that's about the end of it, then," Laney said. She turned to Tucker. "How's about settling up so we can get to the schoolhouse? The judge is meeting us there for Pa's hearing today."

"Well—well, wait just a minute."

Laney cast a glance at Miss DuPres. "Something wrong?"

"Well, it's just that. . .I didn't say I *wouldn't* tell you what was wrong. I just didn't know if I *should* or not."

A shrug lifted Laney's shoulders. "We don't have to know your private business. But if you're done crying, don't forget to give Luke back his handkerchief. I made that for him. He's my fiancé," she said.

"Oh, well, I had a fiancé, too."

Oh, great. Laney could have kicked herself as fat tears once more began to roll down flawless cheeks.

"Is that what has you all upset, honey?" Granny asked.

Miss DuPres nodded.

Granny glanced at Tucker. "She needs another hanky."

The old man pulled a handkerchief from his pocket.

"Not a used one!"

Tucker looked helplessly around, then heaved a sigh and pulled one off the shelf. He mumbled something about folks thinking he was made of money, until a glare from Granny silenced him. "No charge."

"How kind!" Vivienne's splotchy face brightened for a second, then fell again.

"Now, about this fiancé. . ." Laney had just about had all the delays she could handle, and if this Miss DuPres didn't share her troubles soon, she could just forget all about it.

"Are you sure you don't mind listening?"

"Of course we don't mind," Luke soothed, much to Laney's irritation.

"Why else would we have asked?" she said roughly.

Vivienne heaved a great sigh and finally launched her tale of woe. "My Randy heard me singing through the door of my room at his mother's boardinghouse back in Chicago. I declare, the moment I saw him, I fell head over heels in love. Imagine my joy when he proposed. I would have married him right away, but he said he wanted me to have the wedding of my dreams, and we would get married as soon as we saved enough money for a silk gown and a big fat diamond for my finger. Before long, we started traveling to other towns. I sang everywhere." She glanced at Granny a little fearfully. "Some of the places we went weren't very Christian, ma'am."

"That's in the past now," Granny assured her with a comforting pat on her arm.

She sniffed and covered Granny's veined hand with her own. "Thank you."

Laney tossed a glance at the ceiling and sighed heavily. "Then what?"

"Excuse me?" A blank gaze captured Laney's. "Oh. You mean, then what happened with Randy. Well, we finally came here to wonderful Harper, where everyone has been so amazingly kind, coming to hear me sing. We collected more money than ever, and I just knew we had finally saved enough to get married properly. B—but last night I brought it up, and Randy grew quite angry and said we had to wait until we got back to Chicago because his mother would be very hurt unless she could attend her only child's wedding. And truly, I understood. So I told him that was just fine. B—but this morning when I walked downstairs, the hotel clerk told me. . .that is, he said that Randy. . ." She let out a pitiful wail and covered her face with her hands. "I'm so humiliated! How on earth could he do this to me?"

"What is it?" Granny asked, and even Laney had to admit she was a mite curious herself.

"Randy ran off with all the money!" Great sobs engulfed her body, and she clung to Granny. "He didn't even pay the hotel bill, and now the owner is threatening to call in the sheriff. I—I can't buy the gowns I ordered, Mr. Tucker. But if you'll please just not press charges, I'll try to find work here in Harper, and I'll pay you every red cent."

"Well now, how am I supposed to stay in business if people don't pay for what they order?"

"Honestly, Tuck," Laney heard herself say. "It's not like she did it on purpose. You heard her promise to pay you. Don't you think she's been through enough?"

"Leave the poor girl alone," Luke said. "Miss DuPres didn't steal from you.

She can't help what happened."

"Of course Mr. Tucker will wait for the money," Granny soothed. "And if the gowns sell before you pay him back, of course you won't owe him anything."

Tucker gave Granny a look that clearly said he thought she'd lost her mind, but like a man in love, he smiled and nodded. "That's right, miss. You just don't worry about it. I can hardly keep ready-made dresses in stock. Them three dresses you ordered'll sell lickety-split."

"Two dresses," Granny corrected. "The red dress would never suit another woman. Wrap it up, Tucker. You can take our commission off, and Miss DuPres will owe you only for the material."

"What?" Now it was Laney's turn to stare. "Granny!"

"No, I couldn't. Honest. It isn't necessary. I don't need a new gown."

"Yes, you do," Granny insisted. "You are going to be singing again next week, and you need a new gown."

"But everyone has already come to hear me, ma'am. In a town this size, I can only get one, maybe two performances until I lose money."

"Nonsense. God will provide. And you'll come back to the ranch with me to stay until you have the money to move on."

"I just don't know what to say." Vivienne's eyes filled again.

You could say no, Laney thought ungraciously.

"I have no choice but to accept. I just hope you won't regret it."

Laney spun around and stomped to the door. She jerked it open and slammed it shut behind her. That floozy! Weaseling her way into Luke's family's ranch. Laney wouldn't stand for it. No siree.

Planting her hands on her hips, she glanced around the town and tried to gain her composure. What else could go wrong today? Then, with a groan, she remembered the hearing. They were five minutes late.

Chapter 12

Laney's nerves remained taut while the judge listened to the witness seated on his left, his fingers pressed thoughtfully against his graying temple. The prosecutor waxed eloquent, and Laney had to admit if she were the judge, she'd lock up her pa and throw away the key.

She glanced at Mr. Carpenter, the businessman who had been robbed, as he sat on the makeshift witness stand, answering question after question about the awful night three men had invaded his home while he and his family slept only a few rooms away.

He had awakened to the noise of the prowlers and gone to investigate. When he confronted the three men, one of the robbers—Matt, Laney surmised, from the description—fired his weapon and shot the man right in the arm. He still had nightmares about it. And would the judge please make the men pay back his money?

When all was said and done, Pa was found guilty. Laney felt a sense of relief as the judge pronounced a sentence of life in prison rather than hanging. Still, one look at Pa's sickly face, and she knew he wouldn't last a week in prison—even a mild one. As the judge raised his gavel to finalize his sentence, Laney scrambled to her feet.

"Excuse me, Your Honor."

The judge glanced up. "What can I do for you, miss?"

Laney slowly made her way to the front of the schoolhouse. "I appreciate you going easy on my pa. I guess some folks feel like he deserves to hang for stealing a man's hard-earned money. I'm trying to buy a little piece of land and a soddy myself, so I can surely understand their way of thinking. But you see. . ." She cleared her throat and gazed directly into the bewildered judge's eyes. "The thing is, my pa's a very sick man. He's not going to be around much longer as it is, so sending him to prison will be a waste of time. I was thinking maybe you'd just let him come home with me so he can spend the rest of his days with me taking care of him. And don't worry. If he gets well—which Sam says he won't—I'll send him straight to the sheriff so he can take his punishment fair and square."

"I'm sorry." The judge leaned toward her, confusion clouding his eyes. "What are you asking me?"

"Can he come home with me?" What kind of smarts did it take to be a judge, anyway?

"Let me get this straight," Judge Campbell said with a firmness that made

Laney squirm. "You would like for me to suspend your father's sentence and allow him to go home with you instead of to prison."

"Yes, sir."

"I'm afraid that just isn't—"

Laney leaned over the teacher's desk the judge was using as his bench. She dropped her tone so that the occupants of the small room couldn't hear. "Are you a Christian, Your Honor?"

"Now don't start using my faith against me," he said, giving her a stern frown. "Your father must pay for his crime."

"Yes, sir. I know what he did was wrong. But he only has a short time to live, under the best of conditions. If you send him to prison, he'll die in a godless, sinful state. And you know where sinners go when they die. Can you send a sinful man to his death?"

"I certainly can," he said. "The matter is settled." He raised the gavel again.

A sense of urgency tugged at Laney, and she grabbed the judge's arm. "Wait!"

"I beg your pardon."

"Please. Won't you consider my suggestion? What good will it do to send him to prison? He'll be dead in a month if you do."

The judge glanced at her thoughtfully for a moment, then opened his mouth as though ready to relent.

"Excuse me, Your Honor."

The judge sighed heavily. "Yes?"

Laney turned to find Mr. Carpenter approaching the judge. "I will see this man punished for his crime. My family lost a great deal of money that he took and squandered for his own pleasure. He must be made to pay."

An idea formed in Laney's mind, and she addressed the wronged man. "How much did my pa and his partners take from you?"

She started at the amount. "If I give you my pa's cut of your money"—she turned to the judge—"then will you consider it?"

"If restitution is made, I could possibly consider your request, under the circumstances."

"But that's only a third of what was taken from me." The man's whine was beginning to irritate Laney. "I will not stand for it!" He pounded his fist on the desk. "I'll take it to a higher court. I'll write to the governor."

The judge glanced from Mr. Carpenter to Laney. "I'm sorry, miss. This isn't worth the headache to me. My decision stands." For a third time, he raised his gavel.

"Wait. One more thing." Laney gritted her teeth, unable to believe she was about to voice the thoughts twisting through her mind. "I will pay Mr. Carpenter everything my pa and those two no-good scoundrels stole, if you'll only allow him to come home and die in peace."

The judge cast a questioning glance at Mr. Carpenter. "How's that sound to you? The girl pays you the money, I let Jenkins go home to die, and you drop the whole thing and don't raise a fuss about it."

The man rocked on his heels and screwed up his face as though considering the proposition, but Laney could tell by the gleam in his eye that he had already made up his mind.

"I can accept that."

"Good. It's done." The judge slammed the gavel down on the desk before anyone else could interrupt. "And if by some miracle that scoundrel happens to recover, I don't want to hear about it."

Relief coursed through Laney. "I'll head over to the bank right now." She spun on her heel and walked down the aisle toward the door. Luke rose as though he would follow, but she waved him back to his seat. She glared at Pa on the way out. *God forgive me, but I think I hate him. After all the low-down things he's done in his life, now he's off the hook, and I'm paying all I have to buy his freedom.*

She dashed a tear from her cheek. Mr. Garner wouldn't be getting a large lump sum of money after all. Her loan payment was due tomorrow, but there wasn't any possible way she could pay. She would lose her dream.

For the first time, she truly understood how Luke felt about not going west.

Pa wasn't even grateful! Laney kicked at a pebble, sending it sailing into the rippling creek. The cantankerous, ungrateful swindler didn't even care what she had sacrificed to give him a little more time on this earth! Disappointment swelled her chest, threatening to spill over in hot tears.

One month, Garner had said. One month to raise the money to make up for the payment she owed him plus the payment due at the end of that amount of time.

Even with Granny's help, she couldn't work hard enough to raise the money. She sat hard on the damp prairie earth that only now was beginning to turn green with the promise of an early spring. Hugging her knees to her chest, Laney gave a weary sigh and rested her chin on her arms.

A cool, gentle breeze played with the loose tendrils around her face and brought the fresh scents of budding wildflowers to her nostrils, but she found no pleasure in the small reminder that all things were becoming new once again on the prairie. To Laney, all that was new and promising in her life had been taken away with the money she'd handed over to Mr. Carpenter.

Her mind raced with the possibilities of what she could do to save her soddy. She already knew Mr. Thomas at the bank wouldn't extend her a loan, because she had tried that before, asking Garner to carry the note.

Suddenly she lifted her chin, her eyes growing wide at the possibility of the forming idea. What about Luke? He had mentioned before that he had money saved. Laney's heart raced. That was the solution. This was to be their land after all.

Of course she couldn't ask him for the money. But Luke knew what she had done. Once he realized the implications of paying back what Pa had stolen, he would surely offer the money, and they would have their land.

She smiled for the first time in two days, took a deep cleansing breath, and stood. She wouldn't lose her land after all.

⌐

Luke stood on the front porch of the St. John ranch and gaped at Pa, unable to believe what he was actually hearing. "Are you telling me you want me to go?"

Pa nodded. "There's a wagon train pulling into Council Grove in a couple of months. You have plenty of time to get things settled here—marry Laney, get to Council Grove, and get outfitted before they pull out."

"But what about the ranch? You can't. . ."

"Hired Floyd Henderson today to manage the place. He was about to pull up stakes and head back east until I convinced him to stay and run the ranch for me. I'm happy with my decision. Now you're free, Luke. You've done more for me than I can say, and I appreciate it. But I can't let you sacrifice your plans for me."

"I don't know what to say, Pa. I just assumed. . ."

"That you were stuck here running the ranch?"

Luke couldn't deny it, so he said nothing.

"Nothing wrong with wanting to follow your own dreams. Nothing wrong with it at all." He clapped Luke on the shoulder and hobbled into the house, leaving Luke to stare after him.

An hour later, Luke looked across the pasture, his arms resting on the fence he had built just last week. He heaved a sigh. Everything changed so fast. First he was making plans to go west, only to have those plans upset. Then just as quickly, when he'd resigned himself to never making it to Oregon, Pa offered him the chance to live the life he wanted.

A thrill passed through him as all the dreams he'd stuffed down now sprang to the surface. He thought of plush green fields, acres and acres of cattle grazing on his land. A log home that Laney would be proud to tend. He saw children—his and Laney's—running and playing about the place.

Laney. Her image in his mind jolted him back to the present. What would she say? Reality broke through as he anticipated her response. She wouldn't leave Harper. Especially now that her pa and Jane were counting on her. He had made her a promise. Had proposed twice. How could he ask her once more to release him from his promise to marry her? Luke felt pressure overtake him like a ton of water carrying him away against his will.

He couldn't imagine life without Laney. He couldn't imagine life without trying to fulfill his dream. The question he needed answered was, which could he live without the easiest? He knew he couldn't have both.

"It's a lovely piece of land, Luke."

Luke started and turned sharply at the sound of Vivienne's soft voice. He felt the intrusion clench his gut, and he wished he could ask her to leave him alone.

"It is pretty land," he replied. "There's lots of pretty land in the country."

"I heard your pa telling your ma that you're thinking of heading west."

"That's right."

"You won't find anything better, no matter where you run to."

"Maybe. Maybe not."

She placed a gentle hand upon his arm. "There's no maybe about it. Here you have your wonderful family, a woman who loves you and wants to marry you, a town where you're respected. You're extremely blessed."

Luke turned, regarding her thoughtfully. Were Vivienne's observations an answer from God about what he was supposed to do, or was she just butting in? If only he could be sure that whatever decision he made was the right one.

"What will you do, Miss DuPres?" he asked, if for no other reason than to push aside his own quandary for a while and focus on something else.

She shrugged. "Your granny thinks my performance Friday night will be a success. If only it will provide me with the funds to go someplace new. Maybe someplace back east. Or maybe. . ." She cut her glance to his. "Maybe I should go west and see what Oregon has to offer a singer. What do you think? Could you use some company on the trip west?"

Luke swallowed hard. How was he supposed to get out of this without offending a lady or making Laney hate him?

Miss DuPres laughed and gave his arm a playful tap. "Don't worry, Luke. You're too young for me. Besides, I hear in Oregon there are ten men to every woman. I'd have my pick."

A sheepish grin tipped Luke's mouth. "I bet you'd have your pick of men no matter where you go, Miss DuPres."

"Why, thank you. What a sweet thing to say!"

Before he could stop her, Miss DuPres rose up on her toes and gave him a fat kiss right on his cheek. Luke felt his ears burn. He could have taken a little embarrassment. What he couldn't take was the sound of Laney's roar behind him or the look of utter rage on her face when he turned around to face her.

"Luke St. John!" she hollered at the top of her voice. "You. . .I. . .I can't believe. . ."

This was one time Luke was grateful that the angrier Laney became, the smaller her vocabulary.

"Simmer down," he said, knowing full well she wouldn't. "This isn't anything for you to be jealous about."

"Jealous? Ha." She snorted. "You'll never see a day you can make me jealous."

"There's been a misunderstanding." Miss DuPres stepped forward, her tone conciliatory, if slightly fearful. "It's all my fault. If you'll only let me explain."

"You stay out of this," Laney commanded. "The first time my back is turned, he goes and kisses another woman just because she's all soft and womanly. For

335

shame, Luke. How could you go making cow eyes at someone else?"

"I wasn't making cow eyes at anyone. As a matter of fact, she kissed me. What did you want me to do, knock her flat?"

"I would have!"

"Oh my." Vivienne pressed her hand to her bosom, looking as though she might faint any minute.

"Honestly," Laney said, sending her a look of utter disdain. "I wouldn't hit you. I meant if a man kissed me, I'd knock him flat."

"You never knocked me flat for kissing you." Luke moved in closer and took her hands in his.

She jerked away, her face growing pink. "You know what I mean, and don't try to sweet-talk your way out of this."

"Really, Laney," Vivienne pleaded. "Allow me to defend this gentleman's honor."

"Gentleman," Laney said with a sniff. She crossed her arms across her chest. "Fine. Make it quick."

"Very well. First of all, he's telling the truth. He didn't kiss me. I kissed *him*. And not because I have some dream of snatching him away from you. I kissed him out of gratitude because he offered me a few kind words—words that a woman needs to hear after she's been lied to, robbed, and abandoned. Your wonderful Luke merely spoke kindly to me. But you have more than his words, you silly girl. You have his love forever." Vivienne walked past them. She gave Laney a pat on the arm without slowing her gait. "I hope you will appreciate the treasure he is offering you," she called over her shoulder as she made her way back toward the house.

"Well, that was some speech." Laney looked up at him. "I guess I acted a little drastically, didn't I?"

"You must be growing up," Luke said with a chuckle. He swept her around the waist and pulled her close. "I expected a lot worse."

She laughed and punched his chest. "I could always flatten you now."

"I'd rather get a kiss."

She tilted her head and smiled, the look of love in her eyes clouding his senses. Desperation surged inside of him, and he captured her lips, drinking deeply of their softness. He held her tightly, afraid he might lose her if he loosened his grip. Over and over, he kissed her until she wilted against him.

Laney pulled slightly away. "Luke," she breathed against his lips.

Without answering, he covered her mouth once again. He couldn't lose her. He wouldn't!

Not until Laney cried out did he loosen his hold.

"Luke, stop it. You're hurting me!"

He released her suddenly, nearly knocking them both off their feet. Laney gasped and stared at him in bewildered silence. She touched her fingers to her lips.

"Say something, Laney," he said, his voice hoarse.

"I don't understand." She rammed her hands onto her hips, her stance indicating she was ready for a fight. "You'd better explain right now, because I don't plan on being manhandled. Not even by my husband."

He groaned inwardly at the thought of her thinking he would ever purposely hurt her. "I'm sorry, honey." He reached for her, but she quickly stepped away from his arms.

"Don't pull away, please. I don't know what came over me. Forgive me."

"Just don't ever be that rough with me again, Luke. I mean it." Laney's expression softened, and she moved back into his arms.

Relief surged over Luke. "I love you," he whispered and brushed his lips across the top of her head.

"I love you, too, Lukey," she murmured against his chest. "I'll always love you."

They fell silent and watched the sun sink into a glorious orange sky. "Isn't it beautiful?" Laney asked.

"Mmm."

"Just think about all the sunsets we'll watch together for the rest of our lives, Luke."

He knew he should tell her he was thinking about the move west again—give her the chance to rail at him. But he couldn't. Not now. Resting his cheek against the silky softness of her hair, he drank in her sweet smell and knew he'd never watch another sunset as lovely as this one.

Chapter 13

A sense of foreboding gnawed at Laney as she and Luke walked arm in arm toward the house. That was not a mere kiss of passion from a man more than ready to be married. It was something more. Fear railed against reason. What was wrong with Luke? He had gone from passionate to gentle to sullen in the span of thirty minutes. Now she couldn't drag two words out of him.

She had asked him what was wrong, but he insisted everything was fine. He wasn't being honest, and Laney didn't like it one bit. A horrid thought wormed into her mind. What if Luke's mood had to do with a certain Miss DuPres? She was everything Luke had admitted he thought a woman should be. Soft. Womanly. Someone a man could take care of. Laney could just bet that Miss DuPres would never even be tempted to lead a dance. The woman was as curvy as a winding road, too. A man couldn't help but admire that. Laney cast an unhappy glance down at her own figure. She had about as many curves as little Jane.

Before they even reached the house, they were greeted by the heavenly smells of roast beef and freshly baked bread. Laney's mouth watered. Pa had refused to come to supper, so Laney had warmed up yesterday's stew, grabbed Jane, and left him to sulk on his pallet while they were gone.

Guilt pricked her at the thought of him all alone, slurping warmed stew, but she quickly pushed it aside. After all, she thought bitterly, she had given everything for him—even though he surely didn't deserve it. Couldn't she enjoy one dinner with her fiancé and the family without his sourness weaseling in to ruin it for her?

And she tried. How she tried to enjoy the time around the St. John table—like old times. Customary laughter prevailed over the supper table, and the loving looks that passed between Mama Cassidy and Papa Dell filled Laney with longing. How could two people love and laugh so perfectly? She knew the story of Mama Cassidy and Emily coming to Papa Dell by wagon train and how the first few months were difficult between Mama Cassidy and Papa Dell. But looking at them now, no one would guess they hadn't always been in love. Mama Cassidy had shared with Laney once that sometimes love was hard-hitting and fast, snatching your breath away like a sudden wind. And sometimes it happened slowly over the years. Hers and Dell's, she'd said, was like a twister. It came suddenly and brought with it all sorts of disasters until God's peace calmed their storms.

Laney glanced at Luke from the corner of her eye. Theirs was a slow love. It had grown from friendship and had almost slipped by unnoticed. But the way

Luke was acting now, she worried that perhaps he had decided he didn't feel any kind of love at all. Was his odd kiss similar to the one she had given him last year? Some sort of test? Maybe she had failed. A gasp escaped her. What if he didn't want to raise Jane? Or have to put up with her sickly pa?

Luke turned and caught her perusal. He winked, smiled, and captured her hand under the table. Laney smiled, and for a while her fears calmed once again.

Luke gripped Laney's tiny hand, careful not to hold too tightly. Desperation clawed at him, and he feared Vivienne or someone else would mention Oregon at any moment. He intended to speak with Laney soon, but not yet. He glanced at her practically untouched plate and willed her to hurry and finish so he could usher her out of the house before someone spoke up.

"Not hungry?" he asked.

"Hmm? Oh. I guess not."

"Are you feeling all right, Laney?" Ma's all-knowing gaze studied her. "You are looking a mite peaked. Are you working too hard again?"

Relief overtook Luke. If Ma started in on Laney about working too hard and not eating enough, he was safe from anyone bringing up his own dreaded topic before he could discuss it with her.

Laney gave Ma a half smile. "No, ma'am. I'm fine. Just not very hungry. Although the food is marvelous."

Granny harrumphed from her place directly across the table from Laney. "Don't you think I'd make her rest if we were working too hard? That was the whole point of my helping out over there."

"Of course, Granny," Ma said, her cheeks going pink. "I didn't mean to imply you were remiss in your duty to our Laney."

Luke's heart soared when Laney squeezed his hand and grinned at him during the exchange between Granny and Ma.

"I should say not. Besides, if she's peaked, it's not because Mr. Tucker's overworking her. It's because of that pa of hers."

Jane gasped, and Granny cut her a glance. "I'm sorry, Jane. I know we had a bargain, but you know your pa can be quite a trial for Laney."

Luke noticed that the little girl looked ready to argue, then her face softened, and she nodded. "Yes, ma'am. I reckon you're right." She screwed up her face. "But he ain't no rascal!"

"Well, we won't argue about that. Now you children finish your supper. Granny has some licorice sticks Mr. Tucker sent home with me last week."

Cat, Hope, Will, and Jane shared smiles among themselves and went about cleaning their plates.

Luke was just beginning to relax back into the comfort of his family when Vivienne spoke up. "Speaking of your pa, will he travel west, too, Laney?"

Laney gave her a blank stare. "Why would my pa go west? He can barely go to the out—well, he can barely get out of bed—although he does seem to be feeling a mite better these days. But not nearly well enough to travel. I suppose he'll stay with me until. . ." Her gaze darted to her sister. "He'll stay with me," she finished.

"I see. So you'll be joining Luke in Oregon. . ." She followed Laney's example and darted a glance at Jane. "Afterward?"

Luke wanted to slip under the table and slither outside unnoticed, now that Miss DuPres had opened up the topic he most feared. Why hadn't he just talked it over with Laney while he'd had the chance?

"Oregon? How did you know about that? Besides, Luke already decided not to go."

Vivienne's face brightened. "Good for you, Luke! You took my advice after all. I told you, this is a wonderful place to lay down roots and start a family."

"*Your* advice?" Laney said.

Luke squirmed while Laney glanced at him, then turned a scowl on Miss DuPres. "Luke decided not to go west months ago, before he even met *you*."

Pa cleared his throat. Thankfully Luke turned his attention toward the head of the table. "Have you decided for sure not to head west, son? I can always keep you on as manager and pay Floyd what I promised him just to stay on as a hand. Unless you and Laney have decided to go ahead and try to build your own herd. You let me know if I can help."

"Oh, Luke," Ma said, tears choking her voice. "I'm so relieved. I couldn't bear the thought of you and Laney off hundreds of miles from home."

Luke closed his eyes for a moment as Laney slapped both hands flat against the table and sprang to her feet all in one motion. "Everyone stop for just a minute." She turned the full force of her glare on Luke. "Have you changed our plans without telling me? Because everyone here seems to think you're headed to Oregon and that I'm heading there with you."

Luke stood and cupped her elbow. "Let's go outside and talk."

She jerked away from him. "I'm not going anywhere with you. You've humiliated me in front of the whole family—plus one—now you can just tell me the truth in front of everyone, you low-down, low-down—"

Realizing she wasn't going to come up with an appropriate follow-up, Luke interrupted. "I wasn't keeping anything from you. I just hadn't gotten around to telling you yet."

The hostility in Laney's expression gave way to a worried frown. Luke wanted to hold her close and kiss away that fear; but with the family watching, all he could do was be honest and say what she apparently had already figured out.

"Pa hired Floyd Henderson to run the ranch. He suggested I might want to hitch up with the wagon train in Council Grove in a couple of months. I—I wanted to discuss it with you."

Cold brown eyes stared back at him from a now-expressionless face. "Jane, honey," Laney said without breaking their gaze. "We're leaving now."

"But I didn't get my licorice stick!"

"I'll get you one tomorrow from Tucker's. Get your things now."

The little girl moved to do as she was told. Laney's voice lowered in volume and tone. "Hitch yourself to that wagon train, Luke. But you're not hitching yourself to me, too. And don't think you're going to come back and claim me after you've been gone awhile. No matter how much I ache for you, I'll never leave this town."

"Laney. . ."

She shook her head vigorously, her eyes wide, nostrils flared. "I told you before that Harper is my home. It's my sister's home now, too—look at how attached she already is to your family—and it's even my pa's home until he passes on. This is where my life is. I want to spend the rest of my days here. Get that through your head. I am *never* leaving."

Luke reached for her. "I'll stay. We'll get married like we planned."

Evading his grasp, she moved behind her chair. She spoke as though she had forgotten everyone seated around the table. "I never wanted to be your second choice."

"Second choice?" Did she think he loved Miss DuPres? "Laney, there's no one else."

A short laugh spurted from her lips. "There may or may not be another woman laying claim to your affections, Luke, but that's not even the point. I don't want to be second choice to your lost dream. You'd always blame me that you didn't have a chance to build your own dynasty in Oregon."

"That's not true, honey. Let's just forget about Oregon. I don't want to lose you."

Laney continued as though she hadn't heard him. "You would always be thinking of the what-ifs; and I and any young'uns we had would always be responsibilities rather than gifts from God. If I ever marry, I want to be my husband's first dream, after God—not something he settles for because of a promise. Good-bye, Luke. I don't hold any grudges against you, and I truly hope Oregon is everything you want it to be."

Laney grabbed Jane around the shoulders, and the two left quietly through the door.

Luke watched her leave, pain knifing through him in a way he'd never thought possible.

Silence reigned around the table. Even the children refrained from making comments.

"Oh my," Miss DuPres finally said. "I am mortified at my stupidity. Luke, I beg your pardon for speaking when I had no right."

She sounded so contrite, her face ashen, that Luke softened toward her immediately. He smiled. "It's not your fault, ma'am. I should have brought it up before Laney and I came inside."

Luke pushed in his chair and stepped out onto the porch. He sighed heavily and swallowed hard past a lump in his throat. Even if he wanted to stay in Harper, he'd never convince Laney he wasn't doing it out of some sense of guilt or responsibility.

He let out a groan and raked his fingers through his hair. How had he made such a mess of everything? He had always dreamed of going west, but now he wasn't so sure it was worth it if he had to lose Laney in the process. Suddenly all of his visions of lush green fields gave way to a dismal, brown emptiness of a winter with no snow. What point was there to a dream if he couldn't share it with the one person who mattered?

Chapter 14

*I*diot, *idiot, idiot.* The taunt kept up a steady rhythm to Colby's gallop as Laney headed for home. She wouldn't cry. Refused to cry. This was her own fault, and she wouldn't allow herself one tiny bit of self-pity.

The nearer they drew to home, the stronger the dread gnawing her stomach became. She dreaded the smug remarks she was bound to get from Pa when he found out his prophecy about Luke's intentions had come true.

Laney reined in Colby and helped Jane slide from the saddle. "Go inside, sweetheart. I just have to brush Colby down and put him up for the night."

When Laney entered the soddy a few minutes later, Jane was already tucked into bed and snoring softly. Pa was seated at the table sipping a mug of coffee. Surprisingly the dishes he had eaten from were cleaned and put away on the shelf above her rough-hewn counter.

"You must be feeling better," she said grudgingly.

"A mite."

"Good." She cleared her throat. Now what? It was too early to go to bed, and she would rather cut off one of her arms than make polite conversation with Pa while her heart was breaking. She debated going for a walk by the creek, but to do so would be an admission that something out of the ordinary had occurred.

Pa stood. Relieved, Laney walked toward the kitchen. Maybe he would go to sleep so she could be alone with her thoughts. Instead, he grabbed a mug from the shelf, filled it with coffee, and set it down on the table in front of an empty chair. "Sit."

Too startled to rebel, Laney sat. "What's this?" she asked, barely able to keep the sarcasm from her voice. If he was trying to be nice so he could ask for money, he might as well save himself the effort. She'd already given him all she had.

He shrugged his bony shoulders. "Thought you looked like you might like a cup, that's all. Dump it out if you don't want it."

"I didn't say I didn't want it!"

"Well, don't act like I'm about to ask fer somethin', 'cause I ain't."

Heat rushed to her cheeks.

" 'Sides, I know you done gave everythin' you was savin' just to keep me from goin' to prison. Can't rightly say I know why, but I gotta tell ya, I know what ya gave up."

Laney hadn't mentioned her conversation with Mr. Garner to anyone, let alone Pa. "What are you talking about?"

343

He regarded her evenly, and for once his face held not the slightest hint of mockery. "Garner stopped by while you was gone."

Laney's hands trembled as they grasped her cup. "So?"

"So he told me to tell ya he'll wait one extra week for the money, but then he has to sell the land and the soddy to his other buyer." Pa gave a snort. "Sounded like he hated to see ya hafta give up yer land."

Realizing there was no sense in pretending, Laney shrugged and sipped her coffee. She set the mug back on the table. "One extra week isn't going to matter much. It would take me six more months to save enough to pay him off like we agreed."

"Where you intendin' on livin'?"

The note of concern in his voice made Laney glance up sharply. She caught his gaze. Was he merely worried about his own hide and where he would sleep, or did he honestly care? Laney steeled herself against the last thought. She would not allow herself to be fooled again. If Luke couldn't love her enough to stay by her side, she couldn't make herself believe someone like her pa was genuinely concerned about her well-being.

"Don't worry," she said, curling her lip in contempt. "I'll figure out something for us. Maybe we could all find a good place to squat—just like old times. Huh, Pa?"

Pa's face darkened. He slapped the table and sprang to his feet. Then he swayed and grabbed on to steady himself. "I ain't stayin' here to be insulted."

"Oh yes you are." Fueled by the humiliation and disappointment of the evening, Laney's temper soared to rage, and she stood to face him. He could hit her if he wanted to. This time she wasn't backing down, and he was going to take what he had coming! "You're going to hear what I have to say if I have to sit on you and hold you down to make you listen! You drank away any pittance we ever had while Ma was alive. Then you made Ben and me live like beggars and thieves until you sold us like slaves to Tarah and Anthony, the only people who thought we had any value." A sob caught in Laney's throat. She paused long enough to acknowledge the prick of conviction, but bitterness had already pushed her too far. Ignoring her conscience, she allowed her tongue to continue on its destructive path. "Do you know what it does to young'uns when their own pa sells them like they're no more important than stock? For years Ben and me worked hard to prove over and over that we aren't like you. Ben made it. He got away. Got a scholarship to seminary and made a better life for himself. I was going to. I tried. But then you had to come back. Now I have nothing—just like you wanted. I hope you're happy, Pa. Because I sacrificed all I had so you could live."

"Why'd ya do it?"

Expecting the back of his hand or a good tongue lashing at the very least, the calm four-word response shocked Laney. "What do you mean?"

"Ya hate me, and I'm going to die anyway. Why give up your land to keep me out of prison? I deserved to go for a lot of reasons, and you know it. It don't make sense."

Laney shrugged. "I don't hate you," she mumbled, knowing full well anything she said to defend her burst of anger would sound ridiculous. "Hating is a sin."

He snorted. "So ya love yer ol' pa, do ya?"

She shook her head, already regretting that she hadn't listened to her conscience, regretting that she had most likely passed up an opportunity to share the love of Christ with her pa. "To be honest, I don't know how I feel about you. But I do know that God loves you, and He thinks you're worth saving."

"Just like you were worth saving when I sold ya to that teacher and her beau?"

Just like you were worth saving? For an instant, Laney felt the impact of his words. An image of the cross flooded her mind.

Tears sprang to her eyes. If Pa didn't deserve her mercy because of the way he had treated her, she didn't deserve God's. Jesus had paid a much higher price for her than she had paid for Pa's freedom. Remorse instantly flooded her. "I'm sorry," she whispered, her heart reaching toward heaven.

"What fer?"

Surprised, Laney caught Pa's gaze. She had been speaking to God, but as she stared into Pa's suspicion-filled eyes, she knew she owed him an apology, as well.

"I've treated you like you didn't deserve love or forgiveness. No wonder you didn't want to hear about Jesus. I paid the money for you to come home because even though I was mad as a hornet at you, I'm different inside than I used to be. I know I don't act like I care anything about you, but the truth is, I don't want you to die and go to hell, and I knew you stood a better chance of staying alive longer if you came home with me. Even though I wish I wouldn't have had to give up my soddy or my land, I'd do it again for the chance to share Jesus with you before you die."

Heavy silence permeated the air between them as Pa sized her up. Then he cleared his throat and sneered. "That just shows how dumb you are."

Laney blinked in surprise. This was far from the repentant response she had hoped for and even halfway expected.

"You know I ain't never held to no religion. I ain't a-startin' now just 'cause you got religion and gave up yer land fer me. Ya shouldn't have done it. I wouldn't have done if fer you." He left her to stare after him as he shuffled to his pallet, practically threw himself down, and lay with his back to Laney.

Bewildered, Laney turned back to her cup. Her own revelation had been so real and poignant that she couldn't believe her pa could be so unmoved. Nevertheless, she knew something had transpired on the inside of her. If not the feelings of love, then at least the willingness to love. Urgency filled her as she listened to her pa begin to cough. *I'm trying, Jesus. Please give me enough time.*

⌐

True to Granny's prediction, the townsfolk filled the schoolhouse to overflowing the night of Vivienne's farewell performance. Luke watched the door, wishing—without much hope—that Laney would make an appearance. He wanted. . .*needed* to see her, to somehow make her believe that he loved her and would willingly give up Oregon for her.

He took a seat at the back just as Miss DuPres glided to the front, her red dress shimmering in the lamplight.

"Thank you so much for coming," she said graciously, and the room erupted in applause.

Spellbound, the audience remained completely still while she poured out a haunting rendition of "Lorena."

During intermission, Luke joined several men outside. He noticed Laney leaning against the hitching post. Luke's boots led him in her direction as though they had a mind of their own.

She glanced up and smiled in greeting.

"Been here long?" he asked.

She nodded. "Watching from the door. Granny was right. Folks were happy to show up for another performance."

"She has a lovely voice. We don't get that sort of entertainment around here."

"You think they do out west?"

"I don't know, Laney. And I don't particularly care about entertainment." Luke captured her hand in his and held tightly before she could jerk away. "I want you to listen to me."

"Let go of me!"

"Not until you hear me out."

"Say your piece, then, and make it quick."

Before he could speak his mind, an unfamiliar man wearing a fancy suit and bowler hat interrupted. "Excuse me. Is Miss DuPres performing here tonight?"

"Who wants to know?" Laney asked. From the suspicion clouding her eyes, Luke knew she was thinking the same thing that ran through his own mind. Was this the same man who had abandoned Vivienne and broken her heart?

"I am her fiancé," he replied.

Laney stepped forward, crowding the man's space until he backed up, bewilderment plastered on his face. "What makes you think she wants to see you? Any man who would run off and break a lady's heart ain't worth his salt, as far as I'm concerned."

Luke squirmed. He had the feeling Laney wasn't just directing her words at the wayward fiancé. He almost felt sorry for the man.

Laney moved a step closer. "You'd better give me a good reason not to call the sheriff right now and have you locked up, or that's just what I'm going to do, mister."

"I have all the money right here except what it took me to get to Chicago and come right back." Randy hung his head. "You're right," he said humbly. "I'm not worth the dirt she walks on, but I'll make it all up to her if she'll only take me back."

"If you love her," Laney said, her tone softening, "why did you steal all her money and leave?"

"I was a fool. A swindler. The plan was to wait until she had raised enough money, then leave. I'm ashamed to say I've done it more than once with other women. But Vivienne is so wonderful and kind, I couldn't help but fall in love with her. My relationship with her during the past months has changed me. I made it all the way back to Chicago, then turned around without leaving the train station."

"Well, it's not my place to make Miss DuPres's decision for her." Laney heaved a sigh. "Besides, it sounds as though you've learned your lesson. Come on. Let's go find out if she'll speak with you, but I wouldn't count on it if I were you. If you're a praying man, you might want to say one now, and if you're not, you might want to become one."

Stunned, Luke followed along to see how it all worked out. He had expected Laney to run Randy out of town with the sharp edge of her tongue, not find sympathy for a swindler and a cad—even one who claimed to be a changed man.

The room buzzed with conversation while the audience awaited the second half of Vivienne's performance.

"Luke, over here," Pa called as Luke squeezed down the aisle after Laney and Randy. Luke watched them go, then turned toward his parents. This was the first time Pa had been into town since the accident. Ma glowed next to him. He shook Pa's hand and bent down to kiss Ma's cheek. "How are you enjoying Miss DuPres's performance?"

"It's wonderful," Ma said. "Of course, we've had the privilege of hearing her practice lately. But I must say, being at an actual performance is breathtaking."

"Did I see Laney with a stranger?"

Luke nodded. "That was Miss DuPres's fiancé."

"The thief?" Ma asked, her mouth tightening in disapproval.

"He says he's sorry and came back to beg her forgiveness."

"I hope she makes him grovel before she forgives him!"

"Darling!" Pa said, slipping his arm along the back of her seat. "I'm shocked at you."

She smiled and reached up to pat his face. "No, you aren't."

Pa captured her hand and brought it to his lips.

Luke cleared his throat. In moments such as this, he always felt like an intruder. The sort of love Ma and Pa shared was true and lasting. All-consuming at times. A burst of determination fueled a fire inside of him. He said a hasty good-bye and spun around. He was going to find Laney and make her listen to reason.

The lights dimmed. Luke groaned inwardly. He'd have to find a seat before

Vivienne started singing again. He slipped into a vacant space in the third row just as she appeared on stage. Her voice seemed richer as she sang with great emotion. Luke had the feeling she had forgiven the man she loved.

The audience clapped wildly at the end of the evening, until finally Vivienne lifted her hand for silence. "Thank you," she said, her face glowing brighter than the brightest star in the night sky. "I would like to share some wonderful news with you. I'm about to be married."

More clapping. Luke smirked. Randy was wasting no time in proving his sincerity. "How would you all like to be my wedding guests?"

The applause continued as Miss DuPres reached toward the side door, where a slightly bewildered-looking Randy stood. He stepped forward and took her hand while the audience stood to its feet, giving an ovation worthy of a New York opera house.

"Reverend," Randy said, finally finding his voice. "Would you, please?"

Anthony made his way to the front. He faced the audience. "Well," he said. "I don't think I've ever had such a large congregation before. I hope to see you all in church on Sunday and just as enthusiastic over singing hymns to God as you are over Miss DuPres and her wonderful singing tonight."

The room filled with laughter, some nervous, some humorous.

Luke glanced around while the couple said their vows. Where was Laney, anyway? He finally located her watching from the door. Her gaze was focused on the wedding. In the soft candlelight by the door, Luke could see her face clearly outlined. There were no hard lines to make her appear severe. Her lips curved ever so slightly, and her eyes glistened as though she was fighting back tears. Luke swallowed hard. She was so beautiful, he wished he was a painter, able to capture her image on a canvas. He burned her image into his mind, knowing he'd never see another woman as lovely, no matter how long he searched. Suddenly he wanted to tell her so. Ached to hold her. He would never leave her no matter what; and if it took ten years of working on Pa's ranch to convince her he wasn't going anywhere, then that's what he'd do. Because one thing was for sure. . .he wouldn't give up the woman he loved.

Laney felt Luke's gaze even before she saw him. The crowded room faded away, and she saw only the man she loved. She knew he was experiencing the same feelings. She longed to go to him and nearly did so when his lips moved. *I love you*. After only a moment's hesitation, she shook her head, turned, and slipped out the door.

It warmed her to know he meant it. Luke loved her enough to give up going west in order to marry her. But Laney knew what it was like to lose a dream; and even though she'd reconciled herself to her own disappointment, she couldn't let Luke give up on his dream. She loved him too much.

So she hurried to Colby, knowing if she had to face Luke again tonight, amid the romance of renewed love and a wedding, she wouldn't have the strength to turn him away.

"Miss Jenkins."

Laney inwardly groaned at the sound of Mr. Garner's voice. She turned slowly to face him. "Hello, sir," she said.

"I assume your pa told you I was by the other day?"

"Yes, sir." Ashamed, she glanced at the ground. "I'm afraid, Mr. Garner, that even with an extra week, I won't be able to honor our agreement. We'll be clearing out before too long."

"I'm sorry to hear that, Miss Jenkins. I know this isn't your doing."

Tears pricked Laney's eyes. She glanced away and cleared her throat to compose herself. "Thank you."

"Where will you go?"

"Miss Hastings has room for us at her boardinghouse." It was the cheapest place in town. Miss Hastings was a nosy, grouchy spinster without a sense of humor. The thought of paying to live in a place she would never own seemed like a waste of money, but Laney knew she couldn't afford to be choosy in her present circumstances.

Mr. Tucker had offered her the use of his back room to work, and she had gratefully accepted. She suspected the idea of Granny working there every day appealed to him and had prompted his generosity to waive any rental fees.

From the corner of her eye, she saw that Luke had finally squeezed his way through the crowded schoolhouse and was making his way toward her.

"I have to go, Mr. Garner. Have a wonderful evening."

She quickly mounted Colby and rode off before Luke had the chance to stop her.

Chapter 15

L aney! He–l–l–lp!"

Fear gripped Laney at Jane's cry of distress. She hurried across the wooden floor of her room at Miss Hastings's boardinghouse, flung open the door, and made a mad dash toward the stairs.

She stopped short at the sight of Miss Hastings practically dragging Jane up the stairs. Fear widened the child's eyes. Indignation filled Laney, but she bit back angry words. She knew she was in a precarious position, and if she angered her landlady, they'd be out on their ears with no place to go.

Breathless from her swift climb up the long staircase, Miss Hastings stopped at the landing and grabbed her side with her free hand. After taking a moment to compose herself, she turned her furious gaze upon Laney. Laney gritted her teeth as she glanced down and observed her landlady's bony fingers digging into Jane's small arm. The spinster opened her mouth to speak, but Laney halted her. Regardless of the consequences, she would not allow Jane to be hurt.

"First turn Jane loose, Miss Hastings. Then tell me what my sister did to rile you."

The woman's face reddened in anger, and she turned Jane loose so suddenly, the child had to grapple for the railing to prevent herself from tumbling down the steps.

Silently she counted to ten to keep from giving the old hag a quick shove backward. Laney reached for Jane. Once she held her sister protectively to her side, Laney regarded Miss Hastings evenly. "Now what did Jane do?"

"I caught her stealing from me!"

Alarm clenched Laney's gut. "What do you mean?"

"Ask her. She'll tell you."

Laney cupped Jane's chin and forced the little girl to meet her gaze. "Did you steal something?"

Sudden tears filled Jane's blue eyes. "Yes."

Miss Hastings gave a smug nod as though she'd just solved the mystery of the decade. "There. You see?"

Disappointment washed over Laney. Was Jane going to follow in their pa's footsteps? "For shame. You'll have to give back whatever you took."

The child looked miserable. "I can't."

"Why not. Did you break it?" Laney inwardly groaned, envisioning an expensive vase she would have to pay for.

Jane shook her head. "I ate it."

Blinking twice, Laney tried to assimilate the child's words, but she could only conjure up an image of Jane trying to eat a vase, and it just didn't make any sense. "What do you mean, you ate it?"

Miss Hastings stomped her daintily booted foot in a not-so-dainty manner. "Oh, for pity's sake, the child stole a roll from the kitchen."

Jane cast soulful eyes upon Laney. "It just smelled and looked so good, and I was hungry. So I took it. But I tried really hard not to."

Relief flooded Laney that it wasn't worse; still, she knew her sister had to understand stealing was wrong, no matter what the object of desire.

She glanced down sternly. "Tell Miss Hastings you're sorry and promise never, ever to take so much as another bite of food that doesn't belong to you."

Jane obeyed instantly.

Miss Hastings gave an ungracious sniff. "Those were to be served with dinner. Since the child has already eaten her share, she will not be given one this evening. And, Miss Jenkins. . ."

"Yes?"

"Please dress appropriately for dinner. I do not approve of your mannish garb." So saying, she spun on her heel and flounced down the stairs.

Laney released a frustrated breath and ushered Jane into her bedroom. The child hopped up on the bed, swinging her legs along the side. She tucked her chin glumly into her palms. "I don't like Miss Hastings one little bit! I wish I had a fat snake to put in her bed. Or a slug or a mess of worms like the ones Will and me dug up last week."

Laney shuddered at the thought of sliding into bed with a mess of squirmy worms, although she had to admit the thought of Miss Hastings doing that very thing contributed greatly to the mirth rising inside of her. She swallowed down the laughter before it reached her face in the form of even a hint of a smile. Composing herself, she recognized that she was the only guidance Jane had, and it was up to her to teach her sister how to treat others—even those who treated a person unfairly. Plastering on as stern a look as possible, Laney eyed the little girl. "Janey! Do you honestly think Jesus would put a fat snake in someone's bed?"

"No," she mumbled. "But He probably never met Miss Hastings."

"Yes, He has. And He loves her just as much as He loves us, so let's try real hard to say something nice about her."

Jane scrunched her nose and closed her eyes while Laney waited. Finally the little girl shrugged, capturing Laney's gaze. "I can't think of anything nice."

It was quite a challenge for a first try, Laney had to admit. "All right. I'll go first, and then maybe you can think of something." Determined to be a good example, Laney searched for something to say until finally, like a stroke of genius, she found her nice thought. "She keeps a sparkling clean boardinghouse, and Granny always says cleanliness is next to godliness. Okay, your turn."

Jane screwed up her face and thought. . .and thought. . .and thought. Suddenly she brightened and glanced up at Laney with a wide grin.

"You thought of something nice to say?"

"Yep. Miss Hastings makes the best rolls I ever had in my whole life!"

Laughter bubbled up inside of Laney and flew from her lips. She went to the bed and grabbed her little sister, tickling her until their laughter prompted three sharp taps beneath the floor from Miss Hastings's broom. "I will not tolerate such noise."

For someone who couldn't tolerate noise, she could sure yell loud enough to cure a deaf man.

"Shh," Laney said, her eyes still damp with mirth. She laid back and stared at the water-stained ceiling. "Oh, Janey, I promise I'll get us out of here as soon as possible."

Janey cuddled up next to her and rested her silky head against Laney's shoulder. "I don't care where we live, Laney. Just so long as you and me and Pa are together."

"You don't mind living here? Even with mean Miss Hastings fussing at you all the time?"

Her head moved left and right against Laney's arm.

"But what about all the fun you had when we played with the baby chicks at the soddy? And what about all the times we sat on the bank and dipped our toes in the creek?"

"I liked that, but it wasn't as much fun when I had to go play at the creek by myself. I reckon there's lots of fun things we can do even here at Miss Hastings's—as long as she don't hear us. Do you think we could find something quiet to do together?"

"Well, yes. I thought we might ask Emily for a reader so I can get you started on your letters. You can practice them while I'm working. Then we can go over them after supper each night. How does that sound?"

"And maybe Pa can listen to me practice, too. He'll probably get awful lonesome over in that room all by hisself. I sure wish we coulda all been in the same room like we was at the soddy."

Laney tightened her grip on Jane's arm. How could two children be raised by the same man and come away so differently? Laney cared where she lived. She wanted stability. Sameness. Jane wanted love above everything else. Family.

With a gasp, Laney sat up. Awareness flooded her like light pushing through a thick, black cloud.

"Are you mad at me, Laney?"

Laney laughed and grabbed Jane for a tight hug. "Of course not! You're wonderful. How did you know that happiness and security don't come from where you live but who you love?"

Jane's brow furrowed with confusion. "I don't know. Did I do something good?"

"You did something very good, sweetheart." Laney bent and pressed a tender kiss to her sister's forehead.

Luke! Laney would have liked nothing better than to run to him immediately, but the downstairs clock bonged six o'clock, a mere half hour before Miss Hastings ordered they be ready for supper. Laney gladly would have foregone a meal to go to Luke, but Jane needed her nourishment. "We'd best get ready so we aren't late for supper."

Jane shuddered a deep sigh. "Yeah. Miss Hastings might get cross if we're late. What are you going to wear?"

"I have a clean pair of britches in the. . .oh." Inwardly she groaned. Miss Hastings had insisted upon appropriate attire. With a sigh, she opened the wardrobe and yanked out her only skirt. She groaned as a telltale rip filled the room.

Jane gasped. "Laney. You tore it!"

Now what? She knew there was no way Miss Hastings would stand for her showing up in britches. She pulled out the blue gown she had made last year.

Jane's eyes grew wide. "Did you make that?"

"Yep."

"It's so pretty!"

Eyeing the gown objectively, Laney grinned. "It is, sort of, isn't it?"

"You going to put it on?"

"I reckon. Why don't you go over and let Pa know we'll be bringing him a tray in a few minutes. I'll come and get you when I'm dressed."

"Okay." She hopped from the bed and scurried out the door, forgetting to shut it behind her. "Pa! Guess what Laney's going to wear?"

A grin tipped the corners of Laney's lips as she crossed the room and closed the door. Twenty minutes later, she was washed and dressed, thanking the Lord she was small enough that there was no need for her to wear a corset. She'd never have managed one alone. After several futile attempts to pin her hair into something resembling a fashionable style, she gave up and let it flow freely down her back.

With five minutes to spare, she left her room and collected Jane. She held her breath, daring Pa to say something. He did. "Ya look jus' like yer ma." Then he turned his back. Laney blinked in surprise as she turned away toward the stairs. She remembered only one kind thing her pa had ever said about Ma: *"She was the pertiest thing I ever saw."* Laney couldn't help but smile. Pa was definitely softening.

Luke's heart raced until he thought it might beat from his chest. Rusty's hooves pounded the earth. Only one thought hammered in his mind. *Where is Laney?*

He reined in his horse in front of the ranch, slid from the saddle, and skipped all three steps, landing on the porch. Pa opened the door just as Luke was about to barrel through it.

"Slow down, son. What's happened?" Pa hobbled to the bench beneath the front window and sat.

"Laney's gone. Cleared out, lock, stock, and barrel." Panic welled up inside of him. Why had he allowed his pride to keep him from going to her right after the concert? How long had she been gone? How would he find her? "I just came home to grab some gear. I'm going after her."

"I reckon I knew she was clearing out of the soddy."

Luke blinked and stared incredulously. "You knew?"

"Just found out yesterday."

"And you didn't tell me?" How could Pa have done this to him? "I've lost an entire day I could have been on her trail."

"No need to trail her. I know where she is." Pa patted the bench next to him. "Come and sit."

Reluctantly Luke did as he was told. He wanted to go find Laney. The longer he waited, the farther away she would be—even if Pa knew where she had gone.

"I had a visit from Garner a few weeks back, right after the trial. Seems Laney paid off her pa's debt to keep him out of prison."

"Yes, sir. I was there when she offered."

"It was all she had."

The implication of his words hung in the air. "She lost the soddy?"

Indignation washed over Luke. "How could Garner take her soddy away after all the hard work she's done?"

"Now don't go jumping to conclusions. That's why he came to me for advice. He would have offered to give her the soddy or at least have waited until she could raise the rest of the money. But he knew before he asked she wouldn't do it. She's too stubborn."

"So you just let her lose it?"

"Not exactly." His lips twitched.

"Then why is she gone?"

"I bought it from Garner and planned to offer it back to her, but she moved out early."

"You said you know where she went?"

"Took two rooms at Hastings's boardinghouse."

Luke's throat tightened. Laney would go crazy closed up in a musty old boardinghouse. And what about little Jane? A young'un needed a place to run and play.

Pa reached into his pocket and pulled out a document. He handed it to Luke.

"What's this?"

"The deed to Laney's land and the soddy. I talked it over with your ma. This is our wedding gift to you and Laney."

"I can't take that from you, Pa."

"You ran this ranch while I was laid up. You were even willing to give up the idea of your own ranch to honor your ma and me. We want you to have that land to start your own ranch, just like you've dreamed."

"But Laney won't marry me, and I don't want it without her."

"She will when she sees you're serious about not going to Oregon."

A slow grin found its way to Luke's lips. He headed for Rusty. "Tell Ma I won't be here for supper."

Pa chuckled. "I thought you might not."

Trying to formulate the right words to make Laney listen this time, Luke took it easy on Rusty during the two-mile ride into town.

When he reached the boardinghouse, he dismounted, tethered Rusty to the hitching post, and strode to the front door. He knocked with purpose and waited until Miss Hastings appeared. "Yes?"

"May I see Miss Jenkins, please?"

She glared at him with contempt. "I am afraid Miss Jenkins has retired for the evening."

Flashing his most winning smile, Luke leaned closer. "Miss Hastings, would it be too much trouble to ask her to unretire for a few minutes? I need to speak with her."

Apparently unmoved by what Luke had been assured was a handsome smile, Miss Hastings squinted behind her spectacles. "Come back tomorrow at a decent hour, and I'm sure she will speak with you then."

"I'll speak with him now, Miss Hastings."

Luke glanced up at the sound of Laney's voice. His eyes widened and his mouth fell slack at the sight of her. Laney was always beautiful, but in a gown of blue silk, she was almost more than any man could take.

"I thought you had retired for the evening, Miss Jenkins."

"I would have, except that you reminded me to remove my pa's tray from his room and clean his dishes before I retire."

The pinch-faced spinster's face turned red. "I'll just take that so you can attend to your guest. Please go into the parlor and leave the door open. I run a respectable place, and I will not have my name sullied."

"Of course, Miss Hastings," Laney replied graciously.

Luke would rather have stepped onto the porch or gone for a walk so they could be completely alone, but for the moment he wouldn't argue. He patted his shirt pocket where he had placed the deed. Now if only he could convince Laney that he truly wanted to marry her and stay in Harper.

Chapter 16

Laney bit back a grin at the glare on Luke's face. She knew he resented the lack of privacy, but she couldn't afford Miss Hastings's disapproval right now.

"You look beautiful," Luke said, taking her hand as they walked into the parlor.

Laney ducked her head, unaccustomed to such compliments. "Thank you. Miss Hastings doesn't approve of my 'mannish garb.'" She threw him a cheeky grin.

He leaned in close, his tone conspiratorial. "If she ever wants to catch a man, she'd better not insist you wear dresses like this one too often," he drawled. "You overshadow her by a mile."

She laughed, enjoying the glint of admiration in his green eyes, as well as the easy camaraderie they had fallen into as though they had never disagreed. "Why are you flattering me?"

"I'm not. It's all true."

She sank onto the couch. "Have a seat."

He started to sit next to her, but mindful of Miss Hastings pacing the foyer just outside the room, Laney motioned him to a wing chair across from her.

She gathered courage about her like a shield. "I'm glad you've come, Luke. I—I need to speak with you, too."

"What is it?"

Her eyes misted. She longed to sink into his arms, but Miss Hastings's shadow fell across the doorway, keeping them at a proper distance.

"I—I wanted to tell you that I will go to Oregon with you—if you still want me to."

Wordlessly Luke stared at her for such a length of time that Laney thought maybe he hadn't heard her. Finally she cleared her throat. "If you still want me, that is," she repeated.

"If I . . . ?"

"Well?" A frown furrowed her brow. He could say something. Even if he didn't want her anymore.

"No."

"No? You don't want to marry me?" Laney grimaced as her voice reached a high pitch and cracked. She felt the heat rise to her cheeks and wished she could take it all back. She should have let him tell her what he came to say first. He probably would have spared her the humiliation of this rejection by telling her up front he had changed his mind about her.

"I don't want you to go to Oregon."

Laney leaped to her feet. "Yes, Luke. You've made that perfectly clear. Just say what you came to say and get out of here."

"If you don't simmer down and stop that yelling, Miss Hastings is going to be in here throwing me out in two seconds flat."

As if answering a summons, Miss Hastings appeared in the doorway. "Is he manhandling you, Miss Jenkins? Shall I call in Mr. Witherspoon to escort him out?"

Luke grimaced and glared at Laney. "That won't be necessary, Miss Hastings," he said. "Miss Jenkins offered to come west with me. . .and—"

The poor woman's face was instantly stripped of color. "Miss Jenkins, I am afraid I did not realize you were a woman of questionable morals when I allowed you to move into my establishment. Perhaps your peculiar ways should have raised my suspicions, but being a Christian woman, I hesitate to judge a person without proof."

Mortified, Laney flailed her arms at Luke. "Look what you've gone and done, Luke. Miss Hastings, I promise, this isn't the way it appears. I meant I would marry Luke and *then* move west with him."

"Oh, that is a relief." She nodded but didn't quite smile. "You are getting married, then. When will you be moving out? I am afraid I cannot give you a refund for the month in advance you've paid, but I informed you of that fact when you insisted upon paying ahead of time."

"It doesn't matter, Miss Hastings," Laney said glumly. "Mr. St. John has decided he doesn't want me to marry him after all."

"How unchivalrous! I would have expected more from the son of one of Harper's most distinguished citizens."

Something akin to a growl escaped Luke's throat. "Wait!" He took hold of Laney's hand and led her back to the couch. "Sit down," he commanded. Then he strode to the door and extended his arm in that direction. Miss Hastings turned three shades of red and stepped out of the room.

Laney heard her gasp when he pulled the door firmly shut behind her. "Luke, you're going to get me thrown out of here!"

"You don't want to live here anyway." He sat next to her and took her hands. "Now tell me why you changed your mind about coming to Oregon with me. Is it just because you lost the soddy? Because that's exactly the same bad reasoning as it would have been for me to marry you just because I didn't think I'd ever be able to head west."

"That's not it, and it doesn't really matter since you don't want me anymore, anyway. Don't worry about thinking you have to do the right thing by me. I don't go where I'm not wanted!"

"Yes, I know." Luke chuckled. He cupped her chin. "Tell me. What changed your mind?"

Laney gave a sigh. "Jane."

"I don't understand."

"Oh, Luke. Jane made me realize that if you don't have the ones you love around you, it doesn't really matter if you have the best land in the world or not. I can be happier in Oregon with you than I would be on my land, in my soddy, without you."

He bent forward and pressed his forehead to hers.

Laney closed her eyes, savoring his closeness.

"Laney," he whispered, drawing her closer. His mouth moved over hers and clung until she could hardly breathe. All too soon, his lips left hers. He pressed her head against his shoulder.

She wrapped her arms around his waist, resting in the familiarity of his arms. "I meant it, Luke. I'll be happy anywhere, as long as we're together."

"I feel the same way," he said against her hair. "I'd rather stay here with you than go there without you."

Laney pulled away and stared for a moment, trying to wrap her mind around his words. "Then why did you say you didn't want me to go?"

"Because I've already made up my mind not to go west."

Relief nearly overwhelmed her as she looked into his love-filled eyes. Still, she needed to be positive. "But are you sure, Luke? You've wanted it for so long."

"Something changed inside of me when Pa got hurt. What if I hadn't been here to help? I need to stay close to the family. And as far as my land goes, I can raise my own herd right here. It may never be as prosperous as Pa's, but it'll be mine. . .ours, if you'll have me."

"I will, Luke. But where are we going to live?"

"I want to build our herd right here. On your land."

Laney felt the color drain from her face, and she sent him a blank stare. "Didn't you know? I mean. . .why else would I be living here?"

Luke nodded. "I know what you did for your pa." He moved closer and wrapped her in his arms, pulling her close. "I'm sorry I didn't realize the consequences. I would have made sure you didn't worry about your land for even one minute."

She sighed against his shoulder. "Oh, Luke. I think sometimes we just have to be brought low for God to show us the truth about ourselves. I had to realize that my land wasn't the most important thing. God is. And the chance for my pa to come to know the Lord."

"Has he?"

"No, but I'm not giving up. He's softening." Laney gave a short laugh. "He hates it, but he's definitely changing, in spite of himself. I know it won't be long before he accepts Jesus."

"I'm glad to hear it. We'll keep praying for him." He pulled back and studied her, a twinkle lighting his eyes. "How soon can you be ready to move back out to the soddy?"

Was he being cruel? Or had he simply misunderstood? "What do you mean? It's gone. Garner sold it to another buyer already."

Luke grinned broadly, pulled out a document, and handed it over to Laney. "A deed?"

"Read it."

Her hands began to tremble as she glanced down and read the name on the deed. "Luke St. John." She threw him an accusing glare. "You bought my land?"

"Stop looking at me like that. Pa bought it. Garner wanted you to keep it, but he knew you wouldn't accept an extension. Pa wanted to give you the opportunity to buy it, but when you moved out before he could offer you a deal, he decided to give it to us as a wedding present instead."

"A wedding present? We can't take this. We have to make him let us pay for it."

Luke placed his hand over hers. "It's a gift, honey. A gift. I'm not going to hurt Ma and Pa by trying to pay for it." He slid to his knee in front of her. "You never answered me. Will you share it with me?"

Her eyes misted. "Oh, Luke. You know I will."

Mesmerized by her tears, Luke cupped her face and brought his lips to hers for a brief, tender kiss.

"When can we get married?"

"Wh–when do you want us to?"

"As soon as possible, before something else goes wrong."

"But where would we live? With Pa and Jane and me, the soddy's awfully crowded already."

"I can add a room on to the soddy for now, and I can start hauling sandstone from the creek to build a real house as soon as possible. It still might take a couple of years before we can move out of the soddy, though. Is that all right with you?"

Laney flung herself into his arms, nearly knocking him backward. "It's wonderful. If you're sure you can put up with Pa. I—I can keep making dresses for Mr. Tucker, and we can save our money for our herd."

Luke frowned.

"What?" Laney asked. Then understanding dawned. "You don't want me to keep working for Tucker?"

Luke smiled, hugged her, then pulled back again to look into her eyes. "I don't guess it would hurt anything, as long as you promise not to get yourself all worn out like you did last fall."

The corners of her lips tilted upward. "I thought you might fight me on that part of it. I don't *have* to work if you don't want me to."

"There'd be an uproar in town if the womenfolk thought I tried to keep you from making their gowns." He grinned. "I guess since the woman from Proverbs could take care of her family and still buy and sell land, my Laney can sew to help build our herd."

"We'll work together," she said, resting her head against his shoulder. Suddenly she jumped up and reached out for him. "Come on."

"Where?"

"You, sir, have to ask my pa for my hand in marriage."

Luke stood and grinned. "Are you sure you want me to?"

Laney laughed. "It's a risk. He might say no just to get under my skin. Then where would we be?"

"Maybe I'd better not ask, then."

"Come on. And maybe while you're at it, you can let him know he's welcome in our home."

Luke pulled her back and wrapped his arms around her. He pressed his forehead against hers. "You've changed," he said softly.

She nodded. "God changed me, Luke. I'm not sure how it happened, really. But all the fighting and anger, it's just not there anymore."

"So I don't guess I have to worry about you flattening me once a day, then?"

She sent him a cheeky grin. "I'm not making any promises. A girl can only change so fast."

"What about the dress? I kind of like it. Think you might wear it again, even without Miss Hastings around to insist on proper attire?"

"I'll wear a dress to church on Sundays."

"Then I'll look forward to every Sunday for the rest of my life."

"And of course I'll keep a skirt handy to pull over my britches when I go to town."

"Of course, we wouldn't want the town dowagers to talk."

Laney smiled and squeezed his hand. "Oh, Luke. I'm so happy it's all finally working out. Let's go tell Pa and Jane."

Luke pulled her back toward him. Laney caught her breath at the love shining from his eyes. Laney's mind filled with the memory of their first kiss. She smiled.

"What are you thinking?" he asked.

"Just that I'm glad I kissed you last fall, or we might never have decided to get married."

"You kissed me? I kissed you after the harvest dance and then asked you to marry me."

Laney regarded him through narrowed eyes. "Luke St. John, you know good and well that if I hadn't kissed you, you never would have gotten up the gumption to admit you love me in the first place. And that was two weeks before any ol' dance!"

His lips twitched, and Laney felt the heat rush to her cheeks. "Oh, you're teasing. Will I ever learn not to get so riled at you?"

"We have a lifetime for you to figure it out." He pulled her close.

Laney smiled as his mouth closed over hers in a kiss very much like the one that had started it all.

Epilogue

"Ma! Look at the wildflowers I picked for Grandpa's grave."

Laney pulled up the last of the weeds from Pa's gravesite and sat back on her heels. "They're lovely, Jenny."

She swiped the sweat from her brow with the back of her hand and smiled at her firstborn child. The four-year-old couldn't remember her grandfather, but her curiosity over the source of her given name of Jenkins had forged a bond between the absent grandpa and herself. She loved to hear the stories of her first year of life, when he was her favorite person on earth. Laney smiled to herself as the memories came rushing back.

It hadn't taken long after the wedding for Pa to soften and give his life to Christ. To everyone's surprise, God had given Pa three extra years before He took him home. Pa had learned to read but never read anything but the Word of God. In those years, God truly proved that love could change the hardest of hearts and humble the proudest of men. Pa had doted on his granddaughter and spent every waking hour trying to make her smile—which wasn't a difficult task, considering the baby had lit up like a prairie fire every time he was near.

Laney had grown to love her pa dearly and in the end had shed many tears of grief. Jane's presence helped ease the hurt, and the girl had quickly found a cherished place in the bosom of Luke and Laney's family, as well as the St. Johns' large extended family.

The Double L ranch thrived under Luke and Laney's management. No one could say Luke hadn't proven himself every bit the rancher his pa was.

Laney felt a hand on her shoulder, pulling her from her musings. She glanced up and smiled at her husband as he stooped beside her. "You feeling all right?"

"Wonderful."

"Think it might be today?"

She rubbed her bulging tummy and grinned. "This one's in no hurry, is he?"

"Stubborn like his ma," Luke replied and planted a kiss on her nose.

They anxiously awaited the birth of their third child. So far they had two redheaded girls; and though Luke adored his princesses, including Jane, he longed for a couple of princes to join the kingdom and even things out a bit. Laney would just be glad to fit into a pair of britches again. With each pregnancy, she had to put them away and don dresses for the last six months. She glanced at her pudgy fingers. She might have to wait a bit longer this time before she could wear them again. She grinned. At least she had a figure now.

"Time to go in and start supper." She reached for Luke. "Help your wife get off the ground."

He hopped effortlessly to his feet and swept her into his arms. "My pleasure," he murmured against her neck.

A gentle breeze blew across the prairie, carrying the fresh scents of spring. The new grass bowed in reverence, and Laney marveled as she glanced out across the land. "Oh, Luke, just look at what God has blessed us with." The pastures teemed with cattle, from last year's stock to the newborn calves. As far as she could see, the land belonged to them.

"God sure knew that His plans for us were right. Thank God I didn't run off to Oregon."

"No regrets?"

"Not even one, honey. Everything I ever dreamed of is right here in Harper— a beautiful family and prosperous land." He captured her lips for a quick kiss, then he smiled, the expression of love in his eyes taking Laney's breath away. "I wouldn't trade any of this for anything in the world."

Tears sprang to her eyes. How good God was to plant their dreams inside of them and then to make them come true.

EMILY'S PLACE

Dedicated to:
My husband, Rusty Bateman.
You're my kind of hero, honey,
and now you have it in writing.
Special thanks to my crit partners:
Nancy T., Chris L., Pamela G., and Tamela H. M.

Chapter 1

1885, Harper, Kansas

Emily St. John pulled on the schoolhouse door with a firmness that wasn't quite necessary to close it. The finality of the action brought a smile to her lips. She fastened the lock and slipped the key into her beaded purse.

Turning away, she took a large gulp of fresh late spring air. She couldn't help but be amazed at how much better the simple act of shutting out the responsibility and drudgery of teaching made her feel. Lord willing, that door wouldn't be opened again until the beginning of next term—not by her hands, anyway.

Her steps remained light and quick as she began the short walk to the mercantile. The grass looked greener, the prairie flowers more lovely; and it seemed as though the birds serenaded her, no doubt sensing her relief.

No more schoolchildren for months, she thought gleefully. Then a sudden touch of guilt wiggled inside of her. The problem wasn't the children at all, she had to admit, but their teacher. The last five years had proven the worst of her life.

The town had nearly burst with pride when she returned from a year of training at Emporia Normal School with a teaching certificate to her credit—the only schoolmarm in Harper ever to attend school specifically for the position. It proved Harper, Kansas, was becoming a real town.

Emily figured it was just one more instance of life taking her where she didn't necessarily want to go. She'd gone because it was expected of her. An orphan, she was grateful that Aunt Cassidy brought her from Missouri to Kansas when Aunt Cass married Dell. The two had raised her as one of their own. She'd had a secure childhood filled with love and laughter, so who was she to throw that back in their faces by refusing to go?

Her maudlin thoughts invited the all-too-familiar heaviness to return, and she released a frustrated breath at her brief reprieve.

This summer she had another plan. She had every intention of joining Mrs. Thomas and her little band of suffragists. Though Emily had attended her first and only meeting out of mere curiosity, she had to admit she'd been impressed and agreed with Mrs. Thomas—it was high time women were given the right to vote.

Emily glanced up, surprised that her thoughts had carried her so quickly to the mercantile steps. She opened the door and stepped inside while the bell dinged her entrance. "Good afternoon, Mr. Tucker."

"Afternoon, Granddaughter." Mr. Tucker's grizzled face brightened. After being a confirmed bachelor for most of his life, the poor man hadn't stood a chance when Emily's granny had taken a fancy to him. With the approval and well wishes of the entire town, they'd married a couple of years ago.

Their happiness was a bittersweet thing for Emily. Some folks thought reminding her of her new grandfather's age was a comfort—as though her Prince Charming might come along when she was seventy, just like Tucker.

Emily snorted at their ignorance. If Prince Charming wanted to wait until he was seventy, he could find himself a different princess.

"What was that, missy?" Tucker asked.

Emily rose on her toes and pecked a kiss on his cheek. "Sorry, Tuck. Just woolgathering."

"Must not have been a very pleasant thought," he grouched. "I tell a girl hello, and she grunts at me."

"You're right. My thoughts weren't very pleasant, and I'm sorry." All she needed was for Tuck to run home and tell Granny on her for being rude.

"Here," he said, pushing a jar of candy across the counter. "Have a licorice stick, and we'll forget about it."

Emily eyed the sweet temptation, thought to decline, then gave in and grabbed one. Why was everyone always trying to feed her, anyway? Disgusted, but knowing she'd better not make any noises for fear of offending her stepgrandfather, she attempted a smile at the old man. "Got any mail for us? I told Ma I'd pick it up after school."

"As a matter of fact, I do." He shuffled to the postal slots behind the counter and returned with a handful of mail.

"Thanks, Tuck. And thanks for the licorice." Emily turned to go but stopped at the sound of Jeremiah Daniels's familiar deep voice as he walked out of the storeroom.

"Hi there, Emily. Last day of school, huh?"

Her stomach flip-flopped as he sent an easy wink in her direction.

Wishing she could dry her suddenly damp palms, she found the presence of mind to give him a nod and respond. "Did you hear all the shouting when I dismissed?"

"Sure did. I imagine everyone else in town heard them, too." He grinned broadly, flashing even, white teeth. "You leaving now?"

"I was just getting ready to, yes."

"Me, too. I'll walk you out." He removed his apron and hung it on a nail next to the storeroom entrance. "I'm headed home now, Tuck. See you in the morning."

"Hold on a minute," Tucker said.

Jeremiah hesitated. "Yeah?"

The storekeeper cleared his throat. "I—uh. . . The thing is, I thought I'd take my wife on a picnic tomorrow." He pulled at his starched collar and averted his gaze to an imaginary speck of dust on the counter. "Think you can run the store by yourself?"

A grin played at the corners of Jeremiah's lips. "I think I can do that." He winked at Emily again, and her knees felt wobbly. "I didn't know you were such a romantic fella, Tuck."

The older man's face darkened to deep red. "Now who said anything about bein' romantic? Ellen has a notion to eat outside on the ground. That don't make no one romantic." He shifted his outraged gaze from Jeremiah to Emily. "And don't think I didn't see him wink at you like you two was cookin' somethin' up. You'd best not go spreadin' tales about me, else I'll have somethin' to say about it. And that's the truth."

"I wouldn't dream of saying a word, Tuck," Emily said. "Besides, everyone already knows you're an old softy where Granny's concerned."

He released a loud breath. "Now see? That's exactly how rumors get started. Don't you go repeatin' none of that gossip, missy. You hear me?"

"You have my word." Emily grinned and opened the door. "Good day. And tell Granny I said hello."

Jeremiah followed her outside. He paused on the step and leaned close as though they were conspirators. "I guess we shouldn't tease ol' Tuck, should we?"

Emily's heart picked up at his nearness. "I suppose not," she murmured. "It upsets him for anyone to think he has a soft side."

"Can't really blame him, though. After all those years of evading capture, the man surrendered like he wanted to get caught. He never even saw it coming, and now he melts like ice in July anytime your granny is within a hundred feet of him."

"Poor Mr. Tucker," Emily said, laughter bubbling to her lips. "Not only does he suddenly become a husband, but a grandfather to seven children, and even a great-grandfather, as well."

"Well, there's not much a man can do about it. When a woman sets her cap for him, he's bound to end up smitten. He might as well put on his Sunday best and head for the altar."

Emily gave a snort, then immediately regretted it as Jeremiah lifted his brow in a challenge.

"You disagree?"

What could she say now without giving away the fact that she'd had her cap set for him since they were ten and he hadn't "ended up smitten" yet?

"Yes, but let's not talk about it." She quickly descended the steps.

Jeremiah's boots thudded on the wooden planks as he followed her. "All right. Have it your way. How about walking with me to the livery, and I'll help you hitch your team."

"There's no need. I'm walking home today. Ma needed the team to go see Laney. The new baby was born last week, and Ma can't seem to stay away."

"Girl or boy?"

"Another girl." Emily grinned. Her brother Luke—Laney's husband—earnestly prayed for a boy during each pregnancy, but so far, God had blessed them with three girls.

Jeremiah chuckled. "Maybe next time. Anyway, it just so happens that I had to bring the plow in to get it sharpened, so I have the team. Gives me an excuse to drive you home."

"Oh, really?" Emily tossed back her hair and sent him a saucy grin. "I don't recall you asking if I'd like a ride home."

He removed his bowler and pressed it gallantly to his chest. "May I have the honor of escorting you, Miss St. John? It would be a great pleasure, to be sure."

A giggle escaped her lips. "I would be pleased to accept your kind invitation, Mr. Daniels."

He grinned. "Shall we, then?"

The feel of his hand guiding her across the street sent an ache of loneliness and longing through Emily. Why couldn't he see her as more than the girl he grew up with? She'd loved him for so long, it had become a delicious habit—a dream she couldn't live without. If only he could see her the way she saw him, maybe the dream would become reality.

He squeezed her elbow and then let go as they entered the livery stable where he'd left his team that morning. "Afternoon, Mr. Collins." He smiled at Emily. "I'll hitch up the team and be right back."

Emily nodded, wishing her heart didn't go into a tizzy at the smallest of smiles from Jeremiah.

Emily kept quiet and stayed out of the way while Mr. Collins finished grooming a gray mare. He finally straightened up with a grunt. Fishing a handkerchief from his shirt pocket, he swiped at his forehead and the back of his neck.

"You didn't bring the team today," he said, inclining his head toward Emily.

"I know. Jeremiah was kind enough to offer me a ride home."

His eyes shone in amusement. "Oh? You two finally courtin'?"

"No, sir!" Emily's cheeks burned as she heard the forceful words leave her lips. "He only offered me a ride home, and I accepted out of politeness."

"And no one can argue with Emily's manners, can they, Mr. Collins?"

Emily turned at the sound of Jeremiah's voice. She couldn't determine whether it was wounded pride, hurt, or merely embarrassment that hardened his tone; but she inwardly cringed, knowing that whichever had prompted the steely glint in his eyes, she was to blame.

"Ready to go?" She tried to keep her voice cheerful. Relief coursed through her as his expression softened.

"I'm ready. I brought the team around front."

They bid Mr. Collins good day and walked out to the hay-scented yard. Once there, Emily accepted Jeremiah's proffered hand and allowed him to help her onto the seat. She stepped up, so conscious of Jeremiah that she was unconscious of anything else and failed to establish a firm step. The mail she'd collected from Tucker's flew from her hand and scattered to the floorboard and ground.

"Easy does it," Jeremiah said, placing his hands on either side of her waist to steady her.

Her cheeks burned mercilessly, and she settled onto the wagon seat, unable to utter a word. But that didn't stop her vicious self-deprecating thoughts. *Stupid woman, stupid woman, stupid woman.*

Tears choked her.

Jeremiah gathered up the letters and dropped them in her lap. "Here you go." His chipper voice did nothing to improve her mood.

She looked up.

"What's wrong?" His eyes clouded in concern. "Did you hurt yourself?"

"No," she muttered, gathering the pile of mail in her lap. She looked it over, pretending great interest.

He moved to the other side of the wagon and climbed onto the seat. After waving good-bye to Mr. Collins, he flapped the reins, and the wagon lurched forward.

"Emily, about what Mr. Collins said."

"Yes?" she asked, still riffling through the mail, most of which seemed to be business relating to the ranch.

"The thing is. . ." Jeremiah cleared his throat. "You know Tuck is planning to sell the mercantile, right?"

Emily glanced up in surprise. "He is?" What had that to do with Mr. Collins's teasing?

"You didn't know?"

The wagon rolled out of town and onto the rough road.

"I had no idea. Granny never mentioned it." Her heart suddenly softened in concern. Was Jeremiah worried that he would lose his position should Mr. Tucker sell out? Surely he should know by now that Tuck wouldn't just leave him in a lurch.

"The fact is. . ."

Emily was just about to abandon the rest of the mail so she could give Jeremiah her full attention when the inscription on the next envelope captured her interest.

Miss Emily Sinclair.

Emily scrunched her brow. She hadn't been called "Sinclair" in many years, and the name looked unfamiliar and quite unsettling.

"Something wrong?"

She showed the envelope to Jeremiah.

He frowned. "Tuck gave you the wrong mail? That's not like him."

"No. This is me."

"I don't understand."

"Emily Sinclair. That's my name. At least it was my name a long time ago."

"I remember. You look so much like Luke I forget you're adopted." He grinned. "The same red hair and freckles."

Emily sniffed. "At least his hair turned dark."

"Your hair is cute," Jeremiah said.

Emily glanced back over the envelope and gave him a dismissive wave. "If you're partial to orange."

"Maybe I am. And green eyes. And freckles."

If only he were serious! She scowled. "Stop teasing."

Turning the letter over again, she started to tear into it but hesitated. She supposed she should wait and let Ma open it. As if reading her thoughts, Jeremiah quirked his brow.

"Aren't you going to open it?"

"Shouldn't I wait until I get home?"

"Why? It's your name on the envelope. Sorta."

"I know, but. . .well, I suppose you're right." She grinned. "Besides, I can't wait to see who would be writing to me."

She tore open the envelope and took out the letter, carefully unfolded it, and read aloud:

Dear Miss Sinclair,

My name is Andrew Cambridge, and I am the attorney for the Harrison estate. I trust this letter finds you well.

I must first bring you the sad news that your grandmother Harrison has passed away. She died quite suddenly in her sleep several years ago, and her husband, your grandfather, two years earlier.

We have been attempting to discover your whereabouts for quite some time in order to inform you of the provision your grandmother made for you in her will. As it has taken this many years, the money was invested for you and has grown to quite a handsome sum.

Please respond as soon as possible so that we may settle this long overdue matter.

Sincerely,
Andrew Cambridge
on behalf of the Harrison Estate

Jeremiah released a low whistle.

Emily turned to him. "I didn't even know I had a grandmother Harrison," she said, still trying to absorb the information that she had just inherited what appeared to be a tidy sum from a source she hadn't known existed.

"You had a grandmother you didn't know about?"

"It seems so. I feel odd—like I should be sad or something, and guilty because I'm not."

"You can't mourn someone you didn't even know."

"Why didn't they tell me I had a grandmother on my ma's side? I always thought since Ma was dead, any family she had must be, too. Why do you think Aunt Cassidy didn't tell me?"

Jeremiah shrugged and shook his head. "I don't know, but sitting here isn't going to answer any of your questions. I'll drive you on home, and you can straighten all of this out."

"Thank you, Jeremiah. I'd appreciate it."

Emily read the letter over several times during the drive. With each reading, her spirits rose. She wasn't sure what constituted a "handsome sum," but perhaps this inheritance was God's answer for getting her out of the schoolroom. Why, she could travel or enter the university, only. . .or. . . What had Jeremiah said? Mr. Tucker was selling his store? She vaguely remembered a conversation with Granny about Tuck selling out and resettling in central Kansas to be near Aunt Olive and her family. The question was, would Tucker sell to her?

She sat up a little straighter on the wagon seat. With Jeremiah to run the mercantile, she would see him every day, and he would never, ever have to worry about losing his job. And maybe all that togetherness would grow on him until he came to see her as more than the girl he grew up with.

She closed her eyes as if to will it to happen as she'd just imagined. This was her one chance. . .her one chance. It just had to work out!

Chapter 2

Emily handed Mrs. Marshall two bits' change and smiled as the older woman gathered her purchases and bid a cheery good day. Emily forced herself to remain where she stood until the bell above the door dinged the matron's departure, then she fairly flew around the counter and took up her entreaty once more.

"But why won't you stay on and work for me, Jeremiah?"

He shrugged, scowled, and resumed his duties without a word.

Emily followed him around the display of Healy's Magic Elixir. She stopped short of slamming into his broad back as he halted and began to fill in the gaps in the display.

"A man just doesn't work for a woman, Emily," he said without looking away from his task. "I have my pride."

"Oh, honestly." Emily gave a careless wave. "That's the silliest thing I've ever heard. You must be joking."

"No. I'm not." Jeremiah darted a glance at her, then refocused on the task at hand. "I'll stay until the end of the month to teach you as much as I can about running the store, but then I'm moving on."

The thunderous drum of panic beat wildly within Emily's chest as she realized she might be fighting a losing battle. "But, Jeremiah, what difference does it make if you work for me or Tuck? It's the same job."

"It just matters, that's all."

Emily detested her whiny, pleading tone. And she shuddered to think what Mrs. Thomas would say should she hear the newest member of Harper's chapter of the Kansas Equal Suffrage Association begging a man to stay and work for her. But the fact was—votes for women notwithstanding—if Jeremiah didn't agree to manage the mercantile, Emily might as well ask Mr. Tucker to return her money. Then she would have no choice but to hightail it back to the schoolhouse and resign herself to teaching forever.

She gathered a deep breath to steady herself for the next phase of the battle. "Be reasonable, Jeremiah," she said, trying without success to keep her voice even. "I need a good man to run this place. I counted on you to stay on as manager like you have for Tucker all these years."

He quirked a brow and flashed her a wry grin. "You shouldn't count on a fella without checking with him first." He pushed the last bottle into place and walked back toward the counter, stopping midway to straighten a display of dime books. "I'm happy that your real ma's family left you all that money, Emily. But just because you can buy Tucker's doesn't mean I have to stay and work for you."

Emily trailed after him. "Think of your poor mother, Jeremiah. What will she do if you don't have a job to support her?"

His lips twitched. "It's mighty thoughtful of you to be concerned about my ma, but rest assured I can still provide for her without your generous salary."

Heat suffused Emily's cheeks. "It's not very gentlemanly to make a lady beg and then laugh at her efforts." With a huff, she flounced around the counter and reached for the bolt of dress goods she had carelessly left out in her haste to resume her discussion with Jeremiah.

She spun around and lifted her gaze to the empty spot on the top shelf. A tremor slid down her spine, sending a shudder through her body. She hated climbing of any kind. Even short steps up. Emily preferred to keep her feet firmly planted on the ground where God intended for them to stay.

Warmth encompassed her elbow just before she heard Jeremiah's soft voice behind her. "Here, let me put that away for you."

Straightening her shoulders, Emily jerked her chin and climbed the small ladder, willing her hands to stop trembling. "I am perfectly capable of doing it myself." She swallowed hard, her head spinning from the lofty position three steps above the ground. With a firm grasp on the shelf in front of her, she drew a shaky breath and slid the bolt into place.

"Be careful stepping down from there," Jeremiah cautioned, grasping her elbow once more.

Emily jumped at the unexpected contact. A scream tore at her throat, and she tumbled from the step and into Jeremiah's strong arms. She glanced up into his startled gaze.

"Easy does it." He set her on her feet, keeping a steadying hand on her back, the other around her wrist for support.

"Th—thank you, Jeremy." Emily stepped back quickly, smoothing her palms over her skirt. "I'm fine now."

"Jeremy? You haven't called me that since that time I stole a kiss at the harvest dance when we were kids." Speaking softly, Jeremiah took a step closer.

"I—I haven't?" Was he going to try to steal another? Just in case, she kept her chin tilted upward to give him easy access.

He reached forward, and Emily's eyes shut as though of their own accord. Her mind conjured up the memory of his palm against her cheek just before he had leaned in and kissed her all those years ago.

"Here you go," he said.

When no kiss was forthcoming, Emily's eyes shot open. She stared into Jeremiah's amused face.

"This was in your hair."

Emily looked dumbly at the loose thread he held between his thumb and forefinger. Then clarity broke through her romance-filled imagination. She brushed the thread from his fingers and scowled, planting her hands firmly on her hips.

"If you aren't going to work for me, then what do you intend to do?"

All amusement left Jeremiah's face, and a flush deepened his tan. He turned away and opened the ledger, mumbling.

Emily gasped. "It sounded like you said opening your own store. Is that what you said?" Horror of horrors, Jeremy wouldn't do that to her, would he?

He turned to her slowly, gentleness shining in his soft brown eyes. "Harper has grown so much in the last few years, it can easily support two mercantiles. Don't you think?"

"I can't believe you're going into business against me, Jeremy. Of all the spiteful, mean things to do." She glared at him, fighting to keep her tears at bay. "I would never have thought it of you."

"Don't take it so personally. This is about my need to run my own business." His expression grew distant. "I would have done it years ago, but I thought I'd someday buy out Tucker."

"I see. You wouldn't compete against Mr. Tucker, but you have no problem trying to force me out of business."

"It's not like that, Emily." He frowned. "And don't you think you're overreacting just a bit?"

"Overreacting? No, I don't." She grabbed her bonnet from the peg behind the counter and stomped toward the door. "I think you're a low-down, sneaky. . . business stealer; and I don't want to be in the same room with you. Lock up when you leave, please."

Emily yanked the door shut and hurried down the stairs. She stopped short and gasped when she reached the bottom step. Turning, she made her way back to the door. Jeremiah glanced up as the bell dinged her entrance.

"Forget something?" he asked cooly.

"Y—you're still going to stay on until the end of the month, right?"

An indulgent smile lifted the corners of his lips, and the hard glint in his eyes softened. "I won't leave until I'm sure you know everything necessary to run this place."

Relief coursed through Emily, weakening her knees. *Thank You, God, that he isn't abandoning me.*

He glanced at her cautiously, curiously.

Still stinging from the revelation of Jeremiah's plans, Emily wasn't ready to make up with her old school chum. She sniffed. "Well, good. It's nice to see you've retained some semblance of chivalry."

Jeremiah chortled.

"What's so funny?" Emily demanded.

"I thought you 'equal suffrage' women were opposed to chivalry."

Emily's brow furrowed. "That shows how much you know about our cause!

We're simply tired of being treated like slaves and. . .and being kicked around like starving, stray dogs, Jeremiah Daniels."

His eyes twinkled as his gaze traveled over her. "One look at you and anyone could tell you've certainly been deprived of nourishment and kicked around."

Heat rose to Emily's cheeks. Her eyes grew wide, and suddenly she became conscious of her plump hips and thick waist. She stared, so shocked by his reference to her figure that she couldn't even muster enough anger to retort. "Why, Jeremiah. . . ," she finally squeaked. Then, unable to continue, she spun around and left before she made a spectacle of herself by weeping out her humiliation right there in the mercantile.

Tears stung Emily's eyes as she stomped toward the livery to pick up her horse and buggy. No wonder Jeremiah had never looked at her twice. He thought she was too fat! Emily sighed. She had to admit she had filled out quite a bit since graduating from the small-town school seven years earlier.

Still, that was the least of her worries right now. More pressing was the issue of Emily's Place. How could she run the store alone? She had to find a way to change Jeremiah's mind.

It had never even occurred to her that he wouldn't want to stay and run the mercantile. He had worked for Mr. Tucker since his school days when he stocked and dusted shelves after school and on Saturdays. Jeremiah working somewhere else just didn't seem right. He belonged with the mercantile. Besides, Emily needed him.

"Yoo-hoo, Emily!"

Emily turned at the sound of Mrs. Thomas's singsong voice. The older woman pulled her buggy beside the boardwalk. Forcing a cheery smile, Emily tried to push away her troubling thoughts of Jeremiah. "Good afternoon, Mrs. Thomas."

"Hello, dear. You haven't forgotten tonight's meeting, have you?"

"No, ma'am." As if she could forget that tonight she had to stand in front of a crowd of women and give a speech. When she'd signed on, she never intended to be a vocal force in the group, only to support the group and maybe hold up an occasional sign demanding the right to vote. She'd never counted on the knee-knocking experience she was in for this evening.

"We're all very excited to have Harper's newest woman entrepreneur in our little group of soldiers." The older woman flashed a wide grin. "Amelia Bell actually gained permission to cover the meeting for her pa's newspaper. What do you think of that? You're already making a difference for the women of this town."

Emily flushed with pleasure at the praise. "I'm glad I can help the cause, Mrs. Thomas."

"It's too bad we can't convince your mother to join. Cassidy St. John would be a mighty shot in the arm for the Kansas Equal Suffrage Association."

"I—I could speak to her, if you'd like."

Mrs. Thomas beamed as though Emily had made the most brilliant of statements. "Lovely! Just lovely! I knew you would be an amazing asset to our endeavor."

"Thank you, ma'am."

Mrs. Thomas gave a swift nod. "I must be going. I have a million things to do before the meeting tonight." She suddenly leaned toward Emily. "Oh, and, dear, I've been informed that the League of Christian Women intends to protest our cause from right outside the door. But don't let that discourage you. Hold your head high, and remember, God is on the side of right. And we, my dear, are right!" She raised her fist in the air. "Votes for women."

Emily returned the salute. "Votes for women," she echoed weakly, watching the matron drive away at breakneck speed.

Turning back toward the livery, she stiffened her spine and lifted her chin. She was Emily St. John, a woman of independent means. She didn't need a man, least of all Jeremiah Daniels, to make her business a success. She'd show him. Her store would outsell his by a mile. Then the good folks of Harper, Kansas, would see that she was just as special as the rest of the St. Johns, even if she wasn't smart like Sam, or funny like Luke and Jack, or clever like Will, or beautiful like the girls. She would do this on her own, and Emily's Place would be the talk of the town.

⌐

Jeremiah watched Emily through the store window until she stepped into the livery stable and out of his view. What had he said to upset her so? Mulling over the conversation, he suddenly groaned. He'd made a reference to her figure. Wasn't his ma always lamenting her own plumpness? How could he have been dumb enough to practically come out and tell Emily she looked fat? Inwardly he kicked himself. He certainly hadn't meant to imply she wasn't attractive because of a little plumpness—truth be told, he found her round cheeks most becoming. And he'd had to force himself to look away from her womanly curves more than once since she'd been coming to the store every day. Even now, the memory of catching her in his arms quickened his pulse.

He'd have to apologize for hurting her feelings, but for now he couldn't get sidetracked by the only girl he'd ever had any desire to court. If he allowed his feelings for her to rule him, he'd stay here and make her business a success and forget about his own dreams—dreams that for a brief moment appeared to be coming true.

Last month he'd put away the last of the money needed to make Tucker a fair offer on the store. He was on the verge of asking Emily if he could call on her when she received the letter about her inheritance.

He scowled and turned his attention back to the ledger. His ledger. Or it should have been. After his years of working for Mr. Tucker, he couldn't believe Emily would just waltz in and take over. Lock, stock, and barrel. She knew—everyone knew—how much he'd always counted on buying this place from Tucker.

She had to have known. And she had the nerve to call him a business stealer.

He glanced around the familiar room. If he closed his eyes, he could still see every single inch of the place, from the pickle barrel in front of the counter to the ever-present display of Healy's Magic Elixir to the newly arrived stack of dime novels—rubbish to be sure, but amazingly fast sellers.

Since Tucker's marriage to Emily's granny, Jeremiah had pretty much run the place on his own. Like most newly married men, Tucker couldn't focus on much but the love of his life and could rarely be bothered with store business. And that suited Jeremiah perfectly fine.

He paid a neighboring boy a small sum to help him work the farm, and he had been able to save most of his wages from the store for the past several years. Then Emily had swooped down and pulled the rug right out from under him before he could make an offer on the place.

A fire of resentment burned inside of him at the unfairness of it all. He glanced across the street to the empty lot and saw what it would become. A bigger store than this one with JEREMIAH'S MERCANTILE written in large letters above the door. He might even get one of those fake storefronts he'd seen in Abilene. Something fancy maybe. Eye-catching. Something to make folks pass Emily's Place right up and head for Jeremiah's instead.

The look of fear on Emily's face and her pleading tone came back to his mind, bringing with them a prick of guilt. Hopefully his words to her would prove true and Harper could support two stores, but if not. . .

He hated to put her out of business, but she was a St. John, after all. Her store was another hobby. Like teaching school had been. Okay, so maybe she had lasted as a teacher longer than he'd expected her to, but everyone knew she'd never liked the position. And if her pa hadn't been on the town council and county board for the past twenty years, she probably wouldn't have gotten the position in the first place. He knew Emily. She didn't like not getting her way. But he could handle himself just fine. Only he'd better avoid those enormous green eyes of hers, or they'd be his undoing.

Chapter 3

Emily focused her attention on transferring thick slices of ham from the skillet to a platter. She cut a glance to her ma and drew a deep, shaky breath before resuming her plea. "So I hoped you might consider coming?"

"My goodness, Emily. Why didn't you tell us sooner about your speech tonight?" Cassidy St. John pushed back a loose strand of wayward graying hair and leveled her gaze at Emily.

Emily shrugged and looked away. "I don't know. I didn't want you to feel compelled to come if you don't want to. You're not exactly supportive of the cause."

Ma moved toward the kitchen door with a basket of biscuits. She smiled over her shoulder. "And what's different now? Let me guess: Mrs. Thomas asked you to try to get me involved?"

Emily followed, carrying the platter of meat. "Something like that." There was no point in trying to deny it. Mrs. Thomas had been plaguing Ma for months with literature and suggestions that she at least "give the movement a try." Ma politely refused each time, and she had not been happy when Emily announced her intention to join the cause. *But after all,* Emily thought, *I'm a grown woman of twenty-five and own a business.*

Shaking her head in disgust, Ma pushed open the kitchen door with her elbow. "That woman. She never gives up!"

"Who never gives up?" Pa asked from his place at the head of the table.

"Mrs. Thomas. She asked Emily to invite me to the Equal Suffrage Association meeting tonight."

"You're not going, are you?" Pa winked at Emily and slid his arm about Ma's thickening waist as she set the basket of biscuits in front of him. "One independent woman in this family is enough. I prefer my woman at home where she can keep an eye on me."

"Oh, you. Keeping an eye on you is a full-time job in itself. I don't have time to fight for a woman's right to vote." Ma stood still for a moment, allowing him the embrace, then she dropped an affectionate kiss on the top of his head and walked to her chair at the other end of the table.

Will and Jack, the only two boys still living at home, snickered with their pa. Will elbowed his older brother. "What do you think, Jack? Can't you just see our ma carrying a banner and marching down Main Street?" He held up an imaginary sign. "Votes for women!" he said in a forced high-pitched tone.

Emily's defenses rose. Why did they always have to dismiss the cause as though it were mere women's foolishness?

"You boys hush up," Ma admonished, then focused her attention on Pa. "Dell, darling, Emily feels very strongly about women gaining the right to vote. I believe we should both go and support her."

"You expect me to go to a women's rights rally?" he asked in mock horror, but he added with a grin, "I'm afraid my stump's paining me too much to sit through a meeting tonight."

Despite her cause being put up for public ridicule, Emily bit back a giggle. Since losing his leg several years ago after a bull attack, Pa had, on occasion, used the misfortune to gain an advantage.

Only this time it appeared Ma was having none of it. Her brow rose, and she eyed him sternly. "Hogwash. If I can go and put up with Mrs. Thomas, you can sit for an hour or two. Besides, our own daughter is giving a speech."

"It's all right, Ma." Emily set the platter none too gently onto the wooden table and flounced to her own chair. "You needn't bother yourselves on my account. I am perfectly capable of attending alone."

"Let's say grace, please, before the meal gets cold." Ma folded her plump hands and gave a pointed glance to each family member seated at the table. "We'll discuss this matter while we eat."

After Pa said the blessing, he reached out and patted Emily's hand. Emily felt the tears rise and sting her eyes at his gentle condescension. "Now, sweetheart. Don't get upset. We'll go to your meeting."

Twenty-two-year-old Jack coughed loudly. Will pounded him on the back. Once he regained his composure, Jack sent Pa an incredulous look over the rim of his milk glass as he washed down his bite. "You mean you're actually going?"

"Of course. Didn't you hear your ma? Emily's giving a speech. I wouldn't miss it for anything."

Clearly unmoved by the strong show of family support, Jack gave a deep scowl and pressed his side of the issue. "But we won't be able to hold up our heads in decent company if she gets up on the platform and starts shouting about equality and the right to vote. Don't let her do it, Pa."

"That's right," Will echoed. "What kind of example is that setting for the other girls?" He cast a pointed glance at his twin sister, Hope, and their baby sister, thirteen-year-old Cat.

Hope sniffed and raised her chin slightly. "As if I'd set foot in a meeting for that disgraceful movement. I have enough on my mind lately, planning my wedding. What do I care about women who wear bloomers and smoke cigars?"

A gasp escaped Cat's rosebud mouth, commanding attention from her family. "What's wrong, sugarbaby?" Emily asked, frowning.

"I can't believe Hope doesn't support votes for women. And besides, most of the women don't smoke anyway, do they, Emily?" Her wide blue eyes begged Emily to dispel the awful rumor.

"Of course not." Emily settled an affectionate smile on her baby sister—clearly the beauty in a family of attractive girls and handsome boys. Her hair, the color of spun gold, fell in ringlets down her back. "Do I?" Emily asked the angelic-looking child.

A grin curved Cat's lips. "I should think not!"

"I don't see why girls think they have a right to vote anyway," Will said with the wisdom only a seventeen-year-old could muster. "Personally I wouldn't want to live in a country where my president was decided by a woman."

Although she knew better than to have this debate, Emily couldn't help defending her newfound cause. "It's about more than the right to vote," she retorted. "It's equal humanity we want. Women worked just as hard as men to settle this land. Since the end of the war, we have educated the young men who fill the voting booths all across this country; and yet if I were to step foot into one of those very booths and try to cast my vote, I would be arrested. Why shouldn't we have a say in the way things are run?"

Will regarded her smugly. "The declaration says all men were created equal. Not women."

"And who taught you that?" Emily raised her brow.

Ma and Pa each let out a chuckle.

Will's face reddened considerably. He stuffed a forkful of ham into his mouth.

Emily gave him a self-satisfied smirk. "I, a lowly woman, taught you everything you know about our government."

"Those women are disgraceful," he said, obviously undaunted. "And whether most women in the group smoke or not, I saw Mrs. Krenshaw smoking a cigar the other day. And she's taken to wearing trousers and cut her hair off short like a man's. Poor Mr. Krenshaw. I wouldn't stand for it if I were him."

"Now, Will. You know better than to judge a person by outward appearance," Ma admonished.

"Sorry," he muttered and shoveled another bite into his mouth.

Ma scooped potatoes onto her plate, then paused with the spoon still in hand. "Mr. Krenshaw seems to be holding his own. He goes with Mrs. Krenshaw to the meetings."

Will snorted. "She probably threatens him with a good lashing if he doesn't."

"Honestly." Ma shook her head. "Hush and eat your supper."

"And women say they're treated like an inferior class." Will elbowed Jack.

"Yeah, Ma runs this family with an iron hand."

"You two. . ." Ma blushed and smiled affectionately at her sons, then turned to Emily. "What are you going to wear to the meeting, honey?"

"Actually. . ." Emily's gaze darted around the table. She had wanted to ask Ma in private. She cleared her throat. "I hoped you'd lend me your old bloomer outfit."

"My what?"

"You know. The bloomer outfit you wore on the trip from Missouri. Way back when you first married Pa."

"Emily St. John, that's ancient. I wouldn't know where to begin looking for it. Why on earth would you want to wear something so outdated anyway?"

"They've become quite fashionable again. Especially among suffragettes, Mama," Cat piped in. "I planned to ask for one myself, since I'm joining Emily's group as soon as I'm old enough."

Emily smiled at the youngest member of the family. "Hopefully by that time we'll have gained our right to vote, sugarbaby; but if not, you'll be a welcome addition to our cause."

"You can always ask Laney if she'll loan you a pair of her trousers, Em," Hope said, disdain thick in her already-husky voice. "She hardly ever wears them anymore except when she's working the cattle."

Emily scowled at her sister. Like she'd be able to fit one leg inside Laney's tiny jeans. "I don't want to wear men's clothing. Just comfortable women's clothing. Bloomer outfits are still made for women, even if they are bloomers."

"I'm afraid you'll just have to wear a dress tonight," Ma said. "But we'll visit Laney and have a bloomer outfit made for you very soon."

"And me?" Cat asked.

"You'll have to take that up with your pa."

Cat turned her wide, pleading eyes upon Pa. "Please?"

Shaking his head, Pa admitted his defeat with an indulgent smile. "I suppose so. But you are only allowed to wear it at home and on picnics. Is that understood?"

Her hopeful expression dropped, but Cat nevertheless nodded, bouncing her curls around her shoulders. "Yes, sir."

"What is your speech going to be about, Emily?"

Staring dumbly at Ma, Emily felt the heavy weight on her shoulders of what she was going to do. How in the world could she stand up in front of those women and speak? Suddenly ill, she pushed back her plate. "I'm sorry, Ma. M—may I be excused?"

"Of course. Are you all right, Em?"

Emily nodded and fled the room just as her stomach protested her supper. Fighting nausea, she prayed. *Please, Lord. Help me get through tonight.* Oh, why had she ever agreed to speak about women having the right to their own businesses?

The only reason she had even bought Tucker's in the first place was so she could be near Jeremy every day. It had only become a matter of independence after Mrs. Thomas had made an issue of it.

It felt good to do something no one else in her accomplished family had ever done. She wanted to make a difference, wanted to be recognized as more than the girl Cassidy brought with her when she moved to Kansas to marry Dell St. John.

Emily wondered, as she had many times since receiving her inheritance from her maternal grandmother, what it might have been like if her real ma and pa hadn't died, leaving her to be raised by her aunt Cassidy. Not that she didn't love Cassidy and Dell as though they were truly her parents. But in a family where everyone was beautiful and accomplished, it was difficult to be ordinary.

⌒

"And to think, at one time I had hoped you'd marry that Emily St. John. Thank the merciful Lord in heaven He didn't see fit to answer my prayer on that one."

Jeremiah cut a sideways glance at his mother, who sat next to him on the wagon seat. He, too, had been surprised to learn of Emily's involvement with the suffrage movement, but nowhere near as upset as his poor mother. It came as quite a blow for her to discover Emily wasn't fit to be the mother of her future grandchildren after all.

"Her ma and pa must be absolutely mortified at her disgraceful behavior."

"Disgraceful?" Jeremiah couldn't keep the defender in him from rising. "All she's doing is giving a speech about being a woman in business. Personally I don't see why she shouldn't."

From the corner of his eye, Jeremiah saw his mother's cheeks puff out in indignation. "That girl has no business even owning that store. Everyone knows it was rightfully yours, and she stole it right out from under you. Then, adding insult to injury, she joins those radicals. Well, I hope you put her out of business right quick."

"A Christian attitude, to be sure."

"Oh, fiddlesticks. We'll be doing her a favor by putting her out of business. Then she can concentrate on finding a husband, as God intended."

"I see. You're watching out for her soul."

"Exactly," Ma said, obviously missing the sarcasm in Jeremiah's tone. "My league and I certainly have no intention of patronizing her store once yours is opened. Of course, we have no choice until then."

"Of course," Jeremiah said wryly. "Otherwise, where would you buy those dime novels?"

"Don't be smart. You're still not too big for me to turn over my knee."

Jeremiah pulled on the reins, halting the horses in the yard before the meeting hall. Already most of the League of Christian Women had gathered to protest the meeting inside, and his mother was chomping at the bit to join them. He hopped down and offered her his assistance.

"You stay put until I'm ready to leave," she commanded. "I don't want to have to wait on you."

"Yes, Ma." He grinned. Ma had the patience of a hungry puppy. He couldn't resist teasing her. "I'm just going to head to the dance hall for a while. You let me know when you're ready to go."

Her eyes twinkled in the glow of the moon. She gave him a whack on the arm. "You go anywhere near that evil place, and I'll whip the hide off you."

Bending, he kissed her on the cheek. "Go ahead and protest women's rights to your heart's content, and I'll be here waiting for you when you lose your voice and have no choice but to go home."

"Oh, you. You could come with me. I see little Hope St. John joining in the protest."

"Sorry, Ma. She's spoken for. Besides, I think she's headed away from the meeting, toward the Evans's place. She must have come into town with Emily's folks."

Ma's expression dropped. "What a pity."

A chuckle rose inside of Jeremiah. "One St. John girl is as good as another. How about I wait a few more years and try to woo little Cat?"

"You're being smart again." With that she sniffed and headed toward the group of protesters.

Jeremiah turned back to the wagon, wondering what in the world he was going to do for the next two hours. Tempted to sneak inside so he could hear Emily's speech, he glanced at the convoluted entrance to the meeting hall. There was no way he could sneak past Ma, and she'd be humiliated if he showed a hint of support for the suffragettes.

With a sigh, he climbed back into the wagon seat, stretched out his legs, and folded his arms across his chest. Shutting his eyes, he settled in for a nice long wait.

"Psst."

His eyes shot open, and he sat straight up. He twisted, looking from one side of the wagon to the other, trying to locate the source of the whisper. When his search yielded no answers, he frowned and shivered, though the midsummer breeze blew warm against his neck. "Who's there?"

"It's me, Emily."

Turning, he spied her lying flat in the back of his wagon. "What are you doing?"

"Please, Jeremy," she pleaded, her voice trembling. "For mercy's sake, hurry and get me out of here before they find me."

Chapter 4

A quarter mile from town, Jeremiah halted the horses. Emily sat up in the back of the wagon, breathing a relieved sigh to be away from the meeting. "I don't know how to thank you, Jeremy."

"Hang on." Jeremiah wrapped the reins around the brake and climbed down. He walked to the back of the wagon and hopped onto the tailboard. "Now you want to tell me what this is all about?" He scooted in, swung his legs up, and rested his back against the side of the wagon, facing her.

Emily glanced down at her fingers. "All those women. Inside the building, they were chanting about women's rights. And outside..." She shuddered. "A mob. Just like during the French Revolution. I thought my head was going to roll any second."

Jeremy gave a deep chuckle. "With my ma leading the angry pack."

"That's right. She's head of the League of Christian Women. I forgot." It certainly wouldn't do for Emily to spout off anything unflattering about the league. She refused to antagonize Jeremiah before she convinced him to give up his silly idea of building his own store. She had to make him see that teaming up would be more profitable for them both than pitting two stores against each other.

"How did you sneak out without being seen?"

"I told Mrs. Thomas I had to visit the..." Emily felt the heat rush to her face. Thankfully, Jeremiah nodded understandingly. "Clever ploy."

Emily opened her mouth to set him straight, then changed her mind. Better to let him think she'd told a bold-faced lie than to admit she'd actually made a dash for the privy as her stomach churned at the thought of facing those women. That would be too humiliating.

"What else was I to do?"

He shrugged. "You could have stayed and given your speech."

Emily's temper flared. "With all that racket going on outside from your ma and her cronies? I was nervous enough as it was."

"If you're going to be a pioneer, you have to expect some opposition."

The anger sifted from her as she mulled over his words. "Honestly. I don't want to be a pioneer. I just want..."

What did she want? Certainly not to march through town shouting for rights. Not to go to her store every day and haggle over prices or stock shelves.

"Do you even know what you want, Emily?" Jeremiah's tone was gentle, without any condemnation. "Why did you buy Tucker's? You could have taken the money or part of the money you inherited and traveled to England or back east. You could have set yourself up in a nice little house in town and lived comfortably on your teaching salary. Why the mercantile?"

A heavy sigh escaped her lips. "I don't know. After you mentioned that Tuck was selling and I got news of my inheritance, it just seemed like the right thing to do. I never thought you might not stay and run it. That was the sole reason for. . ."

"The sole reason for what? What do you mean?"

"Oh, nothing. I just wanted to buy it and Tucker wanted to sell. So that's that."

"All right. That explains the store—somewhat. What about this Kansas Equal Suffrage—"

"Don't call it nonsense," Emily cut in.

"I wasn't going to," he retorted. "Do you really feel that strongly about women having the right to vote?"

Resting the back of her head against the side of the wagon, Emily stared into the glorious star-dotted expanse above. "Oh, Jeremy. I never thought much about it until I heard Mrs. Thomas speak. But now. . ." How did she explain that she wanted respect, the kind of respect that only came with finding your own place in the world? Having a voice that counted for something? "I believe women should have the same civil liberties men enjoy. Aren't we citizens of the United States?"

"I see your point."

"Do you?" Emily had expected an argument similar to the constant berating she received from her brothers.

"Of course. I see no reason you shouldn't be allowed to cast your vote."

Affection swelled Emily's chest. Jeremiah Daniels was a rare man indeed. Of course, she'd always known that.

"Just don't take to chawing and spitting." He grinned, and Emily thought her heart might stop from the pure joy of being the recipient of such a smile.

"Don't worry about that," she replied, returning his smile. "Besides, they'll probably kick me out of the association when they realize I'm not coming back. I figure I have about another hour before they announce me and realize I hightailed it out of here." Emily's heart sank at the thought. Would she ever succeed at anything?

Jeremiah slapped his thigh and hopped from the wagon. "I have an idea. How 'bout you go back and give your speech?"

Emily gasped. "I can't go back now! How would it look?"

"It would look a whole lot better than running away like a coward. Stay and face it, Em. If you don't want to be in the movement after tonight, then don't be. But at least give yourself the opportunity to be a success. Who knows? Your speech may be the one that encourages some destitute widow to start selling baked goods from her home. And what if it turned into a thriving business and she opened her own bakery right here in Harper?" He reached across the wagon and gripped her hand. "You're the only woman in town who owns a business. Even Laney gave up sewing for Tucker when she and Luke made a go of the Double L Ranch. You have to set a good example for the women who need to be independent. Every

unmarried woman has to be able to take care of herself. You can show them the
don't need to worry if they can't find a husband. It's possible for a woman to go
alone if she needs to."

Emily gasped. Jeremiah didn't think she could find a husband? Is that why h
was being so nice to her? Pity! She focused her gaze on him, hoping the full moo
shining across the back of the wagon afforded enough light for him to catch th
full force of her glare. "You're right. I do need to show the unmarried women ju
how wonderful it is not to be encumbered with a tyrannical man who only wan
a woman to cook and clean and raise a passel of babies. I—I thank you kindl
Jeremiah Daniels, for setting my thinking straight. Only a foolish woman woul
want to marry when she can have a business instead. Please return me to the mee
ing hall so I can give my speech."

Confused, Jeremiah glanced at Emily, who sat ramrod straight and completely sile
in the seat next to him. Well, she wasn't exactly sitting next to him. Rather, she sa
as close to the edge as she could manage without tumbling to the ground. As it wa
he found himself maneuvering the horses with added care so as not to hit a pothol
and bounce her from the seat.

He turned his attention back to the road, puzzling over the sudden change i
her demeanor. He'd been encouraged by their discussion until the bit about wome
in business. Was it possible she didn't want other women to take away from h
position as the only businesswoman in Harper? He dismissed the thought a
absurd. Emily wasn't petty. Prickly at times, yes. But not petty.

When the lamplights of Harper came into view, he'd had all he could take c
her silence. "All right, Emily. Enough is enough. Are you going to tell me what
said that offended you all of a sudden?"

Emily pressed her lips together and jerked her chin upward.

"Fine." Jeremiah pulled on the reins, stopping the horses in the middle of th
road. "We're not going another foot without an explanation."

"I'll walk, then." Emily started to climb down; as she did, her dress caugh
beneath her heel, making her stumble.

Jeremiah reached across the seat and grabbed her arm to steady her.

"Don't you dare manhandle me, Jeremiah Daniels! I may not have a man of m
own, but I have a pa and four huge brothers."

With a scowl, Jeremiah turned her loose, but only after assuring himself sh
wouldn't tumble headlong to the damp ground. "I was only—"

"So you see, even if I can't find a husband, I'll always have someone t
protect me!"

A frown creased Jeremiah's brow. What was she talking about. . .husband
and protection? Protection from him? Then understanding dawned, and h
couldn't help but laugh. "Oh, you thought I meant *you* couldn't find a husband.

"Well, that was your allusion, wasn't it? I'm glad you think it's so funny."

Jeremiah's pulse picked up, and all thoughts of teasing fled as he observed her lip tremble. He reached over, and at the risk of being accused of manhandling again, he took her soft hand and held it. "Emily, I didn't mean you couldn't find a man. I don't figure you want one, or you'd have had some lucky fellow at the altar years ago."

He swallowed past a lump in his throat as she turned her wide, tear-pooled eyes upon him.

"Really?"

"Of course," he said, his voice suddenly raspy. "I only meant for women who are alone, whether by choice or necessity, you're a good one for them to look up to."

Her lips curved into a beautiful smile. She placed her free hand over their clasped hands. "Thank you, Jeremy. I apologize for the misunderstanding."

"I'm the one who should apologize. I seem to make a habit of saying the wrong thing."

"We'll pretend it never happened."

As much as he hated to, Jeremiah slipped his hand free and gathered up the reins once more. "I'd best get you back so you can give your speech."

Emily cleared her throat, then turned to him suddenly. "You know, I don't believe in the cause to the exclusion of marriage and family. I—it's just that the right man has never asked."

Another man might have considered her statement an opening, an offer that she might not reject a proposal or at least the request to court her properly; but Jeremiah knew he was in no position to marry a girl like Emily. Besides, she was the daughter of the most successful rancher in three counties. While he, on the other hand, would always be the grubby little boy who stole sourballs from Tucker's store.

Jeremiah sighed. Perhaps if his business proved successful. Maybe then he'd be good enough for Emily. A month ago, he would have jumped on her statement like a fish on a worm. Now that she'd bought the mercantile, he had no choice but to wait and see how his new store fared in the scheme of things before he'd be in a position to consider courting.

"I'm sure when that lucky man comes along, he'll be praising God that you're not opposed to marrying and settling down."

"Yes," she replied flatly. "I'm sure you're right."

The remainder of the trip into town was uncomfortably silent. Jeremiah knew better than to try to explain. It would only make things worse.

⁓

Emily lay in her bed, mulling over the events of the evening. Her speech had gone off without a hitch; and when she slipped back inside, it appeared no one had even noticed she'd been gone. Afterward, ladies of all ages had surrounded her, flattering her, thanking her for giving their cause another voice in the community.

Emily had the uncomfortable feeling that many of the more mature members of the group only welcomed her in an effort to woo Ma to the association. Mrs.

Thomas fawned all over poor Ma the minute she stepped in the door. Like mos women in love, Ma was content to take care of Pa and the family. While she migh believe in the cause of women's rights, she certainly wouldn't make a habit of leav ing home to attend rallies and marches. And she had told Mrs. Thomas so in n uncertain terms.

Rolling onto her back, Emily stared at the moonlit ceiling. The time she' spent with Jeremiah would remain imprinted on her heart forever—partly a swee memory and partly bitter.

If only she hadn't told him she'd like to get married, should the right man as her! She groaned, feeling ill from the memory of her brazen hinting. What mus he think of her now? He'd been gracious but clearly not tempted to take her u on her invitation.

Despite her glum musings, a grin tipped the corners of her lips at the though of Jeremiah sneaking into the meeting hall to hear her speech. He'd smiled broadl at her and was the first to his feet, leading the ovation as she said the words, "So le us rise up and attend our own businesses. If we can run our homes and raise goo Christian children who contribute to the betterment of society, why can't we ru profitable businesses, void of the management of men? Who is to say that we can remain fine, upstanding citizens of the community without spot or blemish t tarnish our reputations?"

With a start, Emily sat up in bed. Perhaps she didn't need Jeremiah to manag Emily's Place at all! What if she could attend her own business and really mak it a success?

What if she went so far as to move into Tucker's old rooms above the store? / bubble of excitement rose inside her. She would truly be on her own. The bubbl deflated in an instant of new thought. What if Jeremiah decided to court her? H couldn't very well do that if she were living alone.

Releasing a sigh, Emily flopped back onto her feather pillow. Jeremiah ha made it abundantly clear, despite her unabashed hinting, that he wasn't intereste in courting her anyway, so what was the point in waiting around?

For the rest of the night, her mind whirled with activity as she organized he thoughts into what it would take to set up housekeeping for herself. Now hov would she convince Ma and Pa it was a good idea?

Surprisingly she received minimal argument from her parents; and within th week, Emily found herself on her own in every sense of the word.

As she lay in her bed the first night away from home, listening to the lonel silence of her own little three-room home above the mercantile, she couldn't kee the tears at bay. Suddenly all she wanted was a little home of her own and a ma to take care of her and give her a houseful of children.

Independence certainly wasn't all it was cracked up to be, and Emily knev she'd give it up in a heartbeat. . .if only the right man would ask her to.

Chapter 5

Emily planted her chin in her palm and watched the influx of customers at the newly opened Jeremiah's Mercantile across the street.

She'd watched daily for the past two months as the store was built frame by frame, nail by nail—and she'd prayed for a miracle. When no divine intervention seemed likely, however, she'd resigned herself to the competition. Still, with dread, she had anticipated this day. And now the big opening was upon her.

Emily scowled at her empty store. Honestly, the lack of loyalty present in her customers was nothing less than shameful. No one seemed the least bit concerned about how she might feel as they happily entered the enemy's camp and came out with their ill-gotten goods.

Well, she, for one, was not about to let it bother her. Once folks realized that she had better prices and better-quality goods, they'd be back. Only—she stomped her foot—how much was Jeremiah charging anyway? She couldn't very well go over and find out. And if she sent one of her family members, Jeremiah would know they were nothing more than spies.

It wasn't fair. He knew every single item she had for sale, and he knew exactly how much she charged.

Suddenly a huge, marvelous idea entered her mind. Joy bubbled in her soul. She would mark prices down and undersell Jeremiah by a mile. A quick glance around brought a new worry. Only how would she get the word out?

She planted her hands on her hips and released a quick breath as she thought. The *Harper Herald*! With a grin, she closed up the empty store and headed down the sidewalk to the paper office. Amelia Bell, the owner's daughter, met her at the door and ushered her inside. "What can I do for you, Emily?"

"I need to place an ad in the newspaper."

Amelia grabbed a pencil and walked around the counter. "What kind of an ad?"

"Well, I'm having a sale on certain items in the store, and I. . .um. . .need to let folks know about it."

"That's a wonderful idea! The perfect way to steal back your customers."

"I'm not trying to. . ." Oh, what was the point? Of course she was trying to lure folks back to her store.

A look of expectancy crossed Amelia's features. "What items?"

Emily drew in her lip. "I'm not sure. I hadn't thought of it." She shot her gaze to Amelia. "What do you suggest?"

The other woman tapped her ink-stained fingers on the counter, staring a though she were deep in thought. Suddenly her eyes unclouded and she slappe the countertop. "I have it!"

Emily jumped at the sudden movement. "What?"

"You need to lower prices on items folks need for every day. Not boot black o things like that. But things like flour, sugar, eggs, and beans."

"Why, I can't mark all those things down. I wouldn't make a cent! I might a well put up a sign that says, COME GRAB WHATEVER YOU WANT. NO CHARGE."

"That'll bring all your customers back," Amelia said wryly. "All right. Pic two items."

"Flour and. . .let's see. . .how about flannel? Mrs. Moody was just saying th other day the price of flannel is ridiculous and how was a body to afford to dres her men warmly throughout the winter? Yes, I think flour and flannel are goo places to start." Emily grinned and repeated it. "It has a nice ring to it. The Flou and Flannel Sale. What do you think?"

A crescent grin spread across Amelia's mouth. "Catchy. We'll have folks flock ing back to Emily's Place in no time—that'll be five cents to run the ad."

Envisioning a barren Jeremiah's Mercantile while folks made a virtual ru on Emily's Place brought a smile to Emily's lips, and she gladly handed over th money.

Amelia leaned across the counter and grinned conspiratorially. "All right. No that business is out of the way, guess who asked me to the harvest dance?"

Staring at the woman who was commonly referred to as owl-faced—thoug Emily would never call her such—Emily felt her heart plummet. Amelia had bee invited to the dance? By a man? Well, that pretty much secured Emily's fate the only woman who would be escorted by her pa. She fought to squelch the tea burning just behind her eyes.

"Oh, don't look so horrified." Amelia glanced cautiously around; then, appar ently satisfied no one was listening, she whispered, "Clyde Hampton!"

"Oh my!"

"Poor man. I suppose he must be desperate if he's asking me to the dance whe everyone knows how bossy and stubborn I am." She laughed. "I told him sure I go with him but not to even bother asking me to marry him because I'm not read to settle down and become a mother to five kids."

"Well, only two are still at home," Emily replied, inwardly smarting becaus Clyde hadn't asked her. Not that she wanted to go with the red-faced sheep farme And she'd never marry him in a hundred years. Still, if he asked Amelia. . .

"Two are more than enough to convince me not to marry a man. Anywa he rescinded his offer." At that, Amelia flung back her head of chestnut hair an laughed so loud, Mr. Bell entered from the back room.

"What are you doing out here, Amelia? I'm not paying you to stand aroun and talk to your friends."

Emily knew Mr. Bell didn't approve of her association with his only daughter. He'd been aloof with her ever since Amelia cast her lot with Emily and the rest of the suffragists.

"Sorry, Pa. Emily just came in to place an ad in the paper." She held up the nickel. "Bought and paid for—just the kind of customer you like."

He gave Emily a tight smile and nodded before heading back to his presses and inks.

Amelia watched until he disappeared, then turned back to Emily. "Has anyone asked you yet?"

Yet? As if anyone would.

"No. But I always go with my pa and ma."

"I know. Because no one asks you," she said flatly. "And don't try to deny that you'd snatch up the offer to go with a decent man!"

Emily took no offense. Amelia was thoughtless and direct but not intentionally unkind. And besides, no one ever asked the newspaperwoman to dances or out for buggy rides any more than they did Emily. "I suppose you're right. I would like to at least be asked to a dance."

Amelia stared reflectively, touching her pencil to her lip. "Too bad Jeremiah always has his ma to bring everywhere." She stared reflectively. "He'd ask you if he could, I bet."

Emily's heart leaped, though she knew Amelia was wrong. "I don't know what you mean. Besides, I told you, it's easier for Pa to pick me up—the dance is in our barn this year, after all. I have to be there early to help set up the refreshment table and such."

"Whatever you say." But her face showed obvious doubt. "I'd better get this back to Pa so we can get it printed. In the meantime, I'll pass along the word about your flour and flannel sale." She grinned. "It is rather catchy, isn't it?"

Emily couldn't help but return the smile. "Very catchy. I'll be going, then. Thank you, Amelia."

"Don't mention it. We women have to stick together, don't we?"

"Yes, I suppose we do."

Emily left the newspaper office with a light heart. She walked the few feet to her mercantile and paused to stare across at Jeremiah's before unlocking her own door. The parade of customers had died down, and she could see Jeremiah through the window, staring back at her. Her cheeks flamed, but she relaxed when he gave her an easy smile and waved. She returned his wave and smiled. After all, it wouldn't do for him to think she was holding a grudge.

As she stepped into Emily's Place, she pondered Amelia's words. Would Jeremiah have asked her to the dance if he weren't escorting his ma? She allowed herself a few minutes of dreamy what-ifs until she heard the bell over the door ring. She looked up to find Clyde Hampton, hat in his hand, appearing very much as though he might want to ask a girl to a dance.

Jeremiah narrowed his gaze and shot a dark glance over the edge of his cup of apple cider while he sipped. The swirl of gaily-colored gowns circling the dance floor made him dizzy as he tried to keep his eye on Emily and Clyde Hampton.

Emily was beautiful. . .dressed in a gown of emerald silk. Watching her made him ache to cut in on the dance. But he held his ground and gulped more of the cider.

"Thirsty, Jeremiah?" Amelia Bell's voice broke through his thoughts and drew his attention away from Emily and her dance partner.

"Hmm?"

"You must be awfully thirsty," she said, amusement thick in her voice and sparkling from enormous blue eyes peeking from behind her spectacles. "That's the third cup of cider you've gulped down during Emily's waltz with ol' Clyde. Why don't you just go cut in on him?"

Jeremiah scowled at the nosy little reporter. Why didn't she just go away and bother someone else?

She laughed and patted his shoulder. "Go on, Jeremiah. You know you can't bear having another man dancing with your girl. I think she'd be grateful. We all know what kind of a dancer Clyde is—bless his heart."

"What do you mean I can't bear the thought of anyone else dancing with my girl? Em's not my girl."

"Oh, really? Maybe not formally. . ."

Jeremiah opened his mouth to protest further, but Amelia held up her hand to silence him. "I'm a newspaperwoman. It's in my blood to sniff out the things that aren't so noticeable to anyone else. Stop pouting and go cut in on Clyde before he cripples poor Emily's toes." She grabbed the mug from his hands and gave him a little shove.

Jeremiah stumbled forward onto the dance floor. Couples swirled around him throwing curious glances his way.

Locating Emily and Clyde, Jeremiah noted a wince on Emily's face. That did it! He was going to do something about that oaf trouncing all over her dainty little toes. He strode purposefully across the floor and tapped on Clyde's shoulder.

"May I?"

Reluctantly Clyde stepped back. "Th–thank you for the dance, Miss Emily."

Emily's lips tilted in a kind smile. "My pleasure, Clyde. Thank you."

Once the niceties were out of the way and Clyde strode toward the refreshment table, Emily turned expectantly to Jeremiah. He gathered a breath and slid his hand along the silk at her waist, wishing he could pull her just a little closer like the married men held their wives.

"Are you enjoying the dance so far?" she asked him.

"I am now." He stared down into her eyes and smiled. No sense in pretending. "You look lovely."

Red blotches appeared on her neck and cheeks, but he didn't mind. No other woman in the room held a candle to Emily—red blotches or not.

"Thank you, Jeremy. You look very handsome, as well."

His heart soared, and suddenly he was glad Ma had talked him into allowing her to make him a new tan jacket and trousers. His white shirt underneath was new as well, and he'd completed the look with a black string tie at his collar.

He stared down at her, wishing he could think of something else to say. For the sake of peace, they'd better steer clear of any conversation regarding the stores. But what could they talk about? They were enjoying the dance, and they'd discussed appearance.

He cleared his throat. "Nice night, isn't it?"

"Yes, it is. It's warm in here, though."

"It is. Let's go get some air."

"Miss Kitty had a new litter of kittens. Want to see them?"

Personally Jeremiah didn't care where they went as long as they went together. "Sure."

"Let me run and grab my shawl and let Ma know where I'll be. I'll meet you out front in a few minutes."

Jeremiah smiled and took her elbow as he escorted her across the dance floor. She smiled as she left to find her shawl. He stepped outside into the cool autumn evening. Stuffing his hands into his pockets, he rocked back on his heels and stared into the starry sky.

He felt someone join him and glanced, expecting to find Emily. Instead, Harold Baxter stood next to him, smoke from a cigar swirling around him as he took a puff.

"Cigar?" Harold asked, reaching into his jacket.

"No thanks," Jeremiah replied, wishing the other man would take his revolting cigar and go someplace else. Harold had never been what he considered a friend. Even during their school days, they'd never had much in common.

"Saw you dancing with Emily." The man took another puff. "Good idea. Thought I might cut in until the two of you stopped dancing."

A surge of jealousy shot through Jeremiah. "That so?"

"Yep. You two courting?"

"No. Why?" Jeremiah asked, surprised at the hostility rising in him toward the other man.

"I was thinking of asking her if I could come calling."

"Is that right?"

Harold had known Emily forever. He had married young, but his bride had died giving birth to their only child two years after the wedding. Why hadn't he tried to court Emily before now if he was interested?

Why haven't you? The words taunted him as he considered the possibility of losing Emily forever. First Clyde, now Harold. Jeremiah could see he was going to have to do something—and quick.

Jeremiah cut a glance at Harold. "I planned to ask her tonight if I could come calling." And he was going to. He'd have preferred to wait until the store was holding its own a little better, but given the alternative, he wasn't willing to take the risk.

"Well now, I guess we have ourselves a little problem, then." Harold sent him a good-natured grin.

"What sort of problem?" No one loved Emily the way he did, and Jeremiah just figured it was fitting for the other man to step aside and let him court her. If she was even willing.

"Miss Emily St. John has a lot more appeal now than she did before." He laughed. "And I don't just mean more to grab on to. But you already know that, don't you?"

Jeremiah frowned and balled his fists, ready to punch Harold if he was insulting Emily. "What sort of appeal are you referring to?" The other man could very well be innocent, in which case Jeremiah would forgive him. Emily had grown lovelier as she'd blossomed into womanhood, and the confidence she'd gained since owning the store was rather attractive, as well. Perhaps those things appealed to Harold.

"Well, you know. The store. Any man would be daft not to try to marry her now—despite her figure."

Her figure? There was nothing wrong with Emily's figure—unless a man wanted a scrawny stick of a woman. As a matter of fact, Emily was the most becoming woman in town. This man didn't deserve her, and Jeremiah had no intention of allowing him the chance to break her heart by marrying her only for her business. He was just about to say so when the other man spoke up. "Of course, there's that annoying suffragist matter. But I'll keep her too busy with our children to have time for that nonsense." He grinned and elbowed Jeremiah. "Know what I mean?"

Nearly choked with rage, Jeremiah faced him fully. "Listen here, Emily is spoken for. So you can get those ideas out of your head. And as far as the store is concerned, I've worked that place since I was twelve years old. If any man is going to run it for her, it'll be me. Not someone who doesn't know anything about storekeeping and might lose the whole thing."

Harold tossed his cigar on the ground and crushed it with his boot. "I guess we'll just have to see which of us she chooses." He extended his hand. "In the spirit of friendly competition for the fair Emily's hand in marriage and a nice profitable mercantile. . .may the best man win."

Jeremiah ignored the proffered hand and glanced away. Harold gave a short laugh. "Have it your own way."

Unable to speak for fear of saying too much, Jeremiah turned and strode toward the barn just as Amelia walked through the door on Clyde's arm. "Oh, there you are, Jeremiah," she said. "My, it is hot inside. Emily asked me to let you know it's her turn to watch the refreshment table, so she won't be able to show you the kittens after all. She didn't look too happy. As a matter of fact, she looked pretty pale and shaken."

He didn't blame her. Disappointment engulfed him, as well. "Thanks for letting me know, Amelia."

"No problem. Clyde and I were just coming out for a breath of fresh air anyway. Weren't we, Clyde?" The sheep farmer glanced down at the little woman on his arm and grinned broadly.

"We sure were, Miss Amelia."

"Ta-ta, Jeremiah."

Jeremiah watched them go, wishing it were Emily on his arm. He shrugged and headed toward the barn. At least the cider was good.

⌒

Emily stiffened her spine at the sight of Jeremiah heading toward the refreshment table. She'd traded shifts with Hope just for the excuse not to go outside with him, but it appeared she wouldn't be able to escape his presence after all.

"If anyone is going to run Emily's store for her, it'll be me."

She'd been standing just behind the door when Harold Baxter began his insulting discourse. At first she'd thought Jeremiah might defend her, but that statement had been all she could take. Shaking inside from fury and heartbreak, Emily could barely bring herself to meet Jeremiah's gaze.

"I'm sorry we couldn't see the kittens," he said. "Another time, maybe?"

Was this where he asked her if he could come courting?

"I don't know, Jeremiah. After all, I don't live here anymore." She filled a cup with cider and handed it to a thirsty child who smiled his thanks and bounded away.

"That's true, I suppose. Actually, what I meant was. . ." He cleared his throat. "Think I could have a cup of that cider?"

Grudgingly Emily handed him some.

He gulped it down. "Thanks."

"What I actually meant was. . ."

"Evening, Miss Emily." Emily ignored Jeremiah's sudden scowl and forced herself to smile at Harold as he approached the refreshment table.

"Good evening, Harold. Would you like some cider?"

He leaned over the table and smiled what appeared to be an earnest smile, flashing beautifully white teeth. But Emily knew exactly what lurked behind his handsome face. A sneaky, low-down scoundrel out to take away her business. And she'd never forgive him for calling the cause nonsense.

Jeremiah shifted from one foot to the other. "Yes or no, Baxter."

"Excuse me?" The hostility in Harold's tone was unmistakable. Jeremiah stepped closer—an obvious challenge.

Emily had always dreamed of what it might be like for men to fight over her, but there was absolutely nothing flattering about having two men fighting over who got to steal her business out from under her while she stayed home and ironed his shirts!

"Do you want apple cider or not? Emily doesn't have all day while you think about it."

Harold turned his melting smile upon her. She might have found it tempting twenty minutes ago, but now she knew what he was about, and she refused to be taken in by flashing white teeth and a handsome face.

"Did you make it, Emily?" he asked.

Barely able to remain civil, Emily dipped some of the sweet liquid for Harold. "No, I didn't. I am much too busy running my own store to bother with things like apple cider. Now if you two gentlemen will excuse me. I'm afraid I need to attend to others who might want refreshments."

"Of course." Harold took her hand and brought it to his lips. "May I have the honor of dancing the last waltz with you later?"

"Now wait just a minute," Jeremiah broke in. "I already started to ask her for the last dance."

Emily glanced from one would-be husband to the next. "T–to tell you the truth," she said, fighting to keep back tears of humiliation, "I'm not feeling well. I believe I'll just go to the house now. You'll both have to find another dance partner for that waltz."

"All right," Harold said in that silky voice that Emily had always found so appealing until now. "You go lie down. I'll talk to you soon." He strode away and caught hold of young Charity Smythe and whirled her onto the dance floor.

"Good night, Jeremiah," Emily said, hoping he'd take the hint. Instead, he frowned and swept his gaze over her face.

"You do look pale." Before she could move, Jeremiah brought his hand to her forehead. "You're warm, too. Stay here. I'm going to go grab Sam and have him take a look at you."

"Oh, Jeremiah. Don't bother my brother. He's so busy doctoring this town, I haven't seen him having such a good time in so long."

Jeremiah hesitated. "All right, but promise me if you don't feel better tomorrow, you'll let him examine you."

Emily had to marvel at her change in perspective. If Jeremiah had shown this sort of concern before she learned the truth of his intentions, she might have honestly thought he cared. Now she realized he was only watching out for his interests. After all, if something were seriously wrong with her, she might not be around to marry him. Then Emily's Place would never be his. Fighting to hold back tears, Emily grabbed her shawl from the chair behind her and whipped it around her shoulders. "Will you watch the table for me until I can find Hope?"

"I'd rather walk you to the house. You shouldn't be alone." The concern edging his voice was nothing short of dramatic genius, and even Emily was almost fooled into thinking he might actually care. Then reality bit hard as Harold waltzed by and grinned at her, despite the beauty in his arms.

"I'll be fine. And I'd prefer to be alone, if you don't mind." Giving him no chance to further protest, Emily headed toward the door. Let him find his own replacement at the table. It served him right if he had to dip up apple cider for all the thirsty dancers. She fairly flew to the house, fighting to keep the tears at bay until she was alone. Once she reached her old bedroom and threw herself across the bed, full-blown sobs wracked her body.

Oh, Jeremiah, why?

God, why did You make me the way I am? Couldn't You have given me even one attribute that might cause a man to think me worth loving?

Chapter 6

"How on earth could you run out of sugar a week before Christmas, Em?"

Standing before the shelf that only a month ago had been laden with bags of sugar, Emily stared at the barrenness. Her cheeks burned under Ma's incredulous gaze. Why, oh why hadn't she listened when Jeremiah suggested she stock up?

Pride. That's all it had been. Stinking, sinful pride. And now she was paying the price for her stubbornness. But for mercy's sake, how could she possibly have known he was trying to help her, after he'd been underselling her for the past few weeks? She'd thought—and quite reasonably in her opinion—that he was simply trying to get her to overstock.

But she couldn't admit that to Ma. "I can get a shipment the first week after Christmas," Emily said, knowing full well that wasn't soon enough.

Ma drew in her lower lip and shook her head in helpless appeal. "I'm sorry, honey, but I'm afraid I have no choice but to buy what I need from Jeremiah. You know we'll have your brothers and sister and their families at the ranch on Christmas. We simply have to have plenty of goodies for the children."

Tears welled up in Emily's eyes, but she looked away. "I completely understand." She gave an airy laugh. "Jeremiah has plenty in stock. I saw him unloading an extra supply just the other day."

Obviously not a bit fooled by Emily's bravado, Ma gave her a sympathetic smile. "I promise not to spend so much as a penny over the cost of the sugar." She kissed Emily on the cheek and headed for the door.

"Give Jeremiah my best, and be sure to tell him I sent you over." It would do no good at all for him to imagine her sulking because he was getting all her business.

"I will, honey," Ma said, waving.

With resentment, Emily watched her through the store window. Ma stopped to talk to Mrs. Thomas midway across the street. Mindless of the winter chill, Emily snatched up her broom and stomped to the front step, glaring at Jeremiah's false storefront.

My own ma, racing over to help the competition run me out of business. Honestly, the lack of loyalty was shameful. Of course, the thought of Christmas without Ma's sugar cookies or apple tarts was every bit the tragedy as sending a little business to Jeremy.

⌒

With a silent groan, Jeremiah watched Cassidy St. John heading across the street to his store. Sugar. He knew the only reason any of Emily's loyal family would be coming to Jeremiah's would be a shortage of one unavoidable item or another. In this case, it must be the sugar he had quite selflessly warned Emily to stock up on. But she had, as usual, failed to take his advice; and as a result, he'd practically had a run on the stuff.

Even now, he could see Em standing outside pretending to sweep, but anger was evidenced in the beating her broom took against the wooden step. He smiled to himself as a plan entered his mind; and from sheer glee, he extended his wide grin to one of his own loyal customers—compliments of Ma's League of Christian Women and their boycott of the "mannish" Emily St. John.

The last thought brought a chuckle to his lips. Emily—mannish.

"Let me take that crate out to the wagon for you, Mrs. Moody."

The elderly woman beamed up at him from rosy cheeks and lovely, though faded, blue eyes. *She must have been a real beauty in her day,* Jeremiah thought as she slipped a bony, veined hand through the crook of his arm and they walked slowly out the door.

What would Emily look like when she was old? Every bit as lovely, to be sure. He'd love the chance to find out, except that for some reason, ever since the harvest dance, Emily refused to so much as give him the time of day. He'd tried numerous times to have a chat with her, but she consistently evaded his efforts.

Once, he'd drummed up the courage to request the honor of escorting her to Sunday service and she'd politely refused, stating she saw no reason to dirty up the Lord's Day with pretense and deceit.

Still puzzled, Jeremiah shook his head at the memory. He'd been trying to figure it out ever since but still found himself no closer to understanding her meaning than when she'd said it two weeks ago.

"Looks like you're doing quite well for yourself, Mr. Daniels," Mrs. Moody was saying. "We're all so pleased and proud at how you turned out, in spite of your early raisin'."

She patted his arm and let go as Mr. Moody climbed down and held out his hand to help her into the wagon.

Jeremiah stiffened at the reference to his childhood. Would there ever be those in town who couldn't remember his pa? Pa didn't even have drunkenness as an excuse. He had just been mean. That was the hardest reality for Jeremiah to wrap his mind around.

"Good morning, Mr. and Mrs. Moody!" Cassidy's cheery voice hailed the elderly couple as she stepped up to the wooden sidewalk in front of the store. Jeremiah welcomed her with a smile, relieved at the interruption. He didn't want to go down another winding road of dark and oppressive memory. Not now. Not ever. But sometimes the thoughts came; and when they did, he was hard-pressed to remember St. Paul's instructions to bring "into captivity every thought to the obedience of Christ."

"Cassidy St. John. I never expected to see you on this side of the street," Mrs. Moody said with a chuckle.

"I'm afraid my daughter has sold out of sugar; and with the children coming next week for Christmas, I have quite a bit of baking to do." She smiled at Jeremiah. "She sent me to her old pal, with her blessing."

Jeremiah kept his expression as passive as he could, knowing just how hard it had been for Emily to send anyone, let alone her own mother, to his mercantile.

"That's my pal. Not a competitive bone in her body." He offered Cassidy his arm. "Shall we go inside and get you that sugar, Mrs. St. John?"

"Certainly. Good day," she said to the elderly couple before slipping her hand inside the crook of his arm.

Cassidy released him as soon as they entered the store. She looked nervously about, as though she felt like a traitor.

Jeremiah's heart went out to her, and he decided now was as good a time as any to implement his plans. "Mrs. St. John, can you wait until later for the sugar?"

She snapped to attention, her eyes widening. "You're not out, too?"

"No. I have plenty. And I plan to sell Emily half of my stock. So you see, there's no need for you to buy it from me."

The delight on Cassidy's face brought heat to Jeremiah's neck. She touched his arm. "That's quite chivalrous of you. I know Emily will appreciate it a great deal."

Even if Jeremiah were a betting man, he wouldn't take that wager. Emily would be madder than a bull caught in a fence and would most likely refuse his offer, but he smiled and nodded. "Yes, ma'am. Tell Em I'll be over later with half my stock."

"Maybe you'd better just tell her yourself." Cassidy gave him a rueful grin. "And while you're at it, ask her to put back ten pounds for me. I'll send Will in for it tomorrow."

Jeremiah waited until five o'clock and loaded a wheelbarrow with bags of sugar, then gathered a deep breath and headed over to Emily's Place.

～

Emily heard the bell above the door ding. Another customer she would have to send over to Jeremiah. She sighed and headed to the front of the store, stopping short at the sight that greeted her.

"What on earth?" Emily gasped. "Jeremiah! You—you're getting snow all over my floor! I demand you get that wheelbarrow outside this minute!"

Jeremiah let go of the wheelbarrow and straightened his back. He glanced around, then gave her a sheepish smile. "Sorry about the mud."

"What do you think you're doing?"

"Bringing you half my stock of sugar."

"I refuse to accept it!" She wouldn't accept charity from any man. Mrs. Thomas would never let her hear the end of it.

He grinned. "I'm not giving it to you. I'm selling it. At a profit to myself, of course." He named his price.

"Why, that's highway robbery!" Emily planted her hands indignantly on her hips. "I won't make a penny on it."

"At least you won't lose any more business. You know your customers are coming to me for sugar, but that's not all they're buying. I've cleaned up this week, thanks to your redheaded stubbornness."

Emily's temper flared, but she checked it. Even selling the sugar to her at a raised price, Jeremy wouldn't make as much as if he'd kept it for himself. The least she could do was swallow her pride and have the grace to thank him.

"I appreciate your generosity, Jeremiah."

He raised his brow in surprise, then his expression relaxed into a gentle smile. "It's my pleasure."

Emily cleared her throat and straightened her spine. "But remember, I didn't ask for your help." She willed her pulse to slow to normal. She had to remember that Jeremiah's kindness had nothing to do with his feelings for her. He was only trying to woo her in order to get his hands on the mercantile.

He chuckled. "Don't worry. If anyone asks, I'll make sure they know you had to pay a hefty price for the sugar."

Although she tried her best to resist, laughter bubbled to her lips at the teasing glint in his eyes. Jeremiah understood perfectly well. He was more than a hero. He was a silent hero. She watched out the window as he pushed the wheelbarrow back to his store. In moments, he reappeared at his door and headed back in her direction. He waited for an oncoming wagon to pass before he crossed the street. Emily smiled. Yes, he was quite the hero.

She walked across the room and opened the door for him. The snowy air added just the right atmosphere for the Christmas season. She stepped into the frigid December air and frowned. Amelia Bell stood next to Jeremiah, obviously fishing for a tidbit of juicy news to print in her pa's newspaper. Emily wasn't sure how she felt about her so-called friend gaining recognition as Harper's first woman reporter. After all, her claim to fame so far had come at Emily's expense. Staring at the pixie-faced, bespectacled young woman, Emily remembered every article.

> PRICE WAR! Head to Emily's Place for the best price on flour this week; but be careful, if you're looking for grain seed, take a short walk across the street, and Jeremiah's will set you up right nicely.

Or the time Emily had ordered the orange-striped bonnets and material to match. Emily's cheeks burned at the memory.

> Anyone looking for a costume for Mrs. Taylor's masquerade ball next month, consider the new bonnets at Emily's Place. You're sure to win the prize for most atrocious getup.

And Emily didn't even want to think about the time she had decided Harper needed a little refinement. She'd decided to order fresh seafood. Twenty pounds of dead lobsters arrived much overdue after the train carrying them derailed and overturned.

Don't panic, good citizens of Harper. Large, red bugs aren't taking over our town. Hoping to tempt our taste buds, Emily's Place planned to offer lobster as an alternative to our common cuisine. Unfortunately, she didn't take into consideration the possibility of the train derailing.

Emily's humiliation had been complete when three schoolboys had swiped one of the odious shellfish and placed it on their new teacher's chair when she wasn't looking. In an uproar and quite in plain view, Miss Larkins had stomped over, deceased lobster in hand, and flung it on the counter, insisting Emily remove the temptation from her young students before the rest of the unfortunate lobsters ended up cleverly placed in various regions of the school.

Emily had waited until nightfall and grabbed her shovel. Jeremiah arrived and silently took the shovel from her. Without a word, he buried every one of those smelly things—deep enough so the dogs couldn't dig them up. Emily smiled at the memory. When he finished, he handed her the shovel, tweaked her nose, and left, never once scolding her for her unrealistic idea. Times such as those nearly convinced Emily that Jeremiah cared for her. But the memory of his conversation with Harold always brought her back to reality.

Emily watched him now, sidestepping Amelia's questions as to why the proprietor of one store would be bringing a shipment to his competition.

Jeremiah nudged his way around Emily and stepped into the mercantile. He sent her a silent plea for help. Emily grinned, tempted to let him handle the nosy reporter on his own, but her conscience got the better of her. Under the circumstances, the least she could do was head Amelia off.

"Morning, Amelia. Out for another fine story today?"

"Oh, Emily. Jeremiah won't say a word. Tell me why on earth he is bringing you bags of sugar." She raised her voice slightly and cast a glance at Jeremiah as he stepped back through the door. "If you don't tell me, I'll be forced to assume."

"Assume what?" Emily asked.

"Oh, I don't know." Amelia tapped her lip with her forefinger, her eyes twinkling merrily. "Let me see. . . . Emily's Place has run out of a most important commodity during the holiday season and rather than profit at her expense, Jeremiah Daniels has put aside any hint of rivalry in the spirit of the season. . .or has he done so for another reason?"

A gasp escaped Emily's lips. "Don't you dare make implications about Jeremiah in that newspaper. He is helping me out because he's a decent man."

"And because I don't want to be called Scrooge a week before Christmas."

Jeremiah flashed a heart-stopping grin as he unloaded the wheelbarrow.

Amelia gave Emily a knowing glance. "And of course because everyone knows you two are sweet on each other. There must be a headline in that. Sweet. . .sugar. How about, SUGAR ISN'T THE ONLY THING SWEET GOING ON BETWEEN EMILY'S PLACE AND JEREMIAH'S?"

Emily gasped. "Why, Amelia Bell! If you print that, I'll flat out deny it even if I have to place an ad in your pa's paper myself. And. . .and I'll never, ever place another advertisement in the *Herald*."

"Oh, Emily. Don't be silly. I'm teasing. I report real news. What do I care who you're courting?"

Stamping her foot in frustration, Emily glared. "We are not courting." She grabbed Jeremiah's arm as he stepped toward them, obviously intent on ducking out and leaving Emily to deal with Amelia. "Will you please tell her exactly why you are selling me half your sugar stock, Jeremy?"

Looking like an animal caught in a trap, Jeremiah swallowed hard. "Just the spirit of Christmas, I suppose."

"And he's charging me a hefty sum," Emily huffed, rather put out with Jeremiah for forcing her to be the one to mention the price while he stood looking like St. Nicholas bearing gifts. She gave him the fiercest of frowns and then turned back to the reporter. "Make sure you print that."

Jeremiah headed through the door. "Amelia."

"Yes?"

"You were right."

"What about?"

He grinned at Emily. "I am sweet on her. And you can print that, as well." Before Emily could recover, he wheeled down the board he'd thrown over the steps, laid the board across the wheelbarrow, and went back to his store.

Amelia tossed back her head and let out a hearty laugh. "There you have it, Emily. I told you he was smitten. What do you have to say about that?" She followed Emily back inside. "I'll bet he proposes by New Year."

"It doesn't matter when he proposes. My answer will be no."

"Are you crazy?" Amelia grabbed a bag of sugar and slid it on the counter. "Why on earth are you playing coy with Jeremiah? Are you honestly considering playing hard to get at your age?"

Emily sent her a scowl. "You don't know all the facts, Amelia. Trust me when I say I am not playing games. I have my reasons for keeping Jeremiah at bay; and I have no intention of sharing those intentions with a newspaper reporter, so you may as well get that inquisitive look off your face."

The hopeful expression on Amelia's face dropped like that of a disappointed child.

Emily sent her an indulgent smile. "How about telling me about you and Clyde? He's been escorting you to church quite a bit since the dance. Rumor has it you're courting quite regularly."

A pretty blush crossed Amelia's cheeks. "I suppose ol' Clyde's not so bad after all. And he says I can work for Pa two days a week even after we're married as long as the boys are in school."

"Oh, Amelia, how wonderful. I'm so thrilled for you!"

And she was truly happy for her friend, but her heart ached just a little with the knowledge that there seemed to be love for everyone but her. It appeared the best she could hope for was a man who wanted her mainly for her business. But listening to Amelia's happy plans, for the first time Emily was beginning to wonder if perhaps it would be worth giving up the store to become Jeremiah's wife.

But could she honestly live with the knowledge that she was nothing more than a means to an end for him?

Her frustrated huff earned her a surprised glance from Amelia.

Emily gave her an apologetic smile. No, she wanted true love. And while she'd happily share the store with a man who loved her, she refused to simply give it away to a gold digger.

Chapter 7

The day after Christmas, Jeremiah stood in the middle of his store, nostrils flared. Anger tore through him like an eagle's talons as he glanced around the disorderly store. He'd been the victim of a break-in. Who on earth had done such a thing?

He gathered a breath and straightened an overturned barrel. Thankfully it had only been filled with an assortment of garden tools rather than pickles or something equally messy.

As he set the room in order, Jeremiah mentally took stock of the items on the shelves and tables. He sent up a prayer of thanks that he routinely emptied the cash box each night, so there had been no money for a thief to take. Casting another quick glance from one end of the room to the other, he reached back and kneaded his neck.

Not a thing had been stolen. As a matter of fact. . .

Perplexed, he strode the length of the room for a closer look at the bags of sugar piled in front of the counter. He scratched his head, trying to grasp the fact that there were twice as many as when he had left work on Christmas Eve.

Had Emily brought back her unsold bags? Immediately he rejected the ludicrous thought. Why would she break in to do that? And besides, she had sent her little sister Hope over with payment in full the day after he'd made his delivery.

Though it made no sense, he had to conclude someone had broken into both stores—had stolen from Emily and given to him.

He glanced through the window to Emily's Place. Had she found a similar mess when she arrived this morning? Knowing how easily she became frightened, Jeremiah set his lips into a grim line and debated whether he should go over there or not. The thought of her afraid made his heart clench and settled the matter. After making sure the door was securely locked, Jeremiah strode across the street and climbed the steps to the familiar store. He reached for the doorknob, then hesitated as he remembered the look of horror on Emily's face when he'd admitted his feelings. What had possessed him to reveal such a thing, he'd never know. . .not in a million years. But he certainly didn't relish the idea of Emily railing at him about it. It was probably a blessing that she'd have something else upon which to focus her attention.

Taking a deep breath, he opened the door. Emily stood in the center of the store, sweeping up what looked to be sugar from the wood floor.

She glared. "Really, Jeremiah. If you didn't want to sell me the sugar, all you had to do was ask for it back."

Jeremiah gaped. "You think I did this?"

A shrug lifted her shoulders. "Who else? I assume you sold out and didn't want to lose money until the supply train arrives at the end of the week. Now if you'll excuse me, I've lost an hour's business because of this mess. And it appears I have a customer."

Emily leaned the broom against the wall. When she turned around, her face showed about as much warmth as the ice hanging from the barn awnings this morning. "I'll thank you to return your key." To her credit, she lowered her voice as the bell dinged above the door.

Jeremiah scowled at his inability to defend himself as Amelia Bell stepped through the door.

"Good morning, Jeremiah," she said, a smirk tipping the corners of her lips. "Aren't you on the wrong side of the street?"

"Yes, I think so," he said, striding purposefully toward the door.

Emily was the most stubborn, pigheaded woman he'd ever known. How in the world could she imagine he'd steal back his own sugar? With a scowl, Jeremiah snatched open the door. For now, he'd get his own store ready for customers, and he'd come back later to return her sugar—and the key he'd held to Tucker's Mercantile since he was a kid.

"Good day, ladies."

Emily's "harrumph" followed him out the door and down the steps. It stayed in his mind all the way across the street, fueling his indignation into an angry fire. By the time he unlocked his door and grabbed his apron, Jeremiah was downright mad. Who did Miss Emily St. John think she was, accusing him of stealing from her? It was so ridiculous that it might have been funny, except that he never would have dreamed she could think so little of him.

His mind returned to the last time Emily had confronted him for stealing. . . only that time it had been warranted.

They had been ten years old, and even then she was the only girl he cared anything about. During a short devotional at school, Jeremiah had been pricked by the Holy Spirit and had admitted to stealing sourballs from Tucker's.

Emily's shock had pierced Jeremiah's heart like an arrow, but he'd known from that time on he'd never steal again. . . . And he had given his heart to Jesus that day.

Did she think his faith was nothing more than a cover? She must believe him to be a fake, a hypocrite.

The thought cut him deeply.

Throughout the rest of the day, Jeremiah had difficulty concentrating on his customers as he pondered who was behind the silly robbery. More and more, he was coming to believe it must have been a schoolboy prank. Who else but an ornery boy would go to the trouble?

The more he thought about it, the more the whole situation struck a familiar chord. He grinned. From the standpoint of a child, it was sort of funny—a stroke of prank genius, stealing from one store and putting the goods in the other store.

Maybe he could get Emily to see it from that perspective. He doubted it. But maybe. . .

Emily's face warmed, and she tried, without success, to remove the memory of her awful words to Jeremiah. How on earth could she accuse him of stealing anything, let alone something he'd been kind enough to share in the first place? Of course he had charged her a vulgar sum for the sugar when the truly charitable thing to do would have been to give it to her at cost; but then, he was a businessman and a good one at that. A rueful grin tipped the corners of her lips, though there was no one around to witness. Under the same circumstances, she most likely would have charged him the same.

And if she was honest with herself, she'd have to admit that her anger toward him was rooted in the fact that she already resented him for his intentions toward her and the store. She was holding a huge grudge; and while she wasn't quite ready to lower her guard where his pretend affections were concerned, she could at least apologize for accusing him of stealing.

With a glance at the clock, Emily noted there were only three minutes until closing time. She wanted to see Jeremiah before he locked up and headed toward his farm. He deserved an apology.

Emily grabbed her key and walked toward the door. Snow had begun to fall early in the day. Already the ground was quilted in the white fluff.

On a whim, she rubbed a circle on the frosty window and ventured a glance across the street, which seemed eerily still except for the occasional wagon rattling along, forming double trails in the fresh snow. Daylight had faded, giving way to a smoky twilight, which promised another moonless night.

Emily shuddered and debated the idea of going out alone. Just as she made up her mind to stay inside where it was warm, Jeremiah appeared in his window. Emily gasped and stepped back, then chided herself for her own silliness. She lifted her arm and returned his wave.

Observing him now as he watched the snow falling to the street outside, Emily decided to make a trip to Jeremiah's after all. But she'd have to hurry if she was to return home before complete darkness settled over the quiet town. Propriety demanded she not remain alone with Jeremiah in a darkened room. Regardless of the Equal Suffrage Association's outcry that women should have the freedom to decide for themselves what constituted a compromising situation, Emily didn't want to put herself or Jeremiah in that position.

At the thought of impropriety, she was about to change her mind yet again when Jeremiah gave her another wave.

"All right, Lord. Of course I know Jeremiah deserves an apology. I'll take his showing up in the window as Your way of telling me not to put off what needs to be said."

Before she could grab her cape, the bell dinged. She turned to see Mr. Moody stomping snow from his boots against the rag rugs in front of the door. "Evening," he said. "That cold wind cuts right to the bone."

"What can I get for you?"

"The missus says her shoulder's aching something fierce. You know what that means. Means we're about to have a storm, and she's out of yarn for knitting. Says she can't be sitting for days without something to occupy her fingers."

Emily's lips twitched. Mrs. Moody and her aching shoulder had been predicting storms with about a 10 percent accuracy rating for as long as she could remember, but Mr. Moody never failed to believe her predictions.

She finished with the elderly man, then grabbed her cape from behind the counter. Steeling herself against what was sure to be a blast of cold, Emily stepped outside. She wrapped her arms about her waist as the wind bit into her. Mr. Moody had been right about the biting wind. In moments, the snow had gone from soft flakes to a swirling mass of white.

By the time Emily reached the middle of the street, she was shivering violently. Alarm seized her as the wind picked up and whipped mercilessly at her skirts, twisting them about her legs. She stumbled but caught her balance just in time to avoid plunging headlong into the snowy street.

She braved a glance up, the snow stinging her eyes and cheeks. The soft glow from Jeremiah's window provided a beacon for her against the blinding white.

Only a few more steps and I will be there. The thought urged her legs to move forward. The door opened just as she stepped up onto the icy boardwalk.

"Emily!" Jeremiah's voice sent waves of relief through her. "What were you thinking, heading out in this storm?" he admonished.

"I–I'm f–f–fine," she replied, grateful to be ushered inside the warm store, which smelled of saddle oil and sawdust. "I h–have to tell you something."

He led her to a chair next to a beautiful coal-burning stove. "Here, sit down and warm up, then you can tell me what you risked frostbite to say. I'll be back." He walked to the window, looked out, then returned to where Emily sat. He smiled, but not before Emily observed his clouded expression and knew the snow worried him.

Jeremiah grabbed a mug from the shelf behind the counter and filled it with steaming coffee, which simmered on the stove. Emily gratefully accepted the mug, relishing the warmth against her half-frozen fingers.

"Thank you."

Jeremiah perched on a pickle barrel near the stove. He folded his arms across his chest and stretched his long legs out in front of him. He regarded her, his expression soft and welcoming—not at all what Emily would have expected from a man wrongly accused as he faced his accuser.

Emily found herself at a loss for words as she stared into his brown eyes.

"What brings you here on a night like this?" he prompted.

Dropping her gaze to the mug, Emily fought against sudden tears of remorse. "I just. . ." She gathered a steadying breath and raised her chin, meeting his gaze. "I wanted to apologize for my rudeness this morning."

A tender smile curved his full lips, and Emily's stomach turned a somersault. "It's big of you to come by. But it wasn't necessary."

"It was. You're not a thief, and I had no right to make the accusation." She shook her head. "Sometimes I just don't know why I say the things I do, Jeremiah." Emily's gaze sought his. "You've known me since we were children. Why do I always have to be the one who spouts in anger, only to regret it the next moment?"

"I don't know, Em. But if it's bothering you, maybe you should learn to think before you speak. God will help you if you're honest about wanting to change."

Emily stiffened under the criticism but relaxed as she studied his expression and found no malice. Releasing a heavy sigh, she nodded. "You're right."

His brow shot up, and his mouth widened into a grin. "Too bad Amelia's not here to hear you. That has to be newsworthy."

In spite of herself, Emily giggled. "It's probably not as interesting as the crate of dead lobsters."

Jeremiah's pleasant laugh rang throughout the store, filling Emily with contentment. She added her laughter to his, and not until tears clouded her eyes did she gain control of her mirth.

"I don't remember the last time I laughed so hard. My sides absolutely ache." She smiled up at him, relishing the pleasantness of his returning smile.

He cleared his throat and stood. "Well, I'd better get you back across the street before it gets any darker. We don't want tongues wagging, do we?"

Emily's heart plummeted. Though she knew he was right, she couldn't help but feel a little let down. If only it were possible, she could have spent hours sitting in front of the stove and laughing with Jeremiah.

With a nod, she stood and handed him the mug. "Thank you for the coffee."

He set the cup on the counter, grinned, and looked about to speak when a blast of wind shook the store and the door blew open. Emily gasped as the snow swirled inside. Jeremiah hastened across the room and forced the door shut against the strong wind.

"I'd better hurry before that storm gets any worse," Emily said, dreading the thought of going out into the fierce snow.

"Emily," Jeremiah said hesitantly, "you can't go out in this."

"What do you mean? I have to go out, or I can't get home."

"Listen to that wind. I barely got the door closed. You wouldn't stand up for a second out there. I'm sorry, but there's no choice. You'll have to stay here until the storm is over." He motioned her back to the stove.

"It's dark out there! I can't stay any longer." Emily jerked away and headed back to the door.

Jeremiah caught her by her arms and demanded her gaze, his eyes showing fear. "I couldn't see past the walk outside. If you go outside, you'll be lost before you've gone five feet. How many times have you heard of friends and neighbors getting lost in a blizzard, only to be found a few feet from their house when the storm is over?"

Emily wilted against him as though all her fight was gone at the truth of his words.

"But how can you even suggest I stay here, considering your mother is the president of the League of Christian Women? What on earth would she and the rest of the league have to say about me? The things they already say are bad enough." She despised the break in her voice, but pretending the harsh judgments didn't hurt was impossible. Especially when facing the probability of even harsher judgments should she remain alone with a man—let alone Mrs. Daniels's son—for even minutes past dark.

Jeremiah regarded her with a tender smile, then he grabbed his coat, gloves, a hat, and a scarf.

"What are you doing?" Emily asked.

"You're right. We can't stay here together. It isn't possible to get you across the street safely, so I'm going to feel along the wall outside. The jail's only two doors down. I can make it there and pass the time with the sheriff. If you have to stay here until morning, use whatever you need from the shelves to stay comfortable. There's extra coal in back for the stove."

Knowing there was no other choice, Emily walked him to the door. "B–be careful, Jeremy."

He winked, sending her heart soaring. "I'll be fine."

Minutes later he returned, his eyelashes frosted with ice, his cheeks red. His teeth chattered, and he shivered violently as he made his way to the stove and stood as close as he could, trying to get warm. When he could talk, he gave her a soulful smile. "I'm sorry, Emily. Jail's closed up and locked. I couldn't get in. We're going to have to stay here together."

"B–but what about your ma?"

"Let me handle my ma. I'll do everything I can to ensure your reputation is intact when the storm blows over. Maybe the snow will stop soon, and we can get you home before anyone even knows."

The thought was of little comfort, considering how the wind howled outside. "Please, Jeremiah." Emily made no effort to hide the tears welling in her eyes. "You can't imagine what it's like to be an outcast."

He started to reach for her, then apparently thought better of it and dropped his arm to his side. "Honey, I'm sorry, but you've lived in these parts long enough to know a blizzard when you see one. We'll have to wait it out and hope folks understand. And who knows? It could let up soon and I'll walk you home."

Emily heard his words, but she refused to entertain the thought that it was now past twilight and she and Jeremiah were alone.

Chapter 8

To Jeremiah, almost as worrisome as the raging storm outside was the sight of Emily huddled against the far wall. Worse still was the knowledge that she did so for fear he might get too close. She'd sat there for the last three hours, shivering and hugging her body tightly in an effort to foster warmth from her own arms.

"This is ridiculous, Em. Come over by the stove and warm up. You know I'm not going to touch you."

She sat up straighter and spoke through chattering teeth. "If anyone comes to find me, it'll look better if I'm all the way across the room from you." She sent him a knowing look. "Less opportunity for folks to talk."

Jeremiah surveyed the frost-covered wall behind her, wishing for all he was worth that he'd taken better care to insulate the store rather than trying to cut costs. "You'll freeze to death before anyone has a chance to talk if you stay over there."

She jerked her chin up and leveled her green-eyed gaze at him. "At least I'll die with my reputation intact."

"Have it your way." With a chuckle, he grabbed a couple of coats from the table and strode across the room. Allowing for no objections, he placed them over her until she was covered from chin to toes. "But if it's all the same to you, I'd just as soon you live to enjoy the favor of the good townspeople."

"Thank you, Jeremiah." Emily's smile almost undid his resolve to keep his distance. Quickly he moved back to the window and glanced out at the angry storm.

The wind howled with vicious fervor and shook the store, rattling the front window until Jeremiah feared it might not hold up.

"I'm going to have to board up that glass," he said, more to himself than to Emily.

"I think you'd better. I certainly hope my glass holds up. I dread the thought of what I might find when the storm quits." Emily stood and carefully laid the coats in a pile. "In any case, I'll help you get yours covered. That'll give us something to do for a while."

"Thanks," Jeremiah replied, wishing he could gather her into his arms and melt away the look of worry from her eyes. "I could use it."

He strode to the storeroom and retrieved four large slats.

"Where did those come from?"

"Lionel McDonald ordered these. He intends to build a small house this spring."

"He ordered a shipment of wood from you?" Emily's eyes flashed in sudden outrage. "Why, I'd have sold it to him at a better price. I don't see why he's wasting money anyway. Most young couples start off in soddies or sandstone homes."

"The soon-to-be Mrs. McDonald flatly refuses to live in a soddy. And I highly doubt the young groom wants to take time to haul enough sandstone from the creek for a house. He'll gladly part with the money to make her happy."

"Why do you suppose his new bride isn't coming until summer?" Emily asked.

Distracted by her wrinkled nose and brow crinkled in thought, Jeremiah failed to stop and weigh his words. "She's waiting until her sister gives birth and gains her strength, from what I understand."

Emily pinkened, and Jeremiah suppressed a smile. She might be a forward-thinking woman, but even Emily-the-suffragette couldn't escape the modesty of a gentle upbringing. She cleared her throat. "Oh, well, I suppose that's understandable."

Jeremiah handed her the bag of nails and a hammer. "Hold these until I ask for them, okay?"

With a nod, she accepted the items, and they worked together in silence until the window was covered. Jeremiah only prayed that the wind didn't shatter the glass on the other side of the boards. Replacing it would be an expense he certainly didn't need.

"That ought to do it." He stepped back to survey their handiwork. He took the nail bag and hammer from Emily and put them away in the storeroom. When he returned, Emily was standing next to the stove, her hands stretched toward the little warmth offered.

"It's getting colder in here," he mused. "I'm sorry. But I think it's best to conserve coal as much as possible. How about covering up?"

Emily nodded. She grabbed two coats from the pile by the wall and handed him one. "You, too."

His heart lurched, and he knew he could no more have refused to accept the gesture than the wind could fail to blow if God so ordained. His gaze captured hers; and to his amazement, she didn't look away. On the contrary, she seemed as mesmerized as he. Jeremiah drew in a sharp breath, and a shiver slid up his spine as he made a startling discovery. Did Emily care for him? Was it even possible that she felt the way he did?

Her eyes welcomed him to become lost in their green depths, and he knew he was treading dangerous waters. Better to be in the blizzard than faced with the temptation that presented itself to him at this moment—the woman of his heart who could very likely be forced to share the same building for the night, if the storm didn't let up soon.

Suddenly Jeremiah was faced with a weakness he had no idea afflicted him. If Emily had remained haughty or angry or even fragile, he might never have considered the fullness of her lips or the roundness of her figure. He might never have imagined pulling her to him and kissing her, holding her. But his mind grabbed on to the image, and he couldn't let it go. Wordlessly, he stared. He took a step toward her, fully aware he should be moving in the other direction.

"Jeremiah?" Even in a shaky whisper, his name had never sounded so sweet coming from any other lips. "Please don't come any closer."

He closed his eyes to gain control.

Help us, Lord. Deliver us from evil and temptation. We both belong to You, and neither of us would choose to be in a situation where we might sin against You.

In an instant, his stomach grumbled loudly.

He opened his eyes. Emily giggled. And the moment passed.

"I reckon I'm hungry," he announced with a grin. "Let's see what I can find for us." Still fighting to gain control over his raw emotions, Jeremiah surveyed the shelves critically, thankful for the excuse to focus on anything but Emily. "We can open a can of beans."

Emily wrinkled her nose. "There's always candy," Jeremiah said, unable to suppress his grin.

"Licorice sticks for supper. Every child's dream." Emily good-naturedly helped herself from a jar on the counter.

"There's always a chance the storm will let up; but in case it doesn't, we should face the possibility of being here for a couple of days." Jeremiah frowned and released a breath. "There are plenty of canned goods, so food won't be a problem."

"I can even pull together the ingredients for bread or biscuits." Emily cast a quick glance at the shelves. "From the looks of your stock, we could live on that until the spring thaw. Of course, I'd expect you to charge me for my share."

A chuckle rose up in Jeremiah at the teasing glint in her eyes. "Don't think I won't."

She smiled back, and they fell silent once again. Unwilling to be put in the position to allow temptation to get another grip on them, Jeremiah broke eye contact almost immediately. "I'd best go and bring in some coal from the back. I'll build the fire up a bit to keep us warm until the storm passes." Which, from the sounds of the wind, wouldn't be anytime soon. Jeremiah scooped coal into the stove, and soon warmth radiated through the back part of the store.

"Jeremiah?"

Turning at the sound of Emily's voice, Jeremiah's heart picked up. The worry in her eyes filled him with compassion. "What is it, honey?"

"Is your ma going to be okay?"

He'd been worrying about the same thing. But Ma was resourceful. There was plenty of food to keep her, plenty of coal for at least two weeks.

"She has everything she needs." He gave her a wry grin. " 'Course, with no one to talk to until this is over, I might be in for a lengthy conversation when I see her."

Emily giggled, then they fell silent again. Jeremiah gave a satisfied sigh that even with Emily's opposing viewpoints, she had thought of his mother being alone at the farm. He smiled into the silence.

After hours of listening to the howling wind, Emily sat in the chair, silently staring at the wall until Jeremiah noticed her eyelids drooping. A wide yawn stretched her mouth. "You might as well go to sleep, Em. This storm isn't quitting, and there's no sense in staying awake all night. It's already after midnight. Let's make a place for you to sleep."

Emily shot from the chair, eyeing him warily. "I have a place to sleep." She glanced toward the wall and the three coats still piled on the floor.

"It's too cold over there."

"Well, I'm not sleeping close to you, Jeremiah."

After the silent exchange between them earlier, he couldn't really blame her for not trusting him to keep a respectable distance. Still, she'd catch her death sleeping next to the wall in the coldest part of the store. Bad enough that her reputation would be in question after a night alone with him. Jeremiah released a heavy sigh. There was nothing to be done about the situation. "I promise not to come near you."

She squared her shoulders and headed for the wall as though he hadn't spoken. "I've made up my mind, and there's no point in trying to change it. This is for the best."

She made a pallet of coats and started to lower herself. She hesitated. "Do you want some of these?"

"No, I have this one, plus I'm sleeping next to the stove. I'll be plenty warm."

"Have it your way, then." She stretched out and covered up, turning her back to him. "Please don't watch me. It makes me nervous."

Heat crept up Jeremiah's neck. He averted his gaze and settled onto the floor, resting his back against a barrel. From time to time, he found himself watching Emily. She struggled to find a comfortable position; and even under two coats, she shivered.

Finally, after two hours of intermittently watching her fight against cold, Jeremiah stood and grabbed the remaining blankets from a stack on the shelf. When he had made a pallet several inches thick, Jeremiah walked toward Emily.

∽

Emily felt herself being lifted into warm arms. She sighed, relishing the dream. Suddenly reality broke through, and she opened her eyes. Jeremiah stared at her, his face merely inches from hers.

She gasped as she realized this was no dream. "What do you think you're doing?"

"Getting you away from that cold wall whether you like it or not." He spoke without even a hint of an apology.

"Put me down this instant."

"I intend to," he said, his voice clipped as he lowered her to her feet. "Now lie down and go back to sleep."

Emily's eyes grew wide. "What is this?"

"A warm place to sleep. I suggest you put it to good use."

He turned to her, his expression almost pleading. "Please just lay down. I will keep my distance, I promise."

Unable to withstand his earnest appeal, Emily nodded. She lowered herself to the pallet, guiltily settling into the soft warmth. By all rights, Jeremiah should be enjoying this. But she knew it would be pointless to suggest he take it, and of course sharing it was out of the question. Her cheeks burned at the fleeting thought, and suddenly her mind reverted to the moment between them when she'd thought for sure he would kiss her. Relief and disappointment had mingled when his stomach grumbled, breaking off the intensity of the silence that had spoken more than words could have. Oh, if only she could believe he truly cared for her.

Heavy, even breathing reached her, and Emily looked up to see Jeremiah seated on the floor, his back and head resting against a barrel. He still wore his coat, but Emily knew he'd be cold when he woke up after the fire had died down. She peeled off two blankets from her pallet. Walking the few feet across to Jeremiah, she carefully covered him.

She tiptoed back to her pallet and lay down.

"Thank you." Jeremiah's husky, sleepy voice reached her ears like a warm breeze. Knowing she dare not face him, Emily forced herself to remain with her back to him. She drifted to sleep with a smile on her lips.

For the next three days, the wind howled and snow whirled about outside. Utilizing Jeremiah's stock, Emily baked biscuits and even made gravy. Although there was no meat to go with their meals, Jeremiah vowed he had never eaten so well. Emily blushed at his compliments. Gradually they became comfortable in each other's presence, settling into a familiar pattern.

At night they slept much like the first night. During the day, Emily insisted Jeremiah nap on her pallet.

Finally, on the fourth day, the howling wind quieted; and after a few hours, Jeremiah decided to remove the boards from the window. Emily held her breath as the first board came loose. White nothingness stared back at them.

"Oh my." She put her hand to her mouth.

"The drifts must be as high as the window," Jeremiah said grimly. "I can't see anything but snow."

"Do you want to try the door?" Emily heard the shake in her voice.

After several attempts, Jeremiah shook his head and glanced at her helplessly. He tried the back door and met the same lack of success. "I'm sorry. It won't budge. It must be iced over on the outside. But now that the snow has stopped, others will be able to get out, I'm sure. You know your pa will hook up the sleigh and get into town as soon as he can to make sure you're fine. Someone will dig us out soon. If not today, then tomorrow or the next day for sure."

Emily inwardly groaned at the thought of being cooped up for two or three more days. Not that the last few days with Jeremiah hadn't been pleasant enough despite the forced circumstances. But she was ready to breathe fresh air again.

Her shoulders lifted in a resigned shrug. "Well then, I suppose I should mix up another batch of biscuits."

Jeremiah stopped her with a soft grip on her upper arm. "I'd like to talk to you about something. I suppose now is as good a time as any."

Emily returned his gaze, wondering at the seriousness in his brown eyes. "Yes?"

"After this many days alone, there will be no stopping tongues from wagging. You realize that, right?"

Heat rose to her cheeks. "Yes." Tears burned in her eyes. Why did he have to bring up the reminder of her coming humiliation?

He cleared his throat and took both of her hands in his. "I want you to know that I understand my responsibility to you."

"Responsibility?"

Nodding, he squeezed her hands. "As soon as we can get out, we'll head straight to the parsonage. Anthony can perform the ceremony right away."

Confusion clouded Emily's mind. She blinked up at him. "What ceremony?"

A frown creased Jeremiah's brow. "Our marriage ceremony, of course."

Chapter 9

Marriage? Jeremiah Daniels, that's the most utterly ridiculous thing I've ever heard you say!" He understood his responsibility? Emily fumed. He understood a good way to get his hands on her business. That was what he understood! "I have no intention of marrying you now or ever."

Jeremiah's brow rose, and he released her from his grip. "What do you mean? You know as well as I do, we have no choice. Think of the scandal this will cause. What of your pa's position in town?"

Emily gave a sniff. "You mean your ma's position."

"Yes, partly." Jeremiah's steady gaze burned into Emily with a stubbornness she had rarely seen. He meant business. "My ma was the town talk before my pa died because everyone knew how he treated us. And after he died, they talked about her because of my actions before Tuck hired me at the mercantile. The last thirteen years, she's slowly risen to a place of respectability. I won't allow her to lose her standing among those self-righteous hens if belonging there makes her so happy."

"Need I remind you of my standing in the community?" Emily huffed, wishing desperately this proposal of marriage were being made for any other reason in the whole world—especially when her heart raced at the thought of becoming Jeremiah's bride. Still, she had to get out of it with her pride intact. She absolutely couldn't endure the humiliation of anyone knowing exactly why Jeremiah really wanted to marry her. "What would my association think if I let a man force me into marriage simply because we were trapped and innocently spent a few days together?"

"I don't see how that compares, Em. The League of Christian Women is made up of all the respectable women in town. You've been on thin ice with them for the last year, as it is. You'll completely lose your good name if you don't marry me."

"Are you threatening me, Jeremiah Daniels? Because if you are—"

"Threatening? You take my marriage proposal as a threat?"

"Proposal? Your so-called proposal was barbaric. Another example of a male-dominated society!" Emily flailed her arms, pacing the floor and feeling as though she might explode any second. She whirled around and faced him, then deepened her voice in a poor imitation. "You have to marry me. I'm not asking; I'm telling."

"I think you've gone soft in the head from being shut up in the store too long."

"You see? I'm the one who's gone soft in the head because I didn't throw myself into your arms and declare undying gratitude that you want to spare your mother's reputation."

Jeremiah opened his mouth to reply, but Emily continued without giving him the chance to speak.

"Never mind that I might not think it's the best idea. Never mind that we've never once spoken of love. Never mind that you've never asked me to a dance or asked my pa for permission to court me."

Emily's lip trembled. Oh, those tears! Those dreadful, telltale tears.

Jeremiah stepped forward and gently took her hands in his. "Em, look at me."

Stubbornly Emily kept her gaze on the tips of her boots.

A long sigh left Jeremiah's lips. "All right. Don't look at me, but at least listen to what I have to say."

"Say it, then."

"I would have courted you if I had thought you wanted me to."

Emily ventured a glance upward. His eyes held a look of earnest appeal. Her mind screamed for her to stay strong, not to give in to his obvious attempt to ensnare her with talk of courting and romance—especially when she knew the truth; but her rebellious heart couldn't help but venture on, exploring where the conversation might lead.

With tenderness, he studied her face, searching for truth as much as Emily searched for the same from him. "Would you have said yes?"

"I let you kiss me when we were sixteen," she mumbled. "What did you think that was, if not a hint that I'd accept you as a beau?"

He chuckled. "I heard you and Amelia Bell talking by the punch bowl that night. She dared you to kiss the first boy who tried."

A gasp escaped Emily's lips. He was right. "I'd completely forgotten about that." She'd forgotten everything about that night except for Jeremiah's soft, warm kiss. But now her mind conjured the memory of what had led up to the event. "My brother Luke had stolen a kiss from Amelia right under the kissing tree, and she was bragging about it. That was long before Laney lassoed him in, of course."

"If I recall correctly," Jeremiah said wryly, "Laney didn't have to lasso him too tightly to bring him in."

"That's true." Emily smiled. "Some people just belong together." Her heart ached to admit it.

"Yes, they do." Though his voice rang with emotion, Emily refused to try to discover whether his words held a double meaning. Better to take them at face value and conclude he meant Luke and Laney belonged together than to have her hopes dashed. Instead, she continued reliving the memory of the night of their one and only kiss. "Anyway, I told Amelia kissing wasn't anything to brag about, she should be ashamed for letting him do it in the first place, and I had half a mind to tell my ma on Luke." Emily giggled. "I think Amelia's dare was mainly to keep from getting into trouble with her own pa if word got out she'd been kissing anyone. She knew I wouldn't turn down a dare."

"Lucky for me I happened to be listening in on the conversation. I had to force myself to wait a respectable amount of time so you wouldn't know I'd been eavesdropping."

"Why, Jeremiah Daniels, you took advantage of me!"

His face split into a rakish grin. "What else would you expect a smitten young man to do? I'd be a disgrace to the male gender if I hadn't taken the opportunity when it presented itself."

"A smitten young man?" Emily sniffed. "If you were so smitten, why did it take a dare to induce you to ask me to dance?"

"That's pretty obvious, isn't it? Can you imagine Emily St. John, daughter of one of the town's most prominent citizens, courting me? I knew I wasn't good enough for you. And likely everyone else did, too. I could have asked, but I seriously doubt your pa would have allowed me to court you."

Emily's heart pounded furiously. She narrowed her gaze. "Then you don't know the first thing about my family! My pa would no more hold your past against you than he would put one of his grandchildren on a bucking horse."

He released a long breath. "Then maybe I should have asked, but stigma is an almost impossible thing to overcome. Don't you see? That's why you have to marry me. Our families would have to defend us and themselves for a long, long time if we don't make this right."

Disappointment washed through Emily, draining her strength. She turned away and grabbed a bag of flour from the counter. "Forget it, Jeremiah. When I marry, I want a decent proposal from a man who's in love with me. My family would never expect me to marry just to keep tongues from wagging."

Emily heard the clip of quick, booted steps behind her, and her heart picked up. Before she had the opportunity to face him, she felt Jeremiah's hands on her shoulders, turning her around.

He pulled her close, his face inches from hers. "You're too stubborn for your own good." His hands moved up her shoulders and cupped her neck, his thumbs caressing the lines of her jaw. "You have no idea how I feel about you. Perhaps it's my own fault for keeping quiet all these years."

Emily closed her eyes, blanketed in the soft warmth of his hands. For a moment, she pushed aside all thoughts of whether or not Jeremiah had ulterior motives, and she abandoned herself to the pleasure of his closeness. The tenderness.

"So help me, Emily. . ." In one agonizingly long second, their breath mingled, just before his lips claimed hers.

This was no repeat of a long-ago schoolboy's kiss. Soft, but filled with passion, Jeremiah's lips moved over hers until Emily's head swam. Childhood memories fled her mind, along with the reality of the snow outside and the last few days. They were alone in an uncomplicated world where there was no room for worrying about scandal or trying to gauge Jeremiah's reasons for asking her to marry him.

A sudden chill swept into the room, and Emily frowned as Jeremiah's lips left hers.

They turned toward the back door, the direction of the cold air. Emily gasped. Jeremiah pulled her close into the protective circle of his arms. In the doorway stood every male member of Emily's family, glaring and poised for action.

Jeremiah saw his mangled, bruised body reflected in the angry glares burning at him from the doorway. He cleared his throat and tightened his grip on Emily's shoulder.

"Sir," he said, addressing Dell, "I assure you this isn't what it looks like."

Dell stepped across the threshold and closed the distance between them in a few long strides. "That's a good thing for you, son, because let me tell you what it looks like from my perspective."

Jeremiah swallowed hard, fully anticipating the situation from a pa's point of view.

"From where I stood—and correct me if I'm wrong—it looked like you had your arms around my daughter and were kissing her—and not just a chaste peck on the cheek. You were kissing her a little too deeply for my comfort."

"Oh, Pa, really. It wasn't anything."

Jeremiah leaned in and spoke close to her ear. "What do you mean it wasn't anything? It was something to me."

"Would you be quiet?" Emily glared up at him. "I'm trying to save you from getting a behind full of buckshot."

Loud guffaws coming from the doorway pulled Jeremiah's attention from Emily. He frowned.

"I don't see what's funny about this situation." He turned to Anthony, Emily's brother-in-law. "I'm glad you're here, Reverend Greene. It'll save us a trip to the parsonage in the cold."

"It's good to see you intend to do the honorable thing," Dell said, nodding his cool approval. "But I think Emily's ma and sisters will want to be in attendance when you actually say the vows."

Jeremiah scowled, knowing every day that passed would give the gossips more time to talk. "I suppose we could wait a day or two, as long as the townsfolk realize a wedding is going to take place directly and that any delay is your idea, not mine. I'm more than ready to do right by your daughter, sir. And rest assured that the scene you walked in on was the only one of its kind that happened over the last few days."

"It's good to hear that." Dell turned his attention to Emily, who stood red-faced and teary-eyed. "Get your coat, sweetheart. I have the sleigh outside ready to take us home to your ma. You've no idea how worried she's been."

He extended his hand to Jeremiah. "We'll be in touch about the wedding."

"Now hold on just a minute!" Emily stomped one foot on the floor and planted her hands firmly on her hips. "I've never agreed to any kind of marriage. Jeremiah and I were trapped together—but not by choice. The blizzard just came on so suddenly, all we could do was wait it out. Nothing happened between us that would warrant suspicion and the need to marry." Her face grew a darker shade of red. "Well, all right, that kiss happened; but honestly, if the boys had to marry every girl they kissed under the kissing tree, they'd all have a dozen wives."

The boys laughed. "She has a point there, Pa," seventeen-year-old Will said with a wide grin.

"What would you know about it, Little Bit?" Jack asked, elbowing his brother in the ribs.

"You trying to say I've never kissed a girl?" Will's face reddened, and he stood poised to defend his honor.

"I'd bet a month's wages on it."

"Ma would skin us alive if we took to betting, so you count yourself blessed with a month's wages you'd have otherwise lost."

Jack slapped him on the back and laughed. "You have a good mind, little brother."

Dell glared them to silence, then turned to Emily. "The kiss isn't necessarily the point, Em, although I'm a bit disappointed to see you kissing a man you're not willing to marry. The point is that your virtue has been compromised despite your claims of innocence. If one of your brothers spent three days alone with a young lady, whether he kissed her or not, I'd expect him to do the decent thing and marry her."

Jeremiah stepped forward. "Emily, take some time to think about the repercussions of not making this right."

"There's nothing to make right. I've done nothing wrong, and I refuse to get married just to satisfy a town full of people who delight in thinking the worst."

"You're just being stubborn." He gripped her upper arm and drew her close. "No one can kiss a man the way you kissed me—forgive me for bringing it up, Mr. St. John—no one can kiss a man the way you did if she doesn't care something for him."

Emily's face glowed, but she lifted her chin and held herself with dignity. "Don't be so conceited."

"Have it your way." Jeremiah released her arm. "But I won't ask again."

"Now don't be too hasty." Mr. St. John stepped forward and pulled Emily close to his side. "After a few days at the ranch with your family, maybe you'll see things a bit more clearly."

"I see things clearly enough, thank you. My mind's made up. Pa, please give Ma my love and assure her I'm fine, but I can't go to the ranch and leave my store any more days. Why, Jeremiah will get all my customers."

Dell chuckled. "I suppose you have a point there." He gathered a breath and shrugged, sending Jeremiah an apologetic look. "Looks like there won't be a wedding after all. I might be a bit old-fashioned, but not so much so that I'd force an unwanted marriage on my daughter. We'll find some way to make it through this. Come on, sweetheart. I'll take you home and help you get settled back into your room."

"It's only across the street. I can make it."

The relief on Emily's face was downright insulting.

Dell sent his irate daughter a smirk. "The snow is two feet deep through town and higher in drifts, honey. Maybe you'd better let me take you home in the sleigh."

She pinkened and gave a short nod. "Fine then."

Jeremiah's ire rose as she looked ready to leave without so much as a good-bye. "Hold on a minute. I want it made clear that this decision is not a result of my refusal to marry you. You might not care about your reputation in this town, Emily, but I won't have my mother humiliated."

Emily's eyes narrowed. "Rest assured, I will take full responsibility for not getting married. The talebearers of this town will be made aware of the truth. And if any other story emerges, painting you in a bad light, I'll take out an advertisement in Mr. Bell's newspaper."

So saying, she swung around and stomped to the door. Her brothers made a path through the doorway. Jeremiah followed her and watched as Luke swooped her up in his arms and waded waist deep in the snow until he reached the sleigh.

"Good-bye, Jeremiah," Emily said, once she was settled. "Th—thank you for everything. Send me a bill for my portion of the supplies we used up and for this coat."

Too angry to speak, Jeremiah closed the door without even saying good-bye.

Emily might think that was the end of it, but she was sorely mistaken. She had lived all of her life with people's approval if for no other reason than because she was a St. John. But he'd worked too hard to gain a little respectability, and he refused to be made a fool of in his own town.

Jeremiah walked to the counter and started to straighten up. A grin split his face at a sudden thought. After a few days of enduring the town's displeasure, she'd be ready to accept his proposal.

Chapter 10

Emily was amazed at how quickly word spread. The forthcoming scandal weighed heavily on her mind, but she couldn't help but be secretly thrilled with all the business the town's curiosity generated for Emily's Place. Jeremiah's also seemed to be teeming with customers. Emily was glad, for Jeremiah's sake.

Two weeks had passed since the snow had ceased to fall, and business had been practically nonexistent until the past couple of days. But now folks were slowly digging out of their homes and coming into town for supplies. Already she'd practically sold out of household essentials such as lard and flour. Hopefully the supply train would be able to get through soon.

She smiled at Mrs. McDonald. "Would you like that to go on account, ma'am?"

"Yes, dear." The woman turned to her husband. "Take these out to the wagon, Rafe. I'll be along directly."

"Don't be all day about it, woman," he said gruffly, but Emily noted he took the crate of supplies and moved through the door.

Mrs. McDonald turned back to Emily, a look of expectation plainly written on her lined face.

"Do you need anything else?" Emily asked, steeling herself for what would most certainly be the question on everyone's mind.

Pink tinged the matron's cheeks. "I—well. . .I don't mean to pry, but I am curious about the wedding."

"Wedding?" Emily glanced at the counter and brushed away an imaginary speck of dust. "Do you mean Lionel's wedding? I thought your son wasn't getting married until spring."

"No, dear. I'm speaking of you and Jeremiah Daniels, of course. If you don't make an announcement soon, folks won't have an opportunity to get you gifts."

Emily released a sigh. "I appreciate the concern, but Jeremiah and I aren't getting married."

Mrs. McDonald fingered the cameo brooch at her neck. "Oh my. You mean Jeremiah's playing the cad? I never would have thought it of him. True, he started out a bit rough in his boyhood days, but he appeared to straighten right up once Tuck hired him." She shook her head and clucked her tongue. "Don't you worry. I will speak to Mrs. Daniels about him. She'll put him in his place real quicklike. You'll be a married woman before you know it."

Emily knew the only fair thing to do was to explain the truth of the situation. This would only be the beginning of the gossip. But for Jeremiah's sake, she had to be honest. "To tell you the truth, he proposed immediately."

Confusion clouded the older woman's blue eyes. "Well, then—"

"I turned him down."

"You turned him down?"

"Yes, ma'am."

"But why?"

"Because I felt it was the right thing to do. Jeremiah and I did nothing wrong. I see no reason we should have to get married."

A look of understanding suddenly replaced the woman's confusion. "I'd forgotten you hold to all these newfangled ideas about votes for women and whatnot. Times sure are changing, and I'm not altogether convinced it's for the best. Not that I am opposed to a woman having a little independence, mind you."

The middle-aged matron leaned in close and dropped her volume. She patted Emily's hand. "But don't you think you ought to snatch him up while you have the chance, honey? I doubt you'll get a better offer, what with my Lionel spoken for."

Heat suffused Emily's cheeks as her anger rose. She had half a mind to inform the nosy matron she wouldn't take Lionel if he were delivered on a silver platter. Catching her tongue just before blurting out the truth of the matter, she addressed the issue at hand. "No, ma'am, I do not feel I should 'snatch up' anyone."

Customers turned in curiosity at the rise in Emily's tone. She glanced helplessly around, then made a split-second decision. "While I have everyone's attention, I'd like to make an announcement." All murmuring ceased, and the store grew as still as closing time.

"All right, then." Emily took in the fifteen customers in one sweeping glance. "First, let me say that Jeremiah Daniels is as fine a gentleman as Harper has ever seen."

Sudden, knowing grins split the faces staring back at her.

"However," Emily forged ahead, "I will not be marrying him, so you can all just stop wondering when the wedding will take place."

Looks of outrage replaced the humor. Emily held up her hand. "As I was just telling Mrs. McDonald, this decision is not Jeremiah's doing. He asked me to marry him. The choice not to do so is mine."

Her patrons stood, no one speaking or moving until finally Mr. Gregory made his way forward from the back of the room. His wife trailed behind him, her head lowered.

He stared at Emily, eyes glinting hard. The family had moved into the area only weeks before Christmas, but Emily had rarely seen any of them. Mr. Gregory had bought the local hotel, immediately closing the dance hall beneath.

According to Amelia Bell, the man had wasted no time setting his wife and five daughters to work cleaning every corner and crack of the place. His plans were to add more hotel rooms below, take away the gaudy remnants of the former disreputable business, and make it a respectable hotel.

The League of Christian Women, which had been trying to close the dance hall since it opened, had embraced the new family with open arms.

Standing before the disapproving gaze of the stone-faced giant of a man, Emily shook, thoroughly intimidated.

"And why is it that you would refuse a man who is only trying to do the right thing by you?" he asked, his voice gruff, his manner bordering on hostile.

Fearing her wobbly legs might not keep her upright, Emily gripped the edge of the counter so tightly her knuckles grew white. She averted her gaze and found Mrs. Thomas—who had recently taken to wearing bloomer outfits almost exclusively—staring at her. The fellow suffragette nodded her support, bolstering Emily's resolve.

She squared her shoulders and looked way up to meet his gaze head-on. "Because, sir, I don't feel that any woman, or man for that matter, should be forced into doing something just to satisfy the expectations of others."

A sneer marred his face. "Is that right?"

Emily felt her burst of courage failing beneath his condemning gaze. She stared, unable to find the appropriate words, and squirmed uncomfortably at his sardonic smile. "Can't think of anything to say? Let me tell you something, Miss St. John. Women like you are an infection on society."

A gasp flew from Emily's lips. She pressed her palm to her chest.

"That's right. You break down the structure of decent homes and spread your lies to unsuspecting, weak-minded women who don't know any better than to believe they are just as good as the men who provide for them. I'd strongly advise you not to go near my wife and daughters if you know what's good for you."

Quick, booted steps on the wooden floor marked the end to Mrs. Thomas's patience. "Now see here, you big fool of a man. This girl happens to be the daughter of one of Harper's most celebrated citizens. You would do well not to threaten her if you know what's good for you."

Apparently undaunted, he swept Mrs. Thomas with a dismissive gaze. "I am well aware of Miss St. John's family status. Her activities reflect poorly on her family. Even as a new member of this community, I have to wonder what her pa is thinking by allowing her to run a business and live alone in the first place. She would never have been compromised if she had stayed properly at home under her father's care, where she belongs."

At the criticism of her family, Emily found her tongue. "H–how dare you suggest my pa doesn't do right by me!"

The man's lips twitched in a smile that didn't come near his eyes. "I am only stating the obvious. Your pa clearly can't manage a proper household."

"Why, why, you get out of my store this instant. I—I, you are not welcome here again."

"You forget, miss, I am a customer, and I have supplies I'd like to buy."

"That's too bad. I'll not sell you a thing."

His face reddened in anger, and his nostrils flared. "Come now. These items are not to be had across the street. And despite your lack of concern for Mr. Daniels's reputation, he has graciously sent me to your place of business."

"Mr. Gregory, I don't care if you can't buy flour or rice or chickpeas anywhere else. I will not do business with a man who holds me in such poor regard that he would stand in my store and insult my family and my honor right to my face." She waved toward the other customers, who stared in bewilderment at the exchange. "Especially in the presence of so many others. Please leave, and kindly do not return."

From the corner of her eye, Emily noted movement from Mrs. Gregory, who thus far had not looked up. She did so now, throwing a cautious glance to the back of her husband's head, then fleetingly met Emily's gaze. Mrs. Gregory held her gaze for only a second, but Emily noted the look of admiration shining from her eyes.

Mr. Gregory's cold hand gripped Emily's, drawing her attention back to him. "I'm afraid you didn't hear me correctly. I will purchase these items, or I will take them without purchasing them. It's really your choice."

Shaking with rage, Emily found all the courage she needed. She jerked her hand from his, and with a quick sweep of her arm, she cleared the counter of Mr. Gregory's purchases, sending them to the floor at her feet. "No! I will not be bullied, sir. It's really your choice. You may leave, or I'll send for the sheriff. I have a right to refuse service to anyone I choose. And I choose not to serve you."

"I think it's about time you leave, Mr. Gregory."

Intent on the situation at hand, Emily hadn't even noticed the bell above the door ding Jeremiah's entrance. He stood at the threshold. Emily's heart pounded at the sight of him standing poised to defend her if necessary. Relief flooded her, and she willed herself not to burst into tears.

Mr. Gregory looked at Jeremiah, then back to Emily. He sneered and leaned easily across the counter. "You just made yourself an enemy, miss."

In a flash, Jeremiah stood at his side. He grabbed Mr. Gregory's arm and jerked him upright. "Don't threaten her. Ever."

A short laugh emanated from deep inside the burly man. "Are you going to ban me from your store, as well?"

"No, sir. I'll take your money anytime you feel the need to spend it. I'm just telling you to leave Emily alone."

"You'd defend her after she's made a fool of you?"

"I'd defend anyone against the likes of you."

"I'll be taking my business to Henderson's from now on. I'd rather drive ten miles for supplies than patronize either of your stores." He grabbed his wife by her upper arm and pulled her out of the store. Emily watched in astonishment as he practically dragged her down the steps and down the street to the hotel. Never in her twenty-five years had she seen a woman treated in such a manner.

"Oh, Jeremiah."

"I know," he said grimly. "Men like that don't deserve to have families."

"And he had the audacity to criticize the way my pa runs our household."

"Are you all right?" He covered her hand.

The warmth brought an immediate end to her trembling. Keenly aware of the remaining customers' watchful observation, Emily gathered a shaky breath and nodded. She slid her hand out from his. "Thank you for your assistance, Jeremiah."

He glanced cautiously about. "I'd best get back across the street. I left the store in Ma's hands." A grin split his face. "She'll be raising prices if I don't keep an eye on her."

"Your ma's helping out in the store?"

He sent her a wink and leaned in closer. "She's afraid it might storm, and I might get stranded with you again."

Emily's eyes widened until she noted the teasing glint in his eyes.

He smiled. "She was going stir crazy after the last two weeks of being cooped up at home, so I asked her if she'd like to come to town. She spent the morning at an impromptu sewing circle with some of the town women." He cast an apologetic look at Mrs. Thomas, who at least pretended to be studying a bottle of Healy's Magic Elixir, unlike the rest of the onlookers, who stared unabashed.

Giving up all pretense of not eavesdropping, Mrs. Thomas smiled broadly. "Don't worry about my not being invited to their little sewing circle, Mr. Daniels. I wouldn't want to attend anyway." She turned her attention to Emily. "I must be going, dear." Now it was her turn to send a cautious glance at Jeremiah. "Don't bend to society's antiquated opinions. Keep to your convictions. The movement is firmly behind you." She hurried to the door and raised her fist in salute. "Votes for women!"

Emily returned her gaze to Jeremiah's. He cleared his throat. "I guess that's that. I'll talk to you later, Emily." He lifted his hand in farewell to their audience. "You folks have a good day, and keep in mind you'll find a better deal at Jeremiah's."

Emily's mouth dropped open. "That's not true! I'll beat his prices any day."

His laughter followed him down the mercantile steps.

That was the most spiteful thing she'd ever heard! Trying to steal her customers just because she wouldn't marry him. She was glad she'd said no.

But as she tallied Mrs. Adams's purchases, Emily faced the truth. She deeply regretted her hasty decision. Jeremiah had made it clear he wouldn't ask her again, and she felt helpless to right this dreadful wrong. One by one, she took care of her customers, speaking only as was necessary to conclude their business.

She watched the last of her patrons leave and close the door. Releasing a heavy sigh, she bent and began cleaning the mess she'd made.

It was one thing when she, alone, was bearing the brunt of the talk; but if her family had to suffer because of her decision, Emily knew she couldn't live with that. She understood now why Jeremiah had considered his mother's standing in town. Her decision was causing negative repercussions for both families.

She glanced out of the window to Jeremiah's. Jeremiah and his mother exited the store together. Mrs. Daniels waited while he locked the door; then with a grin, he turned and offered her his arm.

Mrs. Taylor, the mayor's wife, walked past with only the slightest of nods. Emily seethed at the deliberate snub. Her heart lurched as Mrs. Daniels watched the mayor's wife until Jeremiah tugged at her. With a nod, they headed toward the livery.

Tears stung Emily's eyes. *They don't deserve this scandal, Lord. How do I make it right?*

Without taking the time to grab a jacket, Emily sprinted to the door, flung it open, and stepped out onto the stoop. "Jeremiah, wait!"

Chapter 11

Don't turn around, son. Just keep walking."

"That wouldn't be very polite." Jeremiah chuckled as he watched Emily race down the steps and pause to allow a wagon to pass. "Where are those fine manners I've always admired in you, Ma?"

Ma snorted in a rather rude fashion. "Where are her manners? That girl made a spectacle of you and then refused your proposal as though she's too good to marry a Daniels."

Jeremiah had thought the same thing more than once when his wounded pride got the better of him. Still, he couldn't very well pretend not to hear her when everyone in town was staring.

Especially when she'd already caught up to them. She stood scowling and red-faced. "Honestly, Jeremiah, you might have stopped and met me halfway," Emily said, pressing her hand flat against her stomach as she tried to catch her breath.

"You should be glad he stopped at all, young lady!" Ma huffed, shaking her plump finger at Emily.

"Indeed?" Emily's eyes narrowed to slits, and she looked like a tabby cat about to spit and claw.

Ma wasn't acting much better, as she coiled like a rattler in the barnyard. Jeremiah stepped between them before she could strike. "Ma, would you go on over to the livery and ask Mr. Collins if he'd mind hitching the team?"

Ma harrumphed and set off without another word.

Emily watched her stomp away. "I guess she's a little mad at me, huh?"

"A little," Jeremiah said wryly.

"I am sorry, Jeremiah. You were right. Our families are going to suffer from this if we don't get married."

Jeremiah took her by the arm and pulled her out of the way of a curious matron walking by on the wooden sidewalk. "What are you saying?"

Emily's face grew red. "I just. . .I know you said you wouldn't ask again, and I don't blame you. So. . .well, I guess I'll have to ask you to do the honorable thing and marry me after all." She glanced at him, hesitating briefly as if to gauge his reaction. Worry clouded her eyes, giving Jeremiah the satisfaction of knowing his feigned nonchalance appeared to be convincing.

"Now you want to marry me?"

A frown creased her brow. "This is for our families. After Mr. Gregory's comments in there. . . He. . .well, Jeremiah, he insulted my pa because of me."

"I see." Jeremiah knew all it would take to alleviate her discomfort was to reassure her everything would be all right and that of course he'd marry her; but the fact was, he rather enjoyed seeing her grovel after what she'd put him through during the past two weeks.

She nodded. "A—and when he insulted my pa, I understood what you meant about your ma having to withstand the town's disapproval. Don't you see? I realized us getting married is. . .it's just the right thing to do. For their sakes."

Jeremiah leaned against the wall and folded his arms across his chest. He regarded her evenly. "What if I don't think it's necessary anymore? Everyone knows I was perfectly willing to do the honorable thing by you. And if they don't, they will by the end of the week. After all, you just made an announcement in Emily's Place that you weren't marrying me even though I proposed."

Emily frowned, clearly perplexed. "How did you know about that? You didn't come in the store until later."

"Mrs. McDonald came to Jeremiah's to buy eggs since you were out. She told me all about it. Said you spoke very highly of me. . .even called me a 'fine gentleman.'" Jeremiah sent her a sardonic grin and shrugged. "I think my reputation is pretty much secure. So you see, marriage isn't really necessary after all. Not for me, anyway."

Emily's eyes widened, and her lips tightened. "You can't just take back a proposal! Once you ask, it's out there waiting to be answered."

"But you forget, Miss St. John. My proposal was already answered. With a resounding no."

She brought her foot down hard on the sidewalk. "And now I'm taking it back. My answer is yes."

He moved away from the wall and headed toward the livery. "I'll have to think about it."

"You'll have to what?"

"I said," he called over his shoulder, "I'll have to think about it. I'll let you know soon."

"Why, you. . ." Her boots clacked on the sidewalk behind him as she hurried to catch up. Jeremiah grinned to himself.

Emily stepped quickly to keep up with his long strides. "I'll—yes—I will, I'll have my brothers after you, and my pa—" She paused to catch her breath. "And every ranch hand working on Pa's ranch and my brother Luke's ranch."

Jeremiah shrugged and kept walking. "You can have all those men come after me if you want, but I figure your pa can handle me without anyone's help—even if he is twice my age. I'm not really much of a fighter." Halting, he turned to her, unable to keep the smile at bay any longer. "Emily, thank you for reconsidering. Let's get married."

Outrage flooded Emily's face. She opened her mouth, closed it, then put her hands on her hips. "You were only teasing? You put me through all that when you had every intention of marrying me all along?"

"Well, not all along. For the first couple of seconds, I considered turning you down; but you wooed me so sweetly, I found myself unable to resist."

Obviously not amused, Emily narrowed her eyes. "If my family honor weren't at stake, I'd change my mind!"

"Again?"

"Yes, again!" She glared at him, then hesitated before asking, "When do you want to get married?"

The sudden question surprised Jeremiah. He sobered. "I don't know. Now?"

"Now?" The look Emily gave him spoke volumes, but Jeremiah didn't figure there were any flattering words to describe him. "I can't get ready for a wedding in two minutes."

"Why don't you just decide when the happy event will take place, then?"

"All right, I will."

Jeremiah tipped his bowler and headed back toward the livery. "Let me know when to show up, and I'll be there in my Sunday best," he called over his shoulder.

"Jeremiah?"

At the softening in her tone, Jeremiah turned. "Yes?"

"I. . .just. . ." She shook her head. "Nothing. I'll speak with my family and contact you in a couple of days."

"I'll look forward to hearing from you."

Her lips tipped upward in a tentative smile. She looked about to turn around, then stopped. "You won't be sorry. I promise." And without waiting for his reply, she spun around and hurried back to the mercantile.

Jeremiah swallowed hard. If only she'd given him a chance to voice the words his heart sang. *I could never be sorry for marrying the girl of my dreams.*

⌒

Amelia Bell's grinning, elflike face greeted Emily as she walked through the door, breathless from her sprint across the street and up the steps.

"So you were talking to Jeremiah?" The lilt in the reporter's voice sent a shiver of annoyance down Emily's spine.

"Do you need something, Amelia?" Emily walked to the counter and gave her a pointed look. "I mean something other than information?"

Undaunted, Amelia crossed the room, as well. She leaned against the counter. "No. Living in town has its advantages. We didn't run out of everything and have to restock like most of the township."

Grabbing a cloth from beneath the counter, Emily swiped at imaginary dust. "Then if you'll excuse me, I have work to do."

"Gracious, I had no idea all the hoopla stealing a little sugar would cause. It's been great for town gossip, though."

Emily's mouth went suddenly dry. "What do you mean?"

An impish grin split Amelia's face. "You two were getting altogether too chummy and providing me with nothing of interest to report. Harper is a very dull town for news, you know. Other than your brother and Laney having a baby, nothing has happened in months."

"Are you telling me you staged the robbery? Whatever for?" Emily's insides ached. All of this could have been avoided. "Was it a trick?"

"Newspaper sales doubled when I started writing about you and Jeremiah's war between the stores. Then Jeremiah got a lovesick look in his eyes and was offering you half his stock. No one wants to read JEREMIAH'S BAILS OUT EMILY'S PLACE— PROPRIETOR OFFERS HALF OF SUGAR STOCK."

"Amelia Bell, I've half a mind to go straight to the sheriff."

Amelia shrugged. "Go ahead. At least if he made an arrest, I'd have a story to report."

Emily scowled. "You're hopeless. Do you realize all the trouble you've caused? Jeremiah is forced into marrying me because of you."

Victory washed across Amelia's features. "So that's what you were discussing. You've decided to marry him after all. I guess after Mr. Gregory's little outburst, you really don't have a choice. Can't have Mr. St. John's name besmirched, can we?"

"How did you know about Mr. Gregory?" Did the folks in Harper have nothing else to do but report on the goings-on at her mercantile?

"I have my sources." She grinned. "So when's the wedding?"

Emily released a defeated sigh. "I don't know yet. Pa's coming in tomorrow night to take me to the ranch. I suppose I'll discuss everything with him and Ma at supper."

"You will let me know, right?"

"Are you going to print it in the paper?"

"Of course. Folks will want to know. You gave us our first bona fide scandal since you bought this store and joined the cause."

"Actually, you gave us this scandal with your little sugar stunt."

"You're right. I guess I owe myself a reward." She took a penny from her reticule and slapped it down on the counter. "I believe I'd fancy a licorice stick."

Emily smiled despite her irritation. Amelia was like an ornery child at times. It was almost impossible to stay angry with the nosy little woman.

"Mrs. Thomas is going to be disappointed," Amelia said with a mouthful of candy.

"What do you mean?"

"That you're marrying Jeremiah, of course."

Emily stared blankly.

"Oh, Emily, sometimes you're too naive for your own good." Amelia's laughter filled the air. "Surely you know you've given Mrs. Thomas something to bolster Harper's chapter of the association?"

"I've no idea what you're talking about." Emily sniffed, pretending she didn't care to discuss it. Still, she was relieved when Amelia continued.

"There were only a handful of women interested in the movement when Mrs. Thomas introduced it a couple of years ago. Five or six at the most, and those were matrons whom everyone already knew bullied their husbands. With only a handful of battle-axes to their credit, the group lacked credibility with most of the women in Harper—especially the young, unmarried women with high hopes for matrimony.

"But when you bought this store and the League of Christian Women voiced their outrage at a woman being in business for herself, why, Mrs. Thomas took up your righteous cause. She immediately became your champion, and it was quite selfless of her. Within a month, our local chapter tripled in size and continued to grow despite the efforts of Jeremiah's mother and her fellow Christian Leaguers."

"But what did I have to do with that?"

"Darling. . . With a pretty young face in the crowd, the suffragettes were finally viewed as more than dried-up, sour-faced dowagers with nothing to do but cause trouble and make their husbands sorry they'd been born. I'd have never joined the cause myself if it hadn't been for you."

"So Mrs. Thomas used me."

"Yep, just like I used you to sell papers." She grinned. "You're an easy target because you're a St. John. People are interested in your family. You're the royal family of Harper."

Emily couldn't help but laugh. "Don't you think you're exaggerating a bit?"

"Not really. Your brother Sam is the doctor, Luke has the second largest ranch in the area—second only to your pa's ranch—your oldest sister is married to the preacher, Jack is studying law, Will is the most popular male among all the young people in town, Hope has an absolute entourage of boys and girls alike, and little Cat isn't far behind. I hear she is top of her class at school and sings beautifully enough to be on the stage. And then there's you."

Yes, then there was her. Listening to Amelia regale the attributes of her family members, Emily once again felt the weight of inferiority. "Let's don't talk about me."

"Why not? You're the St. Johniest of all the St. Johns, Princess Emily."

Emily bit back a grin, not wanting to encourage her ridiculous notions. "I haven't the faintest idea what you mean."

"You, my dear, are making your own way in the world. . .defying the odds of a patriarchal society, firm in your determination to keep yourself free of the domination of a man."

She sounded as though she were formulating a headline. Emily hated to be the one to bring her back to reality, particularly when the subject was rather flattering. However. . .

"You forget. My marriage is imminent."

"Oh, that's right." Amelia gave a troubled sigh. "I suppose it is my own fault for getting you compromised."

"You see what your meddling ways caused?"

"In any case, Mrs. Thomas will be fit to be tied unless you find a way to make it appear you're getting everything you want out of the marriage."

"What do you mean?" What did anyone want from marriage? A home. Love. Children, eventually. Emily's mind conjured the image of holding a child in her arms. She smiled.

"All right, you'll have to get rid of the dreamy look on your face, or we'll never appease Mrs. Thomas—unless you don't care about losing her support. Are you ready to join the ranks of the rest of the mousy housewives in Harper who have no say-so in how they live?"

Emily thought about it for a moment. Amelia was right. The store and the cause were her only achievements that meant anything. She wasn't beautiful, extra smart, or talented like her siblings. All she had was Emily's Place, and the only women who understood her were Mrs. Thomas and the women she led as they fought for their civil liberties. If she let them go, she'd be back where she started a year ago. . .nobody.

Gathering a deep breath, she leveled her gaze at Amelia. "All right. What do we do?"

Amelia smiled. "Let's get to work on a plan of action that insures you don't have to give up any of your independence. You can present it to Jeremiah before the wedding, and we can assure Mrs. Thomas that you haven't compromised your ideals one bit by marrying Jeremiah, after all."

Niggles of doubt twisted through Emily, but she quickly dismissed them. This was the way it had to be. If she hadn't overheard Jeremiah and Harold talking the night of the harvest dance, she might not have agreed to Amelia's bold plan. But as it was, she was taking measures to ensure she never had to give up her store.

Chapter 12

Jeremiah scratched the back of his leg with the toe of his boot while he nervously waited for Emily to arrive at the church. His mother sat in the front row, dressed in her darkest blue dress and dabbing at her nose with a lacy handkerchief. She would have pulled her mourning clothes from mothballs had Jeremiah not threatened to leave her home if she even tried.

He knew she worried. But many marriages began only for convenience, he'd reminded her, and most were successful. He intended for his marriage to be in the latter category. The fact that he loved his bride could only help to ease the situation. Without being too immodest, he believed Emily cared for him, as well. Their shared kiss just before her pa had arrived after the blizzard had been a hopeful indication of that.

He glanced about the room and met the questioning glances of the guests waiting for the ceremony to begin. The suffragettes had turned out to the affair, and Mrs. Thomas even cast off her bloomer outfit in favor of an appropriate green satin gown, although her mouth was twisted, making her disapproval abundantly clear.

The St. John family took two benches on the other side of the church, and the townsfolk filled the rest of the seats. Now if only the bride would show up, the wedding could commence. Jeremiah pulled at his tight collar and cleared his throat.

"Don't worry." Anthony gave him an understanding smile. "Tarah and her ma are helping Emily dress at the parsonage. She'll be here."

"She's a half hour late," Jeremiah growled. "Sorry, Reverend."

Anthony clapped him on the shoulder and chuckled. "I was a young groom once myself. Wedding lateness seems to be a female tradition in this family. From what I understand, not one of them, beginning with Mrs. St. John, has been on time yet. So think of this as a good sign."

"A good sign of what?"

A chuckle rumbled in the reverend's chest. "I have no idea. I was just trying to make you feel better."

"Psst."

"What was that?" Jeremiah asked.

Anthony shrugged.

The two men glanced about.

"Psst."

The sound definitely wasn't coming from the guests. Anthony nudged him and gestured toward the back door. Jeremiah turned. He saw Emily's head and face through an opening only wide enough for her to get his attention. His heart plummeted. Surely she wouldn't call things off now that everyone in town had shown up for the service.

She motioned to him. Amid twitters of laughter, Jeremiah strode to the door, the *clack* of his boots incredibly loud on the wooden planks. He stepped outside and closed the door behind him, then stopped short and gaped.

The sight of Emily dressed in a gown of white silk hit him like a punch in the gut. A matching white ribbon woven through her braided hair added regal appeal to her already breathtaking beauty. Her chin was lifted with an air of dignity, which only heightened the effect of her hair, twisted in layers atop her head. Emily St. John looked like a queen. The honor of becoming her husband shot through Jeremiah, and suddenly he felt kingly himself.

"Are you all right?" she asked, pulling him from his stupor.

Ears burning, he cleared his throat and smiled. "You're beautiful." Bending at the waist, he kissed her cheek, forcing back the desire to take her into his arms and claim those full, soft lips.

"Oh, Jeremiah." Her voice almost seemed to hold a moan beneath the words.

A sense of dread slithered through Jeremiah. He steeled himself against what was coming, determined not to show his anxiety.

"What's the holdup, Emily? We have a church full of guests back there."

From the corner of his eye, he caught movement and cut a glance in that direction. For the first time since stepping outside, he noticed Tarah and Cassidy standing a few feet away, both faces clouded with worry.

Looking from one woman to the next, he scowled, sensing a conspiracy. He focused his gaze on his lovely fiancée. "Are we getting married or not?"

Emily cleared her throat. "That depends entirely upon you."

"Good. Then let's go." Jeremiah snatched her hand and headed back toward the door.

"Wait!"

Somehow he had known it wouldn't be that easy. He halted and turned to face her. Concern washed over him. Her face had gone white as the church house. Instead of releasing her as he'd planned, he pulled her close, pressing their clasped hands against his chest. "What's on your mind?"

Cassidy cleared her throat loudly. "You two certainly don't need us." She held out a document to Emily. "Here you are, sweetheart."

"Are you sure about this, Em?" Tarah asked. "It would be better if you just tear it up."

Emily pulled away from Jeremiah's steady grasp. "I'm sure."

Cassidy stepped forward and gave her a quick hug. "Then I guess we'll run along and wait with the rest of the family and your guests."

Cassidy beat a hasty exit, followed closely by Tarah.

With a raised brow, Jeremiah met Emily's gaze. "I suppose you're going to tell me what that is."

Emily dropped her gaze and unfolded the paper. "Yes. It's a contract of sorts. Between the two of us."

"I thought the marriage certificate was a contract."

"It is. As far as the legality of our actual marriage is concerned. But this. . . Here, just go ahead and read it for yourself."

Jeremiah saw the print, read the words, and still couldn't believe what they conveyed. "You expect me to sign this?" he asked incredulously.

"Yes. Before we say our vows. I have to protect my interests."

"Your interests? I thought they would be *our* interests once we're married."

"I want your word you'll allow me to continue to operate Emily's Place as I see fit. That you won't go behind my back and try to sell it or try to force me to stay home and cook and clean while you take over both stores."

"Why would I want to do that? I have my hands full with one. Besides, legally, your property is yours. Didn't you know that?"

"Yes, but that doesn't stop men from taking over or bullying their wives into giving up what they own."

"Don't you trust me?" Pain knifed through Jeremiah. If she didn't trust him, she couldn't love him.

"Will you sign?"

Jeremiah had hoped to merge the two stores and run them together with Emily as his partner. Now to even mention it would cause her to think he wanted to steal from her. He steeled his heart against the pain and leveled his gaze at her. "You're sure you want to do this like a business arrangement rather than a marriage?"

"I'm sure." Her lips pressed together in a grim line.

"All right. I'll sign. For one reason only—if we call off the wedding now, it will cause more of a scandal than it would if you had just kept your original plan not to marry me."

"I understand."

Her grim, businesslike attitude sent a tremor of annoyance through him. Emily had made her position abundantly clear. Fine, he'd play her game, though he inwardly cringed, knowing that playing games with the holy institution of marriage was a dangerous thing. Still, how could he agree to her terms and expect to have an honest relationship? Until she trusted him, they'd have to keep things at a business level. He gathered a deep breath. "Another thing. . . Once I sign the contract, promising to leave Emily's Place firmly in your care, we enter into a business arrangement—not a marriage."

Emily's eyes grew wide. "What do you mean?"

"Exactly what you think I mean. You'll live at my farm because it would cause too much talk otherwise, but we won't pretend at marriage. This is for appearances only and to protect our families from scandal. That's what you wanted, right? My ma will be the only person aware of our living arrangements, and I assure you she won't reveal it to anyone."

"For appearances only? But what about. . ." Emily's face reddened.

"What? Children?"

She nodded and ducked her head.

Jeremiah sneered. "Why do you need children? You'll be too busy running Emily's Place to take care of them. Or do you plan to hold a baby while you measure dress goods and make change?"

"Well, you don't have to be insulting! All I am asking for is a little respect for my rights as a businesswoman."

"Insulting? Honey, this contract is an insult. All you had to do was ask me to stay out of your business and let you run it, and I would have. Instead, you accuse me of being underhanded. If you had given me the chance, I would have told you how proud I am to have a wife to share my business with—someone I can talk things over with who will understand all the ins and outs of owning a mercantile. I looked forward to the end of the day, sharing that with you."

"But, Jeremiah, we can still—"

"No, you want us to stay competitors. So decide. Right now. Either I sign the contract and we enter into a business agreement; or I don't, and we join our lives in every way. I won't force you, but you can't have it both ways. A man can only take so much."

Jeremiah held his breath and studied the struggle of emotions crossing her face. His hopes dashed to the ground when she squared her shoulders and met his gaze evenly.

He motioned toward the parsonage. "Let's go and sign this so we can get on with it. The good people of Harper don't want to wait all day to watch the most anticipated wedding of the year."

⌒

Emily squinted against the blinding sunset. The wagon rattled, the only sound breaking the thick silence around Emily, Jeremiah, and Mrs. Daniels as they made their way toward the Danielses' farm.

Emily Daniels. Emily Daniels. She'd been trying on the name all day, though she hadn't quite had the nerve to speak it aloud. Heaviness covered her like a thick, suffocating quilt—not the freedom she'd expected to feel over her victory.

Jeremiah had signed the contract in the parsonage and headed back to the church, leaving her with no option but to follow. Somehow she had the feeling she'd made the biggest mistake of her life—not in marrying Jeremiah, but in insisting he sign a contract between them.

She shot a sideways glance and caught a glimpse of her husband's tightly clenched square jaw. His shoulders rose and fell as he stared intently at the rutted ground ahead of them, carefully maneuvering the horses around the worst of the dips and holes.

He turned his head and slowly met her gaze. Rather than condemnation, anger, accusation, or any of the emotions Emily would have expected to find flashing in his eyes, she was taken aback by the smile he gave her. Her throat tightened, and her eyes stung with unshed tears. She would do anything if given the chance to go back a few hours and tear up that hateful contract.

The wagon suddenly lurched, pulling Jeremiah's attention back to the road, the last stretch leading up to the Danielses' farm.

"Well, we're home," Mrs. Daniels said matter-of-factly. Emily could feel Jeremiah's gaze upon her as she studied her new home. The dwelling was made of sandstone like her pa's ranch house. Only this house was very small in comparison. She imagined there was only one bedroom and maybe a loft.

Emily's heart leapt, and she pictured children running about the yard, chasing squawking hens and feeding the hogs penned up next to the barn. She could see a miniature Jeremiah or two and a couple of redheaded girls following after her as she took apple cider to her hardworking husband.

Mrs. Daniels cleared her throat loudly, arresting Emily's attention. Heat crept to her cheeks as she realized she was the only one left on the wagon seat and Jeremiah stood waiting to help her down.

"Sorry," she muttered.

The older woman harrumphed and stomped to the house.

"It's not much after what you grew up living in, I know." Jeremiah lifted her down, then turned to the back of the wagon and started to grab her things.

"Not at all, Jeremiah. It's lovely. W–will you be building a home for us, or. . ."

"Ma stays with us until the house and land pass to me," he said, a note of finality edging his tone. With her bag in hand, he brushed past, sweeping her a sideways glance. "It's not like we're going to need more room, is it?"

When they entered the house, Mrs. Daniels already stood before the cookstove, stoking the coals. "All that waiting at the church killed the fire," she grumbled. "I'm going to have to build it back up before I can start supper."

Emily's face warmed. "I'm sorry, Mrs. Daniels," she said. "May I help?"

The woman turned on her. "I won't have you soiling your fancy clothes," she huffed. "Get yourself settled in. Supper will be ready in a couple of hours."

"Come with me, Emily," Jeremiah said. "I'll show you where you'll sleep."

Following meekly, Emily could feel her mother-in-law's gaze burning into her back. She squared her shoulders and trailed after Jeremiah across the room and into the only separate room from the rest of the house.

Inside, a lovely four-poster bed sat against the far wall, displaying a rose-covered quilt. "Your ma thought you might like to have that."

Emily strode to the bed and sat. She smoothed her fingertips over the soft quilt, picturing it on Pa and Ma's bed for as long as she could remember. "Yes, I've always loved this quilt. Ma promised me years ago that it would be mine on my wedding day. I'd forgotten."

"I'll leave you to start unpacking while I unload the rest of your things. Where do you want your rocking chair?"

"How about in front of the fireplace for cold evenings? Ma and Pa always sit and talk before a fire."

"I'm sorry, Emily. There isn't a fireplace. Pa always said they were a waste of wood. And in these parts we couldn't afford to waste any."

"That sounds reasonable." She sighed and waved. "I suppose it doesn't matter, then. Anywhere your ma would like for it to go is fine with me."

With a frown, Jeremiah closed the distance between them and sat next to her. "Things aren't going to be easy for any of us, but I want you to think of this as your home, too."

"There's only one bedroom," she said flatly. "Where is your mother going to sleep? She can't really climb into the loft at her age, can she?"

Jeremiah chuckled. "You probably didn't notice, but there's a bed in the corner of the other room. Ma will sleep there. I'm taking the loft."

Emily darted her gaze to him and frowned. "Husbands and wives generally share a room."

"That was the original plan, but things changed, remember?"

"I know, but I thought. . ."

"You thought we'd share a room without being intimate?" Jeremiah's face reddened at his bold statement. He stood and walked toward the door. "As I said earlier, a man can only take so much. I'll bring in the rest of your things."

Tears pooled in Emily's eyes as, miserably, she watched him leave and close the door behind him. She stood and began hanging her things in the wardrobe. Jeremiah made two more trips from the wagon, but they didn't speak. When he left for the last time, he informed her supper would be ready in about an hour.

When her things were put away, Emily noted the time. She had forty-five minutes before she was expected for the meal. The thought of facing the awkward silence was more than she could bear, so she stretched out on the soft mattress. She stared at the ceiling, wishing for all she was worth that events had unfolded differently today.

If only she hadn't listened to Amelia Bell!

Chapter 13

When Emily didn't emerge for supper, Jeremiah tapped on her door and waited. After a minute he turned the knob and stepped inside. At the sight of his new bride sleeping peacefully on the bed he'd prepared for them to share, Jeremiah's heart stirred within his chest.

He swallowed hard and tiptoed closer, daring a look at her lovely, pale face. Tenderness washed over him. Tears clung to her lashes as though she'd cried herself to sleep. He understood her tears. He wanted Emily to be happy—he'd wanted to bring her here and begin a life together.

Why did you have to put a contract between us, you silly woman? All you have to do is tear it up. . .prove you believe in me, or this is the first of many lonely nights for us both.

She sighed and snuggled deeper into the fluffy mattress. Jeremiah backed slowly away and gently closed the door behind him.

"Well?" Ma asked, setting a pot of stew on the table. "Is she coming or not?"

"She's sleeping, and I hated to wake her. We'll keep her supper warm in case she's hungry later."

Jeremiah grabbed Emily's bowl, grateful that Ma had at least had the courtesy to set a place for his wife. He dipped out a portion of stew and set it on the back of the stove to keep warm. Then he took his place at the table. Ma snorted. "I can see things are going to be different around here from now on."

"Did you have any doubt of that?"

"No, but I didn't expect her to start running things the moment she arrived."

A grin tipped Jeremiah's lips at her exaggeration. "She's sleeping, Ma; how does that translate to her running things?"

Ma's mouth tightened into a firm line. She clasped her hands in front of her and closed her eyes.

Taking the silent hint, Jeremiah bowed his head and said the blessing. When he looked up, Ma's faded gray eyes were narrowed and pensively staring at him.

"I just hope you don't live to regret your hasty marriage like I did."

With a scowl, Jeremiah dipped a generous portion of venison stew into his bowl. "I don't see any comparison."

"Marriages can be hard for many different reasons. Your pa was a bully and a gambler, but at least we knew what to expect from him." She forked a chunk of meat from her bowl and held it suspended in front of her mouth. "I know you. You've loved this girl since you were ten years old. Suddenly you have an opportunity to marry her, and you jump on it like a cat on a mouse. All of your hopes of a family life are wrapped up in this marriage. I just don't want to see you hurt." She took her bite.

Jeremiah sent her a smile. "I know you only care about my happiness, and I appreciate it. But first off, my hopes are firmly set in Christ and my relationship with Him—not my relationship with Emily or anyone else. You taught me long ago that God is faithful even during times of disappointment and struggle. Secondly, I didn't jump on the chance to marry her. I just did the right thing by her—not that I was complaining at the turn of events. And thirdly. . ." He grinned across the table. "I liked her a whole lot when we were ten, but I didn't actually fall in love with her until we were eleven. She pitched the baseball and hit me in the eye. I've been smitten ever since."

Ma chuckled. "I've never seen a person so proud of a shiner in all my born days." Her amusement quickly drained from her lined face, and her eyes grew solemn once more. "But, son, you're not eleven anymore. The kind of wounds a person can inflict on the one who loves him are a lot more painful than a black eye—believe me, I know all about heartache and black eyes. The bruises were easier to bear."

Jeremiah swallowed his bite of food with difficulty as the old, familiar anger began to burn inside of him. The memory of Ma's bruises, the unreasonable accusations, and the gambling debts clouded his mind, pushing aside dreams of his own marriage.

As though reading his dark thoughts, Ma tapped on the table to gain his attention. "I didn't bring that up to remind you of the bad times, Jeremiah. But I want you to be realistic. Don't set your sights for happiness on Emily. All those dreams you've lived with about her all these years are bound to be a sight prettier than what's to come."

"Don't be such a worrier, Ma. Emily and I will get along just fine."

Ma snorted. "Is that why you moved your things into the loft? I've half a mind to get my Bible out and show that girl a thing or two about a wife's place."

Jeremiah's ears burned. "Ma. . . ," he groaned.

"Oh, hogwash. You're a man now. And I live under this roof, too. Did you think I wasn't going to notice?"

"At the very least, I hoped you wouldn't mention it. It's rather indelicate."

"Well, some things just aren't right. That's all. It isn't right for a married man to sleep alone in the loft while his spoiled wife sleeps away the day in the feather bed he labored to restuff for them to share! I'd say that's more than indelicate. It's downright indecent."

She was going to cry! He could hear the catch in her throat. "Ma, would it make you feel better if I toss my wife's things into the loft and sleep in the feather bed myself?"

As predicted, she chortled, keeping the tears at bay. "If I had my way, that's exactly what you'd do, you silly boy." A deep sigh engulfed her, and she gazed upon him with the glow of mother-love, that comforting, familiar look he'd always seen shine from her eyes. "You've been such a good son. How many boys would work at Tucker's and stay in school, then come home and do farm chores like a man? You took care of me after your pa died, when I should have been taking care of you. I was determined to see that you found a good wife who would make you happy, and look—I failed again."

Jeremiah shifted his gaze to his plate. While he appreciated his ma's confidence in him, he knew she saw him through the eyes of an adoring mother. She tended to forget the fact that he had stolen from Tuck over and over before giving his life to the Lord. And since he was the only comfort she had, Jeremiah didn't remind her. But it still made him uncomfortable to be admired so undeservingly.

"I will be happy. You'll see. Once we get used to one another, I'm sure things will just naturally take care of themselves. Remember, I may have loved her all these years, but that doesn't mean she's loved me. As a matter of fact, other than once when we were sixteen, Emily never even noticed me until she bought Tucker's."

He reached across the table and grabbed a warm dinner roll from the basket.

"Well, she should have noticed you!" The change in Ma's tone arrested his attention. He jerked up to meet her flashing eyes. "I would have done anything to have married such a good man, and just look. . .your wife doesn't even share your first supper together with you. Instead, she sleeps right through it and expects you to keep it warm for her!"

"She doesn't expect anything! She just went to sleep. That's all. You can't hold it against her when you wouldn't let her help you cook."

"Are you taking her side against mine? Is this the way it's going to be from now on? Why, I might as well move off somewhere and live alone. I can ask Miss Hastings tomorrow if she has any rooms available at her boarding-house. I suppose I can take in sewing and washing again to support myself. I wouldn't want to be a burden on you and your new wife."

Feeling like a brute for making his mother cry, Jeremiah went to her and crouched down next to her chair, gathering her into his arms. "Come now, Ma. You know you're not a burden."

"Are you sure?" She sniffed and accepted his handkerchief. "Perhaps your wife wouldn't mind sharing your bed if I wasn't here. After all, even if she is an old maid, every new bride needs her privacy."

Jeremiah heard a gasp coming from the direction of the bedroom.

With a groan, he glanced up to find Emily staring ashen-faced in the doorway.

$\backsim$

She would not give that horrible woman the satisfaction of seeing her cry! Plus, she had half a mind to let her dear mother-in-law know just who decided not to share a bed with whom. Satisfying as blurting it out might be, Emily couldn't imagine actually doing so and ever being able to face Jeremiah again. She simply jerked her chin up and walked to the table, where Jeremiah stood holding her chair for her. "I'm sorry. I guess I didn't sleep well last night what with all the excitement of the wedding."

Jeremiah pushed in her chair, then walked to the stove and brought her a bowl filled with stew.

Emily's cheeks warmed. "I could have gotten it myself."

"As any wife should," Mrs. Daniels huffed.

"Ma. . ."

"Well, I have a right to my say-so, don't I? Wouldn't you say so, Emily, dear?" Her smile was a little too sweet after the conversation Emily had just overheard.

"I—I suppose so."

"You see?" She glanced at Jeremiah. "Your wife is an advocate for the rights of women. So don't try to shush me again."

"Rights are one thing," he shot back. "Bad manners are another."

Emily gasped at his disrespectful tone. "It's fine, Jeremiah. Your ma is right. I should have gotten my own supper, and I would have if I had realized you kept it warm on the stove for me. That was. . .very thoughtful of you, Mother Daniels."

"It wasn't my idea," she replied with an ungracious sniff. "I wanted to wake you up."

The woman was obviously spoiling for a fight, and Emily almost obliged. Only Jeremiah's pleading eyes halted her retort.

She took a bite, determined to pay her mother-in-law a compliment whether she deserved one or not. She chewed with relish and relief that she could praise the cook without deception.

"This is delicious, Mother Daniels," she said. "I'd love the recipe."

"Thank you," she replied curtly. "I'm surprised someone like you would be interested in a recipe."

"Someone like me?" Emily narrowed her eyes and captured the woman's challenging gaze. "What do you mean by that?"

"Isn't it rather obvious? A woman who chooses to work rather than taking care of her husband and home surely has no intention of cooking."

"Independence and domesticity aren't mutually exclusive, ma'am. I have every intention of being a wife to Jeremiah."

Her brow shot up, and her lips twisted into a sardonic smile. "Oh, really? Is that why—"

"Ma. Don't. . ."

"Never mind, Jeremiah." Emily's nostrils flared, and her grip tightened on her fork. "Remember, I am all for civil liberties. Your mother has a right to state whatever's on her mind."

Jeremiah's fork clanked against his bowl, and he stood suddenly. He swept them both with his disgusted gaze. "I don't have the stomach to listen to your bickering. I'm going out to do the chores. Kindly have this over with before I get back." So saying, he stomped to the door, grabbed his hat from its peg, and left.

"Now see what you've done, young lady? He can't even finish his meal."

"What I've done?" Emily closed her eyes, fighting for control. "I think we've gotten off on the wrong foot. I'm sorry for sounding testy. Since we're going to be living under the same roof, I think we had better try to get along—for all of our sakes, but particularly Jeremiah's."

A glint of grudging respect appeared in the woman's eyes, and Emily felt hope rising. "I'll clean up the supper dishes," she offered.

"No need for that. I've been cleaning my own kitchen for forty years. I will continue doing so. You have your store to attend, and Jeremiah has his. I'll attend to the house and cooking."

"But. . ." Emily didn't know what to say. She wanted to do the things wives were supposed to do. Cook, clean, wash her husband's shirts. Share his bed. Give him sons and daughters. But that wasn't the life Jeremiah had offered her. He had offered her a home. Period. A lonely bed in which to sleep at night. And a mother-in-law who clearly despised her.

Fine. Let Mother Daniels make her meals and wash her dishes. Emily was determined to find a way to make Jeremiah see that she could still be a wife to him whether she retained her contract between them or not. She had to make him see that every woman had the right—no, the responsibility—to protect her interests. And she had to do so without Jeremiah finding out that she'd overheard his humiliating conversation with Harold Baxter.

Who knew? She might even win her mother-in-law over to the suffragette movement. The woman certainly had the spirit for it.

Emily's lips curved upward at the thought.

Chapter 14

The wagon swayed with the ruts. Emily pressed against Jeremiah; and even though he knew it wasn't intentional, he couldn't help but enjoy the sensation of her arm against his. She righted herself immediately and resumed her ramrod straight position on the wagon seat. Ma sat on Emily's other side. . . equally silent, equally straight.

Three weeks. . .he'd been a groom for three weeks, and the women in his life were driving him crazy. They didn't bicker anymore. Thankfully. Now they were polite. And at times that was worse than the arguing.

He should have refused to drive them to town tonight and would have, except he wasn't sure they'd both make it home in one piece if he left them to their own devices.

It seemed ridiculous to him that he'd be dropping them off at the town hall so that Emily could give a speech inside while his ma protested from without. Downright embarrassing.

Give me the patience of Job, Lord. Because unless these two women You've placed in my life come to a meeting of minds soon—one way or another—I'm afraid I'll have to move out to the barn.

The wagon rolled onto the street, and slowly they made their way toward the hall. Jeremiah groaned. It seemed more folks had turned out tonight than had shown up to the Christmas pageant. He figured they were curious, knowing his mother—president of the League of Christian Women—would be the first in line to protest the unwomanly behavior of the suffragettes whom his wife supported.

A tug on his sleeve pulled him from his thoughts. He stared dumbly at Emily.

"Where are you going, Jeremiah? You rolled right past the hall. Everyone is staring."

Heat crept up his neck. "Sorry. My mind was in the clouds."

Emily gave him a shy smile. "No harm done."

Jeremiah's heart raced at the upward curve of her full lips. He patted her hand, which still clutched his sleeve. She released it immediately and ducked her head. Inwardly he smiled. Perhaps it wouldn't be long. She cared for him. He knew she did. Soon she'd realize she could trust him. And when she did, she would tear up that contract and come to him, knowing he'd never try to make her do something against her will. He wasn't anything like his pa.

"Just let us out here," she said. "We can walk a few steps back to the hall while you go on and find a place to tether the team."

"That all right with you, Ma?"

"We're already a spectacle," Ma huffed. "Might as well be a bigger one—imagine, the two of us walking together."

"How about if I let Emily off here, and then I can circle the team around and drop you off in front of the hall?"

"Don't be ridiculous. Everyone already saw us ride in together. We'd look even more foolish if you did that. We'll just get down here."

Jeremiah hopped from the wagon and extended his arms to Emily. She slid over without catching his gaze and allowed him to lift her down. So intent was he on the pleasant feel of his wife in his arms, Jeremiah failed to notice a deep crevice in the ground. Just as he turned her loose, she gasped and grappled for him, trying to keep from losing her footing in the wagon wheel rut.

In a flash, Jeremiah reached out and grabbed hold of her waist to steady her. It was a natural reaction, he told himself, to pull her closer—instinctive, really.

"Thank you," she whispered, withdrawing slightly but not actually pulling away.

Jeremiah's heart soared at the way she molded perfectly against him. The top of her head reached just under his chin, so that if she raised her head a bit and he bent ever so slightly. . . So help him, he'd give a front tooth for the courage to kiss her soundly right here and now. He gathered a deep breath, seriously contemplating the temptation, when Ma's loud clearing of the throat brought him back to reality.

"The two of you stop it immediately," Ma hissed.

With a gasp, Emily stepped back. Jeremiah resented the cold, empty void replacing her warmth. When he was sure she had her footing, he walked around and helped Ma from the wagon.

She gave him a cold, silent glare, raised her chin, and fell into step beside Emily.

Jeremiah watched them, each holding her head erect, shoulders straight, and striding purposefully toward the hall. With a sigh, he climbed back into the wagon and flapped the reins. He resumed his earlier silent prayer.

Yes, Lord. I need the patience of Job to get through these trials. Either that, or a nice warm bed in the barn ought to do it.

◈

Emily cast a sideways glance at her mother-in-law and sighed. The Lord knew she'd been trying to get along with Mother Daniels; but honestly, the woman sure didn't make it easy. Honey dripped from her lips when she spoke to her son and turned to vinegar before any words directed at Emily reached her ears.

The Bible said sweet and bitter waters couldn't flow from the same cistern, but Emily had proof that this woman definitely had an inward switch to make that possible. She smiled to herself. No, the Word wasn't wrong; but she couldn't quite figure out how to let those sweet words flow in her direction.

It wasn't as though she wasn't trying. No matter how hard she tried, she couldn't do anything to please the woman.

Tensions had been running high the last couple of days as each prepared for tonight. But Emily didn't want to make an enemy because of her beliefs. She only wanted to have the right to express them and not be ridiculed or despised because of that expression. Didn't they both love God? Weren't they both Christians? Why couldn't they live together without ungodly strife?

She felt she needed to speak candidly, or the woman would be impossible to live with in the upcoming days.

Halting, she reached for Mrs. Daniels. "Wait just a moment, please."

"What is it? Everyone is waiting for me."

"Yes, ma'am. I'll hurry, I promise. But there's something I want to say. I'm not sure how. . .but I want you to know, I don't want us to be enemies. We're family now, and I'd very much like it if we can be friends."

"Why are you bringing this up now, of all times?" Mrs. Daniels scowled. "You have a knack for doing things at the inappropriate time, girl. And I don't mind saying so."

"I don't know what you mean." Emily's stomach tightened at the disappointment of having her efforts thrown back in her face.

"You and Jeremiah." Disgust thickened her tone.

"Did I do something inappropriate with Jeremiah?" Her face warmed, knowing exactly what Mrs. Daniels was getting at but hoping she'd let it pass in the spirit of propriety.

However, as Emily had come to understand all too well, Jeremiah's mother chose carefully the topics she considered proper; and apparently she didn't have a qualm about this particular topic.

"It's ridiculous. You won't kiss my son at home, and yet right there on the street you use the oldest trick around to try and get one from him." She shook her head. "Believe me, you don't have to resort to trickery to get a kiss from a man. Especially one who's as smitten as my son is."

Emily felt the outrage from the tips of her toes to the top of her head. "What trick?" she asked, her voice suddenly shrill.

"Oh, come now. Tripping when you get out of the wagon so he has to catch you before you fall."

"That was an accident!"

"So you say. From where I sat, it looked mighty fishy."

"Then perhaps you need to purchase a pair of spectacles," Emily retorted.

"Well!" Mrs. Daniels pivoted and stomped away.

"Wait!"

The older woman spun around, her lips twisted downward, brow furrowed.

"Wh–what do you mean he's smitten?"

"Oh, for mercy's sake. What do you think I mean?"

Emily let her go this time, her heart about to explode with the joy of the merest hint that Jeremiah was smitten with her. He had told Amelia Bell he was sweet on her and that he wouldn't mind her printing it in the newspaper, but Emily had assumed he was just trying to get under her skin. Now she wasn't so sure.

On the other hand, perhaps Mrs. Daniels was wrong. She hadn't been the one to overhear Jeremiah talking with Harold about running her store. And the woman had certainly been wrong about her recent accusation. Emily fumed. Imagine the audacity! Accusing her of trying to finagle a kiss.

A guilty little shiver rubbed down her spine. Maybe she had taken advantage of the situation. But she certainly didn't cause it. And there wasn't a thing wrong with a woman offering her husband a kiss of thanks for saving her from a tumble in the street.

"Where do you think you're going, woman?"

Emily gasped and stopped short at the gruff voice, then realized the words came from the opposite side of the street and weren't directed at her. She peered more closely, her heart beating rapidly as she spied Mr. and Mrs. Gregory.

"Did you hear me? I asked where you think you're going." He had her by the shoulders and shook her hard until her hair came free from its pins and fell down her back.

"Please don't make a scene," the woman pleaded. "Let's just go home."

"Now you want to go home? I told you you're not to go near that meeting hall tonight, didn't I?"

"I–I'm sorry."

"You're sorry you got caught. Thought I wouldn't be home tonight. Thought I didn't know you sneak off to those meetings when I'm not around."

Unable to look away, Emily watched the exchange, her stomach quivering. She had seen Mrs. Gregory at the meetings and wondered how she'd managed to convince her husband to allow it. Now she realized the truth. Tears stung her eyes, and she debated whether to run across the street and rescue the poor woman. But she knew it would do no good. *Please watch over Mrs. Gregory, dear Lord.*

With a heavy heart, she turned back toward the hall.

"Do you see what your ideas have created, Mrs. Daniels?"

Dread engulfed Emily as she realized that this time, Mr. Gregory was calling to her.

Facing the street, she swallowed hard. "My ideas are creating good things, sir. Hopefully before long, the law will favor a woman and not allow her husband to bully her. Now if you'll excuse me, I have a speech to give. Good day, Mrs. Gregory. I'll pray for you."

Knees wobbly, she mustered her courage and stomped away.

She halted close to the hall, hating the thought of shouldering her way through the crowd of protesting women blocking the steps. She wasn't afraid of bodily harm, for she knew none of them would accost her in that manner. But she detested the disapproving whispers, the stares, the implications about her womanhood. Still, better that than Mr. Gregory's brand of disapproval.

"Come on, I'll walk you in."

Emily turned at the sound of Jeremiah's voice next to her.

"That was fast."

"I found a close spot. I've been following you." He took her chilled hand, warming her as he laced his fingers through hers. "That was some speech you gave already."

"You witnessed my exchange with Mr. Gregory?"

He nodded grimly. "I thought I might have to take care of him."

Emily's heart turned over at the iron in his tone. "I'm glad you didn't." She gave him a teasing grin. "After all, didn't you say you're not much of a fighter? Besides, if I can take on your ma, I can handle a bully like Mr. Gregory."

"Something happen between you and Ma?"

"We had words," she admitted.

He groaned. "What did you argue about? Never mind; don't tell me. It's better if I don't know."

She grinned. "I wasn't going to tell you anyway. Your mother and I made a pact that we wouldn't involve you in our disagreements."

"That explains the unbearable silence at suppertime."

Emily couldn't keep back her smile. "We could stop holding back on your account."

He gazed warmly at her and grinned in return, nearly snatching Emily's breath away. "I think I'd prefer to suffer the silence."

He seemed unaware of the havoc his nearness was wreaking on her—legs trembled, cheeks were warm, and she was quite possibly heading for a dead faint—although she couldn't be sure since she'd never actually fainted before.

Squeezing her fingers, he leaned in close and whispered against her ear, "Time to face the gauntlet. Don't worry, I'll protect you."

His teasing tone eased her tension, and she elbowed him playfully. "The main one you have to protect me from is your ma."

To Emily's relief, the sight of Jeremiah firmly stationed at her side seemed to drain a bit of spunk from the ladies. The crowd moved back, creating a path for them to the door.

"Just where do you think you're going?" Mother Daniels took one step and blocked the entrance. She ignored Emily, focusing her gaze on Jeremiah.

He leaned forward and kissed his mother's cheek, then whispered something into her ear. Concern shot through Emily as the woman's face drained of color, and sudden tears pooled in her eyes before she ducked her head, stepping aside.

Jeremiah ushered Emily inside.

"What on earth did you say to her? You made your mother cry."

"I did?" He looked genuinely surprised. "You must be mistaken."

"I most certainly am not mistaken. I know tears when I see them!"

A scowl marred his features. "You two are driving me to distraction! All I said was that my wife is giving a speech tonight, and I intend to be in here to support you."

"Oh." Emily wanted to say so much more. Just as she opened her mouth, Amelia grabbed her.

"Nice to see you here, Jeremiah." She beamed at him. "I have to borrow Emily, but you can have her back right after the rally."

"I'm counting on it." He kept his gaze focused squarely on Emily. She wished Amelia would go away. As a matter of fact, she wished everyone would go away. She could do without the noisy women gearing up for the rally and the chanters outside expressing their displeasure with those women—including her. They could all just go away!

Who cared about her dumb speech anyway? What did any of it matter?

At this moment, she only cared about one right—the right to be alone with her husband.

Chapter 15

Jeremiah grinned as he helped Emily into the wagon and climbed up beside her to wait for Ma.

"You gave a good speech tonight. Even better than the first one."

The warmth of Emily's smile cut through the chilly late February night and wrapped around him like a pair of arms.

She sent him a saucy look from her cat-green eyes—a flirtatious look, pleasing Jeremiah a great deal. "You're a hero," she said. "I believe every woman in town envies me. I may have to keep an eye on the unmarried girls."

"Jealous?"

She shook her head, her eyes sparkling in the lantern light. "Proud."

Jeremiah chuckled. "Isn't that a sin?"

"Maybe. Although I'm not sure that kind of pride is the same kind that God hates. But just to be on the safe side. . . How about, I'm feeling incredibly blessed and thankful for your support?"

She reached over and pressed her palm against his arm. "Thank you, Jeremiah."

He'd felt incredibly blessed himself as he watched his wife stand before all those women and be admired. Emily had displayed a new confidence as she proudly stated that he supported her efforts to run her own business.

He took her hand and brought it to his lips, capturing her gaze.

She stared back at him, and he recognized the look of love shining in her eyes.

Leaning close, he rested his head against the top of hers. "I'd kiss you if we weren't in the middle of town," he whispered, pressing their clasped hands close to his heart.

"I'd kiss you back." Hearing the smile in her voice, Jeremiah inhaled deeply, taking in the scent of lilacs wafting from her hair.

She released a soft sigh, and Jeremiah's heart beat a rapid rhythm against his chest. Where was Ma, anyway? The quicker she showed up, the quicker they could get home, away from the town's prying eyes. Because he had every intention of claiming that kiss.

Sobering at the thought of what Ma would have to say to him about entering that building tonight, he came crashing back to earth. He might be practically a hero with the suffragettes, but he was far from a hero with the ladies in town who represented the other view. To their way of thinking, he was a traitor, a bad son, and most likely bullied by his aggressive, independent wife. Why couldn't folks tend to their own business and leave him alone?

"What's wrong?" Emily's brow furrowed. "Thinking about your ma?" Her voice rang with sympathy.

"Partly. And partly I was thinking about other folks and their wrong ideas about you and some of the other women who were there tonight."

"Like my brothers thinking Mr. Krenshaw is a sissy because his wife is in the movement?"

Nodding, Jeremiah straightened in the wagon seat but still kept her hand grasped in his.

"But you see how Mrs. and Mr. Krenshaw are together. She adores her husband, and he adores her. He is just a very forward-thinking man. I don't see why folks have to make issues out of things that are none of their affair."

"Well, she does smoke cigars and wear men's britches," Jeremiah drawled.

"True. . ." Emily nibbled her bottom lip. "But that doesn't mean she bullies her husband, does it?"

"No."

"And they never show up to services on Sundays, so I don't believe they know Jesus. That doesn't mean she wears the pants in the family. . .well, you know what I mean."

"I do. And no, I don't think she wears the figurative pants in the family. But I am afraid most folks think so, and there's nothing we can do to change their minds."

Emily sat up straighter in the seat and squared her shoulders. "I intend to do everything I can to change folks' minds. It's just not right for a man to be spoken poorly of because his wife wants to vote. Land sakes, they let us vote for school board positions, why not state and federal officials? It's nonsense."

"I agree."

She regarded him with a raised brow. "You really do? You're not just pretending to save face?"

"Is that what you thought tonight?"

"I considered it. After all, how many of the men inside, other than Mr. Krenshaw, of course, honestly support their wives, and how many are just showing up so they get their suppers cooked and their beds warmed?"

"You probably have a point, but there is always the chance that the men appreciate the value of a good strong opinion coming from someone with a lot of sense." Jeremiah squeezed her hand. "I think this country would do well to allow women like you to vote. As a matter of fact, there are quite a few men whose votes might cause more harm than good."

Emily's laughter rang loudly into the air. She threw her arms about his neck, nearly knocking him backward from the wagon in her exuberance.

"Well, I can see you weren't too worried about my absence." Ma's cold voice pulled them apart. She stood next to Miss Hastings. "Myra has graciously informed me she has a vacancy."

"Ma, what are you talking about? You don't need to move into the boardinghouse."

"I wouldn't stay another night in that house knowing that I'm not wanted. It's obvious that wife of yours has poisoned your mind with all this women's rights nonsense—enough so that you would betray your own mother—publicly humiliate me!"

"Mother Daniels, please. Jeremiah didn't—"

"I am not speaking to you, young lady, and don't call me 'Mother Daniels.' And don't pretend you aren't happy to be rid of me."

"But I don't want you to move out of your home on my account." Emily's voice trembled. She tried to pull her hand away, but Jeremiah kept it firmly grasped in his.

"Ma, how about coming home and we'll discuss all of this in private?"

She raised her chin stubbornly. "There's nothing to discuss. I will get the wagon from the livery while you two are at your stores tomorrow and will pack my things. And don't worry, I intend to hire Billy Simpson to help me, so you won't be bothered."

"You're never any bother, Ma."

Hurt clouded her eyes. "So you're willing to help me move out? I knew you wanted to be rid of me."

Jeremiah released Emily's hand and climbed down. "Ma, Emily and I want you to stay at home where you belong. Give up this silly idea and let me help you into the wagon."

Ma lifted her chin stubbornly. "My mind's made up. Come, Myra, let's get home."

"At least let me drive you and Miss Hastings over to the boardinghouse."

"No, thank you, we'd prefer to walk."

"Then let me walk with you. There are still some icy patches on the sidewalk."

"Then we'll walk on the road."

"Be careful on the road, too. There are deep ruts. Remember Emily stumbled earlier."

"That is a matter of debate."

From the wagon seat, Jeremiah heard Emily gasp.

"Ma, wait. I'm coming with you."

"I am not a child," she snapped. "I can certainly walk a few feet without your help."

"Yes, ma'am," Jeremiah said with a sigh.

He watched her walk away, then climbed into the wagon.

"I'm so sorry, Jeremiah," Emily said, self-condemnation evident in her tone.

"Regardless of our differences, I never wanted your ma to move out."

"This isn't your fault, honey. Ma's got a stubborn streak a mile wide, and I stepped on it tonight when I walked into that hall."

"I wouldn't have been mad at you if you had chosen to stay away," Emily said quietly.

He reached forward and tipped her chin until she met his gaze. "I went because I believe in you, not to keep you from becoming angry with me. And I want everyone to know I believe in you."

Her expression softened, and her eyes looked almost liquid in the moonlight. Drawing a swift breath, he lowered his head. Just as he claimed her eager lips, a scream filled the air.

Heart in his throat, Jeremiah grabbed the reins and drove the short distance to the source of the scream. Seeing his mother crumpled in the street, he felt his heart in his throat. He halted the horses and gave the reins to Emily, then sprinted to his mother's side and fell to his knees.

"What happened?" he asked Miss Hastings.

The woman trembled, and her voice shook. "As you said might happen, she twisted her ankle in one of the wagon tracks. She fell before I could reach out to steady her."

"Ma, I'm going to have to lift you in order to put you in the back of the wagon. We'll take you home while someone rides for Doc St. John, okay?"

Ma nodded and attempted a slight smile, but it fell short and instead appeared as a grimace.

Emily pressed gently on Jeremiah's arm. "I'm going to grab some blankets from my store so she doesn't have to lie down on the wood."

Without waiting for an answer, Emily flew the few feet to Emily's Place and made it back to the street in record time. She quickly spread several blankets in the back of the wagon.

Ma moaned softly when Jeremiah lifted her from the ground. She fainted by the time she was settled into the bed of the wagon. He released a relieved sigh that she was free from pain for a little while. Her leg had felt twisted in his arms, and he knew it was badly broken.

He drove as quickly as he could without jostling her too much. Emily remained quiet next to him. He wanted to comfort her. . .to reassure her that this wasn't her fault, but he was struggling with his own guilt over the matter. Why hadn't he just insisted Ma come home? All she had wanted was some reassurance that he still needed her and wanted her around. The truth of the matter was, he'd been so focused on getting alone with his wife that he hadn't tried nearly hard enough to dissuade Ma from staying the night at Miss Hastings's.

They finally arrived at the farm and settled Ma into Emily's bed. He knew when Ma came to, she'd protest sleeping there, but Emily had insisted.

Emily's brother Sam, the town physician, arrived within minutes. Emily ushered him into the bedroom, and she and Jeremiah paced the sitting room until he emerged a few minutes later.

"How bad is she?" Jeremiah asked. "I reckon she broke her leg?"

Sam nodded solemnly. "I'm afraid so. I need to set it quickly, and of course she'll have to stay in bed until it heals."

"Of course."

"How long until she heals up, Sam?" Emily asked, her eyes soft with sympathy.

"I'm not sure. Quite some time, maybe. She may never regain full use of that leg. As a matter of fact, I'd say it's doubtful she'll ever walk unaided by a walking stick, at least."

He glanced at Jeremiah. "I could use some help setting the leg and getting it in a splint. You up to it?"

Jeremiah's stomach churned, but he nodded. He followed Sam into the bedroom and held Ma still while Sam set the bones. After the splint was on and the leg tightly wrapped, Sam regarded Jeremiah soberly. "She's going to need 100 percent care for a while. Your ma can't even attempt to use that leg for several weeks. If she tries, she may break it worse and lose all hope of ever walking again. Make sure she knows that."

"I will."

Sam snapped his bag shut and headed for the sitting room. He bent and kissed Emily on the cheek.

"How is she, Sam?" Emily asked, her eyes clouded with worry.

"Still sleeping. I used a little chloroform to make sure she didn't wake up while I was working on her leg, so she'll probably sleep through the night. I left a bottle of laudanum for when the pain is too much for her to bear. But use it sparingly so she doesn't come to rely on it."

Listening to Emily question her brother, Jeremiah couldn't help but think that if Ma could only see how much Emily cared about her, perhaps the barbs and insinuations would stop. Perhaps she could meet his wife somewhere in the middle.

Sam clapped his hat on his head and headed for the door.

"Sam—wait. How do we care for her?"

"Jeremiah will fill you in. Just be careful around her leg, and don't let her get up."

With a frustrated sigh, she closed the door after him and turned to Jeremiah. "I wish he could have told us more."

Jeremiah repeated Sam's counsel and instructions. "I'll ask around and perhaps hire a girl to cook and clean and care for Ma."

Emily's face drained of color, and her lips trembled. "You don't think I can do all that?"

"You have the store to run. I was only thinking of hiring someone to do the things Ma usually does around here and to tend to her while we're gone."

"Jeremiah, if you don't mind, I'd rather hire someone to look after the store for me so I can stay and take care of your mother."

His jaw dropped open. Never in a million years had he considered Emily for the job. "Do you think that's a good idea?"

Emily shrugged. "I think it's a God idea. It came to me as I was praying. Work can't come before family. A woman has needs that her son simply can't attend to, so you can't stay home with her. But she needs family, not hired help."

"She'll eat you alive, honey. Are you sure God gave you this idea?"

"Who else?"

Jeremiah didn't want to say who sprang to mind.

Emily scowled. "It wasn't the devil. I know it doesn't look like a good idea. But sometimes the worst ones turn out to be the best. Who knows, maybe your ma will learn to love me like a daughter."

Lacking the heart to further discourage her, Jeremiah smiled warmly. "Maybe you're right."

Emily smiled brightly. "Thank you, Jeremiah. I know this is for the best."

Chapter 16

"Emilee—ee—ee!"

"Just a minute," Emily growled under her breath. She slammed Jeremiah's wet shirt against the washboard and straightened up, stretching her aching back. She sighed. Her every effort over the past few weeks had been met with scorn, and Mother Daniels's constant need for attention nearly drove Emily to distraction. She had truly hoped their time together would improve the woman's opinion of her, but if anything, it had worsened.

Feeling guilty for her sour thoughts, Emily determined to be extra pleasant this trip inside. She dried her hands on her apron and refrained from stomping into the house. "Yes, Mother Daniels?" she asked, entering the bedroom.

"I need another pillow at my back. I'd like to read for a while."

Emily couldn't fault her for wanting a little entertainment. After weeks in bed, anyone would be touchy. But with all of these interruptions, how was a body to get anything done?

She grabbed a pillow and gently adjusted it under the older woman's shoulders. "How's that?"

"A little high."

Irritation niggled Emily's stomach. She adjusted the pillow again. "This?"

"Yes, it's fine now."

"All right, then," Emily said, forcing a cheery smile. "I'll get back to my washing."

A grimace crossed Mother Daniels's face.

"Are you in pain?"

"No. You run along. I don't want to keep you." The grimace again.

Emily hesitated. "Then what is it?"

"What is what?"

"You looked like you wanted to say something." And it didn't look like a pleasant something, she wanted to add, but didn't.

"It's nothing. You have better things to do than take care of an old woman."

Biting back a retort and resisting the temptation to roll her eyes, Emily dug deep inside and tried to find compassion for her mother-in-law. After all, she couldn't imagine having to stay cooped up day in and day out with only four walls staring back at her. "Nonsense," she assured her mother-in-law. "What can I do for you?"

Her mouth tightened into something resembling a grudging smile. "Well, since you insist, I could do with a nice mug of coffee." She gave Emily a sharp glance. "Only, be careful not to get it too strong this time. This morning's coffee nearly choked me."

And yet it hadn't stopped her from asking for a second cup. Emily refused to begin a war of words with the ungrateful matron. Rather, she smiled. "All right, I'll do my best to make it a little more to your liking."

"Thank you. If you're sure it's not too much trouble."

"No trouble at all." *Unless you happen to have piles of laundry to do.*

Emily made her way into the front room and grabbed the coffee beans from the shelf above the stove. She ground the beans, then took the coffeepot to the outside pump to fill it with water. On her way back to the house, she eyed her pile of half-washed laundry and grimaced. At this rate, she'd never have it all finished before Jeremiah returned from town. And she so wanted to prove herself useful in household duties.

While the coffee boiled, she decided to start their supper. Jeremiah had shot and killed two rabbits the day before and had mentioned a "hankering" for some slow-roasted rabbit. Emily had been planning tonight's meal ever since.

She went to the root cellar, grabbed the rabbits and some preserved vegetables, then headed back to the kitchen.

Twenty minutes later, she gave a happy nod and resumed scrubbing clothes. Mother Daniels was occupied with a recent dime novel and her cup of coffee, slightly sweetened as she liked. To Emily's delight, the woman had actually smiled her thanks and expressed her satisfaction with the taste of the coffee.

The house filled with the smell of cooking meat and onions, and Emily's stomach rumbled, reminding her that she hadn't eaten since breakfast; but she decided against stopping for food. She had precious little time to finish her chores without taking time to eat.

A smile touched her lips as her stomach grumbled again. Another blessing that had come from weeks of hard work at home was that her clothes were getting loose on her. And she'd learned to push away her plate after one helping. Though she was far from having the trim figure she'd always craved, she would at least have to take in most of her dresses at the waist before long.

She worked throughout the afternoon, scrubbing the clothes, boiling them, then rinsing. By the time she had hung the last piece of laundry to dry, her hands were red and raw from the soap, wrinkled from the water, and aching from scrubbing and wringing. Still, a sense of satisfaction came over her as she put away the washtub, boiling pot, and scrub board.

Walking into the house, she had to laugh at herself. Over the months of working at the store, she'd become soft to the hard life of a prairie woman. Even before she bought Tucker's, there had been enough women living at the ranch to share the load. Doing it alone was much more of a challenge than she'd ever thought it would be.

She perked her ear to listen for Mother Daniels and breathed a sigh of relief at the silence. The last time Emily had checked on her, the older woman had been sleeping with her book facedown across her chest. She must still be napping.

Emily opened the oven and took in the heavenly aroma wafting out to greet her senses. "Mmm," she said aloud. Jeremiah would be pleased. She felt her cheeks warm at the thought.

Lately her mind didn't seem to stray far from events occurring the night of her speech—before her mother-in-law's accident. . .the near-kiss beside the wagon, Jeremiah's proud grin during her speech, but most of all, what had happened afterward. Jeremiah's lips had touched hers briefly. She could still feel their softness, the sweetness—the longing. Her stomach lurched at the memory, and a giggle bubbled up inside of her.

She'd loved Jeremiah Daniels since she was ten years old, when he'd molded a turtle out of clay during class one day. She'd spied that turtle on Mother Daniels's knickknack shelf soon after she married Jeremiah. The lesson at school had been about allowing God to mold one's life. Jeremiah had certainly turned his life around that day. The change in him from that point on had been noticeable. And soon after that, he'd begun working for Mr. Tucker.

Emily sighed. Jeremiah deserved that store. Why had she been so stubborn? Refusing to share with him just because he hadn't married her for love.

Satisfied that the rabbits were doing well, Emily shut the oven door. How could she keep the store from him when he wanted it so badly? The fact remained that she'd made certain vows before God—that she would love him and be his helpmeet forever. A true helpmeet wouldn't withhold the thing that would make her husband the happiest. Jeremiah wanted Tucker's.

The truth of the matter was that as much as she enjoyed running the store, she also enjoyed caring for the house and Jeremiah. Given a choice, she'd prefer to relinquish the store and stay home. The thought filled her with joy. No matter the reason for their marriage, Emily knew Jeremiah cared for her. How could she doubt it after the tenderness he'd shown her? The desire she saw in his eyes as he watched her go about the house. The long, searching looks he gave her whenever she found the courage to meet his gaze.

She felt her heart race as a collage of memories flooded her. Each brush of his hand against her back or her elbow when he helped her into or out of the wagon filled her with longing, and the warmth of his hand as he held hers during the mealtime blessing made it difficult for her to concentrate on the prayer. She knew he felt the same way.

A plan emerged, and she grinned broadly. Only one thing stood in the way of her and Jeremiah having a true marriage—that contract. And she had every intention of getting rid of the obstacle.

A niggling of worry squirmed inside of her. What of Mother Daniels? She had made it perfectly clear she wouldn't give up taking care of the house. But surely two reasonable women could find an amicable way to share the load, couldn't they? The more she turned it over, the more Emily thought the idea might work.

She practiced a few words in her mind, then tiptoed to the bedroom.

"Mother Daniels?" she whispered, determined to have a heart-to-heart talk before Jeremiah came home. After all, whether she liked Emily or not, the fact remained that she loved her son more than life and would do anything to see him happy. To that end, Emily knew they had to find a way to compromise and work together in regard to the house.

"Yes?" A grouchy, sleepy voice greeted her.

"May I come in? I think we need to talk. . . ."

⌒

Sunday morning dawned bright, the weather just right for a late spring morning. Not too warm, not too cold. Jeremiah climbed from the loft, following the wonderful scents of coffee boiling, bacon frying, and biscuits baking in the oven.

He'd been up for hours, finished morning chores, cleaned up, and now looked forward to a nice leisurely breakfast with his wife before attending services in town.

Their marriage wasn't all it could be, but it wasn't entirely unpleasant, either. With Ma's injury, Emily had certainly proven herself a capable housekeeper and cook. And over the last couple of weeks, he'd noticed camaraderie between the two women that was nothing short of miraculous. He sent a silent prayer of thanks heavenward. An answered prayer.

He had to admit, though, that he'd missed having Emily ride into town with him over the past few weeks. He missed looking across the street and peeking in on her through the large store window. Her sister Hope was doing a competent job of minding the store, but she was no Emily.

Now that Ma was ready to get around with a walking stick, he figured it wouldn't be long before Emily joined him for the daily ride to town once more.

He released a low chuckle as he turned on the bottom rung to find Emily pushing a loose strand of hair from her forehead, leaving a streak of flour in its place.

Her eyebrows shot up. "What's so funny?"

"You." He closed the short distance between them in a couple of strides. "Hold still," he said. Reaching forward, he thumbed away the flour. "There you go."

Splotches of red appeared on Emily's cheeks. "Thank you."

"You're welcome."

"Sit down, and I'll bring your coffee."

Jeremiah sat and watched while she pulled a mug from the shelf above the stove. He frowned.

"What's wrong with your dress?" he asked.

"What do you mean?" She set his cup in front of him, and he caught her around the waist.

"This." He pulled on the material. "You're swimming in this. You feeling poorly?"

"P–poorly? I suppose I've lost a few pounds since I took over the house for your ma. Do I look sick?"

Her eyes flooded with hurt, and her voice sounded strained.

"I guess I didn't notice. You don't look sick. Just different. I'm sorry you're working so hard. Maybe I should hire someone to help you out until Ma's ready to take back over."

"Oh, but. . . Well, if you don't think I'm doing it right."

Jeremiah tenderly searched her face. And suddenly he realized his wife had blossomed over the last couple of months. She exhibited a true joy he'd never observed in her during all the years they'd known each other. Confusion swept over him. That was something he'd have to ponder further to understand. For now, he needed to undo the hurt he'd inadvertently caused her.

On impulse, he scooted his chair away from the table and gently pressed her waist until she had no choice but to pull away from him or take steps toward him. She didn't resist when he pulled her onto his lap.

"What are you doing?" she asked breathlessly.

"Something I've wanted to do for quite some time. Do you mind?"

She smiled and shook her head.

Taking her hand, he brought it to his lips, then nestled it close against his chest.

"In answer to your question, no, you don't look sickly. You're beautiful. You're always beautiful. I just hadn't noticed how thin you've gotten."

Emily laughed. "I'm not thin by any means. As a matter of fact, I could stand to lose more to be like Tarah or Hope. Even Amelia."

"You're perfect." And he meant it. Emily was perfect for him. If only she'd realize how unnecessary that contract between them was. "And the work you do around here is more than acceptable. It's wonderful. I suppose Ma will be taking over again soon," he said, then could have kicked himself as her expression drooped.

"I suppose so." She rose, leaving his arms aching for her to return. He fought the urge to pull her back. "I have to check the bacon before it burns."

"I'll enjoy your company again during our rides to and from town."

She slipped the sizzling bacon onto a platter, then turned to him. "You will?"

"I miss you. I enjoy our talks. Who else in town understands and appreciates talk about running a mercantile?"

"We could talk about it in the evenings, like we do now."

"I know. But I enjoy having you all to myself for a few minutes twice a day. We don't get much time alone at home."

A loud cough caught their attention, and Jeremiah nearly fell from his chair at the sight of Ma standing in the bedroom doorway. He inwardly groaned. Why couldn't he watch his mouth?

"Ma! What are you doing out of bed?"

She leaned heavily on the walking stick he'd whittled for her upon Sam's suggestion. "I think it's about time for me to try this thing out. Besides, I have a hankerin' to join you and your wife for breakfast and then Sunday services."

"Why, that's wonderful!" Emily went to her. "Let me help you to the table."

Embarrassed that he hadn't offered first, Jeremiah stood and strode across the room. He took his mother's free hand. "Here, let me."

"Both of you sit. I can make it alone."

Jeremiah and Emily exchanged glances, and with unspoken agreement, each stayed on one side of her as she moved with painstaking slowness to the table. She was breathing heavily by the time she accepted the chair Jeremiah held out for her.

"Now," she said, "let's have our breakfast and get to the service. You two have plans for this afternoon."

Jeremiah glanced at her sharply.

Emily drew in a breath. "Today? Are you certain you want to be left alone that long?"

"Quite certain. I'm sure I'll be worn to a frazzle by the time we return from the service and in need of a nice long nap. Plenty of time for what you have planned."

"Does one of you want to inform me of our plans?" Jeremiah asked, exasperated at being left in the dark.

"Nope." Ma's eyes crinkled at the corners. "Your wife has a surprise for you, and I'm not going to be the one to spill the beans."

Jeremiah sent Emily a questioning look, but she merely smiled. "Sit down and have your breakfast, Jeremiah. You'll find out in good time."

Her eyes flashed in saucy determination. Jeremiah grinned and complied. From the way Emily and Ma were smiling at each other, whatever the surprise, it was bound to be a good one.

Chapter 17

"Thank you. This has been a wonderful surprise," Jeremiah said.

Emily smiled at her husband. They'd enjoyed a nice lunch together, and now he stretched out on the blanket, resting jauntily on his elbow. She walked the short distance to the creek and rinsed off their dishes, keenly aware of Jeremiah's gaze upon her. He'd watched her all day—every single move she made. The attention sent a thrill through Emily, and the hunger in his eyes made her dizzy and nervous at the same time.

The wind whipped at her skirts as she set the picnic basket into the back of the wagon. Nervously Emily searched the darkening skies. She had planned to produce the contract now and offer Emily's Place to Jeremiah. But she wanted to do so when they wouldn't be interrupted. And from the looks of the clouds, it wouldn't be long before the entire prairie was soaked with rain—including them, if they didn't find shelter soon.

"Jeremiah," she said. "I think we should go home. Look at the sky to the west."

Jeremiah glanced in the direction she pointed and hopped up from the blanket. "You're right," he said, regret thick in his voice. "Much as I hate to cut this day short, we should probably head to the farm."

Emily waited while he snatched up the blanket and pitched it into the back of the wagon. He joined her where she stood waiting for him to offer his assistance. She glanced at him expectantly. He made no move to help her, however. Instead, he reached forward and gently traced a line down her cheek. "Thank you for today. I enjoyed our time together."

"Me, too," Emily said, suddenly shy.

Jeremiah's lips turned upward in a smile that weakened Emily's knees. "And thank you for your efforts with Ma. I know she can be difficult, but it seems as though you've won her over."

Barely able to concentrate, Emily shivered.

"Want to tell me how you managed it?" he asked, his voice hardly more than a whisper as he stared down into her eyes.

"Your ma's a good woman," Emily said. "She just needed to know I care about you. No mother is willing to stand by and watch her child be hurt."

He stepped closer, sliding his hands about her waist and drawing her to him. "And do you?"

Emily's breath caught in her throat at the rush of emotions swelling inside of her. Mrs. Thomas's warning echoed in her head. "Never let a man know how much you love him. It gives him the advantage over you. Keep the marriage on your terms."

She smiled, pushing aside the annoying inward voice.

"I care more than you could know, Jeremiah." Joy sprang to his eyes, bolstering her courage. "I've loved you since we were children. You've no idea the many times I dreamed you'd call on me."

Bewilderment flashed in his eyes. "You've loved me. . ." He shook his head. "I was such an idiot. It never occurred to me back then that you would think I'm good enough for you."

"Good enough?" Emily frowned. "You mentioned that during the blizzard, too. Why wouldn't I think you're good enough?"

A look of disbelief crossed his face, and he gathered her into his arms. "Emily, I should have known better. Look at all the years I wasted feeling like I couldn't measure up to your family because of my pa."

Emily gave a short laugh and pulled away enough to meet his gaze. "Jeremiah, no one measures up to my family. Not even me. But none of that matters. The only thing that matters is I love you."

She gasped at her sudden admission. Jeremiah had never spoken of love. It was rather bold for her to be the first one to bring it up.

He brought his forehead to rest upon hers. "Emily Daniels, the best thing that ever happened to me was that blizzard trapping you in my store. I was too dumb and stubborn to ever admit how I felt about you—how I feel."

"H—how you feel?"

A streak of lightning split the sky, followed by a loud clap of thunder. Emily jumped, barely containing a scream.

Jeremiah released her suddenly. "Come on. Let's go. We'll talk about this later."

Emily nodded and accepted his assistance into the wagon. Jeremiah trotted to the other side. He flapped the reins and headed toward home just as the rain started to fall.

By the time they reached the farm, they were soaked. But that was the least of their problems. The wind had grown to such an intensity, Emily could barely keep her footing against the gusts.

She started toward the house, but Jeremiah grabbed her. "The cellar," he yelled.

Nodding, she turned, but his fingers tightened on her arm. She pivoted back around.

There was no time for more talk! Then, realizing he intended to see that she made it to the cellar, Emily yanked her arm away. "Go get your ma. I'll be all right."

He hesitated, clearly torn.

Rising on her toes, Emily kissed him hard on the lips. "Go!"

With a nod, he gave her arm a squeeze and dashed toward the house.

As she reached the cellar door, images flashed through her mind of when she was just a girl. A twister had demolished their barn and forced the family underground for the night. She stepped into the musty cellar, shuddering at the terrifying memory.

"Keep us all safe, Lord. Please. Watch over my family and all of our friends and neighbors." She kept her focus on the door above her, waiting for Jeremiah to appear with Mother Daniels. She breathed a sigh of relief when they appeared after what seemed like an eternity.

"Emily! Help me get Ma down the steps."

Together they got his mother settled without too much difficulty. Jeremiah closed the doors and set the latch; then they listened grimly as the storm raged above them.

A deafening roar grew louder. A shudder claimed Emily. She knew the sounds of a tornado.

Jeremiah's face remained clouded with worry as the minutes ticked by. Emily reached forward and slipped her hand in his. She leaned her head against his shoulder and closed her eyes; and though she'd meant to make him feel better, she found that she was the one taking comfort from his nearness. He reached up and cupped her head with his opposite hand, pressing her closer.

"I don't have a very good feeling about this," he said.

Emily wished she had words to reassure him, but she heard the banging outside. That twister had gone right over them. If they were fortunate, only the barn was taken. But dread knotted inside of her. And when finally a deafening silence replaced the howl of the angry winds, her fears were confirmed. There was not a building standing on the Danielses' farm. No house. No barn.

Nothing but rubble.

Jeremiah held back tears of frustration, anger, and helplessness as he stood next to the broken boards strewn across the land where his store had once stood. *Why, Lord? First my home and now my business? I don't understand why.* The only possessions left to him were the horses and his wagon, which had somehow been miraculously spared.

He glanced resentfully across the street. None of those buildings had been touched. Emily's Place stood without so much as a missing shingle, while Jeremiah's, the livery stable, and the hotel were all flattened. Other buildings had suffered damage, as well.

Emily stood silently by his side. After the storm, they'd driven over to check on the St. John ranch and found the twister hadn't reached them at all. They'd endured a storm, but nothing had been damaged. They hadn't lost even a single chicken.

Emily's ma and pa had graciously extended an invitation to Jeremiah's ma; and after making sure she was settled comfortably, Jeremiah and Emily had headed to town.

"Jeremiah," Emily said quietly. "We still have the land. We can rebuild."

Shaking his head, Jeremiah crouched down and released a can of bootblack from beneath a board. "I don't have any money to start over. Everything was wrapped up in the store." The good news was that at least he'd managed to break even so far.

"Mr. Thomas will loan you the money to rebuild. Everyone knows what a wonderful businessman you are. The bank will be chomping at the bit to extend the loan."

He stood and faced her. Her sweet face softened him, and he smiled, suddenly happy that her store had been the one left standing. "No credit," he said, keeping his voice deliberately gentle. "My pa got us so deep in debt, Ma almost lost the farm after he died. I don't believe in buying something with someone else's money."

"Do you mean to tell me you paid cash to build your store?"

"That's right."

"But how?" she asked incredulously.

Jeremiah shrugged. "After we paid off the farm, I saved every extra penny over the years. Tuck gave me bonuses at Christmastime and on my birthdays. Fifteen years of that adds up. Plus I sold off some cattle to Luke and Laney a couple of years ago when I decided not to raise them anymore."

A scowl scrunched her freckled nose and furrowed her brow. "Honestly, Jeremiah. If you could pay cash money, why didn't you buy Tucker's in the first place?"

Jeremiah stared at her, fighting the temptation to tell her exactly why. But as he studied the baffled expression on her face, he realized that she didn't know. She truly didn't. How could he tell her he was about to make an offer on Tucker's and offer her a wedding ring, as well, when she swooped down and bought it out from under him with money she didn't even earn?

"I just didn't, that's all. Anyway, none of that matters now."

"But of course it matters, Jeremy! If you had bought Tucker's, you'd still have a store."

"Look, just let it go, all right?"

Hurt clouded her eyes, and she turned away. She gathered a shaky breath, and Jeremiah knew she was fighting back tears.

"Emily. . .I didn't mean to sound curt."

"It's all right. I know this has been a difficult day. I suppose we'll stay in my old rooms over the mercantile?"

"You don't want to go home?"

She turned and gave him a blank stare. "Do you want to stay in the cellar? I guess I don't mind, but we'd be a lot more comfortable over the mercantile."

Jeremiah chuckled. "I meant I thought you'd want to stay with your folks."

"Do you want to?"

"No, I was going to stay in the wagon at the farm. I didn't even think about those rooms."

"We're blessed that we didn't lose everything, Jeremiah. I'm sure there are people who will be starting over with nothing. At least we still have Emily's Place, and it looks like we'll be able to salvage at least a small portion of your stock."

"I lost everything," he said flatly. "You didn't."

"But the store is ours. We'll get along nicely on what it brings in. You'll be able to rebuild the farm in no time. In the meantime, we can live upstairs."

Exasperated by her generous spirit, Jeremiah kicked a board. "Listen, you made yourself abundantly clear from the beginning of our marriage. Jeremiah's was mine, and Emily's Place was yours. We weren't to interfere in each other's business, remember? Well, I've honored my word so far, and I don't intend to go back on it now. I'll make a soddy on the farm and give up storekeeping. But know this, Emily, I'm not going to be supported by a woman. So any money you make will be yours to do with as you please. But not a penny of it will go to our living. Is that understood?"

"No! That's just silliness, Jeremiah. You love working in the store. You should run Emily's Place."

"I told you a long time ago I wouldn't work for you. And I'm not going to start now."

"Work for me? You'll be working for yourself. It's ours. Not mine. Things are different now, aren't they? We're married, and besides, I was going to—"

"Don't pressure me, Emily. I said no."

Tears pooled in her eyes, and Jeremiah steeled himself, forcing his arms not to reach for her.

"Fine, Jeremiah Daniels. Be stubborn, then. I'm going to start supper for us. Shall I rummage through the rubble here for something to cook, or will you accept food from my store?"

Before he could answer, Emily put her hands firmly on her hips and leveled her gaze at him. "Will you please drive to the ranch and let our parents know we will be staying in town? And do me the courtesy of not humiliating me by sleeping in your wagon!"

She stomped off toward the mercantile, leaving him to stare after her. Unease gnawed his gut as he watched her. His mind whirled with the unbelievable events of the day. A day that had started with optimism had ended in destruction.

With a shake of his head, he cast another glance at the fallen store. His shoulders slumped. No matter how hard he tried, it seemed his pa's failures followed him like a curse.

With a heavy heart, he climbed into the wagon and headed toward the St. John ranch. Dread engulfed him as he tried to construct the words to tell his ma. Not only did she lose her home, but he had no means to support her in her old age. Tears stung his eyes once more, but this time he was powerless to rein in the onslaught of despair.

Chapter 18

Without giving it a second thought, Emily broke an ironclad rule for Sunday. She opened the store just in case folks needed supplies—and they did. Once the word spread, it seemed everyone in town headed for the store—if for no other reason than to assure themselves that their friends and neighbors were all right.

Hour after hour, the onslaught of customers continued. Until far into the night, Emily handed out blankets, lanterns, kerosene, and anything else folks were in need of. But rather than profit on the Lord's Day, she extended credit to all; and they promised to pay her when they got back on their feet.

She wasn't alone in her vigil. Anthony opened the church, and Sam set up a small hospital for those in need of medical attention.

From all over the county, reports were coming in of damaged or destroyed homes and property. Some announced animals missing or killed, but not one report confirmed a death among Emily's friends and neighbors. Her heart sang with thankfulness for that. She blessed the Lord for sparing Emily's Place, and even the folks who had been unkind to her came and humbly accepted the goods she had to share.

For a town that had been divided by opinion only a day ago, Harper now united in a common cause—survival. Families who were barely on speaking terms before the storm now doubled up in still inhabitable homes. Few allowed pride to keep them from accepting help.

Emily breathed a sigh of relief when the last customer said farewell. She locked up and headed back through the store to take inventory of her depleted stock.

From time to time she paused in her work to glance anxiously at the clock. Jeremiah still hadn't returned. She hoped he'd eaten at her ma and pa's, because she'd been too busy with the store to cook the promised supper. As the minutes ticked away, she began to worry in earnest. For the first time since her disappointing conversation with Jeremiah on the site where Jeremiah's once stood, she found the presence of mind to mull over the events of the day.

Oh, if only she'd torn up that contract before the storm hit. Now there would be no convincing him. How could a Christian man be so stubborn as to scratch out a living on a farm when he could at least live comfortably with the profits from the store?

The thought of Jeremiah coming home each night, so exhausted he could barely drag himself to bed, filled her with despair. That wasn't the life for him. He was born to manage goods for sale.

A knock at the door pulled her from her musing with a jerk. Cautiously she made her way across the room and peered through the small window. She squinted and was able to make out a shadowy male form. "Jeremiah?" she called through the door.

"Let me in," came the muffled reply.

Relief welled inside of Emily.

She unlocked the door and threw it open. "It's about time. I was beginning to worry. . . ." Confusion clouded Emily's mind as a figure stepped from the shadows and Mr. Gregory's dark face loomed before her.

"Where is she?" He grabbed her arm and pushed her farther into the store.

Every cell in Emily's body shook with fear as pain laced her arm. "Wh–who?"

A growl escaped his throat as he towered over her, his eyes narrowing. "You know who. My wife." He released her arm and shoved her toward the counter. "She's gone, and so are my daughters. I think you have something to do with it."

"Me? Mr. Gregory, I assure you, you're mistaken." He took another menacing step forward, his fists clenched. *Help me, dear Lord!*

"You and your ideas. Owning your own business and working when you should be having sons to carry on your husband's name. What kind of woman are you to encourage married women to go out and work?"

"I—I never. . . I only want women to have the right to do so, Mr. Gregory. I assure you, I would never encourage a woman to go out and work against her husband's will, particularly to the neglect of her family. I—I bought the store when I was single."

"A young woman has no business leaving her pa's home until she is married," he snarled, and Emily nearly wilted to the floor.

"Sir, I—I respect your opinions. Many share your view. But—"

"Shut up. Where is my family?"

"I'm sure I don't know where your wife and daughters are."

A sneer marred his face. For the first time, Emily noticed he swayed as he walked. Was he intoxicated? Although liquor was illegal in Kansas, everyone knew some folks made their own.

Surging toward her, Mr. Gregory muttered an oath, his arms reaching out. Emily stepped out of his way, easily evading his grasp. His face grew white, and he grappled at the air.

Emily gave a bewildered gasp as he crashed to the floor, taking out a display of newly arrived dime novels on the way down. "Help me," he said, though his words were barely discernable. For an instant, Emily froze, torn between the desire to run away and the knowledge that this man was hurt and needed her help—regardless of what had just occurred. She sent up a hasty prayer for protection and sank to her knees beside him. Blood trickled down his cheek from a gash at the side of his head, and she knew he had received the wound before his fall. "Mr. Gregory, what happened?"

He groaned and mumbled something unintelligible.

"I'll be right back," she said, though she knew in all likelihood he couldn't hear her. "I'm going to go outside to the pump and bring some water to clean that wound. And we'll see about getting you to the church, where Sam can have a look at you."

She grabbed a pitcher and dashed out the door and around to the back of the store.

Jeremiah took the steps up to Emily's Place two at a time. Why was the door wide open? He strode inside, his heart nearly stopping at the disarray and the sight of Mr. Gregory sprawled on the floor. "Emily!" he called, terror gripping his gut. "Where are you?"

If Gregory had harmed one hair on her head—

"Emily!"

"I'm here, Jeremiah. Honestly, stop shouting before everyone in town ends up here." Jeremiah turned to see his wife coming through the door, carrying a pitcher of water.

"Oh, thank God, you're all right." He gathered her in his arms and held her tightly against him, mindless of the pitcher gouging into his stomach.

"Of course I am." His shoulder muffled her words.

He pulled back so he could look her in the eyes. Reaching forward, he stroked her face, then bent and kissed her gently on her lips. "I was afraid Gregory might have harmed you."

"Why would you think that?" she asked, dipping her head toward the unconscious man. "He's the one on the floor."

Exasperated, Jeremiah released her and closed the door. "What happened here?"

"Not much, really. May I have your handkerchief, please?"

He fished the hanky from his pocket and handed it to her.

"Thank you." Emily knelt beside Mr. Gregory. She wet the cloth and gently began wiping away the blood from his face. "He must have been injured before he came over here, because one second he was coming after me, and the next he was on the floor."

"You're right. He was already injured."

Emily glanced up and arched a brow. "How do you know?"

He took her by the arm and pulled her to her feet. "Come to the storeroom with me, and I'll tell you."

It wouldn't do for Mr. Gregory to gain consciousness and hear what Jeremiah had to say. Once they were out of earshot, Jeremiah gathered a breath. "I found Mrs. Gregory and her girls walking outside of town. Mrs. Gregory was badly beaten and could barely walk without assistance. I took her to your ma and pa."

Revulsion covered Emily's features. "Did Mr. Gregory. . . ?"

Jeremiah nodded grimly. "He was angry that the hotel was flattened; and when she suggested maybe she could take in laundry to help them get back on their feet, he went crazy and started hitting her."

"Oh my." She glanced up at Jeremiah. "Is Mrs. Gregory all right?"

"She will be. Physically. But that woman has deep wounds on the inside of her, too. Emotional wounds that only God can heal."

"What will she do?" Emily asked. "Will she go back to him?"

Jeremiah shrugged. "Your pa and ma offered her and the girls the use of the old soddy until she decides what's to be done."

"And Mr. Gregory? What should we do about him?"

Anger burned a fire inside of Jeremiah at the memory of poor Mrs. Gregory's bruised and bleeding face. "We should dump the no-account in the street and let him take his chances, but I suppose we'd better load him into the wagon and cart him over to the church so Sam can doctor him."

Emily shuddered. "Let's do it, then. The sooner we get him out of the store, the better, as far as I'm concerned."

The next morning Sam reported Mr. Gregory had left before dawn.

᠅

A week later, the town still looked like a great battle had been waged on Main Street. The desolation was phenomenal; and according to Amelia Bell, even she could find no pleasure in the fact that she had all the news stories she could report and then some. Several families had had enough of the volatile Kansas weather and were packing up anything they could salvage and heading back to wherever they'd come from.

The tried-and-true prairie-dwelling Kansans stiffened their upper lips. They'd suffered through blizzards, crop failures, prairie fires, pestilence, and droughts. A twister would not get the better of them. And that was the crux of the talk around the cracker barrels at Emily's Place—which had become the town central.

The store was packed from open to close every day. Only one person remained absent, filling Emily with emptiness even in the midst of the crowded mercantile: Jeremiah.

Each night he slept on a cot in the storeroom, and every morning he rose before dawn and left for the farm, working until dusk.

Emily knew they couldn't go on this way; but for the life of her, she didn't know how to make things better, so she prayed and cried and prayed some more, hoping desperately that God would soon hear her plea and send help.

Chapter 19

Sunday morning dawned bright, promising to be the warmest day of the year thus far. Emily walked beside Jeremiah as they made their way to the church. Her eyes grew wide at the congested churchyard. She'd never seen so many wagons, indicating a full service.

"Jeremiah, look!" Emily's heart sang at the sight of Mother Daniels leaning heavily on her walking stick with Jack on one side of her and Will on the other. Emily's brothers made a gallant attempt to pretend to be fighting for the honor of escorting her, but anyone could tell they were ensuring she made it to the church without stumbling.

"Good morning, Mother Daniels!" Emily said. "It's wonderful to see you. You're getting along so well."

"That I am," she replied. "Doc says I'll probably have to use this for the rest of my life, but at least I can walk on my own."

She turned to her escorts. "You two run along. My boy is here to take care of me now."

Will grabbed his chest in mock offense. "Come on, Jack. I think we've been jilted."

Mother Daniels shook her head as she watched Emily's brothers race toward the church. "Those two make my head spin." She turned to Jeremiah. "And why haven't you been over to see your ma this week?"

Jeremiah bent and kissed her cheek. "I'm sorry. I've been busy."

Mother Daniels studied his face, her eyes clouded with concern. "You feeling poorly, son?"

"He's been working too hard trying to clean up at the farm," Emily broke in, earning her a scowl from her husband. She didn't care. If anyone could reason with him, it was his ma.

Mother Daniels's face grew pensive, then she shifted her gaze between Jeremiah and Emily. "How about if the three of us take a trip to the farm after services?"

Emily's stomach churned at the thought of having to witness the devastation again, but she didn't have the heart to say no to the woman who obviously needed to see her home. She smiled. "I made a nice ham yesterday. I'll slice it and pack a picnic."

Mother Daniels's face brightened. "Sounds wonderful." She moved slowly up the steps ahead of them.

Jeremiah leaned close and whispered in Emily's ear. "I guess I have no say in the matter."

"I guess not," Emily retorted, then turned to smile brightly at Anthony as they entered the church.

⟜

Jeremiah watched the look of sorrow pass over Ma's face as she witnessed the destruction of her home for the first time since the storm. "I'm sorry, Ma," he said, lifting her from the wagon. Ma accepted her walking stick from his hand and silently walked toward the site where her house once stood.

Turning to Emily, Jeremiah reached out to help her down. She placed her hands on his shoulders, and his senses reeled at her nearness. The scent of soft lavender drifted over him as she slid into his arms. He was nearly overcome with the desire to pull her close and bury his face in the curve of her neck.

She stared up at him. "I miss you," she whispered. She rose on her toes and pressed a soft kiss to his lips. Jeremiah tightened his hold, but she resisted, pulling gently from his arms. "Go see to your ma. She's not steady enough on her feet to walk through that rubble alone. I'm going to get the lunch ready."

Reluctantly he let her go and strode to his ma's side. He cleared his throat. "I've managed to save a few things, Ma, but not much."

She shook her head. "It doesn't matter." She turned to him suddenly. "I want to sell it."

Jeremiah blinked. "What?"

"Myra Hastings came to see me a few days ago. She's answered an advertisement for a position as headmistress at a girl's school in Boston. You know she went to college before her pa forced her to move here."

"I'm sure you'll miss her." Jeremiah shifted. Did Ma want to move off, too?

"I'm sure I will, but that isn't the point. She will need to sell the boardinghouse, and I'd like to buy it."

"And you'd have to sell the farm in order to do that." Jeremiah's gut clenched. How could she even consider selling their home? Without the farm, he would be forced to accept his wife's charity or live at the boardinghouse with his ma. The thought of either gnawed at him. "Are you sure that's a good idea?"

"Yes. I know you should have the right to your pa's farm; but if you're honest, you'll admit farming isn't in your heart. You've only kept it going for me all these years. I'm grateful, but you don't need it, and I do."

"I understand, Ma. But I was going to rebuild and move back out here."

"There's no need for you to do that, and it doesn't make real good sense to consider such a thing. You and Emily are townsfolk. You have your store; and if you don't want to live above the mercantile, use the land where your store was and build a house."

"But why do you want to move to town when I could rebuild your home? It's home. All our memories are here."

Ma released a heavy sigh. "Oh, Jeremiah. The memories here are not good. Your pa and his tirades and beatings, then after he died, memories of my young son working to take care of me. I'd like to start a new chapter, and maybe I can help someone in the process."

"What do you mean?"

"Mrs. Gregory and her girls need somewhere to live, and I need someone to help me run the boardinghouse. Mrs. Gregory and I have traveled the same road. We understand each other and will get along very nicely. It's a good arrangement."

"And what happens if Mr. Gregory comes back?"

She shrugged. "We'll have to deal with that if it happens. But for now, this plan just makes good sense."

"What makes sense?"

Jeremiah turned. The sight of Emily's sunny face reminded him of his options. He groaned inwardly. How could he live off his wife's charity? "Ma wants to sell the farm and buy the boardinghouse."

"Why, that's a marvelous idea!"

Ma chuckled. "And guess who would be Harper's new businesswoman?"

Tossing back her head, Emily burst into peals of laughter and hugged Ma close. "Well, rest assured, my days of giving speeches and going to rallies are over. You may take my place. I'm sure Mrs. Thomas would be thrilled to have you."

Joining in the laughter, Ma shook her head. "No, thank you. We women may have the right to vote someday, but I don't think I'm quite up for joining the suffragists. I'll leave bloomer outfits and cigar smoking to Mrs. Krenshaw."

Emily suddenly turned to Jeremiah. "What do you think of your ma selling the farm, Jeremy?"

Jeremiah exulted in the pleasant way his nickname rolled from her lips. He received it as an endearment, and his pulse quickened. "I don't really know. I suppose I'll have to let the idea grow on me. It's really Ma's decision to make."

"I was just trying to show him how much sense it makes when you walked up. Since that crazy contract is no longer between you two, Jeremiah can run the store. He doesn't need this farm."

"What do you mean, the contract is no longer between us?"

Mother Daniels cleared her throat as Emily gave her a long look, her eyes speaking volumes that Jeremiah was helpless to read.

"Take me to the ranch," Ma said. "Then you two can discuss this in private."

"But what about lunch?"

She shrugged. "Eat while you talk, for all I care. But it's time you work some things out. It's obvious to anyone that you love each other desperately. If any two people are meant to be together, it's you. I've known that since you were children."

"So have I," Emily said, eyes shining.

A lump lodged in Jeremiah's throat at her admission. "Emily. . . ," he began, but Ma interrupted.

"Take me home so I can rest this aching leg. Then you can work it out between you."

The women strode arm in arm, leaving Jeremiah to follow in stunned silence. He had a feeling the upcoming discussion with his wife might just be the most important of their lives.

"Now what's this about tearing up the contract?" Jeremiah demanded. They had made sure Mother Daniels was settled, declined an invitation to lunch from Emily's ma, and were now headed back to town. Still, Emily was surprised he'd brought it up so suddenly.

"Well, that's what the picnic was about, but the storm came before I could give you the document to tear up. I started to tell you while we were standing in the rubble of Jeremiah's, but you wouldn't hear me."

"I'm sorry, Em. I've been acting like an idiot all week. I've just had trouble trying to figure out exactly what God has in mind. It's not easy, losing everything in one day."

Emily pressed his hand with hers. "Oh, Jeremiah. You didn't. Don't you see? You still have a place to live, a business to run."

He snorted. "A home and a business that are yours."

She raised her hands helplessly and let them drop to her lap. "Jeremiah, haven't you learned anything from me? Men have been sharing with their wives since the dawn of time. Why can't you take what I have to offer? Eventually you can use your land across the road from Emily's Place to build us a nice home. For now, let me share the store with you. You were willing to marry me for it at one time; why not just take it now? It doesn't matter to me anymore."

Glancing at her sharply, Jeremiah drew a breath and pulled the wagon to the side of the road. He wrapped the reins around the brake and turned to her. "What do you mean, I was willing to marry you for it? That never crossed my mind. It was you I wanted—not the store. I still had my store at the time."

Emily gathered a shaky breath. "Oh, Jeremiah, let's not start this off with lies. I'll be honest first." Her voice faltered, and tears threatened to choke her words; but she knew she'd gone too far to turn back now. "The night of the harvest dance, I heard you and Harold Baxter discussing who would be the first to marry me and run my store."

The blood drained from Jeremiah's face. He reached for Emily, and she went to him willingly, for she had no strength to resist.

"Honey, you misunderstood. I promise you, that's not what I meant. Harold, yes. But not me. I just meant I planned to court you. Do you remember the day you got the letter from your grandmother's attorney?"

Emily nodded against his chest.

"Before you read it, I was trying to work up the nerve to ask your permission to call on you."

She pulled away and met his gaze, unable to deny the earnestness she saw in his eyes. "You were?"

"Yes. I planned to talk to Tucker about selling the store to me, since I knew he wanted to sell. I wanted to have something to offer you before I courted you. I was going to ask you to marry me inside a month."

Horror widened her eyes. "And I ruined everything!"

"I wouldn't exactly say everything was ruined," he drawled. "God still worked out a way to get us together."

"Jeremiah, if I had known how much you wanted Tucker's, I never would have bought it. I just didn't know you had the money to buy it. I only bought it in the first place to be close to you and because. . .because I wanted to do something. . ."

She stopped. She had never spoken of her feelings to anyone before. In all the years of being surrounded by fantastic St. Johns, she'd withheld the fact that she felt practically nonexistent.

Grabbing her hands, Jeremiah shifted closer to her on the seat. "You only wanted to do what?"

Tears stung her eyes at his gentle concern. She had said she'd start by being honest with him—but what if he agreed that she wasn't special like the other members of her family? It was one thing to quietly hold on to that belief, quite another to give someone the opportunity to agree.

"Don't cry," he soothed. "You can tell me anything."

Deciding to trust his love for her, Emily opened her mouth, and a flood of words began. "It's just that everyone in my family is so handsome and good at everything. Everyone except me, the adopted one. I just. . .Jeremiah, I just wanted to be good at something. I knew I could never be a great beauty like the other girls, but for once I wanted to do something well. I just thought if I ran the mercantile well, maybe people would see that I'm not the only St. John who doesn't amount to anything. I guess that's why I joined the Suffrage Association. I just wanted to do something special."

Jeremiah released her hands. Gently he cupped the sides of her neck, forcing her to meet his gaze. "Now you listen to me. First, I don't know where you got the idea that you're not special, but you are. Who is the only teacher in Harper to get a teaching certificate from normal school?"

Emily smiled. "Me."

"Right. Folks around here think that's pretty special. And who set this town on its ear by giving the two best speeches ever heard in Harper?"

"I wouldn't go that far," she said with a wry grin.

"I would. You're an amazing woman, without even knowing it. You do whatever you set out to do, and you do it well. Even my ma is talking about wanting votes for women. Now who else but a special woman could have won her over?"

A giggle escaped her lips, then she sobered. "I guess I just need to know there's a purpose for me."

"What makes you happy? That's usually a pretty good indication of what God planned for you."

Her cheeks warmed, but she held his gaze, determined to keep her resolve to be completely open with this man she loved. "I've never been happier than the weeks I stayed home and cooked and cleaned for you, Jeremiah. All I've ever wanted was to be near you. It means more to me than running a successful store or votes for women or anything else for that matter, except my relationship with God."

He kissed her then, without saying a word. His mouth moved slowly over hers. Breathless, she clung to him by the time he pulled slightly away.

"I love you," he whispered against her lips, sliding his hands down her neck and arms and finally gathering her around the waist. He cuddled her close and deepened his kiss once more, lingering, leaving Emily's senses reeling by the time he pulled away.

"My purpose in life has never been clearer, Emily." His husky voice sent a shiver down her spine.

"What makes you happy?" she whispered, her lips still tingling from his kiss.

"You should already know the answer to that question by now."

"Running the store? You're not a farmer."

He grinned. "It's what I do best. It gives me satisfaction at the end of the day to know that's something I can do well. But that's not what makes me happy."

"What then?"

"Knowing that God handpicked us to be together." His gaze held her tenderly. "We've wasted a lot of time with stubbornness and misunderstanding. I think it's time to put all that behind us and move forward."

"And you'll let me share the mercantile with you?"

"Yes, we'll run it together."

"Until the children come along. Then I'll stay home and take care of them."

"If that's what you want." A smile played at the corners of his mouth. "Did you mean what you said about not going to any more rallies?"

"Yes. I hope women have the vote soon. We deserve it. I realize now that I took up a cause because I was looking for a place to fit in. But I don't need the Suffrage Association anymore. I know where my place is." She smiled at him, feeling for the first time in her life that she truly belonged. "With you."

Jeremiah pressed an urgent kiss to her lips. "Then let's go home."

A Letter to Our Readers

Dear Readers:

In order that we might better contribute to your reading enjoyment, we would appreciate your taking a few minutes to respond to the following questions. When completed, please return to the following: Fiction Editor, Barbour Publishing, Inc., P.O. Box 719, Uhrichsville, OH 44683.

1. Did you enjoy reading *Kansas Home*?
   ❏ Very much—I would like to see more books like this.
   ❏ Moderately—I would have enjoyed it more if _____
   _____
   _____

2. What influenced your decision to purchase this book?
   (Check those that apply.)
   ❏ Cover   ❏ Back cover copy   ❏ Title   ❏ Price
   ❏ Friends   ❏ Publicity   ❏ Other

3. Which story was your favorite?
   ❏ *Darling Cassidy*   ❏ *Tarah's Lessons*
   ❏ *Laney's Kiss*   ❏ *Emily's Place*

4. Please check your age range:
   ❏ Under 18   ❏ 18–24   ❏ 25–34
   ❏ 35–45   ❏ 46–55   ❏ Over 55

5. How many hours per week do you read? _____

Name _____

Occupation _____

Address _____

City_____ State_____ Zip_____

E-mail_____